The Forbidden Forest

MIRCEA ELIADE

The Forbidden Forest

TRANSLATED BY
Mac Linscott Ricketts
and Mary Park Stevenson

UNIVERSITY OF NOTRE DAME PRESS
NOTRE DAME ~ LONDON

Copyright © 1978
University of Notre Dame Press
Notre Dame, Indiana 46556

Published as *Forêt Interdite*
© 1955 Librairie Gallimard

Published as *Noaptea de Sânziene*
© 1971 Ioan Cusa

Library of Congress Cataloging in Publication Data

Eliade, Mircea, 1907–
 The forbidden forest.

 Translation of Noaptea de Sânziene.
 I. Title.
PC839.E38N613   859'.3'34   76-51618
ISBN 0-268-00943-0

Manufactured in the United States of America

Preface to the
English Edition

While yet a very young man, I realized that no matter how captivated I might be by oriental studies and the history of religions, I should never be able to give up literature. For me, the writing of fiction—sketches, novellas, novels—was more than a *"violon d'Ingres"*; it was my only means of preserving my mental health, of avoiding a neurosis. I shall never forget my first year at the University of Calcutta: from January until the beginning of summer, 1929, I devoted myself exclusively to the study of Sanskrit. I worked some fourteen to fifteen hours per day and did not allow myself to read in any language except Sanskrit, not even after midnight a page from *Divina Commedia* or the Bible (I did read the New Testament in a pretentious, pedantic Sanskrit translation). And suddenly, at the beginning of summer, I sensed I had to escape from the prison in which I had locked myself. I needed *freedom*—that freedom which the writer knows only in the act of literary creation. For several days I tried, in vain, to resist the temptation to put aside the Sanskrit grammar, the dictionaries of Monier-Williams and Apte, and Aniruddha's *Samkhya-Sutravrtti*, and write the novel that was obsessing me. In the end I *had* to write it; I wrote *Isabel si apele diavolului* ("Isabel and the Devil's Waters") in a matter of a few weeks, and only after that did I regain the desire to work. I returned then with enthusiasm to the study of Sanskrit grammar and Samkhya philosophy.

Twenty years later, on June 21, 1949, in Paris, at the time I was drafting a chapter of *Le Chamanisme*, I felt all of a sudden the temptation to begin a novel. This time too I tried to resist. I said to myself, quite correctly, that it would be of no use to write a literary work in the Romanian language—a book which could not appear in Romania and for which I should have to find a translator and above all a publisher. Since I was at that time completely unknown as a writer in France, it would be difficult to persuade an editor to publish such a novel. In my Journal for that summer I noted several desperate efforts I made then to ward off the temptation to begin *Noptea de Sanziene* (i.e., *Forbidden Forest*). For some time I hoped I could continue working on *Le Chamanisme* during the daytime while devoting to the novel only a part of the night.* But soon I realized I could not live concomitantly in two worlds—that of scientific investigation and that of literary imagination—and on July 3 I interrupted *Le Chamanisme* in order to be able to concentrate on the novel. It was to require five years for me to write it, because I did not find suitable time or "inspiration" except for two or three months per year.

I said to myself that my spiritual equilibrium, the condition indispensable to any creativity, is assured by this oscillation between research of a scientific nature and literary imagination. Like many others, I live alternately in a diurnal spiritual regimen and a nocturnal one. I know, of course, that these two categories of spiritual activity are interdependent and express a profound unity, because they have to do with the same "subject," *man*—more precisely, with the mode of existence in the world specific to man and his decision to assume this mode of existence. I know likewise from my own experience that some of the creations of my literary imagination contributed to a more profound understanding on my part of certain religious structures and that sometimes, without my being conscious of this fact at the moment I was writing fiction, the literary imagination utilized materials or meanings I had studied, as if I were repeating formulas under the diurnal regimen of the spirit.

So it was with great joy that I read this observation by J. Bronowski: "The step by which a new axiom is added cannot itself be mechanized. It is a free play of the mind, an invention outside the logical processes. This is the central act of imagination in science, and it is in all respects like any similar act in literature."† This means, however, that literature is, or can be, in its own way an instrument of knowledge. Just as a new axiom reveals a previously unknown structure of the real (that is, it *founds* a new world), so also any creation of the literary imagination reveals a new Universe of meanings and values. Obviously, these new meanings and values endorse one or more of the infinite possibilities open to man for *being* in the world, that is, for *existing*. And literature constitutes an instrument of knowledge because the literary imagination reveals unknown dimensions or aspects of the human condition.

In epic literature (novella, story, novel), literary imagination utilizes narrative scenarios. They may be as different as the scenarios attested in *The Quest of the Grail*, *War and Peace*, *Carmen*, *A la recherche du temps perdu*, and *Ulysses*. But in one way or another, all these creations of epic literature

---

*See *Fragments d'un journal* (Paris: Gallimard, 1973), pp. 107 ff.
†J. Bronowski, "The Logic of the Mind," *The American Scientist* 54, no. 1 (Spring, 1966), p. 6.

narrate something—more or less dramatically, more or less profoundly. Of course the *forms* in which the narratives are presented—from *The Golden Ass* to *Père Goriot*, from Dostoevsky to *Absolom, Absolom!* and *Dr. Faustus*—can appear antiquated; in any event, few contemporary writers would dare to repeat epic formulas used by the great predecessors. But this does not mean, as has been believed, the "death of the novel"; it means simply that many of the classical forms of the "novel-novel" are superannuated, that consequently we must invent new narrative forms.

This is not the place to enter into the recent fervent discussion about the decisive importance (in fact, the tyranny) accorded to language, an importance which, according to some, would justify not only *"la nouvelle-vague"* but also the other contemporary attempts to write unintelligible (or, at any rate, unreadable) prose. I wish only to recall that discoveries made recently in linguistics, in the philology and hermeneutics of language, can help revive lyrical poetry, but they do not annul the importance and necessity of narrative literature. It would require too many pages for me to analyze the function and significance of this literature. The specific mode of existence of man implies the need of his learning what happens, and above all what *can* happen, in the world around him and in his own interior world. That it is a matter of a structure of the human condition is shown, *inter alia*, by the *existential necessity* of listening to stories and fairy tales, even in the most tragic of circumstances. In a book about Soviet concentration camps in Siberia, *Le Septième ciel*, the author, J. Biemel, declares that all the internees living in his dormitory—almost a hundred in number—succeeded in surviving (while in other dormitories ten or twelve died each week) because they listened every night to an old woman telling fairy tales. So imperiously did they feel the need for stories that every one of them renounced a part of his daily food ration to allow the old woman not to work during the day so she could conserve her strength for her inexhaustible storytelling.

Quite as revealing in my view are the experiments carried out in several American universities in connection with the psychology and physiology of sleep.

> One of the four phases of sleep is called REM (Rapid Eye Movement); it is the only phase during which the sleeping person dreams. The following experiments were done: Volunteers were prevented from staying in the REM phase, but were permitted to sleep. In other words, they could sleep, but it wasn't possible for them to dream. Consequence: the following night, the persons deprived of REM tried to dream as much as possible, and if they were again prevented from doing so, they proved nervous, irritable, and melancholy during the day. And finally, when their sleep was no longer bothered, they gave themselves over to verita-

ble 'orgies of Rapid Eye Movement sleep,' as if they were avid to recover everything they had lost during the preceding nights.*

The meaning of these experiments, it seems to me, is clear: they confirm the organic need of man to *dream*—in other words, the need for "mythology." At the oneiric level, "mythology" means above all *narration*, because it consists in the envisioning of a sequence of epic or dramatic episodes. Thus man, whether in a waking state or dreaming (the diurnal or the nocturnal regimen of the spirit), has need of attending upon adventures and happenings of all sorts, or of listening to them being narrated, or of reading them. Obviously, the possibilities of narratives are inexhaustible, because the adventures of the characters can be varied infinitely. Indeed, characters and happenings can be manifest on all planes of the imagination, thereby making possible reflections of the most "concrete" reality as well as the most abstract fantasy.

A closer analysis of this organic need for narration would bring to light a dimension peculiar to the human condition. It could be said that man is *par excellence* a "historic being," not necessarily in the sense of the different historicist philosophers from Hegel to Croce and Heidegger, but more particularly in the sense that man—any man—is continually fascinated by the chronicling of the world, that is, by what happens in his world or in his own soul. He longs to find out how life is conceived, how destiny is manifest—in a word, in what circumstances the impossible becomes possible, and what are the limits of the possible. On the other hand, he is happy whenever, in this endless "history" (events, adventures, meetings, and confrontations with real or imaginary personages, etc.) he recognizes familiar scenes, personages, and destinies known from his own oneiric and imaginary experiences or learned from others.

These preliminary observations do not constitute the most suitable introduction to reading *Forbidden Forest*. But they can be useful to the reader in the sense that they situate the novel in my whole literary production. I am the author of several novels which might be classified under the rubric "realistic and psychological," but I have written likewise a sizeable number of novellas and stories of a "fantastic" type. *Forbidden Forest* presents itself, apparently, as a "historical novel" whose action unfolds—in Romania, London, Portugal, on the Russian front, at Paris—during twelve years, between 1936 and 1948. Some episodes, for instance the bombardment of London on the night of September 9, 1940, are as much as possible exact descriptions of real events.

At other places the reader can guess from the outset that he has to do with something other than the historic flux in which the various characters in the

---

*Mircea Eliade, *No Souvenirs*, Fred H. Johnson, Jr., trans. (New York: Harper & Row, 1977), pp. 279–80; entry for 17 April 1966.

novel are being carried along. The principal character, Stefan Viziru, meets Ileana, the woman with whom he will fall in love, in a forest on the outskirts of Bucharest on the Night of St. John, that is, at the summer solstice, the "magic" night *par excellence* (cf. Shakespeare, A *Midsummer Night's Dream*; Strindberg, *Miss Julie*, etc.). Even from this first meeting Stefan is obsessed by the image of a car which it seems Ileana "ought to have." It is unnecessary to comment on the symbolical significance of the Forest (that *selva oscura* in which Dante wandered), of the Night of St. John (when the sun descends from the zenith to the nadir), of the "car" (vehicular symbolism—which makes possible the passage from one mode of reality to another—is well known). Unnecessary is it also to evoke the many other "enigmas" (for example, that of *doamna* Zissu, the enigma which finds its solution—that is, the role it plays in the economy of the novel—only in the final chapter), and the many "coincidences" (for instance, the physical resemblance between Stefan and the writer Partenie); or to recall the cosmological significance of the twelve years which elapse between the first and last meetings of Stefan and Ileana (cf. the cycle of the "Great Year"—of 12,000 terrestrial years—of ancient cosmologies). Even Stefan's longing—so hard to understand—to love two women at the same time, invites a reading other than the simplistic psychological one: in Stefan's conviction, such a paradoxical experience, impossible to realize in a profane existence, would permit him to transcend the human condition; above all it would help to liberate him from the burden of historic time.

I must insist, however, that all these symbolic meanings have not been camouflaged consciously and deliberately in a narrative of the "historical fresco" type of novel. They were imposed upon me by the process of literary imagination itself. I believe it is an experience known to the majority of writers, no matter to what aesthetic they adhere or the literary method they apply. Actually, in even the most commonplace narrative, *any* event (a meeting, a reading, the recollection of an ordinary dialog, etc.) can camouflage a meaning or a message which the protagonists and the readers—at least those of a certain type—do not discern. There is no more perfect camouflage of "transcendent" meanings than the gray banality of everyday realism.

In reviewing *Forbidden Forest*, I confess that the hidden meanings of many episodes I discovered only after having finished writing the novel. In that sense I can say that this book was for me—and I hope it will be for the readers—an instrument of knowledge. The long, circuitous journey begun on the Night of St. John 1936 and concluded, also in a forest, near the Swiss border in 1948 revealed to me meanings of human existence which I had not known before finishing the novel; or in some instances I knew them only approximately, in such a way that I did not understand their true value.

But there would be so much to say, and not all in relation to this novel or the function and destiny of literary narrative, that it is wiser I stop here.

ix

Commentaries by an author about his own works are justified only to the extent to which he discusses all the problems that confronted him when he was writing. That I am not permitted to do here. *Forbidden Forest* is in itself a sufficiently voluminous book.

Mircea Eliade

La Valette, August, 1977

Translators' Introduction

It gives us great pleasure to be able to make available to English-speaking readers this epic novel of Mircea Eliade, the distinguished historian of religions. While a few of Eliade's short stories have been published in English translations, this is the first of his novels to appear in that language. In the judgment of the translators this novel, so rich in symbolism and resonant with themes drawn from the author's store of mythical, religious, and philosophical lore, is Eliade's masterwork in fiction and as such the novel most deserving of being translated first.

For readers who are not familiar with Professor Eliade's work in the history of religions, it may be said that his researches have had to do with topics as widely ranged as yoga, alchemy, shamanism, myth and symbolism, initiation rites, and Australian religions. He is recognized as the foremost contemporary scholar and theoretician in the field of the history of religions, which includes what is sometimes known as "comparative religion." Eliade has given to this discipline a cohesion, methodology, vocabulary, and direction which it lacked prior to his appearance. His great achievement has been to delineate "structures" and "forms" in the maze of religious expressions and to reveal underlying universal meanings in these forms. While Eliade's orientation is not psychological, many have seen parallels between his work and that of the psychologist Carl G. Jung. Eliade cannot however be catalogued simply as a "Jungian": his methodology is unique, combining as it does perspectives gained from a richly diversified education and a phenomenal breadth of readings and interests.

Born in Bucharest in 1907, Eliade grew up in perhaps the most privileged period of Romanian history, the years between the World Wars. Previous generations had been involved in the struggle for Romanian independence; the generation destined to live after the Second World War would find its creativity stifled by the demands of a socialist state. But the 1920s and

'30s were decades of freedom in which the "young generation" was at liberty to follow whatever impulses might move it. It was in that favored era that Eliade emerged and developed.

Already a contributor to a "popular science" type magazine before his fifteenth birthday, Eliade manifested from then onward a compelling drive to express himself in the written word. His earliest published fiction, a story called "How I Found the Philosopher's Stone," written when he was fifteen, foreshadows his life-long interest in alchemy and fantasy. During his years at the University of Bucharest (1925–28) he contributed on a twice-weekly basis to a daily newspaper with a religio-philosophical orientation, as well as to numerous periodicals. His columns dealt with a variety of topics, reflecting the reading he was doing at the time, the ideas that were taking shape in his mind, and his views on current events and personages, especially in fields of literature, religion, and philosophy.

Thus he was already well known in certain circles when he went to India at the end of 1928 to study Indian philosophy under one of its most authoritative interpreters, Surendranath Dasgupta at the University of Calcutta. While in India he continued to send home occasional reports of his travels and experiences which were published in various periodicals. His first novel, *Isabel si apele diavolului* ("Isabel and the Devil's Waters"), published in 1930, grew out of his early impressions of India and the turmoil of his mind at that time. A second novel was begun in India, *Lumina ce se stinge* ("The Light that Fails"), and was published in 1934. A third, the one which was to establish him on the Romanian literary scene, *Maitreyi* (1933), is based on the author's romance with an Indian girl. Several other novels and novellas followed at a rate of about one per year until 1940. A play of Eliade's, *Ifigenia*, was staged in Bucharest in 1940. But by that time the war was on and Eliade left Romania.

Because he had already made for himself a reputation as a writer of fiction by 1933, the year he became an assistant to Professor Nae Ionescu at the University of Bucharest, it was with difficulty that Eliade persuaded his colleagues to view him also as a serious scholar of Hindu philosophy and the history of religions generally. His dissertation on yoga was published in French in 1936. There followed studies on alchemy, Babylonian cosmology, folklore, and "the myth of reintegration." An international journal for "études religiouses," *Zalmoxis*, founded in 1938 by Eliade, fell victim to the war after three volumes.

Having spent the war years as cultural attaché to Romanian legations in London (1940) and Lisbon, he came in 1945 to Paris to begin a new life among the many expatriate Romanians. In the years immediately following the war he lectured in the history of religions at the Sorbonne as well as other European universities, and wrote the first books that were to bring him worldwide acclaim as a historian of religions: *Traité d'histoire des religions* (1945), *Le Mythe de l'éternel retour* (1949), *Le Chamanisme* (1951), *Images et symboles* (1952), and *Le Yoga* (1954). Eliade joined the faculty of the Divinity School of the University of Chicago in 1957, in which position he has remained to the present. His writings, plus the impact of his students—a whole generation of them now—have carried his influence to all parts of the world in the past twenty years.

While he was still living in Europe, during the time he was writing some of his most significant books in the history of religions, he was working also, intermittently, on the novel translated here, originally titled *Noaptea de Sanziene* ("The Night of St. John"). Eliade has chronicled the creation of this novel in *Fragments d'un journal* (Paris, 1973). Begun in 1949, it was not completed until five years later, when it was immediately translated into French by A. Guillermou as *Forêt interdite* and published in 1955. The Romanian edition appeared only in 1970–71 (Ioan Cusa, Paris) in two volumes.

Those who are familiar with Eliade's writings in the history of religions will recognize in *Forbidden Forest* some of the themes discussed in the author's books on myth and symbol. Most obvious, perhaps, is the emphasis on the sacred revealed in the profane, the conjunction of the otherworldly with the secular. While the sacred is always transcendent, eternal, ideal, it is known to man because it does not remain wholly transcendent, but appears in ciphered guise within the world of time, space, and history. In Christian terms this is the gracious miracle of the Incarnation; but for Eliade *all* religion rests on a similar kind of divine condescension, for which he has coined the term *hierophany*, the "manifestation of the holy." Other themes in the novel include Time as a terror to be escaped, the meaning of death, and motifs derived from mythology and folklore.

This is not to say that Eliade has "used" the medium of fiction to demonstrate his scholarly theses. Rather, for Eliade, scholarly study and literary creativity are two complementary approaches to an understanding of the mystery of the sacred. One might say that the universe created by a literary work is, for Eliade, structurally parallel to the universe created by myth, or even to that created by a god in a myth. Such worlds have a "reality" quite apart from that of the world of everyday, the world of History. In his fiction writing, Eliade turns from myth-study to myth-making. It may be that he is such a perceptive interpreter of myth because he has the gift of creating mythlike worlds of imaginative literature.

In reading this novel, one should bear in mind the historical situation of the Romanian people, for, in large measure, this story is an expression of the Romanian historical experience. Throughout virtually all their recorded existence they have been subjected to control and oppression by conquerors: the

Romans, Huns, various Slavs, Ottoman Turks, and now the Russians. As Vintila Hora puts it in his essay in *Myths and Symbols: Studies in Honor of Mircea Eliade*:

> Like Stefan Viziru . . . the Romanian people live a double drama: on the traditional plane they are forced to remain outside history in order to evade the consequences of historical time . . . ; another force, however, has incited them to participate in history since the time they were integrated into the Western conception of life in 1848. That fragment of the Romanian people which has remained loyal to the traditional conception, and, situated on the mystical plane, refuses civilization (we refer to the peasants), has the opportunity of saving itself from any disaster, since disasters occur only in historical time. The other fragment (the bourgeoisie and the workers), who became entangled in history, are being destroyed by it.[*]

In Partenie and Ioana we see the destructive force of history; but Stefan and Ileana—and eventually Biris—by their openness toward the transcendent world of myth, are able to escape it.

Perhaps the best term to characterize this novel is "epic." In the twelve-year cycle, 1936–48, beginning and ending with the Night of St. John,[†] the hero Stefan pursues through innumerable vicissitudes the hope for immortality. This is possibly the oldest literary theme in the world, being evidenced as early as the third millennium in the Sumerian epic of Gilgamesh. It is, moreover, the theme of one of the best-known Romanian folktales, about Fat Frumos (Prince Charming). Since the quest for immortality is a universal one, the fact that the novel is set in Romania is relatively incidental; like religious phenomena, the universal must of necessity be embodied in some particular historical situation.

Since completing *Forbidden Forest* Eliade has written no other novels, but he continues to produce a stream of short stories and novellas, all written in his mother tongue. The great majority of these stories await translation and publication in other languages. This literary output is no mere "hobby" for the scholar; it is as much a vocation for Eliade as are his researches into exotic religions. He has spoken of his work in the history of religions as involving for him a personal sacrifice—the sacrifice of his literary vocation—made in the cause of inculcating a new conception of *homo religiosus*.[‡] This remark

[*] Hora, "The Forest as Mandala" in *Myths and Symbols: Studies in Honor of Mircea Eliade*, ed. J. M. Kitagawa and C. H. Long (Chicago: University of Chicago Press, 1969), pp. 390–91.
[†] The evening of June 23 until midnight, observed as the summer solstice. St. John's Day is June 24.
[‡] See the quotation in George Uscateascu's essay in *Myth and Symbol*, p. 398.

indicates the high value Eliade places on his work as an author—as well as that of a historian of religions.

A few remarks may be in order here about the preservation of certain Romanian words in this translation. The translators felt that just as *monsieur* and *rue* or *place* in books with their setting in France serve to remind the reader of that setting, so Romanian titles of address and terms for streets, etc., should be retained in our translation for the same reason. A footnote is provided at the first occurrence of these terms in the text. Since these titles are not ordinarily capitalized in Romanian, we have left them uncapitalized in the translation. Certain titles and proper names acquire a final *e* when used in direct address.

It has proved impossible to employ Romanian diacritical marks. Those readers who are not familiar with Romanian will not miss them; those who are familiar will, we trust, understand. We have not altered the Romanian spelling of names to render them phonetically; however, the following may be of some interest to readers unfamiliar with the language: Stefan is pronounced approximately *Shteff-áhn*, Ileana *Éel-yah-nah*, Ioana *Yoáh-ahna*, and Biris *Béer-ish*.

Eliade has used the technique of flashback frequently throughout the novel, and sometimes there are flashbacks within flashbacks. For this English edition we have adopted the device of indentation to indicate where the sequence in time is interrupted.

The translators are grateful to the University of Notre Dame Press and to its director, James Langford, for undertaking the project of publishing this novel. A special expression of appreciation is due to Ann Rice for her painstaking editorial work, and for taking a very personal interest in seeing this volume through to publication.

The Forbidden Forest

PART ONE

1

HE OPENED THE DOOR AS QUIETLY AS HE COULD AND TURNED ON THE LIGHT.
The room was hot and smelled of dust. The blinds at the windows were
lowered. Next to the bed there was a large wooden table laden with books,
almost all of them new, some with pages still uncut. A set of flimsy shelves,
apparently made by an amateur, leaned against the opposite wall. It too was
full of books.

"What would you like to be?" He heard the voice of the woman in the
next room. "Would you like to become a deputy?"

He's with Arethia, Stefan said to himself and went on tiptoe to the bed.
Since Spiridon Vadastra had moved into the room next door, he never entered his own room in the hotel without a feeling of excitement. Almost every
evening Vadastra had visitors. The walls were thinly plastered and Stefan
could hear all the conversations distinctly. In just a few weeks he had learned
many things. He had found out that Vadastra had recently received his
doctorate in law; that he was the managing director of a newspaper, *The
Students' Progress*, which was subsidized by the office of the Police Commis-
sioner; that his associate, the business manager of the paper, a certain Voinea,
had fled to Jassy with the entire subsidy in the amount of 50,000 lei. Above
all, he had found out that *domnisoara** Arethia was in love with Spiridon.
Several times he had seen them together. Spiridon Vadastra was a scrubby
youth with bristly hair who wore an opaque black monocle over his right eye
and had the arrogant walk of a man who was sure of himself. He was just as
Stefan had imagined him to be from his manner of speaking. Arethia seemed
ageless. She was lanky and angular, with colorless hair and thin lips, her
cheekbones accentuated with rouge. When she smiled she closed her eyes
coquettishly. Every time Stefan met her on the stair he surprised her in the act

*Miss.

of tugging at her blouse in order to give some contour to her shapeless breasts.

"I?" responded Vadastra raising his voice. "Anyone can become a deputy. Even someone like Voinea can become a deputy."

"Then a minister?" Arethia insisted.

"Possibly," answered Spiridon after a short hesitation. "But what's so good about being a minister? Here today and gone tomorrow. Then you go over into the opposition and who knows when your turn will come again. . . . Still, it's not bad to be a minister," he added. "Maybe that's what I'll be. . . . Even so, why be a minister when there are so many other things to do?"

"What kind of things?

"Great things!" exclaimed Spiridon with a strange exaltation in his voice. "Things that no one else can do. For example, to discover the North Pole! If it hadn't already been discovered I'd set out alone on an expedition and after years of struggle I'd discover it! . . . This, yes! I'd be written up in all the newspapers. All the kings would invite me to their courts. I'd become a member of all the academies in the whole world! And so many other things!"

He's overwhelmed with regrets, Stefan realized as he became aware of the protracted silence in the next room. It was just like that other evening when he had recounted his great defeat in the *liceu*.* He was playing the *Sonata Pathetique* on the stage of the National Theater at the ceremonies celebrating the end of the school year. The curtain fell unexpectedly because the address of the history teacher had been too lengthy and it was necessary to shorten the program by a half hour. "But why cut short *my* performance?" Vadastra had protested. "Why do that to me, an honor student, a person of consequence? I wanted to surprise them. No one knew I had taken up the piano except *doamna*† Zissu. I practiced with her three or four hours a day and I paid fifteen lei an hour. . . . But they all envied me. It irritated them that I had learned this too: how to play the piano. I was the best in composition and in Latin, and now I'd learned to play the piano too!"

On that evening Stefan had not known that Vadastra wore a glass eye and that two fingers were missing from his right hand. It was several days later that he mentioned the accident: A colonel's son had wounded him inadvertently while the boy was playing with a shotgun. The colonel had given Spiridon a large sum of money. Yet while he was still in the hospital he decided how he would take his revenge. He would learn to play the piano and he would show the others how unimportant this accident was. No obstacles existed for such a man. And it was when he was looking for a piano he could rent by the hour that he had met *doamna* Zissu. . . .

"Well, but what can you do *now*?" Arethia asked after a moment of silence.

---

*A public secondary school.
† Mrs.

"What do you mean, what can I do? If a man really wants something, and wants it with all his might, he'll succeed. And it's not necessary to stay in Romania. What does Romania matter? It's a little country. But imagine being in America and doing something really great! Something that no one has done before, that only you can do! Just imagine discovering something like radium or something even a thousand times more important than radium! I'd become the most celebrated man in the world and the most powerful and the richest, all at once. What would an Edison be then, compared with me? The sound of my name would make everyone tremble! I'd be able to do anything I wished in all the world, even dethrone kings if I wanted to."

"Too bad it's been discovered," whispered Arethia a moment later. "Radium, I mean." And she repeated with more courage, "It's too bad it's been discovered."

"What does that matter!" exclaimed Spiridon. "There are other things yet to be discovered! And besides, there are many great things I can still do! Not just some little invention that anyone else can make. Something extraordinary, something unique that all the world will talk about. Like discovering a new continent, for instance, or some such thing! Or maybe to discover a substance that will transform everything it touches into gold!"

"That's impossible! It's the story of that king who... you know what I mean ... but it's not possible."

"Why isn't it possible?" cried Spiridon, growing more impetuous. "Chemistry can do anything. It's a question of atoms. You just change the number of the atoms. And one day somebody will discover how to do it as they've discovered so many other things. But what good will it do me if someone else discovers it? The wonderful thing would be for me to find it myself! A substance that transforms everything it touches into gold! For instance, I'd just touch this chair and it would be changed to gold! Do you understand what this would mean? I'd become the master of the world! I'd be able to buy anything, all the palaces, all the museums. I'd buy the Louvre and bring it home! And how many other things I could do! Everybody would tremble because of me! If I were walking down the street and someone didn't greet me with sufficient respect I'd call a policeman and order him arrested on the spot! What could he do to me? If I wished I could even kill him!... But I wouldn't kill anyone. I'm only telling you this so you can see what power I'd have and how everyone would be afraid of me. Then they'd know how to behave with me. They'd know who Spiridon Vadastra is! It would be enough for somebody simply to utter my name to make all heads turn. Whenever I went somewhere, like into a restaurant, everyone would stand up... and... oh, so many other things!"

Vadastra had stopped abruptly and all was silent. A lone moth awakened and began to circle blindly around the light globe. So, when he was looking for a piano he could rent by the hour he had met *doamna* Zissu. Vadastra would have been fifteen or sixteen years old at the time. Perhaps *doamna* Zissu was his first love. He spoke of her constantly but he had never described her, never made any allusion to her age. He had not even suggested that she was beautiful.

Stefan was aware that someone was knocking at his door but he didn't answer. It's a mistake, he told himself. Maybe the light in the hall is out and he can't see the number of the room.

"It sounds like someone's knocking," said Arethia.

"It's not for us," Vadastra replied. "It's next door." The pounding, louder this time, began again.

"Come in," called Stefan. It was the porter. He stayed in the doorway politely, with an absent air, his gaze wandering. A pair of gloves lay in his outstretched hand.

"The cabdriver brought them just now. He said they belong to the young lady who was with you, and that he came back from the Bratianu Statue especially to bring them to you. I gave him a hundred lei."

Stefan took the gloves and looked at them a long time, frowning intently.

The porter spoke again. "Why don't you open the window? You'll get sick. It's very hot in here."

"What young lady?" asked Stefan. Then all at once he remembered and his face brightened. "Ah, yes, I know," he said. "Wait. . . ." He searched in his wallet and drew out a banknote, handing it to the porter.

"Thank you. Perhaps you will also let me have a book to read?" asked the porter, folding the bill carefully.

Stefan went to the bookcase that stood against the wall and glanced at random over the shelves. "But is he sure that the gloves are hers?" he asked suddenly.

"He said that he came back from the Bratianu Statue to bring them. He said they belong to the young lady who was with you. . . . I'd like a good novel," the porter added in a lower tone, with a smile.

After the man had left holding the book under his arm with extreme care, almost fearfully, Stefan stood for a moment in the middle of the floor listening. The voices were silent in the neighboring room. Going to the window, he opened it wide. He could smell a garden freshly watered. I have plenty of time, he said to himself, leaning over the sill. It's not yet midnight. . . .

The girl shrugged her shoulders and smiled. In the evening light her face seemed more sunburnt and her hair had taken on the dim luster of old metal.

"I don't understand you," she said. "I don't know if you're joking or if you really believe. . . ."

6

Imperceptibly the sky above them muted its brilliance. A single star gleamed in the transparent air over the forest.

"All kinds of miracles could happen," he continued without looking at her. "But someone has to teach you how to look at them so you'll know they are miracles. Otherwise you don't even see them. You pass right by them and you don't know that they *are* miracles. You don't see them. . . ."

"I'm sorry, but I can't follow you," she said a moment later. "I'd like to be able to understand you. . . ."

"Some say that on this night at exactly midnight the heavens open. I don't quite understand how they could open but that's what they say: that on Midsummer Night, the Night of St. John, the heavens open. But probably they open only for those who know how to look at them."

"I don't understand at all," she said. "I don't understand. . . ."

He gave a start and drew back from the window, much moved. The gloves lay on the bed where he had dropped them. He lifted them for a moment to his face. I don't think they're hers, he said to himself, puzzled. It doesn't seem like her perfume.

When she held the lighter to her cigarette he noticed that her eyes were not as green as he had believed them to be. They had seemed darker because her face was tanned, but their color was really a light green shot with gold. Her lips, very red and slightly parted, permitted the gleaming whiteness of her smile to illuminate her face.

"I've been listening to you all evening," began Ileana, toying absently with the lighter, "and I don't understand why you insist on continuing this joke. Why won't you tell me you're a writer and your name is Ciru Partenie?"

Perplexed, he looked at her and made an effort to return her smile. "I couldn't tell you this because I'm not a writer and my name is Stefan Viziru. To be exact, Stefan I. Viziru. My father's name is Ioan."

Ileana bent her head slightly. The gesture brought to Stefan's mind a sudden effortless answer to the question that he had been asking himself so frequently in the last few days. Where had he seen before the strange color of her hair that was not black nor blue nor silver? Now he knew. It was the hue of a rare species of pansy that he had examined as a child, spellbound, in the park at Cismigiu, shortly after his family had moved to the capital. It pleased him to discover this.

"I've been in Bucharest only a few months," Ileana resumed. "I know almost no one. And I've read nothing by Ciru Partenie. I'd heard about him vaguely, but when we entered the restaurant someone pointed to you with his eyes, saying 'Look at Partenie. I'm surprised to

7

see him here. Probably he has a date!' And the whole evening I've watched all those eyes looking at you curiously. You've been recognized, dear *Maestre!* No use hiding any longer!"

Stefan was content to gaze at her in silence.

"Are you angry? Really?" continued Ileana. "I heard it quite unintentionally at the door as we came in and it's intimidated me all evening. . . ."

"I assure you I'm not Ciru Partenie," he interrupted calmly, earnestly. "Look, if you like I'll prove it." He began to search in both pockets at once. He found an envelope and held it out, but he took it back quickly and handed her a passport. "It has a photograph, too," he said. "It's the best piece of identification."

She opened it and read the name aloud: "Stefan Viziru. Thirty-four years? You don't look it. . . ."

He had approached her without telling her his name or who he was. "Look," he had begun without preface, pointing toward the forest. "In those places there were once marshes." She turned her head suddenly, startled at seeing him so close to her. Since there had been no sound of footsteps behind her, she hadn't realized that he was there. He was a tall man, sturdy yet slender, almost delicate, and the light of his smile disturbed her. "In place of these woods there were marshes. I came here to swim with the boys when I was little. . . ."

He talked continuously, telling her of the marshes around Bucharest, about the trees that he had seen being planted, and especially about his childhood. "When I was in *liceu* there was a hedgehog I made friends with. Whenever I came to see him he sensed me from a distance and ran out to meet me."

He stopped and turned his head quickly, running his hand through his hair, stealing a glance at her with a timid smile. "There's something curious," he added, "but I don't quite understand what it is. You have a strange accent, almost foreign. . . ."

"I spent my childhood out of the country, and it was late when I learned to speak Romanian. I learned it on the farm with the peasants."

"I read a book once," he continued as though he had not heard her, "a book about a young man who called snakes to him and talked with them. I'm sure these things are possible, but someone has to teach you. . . . My hedgehog, for instance, would roll over for me, hide his quills and let me rub his belly. I'm sure I could have learned a lot from him, but I didn't know how to talk to him."

8

The sun went down. A scent of freshly mown hay began to reach them. "If you like we can stay here awhile," he told her. They sat down together on the grass, facing the forest.

"I'm sorry," he began again a little later, "but I have to ask you something." He stopped a moment, embarrassed, and looked at her. She felt his gaze go through her and beyond. He didn't seem to see her.

"*I don't suppose you have a car.* Probably you came to the *sosea** Jianu by tram or bus."

She started to laugh. "By bus. Should I have come by car?"

"I thought so," he murmured. "I didn't think you had a car." He raised himself to his knees on the grass and drew closer to her. Now he didn't seem so young, but perhaps he was more handsome. He had a high forehead, pale and smooth, with the hair receding at the temples. His mouth was large and tranquil, providing a dark contrast to the intense glow of his eyes and the bright gleam of his teeth.

"For some time I have been sure that you didn't have a car," he repeated without attempting to hide his regret, "that you came by bus or tram as far as the *sosea* Jianu. . . ."

She returned his passport with a shrug. Stefan looked at her for a moment and smiled. "Aren't you sorry I'm not Ciru Partenie? Wouldn't you have preferred to sit at table with a famous man, a celebrated personage, admired by everyone, adored by women? Whispers all around you: Look, that beautiful girl is Partenie's latest passion. . . ."

Ileana listened to him with a strained smile. "All this is none of my business," she said, "and it doesn't interest me. But I'd like to point out that your name could very well be Viziru, as your passport proves, and Ciru Partenie your literary pseudonym. Anyway, here in this restaurant, and probably everywhere in Bucharest, you're known under the name of Partenie. . . . But if you wish to continue the game you began in the forest, of course I'll go along with the deception and call you Stefan."

"Probably you don't believe in these things," he said to her as they sat on the grass. "And yet I was sure that *something* would happen. When I saw you at a distance, I felt my heart begin to pound. I was sure a *sign* had been given me. . . . It isn't absolutely necessary to see the heavens opening. *If only you had really come in the car*, as I imagined at first . . ."

"I don't understand. . . ."

*Avenue.

9

"Look, here's what might have happened: We would have walked in the forest. We'd have walked a long time and then when we returned we'd have found no trace at all of the car. It would simply have disappeared. *Exactly at midnight* it would have disappeared."

"Would someone have stolen it?" she asked timidly, bewildered.

"No one could steal it. It was locked. *You showed me the keys.* I saw you show them to me. They were on a ring with many other keys, big and little. And I wouldn't have given them back to you again, I would have kept them."

"I don't understand at all," she had said. "Explain it to me, please. I don't understand. . . ."

Stefan stuffed his passport in his pocket, then burst into laughter. But now it was not the youthful laugh that Ileana knew, the laugh that lighted his face so mysteriously. This time he laughed as some men do when they are alone, confidentially yet harshly, somewhat ridiculously.

"I regret I haven't an exact count," he said. "I should have made note of how many times a year I've been mistaken for this great man, and especially in what circumstances. This above all: *in what circumstances,*" he repeated, stressing each word. "I should also have noted the reactions of the different people who have done me the honor of taking me for the Great Man. Sometimes a terrible disillusionment, at other times doubt, suspicion; or again, even an uncontrolled outburst of fury: How, sir, can you, an ordinary citizen, allow yourself to pass before our eyes looking like the Great Man? How can you permit youself to play such a trick on *us,* who only mark Great Men? You shouldn't be allowed to go about on the main streets or to places frequented by the Master!"

Ileana listened to him with increasing confusion. "I don't know what to think," she said. "You *could* be telling the truth, but you could also be deceiving me. Actually, how do you happen to be walking around with your passport on you? It's as though you expected to be discovered and had prepared for it in advance."

Stefan shrugged his shoulders with a gesture of resignation. "I can see very well how much it costs you to admit that I am not He, the Great Man," he said. "I understand. It's so pleasant to sit at the table with a celebrity, to be stared at by everyone around you, to be envied . . ."

"But really, what's your connection with him?" Ileana interrupted.

"We look very much alike," said Stefan dispassionately. "We're

10

constantly being confused with each other. Sometimes it's exasperating."

"Do you know him?"

"Not personally. I know him only by sight." He paused a moment, then continued. "I mean I've seen him from a distance quite often. Several years ago we lived in the same part of the city, but we never happened to meet on the same sidewalk. From far away one of us would always sense the other approaching and cross the street. And yet. . . . Although I shouldn't complain," he added with a forced smile. "I owe a great deal in my life to this astonishing resemblance. It was through Partenie that I met the woman I love most. She confused me with him. Since then there have been many ties between us. . . ." He was silent.

"To say many ties is perhaps an exaggeration," he went on. "But there is one important bond. My wife was engaged to him. One day on the street she confused me with him and threw her arms around me. She realized her mistake immediately but it was too late. She stayed with me. She claimed I was irresistible," added Stefan smiling. "She said that if a woman kissed me once, she couldn't forget me. But probably she was exaggerating."

"Probably," said Ileana, putting out her cigarette absently.

For a long time Ioana had observed that when he was with her Stefan behaved and talked differently from the way he did with other people. He always seemed to be forcing himself not to take her seriously. "We're not the same as they are," he told her, "we love each other!"

One evening they were returning from a performance of *Miss Julie** at the National Theater. She had been listening to him discuss the play during the intermission and on the way home she had said to him, "I never thought that *Miss Julie* could be explained by the magic of the Night of St. John. You never talk to me about these things." He had put his arm around her waist. "I love you," he told her. "We love each other." She knew what he meant: he thinks that if we talk about *Miss Julie* I will remember Partenie.

Ioana was tall, almost as tall as Stefan. Her hair was blond, her face long with slightly prominent cheekbones (like the German nymphs, Stefan had once told her, like the Rhine-maidens of the Nibelung), and she had unusually large hazel eyes. "You'd expect any other color, but not hazel," said Stefan. "A blond of the Scandinavian type like you ought to have blue eyes,

*Strindberg's play.

11

or green, or even black—but this particular shade you just don't expect. That's what is so unusual about you. I think that here is the source of your magic. . . ."

"The magic of the Night of St. John," Ioana continued insistently. "What happens on that night? What could happen?"

Stefan came close to her again and tried to kiss her. "We two . . ."

"Really, you have a very low opinion of my intelligence," Ioana interrupted. "You think I can't understand anything but love stories. When you're in Bluebeard's room you imagine . . ."

The room that Stefan had rented at the hotel was held in strict secrecy. Ioana's family did not know about it, nor did their friends. Before they were married Stefan had told her about his private retreat. She hadn't understood why he felt the need of such a room in a modest hotel located in a distant quarter of the city, a place that she could never enter. "Just like that forbidden room in the story of Bluebeard," he had said. "No woman has entered it, and none ever shall." "*Alive* . . ." he had added on another occasion. She had lacked the courage to object to his indulgence of this whim. "Other couples," Stefan said, "have separate bedrooms. I need a room of my own to hide in now and then without anyone knowing where I am."

". . . You imagine that I can't follow you into your secret room, that I suppose all you do there is read novels. . . ."

When they were alone Stefan avoided bringing up the subject of literature. He often found her reading when he came home at night. Sometimes Ioana surprised him in the act of glancing at the cover of the book, but he never asked her what she read. At home with her Stefan did not read fiction. Nevertheless Ioana was astonished at the number of things he knew about literature. This knowledge came quite incidentally as they stopped in front of shop windows, or when she happened to mention the title of a book she had run across in a magazine. "That's no good," he'd say; or "I read it. It's rather interesting. I'll bring it to you, if you want it." He thinks I like novels because I was Partenie's fiancée, Ioana surmised.

"And yet," she continued, "a long time ago I found out what you do there in your secret room. Of course, I don't have to tell you. But, really, you think me too naive. I guessed it that evening when you came home with your hands smelling of turpentine. You have a laboratory. It's probably not a room in a hotel at all. You work in a laboratory!"

12

During the first months of their marriage Ioana sometimes had waited for him at the window. She could see him in the distance and assumed from his absent air, from the way he walked, that he had been to his secret room. It seemed to her that Stefan did not really come to until she had held him for a long time in her arms. "Today do I have permission to ask you something?" she inquired once. He answered as he always did when she questioned him in this way, "It's a room two and a half meters by four...." "No, no," she interrupted, still holding him in a tight embrace. "I want to ask you something else. But I won't ask you unless I have your permission." Forcing back a smile, she turned a profound gaze on Stefan's face. Her eyes, so large, so unusually limpid, overwhelmed him again with their mysterious magic. "What do you see from the window?" she asked. "Just tell me this much: when you stand in front of the window, or when you open it and lean out, what can you see?"

They sat down close together on the sofa. "First of all," he began, "this secret room has a great many windows. One of them looks out on the park, another opens toward the sea...." "Stefan!" Ioana chided. He corrected himself, "No, I'm wrong. The secret room has only one window. I think it overlooks a park. I've never seen it. When I go there the curtains are always drawn." "What are the curtains like?" insisted Ioana. "Tell me about the curtains, about the furniture, the color of the walls. So I can imagine them. So I can follow you in my mind when you're there." Stefan was silent a moment. "I don't think there are any curtains," he said. "I don't remember seeing them. When I go into the room, it's always dark because the blinds are closed."

"When we have a child," Ioana had said once, leaning her head back against the sofa and closing her eyes, "when we have a child I'll tell him what I see in Bluebeard's room and I'll let you listen to me. You think I'm completely lacking in imagination. So much the better. Then you'll be surprised at how much I know, how much I've known from the first day you told me about your secret room." She had opened her eyes quickly and looked at him. He seemed very far away from her, lost in thought. "You still haven't decided to take me seriously," added Ioana. "You think that if you love me..." "Give me another year!" he had interrupted, becoming suddenly grave. "Let me try something else. Perhaps there's something else still. You know very well what I mean," he had added, lowering his voice.

Now the Big Scene commences, thought Ioana. Through all her being she felt a sudden unaccountable exhaustion. Vainly she tried to smile, to reassure herself. Long ago she had prepared each reply. She had listened mentally to this dialogue innumerable times. She

13

shouldn't let it trouble her so much. It would be wise for her to begin by suddenly taking him in her arms as she had done a few days before their marriage when she declared, "I only admired him, and I still admire him. I think he's a very great writer, but this doesn't mean I love him. As soon as I met you I knew that I didn't love him, that you were the only one I loved!" She had not been able to say much more at that time, but during the Big Scene she would confess everything. *"Please make an effort to listen to me,"* she would say. *"We torture each other. I've never loved him. Why are you afraid of him? Why are you afraid of my past? You must understand me: there is nothing. I have nothing to forget, because there's* nothing there *for me to forget."*

"You know very well what I mean," Stefan repeated. "Perhaps something else exists besides love. Perhaps somewhere there's an open possibility of miracles, an irreducible mystery, a secret we haven't yet been able to decipher. That's what happened to you."

"You know very well there's no question of any mystery. I didn't love him. I didn't love anyone but you. From the moment I met you, I only loved you!"

"This isn't what I was thinking of," interrupted Stefan. "It's not a question of love. I wonder if there isn't something else. Something that begins with love but leads somewhere *beyond it.* It's very difficult to explain. I'm not clear about it myself. There could be a way out, though—one we don't see. The fact that you met both of us, Partenie and me, could be a *sign,* it could mean something. . . ."

He went on like that for a long time as though he were talking to himself. Ioana wasn't always able to understand him. She noticed that her thoughts wandered and she found she wasn't attentive. In her mind she replied to him: But what connection does all this have with the secret room? She would have interrupted, but she had promised never to question him. "I won't be curious," she had said when they were still engaged. "I trust you. I'll not ask you. If you tell me, fine; but I will never ask you."

"Probably the secret room doesn't exist," she repeated that night on the street as they were returning from the National Theater. "I was sure of it long ago. You work in a laboratory. . . ."

Sometimes when he came home in the evening he was preoccupied. He seemed tired and yet he looked more youthful, his clothes had a strange odor, his hands were stained. "There is no secret room!" she had exclaimed once, triumphantly. "You do experiments in a laboratory. Adela told me that in the *liceu* you liked chemistry. You searched for the Philosopher's Stone. You're

14

still looking for it. It's absurd, now, in the twentieth century, to think that the Philosopher's Stone exists. . . ." From the way he had looked at her and put his arm around her shoulders, Ioana could sense his distress, his diffidence.

And then suddenly Vadastra had appeared. "I've met an extraordinary man—something of a fool, but extraordinary," Stefan said one evening. "He moved into the room next to mine at the hotel. I'm sorry you can't listen to him too."

Baffled, Ioana stared at him. "You do experiments in your hotel room? Don't you work in a laboratory?"

There followed then his discovery of Voinea who had fled to Jassy with the subsidy of 50,000 lei, his discovery of *domnisoara* Arethia and of *doamna* Zissu. "But I can't figure out who this *doamna* Zissu is," he repeated several times at dinner. "I don't understand his connection with this so mysterious lady." And then one day he took her hand and looked deeply into her eyes. "Give me another year! Perhaps there will be some *sign*. Maybe even *doamna* Zissu . . ."

Ioana began to laugh. "Do you really believe what you're telling me? Do you think the recollections of a man you scarcely know . . ."

"I don't even know him," Stefan interrupted. "But I hear him talking all the time. A couple of times I passed him in the hall, but I don't know him personally. And this is exactly what bothers me: that I'm allowed to listen involuntarily to the confessions of a fanatic. Perhaps it's a sign. . . ."

One day he told her, "Here's what happened. Probably a building was being torn down near *doamna* Zissu's house. Probably they were loading the rubbish in a truck just as Vadastra passed by. Anyway some dust got into his eye, under the lid of the glass one. Vadastra said that in the *liceu* he wore blue eyeglasses, pince-nez. When he raised his hand quickly to his eye, he knocked the glasses off. They fell to the ground and broke into bits. The glass eye turned around in its socket. He went back to *doamna* Zissu's, covering his right eye with his hand, and asked her for a basin of water. 'I've broken my glasses and hurt myself,' he told her. When *doamna* Zissu tried to see what had happened he didn't want to take his hand away from his eye. She brought him the water and went out, leaving him alone. He took out the glass eye, washed it and set it aside. Then he began to clean the eyelid and the socket. But *doamna* Zissu came back. She didn't understand what had happened. She began to scream when she saw him with his eyelid all red and pulled out. 'Don't be alarmed!' Vadastra told her quickly, picking up the glass eye and showing it to her. 'It's nothing. I've been like this since the accident.' With pathetic pride Vadastra continued, 'And then I saw *doamna* Zissu begin to cry, and I realized how much she loved me. As I watched her crying because of me I felt I ought to cry too, and I tried. I kept thinking about my broken glasses and I tried hard to make myself cry. But I couldn't. *Doamna* Zissu went on crying and it was very late, so I said, "Excuse me, I must go. . . ."'"

It was late that night when Stefan returned home. He seemed agitated. "You're reading? On the Night of St. John?"

"Is it the Night of St. John? I didn't know."

"It was. Now it's past midnight. Nothing else can happen." He went to her and put his arms around her. "Do I seem so old?" he asked. "It's unbelievable how time can pass." Gently he disengaged himself from her embrace and added, "I hope I won't be tired tomorrow morning at the Ministry."

"What happened?"

"I ran off without telling anyone and went to the forest. The Forest of Baneasa. Suddenly I remembered that this was the Night of St. John. I telephoned you and left. I felt something drawing me there. . . ." After a brief silence he continued, "It made me long suddenly to see the places where I spent my childhood with Ionel. Am I truly so old? Ionel and I went there every summer to swim. The marshes were broad and deep. And now in their place trees have grown. Nothing but tall trees everywhere. My heart kept pounding constantly. . . . I remembered my hedgehog. . . ."

Absently, Ioana began to undress. "You might have taken me too," she said without raising her eyes. "When you called I thought you were going to ask me to go for a walk with you."

Sometimes, especially before the appearance of Vadastra, Stefan would phone her from the Ministry and arrange to meet her in town; but during the past year they had met only once. Ioana had caught sight of him in the distance. He seemed downcast and she realized he had been confused with Partenie again. Someone, some stranger, had greeted him on the street. "I'll have to grow a mustache," he said. "Or maybe it would be better if I shaved my head."

"I wanted you. I really wanted to ask you to go walking with me in the forest, but something prevented me. I felt a need to go back there by myself, to visit the places of my childhood *alone.* . . ." Then he added quickly, "But I have to ask you something, and I want you to tell the truth, whatever your answer may be."

Ioana turned her head and looked at him in astonishment. Stefan's voice seemed dry, unrecognizable.

"Do you believe that now, in our time, a car can disappear without having been stolen by someone? Just dissolve into thin air without leaving any trace at all?" He wrenched his gaze away from Ioana's eyes and continued, embarrassed, "Are you sure you've never spoken to me about something like this? Haven't you read somewhere, in some book, such a tale? A securely

16

locked car that disappears at midnight without having been stolen? It simply disappears. . . ."

"I don't remember."

"I'm beginning to calm down," Stefan said, wiping his face with his handkerchief. He took off his coat and sat down on the carpet, leaning his head against the easy chair. "Then that's not where it came from—some book I've read or a story I've heard told," he continued, becoming more cheerful. "More than likely it's something I imagined."

Ioana seated herself on the low chair in front of the mirror.

"But anyway, do you *believe* that such a thing could really happen?" Stefan insisted. "Do you believe that a car can vanish without a trace?"

"Why not?" Ioana said, turning around in order to see him better.

"Now I know why I love you so much," whispered Stefan, his face brightening.

"But what happened to the car? Why did you ask if I truly believe. . . .?"

"I don't know what's the matter with me today. Maybe it's because I was reminded of my childhood, maybe because I saw those great trees growing on the site of the marshes. I planted a tree there myself when I was in the *liceu.* . . . It seemed as though I *saw* a car. And there was something else: I seemed to *know* what was going to happen to that car. Exactly at midnight it had to disappear. I was obsessed all evening by that car I had seen—although I didn't find it there in the forest—the one that had to disappear at midnight. I *knew* it would disappear and I'd never see it again in my whole life. And this thought made me sad in an incomprehensible way, the thought that I might never see it again. . . . Happily, you exist," he added, smiling cheerfully. "And on July 15 we'll be at Predeal in the mountains. . . ."

Ioana remembered *Miss Julie* as she slipped into the coolness of the bed. Something happened on the Night of St. John, she thought. "Actually, do you really believe in all those things? Do you believe in the Philosopher's Stone, in magic and miracles on the Night of St. John?"

Because it happened frequently, she was not surprised when Stefan did not answer her. He said suddenly as he got up from the carpet, "I long for the mountains."

"Perhaps the decisive year will be repeated." She didn't understand what had prompted her to say these words, but she was glad she had said them and she smiled. Stefan stopped beside the bed and looked down at her.

"Which year?" he asked. "1923 or 1919?"

"The decisive year," Ioana repeated, "when you were alone on the mountain. When you were in the *liceu* and you went alone to the mountains . . ." She realized she was confusing two great events in Stefan's life, but she did not amend her words. She expected him to correct her as he had been in the habit of doing ever since the first days of their marriage, declaring that "This took place in 1928, the summer I returned from Paris. I was then . . ." and he would quickly tell her his age.

17

One day he had shown her his photographs from school days, choosing one that revealed a handsome adolescent with large eyes and hair cut in bangs across his forehead. "This is in 1919," he had said. "I was seventeen then and in the last class at the *liceu*. That was when I climbed up to the cabin with Ionel. . . ." Ioana had held the picture in her hand, studying it for a long time. Quite suddenly she recalled the unreality of the days preceding their marriage. Stefan had told her the story of the incident at the cabin shortly after they had become engaged. It was during the first spring after the end of the war that this adventure had taken place, the spring of 1919. Stefan and Ionel Paraschivescu and three other schoolmates had been too impatient to wait for the summer vacation to climb in the Bucegi. For several years they had dreamed only of seeing the mountains. But Romania was occupied by the Germans and the war went on year after year. When the Armistice was concluded in November it was too late to carry out their plans that year. Deceived by the premature spring of Bucharest, they attempted the climb the following March. They could see the peaks still white with snow, but at the foot of the mountains it was warm and serene. The storm had come upon them when they reached Pietrele Arse,* and they lost their way. It was not until evening that they stumbled upon the cabin of a funicular that transported timber. They broke the padlock on the door, went in and made a fire. Since they had plenty of food and even a large bottle of rum, their spirits rose rapidly. Then they stretched out to sleep in disarray on the bare board floor. Toward midnight they were awakened by the sound of men's voices outside the door. A snowdrift had piled against the door, covering the latch, and only by the most strenuous efforts did the boys inside succeed in opening it. They were afraid at first but the men, who were woodcutters from the valley, became insistent. They were acquainted with the cabin, and were glad to find the young folk there. "We have a dead man with us," they said. "We've been carrying him since six o'clock this evening. If we leave him on the trail the wolves will eat him before morning. So we've brought him here. And it's good you're here, too." After thanking the boys, the woodcutters left. They had to be at work in the valley next morning. "We couldn't sleep, and kept watch all night." Stefan told Ioana. "And in the morning some men came from the village and loaded the corpse on a sled. But Ionel was afraid. He wouldn't look behind him at all, where he knew the dead man was. He finished the bottle of rum all by himself. And he kept saying over and over, 'Oh, don't leave me alone! No matter what happens, don't leave me alone!' Poor Ionel! He had no way of knowing then. . . ."

*Burnt Rocks.

Stefan began to undress absently. "When I was alone on the mountain," he said, "I wasn't in the *liceu*. That was in 1923."

Ioana listened to him with her eyes half-closed, smiling. The decisive year, she repeated to herself.

In 1923, when he was twenty-one and preparing for his degree, Stefan had run away from home. He had even found a freighter to take him secretly to Constantinople. But before he left he had gone to say good-bye to the Carpathians. On their first trip together to the mountains, immediately after their marriage, Stefan had pointed out to her the footpath he had climbed at that time, prior to his departure. "Time seemed not to pass here," he had told her. "The rocks, the pines, the grass, the sky, were always there, in their places. And now every time I evoke such a moment of suspension, of cessation, I feel an inexpressible emotion, almost a beatitude. You can't understand this," he had added. "You're still too young." When he told her this, in 1933, Ioana was twenty-three, eight years younger than he.

"I forgot to tell you something," added Stefan, becoming suddenly animated. "In his own way, Vadastra also believes in the Philosopher's Stone. He was talking with Arethia this evening about a substance that transforms everything it touches into gold. He regrets he hasn't discovered it. . . ."

In the compartment Ioana observed that a young man with penetrating dark blue eyes and receding hair was staring at Stefan, frowning perplexedly. He's been confused with Partenie again, she thought. She was afraid that Stefan would also notice him, but a man with a vandyke, who had taken out his watch to check the time just as the train began to move, had claimed her husband's attention. He had a profile of astonishing nobility. The flawless curve of his brow, the straight nose, the mustache full and yet without arrogance, the beard arched slightly forward—all these gave him a lordly and somewhat old-fashioned air. The rest of his features, however, created a different impression. His broad cheeks with the skin hanging softly over his jaws and the few locks of colorless hair that were stuck across the top of his head were reminiscent of the portraits of doctors and teachers of about 1900.

"In forty-five minutes we'll be at Ploiesti," he said, regarding each of his neighbors in turn. As if in response to a signal everyone began to talk. The gentleman with the beard seemed erudite. He had read the verses of the principal Romanian poets several times and even a Latin text. He spoke particularly with the young man of the deep blue eyes. But soon the conversation became general, and before getting off at Sinaia he bowed politely and introduced himself: Professor Iancu Antim. "I hope we shall have the pleasure of meeting again," he said.

A week later Stefan allowed himself to be persuaded by Ioana to go off for two days alone in the Bucegi. She watched from the window as he vanished in the forest, turning back to the bed with an indefinable sadness. She had grown accustomed lately to returning in her thoughts to the "Great News."

That day had been extremely hot and oppressive. Stefan had shed his shoes and coat at the door and hurried immediately into the bathroom. With a mysterious smile she had followed him, watching patiently as he stood in the torrent of water.

"I don't believe I can climb up to the cabin," she said. And because it seemed to her that Stefan couldn't hear her very clearly with his head always under the water, she repeated, almost shouting, "I can't climb! *I think we're going to have a baby!*"

The next moment Stefan bounded out of the shower as if he had been scalded. His long hair was sticking to his face and he brushed it aside with a frightened gesture. He regarded her for a moment, bewildered. He appeared not to have understood. Then he sprang out of the bathroom just as he was and took her in his arms. That face so cool and wet seemed to Ioana to be bathed in tears. Half-consciously she listened to the water running in the shower . . .

When he returned from the Bucegi he asked her, "Can you imagine whom I met at the Casa Pesterii?"*

"Iancu Antim," Ioana answered readily.

It wasn't the Professor whom he had encountered, however, but a certain Petre Biris. Ioana had never heard of him.

"He's the greatest authority on the works of Partenie," said Stefan in a voice that seemed to be preparing a multitude of revelations, "but he doesn't know him personally. He's only seen him at lectures. And of course he mistook me for him. So we started talking. . . ."

Without giving her time to comment he added, "He was rather critical of the Master. He even criticized him quite harshly. He said that for some time now Partenie has been too hasty. He writes too fast and publishes haphazardly. *For some time now,*" Stefan repeated, emphasizing the words. "What do you think he meant by that, this boy Biris?"

Ioana shrugged.

"I liked Biris," continued Stefan, "but I wonder just what he meant by saying that *for some time now* Partenie hasn't been what he was in the beginning, that he's making almost a mockery of his own work. Have you noticed

*House of the Grotto.

20

any change?" But without waiting for an answer he went on in a more serious tone in an effort to reproduce Biris's exact words.

"He said there's something immoral in Partenie's recent output. That he wants to live as well as write in the same rhythm *as earlier,* but that this isn't possible, that anyone who tries to do this is cheating. A writer can live *before* and *after* he has composed a book, he said, but he cannot live and create at the *same time.* The act of creation absorbs him entirely and so it prohibits him from living. . . . But really, why am I telling you all these things?" He looked suddenly at Ioana. "You must know them and understand them better than I."

"Maybe I don't understand them so well," Ioana volunteered, feeling that she had to say something.

"I only wanted to ask you if you'd noticed too that Partenie's recent work has been written in haste, or, as Biris expressed it, that he wants to enjoy life without giving up his writing? He said people who know his work well are struck by the fact that for some time Partenie has been making a joke of his talent and intelligence. You've never said anything to me about such a thing."

"I haven't been aware of any change."

Stefan studied her thoughtfully for a long time. "But why did you think I'd met Iancu Antim?" he asked.

Ioana smiled. "I don't know what made me ask you that. Perhaps it was because I dreamed about him last night." But she didn't tell him what she had dreamed. Antim had approached the window of their compartment, and standing on tiptoe so that he could see her better, he had rapped anxiously on the glass. "Your husband has met with an accident!" he called. "He's had an accident . . . an accident . . ."

His vacation came to an end and Stefan returned to Bucharest on the evening of the fourteenth of August, going directly to the hotel from the railroad station. Ioana remained at Predeal for fifteen more days. Without her the house on *bulevardul* Domnitei would have seemed lonely and deserted.

The room smelled close and hot, and it was full of moths. Stefan sprinkled the floor with water, changed, and went downstairs to eat at the tavern on the corner. It was quite late when he returned, and since he didn't hear anyone talking in the next room he dropped off to sleep very quickly. Some time later he was awakened by the sound of Vadastra's strident voice.

"I'm not like other men. I don't like to lie. I always speak directly to a man's face.

"I don't understand what you're driving at," Arethia interrupted. "I don't understand and I'm not interested!"

"Wait! I'm not finished! I've a few more words to say to you. . . . You think you know me because . . . You know why. . . . Well, let me tell you

21

something—you don't know me at all! You think I'm weak because I came to your room when Voinea stole my money and asked you to lend me 12,000 lei. You think that I needed assistance, that I called for help. Well, let me tell you, you're wrong! I came to you because you've always inspired me with confidence and I needed someone to consult for advice. That's all. What happened later doesn't matter to me. To tell the truth, I personally didn't think..."

Probably Arethia had started to leave. Stefan heard Spiridon's footsteps as he hurried to the door to bar her way.

"Stop! Why are you angry? I'm not finished! You said that men are liars. Let me prove the contrary...."

"Well, thank *you*!" exclaimed Arethia. "Now you're getting impudent too!"

"I'm not impudent at all," Spiridon continued with the same earnestness. "If I were to tell you I love you with a passion, would you believe me? You'd think I was making fun of you, and I don't want to make fun of you. You haven't done anything to me. We've always been good friends...."

"Please get out of my way!" cried Arethia. "It's my fault for trusting you, a man with no manners. Please let me go immediately!"

Someone knocked on the wall then, in Daniil's room next door. "Finish it up, you two, right now! I can't sleep!" Daniil shouted.

"See what you've done!" murmured Arethia, opening the door a little fearfully. "You've disgraced me!"

"Let's talk some more tomorrow," Spiridon said in a whisper.

For several evenings in succession Stefan did not hear Arethia's voice again. Only Vadastra burst out unexpectedly from time to time, talking to himself. "Just wait. My turn will come too! I'll show them then, all of them! I'll teach them a thing or two!"

One evening Stefan heard someone knocking at one of the doors in the corridor. That's not for me, he said to himself. The day had been unusually hot and he had thrown himself on the bed exhausted, naked, with a towel around his neck. The oppressive heat persisted in his room, on the pavement, over the housetops, radiating hot odors, like furnaces of concrete and metal. The knocking became increasingly louder.

"Come in!" Vadastra called out suddenly. But no one entered. It's not for him either, Stefan said to himself drowsily. It's probably at Arethia's.

He woke up and felt a change in the beating of his heart. All at once he was aware again of the presence of Ileana, like a strange, innocent obsession. It had been with him constantly until the moment when Ioana had followed him into the bathroom and shouted, "*I think we're going to have a baby!*" He remained motionless, with his eyes closed, concentrating. Time turned back. Since the "Great News" he had thought of Ileana on a number of occasions, although never with the same emotion that had accompanied his previous

22

recollections of her. The meeting in the Forest of Baneasa, dinner at the restaurant, the other two brief encounters that followed, had taken on an incidental aspect after Ioana's announcement. Now as he returned in his mind to the earlier days those few moments of companionship came back to him charged with longing. He could see the dress she was wearing on their last afternoon together. It was white with a printed design, and it emphasized the slimness of her waist, giving her a youthful look. He didn't understand how she had managed to be so tanned at the beginning of summer. "As long as there is any snow on the mountains, I stay to ski. And I usually spend the spring at our place in the country."

"Come in!" Vadastra shouted again, almost furiously. Stefan said to himself, It's not for him; he's yelling for nothing. The knocking sounded fainter now, as though the visitor were afraid.

He was sorry he had not had time to find out more about her life. All he knew was that she had been brought up by *Tante* Cecile, who had an estate in Moldavia on the banks of the Siret. It was there that she had spent her adolescence. But he knew very little else about her, except that she had returned to Romania recently and that she was living now with another aunt on *strada* Batistei.

Slowly, timidly, the knocking began again. It seemed very far away at the end of the hall. Stefan heard Vadastra open his door softly in an attempt to catch the intruder off-guard. "There's no one here!" exclaimed Spiridon, somewhat disappointed. Stefan said to himself again. It's not for him. . . .

As he was accompanying her to her home that evening he enjoyed watching her walk. She moved in a manner that was almost boyish, clasping her hands behind her back and shaking her head from time to time in a brief gesture of someone just waking from sleep. Whenever she felt Stefan's long gaze upon her she turned her head and smiled at him with a questioning look. But she also knew how to look at him in another way, gravely, seriously. When she had found out about Ioana she had looked at him like that, and again when he met her a few days later with the question: "What did you do with the suitcases?" She hadn't understood. "You couldn't have locked the suitcases if you had given me that key ring," Stefan explained.

"What key ring?" she asked. She had forgotten and Stefan looked at her for a moment in astonishment. He reminded her. "The car in which you might have come to the forest and which might have disappeared. . . . The keys to your suitcases would have been on the same ring, next to the car keys," and, as he had told her then, he would have kept it. But he didn't tell her anything more.

He didn't tell her the final scene, the scene at midnight as he had witnessed it. *"That's strange!" he had heard her exclaim. "And yet I left*

it here. My car, I mean . . . I remember very well that it was here where I
left it . . ." "Are you sure you came in a car?" he had asked her jokingly.
He saw the way she looked at him in some annoyance, as she searched in
her handbag and held up a key ring. "See," she said, "Here are the keys!"
It was a dull metal ring holding a Yale key and several smaller ones, the
keys to the suitcases. Stefan took it with a strange, secret joy, and looked
at the keys for a few moments, deeply moved.

"I seem to see it," he continued. "A dull metal ring holding a
Yale key and several smaller ones, the keys to the suitcases. . . ." She
looked at him seriously again, then suddenly burst into laughter. "Do
you know that you're beginning to interest me?"

"Who's doing all that knocking?" It was Daniil's voice. He had opened his
door suddenly and was shouting from the threshold, facing the end of the
hall. No one answered. The knocking ceased.

"Is someone there?" Daniil called out again. "Are you looking for someone?"

"We ought to call the porter," shouted Vadastra from his room. In the
darkness, Stefan smiled.

"Do you know, you're beginning to interest me? If you weren't married
I might possibly develop a passion for you. But I'll write to the Valkyrie
about you. The Valkyrie is a former classmate of mine from Lausanne.
I call her that because she's blond, stout, and she sings. But you're her
type. The Valkyrie's a romantic and a spiritualist. You're a little too
healthy for her though. If you were thinner, sadder, almost tubercular,
I'm sure she'd come to Bucharest to sing for you."

She stopped a moment and ran her hand through her hair. "And
yet you're not very well-bred. I could have been angry. I thought you
were flirting with me, but now I understand. You approached me
because you thought I had a car, and you wanted to see how I'd react if
my car had disappeared. I'll tell you how I'd react—I'd report it immediately to the police!"

Suddenly he heard Vadastra talking to himself. "But what can she do to me?
I've kept all the receipts: once three, once three, and once six—twelve
thousand lei in all. If she says anything, I'll ruin her! I'll go to the chief and
he'll fire her inside of twenty-four hours. . . ."

There was no more knocking. Stefan opened his eyes and waited for a
long time in the dark. It was still very hot, but now everything in the room was
different. Everything, even the warm night air that drifted lazily through the
window, had changed.

24

• • •

Once long ago he had wanted to ask Ioana if she, who had loved the two of them at the same time, had felt a *change* in her surroundings then. Or had the world remained for her the same as *before?* But he hadn't dared to ask her. It was not often that he spoke to Ioana about his premonitions and reveries, his secret longings. Now and then he talked to her about Time, and about the open possibility of miracles, but he had never dared to tell her that his deepest wish was to become a saint, to be able to love everyone with the same intensity.

"I have something to confess," he had said to Ileana in the forest. "I don't know you. I don't know who you are. I don't know what you do. With you I can have no secrets. I haven't told this to anyone, but I can tell it to you: everything depends on Time. If you don't resolve this problem now while you're young, life will catch you and crush you inside, and one day you'll realize you're old and the day after that you'll find yourself on your deathbed and by that time it's too late to try anything else. You must search for this now, while you're young. This is a problem for youth. . . ."

"What must I search for?" Ileana had asked.

"To escape from Time, to go out of Time. Look well around you. Signs come to you from all sides. Trust the signs. Follow them. . . ."

He sprang up suddenly from the bed and in a few steps he was in front of the bookshelves. Kneeling, he began to grope behind the books on the lowest shelf and after a few long seconds he found the gloves and pulled them out with great care. In the darkness he could feel how dry they were, dirty and full of dust. I'm almost certain they're not hers, he said to himself. Rising to his feet he became aware that he was naked, aware of his hot moist body. Quickly, he began to dress. "*I think we're going to have a baby!*" He heard Ioana's voice again, but he continued to dress nervously, almost trembling. Turning on the light, he examined the gloves carefully. They were dusty and moth-eaten. "They're not hers," he kept repeating, "but I must give them to her." He picked up his coat and left the room without putting it on.

"Did you hear anything?" The porter stopped him when he reached the head of the stairs. "There was a man knocking on all the doors. Did you hear him?"

"He didn't knock on mine," Stefan answered quickly.

"If he's the one who was here last winter, I know him," said the porter. "He's an Adventist. Selling Bibles. He's been here before and I noticed him when he came in. 'Are you looking for someone?' I asked him. He pretended not to hear me and started to climb the stairs. . . ."

25

At that very moment Ileana could be on the point of leaving. It could be, for example, that right now while he was listening to the porter she was locking the front door, traversing the few meters of gravel path in the little garden in front of the house and preparing to climb into the taxi that awaited her at the gate. Stefan walked faster. Once past the corner of the street he began to run, holding his coat tightly under his arm. She's probably leaving for the country, he reasoned. And he was still obsessed with that absurd question, *"But how could you lock the suitcases?"* His heart began to beat faster. He hailed a taxi and gave the address on *strada* Batistei. "As quickly as possible," he added, leaning toward the driver.

From a distance he saw the house asleep in darkness. When the taxi drew up in front of number 27 the scent of cloves struck him. Just then a cat leaped down from the wall, losing itself in the shadows at the back of the courtyard. All the blinds were drawn. Impulsively he tried the latch many times, then returned to the cab and called to the driver, "The North Station!"

He remembered then a gesture of Ileana's that he had not noticed earlier. Occasionally she rested her cheek on her fist, inclining her head slightly. It was a schoolgirl's pose and Stefan wondered how long she had carried it with her through the world. Probably he would find her in this attitude seated at the window of the train, looking straight ahead, waiting for him. But he discovered that the express for Moldavia had been gone for two hours. There was another passenger train toward midnight. "At exactly 23:45," he was told at the ticket window. He realized that his haste had been in vain and he felt suddenly ridiculous. Undoubtedly Ileana had left long ago for the country— long ago, at least a week or even a month. It was unlikely she would have stayed in Bucharest until the end of August. . . .

Whenever he felt ridiculous he tried not to think of anything. Once again he shook the gloves and squeezing them into a bundle he stuffed them into the pocket of his coat. A hundred lei, he remembered. The driver said he had come back from the Bratianu Statue just to bring them. *"I think we're going to have a baby!"* Suddenly he quickened his pace. As he crossed *bulevardul* Dinicu Golescu he heard someone calling from behind and he turned his head in surprise. It was Biris.

"Where to, *Maestre?*" Biris asked, holding his coat slung over his shoulder with one finger stuck through the loop. It's going to break, thought Stefan. It can't possibly hold. . . . Biris had taken off his tie and opened the collar of his shirt. He was not very tall and still seemed young, although his hair was getting thin and he had a few wrinkles on his forehead. His eyes were without sparkle and lacking in expression.

"My dear *Maestre,*" he continued, lowering his voice. "What can I say—you've disappointed me. . . ." While Biris gesticulated the loop broke, as Stefan had foreseen, and the coat fell to the sidewalk. Both of them bent down to pick it up.

"But I think I've already explained to you that I'm not Ciru Partenie," said Stefan.

"I know, I know," Biris reassured him, patting him familiarly on the shoulder. "You're Viziru. I know you very well. But I like to talk with you like this on a different plane, an *impersonal* one, so to speak." He emphasized the word "impersonal." "On the plane of ideas, as you said very properly in your last article. . . ."

"But I just told you," Stefan interrupted, "that I'm *not* Partenie."

"What difference does that make?" Biris exclaimed, a little vexed. "Let's not confuse planes. You are, and you remain, Viziru. But when I'm discussing *ideas* with you, allow me to occupy the plane of ideas. Or haven't I expressed myself clearly enough?"

Stefan smiled acquiescently and shrugged his shoulders. Biris gave him a long look, then took his arm and urged him toward a bench.

"Wouldn't you like to sit here a minute? I've been walking an awfully long time today, and I feel rather tired."

They sat down together and Biris began to search methodically through all his pockets for his cigarettes. He selected one and slowly passed his hand across his forehead.

"I think maybe I have a touch of sunstroke," he said somewhat hesitantly. "It was terribly hot today. . . ."

It was impossible for Stefan to understand why he hadn't thought again of telephoning Ileana. The last time was . . . *"I think we're going to have a baby!"* That day had been hot and oppressive too, and he had run straight for the shower.

Biris lit his cigarette, choked on the first puff and began to cough, spitting into his handkerchief. "But actually, don't think for a single moment that I confused you with Ciru Partenie. No, God forbid! It's just that I like to speak *directly* with a man when I discuss his ideas. For instance, in your case, when I saw you, I remembered Partenie's article—very intelligent, very amusing, but it didn't come to any conclusions. As I told you before, that man's in a hurry. He seems to be afraid he won't have time enough to say what he has to say."

Biris had told him this in the Bucegi at Cheile Tatarului.* The sun set very late on the rock where they rested. "Partenie wants to live and to write at the same time," Biris had said then. "But this isn't possible. Writing grips you from within, it prohibits you from living. Not every

*The Pier of Tartarus.

27

kind of work seizes you inwardly. If you load coal on a freight car or sign administrative papers your mind can pursue its own course. Your inner time, the only time that counts, belongs to you. You can dream while you work, or reminisce or meditate. Only work performed in the fulfillment of a vocation—especially writing, because its process is the most complex—only this work possesses you completely. Only the act of creation demands of you this sacrifice. . . ." He had paused, then added, "I have to go. The sun sets here too."

"He starts from an interesting observation," Biris went on in a subdued tone, "that there are people who behave all their lives like an organ—like a liver, for instance, or a kidney, or a stomach, an organ of sex, or a brain. What a marvelous insight!" he exclaimed, turning suddenly to Stefan. "One could establish a science of character, or even an anthropology, on his premise. Take for instance a man who behaves like a stomach, who relates himself to the world and to history from the stomach's perspective. We might be tempted to confuse him at first with a man who likes to eat and digest, but this would be a mistake. His very existence being identified with the behavior of a stomach—he might or he might not have the passion for alimentation. But in any case his historical existence will be reduced to the act of digesting *his own universe*. This man will behave with respect to the universe like a stomach. He will try to digest it, to select the fat and the nutritive materials, to measure out the juices he needs, to eliminate the toxins, etc. Now the kidney-man's behavior would be entirely different. He'd filter the universe. His life would be reduced only to this function of separating the liquids, of filtering them. . . ."

A tram approached noisily. Biris stopped abruptly and turned again to look at Stefan, who had just managed to slip his hand into his coat pocket and touch the gloves. Surprised, Stefan nodded.

They couldn't be hers. He didn't recall having seen her a single time with gloves. Tossing her head, she walked boyishly with her hands clasped behind her back. Of course she might inform the police, but all their investigations would be in vain. It was not a case of a theft, a stolen car. It was quite different. Something else had happened. . . .

"What I reproach you for, dear *Maestre*," resumed Biris after the tram had gone by, "is that you have not examined this intuition thoroughly. You could survey the history of the world in the light of this science of character based on physiological structures. You could find nations and states that have behaved like brains or livers or especially like large intestines. And finally those nations and states *perished*."

He stressed that last word with such force that Stefan felt a sudden surge

28

of excitement. "Why did they perish?" he asked. "Why do you say that they perished?"

Biris stared at Stefan. Taking the butt of his cigarette between two finger-tips he flipped it with a jerk of his forefinger far out into the middle of the street. "They perished," he began again, "because the *history* that these na-tions and these states made was in a certain sense a dictatorship of a single organ, a spleen for example, or an intestine. I even wonder if history doesn't seem so absurd just because of these monstrous confiscations on behalf of *a single manner* of seeing the world, a *single* behavior that is necessarily limited and therefore false. . . ."

Stefan observed again that Biris was fond of emphasizing certain words, sometimes without even changing his voice. He would simply raise his eye-brows suddenly or perhaps lower his eyelids and squint.

"You might have called the article 'Universal History, or the Deplorable Dictatorship of the Organs,'" Biris went on after a short pause. "But history doesn't interest you, dear *Maestre.* You are only concerned with psychology. The individual preoccupies you exclusively. . . ."

"It's too bad you don't know him," Stefan said. "Partenie, I mean. You ought to meet him."

Biris began to search for his package of cigarettes. "I know he doesn't like pedants," he said without looking at Stefan. "He especially doesn't like phi-losophy teachers. Partenie seeks 'experiences'—always with beautiful women, in *cofetarii** and deluxe restaurants. But I'll look for him some day. I'll step up to him and come straight to the point. 'Listen, *Maestre,*' I'll say, 'wouldn't you like to have a little talk? But not here. Come to *strada* Macelari.'" Turning to Stefan he explained in a quieter tone, "I live at number 10, *strada* Macelari."

"I know. You told me once when you confused me with Partenie. No, no, I wasn't angry," Stefan added quickly. "But you ought to say it to him too, to Partenie. You'll have to meet him."

"I'll tell him a lot of things," continued Biris. "I'll run into him one of these days and I'll tell him."

"I live at number 10, *strada* Macelari. . . ." After he had visited Biris, Stefan recalled the invitation. He had been somewhat disappointed, almost irritated. Biris had given him his address again, about ten days following their en-counter on the bench, when they met by chance in front of the bookstore *Cartea Romaneasca.*† "I invite you to come and talk with me at my place on

*Pastry shops.
†The Romanian Book.

strada Macelari." But when Biris opened the door and saw Stefan he seemed surprised, as if he were not expecting him. He was in his undershirt, still sleepy and unshaven. With difficulty he suppressed a yawn.

"I hope I'm not disturbing you," Stefan said.

"I was expecting you," answered Biris without enthusiasm. "And we'll go directly to the heart of the matter. This is the custom of the house, to go directly to the heart of the matter."

It was a small, old-fashioned room and sad, almost wretched. Here and there the wallpaper had peeled off and cheap colored reproductions of famous paintings had been stuck on the bare walls. Some had already become yellowed and the edges had curled up.

"What are we supposed to talk about?" Biris had asked. "Ah, yes, I remember. . . ." He had begun to speak about Partenie's article. I don't believe we can be friends, Stefan realized as he listened to him. We're both too old. I'd hoped for a moment we could be friends. . . .

"I have the impression that I'm rather boring you," he heard Biris say all at once, and he felt the other's gaze riveted upon him. Biris had stopped speaking for a moment in order to open a package of cigarettes and light one.

"No, what you're saying is very interesting, but I happened to think of something else. I thought . . ."

"If it was interesting how is it that you thought of something else?" Biris broke in.

"I was thinking that all you're telling me would have been fascinating to Ionel Paraschivescu. We were friends once. I knew him in the primary school."

Biris looked at Stefan a long time quizzically. "You're a strange man," he said.

Just then they heard someone kick the door repeatedly and Biris jumped up to open it. There in the entrance stood an old woman, poorly clad, with a kitchen apron over her faded calico dress and worn woolen slippers on her feet. She had brought a tray of sweets and coffee.

"Allow me to present you to my aunt, *doamna* Porumbache," said Biris solemnly, taking the tray.

Stefan went to her and kissed her hand politely.

"Thank you," said the old lady. She went to the table, walking with tiny steps, and sat down on a chair. Looking at Stefan with considerable curiosity she asked, "What have you been talking about?" Both of the young men had fallen silent.

"We were talking about our affairs," Biris said in a matter-of-fact tone. He lifted up his cup of coffee without saying anything more. Stefan fixed his eyes on a yellowed photograph in a burntwood frame. It showed a young woman seated by a window.

30

"It's my sister, Aneta, Petrica's* mother," said *doamna* Porumbache, following his gaze. "She wasted away with tuberculosis in her youth, poor thing! She'd been to a boarding school, too, at Notre Dame. She even played the piano! But what was the use of it? She never got a chance to enjoy her life! What agony she suffered bringing Petrica into the world! What a hard time of it she had, poor thing! Those days when Petrica was born—they ate her up! After that she never was right! And how she loved him! As she was wasting away she kept saying to me, 'Have you seen, little sister, that I've given you a son?' She knew, poor thing, how much I'd longed for a son too! But it wasn't God's will. . . ."

She kept talking like that a long while, drinking her coffee slowly and smoking three of Biris's cigarettes. He listened to her with unusual interest, as though he were hearing all those familiar details now for the first time. Sometimes he interrupted her in order to add a short explanation for Stefan's benefit. But after *doamna* Porumbache had taken the tray and left the room, he exlaimed in a low confidential tone, "What a gem of a woman! You'll see when you get to know her better." Then he turned abruptly to Stefan and asked, "What did you say is the name of your friend, the one from the primary school?"

"Ionel Paraschivescu. But he died about five years ago. He was drowned at Snagov. His boat overturned and he got entangled in the weeds."

"I remember now," Biris interrupted. "I read it in the papers. I think his sister was also in the boat and she was drowned as well."

"I was with them, too," said Stefan. "It was an absurd accident." So this was why he was on edge. He had mentioned Ionel and Mia. "You see, it was like this . . ." he said, and he began to tell the story. That was what always happened. He told strangers about the most private things, the most intimate matters. He had never told Ioana, never admitted to her how afraid he was when he felt the grass clutch at his legs, how he wanted to call for help and found it impossible. His neck felt constricted, strangled. "You see, it was like this . . ." He had not told Ioana that the last time he saw Mia she was trying to lift her head, but her face had gone under the water so quickly. She seemed to be choking. Once her hands emerged from the surface of the lake groping for something, twisting with unnatural, spasmodic movements. All her fingers seemed to be out of joint. "You see, it was like this . . ." And he told Biris how they searched that night by the light of torches until they found them quite near the shore, and they dragged the bodies out of the weeds with hooks fastened to the ends of poles. . . .

He was startled to feel someone grasp his arm. It was *doamna* Porumbache. "Listen, *maica*,† don't you have a cigarette?"

*Diminutive of Petre (Biris).
†A term of endearment.

31

"I've given up smoking," said Stefan, embarrassed.

"There's a tobacco shop close by. . . . Give me something for a pack."

Stefan pulled out his wallet diffidently, then feeling ashamed he offered to go to the tobacconist's for her.

The old woman held him back. "Never mind, don't bother. I'll go later and buy some." Her eyes sparkled as she took the hundred lei and hid the bill in her apron pocket. She sighed deeply. "But what do you say about my nephew's fine position? I raised him well with my poor little work, and see how he turns out—a pauper! Are you a teacher too?"

"No, I work for the government," Stefan answered, looking down.

"But I see you are well-dressed," said the woman, examining him from head to foot. "Have you done some politicking? Do you get a big salary?"

"I have enough." Stefan's embarrassment was increasing.

"Why don't you get my nephew into politics? I've tried to pound it into his head, but does he listen to me? I've lived a while and seen a few things! My dear departed husband, God have mercy on him, was in politics on the side of the Takists. Who didn't come to our home in those days! We had those big houses on *calea* Mosilor, but we lost them later because we had a no-good, thieving lawyer. He had an understanding with the others and in the court-room he was silent as a fish. A certain Dumitrescu—Mitache, we called him. Maybe you've heard of him?"

"No."

"A no-good, a thief, and a drunk besides! What we've suffered on account of him! All my hope, after my husband died, was in Petrica. And look what he's come to! A teacher, starving to death. And when he gets a penny extra he buys books! What'll he do with them? And with these new laws we stay poor all the time! If only you'd known me before the war! Hei, hei! . . . Who else was like me in Ferendari? I was beautiful and everyone turned around to look when I passed by. And what luxury! I had a cabriolet with a gray horse. I even drove it myself. Everyone called me the Princess. When I came from Sosea,* nothing but sighs all around me! And how many hearts I broke! Alas! And what have I come to? Everything's gone! It's as though it had never been. . . ."

She sighed, paused, then added in a different tone, "But I don't want to keep you. You may be in a hurry. . . . Thanks, *maica*, thanks for the cigarettes!"

*A fashionable section of Bucharest.

32

2

SPIRIDON VADASTRA JUMPED OUT OF BED AND HURRIED TO THE MIRROR ON THE wall. He began to inspect himself, probingly, soberly. As usual his one good eye burned darkly while the other displayed only a moist, red, collapsed eyelid. Every evening he removed the glass eye for the night, restoring it to its socket with meticulous care only after he had washed and shaved in the morning. When he finally set the smoked-glass monocle in place his appearance changed dramatically.

"Today I move to a new house!" he exclaimed aloud to the image in the mirror. He dressed in haste but with some difficulty because the room was in great disorder. An overcoat lay on the sofa, together with a mackintosh, a rain cape, and two summer suits. Beside them on the floor two cheap suitcases, almost new, were lying open, revealing the piles of shirts and underwear within. There was a trunk too in which he had placed shoes, boots, books, and various miscellaneous items. And still everything had not yet been packed.

"Thank God!" he exclaimed when he had finished dressing. "Most of it's done. There's not much left!"

He approached the mirror again and deftly replaced his glass eye. Then he began to pick up the things that were scattered about, trying to squeeze them into the trunk. He was attempting to close the lid when the porter entered. It was obvious that he brought unpleasant news: he went to Spiridon and whispered in his ear, "The old man has come!"

Spiridon raised his hands in a gesture of exasperation and weariness. "Did you tell him I was in?" he asked.

"He knows. He says he knows too that you're going to move today."

A man entered the room then with a heavy, unsteady tread. He was rather elderly and dressed somewhat like a peasant in a tunic closed at the neck, a type of garment worn by village schoolteachers. On the back of his head rested a large round hat.

"What do you want, Father?" Spiridon asked, going up to the old man. "When did you come?"

His father did not answer. He only stared at Spiridon, shaking his head and frowning. "Where's your glass?" he asked presently in a hoarse voice. "The glass . . . your monocle, or whatever you call it?"

Spiridon began to laugh, but he was visibly embarrassed. "Better sit down!" he said indicating a chair. "Sit down. I can see that you're tired! Please excuse me for rushing. I have to pack these things." He indicated with a wave of his hand the trunk, the boxes, the desk. However, the old man did not sit but continued to stare at his son, remaining on his feet with difficulty, pretending to be perplexed.

"When did you come?" asked Spiridon again, paying no attention to his father's gaze as it followed him about the room. "On which train?"

"What do you care?" the old man responded. "What difference does it make which train I came on? The fact is I came to see how you are. . . . To see how things are going with you," he added as if to himself, with a crafty smile.

"Very well, thank God."

"*Bravo!*" exclaimed the old man thickly. "I can say I'm glad that things are going well for you. And things are going well for me, too," he lowered his voice and smiled, "better knock on wood. . . . But with politics, how do we stand? Did you or did you not become a deputy?"

Spiridon passed in front of him quickly with several books in his hand, his attitude solemn and preoccupied. "What is it anyway to be a deputy? Any idiot can be a deputy. . . ."

"*Ei,* but if you just didn't want to change the world," reflected his father. "It's a question of first becoming . . ."

"I've more important things to do," Spiridon replied, a little irritated. "You'll see, later on—" He stopped abruptly when he noticed that Arethia had entered the room unexpectedly. Searching nervously for his monocle in the upper pocket of his coat, he approached her with a confident stride and asked very coldly, "Do you want something, miss?"

"I came to see if you'd moved," Arethia said. "I see that you still have . . ." She seemed to be even thinner and aged before her time with her cold spiteful expression. Surprised, she stared at Spiridon's father. The old man smoothed his tunic, bowing politely before her.

"Pardon me, I'm Gheorghe Vasile, teacher, and father of the gentleman. An apostle, you might say—one of the apostles. I carry the light to the village."

Arethia turned to Spiridon, who pretended to be occupied with previous business.

"And we give the country its great men," the teacher continued. "This is our vocation: to raise our nation's great men. The gentleman whom you see here, my son, will be a deputy tomorrow or the day after. And who raised him? I ask you, who could raise him? He grew up almost at the center of the light . . ."

"Father, will you please shut up!" interrupted Spiridon sharply. Perhaps *domnisoara* Florian is in a hurry and isn't interested in such matters."

"On the contrary I'm very much interested," retorted Arethia. "I didn't know your father was a teacher."

"An apostle, lady, an apostle!" the old man said with an ironic smile and a meaningful wink. "The gentleman my son has not perhaps had an occasion to speak to you about me. But I too, in my own way, am somebody. I, my dear lady, knew Haret, the great man Spiru Haret. You must have heard of him. And in his honor I christened the gentleman, my son, Spiru Gheorghe Vasile. Not Spiridon, as he called himself later, but Spiru, in honor of the great Spiru Haret. . . . And not Vadastra. He also added that name himself. My name is Vasile. We don't have any Vadastras in our family, neither I nor his mother, who was the daughter of the priest Florea, of Dobresti . . ."

"Now why have you started talking about these things that don't interest anyone?" Spiridon interposed again, quite obviously annoyed.

"How can they be of no interest to anyone?" barked the old man. "Just what is it that is of no interest to anyone? Your being my son? That, I'm sure, interests *me!* But who will know later on that Vasilescu-Vadastra is the son of Gheorghe Vasile, the teacher from Dobresti?"

"My father regrets that I didn't add to mine the name of the town where he has been a teacher," Spiridon said to the girl with a smile. "As you can see, it's purely a family affair."

"So-o-o," said the old man, blinking his eyes at Arethia. "It has always pleased me to speak of family affairs. I like them. Maybe he's ashamed of me. Who knows? Maybe he's ashamed that I'm only a modest teacher in Dobresti, and have been for the past fifty-three years."

"Father, I asked you to shut up!" said Spiridon in exasperation. "Why do you want to make a scene in front of *domnisoara* Florian, a stranger?"

"Perhaps the lady isn't paying attention to me," the old man mumbled to himself. "She doesn't see that I'm a little tipsy! For the past fifty-three years . . . I who knew Spiru Haret am now, I can say, a man on the outside of society. . . . But why, pray?"

"I'd better go get a cab," Spiridon said suddenly.

"What do you want a cab for?" asked his father, surprised.

"To take these packages with me. I'm moving. Can't you see that I'm moving? And *domnisoara* Florian is burning with impatience to see me leave. Not that she has any more right than I to live in this hotel, but that's the way she is. She regrets that I have kept certain receipts."

"Oh, you're so sarcastic!" Arethia shrugged and left the room, slamming the door behind her.

Spiridon looked at his father, his face expressing a fury that he restrained with difficulty. The old man dropped into an armchair and began to scratch his head thoughtfully.

"You've made me appear ridiculous!" the young man hissed through his teeth. "What will everyone think about me? I've asked you I don't know how many times not to come here anymore. When you have something to say either write to me or make an appointment to meet me in town."

His father looked at him soberly with a bitter smile and sighed deeply. "I want to read a book," he said. "Maybe you have it. An astronomy book, *Wonders of the Heavens*, I think it's called."

"I don't have it but you'll find it at the bookstores," said Spiridon, pulling out his wallet. He selected from the bundle of bills three 100-lei notes and held them out hastily.

"Does it cost that much?" asked the old man.

"I don't know how much it costs, but this is enough money in any case."

"Good. I'll bring you the change."

"Forget the change," Spiridon interrupted. "Tell me, how much longer will you be staying in Bucharest?"

"About two days. I've come on business."

"That's good. Let me give you some money." Spiridon searched wearily again in his wallet. "But look, finish your business as quickly as possible."

"That depends!" remarked Vasile ironically. "It depends on the authorities. Good-bye! Good health!" He turned around in the doorway and inquired, happy to have remembered it in time, "I forgot to ask. Where are you moving?"

"For the present to *calea* Victoriei 119. With a friend," Spiridon lied. "But I don't know how long I'll be staying there. If you need something write me at the same address as before."

One evening during the Christmas season Stefan heard strange voices in Spiridon's room. He listened alertly for a few moments but failed to recognize any of them. An obscure feeling of sadness filled his heart when he left later that night, and on returning to the hotel the following morning, the first thing he did was to knock at Daniil's door. They were only slightly acquainted, but Stefan knew that Daniil was a man who liked to talk and would answer his questions about Spiridon.

"He moved," Daniil said, inviting Stefan to come in. "He moved downtown. He has an apartment there and he's put up a nameplate on his door because he's a lawyer now. He showed me his visiting card too, but he didn't let me keep it because he said he didn't want his address to be discovered." Daniil chuckled quietly to himself and added a moment later, "He probably has his reasons."

Stefan found himself thinking, I'll have to move too. I'll have to find another hotel.

"Some young people have come here looking for him," continued Daniil. "But since he didn't leave an address they hadn't any way to find him."

Suddenly Stefan resolved to question Daniil further. "What do you think about *doamna* Zissu? What was that woman to him?"

Daniil's eyes gleamed for a moment. He took his tobacco pouch from his pocket and rolled a cigarette in eloquent silence. "That lady's a great mystery," he began, lowering his voice. "No one knows her, not even Voinea. Yet Vadastra talked about her constantly. And whenever anyone mentioned her name he'd fly into a rage. Once they quarreled over her. And because of her Vadastra didn't dare to bring charges against Voinea when he took the newspaper funds. It was enough for Voinea to say, 'Now the others will find out about you and *doamna* Zissu!' and Spiridon hushed right up. But what that affair might be I haven't been able to determine. This is a great mystery. . . ."

"This is a great mystery. . . ." Those are the words of St. Paul, Stefan suddenly remembered, and he was troubled. That's how he should have answered Ileana: "This is a great mystery. . . ." That was what he should have told her before he squeezed her hand and ran off again in the rain.

He had caught sight of her by chance from the window of the tram on a rainy afternoon toward the end of October. She was wearing a short waterproof coat gathered at the waist with a belt, and she had taken refuge under an immense black umbrella. Although the effect should have been ridiculous it only seemed slightly unconventional. Stefan got off at the next stop and turning up his collar on his rain cape he began to run with long strides along the boulevard, searching for her. The rain grew heavier. He was soaking wet when he reached Ileana as she stood in front of a jeweler's window. Without hesitation he stepped under the umbrella and took her arm. "I've been trying to find you for a long time," he said.

Ileana looked at him, feigning indifference.

"Wherever did you get this umbrella?"

"It's not mine. It belongs to *Tante* Alice. She got it at the Exposition. It was patented, and it's called '*Famille nombreuse.*' But we had to cut off part of the handle. It was much too long for just one person. . . ."

"I looked for you at home too," interrupted Stefan, "but no one was there. You'd gone to the estate in the country."

"When were you looking for me?"

"About two months ago. On an evening in August. The twentieth, to be exact."

"Please hold the umbrella for a moment," Ileana requested. She opened her handbag and took out a handkerchief. Smiling she stood on tiptoe and began to wipe the rain from Stefan's forehead, from his eyes and cheeks.

"Thanks," he said.

Ileana wrung out the handkerchief, put it in the pocket of her raincoat, and took back the umbrella. "What was on August twentieth?" she asked. "Some anniversary?"

"No, nothing special," answered Stefan quickly. "Just a day like any other. But I always remember certain days. I have this mania of never forgetting the days when something happens to me, or when I meet someone, or . . . ."

"What day is this?" Ileana broke in. She spoke earnestly.

"October 27."

"Doesn't it have any significance?"

Stefan regarded her profoundly, his gaze laden with a naive seriousness.

"Don't the heavens open on this night? Couldn't an automobile disappear, supposing it had been left somewhere at a street corner?"

"That's just what I wanted to ask you about." Stefan's face brightened. "I wanted to ask you then, on the twentieth of August when I was looking for you, what did you do with the keys to your suitcases? Don't you remember? . . . ."

"I know. That key ring that you kept. . . . ."

"That I would have kept," Stefan corrected. "I could have kept it. . . . ."

"It's virtually the same thing. As I told you . . . ."

"And there was something else, too," Stefan broke in with a smile. "There was also the pair of gloves. The taxi driver brought them that very night. He said he came back from the Bratianu Statue to bring them to me. But in my secret room there are always moths and when I came back from the mountains the gloves were full of holes, even though I'd hidden them very well behind a shelf of books so no one would find them. And then I caught a cab—I was afraid that you were leaving at that very moment for the station—and I brought them to you. On August twentieth! Probably you'd gone to the country long before. . . . I don't have them anymore!" he exclaimed finally, exhausted.

"You went to all that trouble for nothing," Ileana asserted. "They weren't mine. I don't wear gloves."

38

"I was almost sure you didn't. I looked them over, I held them in my hands, and I didn't feel you any nearer. . . ."

"But don't you think this has some significance?" Ileana demanded suddenly. "It must have! As I told Partenie. . ." The look of astonishment on Stefan's face was unmistakable, but she continued as though she had noticed nothing. "As I told him, really you have a creative imagination. Partenie is just an observer of people. He doesn't have your imagination. It's quite obvious that he doesn't believe in myths."

It began to pour again, and a cold sullen wind started to blow, carrying with it a hint of winter. Ileana brought the umbrella closer over their heads and they moved gradually nearer to the window of the jewelry store.

"He kept asking me if I knew you very well, if you're really the bizarre fellow that people say you are. 'Bizarre, no,' I answered, 'but he has imagination. For instance, be sure not to be with him on the Night of St. John, because if you have a car then, it will disappear—and if you don't he'll tell you what might have happened if you had!' "

Stefan seemed to awaken then from a long reverie. He took her head between his hands and kissed her hungrily on the mouth. Ileana tried to pull away but she only managed to bring the umbrella down still farther over them. It seemed to her that some stranger was kissing her in a dream dreamed long ago of which she could remember nothing except this sudden embrace, unreal, menacing. Finally she felt that she was suffocating and gave a low moan, struggling to free herself. Stefan relaxed his grasp and let her go, supporting her for a moment with a timid, embarrassed gesture. He tried to lift the umbrella. Breathless, Ileana ran her hand through her hair, then rested it against her forehead and looked down at the pavement without speaking.

"I'm very glad we met today," Stefan murmured, drawing nearer. "I'll come to visit you some evening." Quickly he sought her hand and held it tightly, prolonging the moment of contact. Then without looking at her again, he stepped from under the umbrella and ran off through the rain. . . .

"But I should have said to her, 'This is a great mystery!' " he repeated over and over to himself as he watched Daniil smoking. "That's what I ought to have told her. . . ."

Ileana had not met Partenie, as Stefan had surmised when she was talking to him. During the summer she had read several of the writer's books, and on returning to Bucharest she had tried to make his acquaintance. She had decided·impulsively one morning to call him on the telephone. But Partenie was not at home.

"Who is calling?" a woman's voice queried. To Ileana she sounded somewhat harsh.

"An admirer."

"Try another time. . . ."

He's well protected, Ileana said to herself as she replaced the receiver, although later she recalled that the author was not married, that he was not even known to have a mistress. On the contrary she had found out that he was almost always seen with a different woman. "He's looking for the ideal partner," someone had told her once with a smile full of implications. That was at the Stavropoulos' estate. "We ought to pay them a visit," *Tante* Alice had proposed. "Their nephew's there, the magistrate, the one who took his doctorate in Paris."

"He's looking for his ideal partner, if you know what I mean," the magistrate repeated, continuing to smile.

Who's this Partenie that everyone talks about?" *Tante* Alice had asked as they were returning home in the car.

"A Don Juan," Ileana had said thoughtfully. "I should like terribly to meet him!"

"*Mais tu es folle!*" *Tante* Alice had exclaimed, exactly as she had on the morning Ileana had told her that she had telephoned him and that a woman had answered. "Probably his mistress," Ileana had said. "I wonder how many days he'll keep her? If he gives her up before Christmas, I'll offer myself in her place and I'll take him with me when I go skiing. I'd like to have a famous man for a lover. I'd show him off to everybody, but I'd keep him on a chain all the time!"

"*Mais tu es folle!*" *Tante* Alice had exclaimed.

"Not on a chain," Ileana went on thoughtfully. "I'll have to find something else. But anyway I'll tie him up and lock him with a padlock, no matter how small, and when I go away from home I'll take the little key with me—a tiny key, quite small, that I'd carry with me all the time." She began to laugh suddenly because she knew very well that although she spoke about Partenie, she was thinking of Stefan. Even so, I don't think I've lost my head entirely. I don't love him. Perhaps it would be amusing to love a man at first sight; a veritable *coup de foudre*. . . . But I don't love him. He really is bizarre, not at all my type. He's a dreamer. . . .

And yet sometimes on that evening at Baneasa she had felt tremendously disturbed. She was ready to believe that all those things he told her could have happened. Like the time at Lausanne when the girls had a séance at examination time and had invited her to attend. In a way, she had gone as a joke. It was hard for her to believe that the dead would approach their table and talk to them. Yet in the depths of her soul she was hoping against hope for just such a thing to happen. When she had rested her finger on the glass she had thought, Now *duduca* Ralu* will come. . . . But instead they had been visited by a teacher, a woman who had died that winter. The glass had dictated several complicated sentences, hesitating briefly from time to time. The visitant told them to wish with all their power for the good of humanity. Ileana had been sure that one of her classmates, probably the Valkyrie, had been moving the glass all the time, but she was sorry it had turned out that way. She wished that it really had been moved by a dead person, even if such a thing did seem impossible.

In the same way, as she listened to Stefan she wanted to believe the heavens could open in the middle of the night. Stefan was a strange man. He had a virile handsomeness that was also tender and childlike. It troubled her. She couldn't explain very well what it was that attracted her to him. Was it perhaps his complete lack of vulgarity, his somewhat mysterious alien nature? There were times when he looked at her intently and smiled as though he read who knows what thoughts hidden behind her brow—thoughts of which she herself was not aware. She felt drawn to him too when he was preoccupied and silent, betraying an incomprehensible sadness. Stefan was different from all the men she had known. She couldn't predict what he would say from one moment to the next. Sometimes he would interrupt her with an absurd question, as he had done once when they were coming out of the restaurant. She was telling him about the estate at Zinca and he broke in with a self-conscious smile, "Do you have an old deep cellar at Zinca?"

All these things—and many more—flashed through her mind in a pre-posterous jumble at the moment when Stefan had squeezed her hand quickly and abandoned her there under the umbrella, running away like a blockhead through the rain. It was only later, when he was out of sight, that she remembered the remark he had made in the restaurant. She blushed. He imagines he has only to kiss me and exactly the *same thing* will happen again. I'll lose my head over him. He fancies he's irresistible, that it's enough for him just to kiss a woman and she'll never be able to forget him!

She understood then, too, why he hadn't looked for her anymore, why she had seen no sign of him all summer. Perhaps he expects me to look for him! He appears now and then on the street and says a few words. He asks you about the cellar at Zinca and then he vanishes. "We'll meet again. . . . I'll come by to see you some evening. . . . How could you lock the suitcases? Those keys were with me. That ring of keys you showed me, I mean. I kept it."

"Look where you're going!" a matronly woman shouted at her.

"Pardon me!" Ileana said with a timid smile. The rain had almost

---

*Mistress Ralu, youngest daughter of Ioan Gheorge Caragea, founder of the Romanian theater. The daughter died at age six in 1818.

41

stopped. It was now a fine drizzle and the *Famille nombreuse* umbrella seemed to her suddenly absurd, provocative. She stood in the middle of the sidewalk for some time, undecided, but finally she shrugged her shoulders and went on her way, leaving the umbrella open.

It had begun to snow and Ioana felt afraid no longer. Gradually a great peace surrounded her completely. The fir tree laden with snow, which she could easily see without raising her head from the pillow, seemed suddenly familiar. It was the same fir that she had known in the garden of her childhood.

"How much I love you just the way you are!" Stefan had whispered to her on that evening when he had returned home unexpectedly, surprising her without powder and paint. "You're so ugly! Uglier than I ever thought a woman as beautiful as you could become!"

This was before Christmas and she was in the seventh month of her pregnancy. Sometimes Ioana found herself looking fearfully in the mirror. Her cheeks were covered with big faded red blotches and her lips felt pale and dry. "You're very ugly," Stefan went on, lifting her hand and giving it a long kiss. "And yet you've never been dearer to me than now! Now you're mine alone. Now I'm not afraid of anyone. . . ."

He's always thinking about *him.* She had realized however for a long time that the two men were not in the least alike. They couldn't be confused except from a distance and only by someone who knew neither of them very well—as she had not known Ciru at first. She had seen him perhaps ten or a dozen times, but she knew him better from the photographs. When she had attended the "Book Day" with a stack of books for him to sign she had brought a photograph too. "I don't autograph these things," said Partenie, throwing the picture aside indifferently. Then without raising his head he had asked, "*Doamna* or *domnisoara?*"

"*Domnisoara.*"

That was how she met him. He was not as good-looking as his photographs. He seemed more surly, more gloomy. And he lost patience very quickly. "Don't you want to discuss something besides literature?" he had interrupted her at the beginning of their first date. "I write enough literature, and what I write is infinitely better than what you read." And at their next meeting, when Ioana had mentioned the name of a great contemporary writer, he had silenced her with "He doesn't exist! I'm very sorry to shatter another illusion but this gentleman doesn't exist." "But we studied him in school," Ioana had said timidly.

"So much the worse for you! The only Romanian writer at the moment, unfortunately, is myself. I say unfortunately because I'm second-rate— third-rate even. Next to Aeschylus, Shakespeare, Dante, I don't exist. So how can you expect your idol to exist?"

"My literary idol is you," Ioana had said with effort. "I've read everything you've written. I've kept all your articles, everything the critics have written about you . . ."He regarded her with amusement. "Then you're probably in love with me," he said. "Yes," Ioana whispered. "I've loved you since the fourth class of the *liceu** when I read *The Girlhood of Melania.*"

How did I dare? she had wondered time and again since then. I loved Gary Cooper more. Partenie I only admired, as I admire him now. I couldn't confuse him with Stefan. She had thrown her arms around Stefan—believing that he was Partenie—because he smiled at her from a distance, as Ciru had never smiled before. Suddenly she had seen how handsome he was when he smiled and she had wanted to show him how much she liked him that way—as of course Partenie never could be. "Pardon me!" she had murmured, embarrassed. "What should I say?" Stefan had asked her. "Please forgive me," she had stammered. "I confused you. . . . You look like someone else . . ." "Well," he had interrupted, "but what should I say? I ought to say something, too, shouldn't I? What will you think of me? That I'm an imbecile? That I'm incapable of making a single intelligent reply? You can't leave me like that! We'll have to find an answer!"

"Of course I love you too," Ciru had told her. "But how meaning-ful can a love be? How durable is it? Nothing in this world lasts. Everything comes to an end, everything is transformed, everything dies in order to be born again in another way, another place, with other people. . . . But why are you sad? Did you perhaps expect me to speak to you of eternal love? I'm not a poet. Unfortunately, I'm nothing but a novelist and a dramatist. I've specialized in this commonplace and remarkable subject: ordinary man. Man with a small *m*. Don't ever let me hear you speaking in capitals, don't write or utter the word *man* with a capital *m.* . . ."

"Each of the Fates will urge upon him the same capital letter," Stefan had said yesterday on the way to the clinic. Holding both of her hands in his he had talked to her all the time in the car, his voice full of mystery and enchantment.

"If it's a girl we'll call her Regina," he said. "It's not absolutely necessary for her to have a throne of her own, to be part of a dynasty, I mean. But she'll be queen of something that hasn't existed before—queen of difficult geomet-

*Equivalent to the eighth grade.

43

ric spaces, for instance. She'll move in a universe of her own, controlled by her, perhaps even founded by her. It will be a universe inaccessible to common mortals like us, and one in which revolutions are impossible except from top to bottom, starting from other still more difficult geometric spaces. If someone should overthrow her, it would have to be another queen or a king with a more audacious mind. . . . But if it's a boy he will be a Musician, a Mathematician, or a Metaphysician. Each of the Fates will urge upon him the same capital letter, an M. . . ." After a moment he had added with a hint of regret in his eyes, "If not, our son will be worldly minded. . . ."

Ioana's smile persisted. She was not at all afraid. The dream about Antim seemed like something dreamed in a long-distant past—Antim, who had come once more to the window of the train and rapped, raising himself on tiptoe as he had the first time, shouting, "He's had an accident . . . an accident! . . . But it wasn't your husband. I confused him with him. . . . I confused him, he confused him, we confused him. . . . We confused him, confused him . . ."

Stefan said to himself over and over, 17 February 1937, 17 February 1937, as if he were trying to discover what destiny was hidden in this date. He added up the numbers, he divided them arbitrarily, he considered carefully every combination. Then he recalled suddenly that he and Ioana had not yet agreed upon the name, and he made an attempt to think of one, but a certain expression kept hampering him, coming into his mind automatically and repeatedly: a child of the masculine sex, a child of the masculine sex. . . . He would have to state this at the town hall and sign the paper. And again he felt his responsibility, but to whom? For what?

He was almost home. How much he would have liked to have been in a compartment with many other people, to have someone ask him—on finding out that he had been married for four years—Have you any children? Yes, he would answer, a boy. How old is he? Stefan would look carefully at his watch and answer, after a quick calculation, three hours and twenty-three minutes!

But he felt that he had made a mistake somewhere. As he climbed the stairs he computed it again and found that at that moment his son was three hours and thirty-eight minutes old.

The next day when he returned from the clinic he found Biris waiting for him on the stairs, smoking. "We haven't seen each other for a long time," the teacher observed. "I thought you were annoyed that evening on account of Bursuc. . . ."

Stefan had gone into the coffee shop only because he had caught sight of Biris through the window, and he thought that Biris had noticed him.

44

But Biris was listening to Bursuc and hadn't seen Stefan. The teacher promptly made a place for him at the table, presenting him vaguely to the group, *"Domnul** Viziru."* Then he turned back to the speaker, a fat man, rather young, with a shiny round face and thick, slack lips. His little eyes, deep-set, laughed at them from far back in his head. "Go on, Bursuc!" urged Biris. "Go on with what you were saying."

Stefan discovered that Bursuc had a degree in theology and was telling about his ordination. His family had found a wife for him in a village near his own, in the vicinity of Brasov.

"I gave it up," he said, resuming his story. "I don't like people who don't keep their word. We agreed that in addition to the girl's dowry they would buy me a motorcycle. Her father was against it at first. 'What will the faithful say when they see their priest on a motorcycle?' 'We're also modernizing ourselves, in the Holy Church,' I told him. 'We're motorizing ourselves!'" And with his eyes half-closed he burst out laughing—a short laugh, thick and coarse.

"And why shouldn't we modernize? You could serve the Church better with a motorcycle. A parishioner calls you at midnight to confess him and administer the last rites—with a motorcycle you could be there in an instant. You'd be sure to find him alive, with plenty of time to forgive him all his sins!" He laughed again.. Everyone listened to him in fascination. Other people at nearby tables were listening too.

"And on the last day, the day of the wedding, he told me that he hadn't bought the motorcycle, that he was ashamed, that he didn't have any money. That in seven surrounding towns he was known as a just and worthy man, full of the fear of God. . . . I didn't say anything. And that evening when the bride was waiting for me at home, I was tending to my own sweet affairs! I shaved my beard, changed my clothes, and left. After that I don't know what they decided to do. . . . I didn't send a man to take my place!"

"I wasn't annoyed," Stefan said, leading Biris into his study, "but I was in something of a hurry. And I wonder now what you found out about Bursuc. All I know is that for a long time he's been considered both a genius and a devil. I've even heard about him at the Ministry."

Biris stopped for a moment in front of the bookshelves, then went on to the window and looked out at the roofs of the houses. Here and there in the distance he caught a glimpse of church towers. "This story of Bursuc," he began quietly, returning to the middle of the room, "is a long tale. We'll talk about it another time. Meanwhile, I'm glad you weren't angry. I didn't see a sign of you, you didn't walk down *strada* Macelari anymore, and I wondered what had happened to you, if perhaps you might have been angry."

* Mister.

He stopped suddenly. One of the two paintings hanging on the wall attracted him. It depicted a bouquet of wildflowers with a woman's long black glove lying nearby. Without comment, Biris contemplated the picture for a long time.

Finally Stefan inquired, "But why should I have been angry?"

"I was afraid you were offended by his talk about motorizing the Church," said Biris, sitting down in an easy chair.

Musing, Stefan began to laugh. "I'm not an orthodox churchman. But even if I were, I shouldn't have felt offended by the adventures of a seminarian who let his beard grow for a parish and shaved it off for a motorcycle. One meets with this sort of aberration in all the religions of the world."

"Don't talk like that," Biris declared soberly. "This Bursuc is a much more profound person than you realize, much more satanic. You learn to be afraid of him. Now if I were devout—that is, a true Orthodox Christian—I should tremble at the thought that Bursuc *exists!*"

"But why?" questioned Stefan, leaning on the desk.

Biris hesitated, inspecting the top of his head with his fingers. He seemed perplexed. "It's a long story. But Bursuc has his star, he'll go a long way. . . ." Then with a sudden change of tone he added, "But anyway he's an interesting man. He's a failure and a one hundred percent nihilist. He's interesting— from a literary point of view, I mean. I'm even surprised our writers haven't already used him in a book. Partenie ought to know him. But of course Partenie doesn't meet interesting people. He's always looking for 'experiences.'"

"Listen," Stefan cut in, "I haven't given you the great news. I'm a father. I have a son. Since yesterday, I have a son. . . ."

"My congratulations," said Biris without very much enthusiasm. "My congratulations." He turned to look again at the painting hanging above the chair. "But don't tell my aunt," he added. "She thinks you're not married and she wants to find you a wife. . . . But it isn't important," he continued quickly, seeing Stefan start to interrupt him, "it's not important that you have a wife and child. It gives her so much pleasure to match you up with a girl. She's been making matches for me for several years. This is her great joy, so why should I spoil it for her?"

Stefan smiled and said, suddenly cheerful, "And I still don't know what name to give him!"

His face expressionless, Biris stared at Stefan. He looked for his package of cigarettes and holding it up he called it to Stefan's attention. "This is your pack. She sent me to buy it and she said to me from the doorway 'And maybe you'll go to see how *domnul* Viziru is.' She's awfully good-hearted." His tone changed. "She's never forgotten that last summer you gave her some money to buy a pack of cigarettes."

• • •

Vadastra kept his secret well. His father was not able to discover the new location. He and Lieutenant Baleanu had rented the apartment of a diplomat who had gone abroad. Baleanu was a tall broad-shouldered man with a relatively slender neck, and the expression in his eyes was one of childlike happiness. In the evening he rarely remained at home. "A family has invited me for dinner," he would say.

These absences had begun to intrigue Vadastra. They seemed mysterious to him. Once when he was bored of staying alone he had taken the opportunity to search Baleanu's room thoroughly. He leafed carefully through every book, expecting to run across a sensational letter, but he found nothing. The desk drawers were all locked, but he began to pull open the drawers of the wardrobe, examining the underclothing with great care; and then he inspected the *eau de cologne,* the handkerchiefs, and finally the uniforms. Selecting the most elegant one he lifted it out. When he was a child military costumes had filled his dreams, and they still held a powerful attraction for him. He regarded the garment with great excitement. The one thing that even his most audacious imaginings could not give him was the rank of a military officer. Eventually he was no longer able to suppress his impulse and almost trembling he took off his coat, replacing it with the lieutenant's tunic. Then he approached the mirror and gazed at himself avidly. The tunic was very nearly his size. The broad shoulders would have made him look like a giant of a man had they not dropped a little, giving him instead the appearance of a poorly dressed mannequin. But Spiridon did not tire of admiring himself. He stepped backward and forward in front of the mirror, his neck stiff, martial. He observed his face in full and then in profile, with and without the monocle. In this uniform with its enormous shoulders cut on such masculine lines he found the man he had always pictured himself to be. Now he beheld in flesh and blood the figure that he had formerly seen only in his fancy. His mustache, clipped short, and the black monocle added a piquant, impertinent touch to the tremendous military figure. A moment later he took off the tunic sadly, but his heart was filled with a secret joy.

The next day he was startled when Baleanu came to see him. Maybe he noticed something, he said to himself. Indeed the lieutenant's face held a curious expression. He seemed to be endeavoring to hide his nervousness under a smile somewhat more insistent than usual.

"You know," he began, after making excuses for disturbing Vadastra, "I want to tell you a secret. . . ."

Spiridon's one eye brightened instantly. While Baleanu paused, awaiting encouragement, the other pulled up a chair and motioned briefly for him to sit down. "Now, tell me. . . ."

"You see, I'm studying German," confided Baleanu.

For a moment Spiridon thought that his companion was joking, but the lieutenant resumed in all seriousness, "I've been thinking of spending a year or two at a German school and it would be well to learn German now. But it's a very difficult language. So many declensions!" he exclaimed in fear and admiration.

Spiridon felt overwhelmed with pity for this handsome officer who considered the learning of a modern European language a fact that deserved to be held in the greatest respect and confidence. "And after you've finished the school in Germany what will you do?" Vadastra's voice was sarcastic.

"What do you mean, what will I do? I'll be a captain then. . . ."

"And after that?'" insisted Spiridon relentlessly.

"What do you mean?"

"What will you do after you become a captain?"

"Why, what all soldiers do. . . ."

"Please, where does all this lead? Ultimately, what will you be?" Spiridon had become agitated. "The road that you follow should have a goal. Well then, I'm asking you, what *is* this final goal to which you aspire? If everything turns out to be eminently successful, as I wish it to turn out for you, what will you have accomplished?"

"I'll be a general," replied Baleanu soberly, somewhat offended. "A general—division general, or perhaps even General of the Army."

"Would you say that you might even become Minister of War?"

"No, that's hard. You have to have connections."

"Please. Let's just suppose however that someday you will be Minister of War. So? What have you achieved by that? What does it mean to be Minister of War? First of all, Romania is a little country and our governments change often. . . ."

The lieutenant looked at him with considerably more attention than usual, closing his eyes a little in his effort to understand better, striving to guess the hidden significance of Spiridon's remarks from his gestures, from the way he stressed certain words. But when he heard him talking about the contingency and futility of the post of Minister of War he could not believe his ears. He no longer understood. "Well then, according to you, what should I do?" he inquired, not knowing what else to say.

"No, I'm not suggesting anything," declared Spiridon, his voice becoming more calm. "I don't say that this career you've chosen isn't a fine one. On the contrary, I admit that I also dreamed of being an officer, when I was a child. I'm not saying you've done badly in choosing this career. Only actually, what satisfaction can it give you? What does it mean to be a general? If you had the possibility of becoming a second Napoleon, then I would understand. By means of a career of arms you would capture for yourself a unique position in Europe, and after that you could do as you wish. I can understand this. But you see, it's hard for us to become something like that. We're a little country. . . ."

"I don't understand," Baleanu repeated, troubled.

"I mean that no matter how far you go, it doesn't amount to much.

48

Don't think that I mean to offend you. The majority of careers are like that. You have the impression they give you something, and on reflection you find they have nothing to offer. . . . Now when I was a boy in *liceu*," he went on in a different tone, smiling, "I dreamed of someday becoming the greatest Romanian pianist. The dream of a seventeen-year-old! When you consider it well, what satisfactions would I have received? Only work from morning till evening, and as a final reward nothing but intrigues and slanders."

"Then for you what career *is* worth embracing?" Baleanu asked. "What do you want to do with your life?"

With a smile Spiridon replied, "For the present this remains my secret. I can congratulate myself for discovering the way toward a goal that merits attainment. I admit it's not an easy thing. It's not for everyone."

"I know what you're referring to," ventured the lieutenant. "The legal profession. . . ."

Vadastra laughed. He smoothed his mustache with the index finger of his right hand. Even if only for a few seconds, it pleased him to prolong this pause, this moment of mystery and suspense.

"The legal profession is only an instrument," he declared slowly, deliberately. "An instrument, or to be more precise, one of the instruments for approaching the goal I have chosen. The legal profession in itself is no more interesting than any other career. Everything depends on what you do with it." Vadastra's tone became enigmatic and confidential. "*What you do with it. . . .*"

On a chilly evening early in March Ileana met Partenie. After many telephone calls she had succeeded in finding him at home and had invited him to tea at the Cofetarie Nestor. *Tante* Alice always invited her friends to the Cofetarie Nestor, especially foreign visitors, friends of her relatives, and friends of her friends. Now and then some stranger telephoned on behalf of *domnul* Economu of Jassy, or *doamna* and *domnul* Ifrim of Barlad, whom *Tante* Alice had met a year or two before on the Cote d'Azur or in Italy or in Switzerland. *Tante* Alice invited them that very day to take tea with her at the Cofetarie Nestor. Quite frequently her relatives stopped there. *Tante* Alice came by taxi, almost always alone. Either Ileana was out, or she found some excuse to stay at home. Her aunt looked for a table by the window and conferred with the proprietor. Assiduously they selected together the cakes and cookies for her guests, whom she then awaited, refreshing herself with her fan in summer, or incessantly arranging her fur coat in winter—putting it on, taking it off, putting it around her shoulders. Alone, she could never remain still. She had to do something with her hands. Soon the friends of her

49

Moldavian relatives appeared and *Tante* Alice immediately began to tell them about her travels in Italy if they were Italian, about Lausanne or St. Moritz if they were Swiss. In this way she held them with her chatter until late evening, tempting them with cakes and describing to them their own country.She cited the names of hotels and pensions, reproduced conversations she had heard on the train, recounted events that had been told to her thirty or forty years previously—especially the one about the adventure of taming tigers that Prince Moruzov had related to her in 1905.

When Ileana invited acquaintances to the Cofetarie Nestor, *Tante* Alice gave her without hesitation the several thousand lei that otherwise would have been refused her. One of Ileana's sources of income was her imaginary guests at the Cofetarie Nestor. In this way she accumulated money for short skiing escapades, telling her aunt on those occasions that she was invited to go to the mountains with friends, or that she didn't have to pay the train fare because she would go with them to Predeal by car. Actually she almost always went alone, third class, choosing cheap lodgings and economizing on her food and cigarettes. She would have liked to have been able to stay all winter at the ski resort, which was in fact what she boasted of to her friends: "As long as the snow stays on the mountains, I stay to ski. . . ." But she could never remain more than eight or nine days. And because she didn't like to live in Bucharest, she spent weeks and months at a time at the country estate at Zinca.

Ileana found a seat at a table in the back of the *cofetarie*. When she saw Partenie enter she started. She could have believed he was Stefan. She motioned to him with her hand and he came toward her briskly, but without haste. As soon as she observed him close at hand, however, she could see he did not resemble Stefan so much after all. Partenie's neck was somewhat shorter and thicker, his face more mature, more intent, his expression a curious blend of irony and resignation. He bowed and kissed her hand. After he was seated at the table he took a moment to glance around him.

During the winter at Zinca, Ileana had often pictured this meeting with Partenie. It was partly curiosity that made her want to know him, curiosity about an author whose books she had liked—although sometimes, she thought, he seems to want to prove how intelligent he is, how different from everybody else, and this gives me an antipathy toward him. But above all she wanted to revenge herself on Stefan. His behavior had begun to irritate and offend her.

He had come to see her once before Christmas when she was at home alone. "You know," he began, "I wanted to tell you something that evening when we met on the street, but I didn't dare. Now I have to tell you. I think I'm going to love you very much." His smile illuminated his entire face. "I think I already love you very much. . . . Don't laugh at me. I told you that I love my wife and that soon we're going to

50

have a baby. And even so, I feel I love you more and more. I wanted to tell you this so there would be no ambiguity between us. I'm in love with you, and sometimes I feel as though this love forbids me to live. I go around like a fool, talking to myself, talking in my mind with Vadastra. I'd like to tell this to Ioana, but I'm sure she wouldn't understand what's happening inside me. Neither do you understand, and I don't understand it very well myself. But this love could reveal something to me. Perhaps I met you and fell in love with you so you could teach me something. Teach me, then! Tell me why you've appeared on my path. We didn't meet by chance, just so I might flirt with you. I don't like to flirt. I've never deceived my wife. But when I met you I felt it was a sign. Then at that moment I saw . . ."

"I know, I know," Ileana interrupted him with a gesture of annoyance. "I know your story: the car, the keys, the hedgehog, the butterflies, the heavens—I know them, I know them. You don't need to repeat them again!"

She had felt overwhelmed with indignation and had been unable to control her impatience any longer. He speaks to me about flirting, he repeats that he has never deceived his wife. He thinks I'm waiting to flirt with him, that I'm even willing to go to bed with him, only he hasn't decided yet to honor me with this. He kissed me once on the street and now he imagines. . . .

Allowing him no time to respond she went on, "I know all these things, I know them. Only now there are two new matters you haven't told me about before. One, not so interesting: you seem to think you could be in love with me. Men have made declarations of this sort to me before and I've paid no attention to them. But you said something else." She smiled. "You mentioned a name . . ." "Vadastra," said Stefan. "Exactly. . . What about him?"

Stefan looked at her wistfully for a long time with a sorrowful smile, then, profoundly disturbed, he began, "I came to tell you a great secret. You mustn't think I'm joking. Don't think it's so easy knowing that you love two people, two women, with a love that's new, beyond measure." "Who's this Vadastra?" Ileana repeated, interrupting him. "Sometimes I talk with him. I don't know him and yet I feel drawn to him. Perhaps because he's concealing a mystery too. Perhaps because he was my neighbor for some time . . ." "But what sort of man is he?" Ileana insisted, lighting a cigarette. "Tell me about him. He interests me."

Stefan stared at her again with an intensity that frightened her. Suddenly he got up from his chair. "I'll tell you." His tone changed and he began to pace around the room. "Without his knowledge I was his confidant for almost a year. Now recently he is my confidant, still

51

without his knowledge. I talk with him in my mind when I'm walking alone on the street. . . ."

All at once as she was listening to him Ileana felt her heart begin to beat more rapidly. I'm crazy, she said to herself, blushing. I'm beginning to get it into my head that I love him. Tristan and Isolde! She was sorry she hadn't let him say more, hadn't let him tell her how he loved her and how much he loved her. Stefan was speaking about Vadastra as he walked anxiously around the room, but she was not listening to him. She did not even look at him. Her eyes were fixed on the window. She continued to smoke. He told me he's in love with me. He's absurd, grotesque, but he told me he's in love with me. Again that interminable kiss from which she had awakened struggling! He's in love with me. . . .

Fortunately *Tante* Alice had entered at that moment. Ileana presented him, *"Domnul* Stefan Viziru." "Which Viziru are you?" *Tante* Alice had asked, looking him over from head to toe. "I also knew a Viziru, General Viziru. I knew him at Jassy during the war." "He was my grandfather," Stefan said.

A half-hour later when Stefan had risen to leave Ileana detained him. "I still haven't found out the end of the story about Vadastra," she reminded him.

"I'll come by again and continue it," Stefan had remarked. "I'll come by some day."

At times Ileana thought, He'll come today. And all that day she would stay at home. He'll come today. . . . One evening, surprised, she caught herself gazing absently at the snowflakes that fell slowly against the window, melted, and ran down the glass like tears. Suddenly she decided to leave the next day for Zinca. Early in February when she returned *Tante* Alice had said casually, "The grandson of General Viziru was here the day before yesterday. He was sorry not to find you, but he said he'd come by again."

"Have I perhaps come out without my tie?" Partenie asked, noticing that Ileana was staring at him insistently, but with a friendly smile. He put his hand to his throat, unconcerned and without haste.

"You resemble a friend of mine very much," Ileana said. "Stefan Viziru. I believe you know him."

"I haven't had the honor," said Partenie, looking at her placidly, almost with indifference. "I just knew his wife casually, the way you might know someone to whom you were engaged for sixteen days. . . . No, thank you, without lemon," he said raising his hand to cover his cup of tea. "Are you a friend of his or of his wife?"

"I'm a friend of Stefan's," Ileana said, suddenly embarrassed. "I don't know her."

52

"Ah, I understand," Partenie said, and he glanced again around the room. He smiled and nodded his head in greeting to a young couple passing by on the way out. "Still it's delightful to be invited to Nestor's by such a beautiful admirer," he went on. "I'll be rated very highly after this! I believe I understood you correctly on the phone. You did say 'an admirer'?"

When she was at Zinca Ileana had thought that she could even offer to be his secretary. I've never done it, I'd say to him, but I'd do an intelligent job. I'd especially like to be secretary to a writer. That's why I telephoned you. Perhaps you'll recommend me to a colleague. Or maybe you yourself have need of a secretary. I know how to type and I can handle correspondence. But as she listened to him she felt all at once that she needed to speak to him of something else and she interrupted him abruptly.

"I wanted to tell you a very interesting thing," she said hastily. "That's why I phoned you. I wanted to tell you about a subject for a novel."

Partenie picked up a cookie very carefully and bent slightly over his plate. He did not appear to be surprised.

"I don't know if you've ever heard about a gentleman named Vasilescu-Vadastra," continued Ileana in the same precipitate manner. "Stefan Viziru told me about him. He's a very interesting man, full of mysteries. More than that, he's a veritable enigma. Stefan doesn't understand very well what he's up to. And I thought that you could find the answer to this puzzle. A writer always has much more imagination than the rest of us common mortals. I thought you could write a novel. . . . It's a very interesting theme. . . ."

Partenie had eaten the cookie without uttering a word and almost without looking at her. Ileana felt disconcerted again and made an effort to smile. "In so far as I've understood it," she resumed after a long pause, "I think it might be a very interesting subject for a novel. Imagine a small, ugly man with a black monocle who has a room in a hotel . . ."

Suddenly she felt ridiculous. She stopped speaking and blushed. Partenie continued to drink his tea absently. Now and then he let his glance roam around the room, finally fixing it on his cup of tea. The silence lengthened painfully. I must say something, I must say something else. . . .

Ileana began again, "I have another theme for a novel too." She was beginning to be gripped by panic. "I mean he kissed me. He, Viziru. He kissed me. I was with my *Famille nombreuse* because it was raining and all at once he kissed me. He didn't say a word. He simply kissed me. He has this obsession for kissing women on the street. He's obsessed with this. He's an obsessed person. When he was little he used to talk with butterflies and lizards. Only he never knew how to talk with hedgehogs. . . ." She stopped and bit her lips. Almost in desperation she cast at Partenie a long imploring glance. "He never succeeded in conversing with hedgehogs," she repeated without thinking. "Never."

53

After that evening Ileana simply could not forgive Stefan. Because of him she had made a fool of herself. Partenie's charitable smile when he had stood up to leave, the words he had said as he held her hand in his a long time before kissing it—all these humiliations were due to Stefan. Now she waited for him, her impatience rapidly growing intolerable. Already she saw him before her, talking about Vadastra or about his childhood or his loves, and, delighted, she saw the smile with which she would interrupt him. *Domnul* Viziru, she would say, I discussed you for a long time with *Maestre* Partenie. . . . She abandoned this thought. No, that wasn't quite what she ought to say. She must find something more insolent, more galling. *Domnul* Viziru, because you've brought up the subject of love, I'll tell you what the *Maestre* thinks about you and his former fiancée. . . . No, no, this wasn't right. Something else, more cruel, something that would make him suffer. . . .

The bell rang one afternoon and she went to open the door without enthusiasm. She knew that *Tante* Alice was expecting callers. Stefan greeted her from the doorstep, wan, smiling darkly. "Wouldn't you like to go for a walk?" he inquired. "I've come to take you for a walk."

It was a serene April day and unusually warm. Spring seemed to have arrived that morning. For weeks on end it had been cold and rainy. At times during the last days of March it had snowed heavily, blocking the streets. It seemed like midwinter. Then a fine cold rain had begun again and the snow had turned to dirty slush mixed with mud. Suddenly in one day the sky had cleared. Spring had come. Smiling, Stefan awaited her on the doorstep.

"I can't. *Tante* Alice is having guests. They haven't arrived yet. But if you wish, come in a moment. . . ."

Later when they had entered the salon she asked him, "How is your baby?" Of course she had to say this. She had to talk to him this way, to ask him about his wife and child in a detached, polite, matter-of-fact tone. She had to consider him just an acquaintance, to let him understand immediately that he was only an ordinary person, someone she might have met on a train or at the baths, someone with whom she would exchange a few words in passing when she met him by chance.

"How does the young mother feel?" She questioned him again, sitting down in the armchair by the window.

"Fine. She's really very well," Stefan replied properly. "It's strange how suddenly spring has come," he added, standing in the middle of the room and letting his eyes wander to the window. "It's a pity we can't go walking."

A pity, a pity. This light won't wait for you. It will never be like this again. Never. When he had left Biris, Stefan had been sad, close to discouragement. Suddenly there was this lovely light, fragile and unearthly, and he had taken a deep breath. Time is irreversible, without a

54

doubt. The moments fly and with each moment we move nearer to death, as Biris had said. Stefan knew. Everyone knows. But there's something more than this, something besides this hastening toward death. This light is hiding something different. All of life conceals something different. Each of us, I, and Biris too, conceals something other than this. Somewhere within us in the depths of our being it lies hidden. Something different. . . .

"It's a pity we can't go for a stroll," repeated Stefan in a subdued voice. He seemed to be talking to himself.

He had said the same thing to Ioana just a half-hour before. When he returned from *strada* Macelari he found her nursing the baby. His sister Adela was there, representing his family. They couldn't go walking now as they used to do before the baby came. And he couldn't even tell her about his visit with Biris because of Adela's presence. As soon as he said a word Adela would interrupt him. You're still the same, she would have said. You've a talent for discovering boors and maniacs. Jeannette,* she would have declared to Ioana, he's still the same. He hasn't changed a bit since the *liceu*. He has a talent. . . .

After a moment Ileana inquired, "To what happy circumstances do I owe the pleasure of this unforeseen visit?"

Stefan turned toward her slowly. Something disturbing, something inscrutable, was in his gaze. "I came to take you for a walk. I wanted to tell you something." He hesitated a moment, then began again, "That is, I wanted to ask you something, but I don't know how. It will be hard for me. I don't know exactly what I ought to say." He was suddenly anxious and he smiled.

"Come over here by the window," said Ileana pointing to a velvet stool. "Perhaps you won't regret so much that we can't go out. You can see the whole garden from here. . . ."

Biris had said, "Come here to the window and I'll show you my point of view. Here by the window and you can see better. . . ." He had stopped solemnly in their midst and had opened his mouth wide, tipping his head back a little. With his finger he indicated a tooth.

"Did you see it?" he asked and he pointed it out to them once more, tapping it gently with his fingernail. "Did you notice anything?" he asked again, looking at them one after another. "It's only a little more yellowed, that's all. And yet it is radically different from all the others, because the others are living teeth. But that one, the one I

*French equivalent of Ioana.

55

showed you, is a dead tooth. They took out the nerve three years ago. Since that time it hasn't belonged to me. It's just a mineral, a dead bone. Nevertheless I keep it in me, it's still integrated into my life. I don't know if you understand what I mean."

"No," the poet from the provinces had admitted. Stefan had not quite caught his name, but he had found out that the man had published a booklet of verses and that he lived in the provinces.

"Just the same I'm not profound," said Biris, returning to his desk. "This bone seems to me symbolic. Not because it's a first detachment of mine arrived already, at the age of thirty years, in the land of the dead. It seems symbolic to me because it's *more true* than its neighbors, the so-called living teeth. This is what I am really—a dead bone, a certain kind of mineral. So far, what is it that distinguishes the living me from him, from the true Biris Petre?"

He had not permitted them to respond. Sternly he had lifted his hand, commanding silence, and at the same time he motioned to them to approach the desk. With a gesture of warning he bent over and placed his ear against the wood, listening. He shook his head and moved his ear several centimeters away. He listened again.

"It's not here," he whispered. "I heard it a little while ago, but now it's gone down. That's its habit. It comes up to the surface from time to time, then it retreats quickly at the bottom. I think it's down in the bottom drawer now. It has a direct passageway from the spot just in front of the inkwell to the lowest drawer."

Suddenly he bent his head again and signaled to them not to talk, his finger on his lips. "Do you hear it?" he whispered a few moments later, smiling.

Stefan heard three short clicks, unusually clear, followed by a silence that was broken only by their breathing. "Did you hear it?" inquired Biris again. "It's a beetle. The Death-Clock some call it. And it truly is a clock of death. Its ticking alone reveals to me the Death-Time, the time in which we live, we mortals—at least when we say that we are living, that we are alive. Any other beat—of watches or clocks, or the striking of chimes—seems to me a camouflage. We are deceived. They tell us that a half hour has passed or that it's six o'clock, as though this had some importance. What matters is the fact that our time, the Time that we call our Life, is a Time of Death. No clock in the world tells us this. But my clock tells me, this beetle that nibbles away day and night. And someday it will put an end to my desk. Perhaps after my death, but without a doubt the beetle will kill it. . . ."

He stopped, his energy spent, and looked at each of them in turn with a bitter smile. "I don't know if I've made myself clear enough," he resumed after a few seconds. "I bought this desk a little while before the

56

nerve was removed from my tooth. On the very first evening I heard the beetle. It wasn't a premonition, it was a revelation. I listened and I couldn't tear myself away. When I got up from my desk I didn't feel any older, I only felt closer to death. . . . The most profound philosopher I've known—whom I've had the opportunity to know personally I mean—is my dentist, Dr. Zamfirescu. 'It's nothing serious,' he told me after he had extracted the nerve, 'It's just that from now on you'll be carrying a dead bone around with you.' *A dead bone!* The very words terrified me. And what difference is there between the dead bone and my other bones? The radical difference I mentioned a little while ago? The difference between Life with a capital *L* and Death? Look here, look in this desk: the beetle clicks a certain number of times. It clicked several hundred times and a bone died. It will click again some tens of thousands of times, or maybe (I hope) several hundreds of thousands of times, and all my bones will be dead. Still other tens or hundreds of thousands of times and this desk will one day collapse into dust. In this way everything will enter eternity: bone, desk, and I, the student of Heidegger. . . ."

He stopped a moment to light a cigarette with his habitual slowness and then added, "Because you mustn't believe that all I've been telling you is my own idea. Not in the least. Only the beetle and the dead tooth are mine. The rest—Death-Time, Time-hastening-toward-Death—are from Heidegger. . . . And I haven't finished reading him yet. I'm not even sure I understand him well. But this is Time, *domnule* Viziru." He turned to Stefan. "This is *true* Time, from which you want to escape, from which you wish to save yourself and which you want to evade."

"You don't seem very inspired today," Ileana resumed. She was sorry that he was so sad, so helpless, so silent. His long glances and his weary smile implored her for sympathy. She regretted that he had found her home on a day when he was so discouraged.

"I was thinking. . ." he began when he had sat down on the footstool. "I was thinking how naive philosophers are. . . . Biris, for instance, with his desk eaten by a beetle, with his dead bone, his tooth that has already arrived in the land of the dead, and with his readings of Heidegger. . . ."

Ileana looked at him again and smiled. I don't understand any of this, she started to say, but she reconsidered and allowed him to continue. He was like someone talking in his sleep and you can't bear to wake him because he'd be ashamed that you had heard what he said.

"He maintains that this is true Time, as if we don't know this thing, each of us, this thing so obvious: that Time passes, that it's irreversible. But I asked him: 'How does it happen that Time *doesn't pass* for saints? How does it

57

happen that a saint doesn't feel this thing that we feel: that Time passes? A saint doesn't live in Time as we do. He lives only in the present. He has no past. For him Time doesn't flow. In some mysterious way it stands still.' And I asked him this: 'How does the saint contrive such a miracle? How can he no longer feel within him the passage of Time, Time grinding him down, gradually killing him?'"

Who is this Biris? Ileana wanted to ask Stefan, but then she remembered Vadastra, Partenie, and all that had followed, and smiling wryly she remained silent.

"I don't know if I ever told you why I have a secret room." Stefan's tone changed abruptly. "I don't think I did. I haven't told anyone. But one day I felt I had to have a second room, one entirely my own, protected from intruders, where I can satisfy one of the desires that have obsessed me for a long time: to paint."

"Are you a painter too?" interrupted Ileana.

"No, I'm not. I soon realized I haven't the slightest talent. But this wasn't important. What was important was to have a room to myself, a secret room in which I could gratify my desire. I bought everything I needed and began. I can't tell you what a revelation it was for me, this thing apparently so simple. I hadn't even the most elementary knowledge of painting, but I sat down in front of the easel, took the brush, and began...."

"What did you paint?"

"As a matter of fact, I didn't paint anything in particular. I simply took the brush and began to paint. It's hard to explain. I felt a great tranquillity, almost a beatitude. It seemed that I was no longer I, the I of everyday. Another I reappeared on the surface from somewhere, from the innermost depths of my being. It was the true I, without worries or desires, even without memories. I was particularly impressed by this fact—that when I was painting I no longer had any memories. I saw, I felt, I thought all kinds of things, but they didn't seem to belong to me anymore, they didn't come from my past. Painting, I had no past. I lived differently from the way I lived at home, or at the Ministry, or on the street. I lived in the present... like the saints," he added, smiling. "I was reading at the time a book about saints and I realized that while I painted I was living as they did. I lived only in the present.... Somewhat later, before Vadastra moved next door, I also discovered another thing: that in the secret room even when I wasn't painting I was living *differently* from the way I lived at home or at the Ministry. Anything I did I did differently. I don't know how to explain it, but Time was *different* there, it flowed differently. When I returned home, sometimes very late at night, I seemed to be returning from a journey to a distant place. I seemed to have come from another city where the customs were different and where I met other kinds of people.... In other words, it's possible to live some other way than with a bone that has already arrived in the land of the dead, as Biris says.

58

It *is* possible! And I wonder why he calls this time—time which is more true for me than the time spent at home or the time at the Ministry—why he calls it an evasion. . . ."

While he was speaking his demeanor changed completely. At first he had seemed absent, pale and depressed, but now Ileana saw him become again the man she had met on the Night of St. John—a man consumed by an inner flame, with the same indescribable smile steadily lighting his face.

The doorbell sounded and Ileana rose quickly from the armchair. "It's *Tante* Alice's guests," she said, her voice low. "Please don't go yet."

Stefan stood up also and went to the window. The light outside was no longer the same. Although its transparency remained, it seemed to have lost some of its intensity. It was no longer the same.

"Please come in," he heard Ileana say a few moments later. "Let me present a good friend of mine, a painter. Stefan Viziru, a painter," she repeated, emphasizing the words. "Surely you've heard of him. He's a painter with great talent."

"Well, of course! Of course!" said an elderly gentleman who was leaning on a cane. "I know. My congratulations. It's a pleasure to meet you." He grasped Stefan's hand vigorously and turned to the woman beside him. "He's a painter," he repeated very distinctly. "A painter. He paints." He pronounced the first syllables with unusual force. "A *painter*. He paints *pic*tures." The words sounded like short sudden explosions quickly suppressed. The lady extended her hand and bowed respectfully. She was a very old woman and seemed timid.

"*Doamna* and *domnul* Theodosiu," Ileana continued the introductions. "Good friends of *Tante* Alice. *Domnul* Theodosiu was an important landowner. They're good friends of *Tante* Alice. I must go wake her now." She smiled. "My aunt's been expecting them for some time and I'm afraid she's fallen asleep." Ileana left the room quickly with a wink at Stefan.

"How is the painting going, young man?" *Domnul* Theodosiu asked as he looked around for a chair.

"Fine. I think it's going just fine," Stefan said, attempting to smile. All at once he felt exhausted and ridiculous. He didn't know what else he could have said to dispel the disagreeable impression of being a thief caught in the act, a villain who has managed to hide his sins for years only to be discovered suddenly in the midst of a crowd, just when he is least expecting it.

"My congratulations!" said *domnul* Theodosiu, sitting down.

"What is he saying?" *doamna* Theodosiu asked, leaning toward her husband without daring to lift her glance in Stefan's direction. "I thought he said something. . . ."

"He said he's getting along fine!" *domnul* Theodosiu shouted. "He's a painter. He paints. He's a talented painter. He says the painting is going well. He says that it's going well. . . ."

59

During his free hours Vadastra had a habit of following women who looked beautiful and elegant. Before nightfall he would walk along *calea* Victoriei to the intersection of *bulevardul* Elisabeta, boldly inspecting those who passed by. Most of the time these cutting, insolent stares contented him, since he succeeded then, if only for a fraction of a second, in expressing his desire for possession.

When he thought a woman was exceptionally good-looking he began to follow her. Once she emerged from the torrent that poured into *calea* Victoriei at that hour, he approached her, fixed his eyes on her, and smiled. He repeated this maneuver many times. Sometimes he spoke, always using the same phrases, "Permit me to accompany you, *domnisoara?*" or, "So beautiful, yet so alone?" He rarely added anything more, since he expected the young woman to answer him. If she delayed her response he assumed that she had not heard clearly and he repeated his question. But ordinarily the conversation never began because the girl would get on a tram, or meet someone, or reach her home.

Once on an evening at the beginning of May a woman who seemed especially beautiful paused in front of a lighted shop window. This one stopped just for me! Spiridon said to himself, but he did not dare to approach her. If he had known what to say to her he might have been bolder. However, he had not prepared anything to say except those stereotyped lines, and his only hope was that the girl would ask him something; for instance, "Why are you following me so persistently, *domnule?*" To which he would have replied, "Allow me first to introduce myself, *domnisoara.* I am the attorney Vasilescu-Vadastra, doctor of law, and you wouldn't suppose that a man of my position would have permitted himself to be so indiscreet without a rather serious purpose. Let me tell you, *domnisoara,* that I noticed your face, especially your expression, several days ago when I caught sight of you for the first time. . . ." And he didn't doubt that the conversation would have followed at a very lively pace. Or else the young woman, on hearing him call her *"domnisoara,"* could have turned and said, "Don't be angry, but I've been married for"—let's say—"two years." To which he would have replied immediately, "Let me confess, *domnisoara,* that I don't believe you. You seem so girlish and delicate that. . . ." He was sure that a young married woman would have resisted him no longer. Spiridon had an infinite faith in the seductive power of his words. But now he was helpless to know what to say. The woman appeared to be studying the window with considerable attention. She's waiting for me! Spiridon reflected again, and almost without being aware of it he took a step in her direction.

"Beautiful things!" he began tentatively, persuaded that the young woman would say something, since she had waited so long to rouse him to action. She did indeed turn her head but Spiridon's expression was so comical—his monocle seemed to have been put on for just such an occasion, his one good eye regarded her with such frightening avidity, in contrast to the inertness of his face where only a faint trace of a smile showed in the corner of his mouth—that the woman burst out laughing and moved away with a gesture of mild disdain. Spiridon stood there light-headed, not knowing if he should follow her any longer or if it would be better to give up. Then he recovered his senses and called out to her:

"You don't know who I am! Someday you'll hear about me!"

Amused, the woman turned her head again, but when her glance fell on that monocle, so pretentious for a man with Spiridon's face and clothes, she began to laugh again and hurried away.

"You'll be sorry!" Spiridon shouted, running after her. "Later you'll see who I am! Keep that in mind!"

But at the first street corner he stopped following her and came back. The truth is she doesn't know who I am, he said to himself. She takes me for a very ordinary man, and it's not her fault, because she doesn't know me. If she knew me she wouldn't laugh like that anymore. But eventually I'm going to meet her anyhow—or perhaps she'll even want to meet me. And then she'll see!

At other times Vadastra lay in wait on the side streets for the young girls going home from work, especially the milliners and seamstresses. He would never have thought that he could bear to have a liaison with such a girl, but he liked to exercise his power over them, to verify his charm. He didn't always succeed in entering into a conversation because the girls would start laughing or else leave hurriedly. But there were some who let themselves be accosted and then Spiridon arranged to meet them on an obscure street where he knew he did not run the risk of being recognized. Besides, he never encouraged the establishment of a more permanent relationship, and after a certain number of dates he disappeared without a trace. What he was looking for in such adventures was the initial sensual excitement of proving to himself his power to seduce a stranger, as well as those first hours of verbal intoxication when he was permitted to reveal wholly the self that he usually hid or disclosed only fragmentarily to other people.

After the first date, Vadastra was accustomed to inviting his companion to one of the *cofetarii* in the neighborhood or to a very secluded tavern where he had not infrequently requested a private room so that he could talk freely. Moreover he was rather generous, ordering expensive things that were not always to be found, and demanding the best wines. When it came time to pay he pulled out his billfold with the gesture of a millionaire, scarcely glancing at the bill, and leaving on the plate a tip that was unusually large for that kind of place.

"*Hei, fetito,** I'm not like the others you know," Spiridon began with a

* Little girl.

61

frown, "those loafers and dolts! I'm a man of personality. . . . I can't tell you everything, you understand . . . but if you knew who I am. . . . I don't pay any attention to money. What can fifty, a hundred, or even five hundred thousand lei mean to me? If I had wished, I could have been a millionaire by now. But I didn't want that. It doesn't interest me. What does that mean, a millionaire? There are so many millionaires and look at them. What do they do? They lead the same life as other people. All these things don't interest me. I'm pursuing something else. I have an ideal in life. If you only knew! But I can't tell you. . . ."

The girl listened to him, believing only part of what he told her but no less impressed by his volubility and his assurance. Vadastra hesitated a long time before making his revelations. He began something, stopped, then looked at her in suspicion, laughing nervously. With a certain desperation in his voice, he repeated, "I can't tell you everything, you understand. . . ."

"You'll get nowhere looking at me like that. It's hard to know who I am. It would never enter your head. . . . From time to time, just to amuse myself, I greet a pretty girl on the street. I also need to breathe, you understand. . . . But otherwise I scarcely take my mind off my work. And thank God, if I have need of women, all I have to do is lift my finger. And well-bred women too, from high society. . . . What d'you know? This life's full of surprises. Look at us. Instead of being in a fashionable salon right now, surrounded by the most distinguished people of Bucharest, I've come here with you to a sordid tavern. Why? Ah, I can't tell you, but you'd be amazed if you knew!"

At other times, with a more ostentatious woman who urged him to take her to a fine restaurant or to the movies, Vadastra refused. He led her to believe that he must not be seen by certain of his acquaintances or by a "lady friend."

"I can't tell you the name—you understand why. All I can say is that she's one of the most beautiful and elegant women in Bucharest. I don't want to have an argument with her. She's an intelligent modern woman who wouldn't try to control what I do or whom I meet. But you understand that she's a woman. She's very fond of me, and someone might tell her he saw us together."

Or if the girl changed tactics, threatening him with her finger and trying to tease him about how many times he mentioned his love affairs, Spiridon encouraged her. "Yes," he said, stroking his mustache with his fingernail, "you've got me there! I'll have to admit you've guessed it. I like women. If I had the time to spend with them, I'd never do anything else. But I don't have time. I have other things to do in life."

Sometimes in the course of such a conversation Vadastra began to explain to his companion the secret of his success with women. "You yourself have observed that it's not necessary to be as handsome as a mannequin in order to please them. An intelligent and refined woman isn't attracted by such men. They like interesting people, men who have personality, strength of will, and a goal in life. Such a man impresses anyone, but especially well-bred women, women who are cultured, distinguished. Now I can't say that I'm handsome. It's true I have a very interesting face and this always attracts. But there's something more than the face—the personality. Me, I have personality. This is a very rare thing in our day. Wherever you look you see nothing but men lacking in ideals, without willpower, uncultured, stupid. They think they're someone if they become deputies or heads of bureaus in a ministry. What does it mean to be a deputy? What have you gained by it? There's something more interesting, something that deserves . . . No, I can't tell you everything. But you understand. That's why a distinguished woman always looks for something exceptional in a man—a personality. The woman who loved me, the distinguished *doamna* Zissu . . ." But the next moment he regretted that he had pronounced her name. He hesitated, and then began to talk about personality again.

"Guess who I met today," asked Stefan.

"Professor Antim." But she had not dreamed about him the night before. Just by chance she had answered with his name. And yet this time it was Professor Antim whom Stefan had encountered.

"He asked me to come and see him some day to look at his collections. He says he has some extraordinary things."

Antim. Ioana recalled her first night at the clinic and the dream that had terrified her. It seemed that a long, long time had passed since then: the baby (17 February), the milk-fever, the return home, the big scare—she had heard him coughing, suddenly choked, and she had thought he had stopped breathing. And afterward, one morning, she had discovered that she had become very beautiful. It was Stefan who had discovered this—that she was beautiful again, that she had become even more beautiful than before. Looking at herself, naked, in the full-length mirror she saw that she was tall and fair. She seemed to have gained weight. Her eyes were clear. Only her face appeared to have changed. Something had happened. A feeling of victory, of pride even, shone in her face with a gentle light that transformed her in a way she did not understand.

"It would have been better if I'd gone to see Antim," Stefan said on that evening in April when he returned home depressed. "Instead of going to see Biris to discuss the problem of Time, it would have been better if I'd gone to Antim's."

Ioana sensed that he was dejected, but the baby had a fever and she was preoccupied. "He seems to have a little fever," she said. "I don't think it's anything serious. He had the same thing the day before yesterday, too. What happened at Biris's?"

"I'm sorry I went," said Stefan. He stepped into his study, but returned almost immediately. A strange, troubled gleam was in his eyes. "I'm sorry I went," he repeated. His voice changed. "We started a discussion about Time. Biris maintained... But, after all, what he maintained isn't very important. I'll tell you another time. I just wanted to ask you if you think that it's possible for someone to love two people at the same time...."

Ioana stared at him a long time, paling slightly. It seemed to her that she had been flung back into a time whose disagreeable taste she was beginning to forget. The Big Scene, she remembered suddenly. Now the Big Scene begins.

"Of course," Stefan went on in the same tone. "You don't have to answer now, right here. If you like we can talk about it after dinner or tomorrow at lunch...."

"Raducu and Adela are coming to lunch tomorrow," Ioana said slowly. "I had to invite them. Adela would be here still if I hadn't asked them to come to lunch tomorrow."

She was astonished as she listened to herself speaking. Her arms hung limply. Now the Big Scene will begin. But Stefan did not seem to have heard what she said. He looked at her very intently and began to smile.

"Did you see too what a wonderful light there was today?" he asked. "I came to take you for a walk."

"So I imagined," Ioana murmured, smiling. "I was sorry..."

"What a wonderful light," repeated Stefan, his voice becoming more subdued. "You could understand anything on a day like this. You could penetrate any secret. You seemed to see straight into the essential nature of things. Those hours weren't the same as all the other ones are. That's why I asked you: Do you think it's possible to love two people at the same time? Or rather, I wanted to ask you that this afternoon. Now it may be too late. Perhaps I wouldn't understand you if you tried to explain."

He sat down on a chair and continued his monologue without looking at her. "If I had been a painter, I think I should have tried to understand this question: How can one preserve in a painting a certain time, one wholly favorable to revelations, a certain moment qualitatively different from the rest of the moments that constitute Cosmic Time? How could I have kept, at least for my own use and blissful enjoyment, the hours of this afternoon, their light, their taste, their mystery? That's why I thought that you, having known directly, immediately, this mystery of loving two people..."

Just then Ioana heard the baby whimpering and she ran to the cradle. She scarcely had time to say, "Excuse me, please...." Absently Stefan went back to his study.

She waited in vain, trembling, for him to ask the same question again in the days that followed. Stefan seemed to have forgotten. There was just one time when Ioana was frightened. It was almost two months later on a day in early June. Stefan had returned from the office weary and somewhat dispirited, but this time it was a different matter. He had to leave the very next day for Sighisoara. "I don't understand why they're sending me, of all people, but I have to go."

He often went on missions abroad when commercial agreements were in preparation, but never before had he been sent to the provinces. A question of arbitration, Ioana thought he had said, but she wasn't sure she had understood correctly.

Stefan left the next morning and was gone almost a week. Every evening when he telephoned her Ioana did most of the talking, but there was one time when he seemed excited and happy, and he alone had talked. "I think I'll try to paint," he said. "I'll teach you too. I think we'll both be very happy." And rapidly, precipitately, he had continued, telling her about spring and about "a remarkable man," Anisie, and his orchards.

When she greeted him on his return, Ioana was surprised at his appearance. He seemed to have grown younger. His face was bathed in a strange and constant glow.

"I've met a remarkable man," he began, "and now I tell you that in my own way and without realizing it I had discovered something. I'd begun to profit from an open possibility. . . ." He went into the bathroom, took a shower, and putting on a bathrobe, he came out to look for a suit. It was a clear morning and brilliant, announcing intense heat.

"I must become one with the cosmic rhythms," he said as he passed in front of Ioana. "This also is a great secret. I learned it from Anisie. I have to select a suit that harmonizies with the cosmic rhythm." He smiled.

He dressed and left for the Ministry. More than two hours later he phoned to tell her not to expect him for lunch. He seemed depressed. Maybe he's tired from the arbitration at Sighisoara, Ioana told herself. But when he telephoned again in the evening, informing her that he wasn't coming home for dinner either, Ioana was worried.

"What's happened?" she asked in a whisper. "Nothing serious, I hope. . . ."

But Stefan had not heard her. The operator at the Ministry switchboard had cut them off.

That evening, after leaving the Ministry, Stefan went by the coffee shop to look for Biris. He stood a moment in the doorway and glanced around the room. Biris was not there and Stefan set off at a leisurely pace toward *strada* Macelari. *Doamna* Porumbache met him at the door. Biris had not yet returned home, but she invited Stefan in to wait for him and drink a *tuica*.*

"I'm in rather a hurry," he said evasively. "I'll come back in about an

---

*Romanian plum brandy.

hour." He left and went to the tram station to wait, walking up and down the street. It had been a hot day and now at nightfull the courtyards and gardens were lavishly sprinkled. From everywhere around him came the smell of wet earth and roses, and many windows had been left open. He heard someone playing a piano at the end of the street. A *liceu* boy went by, stopped a moment to listen and then furtively lit a cigarette, hiding it in his fist as he walked on down the street. Strains of the *Sylvia Valse* drifted through the open window and Stefan went nearer, but whoever was playing kept stumbling over the same measure and starting again, diligently but without much enthusiasm. Stefan noticed that he was becoming hungry and turned to go back to the tavern. A moment later someone laid a hand on his arm.

"So you're here, *maica!*" *doamna* Porumbache exclaimed. "I say, why didn't you tell me you like that girl? She's the daughter of *'Trei-ochi-sub-plapuma.'** We call her father that because he's blind in one eye. But he has a beautiful fortune! All these houses are theirs. And they have a new shop on Lipscani, too. La Trei Fazani† they call it."

She paused, then added, "I came out to get some cigarettes, but if you're not sleepy. . . . Let's go in the tavern on the corner where we can talk at leisure. He's an honest merchant. . . . Will you treat me to a glass of wine?"

"I'll treat you."

They sat down at a table near the door so that they could see Biris when he came home. "He has to pass by here," said *doamna* Porumbache, "since he comes on tram number fourteen." She sighed, and emptied her glass of wine quickly. "It's a pity about him. He's not a bad boy, if only he'd listen to me! I've been drumming it into his head to marry a rich girl! How many I've found for him! Honest girls, merchants' daughters, not those student tramps. For instance, take the girl I was talking about, the daughter of *'Trei-ochi-sub-plapuma.'* She knows French, plays the piano—and what wealth she has! Her father was a poor wretch when I first knew him. He came to us in Ferendari to get my husband to endorse his note. He had a hardware shop—so to speak. Really it was just a shed with a few boxes of nails and a bundle or two of sheet-iron. Now he has I don't know how many millions! Did you ever see anything like it? Anywhere in the whole world?"

She filled her glass for the third time and began to sip it slowly, pensively. "Only, every man has his troubles. That girl, the one who's playing the piano, she's not his own daughter. His wife had her by a lieutenant. That one's done well too. He's a colonel. He's married and has other children. . . . 'One-eye' knows she's not his daughter but since he didn't have any children of his own he was happy, especially now that things have gone so well with him. He opened a shop in Lipscani near us. My man said to me, 'Look at that

---

*Three-eyes-under-the-blanket: the name of the tavern as well as the man.
†The Three Pheasants' Place.

wretch, come to Lipscani!' But he did well. He plotted with someone from a big company and they made a deal. They raised the prices on the invoice and divided the surplus between them. They robbed the government, so to speak. But so what? Don't others steal too? What good does it do us to be honest? Look at Petrica! Starving to death! Wouldn't it be better for him to play politics too, like the tenant's son does?"

For a moment she stopped and closed her eyes, smiling, captivated by her thoughts. "For only a year or two I'd like to be rich again!" she sighed. "To be somebody again, along with other people! To have a carriage with two horses and in the summer I'd go to the baths at Calimanesti!... *Hei!* But I don't go in for all that any more. I haven't had any luck! That is, I had it once but I didn't know what to do with it. I thought if you have something once it's yours till death, that once you're rich no one can touch your wealth. I was young, I was beautiful, I had everything. I thought I'd have all these things as long as I wanted them.... And now they're all gone. I hadn't even rightly come to my senses before they were gone.... I couldn't believe it! As though they'd never been!"

She brushed away a tear, hunted in her apron pocket for a handkerchief and blew her nose. "But you haven't told me if you want me to speak to the girl."

"I'm married," confessed Stefan.

The old woman looked at him in surprise. "But I see you don't wear a wedding ring," she said suspiciously. "Too bad!" She was silent, then after an interval she added, "Since she is, you could say, the daughter of the colonel."

Just when he had decided to go home Stefan met Biris getting off the tram. "I've been looking for you for two hours. I wanted to talk to you by all means...."

Biris seemed preoccupied and tired. He puffed wearily at his cigarette. "I went to see someone, a certain man, Mihai Duma, all the way to Cotroceni. I walked all day. Let's sit down somewhere for a moment." He looked around for a bench.

"We'd better go to the tavern," proposed Stefan. "I have a lot to tell you." They found a table in the back of the garden.

"I went all the way to Cotroceni," Biris said again, wearily tossing away the butt of the cigarette that still hung, burned out, in the corner of his mouth. "What a lot of walking I did today!"

"As I said to Ileana when we were discussing the problem of Time," Stefan began abruptly, after he had filled the glasses, "neither the beetle, nor the tooth already in the land of the dead, have convinced me. I've known this for a long time. I've known it ever since I began to paint. But now I have a positive proof. I have Anisie...."

Biris was thirsty and drank half the contents of his glass, filled it with soda and drained it quickly. "Say that again," he demanded. "I didn't understand

67

you very well. It seemed to me that you mentioned something about painting. . . ."

"This was a secret," continued Stefan, still animated, "but now I can tell you, too. In my spare time I paint. But I didn't come to see you about that. I came to tell you about Anisie."

Biris gave him a penetrating glance and ran his hand lightly over the thin hair on the top of his head. He asked in a tired voice, "Who is this person?"

"He's the most remarkable man I've ever known! He lives near Sighisoara. Now that I've met him, I don't regret so much telling Ileana about my painting. . . ."

"Is Ileana your wife?" Biris asked, refilling his glass.

"No," responded Stefan, casually. "My wife's name is Ioana. Ileana is a girl I've known for the past year, and I think I'm in love with her." Lost in his thoughts, he stopped a moment and smiled. His voice changed as he resumed, "It's strange, but now that you've mentioned it, I suppose Ileana could have been my wife too. I'd never thought of it until now," he added dreamily. "Not that I'm sorry I'm married to Ioana. On the contrary, I love her very, very much. But I feel I love Ileana too. . . . Although after she introduced me that day as a real painter, I almost hated her. She seemed to have betrayed my dearest secret. And indeed my painting is a very great, a very dear secret. . . . But fortunately I met Anisie. And it's about him, about just this man Anisie that I want to talk to you."

"Get to the point," urged Biris, noticing that Stefan had stopped again, his gaze lost in space. "Who is this person?"

"He's discovered a great secret," Stefan whispered, leaning over the table. "This man has learned how to live. *He* lives as a *man*, as a total being. He doesn't let himself live by his tissues, his glands, his reflexes, the way all the rest of us do."

"But how do you know he lives in a different way?" Biris inquired, beginning to search for his cigarettes.

"I've seen how he cleans the trees in his orchard," began Stefan with a mysterious smile. "I sat on the porch and watched him. Then I understood. I was convinced that his work is of a different quality from ours. Besides, I was prepared for this because I had known something of the same bliss too when I was painting. Only in my case it's not a matter of serious work with a definite object as it is with him. He cleans the trees of caterpillars. I watched him carefully and I felt that he was *present* in every motion. He wasn't thinking of anything else when he was working on a tree. His mind didn't wander. I perceived that the tree revealed itself to him in its totality. For him it wasn't a simple object, one among thousands of others of its kind, as it would appear to us, to the majority of men. To him, at that particular moment, the tree that he was cleaning revealed the entire Universe. He saw it in its totality: roots, branches, leaves, parasites. . . ."

68

"Are you sure *he* saw all this?" interrupted Biris. "Are you sure that all this you're telling me isn't a sort of mythological invention provoked by your own ecstasies?"

"He saw all those things and many others besides, things we can't see," Stefan said gravely. "I had a long conversation about him the evening before I met him. I went to see a classmate from the University and he told me Anisie's story. He's a few years older than we are. He's studied a great deal. He went through the course of study at the Conservatory in Vienna, then he took up theology and studied mathematics, physics, and biology. But he never wanted to finish anything. He never received a degree. About five or six years ago he had an accident. He slipped climbing a mountain and was laid up I don't know how many months. They thought at first he'd broken his spinal column, but it wasn't that serious. Anyway, during those months he spent in a cast, you might say he had a revelation. He was conscious of *how time passes*, and he discovered at the same time what to do to prevent time from passing."

"This begins to be interesting!" commented Biris, raising his head. "Go on!"

"Since then," Stefan continued with sudden fervor, "he no longer lives as we do, according to a more or less complex time table. He no longer has a personal schedule, so to speak. Nothing counts for him but cosmic time: day and night, the waxing and waning of the moon, the seasons. And he told me that for him even this cosmic time will be abolished someday. But meanwhile he has need of time in order to find himself again; that is, to find himself in the metaphysical sense of the words, to take cognizance of his full integral being. Now he doesn't let anything distract him from living each essential moment of this cosmic time. For him the new moon or the full moon, the equinoxes and the solstices, dawns and twilights, don't have the simple function they do for us, of marking dates on a calendar. Each event reveals to him a new aspect of the whole, of the cosmos. He accepts no time other than cosmic time, and he especially rejects historic time; for example, the time during which parliamentary elections take place, or Hitler's arming of Germany, or the Spanish Civil War. He has decided to take account only of the time in which cosmic events occur: the phases of the moon, the seasons, the rotation of the earth. He's content to exhaust the significance of each of these phenomena, living thereby an uninterrupted revelation. You'd have been convinced too if you had heard him talking about a moonlit night, or noonday in summer, or about the meaning of all the songs of birds and insects at different hours of the day. For him Nature begins to become not only transparent but also a bearer of values. It's not a case of a regression, let's say, to the animal-like state of primitive man. He's discovered in Nature not that absence of the Spirit that some of us seek, but the key to fundamental metaphysical revelations—the mystery of death and resurrection, of the passage from nonbeing to being. And this man, who is scarcely at the beginning of this experience, has already succeeded in escaping from time. He escapes not only from historic time—anyone who decides to live apart from the world, without newspapers or radio can do this—but also from physiological time. He's several years older than we are, but he looks ten years younger! He looks like a youth of twenty-five. . . ."

"Now, listen," exclaimed Biris. Irritated, he shoved his empty glass to one side. "Either you're making fun of me, or else a miracle has really happened to you. You've met in flesh and blood one of Ciru Partenie's characters!"

"What do you mean?" Stefan asked with indifference.

"Don't you read *Viata Romaneasca?** Partenie published a very strange story in the last number. He called it 'The Sheepfold Is Far?'"

"I don't see the connection."

"You'll have to read it. It's your story exactly, with the single exception that Partenie's character doesn't live in Sighisoara, but in the mountains of Moldavia. The author relates how he met the man one evening and stayed to talk with him until late that night. And the episode of the accident to the spinal column, his withdrawal to the country, his technique of integration into cosmic time, and all you've told me, everything, I read two or three weeks ago in Partenie's story."

"It's impossible!" Stefan whispered.

"Only the detail about cleaning the caterpillars from the trees and your interpretation of it—I don't recall reading about this. But of course," added Biris with a touch of irony in his voice, "it wouldn't have made sense in the story, since their meeting had taken place on an evening in autumn, and besides, Partenie's character didn't have an orchard. Apparently he lived a more solitary life in the mountains. His only neighbors were shepherds from a sheepfold!"

He stopped and raised his eyes to Stefan, who seemed to be again lost in his thoughts. He was resting his chin on his fist and looking straight ahead without a word. They were both silent for a long time.

"It's incredible!" said Stefan at length, and quickly filled his glass.

"And yet it's nothing remarkable. You've both met the same individual; a rather bizarre man, it's true, but nevertheless a flesh-and-blood man. . . ."

"It's strange that he, the Great Man, met him first," Stefan remarked with a forced smile.

Biris continued as though he had not heard. "Indiscreet as he is, Partenie has written a story inspired by that meeting. As a character in the story, the man's been changed, while you've taken him more seriously. And basically I think you're right. This man deserves to be known. Whoever he is, one can certainly learn something from him!"

Romanian Life, a literary review.

Stefan shook his head. "Not I, at any rate. And I'm sorry. I'll have to be satisfied with painting." Violently and in haste he drained his glass and refilled it. "With painting," he repeated presently, as if to himself. "I'll have to be satisfied with painting." He passed his hand over his face and tried again to smile. "*Anch'io sono pittore!*"* he exclaimed. He picked up Biris's cigarettes from the table and absently lit one. "I haven't smoked for several years," he said, letting the match burn down between his fingers.

Biris sat with his arms crossed and gazed at Stefan. Both were again silent for some time.

"I think it's late," began Biris. "I feel rather tired . . ."

"What did you say is the name of the story?" Stefan demanded. He seemed to awaken from a long reverie. "What did you say it's called? 'The Sheepfold Is Far?' With a question mark?"

"With a question mark," said Biris. "Because that's the way the story begins. The narrator approaches that mysterious character and asks him, 'The sheepfold, is it far?'"

"And do you think the question mark has some significance?"

"No, I don't," responded Biris thoughtfully. "It's a simple question, a question like any other. The narrator meets a solitary man in the mountains and asks him 'Is the sheepfold far?'"

"Nevertheless I believe it does have significance," insisted Stefan with a shiver of excitement. "*Apparently* it's a question like any other. But if that solitary man Partenie met is one and the same person with Anisie, then the question could also have a hidden meaning. For instance, 'Is it much farther to Paradise?' or 'Is God far?' or 'Where is God?' 'Is it much farther to God?'"

"I don't think so," Biris demurred. "Partenie's a realist, a realistic psychologist. His works have no mystical significance."

He paused. He felt that Stefan was not listening to him anymore and he remained silent, sipping now and then from the glass that he had filled too full. "And now, since you've brought up the subject," he resumed a little later, "I can tell you something more. I can tell you in addition that this Anisie of yours hasn't convinced me. Integrated or not into cosmic time, still the land of the dead lies in wait for us all. Time is still driving us toward death."

Embarrassed, Stefan raised his hand to his forehead, then began to rub his cheek. "It's a shame about Anisie," he said. "It's too bad the Great Man discovered him, too."

He stopped speaking and frowned. Biris fixed his gaze on the bright lamp in the middle of the garden. Innumerable moths and diaphanous green insects had gathered there, flying around it blindly. Their wings beat in endless spasms as they hovered for a moment close to the heated lamp chimney and then flew away, only to approach again with the same obscure and pathetic

*"I too am a painter" (It.).

indifference to their fate. They returned countless times, fluttering their wings ever faster and repeatedly striking the glass of the lamp with a muffled sound, finally dropping stunned and exhausted on the gravel.

"What amazes me," Biris said without looking away from the lamp, "is that Partenie went as far as Sighisoara and met a character so different from those who usually interest him. He, who only looks for 'experiences' with women in high society. . . . Now, he ought to meet Bursuc too. . . ."

"Only this time I'm not withdrawing from the game so easily," interrupted Stefan, his voice harsh and cutting. "*Anch'io sono pittore!* I've been to the sheepfold too, and I have also met Anisie. *Et in Arcadia ego.* I haven't asked him the question, but I will ask it. . . . A *propos* the question mark," he added after a brief pause, a strange light flaring suddenly in his eyes, "wouldn't you like to see my paintings? I've never shown them to anyone before, but I must show them to you. . . ."

"It's rather late, and I'm quite tired. I've been all the way to Cotroceni . . ."

"It's not eleven yet," Stefan said, getting up abruptly from the table. "It's not late, and this business won't take more than a quarter of an hour. We'll go by cab. Wait just a moment. I have to make a telephone call."

After about ten minutes he returned in very good spirits. "Excuse me please. I didn't know the number and I had to look it up, and at first I couldn't find the directory. But fortunately she was at home. We'll go by and get her in the cab. She'll meet us in a quarter of an hour in front of her house. You know," he added, signaling the waiter for the check, "it's the girl, Ileana, the one I told you I'm in love with."

"*Anch'io sono pittore!*" he had said on the telephone. "Come, I'll show you my paintings. And I'll show you that car that disappeared." Ileana had hesitated a moment and glanced at her watch: eleven o'clock. "It's General Viziru's grandson on the phone," she said to *Tante* Alice. "He's inviting me to a preview of his exhibit. I can't refuse him. . . ."

She heard the horn in front of the house and went down the stairs. Outside, the freshness of the night struck her. It was filled with fragrance from the flowers in the garden. All at once, without any reason, she felt happy.

"This gentleman's a philosopher," Stefan introduced Biris. "I told you about him once. He's the one with the dead bone, the vanguard already in the land of the dead. . . . Take us to the Hotel Boston on *strada* Bucovinei," he said to the driver. Hastily he lit another cigarette and settled himself in the back of the car.

"Allow me to speak familiarly," he said to Ileana, taking her arm. "This is a very important day in my life. Today I found out that, although I had met Anisie, the Great Man met him before I did!"

"Who's Anisie?" Ileana broke in with a smile. Again she had that disturbing feeling, so hard to define, that Stefan was beginning to play an absurd game that only he understood.

"He's a remarkable man."

"Very remarkable," seconded Biris mildly. "He's even more interesting than Partenie's character. . . ."

"And yet I'm sure that question mark has a symbolic significance," Stefan interrupted. "I'm sure that the whole meaning of the story lies in that question mark!"

Ileana wanted to say something but Stefan gave her no opportunity. "We've arrived. My secret room is here. I beg you not to mention this visit to anyone. Some other time I'll tell you why." He paid the driver and invited them to go in. Annoyed, the porter raised his eyes in astonishment from the book he was reading and handed Stefan the key to the room. They climbed the stairs silently to the second floor. The hotel was new and clean enough but lacking in taste. Its poverty was scarcely concealed.

"Come in," Stefan said, standing in the doorway after he had turned on the light, "and please speak very quietly because the walls are thin and everything can be heard."

"Vadastra?" Ileana murmured.

"He lived over there," said Stefan pointing. "Now the room is used for transients. The last occupant was a traveling salesman from Brasov. Fortunately, on the other side I don't have a neighbor."

Ileana, amused, looked about her. It was the banal interior typical of rooms in cheap hotels. The bookcase looked ready to collapse and the wooden table piled with books seemed strange and lonely as though it had been brought there out of some other world.

"You should know that you're the first people ever to have entered my secret room," Stefan continued in a whisper. "You can't realize what this place means to me. This is *my secret*. Even if I were to tell you, you wouldn't understand." He went to the window and opened it, leaning far out over the sill and turning his head to look at the next room. "You can talk. I see it's dark next door. My neighbor hasn't come in yet."

Ileana sat down on the chair in front of the bed. Biris continued to examine the titles of the books on the shelves.

"*Anch'io sono pittore!*" Stefan began, returning to the middle of the room and heading toward Biris. "Give me a cigarette, please. This is my fourth in less than an hour. I stopped smoking several years ago, but tonight I feel the need of it. . . . I'm sorry that I can't offer you something," he added after lighting the cigarette with a trembling hand. "I don't eat or drink anything when I'm here. Sometimes if I'm very thirsty I drink a glass of water from the

73

faucet. That's all. Inside my secret room, just as in the room *Sambo*, all physiological functions are somehow suspended. When I get hungry I go down to the street and buy a biscuit. But I can't eat it here. I can't come up to this secret room with a biscuit, or a yogurt, or a bag of fruit. It was like that too with the room *Sambo*," he added with a smile, "Before I reveal the great secret to you, I must tell you the story of the room *Sambo*."

He sat on the edge of the bed and looked at them both intently. "Please don't interrupt me. Now that Anisie has become a literary character, I too can reveal the secrets of my childhood. I'll tell you the story of the room *Sambo*.... I was about five or six years old," he began, his voice hushed, "and I found myself with my family at Movila. We were living in a kind of villa-hotel that had two floors and about fifteen or twenty rooms. In the dining room we sat next to a group of very mysterious young people. They seemed mysterious to me because although they spoke Romanian, I couldn't understand very well what they were saying. From time to time one of them pronounced a foreign word, without significance for me, and then they all began to exclaim, to become excited, and to raise their voices. Their mysteriousness fascinated me. And one day I turned my head suddenly toward their table at a moment when the discussion had become exceptionally animated. I heard one of them—the one who seemed oldest because he had a mustache—say something, and I saw him raise his arm toward the ceiling, apparently to indicate a direction. I heard him utter in a solemn voice the word 'Sambo.' Suddenly they all fell silent. They bent their heads and looked down at their plates. Then one after another they repeated: 'Sambo!' 'Sambo!' ... At that instant I felt a thrill I had never known before. I felt that I'd penetrated a great and terrible secret. All the mysteries of the men at the nearby table were concentrated in those two syllables, 'Sambo!' Through a providential circumstance I had turned my head at the exact moment when the man with the mustache pointed out the place where their secret, *Sambo*, was found. It was above us, somewhere overhead on the second floor. And of course I set out that very afternoon to discover it.

"We children slept with our *doica** in a separate room next to that of our parents. I pretended to go to sleep and when I sensed that the *doica* was dozing I went out. I ran down the hall as fast as I could and climbed up to the second floor, my heart pounding. I didn't know where to go but I felt my heart beating harder and harder. I closed my eyes in fright and began to walk softly on the carpet toward the end of the hall. I don't know how far I went, but I found myself in front of a door, and just at that moment I knew that there was where *Sambo* was! I wondered later how I found the courage to put my hand to the latch and go in. I was trembling all over and if I had heard a loud noise at that moment. or a scream, I probably would have fainted. Nevertheless, I took hold of the latch and went in. . . .

*Nursemaid.

74

"I can see it now. The shades were drawn and in the room there was a mysterious half-light, a coolness of a totally different nature from the coolness of other rooms I had been in before. I don't know why, but it seemed to me that everything there was suspended in a green light—perhaps because the curtains were green. The room was full of all sorts of furniture and chests and baskets of papers and magazines and old newspapers. But to me it seemed that it was green. And just then, at that moment I understood what *Sambo* was. I understood that here on earth, near at hand and yet invisible, inaccessible to the uninitiated, a privileged space exists, a place like a paradise, one you could never forget in your whole life if you once had the good fortune to know it. Because in *Sambo* I felt I was no longer living as I had lived before. I lived differently in a continuous inexpressible happiness. I don't know the source of this nameless bliss.

"Later, when I would think about *Sambo* I was sure that God had been waiting for me there and had taken me in his arms as soon as I stepped across the threshold. I have never, at any place or any time, felt such happiness; not in any church or art museum—nowhere—ever. Each time I went, I must have stayed there for hours, because whenever I returned to my family I found them upset and worried, occasionally even furious. 'Where have you been?' they demanded. 'We've been looking for you for three hours!' 'I was playing,' I lied, and no amount of threatening, no punishment, frightened me. I accepted everything with a smile, comforted by the thought that I would be able to return to *Sambo*. . . . Once I went there with several pieces of candy in my pocket. Without realizing it I put one in my mouth and began to suck it. Impossible! It had no flavor. I couldn't suck it. My mouth was dry. I couldn't move my tongue. I couldn't do anything in *Sambo*. I wasn't hungry, I wasn't thirsty, I wasn't sleepy. I lived, purely and simply, in paradise. . . .

"On the evening of the day when I had gone there with the candy I noticed that the men at the table beside me looked at me furtively and talked in whispers among themselves, pointing at me. Of course I realized then that they knew about my crime. They knew that I'd entered *Sambo* with candy in my pocket and had even tried to eat a piece. I believe the sense of shame and the fear that I had been discovered were the cause of the indigestion I had. For two days I lay ill. The *doica* told me later that I talked in my sleep, that I was delirious although I didn't have very much fever. I had an idea of what I might have talked about but I didn't think I'd betrayed myself. The rest of my family didn't know about *Sambo*. They hadn't turned their heads in time to see the direction indicated by the man with the mustache. . . . I waited impatiently to be allowed to get out of bed.

"On the third day as we were returning from the beach I managed to slip away from their watchful eyes and ran to the second floor. But I couldn't get in. *Sambo* was locked. I was crushed. I stayed there for a long while, trying the latch from time to time. In vain. *Sambo* remained locked. I prayed in my mind as I had been taught to pray. I recited all the prayers I knew, to God, to the Holy Mother, to Jesus Christ, and to my Guardian Angel, but *Sambo* remained locked. I prayed in my mind to the man with the mustache. I prayed to everyone at his table, those powerful men who knew unintelligible words, who were initiated into mysteries—and then trembling I put my hand on the latch. In vain. The door still didn't open. I had been forbidden to enter. *Sambo* had become inaccessible to me.

"I came back the next day and the day after. I came back every afternoon, as long as our holiday at Movila lasted. I came in vain. It had been forbidden me to enter *Sambo*. I was aware of this besides when I spied on my neighbors at the next table. They didn't look at me anymore. They stopped raising their voices, and always spoke in whispers with their heads bowed. I found out the reason for this from the *doica*. The man with the mustache had been drowned on the beach at Tuzla. They didn't bring him back to Movila. He was shipped directly to Constanta. I didn't tell them anything, but I knew why he had drowned. . . ."

"In other words, you had a guilt-complex," interrupted Biris.

"No, I don't think it was that. I didn't have any feeling of guilt, but it seemed to me I knew something. I had participated in a mystery along with all the others at the neighboring table. And this mystery involved, among other things, a death. . . . That's all. . . ." He stopped, exhausted, and lit another cigarette.

"But, actually, what was *Sambo*?" Ileana asked. "Whatever could this word *Sambo* have meant?"

Stefan smiled. "I don't know that myself, but it's not very important. Later when I was in the *liceu* I wondered if perhaps those young men had been discussing literature, and if all those foreign words that had thrilled me weren't titles of books and names of authors. Maybe the man with the mustache had uttered the word *Salammbo* emphatically, and had raised his arm high at the same time. I might have thought that he had said *Sambo* and that he was pointing to the second floor. . . . But even if this were so my experience of the mystery remains no less valid. Actually, perhaps all those literary discussions had only one purpose—of which the men who took part in them were unaware—the purpose of revealing to me the experience of the mystery. I don't want to go into the details now. . . . I've told you the story of the room *Sambo* so that you'd understand why I can't offer you anything in this secret room, why I can't even give you a sweet. Here in the secret room I cannot eat."

"If I understand you rightly," commented Biris, "this room is a replica of the room *Sambo*. You're trying now as an adult to find again that ineffable experience of childhood. . . . A psychoanalyst might call it a case of infantile regression."

"No, I don't think you're right. This secret room has another story. It's too long to tell you now. Besides, I don't know if I could tell it successfully.

76

But I'm sure it's a very different matter. I recall a thought which obsessed me when I was very young: what could I do to acquire a different identity? That is, to be a different man from the one I knew I had begun to be; a man endowed with certain intellectual tendencies, conditioned by certain social and moral complexes, with certain tastes and certain habitual reactions. What should I do, I asked myself, to be able to live in a way that was different from the way I felt myself obliged to live, obliged not only by family or society, but even by myself, by my own past, by my own *history*, as Biris would say? To give you an example: I liked certain authors and consequently I felt obliged to like them all the time. I had convinced myself that I liked them, and I felt I'd be contradicting myself if I should declare some day that I didn't like them anymore. On the day I did that I'd have the feeling that I had repudiated myself, that I was inconsistent, so to speak, that I had no continuity of ideas. Well, now, in this secret room I'm free to contradict myself, free to believe what I like, even if those beliefs and opinions are ephemeral...."

"It is, you might say, an extra-historical and atemporal room," said Biris, beginning to laugh cheerfully.

"It is that indeed," Stefan continued fervently, "but it's also something more. I won't be able to tell you everything because I don't know how to express such obscure thoughts...."

"Better show us your paintings. Maybe we'll understand what it's all about when we've seen them."

Gravely Stefan looked first at one and then the other. He ran his hand across his face and smiled. "This is the very thing that's so hard to explain," he began after a long silence, "because these paintings I want to show you conceal a great secret, and if I don't reveal it to you beforehand, I doubt you'll be able to see them."

"I don't quite understand what you mean," said Biris, "but all the same I think it might be better for you to begin by showing us the paintings."

Stefan was silent again, embarrassed.

"You told me you'd show me the car," Ileana said suddenly. "And if you want to know the truth that's what I came for—to see the car. If it had been a matter of any other kind of pictures perhaps I'd have refused. I could have come to see them some other time. But, I said to myself, maybe that midnight car can only be seen at night. That's why I came...."

Stefan continued to look at them in deep silence, almost frowning.

"You told me, '*Anch'io sono pittore!*'" Ileana insisted.

"And I am!" Stefan exclaimed all at once. "In my way, I also am a painter. But it's a very special picture. In order to understand it properly..."

At that moment they heard a voice from the room next door, a powerful voice with a provincial accent: "Show them the painting, *domnule*, and cut the gab! Show them right now, get it over with! It's midnight. Let us sleep!"

Stefan stood petrified in the middle of the room. Amused, Ileana smiled

77

and motioned toward the next room. "Answer him something," she whispered quickly. "Tell him something to quiet him."

Stefan approached her on tiptoe. "Do you think he heard it too?" he asked in an excited whisper. "Do you think he could have heard the story about the room *Sambo?*"

"No, he couldn't have," Ileana soothed him, still whispering. "I know when he came in. I heard him. It was just a few minutes ago."

"You're sure he didn't hear?" Stefan asked again, greatly disturbed.

Ileana nodded.

"Show us now, before he goes to sleep," whispered Biris, approaching Stefan.

"Impossible," Stefan said very softly. "I have to explain."

"Hang the explanations!" Biris interrupted impatiently. "It's late. At least show us one canvas. . . ."

"Just show us the car," whispered Ileana.

Stefan passed his hand over his face again, shaking with excitement. "There's only one canvas," he said at length. "There's just one and the same canvas for all my pictures. That's why I said I have to explain it to you, so you'll know how to look at it. Ileana's car, for instance, is the last picture I painted, but I painted it on the same canvas with all the other pictures. And as you can see, it's necessary I explain to you how to look at it. Otherwise you won't be able to recognize it."

"What does that matter?" exclaimed Biris in exasperation. "Show us the canvas—we'll figure it out for ourselves. We'll find the car, don't you worry. . . .!"

"But if I tell you it's one and the same canvas?" Stefan raised his voice.

"Then why did you call me?" Ileana asked. "You told me you'd show me the car."

"I'm going to show it to you, "Stefan insisted, "but only after I explain what I painted before I painted the car."

"What a stubborn man he is!" came the voice from the next room again. "God really made a stubborn one this time!" and he pounded furiously on the wall several times with his fist. "Will you show it to them, *domnule,* or shall I go call the porter?"

"I can't show it to them," cried Stefan, "because they don't know how to look at it!"

"Then turn out the light and go to bed," the man shouted at the top of his lungs. "Because if you don't, I'll call the porter!"

Ileana had risen and gone to the door, much amused. "Let's go," she whispered. "You can explain it better on the street."

"Count me out," said Biris irritabily. "I'm going home. I'm very tired. . . . I've walked all day. I went all the way to Cotroceni and I'm very tired. . . ."

3

WHEN VADASTRA RETURNED HOME AFTER THE MEETING WITH VOINEA EVERY-
thing around him—the furniture, the light, the carpets—seemed wonderful,
enchanted.

"I'm at Jassy now, *draga*,* I'm established at Jassy," Voinea had said
quickly with lowered glance. He no longer laughed with the insolence
he had displayed a few years ago. He had grown fat and next to him the
woman seemed thin. She had the timid air of a provincial.

"I have a pharmacy there. It's her property." He pointed to his
wife. "She's also a pharmacist. We do the best we can. Things haven't
been going too well recently. But as you also know, it's like that at
first. . . ."

Vadastra leaned back in the armchair in front of his desk and smiled. "A
pharmacy at Jassy. . . . We get along but it's rather hard. . . ." Poor Voinea!
How much he had been made to suffer in the past few years. . . .

He remained motionless, staring vacantly. Would Ford's answer be
delayed much longer? he found himself wondering. Two months previously he had written to the famous manufacturer a long memoran-
dum in which he had communicated his daring plans to control the
public opinion of the entire world through an extremely secret association of Catholic and Protestant bishops, scholars of universal renown,
politicians and writers of all countries—an association which he offered
to organize and lead. His letter to Ford had been written in great secrecy
and the address he gave was General Delivery. He acknowledged his

*Literally "dear." In this context "my dear fellow," "my good man."

79

own experience in the Secret Services but insisted especially on the worldwide importance this organization could have. It would bring peace to mankind and would make the name of the American industrialist immortal. For several years Vadastra had been preparing in the most minute detail a plan for secret establishments to be located in all the capitals of the world. Having read Ford's autobiography he was certain that only with a considerable fortune and a great spirit of initiative could this plan be successfully carried out. After he had hesitated endlessly over the numerous rough drafts and mental outlines he had finally made a decision and had written to Ford.

He did not doubt that one day he would go up to the post office window with his usual question and the woman would look at him with puzzled curiosity and would say, "Yes, *domnule,* you do have a letter from America!" Not a muscle of his face would move. He had long been anticipating this event. Somewhat bored, he would simply frown, and say, "Oh, is that so! I thought there might be something more interesting." Then very calmly he would put the letter in his pocket and continue to look into the faces of the women, as he always did when he found himself in the large hall of the post office. And, still quite calmly, he would descend the steps, hesitating over which direction to take. Finally he would decide to head for the *cerc* Militar, walking in a leisurely manner, his expression one of complete unconcern. And then . . .

He found it very hard to choose among so many enticing alternatives. Perhaps he would have to move to the United States, and in that case he would go to *domnul* Protopopescu's office and, lighting a cigarette—something he had never done there (and in fact he seldom smoked at all)—he would say, "I've been called to the United States. An important check has been put at my disposal. It's a matter of a very delicate mission. I can't tell you much about it, you understand. . . ." Or if he remained in Bucharest he would be notified by some bank that an account had been opened in his name for, let's say, fifty million lei per year with the request that he be discreet and make checks payable only to persons of great reliability. "But where did you get so much money, Spiridon?" *domnul* Protopopescu would ask one day, humiliated that he had not been able to find out through his own channels of information the inexhaustible source of the checks. Vadastra would look him in the eye, smiling sarcastically. He would puff on his cigarette and ask, "*Hei,* chief, do you still remember when you complained that I was a good-for-nothing who ate up the government's money? Well you see, I've found others more perceptive than you, people who appreciate my talents. I can't tell you who they are, but you'll find out someday!"

And after that he would set to work. First a trip to America to meet Ford, in case he was not asked at the outset to establish himself in the United States. Then he'd rent some elegant house in Sosea, with modern furniture, a library, secretaries (all foreign, for correspondence with illustrious persons in other countries). He would appear rather rarely in society. From time to time he would ask to be invited to the reception of some embassy or to the Foreign Minister's ball. He would dress in very severe formal attire and condescend to speak only with the ministers. But even to them he could not talk of great things. He would always hide behind the same formula: "I am not authorized to say more to Your Excellency, but if I receive new instructions, I will ask Your Excellency to come to our office someday. But I beg you—I even insist—be very, very discreet! The matter is one of utmost delicacy!"

Or so that he could savor the surprise of his former friends and acquaintances, he would sometimes go to eat in the restaurants he had frequented for so many years. And with an air of boredom he would call the waiter. "Jeane, *draga*, I'm fed up with cosmopolitan menus that begin inevitably with caviar and end eternally with champagne. *Draga*, give us something Romanian, something of our own. . . ." Then, adjusting his smoked monocle, he would look around with an air of pleasant weariness touched with melancholy. He would catch sight of an acquaintance. "How are you? . . . Ah, *draga*, what about me? . . . I shall tell you some other time. Projects, trips, a busy life, great responsibilities. But let me tell you I don't complain. It's extremely interesting work; it could have international consequences of the greatest importance for us Romanians and for all of Europe! *Draga*, our continent is too small! What Titulescu does at Geneva is interesting, I don't deny, but it's insufficient. The problem is much more vast; it calls for a spirit of initiative, of perspicacity, and discretion. . . . And that's precisely why you must forgive the fact that I cannot tell you very much. You will understand too that my mission is laden with responsibilities. It's not a matter of Romania only. The problem is infinitely more vast. I am gratified to have been entrusted with this mission because for years and years when you thought I was doing nothing . . . but forget it, forget it! Besides, I don't blame you. You understand very well that I had· to maintain the greatest secrecy, and you had no way of knowing with whom I was working. . . . All I can tell you is that this mission has been entrusted to me by an international organization. . . ."

Or if he saw a distinguished-looking woman enter the restaurant in the midst of a group of well-dressed gentlemen, he would gaze at her absently until he observed the beautiful stranger leaning toward the ear of her companion at the table to inquire about the gentleman with the dark monocle. Then he would allow his glance to slip indifferently over the whole group. "In my situation," he would say to the friend sitting beside him, "I can scarcely glance at a beautiful woman anymore without running into complications. Telephone calls, invitations to tea, and all the rest. You can imagine how discreet I have to be! . . ."

"A pharmacy at Jassy. . . . We get along but it's rather hard." Poor Voinea! If he only realized what a life he leads! Just then he heard the elevator door opening, a sound of footsteps, and next the brief excited laugh of a woman. He gave a start of surprise and strained his ears to listen. For the first time since they had begun rooming together Baleanu was bringing a woman home with him! She's probably one of *those*, thought Spiridon. He glanced at his watch: past midnight.

On the following morning Vadastra lay in wait vainly for the unknown woman. Only once did the door to Baleanu's room open. Spiridon, who was waiting for that moment so he could go out at the same time, pretended to be starting for the kitchen. His eyes fell on the lieutenant who was ready to leave, and he stared at him in astonishment.

"Are you surprised to see me dressed this way?" asked Baleanu smiling. "It's a regulation uniform. I'm on duty at my regiment today. I won't be home until tomorrow morning. So long!"

As soon as he saw him leave Vadastra could restrain himself no longer. Sending the orderly to buy a package of cigarettes, he boldly entered Baleanu's room. He carried several books, giving the impression that he had come to return the volumes. In the doorway he paused, preparing to apologize, but a quick glance into all the corners convinced him that the room was empty. Disappointed, he set the books on the desk and began to search for traces of the visitor. Indeed, a vague suggestion of a woman's perfume still lingered in the room, and this irritated him still more. He looked under the pillows, drew back the bedspread, glanced under the bed and in the wardrobe, but he found no clue of any kind anywhere, not even a flower, a handkerchief, or a cigarette stub stained with lipstick. Vexed, he leafed through the German-Romanian dictionary and grammar that Baleanu always kept close at hand on a little table beside the bed. Here, too, there was not a letter, not a note, not even a visiting card. He heard the orderly coming in through the kitchen and with the books under his arm he left the room quickly. When the orderly brought him the cigarettes Vadastra couldn't refrain from asking, "Listen, when did the lieutenant's girl friend leave?"

The soldier looked at Spiridon in surprise. "I know nothing, *dom'* Vadastra. I didn't even know the lieutenant had a woman with him."

That morning Spiridon went to the post office again. He was startled when the woman held out an envelope to him, but he found it difficult to arrest a gesture of irritation after looking at it. The letter was from his father. He waited until dinner to open it, when he had finished eating the roast. "I must inform you about us, we are well, in good health, and we wish the same to you from the heart, as our old men say when they address their offspring in the military service." He intends to be ironic, Spiridon commented mentally, skimming over the lines. "I was in Bucharest again—the capital of *Romania Mare*—but I did not find you at the old address, while at the new one—if it was correct—apparently we peasants don't even have entrance to the back stairs. . . ." Etc., etc., etc., Spiridon thought, turning the pages in annoyance. Let's see what he wants. . . . "Soon I shall come to bring some business for Your Majesty—trouble with our land at Saraceni, and with a fine imposed on your sister. I should like for us to meet then, so that we can talk to each other about our needs and difficulties. With the money you sent us last month, I have repaired my jacket, I have paid a part of the taxes, and there was enough left for some better tobacco for me. But also I should greatly like to read some of the books that, from what I hear, appear in abundance in Bucharest, each one more beautiful than the last." I understand, concluded Spiridon as he folded the letter and put it carefully in the upper pocket of his vest. Upon reaching home he proceeded to destroy it, lest it be seen by someone indiscreet.

After lunch he returned to the post office and sent a money order for two thousand lei, giving his address at the courthouse as usual. He began to be obsessed by the woman's voice that he had heard on the preceding night. He couldn't understand how she had managed to leave Baleanu's room without his learning about it. Toward evening his curiosity overcame him anew, and he returned home determined to search the lieutenant's room once again. On the way he had bought a ticket to a motion picture. He gave it to the orderly, telling him he was expecting a visitor and that it would be better if he didn't come back before midnight and after that to stay in the kitchen. Left alone, Spiridon entered the lieutenant's room and started his search again. The windows had been standing open for a long time and all trace of the woman's perfume had disappeared. Nevertheless Spiridon did not lose hope. He opened the wardrobe but found nothing unusual to attract his attention. He began to search through the pockets of the military tunic and trousers, but while rummaging around he found himself suddenly excited, almost trembling with pleasure. He paused for a moment in front of the mirror. The temptation was very strong to put on the officer's uniform and go for a walk on the street. Making up his mind suddenly he pulled out the suit, turned off the light, and although he knew that the orderly had gone out he crept stealthily back into his own room.

He did not dress in the tunic alone but first he put on the pants. They gave him some difficulty since Baleanu was stockier than Vadastra and a little taller. Spiridon was forced to shorten the suspenders and pull the belt as tightly as he could. At last, rearranging his monocle and pulling the cap down on his head, he looked at himself in the mirror. Unconsciously he breathed deeply several times and emitted a long sigh, not daring to take his eyes from the image in the mirror, the image that restored the childhood dream of himself: imposing, martial, seductive. He frowned, raised his head higher and turned it slowly until the monocle disappeared almost completely. Out of the corner of his eye he followed his reflection in the mirror, preening himself in the light of the lamp. Then abruptly he took off the cap, stepped back, and broke into a brief laugh, dry and rough. He laughed in an effort to master his emotion. Uncertain as to what to do he dropped into an easy chair and stretched. He admired the military trousers and examined himself from head to foot, but gradually his excitement got the better of him again and he sprang to his feet. In haste he put the cap on and stood soberly before the mirror. He waited indecisively for a few moments with the fingers of his right hand pressed stiffly together, pausing in a position of attention. Finally he saluted himself. That gesture seemed to free him from a burden that until then had made breathing difficult. His face lighted up and he repeated the salute mechanically, perfecting his stance of attention, standing now very close to the mirror, now back in the middle of the room. And then he became aware that he was taking several steps to the left, several to the right, and making an about-face. Each maneuver was more difficult than the last and was followed by a solemn presentation in front of the mirror and a salute.

Absent-mindedly Vadastra walked around the room for half an hour. He walked as he would walk on the street, but whenever he passed the mirror he saluted. Sometimes his salute was respectful and formally correct, at other times friendly, and at still other times it was indifferent or even weary, given grudgingly. He was imagining that he was meeting superiors, comrades, and underlings on the street. He did not think for a single moment that his uniform, too large and with the shoulders drooping, would attract glances, nor that the black monocle might be suspect. From the moment of his first salute in front of the glass his decision had been made. He would go downstairs and take a stroll dressed as an army officer.

He had hardly stepped into the elevator when he began to feel anxiety. It was just eleven o'clock and he might be recognized by one of the neighbors. He removed his monocle quickly and hurried across the lobby with his head bent, preoccupied. Once he reached the street he set off with great strides toward the area of the sidewalk that was not so brightly lighted. For some time he hesitated over which direction to take, then he headed resolutely toward a taxi stand. It was not until he found himself a few steps from the cab that he resumed his military air and looked calmly around him.

84

The driver was dozing. Waking at the sound of Spiridon's voice he turned around suddenly and said, "At your service, *domnule* Captain!" Spiridon mechanically brought his hand to his cap.

"Take me to Sosea, fellow! And there's no need to hurry. We've plenty of time!" The night was clear and not too hot. On *bulevardul* Lascar Catargiu near the Bratianu Statue the crowds still had not diminished. Vadastra looked calmly to right and left with an indescribable happiness bubbling in his soul. As they approached a newsstand he signaled to the driver to stop. He hopped out nimbly and raising his hand momentarily to his cap, he asked for a package of Regale cigarettes. He thought that the woman looked at him somewhat suspiciously but he was not intimidated. He paid her, saluted again, and returned to the cab, whistling.

"To Sosea, fellow!" He lit a cigarette, chiefly for effect, and sprawled in a more comfortable position in the back seat. When they reached Sosea he paid the driver, saluted, and began to stroll along the avenue, full of confidence. He met almost no one, but if he saw a couple approaching in the distance— and if the man were a civilian—he slackened his pace and regarded them provocatively, smiling. He started once when he heard behind him in the semidarkness the noise of spurs. His hand was readied for a salute but it was only a police sergeant who walked by without seeing Spiridon.

At midnight he decided to go back. Only then did he notice that he had walked a long way. It took him twenty minutes to reach the *piata* Victoriei. Here the lights frightened him. There were still several groups of people waiting for trams, and some drunks were singing as they headed for the Filantropie. Spiridon waited a little while to see if any army officers might be nearby, then set out in haste toward the taxi stand located on the other side of the *piata*. However, as he was crossing the street a major got off a tram and Spiridon found himself unexpectedly face to face with him. He felt a cold sweat break out all over his body, but he saluted with such promptness that the major was taken by surprise. When Vadastra had passed, the major turned his head inquisitively, and at the same moment Spiridon also turned to look at him. Not knowing what else to do, he saluted again, his shoulders sagging weakly, and then hurried on. He thought someone had started after him, and since he was afraid to run in the middle of the *piata*, he changed his direction and turned back across the street with the same zeal, heading toward the dark area from which he had come. He could still hear the footsteps behind him. When he reached the shadow of the trees he stopped a moment, looked at his watch, and then as if he had just noticed that he was very late for an important appointment he set off on the run. As he fled he took off his monocle, clutching it nervously in his fist. He crossed several streets and did not stop until he saw a couple coming toward him. The sound of footsteps had ceased. Somewhat tired and perspiring he continued on his way, forcing himself to control his respiration by keeping his mouth closed and breathing only through his nose. He walked back along the *sosea* Jianu and climbed into the first taxi he met on the way.

But as soon as he had found a refuge his fear subsided and he began to laugh. What could he have done to me? he asked himself. How could he have known who I am? It was more difficult for him to make up his mind to enter the apartment house. Dismissing the taxi on a nearby street he walked close to the walls without his monocle, glancing furtively at every shadow. The facade of the building where he lived was brilliantly illuminated by a street lamp. He waited on the corner for some time in case someone might be going in, then he strode forward and opened the door nervously, his head bent. Once he reached his room he replaced his monocle and looked at himself triumphantly in the mirror. He smiled and saluted himself repeatedly. Then very carefully he began to take off the tunic, searching in each pocket to be certain he had not unwittingly overlooked something. He shook it thoroughly to remove the dust, straightened out the pants with care, brushed the cap. Then with a pleasant feeling of excitement he tiptoed barefoot into Baleanu's room, scarcely opening the door. He was shaking as he put everything back in place.

Next morning Spiridon awaited the lieutenant's return with some anxiety. It was nearly eight o'clock when he heard him enter, and Baleanu went immediately to take a bath. Then he retired, commanding the orderly to awaken him at three in the afternoon. Vadastra left for town with a light heart. He only wondered now how he could find out from Baleanu, without arousing suspicion, the days when the lieutenant was on duty with the regiment, so that he could plan ahead of time for his walks in the military uniform. He intended to make a date with one of his casual acquaintances—seamstress, milliner, apprentice—to dine with her in a rather secluded tavern where he knew he would avoid the risk of being recognized or examined with too much suspicion.

He envisioned himself clearly and in precise detail strolling down the street on the arm of the girl, saluting right and left, and all the while continuing his monologue.

"I imagine you're surprised to see me in uniform," he would say, "because you never would have suspected from my appearance what my true profession was. Even now you can't be informed about all of it because—you understand why—I can't reveal everything to you. There are officers and *officers*, dear girl. You know most of them—the ones you see on the street who are so frivolous, with an eye for the girls. 'Officers of the troop,' as we call them at Headquarters. Some are uneducated, devoid of ambition, preoccupied with petty things. But in addition to these an elite exists, the brain of the entire army. The whole

86

burden lies on us. We make the secret plans, we're concerned with espionage and counterespionage. Some of us—a very few you understand, the most gifted—have extremely delicate assignments. Sometimes not only our own lives—this would be nothing, what does one life count for?—but also the existence of the whole nation, even the peace of Europe, hangs on such a mission.

"Naturally our missions impose upon us the greatest discretion. We two are walking now on the street as if nothing could happen. And all at once I see passing in front of me a *certain* man who signals me in such a way that you can be sure I alone will see it. On that signal might hang the life of some important personality in our nation. I say *might* because as you understand I can't tell you more. This is just an example. It might be something quite different—for instance, the capture of a dangerous spy, or a declaration of war, or the theft of a secret document, and so forth. . . . Then at the signal I should pretend that I had suddenly remembered something. I might, for instance, look at my watch, or I might thumb through my date book to check an address or an appointment. This example is just so that you'll understand how things happen with us. Then I'd beg to be excused, telling you some kind of lie, and I'd disappear. Where, I can't tell you, but you couldn't conceive of the extraordinary places in which we gather, those few of us in the military counterintelligence. The reality surpasses the imagination by far, believe me! There are instances when we don't even know one another, because each of us is the head of a special secret service and we come together only when there are grave and urgent questions to be resolved. But we are dressed in such a manner—I can't tell you more—that even if we knew one another, we couldn't be recognized. Some change their voices, while others don't speak at all but write what they have to say on a little tablet. They write of course in capital letters so they won't give themselves away. . . . And so on!

"If you had any idea of the dangers that each of us has to pass through just to get to the meeting place! . . . and the secrets we know! It would be enough for us just to pronounce a few words and a man would disappear—not just anyone, but an important figure. Actually we few leaders really hold the destiny of the country in our hands. The government, the ministers, all the dignitaries of whom you hear talk to the right and left or read about in the newspapers, they're nothing but our instruments. Puppets, my dear girl, mere marionettes in my hand or in the hand of another of our leaders! What does a government matter? If we wish, I or one of the others, we can change it as easily as you say 'hello!' The only thing is that no one knows us. We guide from the shadows. This is our strength. Even if someone should wish to do us harm he wouldn't know how to strike us because we're invisible. But when we feel that a minister, or even a prime minister wants to harm us, we overthrow him immediately. People read the next day in the paper that *domnul* So-and-so has resigned, but no one knows that he was our victim! And so forth. . . .

"You wonder perhaps why I'm walking with you right now when I could be going to the most elegant salon, and especially why I'm telling you all these important things. First of all be assured that I haven't told you a thousandth part of our secrets, and all that I've told you is only an approximate example of how things happen in our life. And in the second place it wouldn't enter your head what my mission is at this very moment. Perhaps—I say *perhaps* just to give you an example—I have to be found on a certain day at a certain hour on a certain street in expectation of a message of extreme importance. You have the impression that we're going together to eat and you wonder why I've chosen this particular remote restaurant when we could be dining in the most elegant place or in a private room in Sosea. This is, let's say, your impression. In reality, to give you an example, I've selected this street or this tavern because I'm *expecting* something—*what*, I can't tell you. . . ."

For a long time Vadastra reviewed this film of himself dressed as an officer walking with a girl friend, imagining the conversation that undoubtedly would have taken place. Ordinarily he abandoned himself to these reveries only after a certain amount of resistance. Their delights were too intoxicating. But this time the events of the previous night justified any fancies. At the first opportunity when Baleanu would go to the regiment for the whole night, he would really make a date with one of the girls and they would go walking together until far into the nighttime!

Only when they left the train at the station in Ulm one cool evening in late August was Ioana happy again. At that moment she forgot everything and clung to Stefan. She felt again as she had felt before—prior to the Big Scene.

She had not been able to read that night when she was waiting for him. She heard him opening the door at two o'clock in the morning and she got out of bed quickly to meet him.

"What happened?" she asked fearfully. "What happened to you?"

Stefan looked at her absently, making an effort to smile. His skin looked sallow and he appeared to be extremely tired. He passed by without kissing her and dropped into an easy chair.

"What's happened?" Ioana inquired again, going to him and taking his hand.

"Have you read *Viata Romaneasca?*" asked Stefan with difficulty. "Do you ever read *Viata Romaneasca?*"

"Now and then. But why do you ask? What's happened?"

"*He* knew Anisie too. He's also met him." Stefan forced himself to smile. "He's the prototype, he creates the model. I don't do anything but walk in his tracks. I imitate him. I model myself after him. . . ."

Ioana sat down beside him on the arm of the chair, putting her arm around his shoulders. "Oh, Stefan!" she whispered, "Stefan!"

"Like that time on the street," he continued with the same forced smile. "If he hadn't existed, my existence too would have been different. . . ."

Holding him close Ioana tried to make him stop talking but Stefan gently freed himself and started again.

"Any man's life is in a large measure the work of chance, but it's not a matter of chance in our case. We didn't meet each other by chance in the way that everybody else does. You confused me with him, and Anisie probably did the same thing. You confused me with someone you already loved. . . ."

"That's not true!" cried Ioana standing up. "I've told you so many times, it's not true!"

"And Anisie," Stefan continued, "he probably confused me with someone he knew already, someone with whom he had once conversed, and with whom he got along well enough to be able to reveal himself. . . ."

"It's not true!" Ioana interrupted, realizing that she could no longer avoid the Big Scene. "I never loved him the way I loved you, once I'd seen you."

"But that's just the tragedy of it," said Stefan, his voice strangely calm. "You didn't see *me*, you saw him. It wasn't a *coup de foudre* but a case of mistaken identity. Why won't you understand? I didn't exist for you and I wouldn't exist even now if it hadn't been for him. If you'd seen me before you knew him, you wouldn't have noticed me. . . ."

"But then you wouldn't have noticed me either," Ioana interrupted again with restraint.

Baffled, Stefan stared at her. "That's true," he said finally. "And that's just as serious. This means that our love and our life together are founded on an ambiguity. We wouldn't have been brought together if it hadn't been for a confusion. We'd have passed right by, perhaps without even looking at each other. We never would have met, we wouldn't have loved each other. . . ."

"How do you know? How do you know we never would have met?"

89

And seeing that he was silent she held him in her arms again, frightened. "My darling, my darling," she whispered. "I'd have searched to the end of the earth until I found you!"

"If he hadn't existed you wouldn't have known how to recognize me," Stefan said, suddenly becoming animated. "In order to be able to love me you needed a model, of which I was a more or less perfect copy. If only we had been different!" He was almost whispering. "If only we had been as different physically as we are in mind and spirit! But as it is I always feel guilty toward him, as if I had forged a signature and received an inheritance that was his, not mine. . . ."

"Be quiet!" cried Ioana terrified. "Be quiet! You'll drive me insane!" She burst into tears, drooping limply on the arm of the chair. Stefan began to stroke her hair wearily, absently.

"And yet I love you very much," he whispered at length. "I love you much more than the other. . . ."

Ioana started and raised her head abruptly.

"I met her last year," Stefan continued without looking at her, "and I thought I could love you both just as you also loved each of us, Partenie and me, equally. But it's impossible for me. I love you much more. . . . Sometimes I think I'm in love with her, but I soon realize that I'm not, that it only seems that way. It seems so to me because I want a miracle to happen. I want to love a great many people in the way that the saints do, with a love as strong as my love for you. But I can't. . . . I can't love anyone but you! . . ."

Ioana had hoped vainly to find out more that night, the next morning, during the days that followed. "She's a girl I met last year," Stefan would answer. "But I can't love her, I can't love anyone but you." And one day he had added, "You've been more fortunate than I. You've been able to love two men at the same time." Ioana had stared at him for a long while. Sadness filled her eyes, and weariness. She had wanted to respond but she felt exhausted, almost indifferent. Then all at once she realized what a failure the Big Scene had been. It was even grotesque. She had not been able to control herself. She had not had time to say all those things she had prepared for years in advance. She had begun to cry too soon. In the Big Scene as she had repeated it mentally innumerable times she was supposed to burst into tears much later. But after that night everything seemed futile and without meaning. Throughout her entire being only an indefinable lassitude remained, an unnamed wasteland. She felt that something deep within her had been shaken, something around her had changed, but what it was she did not know.

"Here on this foreign soil," Stefan had told her in Yugoslavia, "I know that you're mine alone. In Romania there are places you

90

enjoyed before you met me, places we haven't seen together. But here the first step you take on these streets is at my side."

She liked to hear him speak to her in this way, yet something deep inside remained passive and inert. It was only when they had crossed the Swiss frontier, when she knew that they were approaching Ulm, that she began to recover. We've reached Ulm! she thought, repeating the words over and over to herself as if she could not quite believe it.

When she was a little girl her mother once showed her an album of picture postcards. Ioana put her small hand first on one card then on another, asking what each one was. "Ulm," her mother answered after one such request, and this name was the only one that she remembered later. She did not understand why. Uncle Liviu, her father's brother and the only wealthy member of the family, had been to Ulm once. He died when she was three, so she had never known him. Ioana's father was a history teacher at the *liceu* for boys in Targoviste, and his sisters had stayed in Ardeal, where the elder had married a notary and the other a priest in a village near Sibiu. Uncle Liviu had studied engineering in Germany, returned to Romania, and had set up a refinery at Campina. When he was still quite young he had been killed in an accident. After his death Ioana's father inherited enough money to buy a vineyard near Targoviste; and a few years later, when he was transferred to a *liceu* in Bucharest, he bought a house in the Cotroceni section. "What city in the world would you like most to live in?" This was the popular game at the Regina Maria Liceu when Ioana went there that fall. The other girls answered, "Paris," "Venice," "Naples," "Bombay." Ioana's response was always "Ulm." "But why?" they asked her. "The tallest cathedral in Germany is at Ulm," was her prompt reply, yet she knew very well that it was not for this reason that she would like to live there.

To correspond with a girl in Ulm who would invite her there to spend a summer vacation was Ioana's dream during the first year of *liceu*. That was why she enjoyed studying German. Then one day she met Dan, the brother of Stella Ciuceanu, who sat next to her in the fourth class. Dan was in the sixth. He was a poet. He published verses in provincial reviews and sometimes Stella brought the magazines to school to show them to Ioana. Often Ioana thought she recognized herself in those sweet and solitary girls of whom Dan sang. This was especially true of a poem that began "You walk, melancholy, in an old German town. . . ." "It's Ulm!" she had exclaimed, and felt her heart leap. She wanted to ask him about it the next time they met, but that day Dan was talking about *The Girlhood of Melania*, the novel of a young writer, Ciru Partenie.

91

"What an odd name, Ciru," Ioana had said. "I've never heard of such a name before—Ciru!" And *The Girlhood of Melania* was not at all like anything that she had read before either. It was a simple story, yet strange and disturbing. It haunted her. Ioana felt that she was already in love, that only a love like the one in *The Girlhood of Melania* deserves to be lived, that only a woman like Melania could know true love. She had been particularly disturbed by the way the novel began. One morning a young man entered a girls' primary school in a town on the banks of the Danube. "I want to consult the catalogues of eighteen and nineteen years ago," he said. "I want to find out about a girl who studied here at that time. Her name was Melania. . . ." That was the way the novel began. "No, I didn't know her," he said. "A good friend of mine who is now ill at Davos asked me to inquire about this girl, Melania. He doesn't remember the name of her family anymore. All he knows is that her first name is Melania. No, I don't know anyone in the city. I arrived this morning and came directly here to the school from the station. I want to leave by rail tonight. There's a train at five of nine. . . ."

"There's a train at five of nine" had become the customary expression at Regina Maria when one of the girls wanted to say that there was nothing more to be done, that it was vain to hope for something else, that a situation had been definitely decided. *"Rien ne va plus!"* was what Ioana had heard the croupiers shouting at the casino at Sinaia sometime later. This means that there's a train at five of nine, she had interpreted mentally. It means that there's nothing more to be done. *Les jeux sont faits!* Sebastian, the hero of *The Girlhood of Melania*, had not been able to catch the evening train at five of nine.

She had been in Sinaia the summer after she had taken her baccalaureate. She knew then that she loved Ciru Partenie. In the following autumn she would enroll at the Faculty of Letters. During that same summer at Sinaia *doamna* Bologa received the first proposal of marriage for Ioana. It was from a medical officer, a captain, who wanted to set up a practice in the fall in Bucharest. "It is better for the health this way, dear lady," Ioana heard him say on the veranda. "Seventeen to eighteen is the ideal age for marriage. What does she need of more studies? She's not a poor girl who has to work for a living. If I open an office in Cotroceni, I'll be assured of a clientele." "The captain covets our house," old *domnul* Bologa said that evening, smiling placidly. "That's why you must decide quickly. He wants to open an office in Cotroceni." "It's useless to ask me," Ioana had answered. "I'm enrolling at the University. I don't care what the captain's hopes are. . . ." (He had said on leaving. "I hope that *domnisoara* Bologa will change her mind.") But mentally Ioana had added, There's a train at five of nine. . . .

She had read and reread all Partenie's books. She read constantly. In the Seminar on Romanian Literature she probably had read more than any other. But she was timid and it was difficult for her to find words when she had to speak extemporaneously. She felt sure of herself only when she had prepared the assignments at home for the seminar and had written them out. One day she presented a paper about the female characters in Partenie's works. When the professor's assistant stood up and began to criticize it, Ioana shuddered. Her whole interpretation, said the assistant, was wrong because she had disregarded the influence of Hamsun and Rilke on the author. "His women, beginning with Melania, show the effect of his reading of Hamsun and Rilke— read to be sure in French translation because, as he has admitted in an interview, it's the only foreign language he knows. But all his works are inspired by Teutonic motifs. . . ."

"You walk, melancholy, in an old German town. . . ." Ioana had remembered Dan's poem. Later, when she knew Partenie, she asked him once who his favorite writers were. "There are so many that I couldn't list them all," he had replied. "What about Hamsun and Rilke?" "Yes, those, and others greater than they." "Would you like to live in Ulm?" Ioana asked him unexpectedly, looking in his eyes. "In Ulm?" he had responded in astonishment. "That doesn't make sense. Why in Ulm?" "The tallest cathedral in Germany is there," Ioana said quickly. "But it's not only that. It seems to be very, very beautiful. My dream is to be able to go to Ulm some day. . . ." "Fortunately," Partenie had said, smiling, "You've chosen a dream that's very easily realized. . . ."

"Of course the first place we'll go is to Ulm," Ciru had said on the night of their engagement. He had been nervous and out of sorts all evening. This was only the third time that he had visited her at her home in Cotroceni. The first time he came he had said to *doamna* Bologa abruptly, "I should like to inform you of something, and I don't dare anticipate your reaction. Ioana and I have decided to get married. I've come to ask for your consent. . . ." The second time he had been invited to dinner. On the evening of their engagement *domnul* Bologa tried occasionally to talk with him, but Ciru listened for a few moments absently, nodding his head, then turned to speak to Ioana. No one but the two of them knew that they were going to become formally engaged that evening. They had brought the wedding rings, and shortly after Partenie arrived several bottles of iced champagne were delivered to the door. Then they had announced it. "We're engaged!" *Doamna* Bologa began to cry. Probably it was this that upset Ciru, Ioana said to herself. She saw that he had become silent, smoking cigarette after cigarette, and he stared fixedly at them one after the other, looking almost stern.

93

He seemed to be making a great effort to recognize them. They decided to have the wedding six weeks later, just before vacation. "Of course we'll go to Ulm first," Partenie kept saying. "But I'll let you do all the talking. I don't know any German. . . ."

Her honeymoon with Stefan had been to Italy. "You'll go to Ulm another time," *doamna* Bologa had consoled her. "You have plenty of time. You're young. You'll be traveling all your life."

It had become completely dark by the time they reached the back of the cathedral. They caught sight of a number of stained glass windows lighted from within. As they approached they heard strains of organ music coming to them very softly from a source that seemed to be a great mystery.

"Let's not go on," Stefan said. "It's nicer here."

"It seems as though it's being played for people of another age," whispered Ioana, deeply moved. "Maybe we shouldn't listen. We might be committing a sin."

For a long time Stefan had noticed that Ioana's replies sometimes corresponded with his own thoughts to a remarkable degree. The organist did indeed seem to be playing for people of another age.

"I hope you'll stop at Nuremberg," Biris had said to them before they left. "Forget about the Black Forest, Ulm, Heidelberg, and the castles of the Rhine Valley. These are all from another age. You need to bathe in contemporary history to wake yourselves up! Go to Nuremberg, go to Berlin to realize what sauce we'll be eating tomorrow, to look at history on the march. But after all why Ulm?" he had asked them. "It's Ioana's dream, a dream of hers since childhood," Stefan had said, "and I want to make it come true." Biris had begun to laugh. "You should sever yourself from childhood dreams," he had said. Ever since that night in Stefan's room Biris's crude tormenting jokes had not lessened. He called Stefan's painting Le chef d'oeuvre inconnu, and he described it as he imagined it. "A canvas covered to the saturation point with all kinds of colors in which one can no longer distinguish anything. Only your eye, which has grown accustomed to the supernatural light of the room Sambo, can decipher the lost myths of childhood in that multicolored mess! Better go to Nuremberg," he added, "so you can see how myths are being motorized in our day. . . ."

"We'd better go now," Ioana whispered. "We might be committing some sin."

94

A few steps away on one side of the cathedral there was an ale house. They went inside. Stefan liked it from the start. It too was from another age, at least from the time of his grandfather. Swept by a feeling of melancholy happiness Ioana had the impression that she was listening to the story of her own dream told by another. She heard Stefan talking about the man with the thick mustache like the Kaiser's, the one whose sleeves were rolled up and who sighed from time to time into his mug of beer. "He looks like Tazlaoanu, the tenant of our vineyard at Ramnicul Sarat."

He began to relate an incident concerning Tazlaoanu, but he stopped with a puzzled frown after a few moments. A young man from a neighboring table had stood up and was approaching them. His face seemed rather familiar but Stefan could not place him.

"Excuse me," he said. "I heard you speaking Romanian and I even have the impression that we've met; this past year on the train, if I'm not mistaken. Professor Antim was there too. . . ." He introduced himself very properly. His name was Ioachim Teodorescu, and he had come to Germany to study archeology. He had not encountered a Romanian for a long time and he asked permission to stay at their table for a moment. Stefan invited him to sit down, hiding his annoyance with difficulty. Ioana looked at him in desperation, wordlessly imploring him not to accept the invitation but just to disappear. She had recognized him instantly. He was the young man with the dark blue eyes that were fixed on Stefan in the train last summer when they went to Predeal, the youth with whom Professor Antim had talked steadily. But Ioachim Teodorescu did not notice anything and sat down with delighted gratitude.

"When I heard someone speak Romanian," he told them, "I wondered who it could be. Not many Romanians stop here at Ulm. It's a beautiful city but there are so many other beautiful cities in Germany. . . . Actually, what was it that made you come here? . . ."

He heard the elevator stop at their floor, then the sound of Baleanu's footsteps, followed by some very indistinct whispering. Spiridon Vadastra turned off the lamp on his desk so they would not see a light under his door when they came in. He tiptoed to the wall. There was no doubt about it, a woman was with the lieutenant. He could tell by her step. Spiridon held his breath. He heard Baleanu whisper, "Wait until I turn on the light, so you won't stumble over something." Vadastra remained expectantly near the wall, not knowing what to do. It would be impossible to go to bed, yet on the other hand he did not dare to light the lamp and start to work again for fear of attracting attention. At last he made up his mind to wait there in the darkness, but after about an hour he became bored. He pressed the light switch and went down the hall to the bathroom, walking naturally as if he had just got out of bed. There was no sound of voices as he passed Baleanu's room. The lamp was not burning and this fact baffled him. He had expected to see a light under the door. Then he would have cried out, "What, haven't you gone to bed yet, *boierule?*"* But since he had no such pretext he could say nothing. He returned to his room walking heavily in his house slippers. Chewing his nails in irritation he waited a little longer, but finally he undressed and stretched out on the bed, determined not to fall asleep.

Nevertheless drowsiness overcame him after half an hour. He did not realize how long he had slept and he awoke in a panic. He looked at the luminous dial of his watch, which he had placed on the little table beside his bed. It was a quarter to four. Just then he heard someone open the door of the lieutenant's room. Excitedly he got out of bed and went again to the wall. He heard them walk along the hall and this time they did not take so many precautions. Baleanu whispered something to the woman, but in spite of all his efforts Spiridon could not catch the sense of the words. When the lieutenant opened the entry door, Vadastra could restrain himself no longer. Taking a step back toward the bed he called out, "Who's there? Who is it?"

The lieutenant hesitated a moment, but when he heard Vadastra repeat his question as he fumbled to find his doorknob, he answered, "Don't be alarmed. It's I."

"But who are you talking to?" asked Vadastra, not daring to appear in his pajamas.

"I wasn't talking to anyone. You're mistaken." The lieutenant opened the entry door and pulled the woman after him. A few moments later Vadastra heard the elevator descending. He thought Baleanu had gone with her simply to escort her downstairs, but after waiting for ten minutes close to the wall he became aware of his error and went back to bed. He was sorry now that he had not dashed into the hall and surprised them. Disappointed, he let himself fall asleep and did not hear the lieutenant when he returned later in the morning.

The next day Baleanu came looking for Spiridon in his room. "You were rather frightened last night," he began with a big mysterious smile. "Now I can tell you. You weren't mistaken. I wasn't alone. I was with a woman."

"Oh?" inquired Spiridon, pretending to be surprised.

"It's not what you think," said Baleanu defensively. "She's not one of *those* women. You know what I mean. She's married. I've loved her for a long time. To tell you the truth we love each other. It's really a pure love, I assure you. I want her to get a divorce, to separate from her husband, but she keeps putting it off. It's especially hard for her because she's from a very good family

---

*Boyar, nobleman.

96

and her husband is a rich man. And I mean very rich. He's in oil, and he has factories too, although she herself isn't from a wealthy family. With my pay as a lieutenant... You understand. Perhaps later on..."

He stopped abruptly, choked by his great emotion, and drew deeply on his cigarette.

"*Ei*, my congratulations!" Vadastra exclaimed, not knowing what else to say. "But when did you meet her?"

"I've known her for a long time. I didn't dare tell her, you know, that I love her. I went to her house often, especially since her husband spends most of his time at Ploiesti or Campina. But I didn't tell her. I wanted to see first if she felt the same way about me. I realized, by her glances and by the way she spoke to me, that she loved me. Then I told her. She told me, too. And, you know, I've persuaded her to come here to my place when her husband's away on business. It's safer that way...."

"Does she know anything about me?" asked Spiridon, suddenly excited.

"Why not? I told her everything, from the beginning. Who you are, what abilities you have, etc. I assure you, I spoke of you as a friend."

"Thank you very much." Spiridon moistened his lips. "I believe you gave her a good impression of me. Did you tell her what connections I have, about the good families I go around with, about my intellectual preoccupations?"

Delighted that the discussion was no longer concerned with the visitor of the night before, the lieutenant revealed to Spiridon all that he had said about him, even from the time before he had confessed his love. He had told her that Vadastra was a man who sees the world in a different way from the rest of mankind, who has different interests and a vast learning, a great capacity to work—he is able to do many things, avocations, philosophy, politics....

"You told her this?" Spiridon whispered, with a shiver. "And what did she say?"

"She knows you now better than you could imagine," said the lieutenant firmly, "seeing that I talk about you all the time."

"Yes, but she doesn't know what I look alike," Spiridon interrupted with a note of regret in his voice.

"She'll meet you someday. Later on, because now she's embarrassed. It wasn't easy for her to admit she loves me and to come at night to my place."

"Is she beautiful?" inquired Spiridon.

The lieutenant gave him a long serious look. He dropped his glance and seemed to be speaking to himself. "She's the most beautiful woman in Bucharest!"

Overcome, Vadastra could not refrain from sighing. "Bravo! I congratulate you with all my heart!"

Baleanu, however, seemed preoccupied. He lit a cigarette and made an effort to smile again. Spiridon regarded him very intently.

The lieutenant said gravely, "All the same, even though we love each other, this is adultery, it's a sin."

"What difference does that make?" Spiridon interrupted nervously. "Who pays any attention to such nonsense nowadays? If her husband neglects her...."

"Of course he neglects her," Baleanu said, "but such is his life—always at Campina, at Ploiesti, in foreign countries. . . . One doesn't acquire a fortune of close to hundred million by staying home all the time!"

"How much did you say he has?" cried Vadastra springing up from the chair. "A hundred million?"

"Maybe not quite that much, but almost. He has I don't know how many parcels of land at Campina, which are just now beginning to be developed, plus stocks, plus being on the boards of directors of I don't know how many companies. . . ."

"A hundred million!" Vadastra kept repeating over and over. "Do you hear that, man, a hundred million!" All at once he felt overwhelmed with hatred and he began to pace the floor in a rage. "How is it possible for an ordinary man to have a hundred million?" he exclaimed indignantly.

"He's not ordinary," Baleanu defended the man soberly. "He's clever and able and he had good luck with an uncle who bought the parcels of land before the war and left them to him in his will. Then too, he works from morning till night."

"But think how many other people work, and what do they get for it? And capable men too who have an ideal in life, not just to be millionaires. . . . What does he do with so much money? What does he use his millions for? Man, if I had his money, what wouldn't I do!"

"It's not so easy as you think," said Baleanu. "You have to keep youself occupied with your millions. A fortune doesn't come to you all by itself! And then too don't think that a man as rich as he is lives better than we do. He has many more cares than we, and besides this, others live off his money. There are all sorts of benevolent societies and institutions and I don't know what else that come to him continually asking for support."

"What does that mean, benevolent societies?" Spiridon exclaimed, exasperated. "A pretext, in order to avoid saying you don't want to help other people. For instance, if I should come to him and tell him my plans, do you think he'd give me ten or fifteen million?"

"That's rather a lot," the lieutenant said, smiling. "I've heard that he gives scholarships to some students in the villages where his lands are, but they're small sums."

"And I can well believe it! A charity of a few thousand lei per month! He wouldn't find the money for a great work, for a capable man with bold plans. . . ."

He paused briefly then added, "Oh let's drop it. Maybe the wheel will turn eventually, and maybe someday I too will find the money I need to put my plans into operation. Then I'll show them, those gentlemen, and I'll teach them all a lesson! It's nothing. I've waited and I can wait longer. But someday my chance will come too! Then you'll see all of them bowing down to me, offering me millions to forgive them. But I won't forgive them, not one. Listen, man, a hundred million! And if I should ask for fifty or sixty million, he'd say I was crazy. And what great things I'd do with that money. *Great things*, unique things, that everybody would talk about—not such things as oil wells and refineries!"

Suddenly he stopped, worn out, with an infinite sense of longing in his heart. This man next to him knows a millionaire, the master of a fortune of a hundred million lei. And instead of introducing them, instead of trying to convince him of Vadastra's worth, instead of asking the millionaire to help him borrow an important sum—this man, his so-called friend, is content with a love affair that will lead to a fatal rupture of relations with the possessor of all that money! No one wants to help him! On the contrary if they could they would put obstacles in his way for the sole purpose of robbing him of fame, of preventing him from realizing his plans. Like *domnul* Protopopescu, for instance. But never mind. . . . It's nothing. . . .

"It's nothing," he resumed in a low serious voice, gazing at the floor. "Some day my chance will come too and then I'll know whom to thank and on whom to take revenge. When others are wallowing in their millions someone like me, rising through work and willpower, has to appeal to foreigners to be understood and helped. . . ."

A moment later he regretted that he had betrayed, even only partially, his great secret. The lieutenant had been listening with wonder and curiosity, but he had not interrupted nor asked for explanations.

"*Ei*, but it's not important!" Spiridon exclaimed deliberately changing his tone. "These are personal matters. I'm sorry I interrupted you. . . . And you say she's beautiful, eh?"

Pensive, the lieutenant nodded his head. He found himself no longer in the mood for revelations.

"*Ei*, bravo! I'm glad," Vadastra began again, seeking to re-establish the tone of the beginning of the conversation. "I too understand love. A woman who appreciates you, who realizes that you are somebody—a distinguished man, a man of character and not an ordinary person. Such a woman would be just the one for me, too—a woman of distinction who loved me, who realized . . ."

He broke off with the recollection that on numerous occasions he had confessed his adventures to the lieutenant—experiences with women of high society. The regret with which he spoke now could put him in an unfavorable light. He reversed his position and continued in a more matter-of-fact voice.

"But of course I've met plenty of distinguished women in my lifetime.

There was one in particular, a remarkable woman—I've told you about her. She's been here, in this apartment. She loved me and I can say that she still loves me. She even loves me very much. Not because I'm handsome or anything of that sort, but she loves me for my personality, my character—in the last analysis, because I'm different from other people. She's a woman who truly understands me, and she's aware that I'm somebody. But anyhow I don't like the life she lived before she knew me. She's very rich and comes from an extremely good family, perhaps the best in Romania, and she's asked me— even begged me—to marry her. But I didn't want to. Marriage is a serious thing. In my case, I mean. I'm not an ordinary person, one who marries for money or for love. I want a wife who knows who I am, one who'll never look at another man again. For this reason I didn't want to take her as my wife. I didn't like the kind of life she led before she knew me. . . ."

The lieutenant listened thoughtfully. After a while he realized that he should have gone some time ago, and he stood up in embarrassment, without knowing how to excuse himself and leave.

"It'll be hard for you to recognize me, you'll see!" he repeated with animation. "Don't insist that I tell you more, because I can't, but you'll see tomorrow. Be on time, don't keep me waiting, because I'll not be able to wait. You'll understand why tomorrow evening. . . ."

They had a date at nine-thirty on the corner of *sosea* Bonaparte. An hour earlier he sent the orderly to the cinema, telling him not to come home before midnight. When the man had gone, Vadastra entered Baleanu's room and headed straight for the wardrobe. He had a bit of excitement when he pulled on the door handle. It seemed to be locked, but it was only stuck and he made a mental note of this detail to be sure that he left the door stuck when he returned the uniform. Then taking the clothes in his arms he went to his own room and put them on, whistling. He did not once glance at himself in the mirror because he had taken off his monocle, and he disliked seeing his face without it, especially in the light of the lamp. The unnatural sparkle of his glass eye gave the impression that the other eye, the healthy one, was dim and without life. When he had finished dressing he approached the mirror, put the monocle in place with meticulous care, and standing at attention he saluted. Since he was not wearing the cap his fingers touched his temple and the gesture seemed strange to him. He dropped his hand quickly and stepped closer to the mirror, looking at himself in wonder. He was indeed another man. The bony irregularity of his face was adorned by the precise and youthful line of the mustache, freshly trimmed by the barber. His dark monocle introduced an improbable accent into the configuration of hard and com-

100

monplace contours of his face. This evening his hair was not combed down over his narrow forehead as usual and it gave added height to a visage that was already long enough. Still, the appearance of morose seriousness that was generally Spiridon's was diminished by this change.

"Lieutenant Vadastra!" he pronounced solemnly, following the movements of his lips in the mirror. "Lieutenant Spiridon Vasilescu-Vadastra of the Red Hussars! I have the honor of presenting myself, *domnule* Colonel: Lieutenant Vadastra of the General Staff. I have the honor of saluting you. I am Lieutenant Vadastra Spiridon of the Regiment of the Royal Guards."

He stopped and smiled at himself a long time, familiarly. Then with a hasty motion he put on the cap and stood at attention again in front of the mirror, his face impassive. He saluted, declaiming, "I have the honor to present myself to Your Majesty. I am Lieutenant Vadastra Spiridon, Your Majesty's Adjutant. I have the honor of saluting you! Long may you live! . . ." His tone altered and he added, "Anyone who can, does as he wishes!" He stood at ease.

But he remembered that he did not have much more time before his date and he took a deep breath, checked the number of bills in his wallet and turned out the light without stopping again in front of the mirror. He summoned the elevator and went down to the lobby as cautiously as he had the last time, hurrying through it, taking advantage of the fact that the light was out. Once he had reached the street he made straight for the taxi stand. He did not dare to look to right or left but got into the first cab that he saw.

"Take me to *sosea* Bonaparte!"

He saw her from a distance waiting for him and he signaled the driver to stop. He paid the fare, giving the man a tip of eighteen lei and saluting him amicably. The girl did not recognize him when he first approached, in spite of his black monocle. Spiridon planted himself before her and saluted seriously.

"I have the honor of saluting you! How do you do, *domnisoara?* Are you alone? I have the honor to present myself. I am Lieutenant Dimitrie Cantemir of the General Staff!"

"Oh, no!" cried the girl. "Are you an officer? Why didn't you tell me?"

"*Ei,* but I warned you that I had a big surprise for you! And this isn't anything yet. You'll see a lot more. . . ." He took her arm masterfully and started for the Moara Rosie* where he had planned in advance to go for dinner. A gendarme passed them and saluted in time with the rhythm of his walk. Vadastra returned the salute with a certain display of zeal.

"He's a recruit. I could tell by the way he taps the soles of his boots." Spiridon looked at the girl with an expression of triumph and gave her arm a meaningful squeeze. He smiled.

"Do you know that you've become more beautiful since I last saw you? I

*Red Mill.

101

didn't want to tell you this yesterday. I thought it might make you lose your head and not keep our date."

"But you sweep me off my feet!" she said provocatively. "As if I didn't know how you officers are!"

"We'd better get down to business," interrupted Spiridon. "I'm hungry and I know a place near here, a first-rate tavern where we officers from the General Staff ordinarily go. You know, of course, we don't like to frequent common pretentious restaurants where all the riff-raff congregate and you can never find a table and the service is abominable. When we want to have a good time we gather where it's more isolated, where the wine's good and we can sit and talk without being disturbed. Maybe now they'll have brought in some musicians."

On the way to the tavern Spiridon was suddenly seized by a strange anxiety. What if he should meet some officer there by chance? What if the other should start a conversation, introduce himself and ask Vadastra about his regiment, and so on. It would be better to check the place first. When they reached the entrance to the tavern he dropped Marioara's arm. He removed his monocle so that he would not be so conspicuous and resolutely went inside alone. There were no uniforms in sight. The proprietor came forward to meet him, surprised but deferential.

"Please come in. We have a private room near the garden. Come in, *domnule Capitan*. Our specialty is carp, freshly caught."

Vadastra saluted and motioned to him playfully to indicate that he had someone else with him who was waiting outside on the street. When he entered again with Marioara the eyes of the other diners followed them suspiciously. Her head bent, the girl stepped forward shyly but with pride as they accompanied the proprietor to the private dining room.

"It's too bad there aren't musicians as well." Spiridon took his seat and continued, "It would have been more interesting."

The room was a simple one. There were two tables, a thick curtain, and several vases of flowers. A half-screen leaned against the wall, to be used if necessary to cover the window that overlooked the garden. The girl examined all these things calmly and smiled. She expected Spiridon to become more familiar or even bold as soon as they were alone. He was content however just to take her hand and press it and to ask her what she was thinking. Then, since she only smiled in embarrassment, he began to talk.

"Say, was it hard to recognize me when you saw me dressed as an officer? I can believe it! And if you only knew what's coming!"

He continued to talk in his usual manner, interrupted only by the proprietor when he brought the glasses of *tuica*, the little basket of bread, and plates for the fish. From time to time Marioara gazed at him in wonder, on the point of laughing. She could not turn her eyes away from his black monocle. His voice, so grave, so monotonous, dropping now and then with a mysterious inflection, began to tire her. She did not always understand what

102

he was talking about. Sometimes she found that she was unable to listen any longer, and so turned her attention to eating. As the evening progressed there were fewer interruptions and Vadastra's volubility increased. In this respect the roast was a great help. While his companion struggled to cut it into pieces small enough to eat he contented himself with swallowing a chunk now and then almost without chewing it. In the meantime he refilled his glass continually with wine and soda. Ordinarily he did not like to drink but this evening his throat and lips felt dry, and he was exasperated by the frequent appearances of the waiter.

"Don't keep buzzing around me! I'll be sure to call you when I need something," he told the boy at last, vexed.

"Maybe he'll think you have designs on me," Marioara whispered after the waiter had gone. "He'll think that's why you sent him away."

"*Ei*, how about that?" said Spiridon in high spirits. "I'm a devil of a man! Just when you least expect it you'll find yourself caught in my arms and kissed!"

"You don't say!" Marioara exclaimed in surprise.

"You can laugh, but you don't know me. I've turned the heads of a good many girls like you! And they bragged terrifically, too . . . and so on . . . if you know what I mean."

The girl began to laugh, and just then the door opened. A stranger stood reeling in the entrance. Vadastra turned his head in irritation, assuming that the proprietor or the waiter had come back again to refill the wine glasses. But he felt suddenly paralyzed, his veins seemed to have been drained of blood. The man who hesitated on the threshold, struggling with intoxication, was the teacher Gheorghe Vasile! Spiridon could not believe his eyes. And yet it seemed absurdly natural that his father should be standing there in front of him. His sudden pallor and silence prompted Marioara, surprised, to turn and look too. The man in the doorway did not seem at all offensive as he leaned on the doorknob smiling, his large hat pushed drunkenly back on his head, his country schoolteacher's tunic unbuttoned, his homespun trousers stained and dirty. The proprietor appeared beside him a moment later and tried to pull him back, whispering something in his ear. But the man was tipsy and jerked his arm away, taking a step into the room. He pulled off his hat and respectfully saluted Spiridon.

"He's drunk!" whispered Marioara, a little frightened.

But Vadastra did not permit himself to respond. He brought his hand to his forehead, swallowed with difficulty several times, then seized his drink and sipped it. Father! Father has caught me! resounded in his mind. What do I do now?

"I see that this table's free," the teacher said thickly to the proprietor, who was still standing embarrassed in the middle of the room, looking now at Vadastra, now at the newcomer. "If *domnul* Colonel won't mind . . ."

Lieutenant! I'm a lieutenant! Vadastra thought. He doesn't even know

103

the ranks! You can tell he's soused all right! Such thoughts were absurd at a time like this, but they soothed him and Spiridon clung to them, repeated them to give himself courage, filled his terrified consciousness with their accumulating resonance.

"Or perhaps he's not a colonel," the old man added, seeing that Spiridon did not reply, nor even venture to look at him. "He's too young to be a colonel. Maybe he's a major. What do you say?"

"*Domnu'* Vasile, please!" the proprietor said, trying to quiet him. "Let's go over there. You're making a disturbance here. . . ."

"If the gentleman isn't angry," the teacher continued, "and the young lady isn't either . . ." He took another step toward their table and saluted again with respect. "I should be pleased to sit with them."

"As a matter of fact we're leaving," Vadastra said brusquely to the proprietor. "The check please!"

"No, no, if you please, not that!" the old man protested, emphasizing his words. "I would consider that an insult, and we teachers, we apostles to the nation, we don't accept insults. . . . Not even from officers. . . . I said, not even from officers. . . ."

"Don't start a conversation with him, he's drunk!" Marioara whispered again. Vadastra shrugged and poured another glass of wine. His father stared at him for a long time, then sat down at the other table, facing them.

"This is a great infamy!" said the old man, crossing himself. "Just think, *domnule*, what got into his head . . ."

Again Vadastra felt a shudder of terror cutting off his breath. He made a great effort to speak. "As I told you," he began precipitately, "you can't depend on anyone. . . . However, you have to do your duty. You look straight ahead. . . . What does it matter what anyone says?"

"Bravo! I like that!" the old man said approvingly, pulling his chair closer to their table.

"*Domnule*," intervened Marioara at that point, "why are you interfering in our conversation? An old man like you ought to be more serious!"

"Mary, don't get into a discussion with him," Vadastra interrupted nervously.

"What did you call her?" said the old man, facetiously putting his hand to his ear and leaning toward them. "Mary? Say it again! Just imagine, *domnule!*"

"Please, what concern is it of yours?" flared Marioara. "You'd better look at the sorry state you're in! Why, you can't even stand on your feet!"

Vasile passed a dry hand across his forehead, clicked his tongue a number of times, then sighed deeply, looking eloquently at Spiridon.

"Mind your own business! No one asked you anything!" Marioara continued furiously.

"Well, now, isn't that just what I'm doing? Minding my own business?"

asked the old man. He seemed to awaken suddenly. "If I'm not a man who tends to his own affairs, then who is? Do you know who I am, *domnisoara?*"

"I don't know and I don't care!"

"It's too bad that you don't know," the teacher began glibly, drawing his chair still nearer to their table.

"What the devil is that man doing with the check?" asked Spiridon, considerably annoyed, turning toward the door and beginning to beat on the plate with his fork.

". . . that you don't know, and you don't care!" continued Vasile. "You're making a mistake! I'm not an ordinary person. He'll tell you. After all, we know each other!"

The proprietor came in then with the check. Seeing that the teacher was talking with the others, his chair pulled up between the two tables, the man was at a loss to know what to do.

"The bill, mister, I'm in a hurry!" said Vadastra rudely.

"Pardon me!" cried the old man, getting up from the chair. "The bill can wait. First let's have a glass with *domnul Capitan* and *domnul* Ioan."

"*Domnu'* Vasile, please, why don't you go over there?" the proprietor tried again to persuade him. "The gentleman and the lady are in a hurry."

"Shut up and bring me a glass! If you don't, I'll make a scene." He looked at the proprietor with such determination that the man disappeared to get the glass. Vadastra, intimidated, moistened his lips and stared straight ahead. The old man moved his chair from the middle of the room and sat down at their table.

"I, *domnisoara,* am a teacher. . . . I also had learning, enough for my time. . . ."

"You'd hardly notice it!"

"You don't notice it, *domnisoara,* because it's gone," said Vasile, bursting into a sad, stifled laugh. "You know what they say, I'm a has-been," and he laughed again, lifting his hand to his face. "It's my misfortune, that I make children laugh!" he added as if to himself. "But they're right," he resumed firmly. "They're right to laugh at me. I, who knew Spiru Haret. Do you know who Spiru Haret was, *domnisoara? The great* Spiru Haret? Let the lieutenant tell you. Please, I haven't had the honor of meeting . . ."

"I thought you said a little while ago that you knew him!" objected Marioara, who had begun to be amused by the teacher's stumbling speech.

"So it seemed to me," replied Vasile. "I thought that I knew him. He resembles a relative of mine, but that man isn't an officer."

Vadastra breathed more easily as he listened to his father's last words. It seemed that the danger had passed suddenly. He raised his eyes a little. The proprietor had just entered with the third glass on a plate, and seeing that the three were sitting calmly at the same table talking he did not wait to be paid but disappeared immediately, closing the door after him.

"It's a good thing that Greek condescended to bring me the glass," the teacher said, smiling heartily and grasping the bottle of wine. "Now, *domnule* Lieutenant, although I haven't had the honor of meeting you, allow me to drink this glass to your health, and that of your lady! Long life!" he said, draining the glass and setting it decorously on the table.

"And long life to you!" said Marioara, raising her glass. "When a man behaves politely, I can get along with him very well. You're not drinking?" she asked Spiridon.

"Drink, *domnule* Lieutenant," the old man said. "The old lady has asked you to, and it won't do for you to turn her down, as you people say here in the city."

Vadastra forced a smile, filled his glass, and drained it thirstily. The old man looked at him in astonishment, then started to refill his own glass but the bottle was empty.

"*Ei*, I say," he cried, pounding the table with the glass. "A bucket, I say, with ice!"

Marioara, astonished, looked at Spiridon, but he only sucked his lips and smiled furtively from time to time.

"Like I was saying, young lady, I was somebody in my day," the old man began again. "Not everyone has shaken hands with that great apostle, Spiru Haret. I've considered my life to be a mission—a very painful and difficult mission, I can say. . . . I've had my troubles too . . . and I have my pride, the pride of a man who has understood his calling and has had no reward. Take the lieutenant here, the gentleman is a witness . . ."

Vadastra gave a start and stared at his father in fright. The thought flashed through his mind, What if he's loaded enough to call me by name and make a fool of me?

"He's a witness to our sufferings, the sufferings of country school-teachers," the old man resumed with determination, "because any intellectual is a witness to us, and he's an intellectual. You can see that just by looking at him. An intellectual is a subtle man, a man of much learning. I haven't had the honor of meeting *domnul* Lieutenant, but as soon as I entered this little room I said to myself, 'Here's this officer. He's *somebody*, he's an intellectual!'"

Casting an expressive glance at Marioara, Vadastra solemnly raised high the glass that he had just filled. "Your health!" he said, taking them both in with a single glance.

"Yours too!" The old man downed the contents of his glass quickly in one ample gulp. "Although I haven't had the honor of meeting *domnul* Lieutenant. . . ."

"*Ei*, look here! You know him now," said Marioara.

"You only say you know someone when you know with whom you have

106

the honor of speaking—that is, when you know the name of the person with whom you have the honor of speaking. . . ."

"Well, I'll tell you and make a long story short," the girl interrupted with a smile. "The gentleman's name is Cantemir and mine is Marioara."

"What's that name you said? Cantemir? It wouldn't be Dimitrie Cantemir?"

"Yes, that's so!" Amused, the girl glanced at Spiridon.

Vasile broke into a noisy laugh that caused him to cough, and convulsed by deep hiccoughs he brought his hand to his mouth. Vadastra stiffened and gave the girl a look that was ominous and threatening.

"Why did you tell him my name?" he whispered, choking with anger.

"But *domnule* Lieutenant," said the old man, controlling his laughter, "He was a great man, a prince, *domnule*, not a man of the people such as we are!"

"I don't understand what you mean," Vadastra said nervously. "I'm from another family, not that of the Prince . . ."

"That's the only thing that's missing!" The old man laughed and filled his glass again. "So! I have the honor of sitting at the same table with Lieutenant Dimitrie Cantemir. . . ."

"*Ei*, and what if he is a Cantemir?" Marioara intervened, becoming argumentative again. "It's a nice name."

"You must forgive people like us," said the teacher blandly. "At our age and with all our troubles we don't know what we're saying! We're the outcasts of society, as the great writer Maxim Gorki says. We are, I might say, the scum of the wretched. A man talks too much when he's drunk. You mustn't be angry. Who pays any attention to the babbling of an old country schoolteacher? Our day is past as though it had never been! Look at me now, this is what's become of the eminent teacher, Gheorghe Vasile, disciple of the great Spiru Haret! A man outside of society! But why, pray? Why, a man like me? A man who could be said to have been someone in his time, famous in his district. . . . Why have I now become? . . ."

"Let's go," Spiridon said, starting to rise slowly from the table.

"Wait, *domnule* Cantemir," the old man cried, and seized Vadastra's arm. "The Turks are not at our gates. Stay and drink another glass with me. We haven't drunk together in a long time. . . ."

"I can't. I have business! And the lady's in a hurry."

"Leave the lady alone. She's one of us, one of the people. Come over here beside me and we'll have a talk. Who knows if I'll meet you again? How's the army getting along?"

"Fine, thanks," said Vadastra, avoiding his father's gaze.

"Then if everything's going well, I say let's have another drink!" He filled his glass to the brim. "D'you have parents? Brothers? Sisters?" He smiled.

"I have."

"May they live long!" the old man said bringing the glass to his lips.

"God grant it!" Vadastra muttered, confused.

"They're lucky to have such a clever son, and a lieutenant, too. Not everyone can become a lieutenant nowadays!"

"Yes, that's so," said Vadastra seriously. "For a long time I wanted to be an army officer. Even when I was a little boy. . . . This was my ideal in life—to wear the uniform of a soldier."

"And now you've 'seen your dream with your own eyes,' as the saying goes," the old man observed.

"Yes, but what's the good of it? It's not what I dreamed! That's something of the past. My profession is not what I imagined. I can work at Headquarters, but I can't go to the front. You can see why!"

"God willed it," said Vasile solemnly.

"What's that mean, God willed it?" Spiridon said with a scowl. "Why has God inflicted me with this, just me, and not others as well? I mean why can others be officers and not I? What have I done? What am I guilty of?"

"It's because of our sins, the sins of the fathers," said the old man wistfully. "It's been that way since the world began. You're struck down without knowing why, and you're rewarded when you don't deserve it."

"But why do I have to pay for the sins of others? I don't feel guilty about anything. Ever since I can remember I've always done my duty. I always prayed to God at night when I was little. I was first at school. You don't know. . . ."

"Yes, I know," declared the old man, filling his glass again.

"What you know is very little compared with what I've done. You have no way of knowing what willpower was required in order to get where I am. But why did this have to happen to me of all people? For others to come along later and laugh at me? That's easy to do! They didn't have to endure what I've endured. I know too how easy it is to laugh! But to do something—that's more difficult! Thank God I've done something in my life! I haven't wasted my time like so many others."

"Like me, for example," said the old man, sipping from his glass.

"You had your reasons," Vadastra continued in the same agitated tone. "But there are others who don't have any excuse. And even so, nothing happens to them. . . ."

"*Ei*, what d'you know?" Marioara interrupted. She had not entirely managed to understand this strange conversation. "The teacher is right, let's have another drink. To your health!"

"We'll have just one more glass, and then we'll go!" Vadastra said, pouring a round of drinks. He was unaccustomed to wine and felt a pleasant giddiness tinged with a gentle sorrow. At the same time an unfamiliar impulse

108

was driving him to talk, to indulge in confessions. Since he had begun to earn more money and to help his father every month he had been treating the old teacher like a stranger. He didn't love him. He didn't hate him. The man simply did not seem to be his father. This evening, however, after he had recovered from his initial fright and realized that the old man was not going to expose him, he was overcome by emotion. He felt a kind of pity, even affection; but he did not know what might happen next and preferred not to stay any longer.

"Long live the Romanian Army!" he said, his voice trembling with emotion.

"Long live the Romanian Army! But what have I to do with the Army?" asked the old man sadly. "I'd rather drink to your health, to you who are here in front of me, you who honor me by drinking with me—drinking with a poor unfortunate country schoolteacher who comes into your midst and spoils your fun. . . . A man you don't know," he went on, an uneasy fire burning in his eyes, "who sits down at your table and demands a glass of wine. He asks for a glass of wine before he knows with whom he speaks. . . ."

"*Ei*, what does it matter?" Marioara tried to calm him.

"It does matter!" replied the teacher glumly. "It matters very much! When you don't know anyone you have no one to drink with. You go into a tavern and drink with the first people you meet. But they're not yours, not your friends. How would you like to be a friend of a man who no longer counts in the ranks of society? Such a man doesn't exist. He has no name. He's a drunk . . . an outcast from society. . . ."

"Do you have any children?" asked Marioara gently.

"I have, but what's the good?" the old man murmured. "I might as well not have any. Because it's as if you don't have children if they don't bear your name."

"Things are different nowadays," Vadastra said with a nervous smile. "Names don't matter now; people matter. It's a question of whether your children are good. . . ."

"How's that? Names don't matter?" said Vasile frowning. "A man's name is his holiest possession on earth. His name is his and his alone. It belongs to no one but him and his children. Only God can change his name. And if you bear that name, if you bear the name of your parents, of those who gave you life . . . and your parents are proud of you because you bear their name . . ."

"Don't fret yourself anymore for nothing!" Marioara consoled him, seeing that the old man, choked by strong emotion, had lost the thread of his thought.

"How can I help fretting, since it's as if I have no children anymore? And since I am as you see a man of fifty-four years, going on fifty-five, a man outside of society? I might have been someone else in my lifetime. *Someone else*, not this man here before you, a nobody, a spineless creature. What am I in fact if not an outcast of society? Who are my companions? Who can I talk to? Those poor souls you see in the taverns. . . . Instead of being somebody today, instead of being proud of the name that we bear, I and my children, Gheorghe Vasile, teacher from Dobresti . . ."

His last words were lost in a sob that welled up slowly until it silenced him. Unable to say more the old man buried his face in his hands and remained in that position, ashamed of his own weakness and overcome by grief. Marioara regarded him with pity. Vadastra wanted to stand up but he did not dare. He too felt humiliated, nailed to his chair as though awaiting the final scene.

". . . . Teacher . . . apostle to the nation . . ." The old man sighed profoundly, his head still resting on his hands.

"Let's go!" Spiridon whispered then, motioning to the girl. "It's better to leave him alone."

Rising from the table Marioara stopped a moment beside the teacher and put her hand on his shoulder. He continued to sigh, shaking his head slowly in mute despair. Vadastra looked at him, embarrassed, wondering whether he should leave without saying anything, or if he ought to speak to him. As the girl opened the door the old man lifted his head.

"Where are you going?" he asked anxiously.

"You go on. I'll come directly," Spiridon said to his companion, pushing her out and closing the door behind her.

"Maybe you need some money," he whispered, approaching the table and pulling out his billfold.

"What would I do with money? I've drunk enough already! I won't drink any more tonight! But where are you going?"

Vadastra wanted to tell him that he was going home, but it occurred to him that perhaps his father might ask to come too, or that he would at least want to know where he was living. Spiridon replied uneasily, "I have to take the young lady home."

"What young lady?" asked the old man suspiciously.

"The one who was here, Marioara."

"But what do you have to do with her? You haven't been associating with her, a man of your position? Have you come to this?"

Vadastra, although giddy from the wine and touched, until a moment earlier, by a wave of filial love, felt himself blushing in humiliation. "It's my business what I do and whom I associate with! What do *you* know? I might have my reasons, too," he murmured in a brusque and arrogant tone.

"You'd better tend to your business and become a deputy. Look at Varzare's son, he'll be a deputy in a day or two, and the whole village will laugh at us."

"I'll teach old Varzare a lesson!" Spiridon said, grinding his teeth in his

110

irritation. "Just tell me, do you need anything? Tell me now. I have to hurry. I must go."

"Then go! I don't need anything!" cried Vasile. "And see you don't get caught dressed like that. They'll throw you in jail!"

"Good night!" said Vadastra, humiliated, and headed for the door.

"They'll throw you in jail!" the old man repeated, overwhelmed with bitterness. "And you'll make our name a joke!"

Although Vadastra had left the room the old man kept on talking to himself for a long time. "You'll make our name a joke. They'll find out your real name and where you come from. You won't go around there the way you do here, with one name today, another one tomorrow. There, it's the legal names that count. The names you were born with, those you were baptized with—today . . . and tomorrow. . . ."

4

STEFAN STAYED FOR A LONG TIME AT THE WINDOW WATCHING THE SNOW AS IT
drifted down. It had been falling steadily for two days. In the yellow light of
the street lamp the flakes descended heavily, without haste, seeming to be
seized with a brief flurry of liveliness as they neared the ground. He pulled
down the shades at last and returned to the salon, twisting the dial on the
radio, proceeding then to the bathroom. Each year on the thirty-first of
December Stefan shaved as late as possible in the evening. Now he turned on
the faucet and waited a few moments for the water to become hot. Humming,
he began to lather his face. From the salon came the voice of Tino Rossi,
"Ca-ta-liine... Ca-ta-liine...." The Mediterranean resonances of the
melody struck Stefan as especially unreal in this snow-covered Bucharest,
muted under the drifts. "Ca-ta-liine... Ca-ta-liine...."

"Catalina's face—it haunts me," Stefan had said to Biris. "I keep wondering where I've seen those eyes before and I can't quite manage to
remember."

"You haven't seen them anywhere," had been Biris's reply. "She
wears them only once a year on October nineteenth."

On the nineteenth of October, Biris had taken Stefan to the home
of Dan Bibicescu, actor, director, and disciple of Gordon Craig. The
philosopher had told him, "Come with me and you'll see an interesting
chap—a fascinating failure of a fellow. Like you, he's preoccupied with
the problem of Time."

Me? I've never become involved with the problem of Time, Stefan
had started to say, in order to set him straight. That's a problem that
occupies you philosophers. The *flow* of time is the only thing that
obsesses me.... But he had said nothing.

"Just the same he's an interesting man," Biris had gone on to say.

112

"Observe him closely, watch him when he's talking to you. He plays his best roles in real life, among his friends. On stage he has no talent."

"Ah," exclaimed Bibicescu soon after Biris had completed the introductions. "Why didn't Ciru Partenie read Shakespeare before writing his plays?"

Stefan had tried to hide his embarrassment behind a smile. Bibicescu stared at him for a long time, frowning. I'm sure he's made a special effort to learn that penetrating gaze, Stefan said to himself. Perhaps it's the expression he assumes at the conclusion of a current role. . . .

"You guessed right, sir!" Bibicescu continued without looking away from Stefan's face. "I thought when I saw you coming in, 'What a shame that dramatists don't read Shakespeare anymore.' Because probably you're a playwright, too. You have several plays in your dossier, and you've prevailed upon Biris to introduce you so I can give my opinion of your works."

"No," said Stefan, recovering his good humor all at once. "I came . . ."

"Allow me, please, to finish," Bibicescu interrupted, fixing him with the same probing stare. "I want to inform you that I never read a play by a beginner until he convinces me he's studied and assimilated Shakespeare. Look at the case of Partenie, whom I know well, and to whom, parenthetically, you bear a disturbing physical resemblance."

"I'm not a playwright," Stefan broke in again. "I've never written anything in my life except economic reports."

"So much the better," continued Bibicescu. "I like men who are precise, rigorous. But to come back to what I was saying—and I'm speaking especially to you," he said, abruptly turning his frowning gaze upon Biris, "to come back to what I was thinking when you came in, it's regrettable that Ciru Partenie hasn't read Shakespeare! How much talent and perhaps even genius is lost forever only because he didn't understand that a play represents a performance that takes place in Time, a time concentrated in a few destinies."

Like you, he's preoccupied with the problem of Time. As he listened Stefan recalled what Biris had said. Bibicescu bounded from his chair as if projected by a spring and began to walk about the room with one hand in the pocket of his vest. The other gesticulated rhythmically with short circular motions. He talked about Shakespeare. "Only the *performance* completely reveals his genius." He stressed the word "performance" pompously. "The text of Shakespeare, in order to affect us, must be performed, that is, introduced into Time, into a duration that flows. Shakespeare didn't write to be read. He didn't write to stir the solitary reader with poetic emotions. He wrote to be *played*—in other words, to mount a *performance*. The performance, gentlemen, the performance is the great supra-temporal bliss that is allowed us. . . ."

He kept up this monologue for about a half hour, interrupted only by Biris's brief observations. Stefan said nothing. Then he saw Bibicescu turn to them suddenly with both hands extended.

"Gentlemen," he said, "I've been most charmed by the visit you've paid me. I hope I shall have this pleasure again soon. But today is the nineteenth of October and the hour is approaching, the fatal hour for me—six o'clock in the evening. Every year I'm terrified on this day and at this hour. A very serious event has been foretold for me on an October nineteenth at six in the evening. I've been anticipating it for several years. I'm awaiting it . . . in a manner of speaking. Actually I tremble at the thought of its happening. . . ." Then he had led them hastily to the door and opened it with a sigh.

"It's only a few minutes to six," Biris remarked when they had reached the street. "Let's hang around here a little longer. Maybe we'll find out something." But a few moments later he added, "And yet I can't believe him. He seems to me to be false, strident, lacking in authenticity. Even if he knew how to play Shakespeare well . . ."

[Two weeks later Stefan had gone to see him perform. "That's he!" he whispered, leaning toward Ioana. "Biris's friend, the one I told you about." Bibicescu walked out on the stage, a bitter smile lingering in the corner of his mouth. Putting his left hand in his pocket he began to gesticulate with the other. In the darkness of the theater Stefan seemed to see him better than before. When he had met him on October nineteenth, he had been struck by the actor's rather broad face, brownish yellow, with its bulbous nose and large gray eyes the color of ashes. Now on stage he seemed less vulgar. The beginning of baldness on his temples even gave him an air of melancholy nobleness. But his voice had the same artificial quality of being reduced to pure diction.]

". . . But he doesn't know how to act," Biris had continued. "Not just Shakespeare—he simply doesn't know how to act in general. And what's worse, I believe he's beginning to realize himself that he has no talent. He's a failure who's becoming aware of being a failure. . . ."

"I wonder what might have caused his preoccupation with the problem of Time," Stefan mused, his voice touched with irony.

"He may have read about it somewhere," said Biris.

At that moment his face lighted suddenly and he raised his hand, beckoning to a couple who appeared to hesitate on the other side of the street. The man, short, blond, and slightly stout, had a round face and a cordial smile. His companion was a pale young woman with disheveled hair hanging to her shoulders. She looked at them with dull, expressionless eyes. The couple came toward the two men.

114

"Everything's in order," the man exclaimed, clasping Biris's hand warmly. "It's been arranged again for this date. Aren't you coming? Maybe we'll drink a bottle of wine!" And turning to the woman who had stopped a step behind him, he asked, "What do you say, Catalina?"

She made an effort to smile. Her teeth were very white and their brilliance heightened her pallor. "What is there to say? Whatever you wish, *coane** Misu. . . ."

Stefan had remained apart from them, embarrassed. Biris wanted to introduce him but the two had already started for Bibicescu's house.

"Come in a quarter of an hour," called Misu, turning around. "By all means, come! I know what I'm talking about!" Then he went on, grasping Catalina's arm forcefully and pulling her after him.

"I'm surprised that you don't know him," Biris said. "Everybody knows him. He's Misu Weissman, the friend and protector of intellectuals. He has a great weakness for actors, especially for Bibicescu. Bibicescu hopes someday he'll build him the theater he's dreamed about for years. It's his own design, or more accurately it's one that follows the conception of Gordon Craig. And if Misu's business is very successful I don't doubt he will build the theater. . . . But why are you standing there looking so dreamy?" He turned to Stefan with a smile.

"Catalina's face—it haunts me," said Stefan. "I keep wondering where I've seen those eyes before, and I can't quite manage to remember. . . ."

"You haven't seen them anywhere. She only wears them once a year on October nineteenth. If you should meet her tomorrow on *calea* Victoriei, you wouldn't recognize her. Catalina's a beautiful woman. She has extraordinary charm. You understood, I'm sure, that she's Bibicescu's mistress?"

Stefan had been a little surprised by the expression that he had discerned on his friend's face momentarily. It was something new, inexplicable. "But what happens on October nineteenth?" he inquired. "What happens at six o'clock in the evening?"

"I don't think anything happens or ever will. Catalina has simply declared that someday, on some October nineteenth at six in the evening, she will kill herself. That's all."

"But why exactly on the nineteenth of October?"

"I haven't yet found out why," Biris, said musing. "But I will someday, and I'll tell you. That Catalina is a truly interesting girl. She's worth knowing. It's a shame she's fallen in with such a fool as Bibicescu."

*Coane and *conu*, a form of address: *coane*, direct (vocative); *conu*, third person. Used before first names.

115

[One evening during the week of Christmas Stefan had gone to see Biris. *Doamna* Porumbache took him aside and asked in a whisper, "Listen, *maica*, is it true that Petrica is going with a tramp of an actress, someone called Catalina?" Stefan hastened to put her mind at ease. "No, not at all. Catalina is the girl friend of an actor named Bibicescu." "Yes, I know that, but I found out that tart runs around with Petrica too. He doesn't come home evenings now till one or two in the morning. He's squandering his youth on a no-good actress. . . . Look what he's come to! The great teacher running around with one of those women! They'll throw him out of the *liceu*. . . . We'll be paupers. . . ." She wiped away a tear with her sleeve.]

"I think a quarter of an hour's passed," commented Biris. "Don't you want to go and see what's doing? Maybe we'll find out something. . . ."

Stefan had let him go alone. But Biris didn't find out anything that evening. When they met again and he brought up the subject of Catalina, Biris shrugged his shoulders wearily. "They're two of a kind—born losers, idiots," was all that he would say. "It's not worth wasting our time even to talk about their tics and superstitions. The elections are coming up. Don't you have anything to say about them? Aren't you interested in what's going on around you? Aren't you interested in politics? Don't you think about anything but your room Sambo?"

Tino Rossi had finished the song long since and had begun another. Stefan was not listening anymore. He had closed the bathroom door and gone into the shower. "Still, I should contact her," he found himself thinking. "On this night, at least, I should contact her some way."

Dressed, her fur coat thrown over her shoulders, Ioana waited at the top of the stairs for Stefan to come back with a taxi. She was getting cold. The snowstorm seemed to have intensified, threatening a blizzard. Once again she looked at her watch. It was after eleven. Stefan had been gone almost an hour. If only he can find a taxi, Ioana said to herself. If he couldn't it would be necessary for them to go by tram and to change twice in order to get to Cotroceni.

That year they were to share the midnight supper on New Year's Eve with the elder Bologas. It was what they had done the first year of their marriage. Once more Ioana realized that she felt truly happy on this night only when she was in her old home at Cotroceni.

116

Last year they had gone to be with Adela and Raducu, but she had spent most of the time hidden away in the bedroom. She had not felt well all evening. "At least we ought to give them the satisfaction of seeing you at your ugliest," Stefan had said, "after a pregnancy of seven months. This was the reason they invited us. We can't refuse. . . ." The year before they had been at the home of the Undersecretary of State, Stefan's superior and protector. It had seemed to Ioana that the Undersecretary's wife danced a little too much with Stefan, keeping him close to her all the time, holding his arm. For the first time Ioana had suffered from jealousy. She was especially piqued because Stefan was not even aware that she suffered, that she was taciturn and irritated. He simply inquired, "What's the matter?" and put his hand on her shoulder. "Are you cold? You should drink a cognac. And you ought to dance more. That will warm you up. We'll dance the next dance together." But she had accepted the invitation of one of Stefan's colleagues for that dance, hoping her husband would see that she was provoked with him. However, he waved to her as though nothing had happened and looked around for another partner. "I don't know how to dance," he always said, "but if you have the courage to abandon yourself in my arms . . ." Ioana didn't understand how Stefan could be so inattentive, even indifferent. "What's the matter?" he asked her again. "Are you cold? You should drink a cognac. . . ." And then he disappeared, dragged away quickly on the arm of the Undersecretary's wife.

It was like a miracle that I found it," Stefan said, hastily opening the door. "I'd lost hope. I went all the way to *calea* Victoriei, and I was coming back to take you to the tram when I noticed a taxi that had stopped at the third house from us."

It was almost midnight before they reached Cotroceni because the cab had difficulty moving through the snow-blocked streets. They found the family all seated around the table waiting for them impatiently. *Doamna* Bologa went quickly to the kitchen, followed by her two nieces, to get the bottles of champagne.

"*Ei,* what do you say?" Professor Bologa asked from the head of the table. "What do you say about the new government?"

Stefan shrugged and looked at Ioana in despair. For several weeks he had been hearing nothing but the same question, "What do you say? . . ."

"Don't you have anything to say?" the provincial poet had asked him in the entrance to the coffee shop on that evening in December when he had gone there to find Biris. "Don't you have anything to say about the results of the election?" The poet looked like a different man, taller, thinner, more pale. He seemed to have aged overnight. He hasn't

117

shaved, Stefan realized suddenly. And perhaps he hasn't eaten lunch. Maybe he doesn't have any money to buy food. Stefan looked at him with sympathy that was deep and genuine. "It's grave," the poet continued, shivering. "The success of the Iron Guard* means a new victory for Hitler. And the triumph of Hitler means our death—our spiritual death, and possibly even physical death for all of us." He's right, thought Stefan, and he smiled. But he felt he had nothing to add.

["I refuse to discuss it," he had repeated over and over that evening at the Ministry. "I refuse to discuss the results of the election." But all day long he had done nothing else. At intervals his door would open and he would hear the voice of a colleague, "Viziru, are you here? What do you say? What have you to say?" He promised himself not to read the newspapers anymore, but as soon as he reached the street he made straight for a kiosk and asked for all the evening editions. He leafed through them feverishly, almost terrified, standing under the streetlights. Then he wadded them all together, tossed them into a courtyard, and set off toward the coffee shop to meet Biris.]

"Don't you have anything to say?" the poet asked him again, seeing that he remained silent. "I've been talking about it all day," Stefan said, apologetically. "I can't talk about it any more. Please forgive me but I just can't!" The next moment he was ashamed of his timidity and he added with a certain challenge in his voice, "The truth is I can't allow myself to be possessed by an event, however real or catastrophic it may be. I discuss it for an hour or two and I try to understand it. I adapt myself to it or else I don't, but then I go on and get busy with something else. Let's at least enjoy what freedom we're still permitted—the freedom to choose the subjects of our reflections, our conversation, our jokes. . . ." Biris said not a word. He seemed lost in thought, preoccupied. "That's why we're in the situation we're in now," the poet said, suddenly overcome with emotion, "because people like you and me refuse to discuss political realities. We take refuge in the clouds, in poetry, in dreaming. . . ."

"Why do you sit there dreaming?" Bologa appealed to him from the other end of the table. "Look at him! He doesn't seem to know what world he's in. . . ."
"He must be in love!" someone said.

Suddenly Biris had re-entered the coffee shop saying, "I'll be back in a moment. I forgot to tell Bibicescu something." Stefan remained standing in the doorway with the poet, watching the large flakes of snow that were beginning to fall. The poet turned up the collar of his overcoat. "Good night," he said. "It's getting late. I still have to go by the news-

*A fascist organization, properly the Legion of the Archangel Michael.

118

paper office." Stefan watched him as he hurried across the street, hatless, head bent, hands thrust deep into his coat pockets. Stefan was sorry now he had not invited him into the coffee shop, had not thought to offer him something, if only a crescent roll with black coffee. "He's a bohemian," Biris had once said. "He's very proud, but in his own way he's an aristocrat. . . ."

Biris had not come back and Stefan went into the cafe after him. "But let's see what England says," he heard a shrill voice commenting. "England has to say something, and her word. . . ." At a table in the rear Biris was talking nervously with Bibicescu. Stefan went toward them slowly, compelling himself to look straight ahead. "We must bestir ourselves more," said someone at one of the tables, "to make contact with the masses, to explain to people that fascism means war, and war means the occupation of Romania. We've let the Iron Guard do their work, and you've seen what success they've had." Biris held out his hand to Bibicescu. "But why are you in such a hurry to leave?" the actor inquired, surprised. "Wait a little longer. *Conu* Misu will surely come. . . ."

Stefan and Biris met Weissman at the door as they were going out. He appeared vaguely preoccupied but seemed as jovial as ever. "What'll we do, *coane* Misu?" cried someone from a nearby table. "Don't you worry," Weissman exclaimed. "Everything's going to be all right!" He approached Biris and whispered, "Go to her house. Maybe you can persuade her. Tell her to come straight to the restaurant, not to be a fool. I've invited the director of the theater too. . . ."

When they went out on the street Stefan brightened immediately. The large snowflakes were still falling thickly. Although it had been snowing only a few minutes the street had already become white. He raised his head and breathed deeply, suddenly filled with peace. Biris walked silently beside him, paying little attention to where he placed his feet. "I have the impression I came at the wrong time," Stefan remarked. "You're on edge. What's wrong?"

"It's Catalina," replied Biris. "She hasn't been feeling well again today. It was to be expected with that crazy Bibicescu. It's a good thing he has poor Misu. That man gives up his time and sets aside his business just to reconcile them."

"*Ei, sa traiti!*"* cried *doamna* Bologa, raising her goblet of champagne and addressing each of them in turn. "Long life to everybody!"

"*Sa traiti!*" said Bologa from the other end of the table. "A happy and prosperous New Year! May there be nothing but good for everyone in 1938!"

Several of the guests echoed his words, "Nothing but good!" They got up

*A toast: "May you live!"

from their chairs and began embracing one another. "Happy New Year!" Good wishes were exchanged. "*Sa traiesti!* Good luck and health for the New Year!"

"Silvia, my little girl," Bologa said to one of his nieces, "turn up the radio so we can hear the King's address. It was announced that it would be broadcast from the Palace," he explained to Stefan. "It ought to be starting at any moment now. . . ."

They began to eat while they waited for the speech. Ioana observed that Stefan had said nothing. She left her place and went to him.

"What's wrong with you?" she spoke softly in his ear. "Why are you upset? Do you think it's something serious?"

That month after the announcement of the election results she had asked him this question time and again, seeing him return home tired and anxious, absorbed in thought. "Do you think it's something serious?" Sometimes Stefan answered, "It could be. But it exasperates me to have to think about it, to think about what might happen." Then for a long time he looked deep into her eyes in his usual manner, and he smiled. "You can see what amazing progress I've made, how much wisdom I've gained, if I can't even look at events with some degree of detachment!" He tried to laugh. Ioana guessed that he was thinking again about Anisie and she regretted having questioned him.

"I'm not upset," whispered Stefan, "but I think I should go and telephone my boss. . . ."

"Shhh!" interrupted Bologa. "The address is beginning. . . ." Like the rest, Stefan listened to it in thoughtful silence, but he made no attempt to grasp the sense of the words. He was no longer in doubt about that taxi. When he had seen it standing in the snow in front of the third house up the street from theirs he knew that it resembled Ileana's car. He could not say where the resemblance lay. The automobile he had seen in his imagination on the Night of St. John was entirely different from the old taxi, white with snow, that seemed to be waiting before that other house. But the excitement he felt when he saw it, the bliss that swept over him when he entered it, suddenly brought to mind the vision of that summer night.

"Splendid!" exclaimed Bologa. "He made a splendid speech. What do you say, gentlemen?"

At once they all began to discuss it, becoming very agitated. The sound of their voices mingled with the confusion of scraping chairs, rattling dishes, and the constant visits of the nieces to the kitchen to get more bottles of wine.

"Excuse me a moment," Stefan said, getting up from the table abruptly. "I have to make a telephone call . . ."

120

"There's a *berarie** just beyond the school," suggested *doamna* Bologa. "If only it's still open."

Ioana accompanied him to the door and watched sadly as he put on his overcoat. "Don't stay too long," she told him as she closed the door.

Upon entering the dining room Ileana noticed that some of the men were in the midst of a heated discussion.

"Why are you hiding in here?" she demanded, glancing around in surprise.

As though they hadn't heard her several of them continued their argument, gesticulating and moving slowly toward the farthest corner of the room.

She questioned them again. "What's going on? Why do you stay in here?"

"They're talking about the King's address," a young man explained timidly. "It was broadcast just now from the Palace."

Annoyed, Ileana was silent for a moment. Then she forced a smile. "Can't you forget politics even at a New Year's Eve party? Can't we get away from this calamity at least one night in the year?"

There was some laughter but it was rather reluctant. A colonel who was becoming gray at the temples approached Ileana and gallantly kissed her hand. "You chose the right word, *conita,*† it is a calamity!"

Several young girls came in from the parlor. "Is this where you're hiding? What about us? Who do you expect us to dance with?"

"All right! The discussion's over!" the host intervened. "Let's drink once more to the New Year." He approached the table with a bottle of champagne in his hand. "*Sa traiti!*" he cried, lifting his glass. "Nothing but good for everyone in 1938!"

"God grant it! Nothing but good!" Several of the guests reiterated the words.

Ileana suddenly brightened. "Nothing but good!" she echoed.

"And believe me, it will be good!" the colonel cried. "The King has said so. All will be well. . . ."

The door opened slightly and a girl's head appeared. "Ileana!" she called. "Come quickly. It's Bucharest on the phone! . . . Hurry!" she cried again, seeing that Ileana just stood there, puzzled, with her glass of champagne in her hand. She seemed to be wondering if it might be a prank. "We're trying to call Bucharest too, and we'll lose our turn. . . ."

*A place to drink beer.
†Young lady, miss.

121

She recognized Stefan's voice immediately. In her excitement she leaned weakly on the desk. "Happy New Year!" she heard him saying over and over.

"But how did you know where I was? How did you find out the telephone number?"

"From *doamna* Cretulescu," said Stefan, "from your *Tante* Alice. I went to visit her this evening, or rather, I went to see you." He hesitated briefly and added, "I wanted very much to see you."

"I too," Ileana said. "I'm sorry you missed me. I wanted to give you some news..."

"And I have news for you," Stefan interrupted. "When I came home this evening from your place, I thought I saw a car like that other one. You know, the car that might have disappeared...."

"I know," said Ileana, smiling sadly. "Thanks for calling. Maybe you could come to see me after I come home.... I'll hang up now because we're expecting a call from Bucharest."

"What news did you have for me?" Stefan asked quickly.

"I've changed my mind," said Ileana. "I thought I was going to become engaged tonight, but I've changed my mind...."

"That's good. I'll come to see you."

That winter Stefan went to *strada* Batistei a number of times but he did not find Ileana. "She hasn't come back yet," *doamna* Cretulescu told him. "She's still at Jassy. I had a phone call from her last week. She told me she's changed her mind again, that perhaps she'll become engaged this month...."

The thought that Ileana might become engaged, that she could be engaged already without his knowing it, isolated Stefan from all that was taking place around him. The change of government, the royal dictatorship, were only very ordinary events like thousands of others happening all over the world. They did not concern him. "I don't know what she has in mind," *doamna* Cretulescu told him one evening in February. "She's gone to Zinca again."

That night Stefan returned home late from his room at the hotel. He found Ioana waiting for him anxiously. "The day after tomorrow is the baby's birthday," she told him. "Shall we just ask the family? Or shall we include friends, too?"

They decided to invite only the family. Stefan knew that old *domnul* Bologa would spend the evening talking with Raducu. They had the same political views. "He'll liquidate the Iron Guard," Raducu said. "I tell you, I know Armand Calinescu well." Then, turning abruptly to Stefan, he asked. "How long has it been since you had a smoke?"

122

"Several months," replied Stefan, lighting a cigarette. He recalled Anisie, the car, the painting he had not displayed. I ought to have destroyed it that very night, he thought. Recently he had felt tempted to paint again, but in another way, something different.

When it was nearly midnight *doamna* Bologa exclaimed, "Enough of this nuisance of politics!"

One of the nieces, Daria, kept looking at Stefan all the time. "I'm sure she has a crush on him," Ioana said to herself, feeling her heart on fire with pride and jealousy. Stefan seemed more charming than ever as he leaned back in his chair, a smile lingering on his face. He gazed at nothing in particular and allowed himself to become surrounded by a cloud of smoke. Passing near him Ioana bent down and gave him a quick kiss. Daria blushed and smiled. That kiss brought to Stefan's mind the taxi they had taken on New Year's Eve. It recalled him to a bliss that did not arise from the nature of things, but was nourished by other essences, mysterious in origin. Might they be called angelic? Ioana left the room to see what the baby was doing.

"It's too bad your father isn't with us," *domnul* Bologa said to Stefan.

Adela shot him a quick, hostile glance from the other end of the table. A few years earlier Viziru senior, who suffered from gout, had remarried. His new wife was a robust and rather attractive young Bucovinian whom he had met at a bathing establishment. "She's a peasant," Adela had declared, "and I'll never agree to receive her in my house!" "She's a nurse," said Raducu. "Your father is old and ill and he needs someone who can take care of him. Who do you want to do that?" "Us, his family," Adela said. "What does the *Doctorita* do? Ever since she got her divorce she acts as though she didn't know us!" The *Doctorita* was their sister Sofioara. Stefan was on better terms with her, but he saw her only rarely, although after her divorce she had settled in Bucharest. Sofioara had received several years of medical training. She had not finished her studies because she had married an engineer from Resita and had left the capital. All the family had called her the *Doctorita* from the time she had entered medical school. "The *Doctorita* claims that Eleonora is neither a peasant nor a nurse," said Stefan. "Her father was a postal clerk. It's her sister who's a nurse, and it was through her that she met Father when he had his serious attack four years ago." Four years ago, Stefan remembered suddenly; I had just been married. . . . How strange!

It was not until an afternoon early in March that Ileana called Stefan on the telephone. "I'm back," she told him. "If you like, come and see me."

"I'll come right now," Stefan answered quickly, but as he put down the receiver he remembered he had an appointment that afternoon with Vidrighin, the Director of Economic Accords, who had just returned from abroad. "They've recalled him to the Central Office because he's been stealing shamelessly," the Secretary General told Stefan. "We haven't been able to

123

conclude any of the agreements he prepared. It would've meant making him a gift of five or six million! . . . He's a real bandit. And he's not working alone. He's working for others, powerful men in high places. He has connections with the Palace and protectors in all parties. He's always covered. . . ."

Stefan rang Ileana's number but the line was busy. He tried again ten minutes later without success. Then he decided to go to the office of the Director of Accords.

"I'm glad you've come," Vidrighin welcomed him. "We'll be working together from now on." With a wave of his hand he invited him to be seated.

He was a stout man and not very tall, with slow movements that implied laziness. His eyes were expressionless. The sleeves of his coat were shiny at the elbows, and his shirt seemed worn and faded without actually being dirty. He looked at Stefan and smiled, revealing momentarily that some of his yellowed teeth were missing.

"What's a smart boy like you doing buried here in the Central Office?" Vidrighin began, leaning far over his desk. "I've seen the agreements you drew up with Belgium and the Netherlands. My word, you're terrific! And yet you weren't bored with this countinghouse here? Are you waiting for someone to recognize your talents?"

He got up from his desk and sat down in an easy chair, facing Stefan. "You don't say anything, I see," he continued. "I like that. We're going to get along just fine! Are you married? Any children? Are you wealthy?"

Stefan answered each question politely and without enthusiasm, as though he were being cross-examined.

"I don't know why," Vidrighin interrupted, "but I feel a great sympathy for you. This happens with me very rarely. People are usually worthless and uninteresting. Or haven't you learned that yet in thirty-six years?"

Rising, he walked over to Stefan and placed a hand on his shoulder. "Listen. I wish you well. You give me the impression of someone living in the clouds. As if you were a young fellow and single at that. But you have a wife and child. Don't you realize what kind of a world we live in? Don't you realize what's coming?" And because Stefan continued to look at him in silence with the same uncertain smile on his lips, Vidrighin slapped him once more on the shoulder, perhaps in an effort to rouse him.

"I sense the coming disaster as a bird senses the coming of a storm. The great conflagration is approaching, believe me! We'll be reduced to dust and ashes! And you sit here in this countinghouse making a few thousand lei a month! When you have a wife and child! Now's the time to take shelter! And quickly . . . because there's not much time left!"

"What should I do?" inquired Stefan, half joking.

"Make arrangements for yourself. Take a post in a foreign country as far from here as possible. Lay aside some money. Or don't you understand?" He

124

looked at Stefan with an expression that held a mixture of pity and contempt, and lurching backward, he leaned on the desk.

"Maybe you really don't understand! So much the worse for you! You'll be swept away in the days to come. . . . That's too bad! I find you very likeable, and you're clever too. But wealth also pays off in life. . . . Sooner or later it pays off."

"I'm not rich," said Stefan.

"I'm not talking about what you are now," Vidrighin interrupted, frowning. "I'm talking about what your parents were, about what you saw in your house when you were a child. . . . Would you like me to tell you what I saw? An iron kettle for mush, empty most of the time, and a water barrel. My old man was poor. I didn't starve to death, since no one died of hunger in Romania in those days. When my mother gave birth to a child a neighbor would take pity on us and give us a bushel of cornmeal. Once, when my sister was born, they gave us some milk too. And there you have my childhood!"

He sighed deeply and settled himself more comfortably on the corner of the desk.

"But what can I say? It was good for me!" he resumed in a quieter tone. "It cured me of philosophy, idealism, virtue. I've had a good understanding of life ever since my first year of school, when I saw that I couldn't win a prize because I went barefoot. I understood, and I've adapted myself as necessary. . . ." He laughed, lifting his head a little. Stefan caught sight of a glint in his eyes that was evil and venomous and chilling.

"My children are being raised by a governess," Vidrighin added. "Wait, I'll show you. . . ." He searched in his billfold and held out a photograph, with a smile that softened his whole face. Moved, Stefan studied the picture of two fair-haired children laughing and tumbling about on a beach, half-naked in the sand. "This one is called Enrico, the other, Theobald. They don't know Romanian, and they'll never learn it. I've forbidden them to!"

While she waited for Stefan that afternoon Ileana realized that it was because of him she had surrendered to Tony. If Stefan had not come into her life she probably would have held out against Tony's entreaties. She would not have had an opportunity to become better acquainted with him because her Christmas vacation would not have been spent at Jassy. She would have gone to ski at Predeal as she had always done. But she had decided to forget Stefan by flirting and amusing herself in other ways, and for that reason she had accepted with joy the invitation of the Melinte sisters to come to Jassy. Tony was their cousin. His regiment was stationed at Galati, but he had come to

125

spend the holidays with them. On the evening when he met Ileana he told her
that he wanted to celebrate his promotion with his family. At the beginning of
December he had been made captain, and now he had three stripes on his
epaulette.

He was not especially handsome, but he was intelligent and entertaining
and a tireless dancer. Immediately he had started to flirt with Ileana, and
even on that first night he tried to kiss her, but she had promptly slipped
out of his arms. The next night he began to talk about the novels of Ciru
Partenie, and Ileana was reminded of Stefan. She suddenly lost her high
spirits, left Tony's side and went to put a record on the phonograph.
Maria Melinte begged her to play *J'attendrai*, but Ileana pretended not
to have heard and selected a tango. Tony approached her and invited her
to dance, and she slipped into his arms, swaying slowly and humming.
After a few measures Maria stopped the machine and replaced the record
with *J'attendrai*. Maria was in love, Ileana knew, with a student at the
polytechnic school, and she supposed that listening to the haunting song
brought him closer. But their sorrowful romance saddened Ileana still
more, reminding her again of Stefan in a way that she did not understand. Furthermore she felt humiliated because she had made up her
mind to amuse herself, to forget him. And now the voice of the woman
on the record was telling her how beautiful and sad it is to wait for
the man you love! But I don't love him at all, Ileana said to herself.
She had repeated it so many times that winter. Yet now she felt
mortified and irritated, and she rushed out of the room. Some minutes
later Maria followed her. She found Ileana stretched on the bed, in tears.
Begging her friend to forgive her, Maria threw her arms around the girl,
her eyes also wet with tears. That she might be crying for the man she
loved occurred to Ileana, and this thought was consoling to her. When
she rejoined Tony later in the evening he asked her in a voice somewhat
muted by emotion if she would be his wife.

Ileana went slightly pale when she saw Stefan enter and she turned to him
with a smile, lifting her head a little as if she expected to be embraced. But
Stefan simply kissed her hand and held it for a long time in his own.
  "You can't imagine how glad I am to see you," he said very softly.
  Ileana felt her heart begin to pound again, and all the blood seemed to
drain from her body. She sat down quickly on the sofa. Fortunately, she
realized, Stefan had not noticed anything. He's impossible, she repeated
constantly to herself. He's impossible, but still I love him.

She had said the same thing that night in Tony's room, very late, when
she sensed that the man beside her had fallen asleep. "Do you love

126

me?" he had demanded once more with difficulty, fighting to stay awake. She had responded softly, "I beleive I do. . . ." But probably he had not heard her because the next moment he was sleeping. She felt sorry for him. It was extremely late and he had danced a lot and had drunk considerable champagne. She had decided suddenly to tell him how she felt, since she knew that she would postpone the engagement again. She knew too how much Tony would suffer. "Next summer we'll buy a car," he had said to her, "and we'll take our honeymoon in it. First we'll go up to Transylvania, then down into the valley of the Olt. I've made a partial payment on the car and as soon as I receive my share of the inheritance from *Mos** Toader, I'll buy it. . . ."

". . . It's strange how I recognized the car from a distance." Suddenly she was aware that Stefan was speaking. What's he been saying all this time? she wondered anxiously. "I had that same indefinable feeling I had when I first saw you. The snow was falling thickly in a heavy curtain of flakes and within the circle of the streetlight I saw the back of the car half-buried in the drifts. . . . Of course it wasn't your car. It was just an old taxi, almost an antique, but when I opened the door to get in I had the impression again that it was yours. I can't explain why. Even though Ioana was with me an obscure intuition persisted that in a certain inexplicable way that car had once belonged to you. . . ."

After she had decided to postpone her engagement again Ileana had remembered Stefan's wife. It was this, perhaps, that had caused her to submit to Tony. He's married, she thought. I'll take a lover and everyone will be satisfied. Already she had put off the engagement three times. "But don't you love me at all?" Tony had asked in despair. An hour later in his room she answered his question with another, "Do you need more proof than this?" And to herself she explained, As a husband he would be intolerable, but I could prolong this adventure until I get tired of it and his love dies. Unfortunately Tony's body offered no solution to her dilemma, and she had lost hope by the time he unknowingly came to her rescue, saying regretfully, his speech somewhat thickened and halting because of the champagne, "But are you not a virgin? . . ." All at once Ileana had felt free of remorse, of regrets. "Oh, no," she had said in high good humor. "I'm a loose woman. That's why I didn't want us to become engaged. You ought to marry someone who's chaste." "But do you love me?" Tony had asked again, perplexed, overcome with fatigue. "I believe I do. . . ."

*Grandpa.

127

". . . Do you really believe it?" Stefan asked. (But my God, what have I said? Ileana thought in alarm, and she shook her head, forcing herself to smile.) "I can't believe it. It would be too simple. If we wait for our liberation to come with death, then we haven't gained anything. The problem is how to be freed from the belly of the whale as living beings, alive, in Time, in History. . . ."

"But why do you say 'the belly of the whale'?" Ileana demanded, rousing suddenly from her reverie.

Stefan stood up from his chair and broke into a laugh that was gentle and childlike. "It's an image I use sometimes when I get too absorbed in political economy," and stepping closer to Ileana he continued, "when I have the impression that I'm in the stomach of a gigantic cetacean, big enough to cover the whole earth. In the belly of the whale I assist with the ingestion of the raw materials and their digestion, with their removal, even, in the form of by-products. And when I'm lost there in the belly of the whale I pray to God to keep me alive and whole, undigested by the processes of political economy, until the moment when I can escape and see again the light of day out-side. . . ."

"If you say that your whale covers the entire earth, how can you ever hope to escape alive from its belly?" She hesitated a moment, then added quickly, looking down, "Through death, yes. That I can understand. Through death perhaps we are set free. . . ."

Stefan stared at her. "This is just what I asked you a few moments ago. Do you really believe that only through death can we be freed from Time and History? Then human existence would have no meaning! Then our being here in life, in History, is a mistake! If only death allows us to go out of Time and History, we really go, in fact, nowhere. We just rediscover noth-ingness. . . ."

"But why are you telling me all this?" Ileana asked with sudden irritation in her voice. "Why do you speak to me about death and nothingness, about the belly of the whale? I'm a woman. I'm young. I believe even that I'm a good-looking woman. You told me so yourself once, when you thought you were in love with me."

"And I'm still in love with you," said Stefan quietly.

Ileana looked at him in despair. He seemed taller and more remote as he stood there in front of her, his eyes blazing and his face very pale, a vague smile hovering in the corners of his mouth. They looked at each other in silence for some time.

"Then I'm sorry," Ileana said finally, standing up. "I think I've had a certain strange feeling of great sympathy for you that I didn't understand very well, one that might have been called, if you like, a beginning of love. I wouldn't have acknowledged it a few months ago, but because the feeling no longer exists I can tell you about it now."

"I've waited a long time for you to say this," Stefan said very softly.

"It's a kind of posthumous declaration," Ileana continued, lighting a cigarette, "a sort of official report of a demise. A few months ago I found you very attractive. I was almost fond of you. But now I can only regard you as a friend. . . . I don't believe, anyway, that this is going to bring about a change in your way of life, in your behavior. We'll still see each other three or four times a year. . . ."

"But you're not engaged," Stefan interrupted.

Surprised, Ileana gazed at him. She smiled and let the smoke from her cigarette rise slowly, idly upward, brush her temples and lose itself in her hair. Then she sat down on the sofa.

"You're not engaged," repeated Stefan with the same urgency. "What I'm saying to you is very important. You're not engaged, are you?"

"I'll answer that later. Meanwhile tell me how you've been. Talk to me about yourself, about your friends. Tell me how Biris is."

"I think he's in love with Catalina."

One day Bursuc came to the Ministry to talk about Biris and Catalina. It was the first day that year that really felt like spring. When Stefan saw him come in he could not hide a gesture of annoyance.

"Didn't Petrache warn you that I was coming to see you? He forgot, of course," Bursuc exclaimed with a knowing wink. "Ever since he lost his head over Catalina he doesn't even know his own name. He hardly ever goes to the coffee shop any more, and then only when he has to meet Bibicescu." He stretched out full length in the easy chair.

"This is just right for you, you high officials!" he commented admiringly. "Leather armchairs! And we pay for all this, we poor taxpayers! We pay for your luxuries with the sweat of our brows. But when the Revolution comes everyone will be swept away. We'll liquidate this state too, Mr. Budgeter. . . . You'll see!"

"Since when are you a revolutionary?" Stefan asked.

"I've always been a revolutionary. The trouble is there aren't any people to get the Revolution underway. They're all blockheads—and if they're not blockheads, they're cowards. . . . Don't you have any cigarettes?"

Stefan pulled open a drawer and held out a package. Selecting one, Bursuc lit it and calmly stuffed the rest into his pocket. "I've heard that you're on good terms with the Secretary General," he resumed in a different tone. "Couldn't you wangle something for me, a sinecure of some kind or other?"

"But you have a degree in theology and this is the Ministry of National Economy!"

"What difference does that make? If there's good will it can be arranged.

129

When this government was formed I was promised a post as sub-prefect but, infamous as all politicians are, they didn't keep their word. What do you want me to do, starve to death? Everyone in Romania has a job. Why shouldn't I have one too? But," he hastened to add, "let's get this clear. I don't need a serious job with regular hours behind a desk. I don't have time to come to the office. I've things to attend to all the time in town. Besides, my family lives in the provinces and I'm a family man. I can't just leave them there. I have to go to see them now and then."

Stefan began to laugh.

"No, really," protested Bursuc, "I'm serious. You may not think so, but I'm in no mood for joking. I have only a few twenties in my pocket. I haven't paid my hotel bill since I don't know when. Find me a sinecure and I'll offer a prayer for the repose of your soul. Because I see that you're rather restless. You're beginning to get thin. You look bad. Someone ought to pray for you. As a graduate *magna cum laude* in theology I know some prayers that won't fail! So, what do you say?"

"Impossible."

Bursuc regarded Stefan for a moment with his eyebrows drawn together in a frown. He pulled the package of cigarettes out of his pocket, lighted another one and continued. "Fine. I see you're incorruptible. You're possessed of this great antirevolutionary vice. It's your affair. But I warn you, you'll pay dearly when the Revolution comes!"

"What revolution?" asked Stefan. "The Iron Guard will soon be liquidated, and as for the Communists, they're still trying to gather their one or two hundred together so they'll know one another. So what revolution are you talking about?"

Bursuc looked at him in amazement and put his hand to his mouth to stifle a laugh. "They told me you were naive, but I didn't think that you were in this state! And naivete is another antirevolutionary fault. Now then, what do I care who starts the Revolution? One thing matters—to be with it and not against it!"

"Agreed. But I ask you once again, according to you who'll make the revolution?"

"As though someone has to make it! That's good! The Revolution comes and goes. No one makes it. First it was in Russia, then it came to Italy, Germany, Spain. Communist, Fascist, reactionary—the point is, it came. And it will come to us too. And I warn you, I'm with the Revolution and therefore against you. Politically I consider you my enemy. My personal enemy. Because you've endangered my fundamental interests. I ask you for a sinecure of ten or twelve thousand lei a month and you refuse me for legal reasons. As if legality matters in the times we live in! But you're an antirevolutionary by nature. Mark my words, things will go hard with you. . . ."

After a pause Bursuc continued. "I've had bad luck. The Iron Guard was

130

led by naive people without political spirit. If I had been in their place I'd be in power today. And I'd have led the Revolution. I'd have liquidated everyone else. The essential thing to do is to liquidate the adversary. After that the Revolution proceeds by itself. . . ." But as I said, I've had bad luck. If I'd seen that they had courage and political spirit I'd have gone over to their side. I have a lot of friends in the Iron Guard. It could have been arranged. By now, I'd have been in your place. I'd be sitting at this desk instead of being forced to go to one or another of my acquaintances just to put my hands on five hundred lei. . . . And by the way," he added, changing his tone, "could you lend me a thousand lei? I said that I'm running around after five hundred, but I was just being modest. The truth is, I'm after a thousand lei, five hundred for myself and five hundred for the others. I can't tell you who. Important people. Meanwhile keep this to yourself. . . ."

He took the bills that Stefan offered, thanked him and started for the door. But after a few steps he turned around. "I forgot to tell you the most important thing. Don't think Petrache's been going to bed with Catalina. No, God forbid! He loves her in a platonic way. He's an idealist. Catalina sleeps with Bibicescu. And with anyone else besides. . . . You don't say anything? Maybe you like her too, you look so unhappy. But don't get upset about it. Give her a call on the phone!"

The housemaid entered just as he began to raise the lid of one of his glass cases with the intention of removing a first edition of the poems by the Vacarescu brothers. Approaching him with her mincing walk the girl announced, "A gentleman is asking for you. He says it's urgent. He won't give his name. He says you know him."

Stefan smiled. This was just what had happened when he had visited Antim two months before. Again the professor would not have time to explain why the period when "the country mourned under the heel of the Turk" had no heirs. Antim wearily gathered up the few small books from the table and went to put them in the glass case.

Iancu Antim's house was situated at the end of a lane, behind the Foisor de Foc.* A massive and rather ugly building, it dated from 1900, and in the harsh light of the March afternoon when Stefan had come for the first time the house took on a stern nobility. It might have been lifted from an old engraving. A young servant girl had opened the door and invited him into an immense salon. Its walls were so overlaid with

*Firetower.

131

paintings that they could no longer be seen. Several bookcases with glass doors stood in one corner, while another held still more display cabinets, some of them covered with linen cloths.

"*Domnul* Professor is resting," the girl said. "But he ought to be getting up soon. He never sleeps more than an hour."

Stefan gazed around him in astonishment. Paintings, antique furniture, stands bearing open folios, church stalls, odd chairs whose backs were draped with fabrics of faded colors, stoles, bridal veils—all these together constituted a strange mixture of museum, antique shop, and chamber, like that of an elderly spinster. The two large windows that faced the garden were so narrowed by their green velvet drapes that the light could not reach all the corners of this crowded salon. Although the fire was still burning in the terra-cotta stove it was colder in the room than it was outside. Stefan put his hands in the pockets of his overcoat and walked around slowly, examining the pictures. There were portraits of old, bearded boyars in velvet mantles, ladies from the beginning of the past century, and dark, gloomy landscapes, painted amateurishly, quite without charm.

"Has that addlebrained girl brought you in here?" he heard Antim's voice suddenly from the doorway. "You'll freeze! Come quickly and warm up!" And Antim had ushered Stefan into a room that was not so large but just as crammed as the other with glass cases full of old icons and prints, sketchbooks, little tables piled with trinkets and bits of coral and mother-of-pearl.

"Don't look at anything!" Antim exclaimed. "Don't look at an object until I explain it to you. Because each one has to be explained. All the things you see here are relics of the time when 'the country mourned under the heel of the Turk' as the poet says—the eighteenth century and the beginning of the nineteenth."

He began to show Stefan engravings, first editions of Muntenian writers, portfolios of manuscripts and letters.

"I told you that the Vacarescu's are my great weakness. In particular, Iancu Vacarescu, the one with 'The power of evil fate,' and 'My accumulated years. . . .' Or aren't you familiar with Iancu Vacarescu's poems?"

"No, I'm not," Stefan admitted with a smile.

Antim glanced at him questioningly then shrugged his shoulders in a gesture of discouragement. "How can you be interested in what I've collected here? You must be initiated first. . . . I warned you, I have things that are not often found in Romanian homes. I have relics from a past which is not only dead, as any past is, but one which has left nothing to the ages that have succeeded it. A past without heirs, celibate," and he had added, blinking his eyes, "like me."

With a brief rap on the door the maid entered, bringing the coffee.

132

She went to Antim and whispered, "*Domnul* Nichita has come. He says you know what for. . . ."

Antim blushed suddenly and left the room in haste. Alone, Stefan felt his heart stirred by a vague sadness. A past without heirs! he repeated to himself. A time that once existed. A time when the people loved and suffered just as we do now. They had a certain language in which they tried to write according to a certain manner. And then that time vanished as if it had never been because the people who came after it ignored everything that had been done "when the country mourned under the heel of the Turk." A celibate time, without heirs. . . .

"You're a herald of good luck," Antim said when he returned to the salon. "You've brought good fortune to this house!" He saw the cup of coffee and ceased the constant rubbing of his hands in order to pick it up and sip from it thoughtfully. "I must explain to you about all that I've collected here. I've given a lifetime to it. . . ."

Stefan inferred that the Professor's mind was on something else, and when he had drunk his coffee he stood up to leave.

"You must come again," Antim said. "You're a man of good luck. I'll tell you why some other time. But believe me, you've brought luck to this house!"

"Some rare edition of the poets Vacarescu?" suggested Stefan from the threshold.

"I have them all!" Antim exclaimed. "No, it's a much more important matter." He stroked his beard. "I'll tell you someday. I'll tell you and maybe I'll even show you!"

Stefan's second visit was on an afternoon in May. Antim began to show him the first editions of the poems by the Vacarescu brothers. He had just recited some lines by Iancu when the maid entered with the announcement, "A gentleman is asking for you. . . ."

Antim closed the glass case with care and started to go out of the room. His eyes fell on the man in the entrance and his face brightened, but Stefan did not recognize the visitor at first. He had let his mustache grow and he was wearing dark glasses.

"How are things with you, *boier* Ioachim Teodorescu?" Antim greeted him jovially. "What wind brings you from the Scythians and Agatirs to the lands of the Turkish conquest?"

Teodorescu hesitated a moment, wiped his perspiring forehead with his handkerchief, and casting a glance at Stefan he responded, "I've come to ask you for hospitality for a few nights, *domnule* Professor. Just until I get another place. I may find one tomorrow or the day after. . . ."

Antim stared at him in amazement. "Is someone after you perhaps?" he asked, a note of fear in his voice.

"Yes," Teodorescu admitted. "But I assure you, you won't have any trouble. I won't receive visitors. Just let me sleep at your place tonight and I'll leave tomorrow."

Antim wrung his hands, perplexed. "It's impossible, my friend," he said. "Impossible! I have a new servant girl, a peasant who's a little stupid. She'll fill the neighborhood with rumors that I'm harboring Iron Guardists. And of this I'm sure, they'll come here to search! Look at all these things! All these papers and books!. . . I've heard that the police scatter everything around, and what they can't read on the spot, they load in their trucks and take with them. . . . And then, really, do I have any place for you to sleep? Look around! Nothing but books and paintings and papers everywhere!"

Teodorescu regarded him with a smile. He put on his dark glasses and prepared to leave.

"Wait a minute," said Stefan. "If it's a matter of a few nights I can put you up. I have, besides my apartment, a room in a hotel. A place where I hide away occasionally when I'm in the mood. I'll let you have it."

Iancu Antim was delighted and rubbed his hands together. He insisted that Ioachim not leave immediately, urging him to stay and drink a cup of coffee. When he went to tell the maid, Teodorescu turned suddenly to Stefan.

"You know the new law? You're not permitted to rent a room or take in someone without first informing the police."

Stefan shrugged. "I know," he said.

An hour later Teodorescu sat down exhausted on the edge of the bed in Stefan's room. "Tell me frankly, how many days can I stay here?" he asked. "Could I stay until Monday?"

"Certainly."

"Do you think anyone saw us coming in? I mean someone other than the hotel porter? This is very important."

"I don't think so," replied Stefan casually.

Teodorescu sighed with relief and asked permission to stretch out on the bed.

"Of course! I have to leave anyway. Is there anything else I can do for you?"

Teodorescu looked at him a few moments with indecision, then he asked, "Could you make a phone call from town to a number I'll give you?"

"With pleasure, if it's a personal matter," answered Stefan, "but if it's political, no. And not because I'm an opponent of your ideas and your ideals, although I am, politically, but because in the struggle you're carrying on with the police I want to remain neutral. Just as I refuse to denounce one of you, so also I refuse to give him aid."

"I understand, but I don't quite know what to do. I want you to let my fiancée know where she can find me. You might say that this is a personal matter. But on the other hand, she shares my political views. In addition she

134

has to let me know if she finds another place for me to stay." Smiling, he added, "You see, things are rather complicated."

"What should I tell your fiancée?" Stefan asked.

"Just this, but please repeat it word for word: 'Drop out of sight. Come Monday at the same time to the place where we were supposed to meet today.'"

'All right," said Stefan, preparing to leave. "I'll repeat your words exactly as I heard them. Rest easily . . . and good luck."

As he rose to extend his hand Teodorescu brushed a book from the nightstand where it had been lying under the newspapers and magazines. He read the title and smiled. *Encore un instant de bonheur* by Montherlant. "A beautiful title," he said.

It promised to be a hot summer day and Spiridon Vadastra already felt tired as he was caught up in the torrent of people that erupted into *calea* Victoriei during the lunch hour. Nevertheless he went on, his steps firm, glancing around with an expression both stern and aloof.

The woman at the post office searched a moment and finally smiled, shaking her head. "Nothing!" It was not the first time she had given him such an answer, and yet on this day Spiridon seemed to detect a hidden irony in her response. He left, his irritation growing, to go to the restaurant, where he ate very little. At two o'clock he went to the courthouse. Certain tedious matters of business drew him there from time to time, but he also liked to linger in the halls, where he would meet acquaintances and friends and converse with them. Today however he was in no mood to loiter. Without interest he shook hands with several of his colleagues, replying sullenly to their queries and shrugging his shoulders drearily. At five o'clock he went to *domnul* Protopopescu's office, but the moment he entered and held out his hand he regretted having come. *Domnul* Protopopescu greeted him with a contemptuous smile—a rare occurrence and a sure sign he was preparing to impart a bit of unpleasant information.

"Hold your chatter, Vadastra!" he said, opening a desk drawer and searching through the papers, the same ironic smile remaining on his lips. "You've made a mistake to show your face here!"

"What do you mean, *domnule* Protopopescu?" said Spiridon, flushing suddenly.

"You'll see directly. Look here, Ford has answered you. He's returned that nonsense of yours, that plan you had to change the world. . . ."

Spiridon felt as though his veins had been drained of blood. A terrible emptiness yawned in his chest. His throat became dry, his lips white, burned

135

by the heat of his breath. Incredulous, he stared at the long-awaited envelope from which *domnul* Protopopescu now withdrew those pages he had written months before, together with a sheet of heavy paper bearing several typed lines. It was undoubtedly Ford's reply.

"Look here! This is it," *domnul* Protopopescu said, holding it out to him. "He tells you that your proposals are very interesting, but he regrets that he cannot take them into consideration. Look! Read it—if you know English," he said, still with the same mocking smile. "Since I don't know English, the girl translated it for me," he added, joking, running his tongue around the roof of his mouth.

"I don't understand." Spiridon's faint whisper was barely audible. "I don't understand how the letter came to you."

"*Ei*, bravo! As if we weren't always on guard?! Otherwise what's the good of having these services?"

"But the envelope was addressed to me," Spiridon said, his voice still weak. "I gave my address as General Delivery."

"Ah, yes, that's it precisely!" exclaimed *domnul* Protopopescu happily. "I have to know, too, who it is that writes to you from America and what he says to you. . . . We're always on guard!"

Spiridon took the envelope and slid it mechanically into his pocket. He kept in his hand only the sheet of paper that *domnul* Protopopescu had held out to him. He could not bring himself to hide it, yet he did not dare to try to read it. The chief was staring at him with that contemptuous smile, smoking his cigarette in great good humor.

"Have a seat and read it," he said, seeing that Vadastra was still standing uncertainly in front of the desk. "After that I have something else to say. . . ."

Spiridon sat down in the armchair but as soon as his glance fell on the signature he started up and cried, "It's not from Ford! He didn't sign it! A Mr. P. G. Wood wrote it! It's not from Ford!"

"What did you expect? That Ford would sign it himself? As though he has time to read all the junk that comes to him from all over the world! The man who signed it must be one of Ford's secretaries."

Vadastra listened, stealing a furtive glance at the signature, P. G. Wood, which for a moment had restored all his hopes. Then he ran his eyes over the letter. With his slight knowledge of English he gathered that P. G. Wood thanked him in the name of Henry Ford and returned the text of his interesting statement. *Domnul* Protopopescu was right. The copy of the statement, which he had just stuffed in his pocket, was the most convincing answer. Ford was not interested in organizing and guiding the public opinion of the world.

"Now, let's talk seriously," said *domnul* Protopopescu, mashing his cigarette in the grounds that remained in the bottom of his coffee cup, and lighting another. "Vadastra, I see that you consume state money to no purpose. And you do stupid things besides. You disgrace us."

A surge of blood flushed Spiridon's cheeks again but he did not dare to

136

answer. *Domnul* Protopopescu spoke with the voice of a master who did not permit a reply, a voice that invariably brought with it bad news. He crossed his arms on the desk and spoke as though he would rid himself of the bitter taste that poisoned his mouth. His jaws were clenched and he snapped his tongue furiously after each word.

"You disgrace us!" he repeated with disgust. "Instead of working seriously you do such stupid things. All the information you've furnished us is foolishness. Uninteresting. Tales for children. I'm paying you for nothing. . . ."

Spiridon raised his head and was confronted by *domnul* Protopopescu's exasperated face, his habit—so familiar—of shaking his head constantly while he was speaking. Vadastra did not understand. He sensed that something painful was going to happen but he could not imagine what.

". . . consequently you can collect your pay for this month and wind things up. We don't need your services anymore. They don't interest us. . . ."

It was difficult for Spiridon to comprehend. Was he fired? This thought seemed absurd. For five years he had been planning to leave the Service, but only at a time of his own choosing. Never for a moment had it entered his mind that *domnul* Protopopescu would dismiss him. It was utterly absurd! He had never taken his chief's moods seriously. He always did what he had been doing—almost nothing—since the time when he was still in the University and had been engaged to supply information about student movements. He restricted himself to meeting a few times a week with *domnul* Protopopescu or other employees of the Service, discussing what he had heard, even lying sometimes in order to appear well-informed. But most of the time he talked about himself, his successes, and about how he would surprise everyone soon.

". . . Then we understand each other fully," *domnul* Protopopescu concluded. "And now, if you'll excuse me, I'm busy," he added, getting to his feet.

Spiridon stood up too, but he was not at all ready to leave. "I don't understand what you mean," he began emotionally. "I'm a proper and discreet man. I've always done my duty. I don't believe you have any reason to complain. . . . With respect to the proposal I submitted to Ford, that's a personal matter. And I'm surprised that you, a man of elegant manners, would have countenanced such—what shall I say?—a thing so indelicate as confiscating my letter and reading it although it was addressed to me. . . ."

Domnul Protopopescu stared at him in perplexity, as though he could not believe his ears. "I say, you *are* a lunatic!" he exclaimed at last, frowning. "You really are crazy! You ought to get help. . . ."

"I might answer that but I prefer to remain silent," said Spiridon, reddening. "I should like to think that you were joking, because otherwise I should consider it an insult, a grave insult. And I don't stand for insults from anyone—even from one of my superiors in the Service."

137

"You're no longer a part of the Service. I told you that fifteen minutes ago."

"Buy why, please?" Spiridon said, aroused. "Have I committed some error? On the contrary as far as I know, I was always the brain of this Service. I alone know the others. I know who they are—they're ignoramuses, worthless men. I was the only man with personality. . . ."

"Why prolong this conversation?" said *domnul* Protopopescu, sitting down and lighting another cigarette. "The orders are executed. Good day!"

"Do you think you can fire me like a servant after five years of service?" cried Spiridon, furious, approaching the desk. "A man like me, who's always done his duty? You'll be sorry later on!—When I begin to tell those who are concerned about how the state's money is being squandered!"

"Are you trying to blackmail me?" *domnul* Protopopescu asked with a sugary smile, his voice abnormally calm.

"Not blackmail!" Spiridon continued, still fuming. "It's the pure truth! Do you think I don't know anything, that I haven't seen or heard anything? Someday I'll tell it where it should be told!"

"See if they believe you!" said *domnul* Protopopescu, releasing a smoke ring from his lips. "You stupid fool, don't you know I can disgrace you in twenty-four hours by announcing publicly that you have been, or still are, in my service? They'd throw you out of the bar association before you could so much as turn around!"

"Just wait, I'll tell them! I'll tell them!" Spiridon kept repeating. But *domnul* Protopopescu's threat had struck home. The sudden thought of a scandal in the bar made him feel that the earth had dropped away beneath his feet. His self-control gone, exhausted by all the blows he had received in the last half hour, he continued foolishly to repeat the same words, "I'll tell them everything I know," over and over, trembling, clinging to them in his despair.

Domnul Protopopescu regarded him once more with crushing contempt that was not, however, unmixed with pity. Then he said softly, "Get out!"

Spiridon was suddenly speechless. He passed his hand over his dry lips and tried to smile, but his face was stony with hatred, humiliation, and fear. Then with a trembling hand he put the letter from America, which he had been clutching during the conversation, into his pocket. He started to the door.

"You'll regret this, you'll see!" he muttered from the threshold in a last attempt at a threat. But *domnul* Protopopescu was looking for something in one of his desk drawers and did not reply.

Someday when he became powerful he would meet *domnul* Protopopescu and he would repay him with a vengeance for all he had said. *Domnul*

138

Protopopescu would fall on his knees before him, begging Vadastra's forgiveness, but in vain! In tears and beating his breast, *domnul* Protopopescu would try to kiss Spiridon's feet, but he would kick the prostrate man in the face and cry, "Get out of here! Out!" Then he would go to visit him in prison in his stone cell, finding him sprawled on a bed of dirty straw, in chains. "Do you still remember when you told me that I was crazy, that you could ruin me if you wished in twenty-four hours? Do you still remember how you fired me? *Ei*, yes, and now your life is in my hands. Look, this is your pardon!" and he would tear it into little pieces and throw them in *domnul* Protopopescu's face. Then he would spit at him and shout, "Get out of here!"

But Vadastra had awakened from his dreams of violent revenge by the time he reached home. He felt dejected, all energy spent. Wondering what to do next he collapsed in the easy chair and removed his monocle with a gesture of immense weariness. Being in no mood to go out to the restaurant to eat, he decided to retire. He slept heavily, a feverish sleep, broken by nightmares from which he awakened shaking. During one of these intervals of rousing between nightmares he thought he heard the door to the apartment open, followed by the sound of footsteps, familiar now, whispers, and a woman's laughter. But this time he did not get out of bed to lie in wait for them. The knowledge that Baleanu was in the next room in the company of a woman quieted him and he made an effort to go back to sleep quickly.

The next morning when he took his watch from the bedside table to look at the time, he heard again the sound of a woman's steps in the hall. The entrance door opened swiftly and the elevator began to descend. He noticed with surprise that it was almost nine o'clock. Surely Baleanu had long since left for the regiment. On any other day Vadastra would have bounded from his bed to see what the woman looked like. But, although at the moment of awakening the dismal incidents of the day before did not immediately come to his mind, his whole being was pervaded by a disconsolate exhaustion that weighed him down. He was out of sorts, irresolute. For a few moments he reflected on the woman who had left so late in the morning, but he soon recalled his troubles and began to wonder how he could cope with them.

It would be necessary to return to the serious practice of law. Unfortunately the only aspect of his profession that he liked was the trial work, the pleading of cases in the courtroom. All the rest bored him—the time lost in endless waiting, the work at the secretariat, formalities, consultations with the judges, copying from judicial acts and decisions. "What if I lose my job in the solicitor's office too?" he wondered, suddenly gripped by panic. The thought was so terrifying to him that he sprang out of bed and began speedily to dress. His work with that agency was negligible. Eight other lawyers were employed as well as numerous secretaries. Only infrequently was he given a dossier to study or a case to prepare when he visited one of the offices to ask what was new. "If they take that away from me," Spiridon said to himself in dismay, "I'll cause a scandal that will make all Bucharest howl!" But that threat was not sufficient to restore his tranquility. He imagined *domnul* Protopopescu in the act of lifting the receiver and calmly calling the director of the agency. "Fire him," the man would say, shaking his head and smiling. "Fire Spiridon immediately! That's an order!" "I'll cause a scandal!" Vadastra repeated to himself many times, continually moistening his dry lips. "I'll cause a scandal!"

The plan occurred to him that night as he was struggling with insomnia and visions of the disaster that awaited him if he lost the solicitor's job. He heard the elevator stop at his floor. He heard Baleanu open the door with less caution than previously, and he could hear the whispers. An hour later someone walked down the hall to the bathroom, and several minutes after that Baleanu rummaged about in the kitchen, probably looking for glasses. Her husband has a hundred million and she spends the night in the apartment of a lieutenant! said Spiridon to himself. With a hundred million who would refuse to give a million or two? He wouldn't even miss it. In a few days he'd earn as much again and replace it. . . . If only I knew her name. . . .

The simplicity with which he could acquire one or two million lei took his breath away. It frightened him. He would lie in wait one day when she stayed in Baleanu's room after the lieutenant had gone to the regiment. Then he would step out of his room and suddenly confront her. "Don't be angry, *doamna*," he would say, "but please come into my office for a few minutes. It is in your interest. . . ." What she said didn't matter, nor how much she protested. Once they reached his office he would close the door and, approaching her, he would speak with great severity. "You may believe anything about me that you wish, my dear *doamna* So-and-so, but I intend by this evening to inform your husband where and with whom you spent the night"—let's say—"of June fifteenth. You may not like the idea of his finding out, but I don't mind telling you that I shall reveal this gross offence of adultery to all your acquaintances. I don't think you'll like them to know who your lover is. Moreover you'll disgrace Baleanu and ruin his career. He will have no choice but to put a bullet in his head or flee across the border. As far as I'm concerned, I'm not afraid of anything because I've taken full precautions." (That's not true but how will she know?) "However there is a possible solution for you. I believe my friend Baleanu has told you in considerable detail about me and you realize I'm a person of some importance in Romania. *Doamna* So-and-so, I have great plans. Unfortunately until now I haven't found a capitalist who will understand and

140

help me. I say unfortunately, because I am forced in consequence to appeal to you for help. I need about two million lei in order to bring to a successful conclusion a sublime work, useful not only to our country but to humanity in general. Although it is a deep secret I might be able to tell you more about this sublime work on another occasion. Your husband is very rich, as you know better than I. If you don't want me to reveal anything about your relations with my friend, pleace place this sum at my disposal. I don't care how you do it. You could recommend me to your husband—ask him to accept me as an associate in his business. Or you could even bring me the two million yourself in jewels or in cash . . . but don't try to betray me by saying anything to Baleanu about it. You'd regret that very much. I've taken full precautions. I warn you, don't try anything. Set a time to meet me tomorrow. . . ."

He had not been mistaken. The lieutenant had gone to the kitchen for glasses. Now he heard laughter from the bedroom, the sound of a cork being drawn with difficulty from a bottle, the beginning of a song. He tossed about in his bed, expelling all thoughts alien to his plan, and resumed with new vigor the drama of his meeting with the beautiful stranger. Such women always have money and a great many jewels. If her husband should refuse to receive him into his business at Campina, she would only have to sell some of her jewels in order to pay the amount—if not two million, then he'd be content with one. But what was her name? He absolutely must find out her name in order to appear well-informed about her situation, about her husband's fortune!

Toward morning he fell asleep, long after the strains of the last song from Baleanu's room had died away.

Early in the afternoon of the fourteenth of July Stefan climbed the stairs to his hotel room and stretched out wearily on the bed. The day was very hot. He hoped he would be able to rest for a while before returning to the Ministry. His appointment was to be signed that afternoon. He was going to Japan.

A long time before Stefan had learned by chance that this assignment might be his, but the mission was not defined until the middle of June. He would be an observer at the Economic Conference of the Far Eastern Nations. The Secretary General had sent for him one hot rainy morning. Stefan found him nervous and preoccupied.

"You'll leave in five or six weeks," he said. "Be very careful! It's a more important matter than simply being an observer. The Japanese need oil and they're prepared to send their tankers to pick it up at Constanta. Out of all the things they're offering us we need only rubber. But they don't have any. For the present they're buying it from the Dutch Indies. Nevertheless they've offered us rubber—and at an advantageous price! Their proposal seems very suspect to me. Besides, it came through a company recommended by Vidrighin. Also the Germans are involved somehow. The important thing is to prevent Vidrighin from taking the business into his hands. I've sent him on a mission to Switzerland and I'll try to keep him there as long as possible. In the meantime get ready to leave. Be very discreet. Don't discuss it in town. . . ."

He stared at Stefan for some time, hesitating, then he added, "Your stay there could be lengthy. God knows what may happen in the fall. Perhaps it would be well to take your wife with you. Think it over. . . ."

Stefan had left the office of the Secretary General with a vague sadness in his heart. He would take Ioana, of course. But at the same time he thought of Ileana.

He recalled their last meeting on the eve of Palm Sunday. "I'm going to church," she had told him. "I don't know why but all at once I felt the need to go into a church." She had looked at him anxiously, then with that brief boyish gesture she had shaken her curls and asked, "Do you believe in God? Do you really believe?"

Stefan got up from the bed and went to the window. When he opened the blinds the room was flooded with light. I simply won't be able to sleep, he said to himself, lying down on the bed again. Nevertheless he closed his eyes.

"Do you really believe?" Ileana had asked at that time. "Do you believe that car existed?" (Or maybe it only seemed as though she asked that, Stefan had thought later. Perhaps I didn't understand her very well. She spoke about God and asked if I believe that God exists. In her way she was asking, "Is the sheepfold far?") "Or are we condemned to remain forever in the belly of the whale?" She tried to smile. It was the first time he had seen such a strained expression on her face. The spontaneity was gone. It was as though she were smiling for her own benefit, to console herself in her solitariness.

Then one morning at the Ministry several weeks later he answered the telephone and heard a voice that seemed to come from very far away, crying, "Stefan! Stefan!" "Where are you?" he had asked. "In a tobacco shop in Sosea. I went to the forest. I was possessed by a longing for the forest." "But aren't you engaged?" he demanded suddenly, startled. There was a very long silence. "Aren't you engaged?" he asked again, and repeated it several times. "I don't understand what's hap-pened between us," she said tardily. "I simply can't understand you. I don't know what you want or what you expect. . . . I'm sorry I ever met you—very sorry. . . ." "But you still haven't told me if you're engaged, or if you're going to get engaged," he insisted. "Sometimes I wonder if I really met you, or are you just a hallucination? Perhaps you really are lost in the belly of the whale. . . ." Then she added softly, almost whispering, "Good-bye, Stefan, good-bye. . . ." The connection was broken suddenly, perhaps inadvertently. He could hear the sound of it, dull and metallic.

That evening when he left the Ministry he went straight to *strada* Batistei. He rang the doorbell insistently and long, before *doamna* Cretulescu finally answered. She seemed surprised to see him standing in front of her with a bouquet of lilies of the valley in his hand. "She left this morning for Jassy," *Tante* Alice told him. "She telephoned you from the station. Didn't she speak with you? She said she was going to phone you to let you know she was leaving. She made up her mind unexpectedly. . . ."

"But she's not engaged?" Stefan asked anxiously.

"Only God understands her!" exclaimed *doamna* Cretulescu. "He came here to see her once, Captain Melinte. He begged her, he fell on his knees before her, and before me, too, Captain Melinte. 'Doamna Cretulescu,' he said to me, '*Tante* Alice, I implore you, persuade her!' I felt sorry for him, a sensible man, pleading with us both as if he were praying to a god. . . ."

Stefan had smiled, embarrassed, and held out the bouquet of flowers.

Do you believe in God? Do you really believe? Do you believe that car exists? . . .

He heard the sound of rapid footsteps in the corridor, and voices. The doorknob was shaken repeatedly. Someone began to knock vigorously. It's an Adventist selling Bibles, Stefan recalled, and jumped from the bed in fury. He had scarcely turned the key in the lock when the door burst open so violently that it hit the wall. A group of strange men surrounded him, some carrying revolvers. He did not have time to grasp the significance of what was happening before he heard the first man shout, "Police officers!"

Two armed agents flanked Stefan while a third felt of his pockets. The others overturned the bed and chairs and searched the wardrobe.

"Where's Teodorescu?" asked a man who stood by the door, taking a step toward Stefan.

"I don't know. I haven't seen him since he left. He thanked me for putting him up and he left. I don't know where he went."

The leader looked at him with a skeptical smile. "Were you friends?" he asked.

"No, not really. I met him in Germany a year ago. . . ."

"Come to the police station," the leader said. "You can make a statement there."

143

. . .

"I realized how much you love each other," said Vadastra, "when I heard you singing that evening. I must say that *doamna* Macovei has a lovely voice!" He pronounced the final words with a certain awkwardness. The lieutenant raised his eyes and blushed.

"It isn't she," he said. "That's not her name."

Spiridon moistened his lips. "I supposed it was she because I know that Macovei is a big oil man and has a very beautiful wife."

"No, it isn't she," repeated Baleanu, smiling. "That's not her name."

"Forgive me, please, I didn't mean to be indiscreet," Vadastra excused himself, and a moment later he added, "although I might have been angry. We're friends, and we live in the same house."

"I'll tell you later. On my word of honor, I'll tell you. But I can't now! A difficulty's arisen in our relationship, and I don't know how it will end. . . . But when the day comes that I'm able to, I'll tell you first, you have my word of honor. . . .

After the lieutenant's departure Vadastra felt a little less secure. How was he going to find out her name if Baleanu continued to defer his confidences? And he had spoken vaguely of a difficulty. What if something should happen between them and the beautiful mystery woman would cease to visit their apartment at night? For two evenings Vadastra remained vigilant, but Baleanu returned home alone. I know they've quarreled and she's not coming again! Vadastra said to himself, alarmed. It seemed catastrophic to think that the millionaire's wife might have parted from the lieutenant. He slept poorly, startled by every sound made by the elevator, although he knew that Baleanu was asleep in his room. The next day he tried to find out from one of his co-workers at the courthouse the names of the important oil magnates, but he soon realized the futility of this inquiry. He did not know how he could get Baleanu's confirmation of any name he might propose. If he were to ask him again, the lieutenant might become suspicious. During their brief encounters Baleanu did not speak again about his friend and the possibility of marriage with her.

"And what if I should try it even without knowing her name?" Vadastra wondered one evening. "I'll just say *'doamna'* all the time. She'll be so upset she won't notice. . . . If only she won't speak to Baleanu. In her fear she might be capable of it. If I just had some guarantee in my possession, a letter, a document—in short, something sure. . . .

But when he searched Baleanu's room one day after sending the orderly to town, he found, as before, nothing. Anxious, he returned to his own quarters. He was certain the woman would denounce him to Baleanu if he could not produce something that she feared, some proof that would involve no risk to himself. What good would it do to know her name if she were to tell everything to Baleanu that same evening?

He remained slumped in the easy chair beside the desk twisting his monocle nervously between his fingers. Suddenly he realized that *he had found it*. He had discovered a solution, a means of great simplicity. For several moments he sat with his mouth open, his hands limp. His monocle slipped unnoticed to the carpet. A wave of blood surged violently to his face. He stood up suddenly and raised his hand to his brow. Picking up the monocle he left in great haste.

Doamna Porumbache heard him singing in the street.
  "In the mill the wheel is turning, tac, tac, tac,
  And the miller wields his hammer, tac, tac, tac..."
She got out of bed, slipped into her dress and went into the hall to welcome him. Although it was long after twelve the night was still very hot. Biris had pulled off his jacket and had thrown it carelessly over his shoulder. He stood in front of the door and tried many times without success to insert the key in the lock.

"You're drunk again!" *doamna* Porumbache exclaimed as she opened the door. "You've lost your mind drinking with Catalina!"

"I don't think I've exactly lost my mind," said Biris, "but undoubtedly I've drunk a lot. And now I'm sleepy. Good night!"

He wanted to go to his room but *doamna* Porumbache caught his arm. "It's a shame she's bewitched you, *maiculita*,* that tart! She's driven you out of your mind!... Alas, poor old woman that I am! They'll catch you running around with an actress and they'll kick you out of the *liceu!* We'll be paupers...."

Biris took a package of cigarettes from his pocket and held it out to her. "Would you like a smoke?" he inquired mildly.

The woman sighed. She moistened her lips and placed the cigarette in the corner of her mouth. Biris lit it for her and then lit one for himself, giving her the pack.

"Do you have any money left?" she asked.

"I do. Do you need something?"

"No, I was just asking. Did that woman give you some money?"

"No, I earned this with a translation."

The woman was silent, drawing deeply on her cigarette. "Why don't you want to get married?" She was more calm now. "Only don't take Catalina...."

Wearily Biris shrugged his shoulders. "I've told you before that there's nothing between Catalina and me! Whoever put that idea into your head?

*A term of endearment.

Everybody knows she's Bibicescu's girl. We're only friends. Or perhaps this also is disgraceful? To be friends with an actress?"

"It would be better if you'd get married," continued *doamna* Porumbache, as if she had not been listening to him. "There are so many girls who are rich and beautiful! Why don't you want to get married? Aren't you sick of poverty? Maybe we could move to another house. I'd see people again, I'd have someone else to exchange a word with. . . ."

Biris gazed at her for a long time and a sudden pity for her overwhelmed him. "All right. We'll think about it," he said. "Keep on looking. Maybe eventually I'll get married and even, perhaps, play politics! And now good night!" He lifted her hand and kissed it.

"Petrica, you wouldn't have about five hundred bani you could give me, would you! I thought I'd fix chicken with sour cream tomorrow."

Biris produced his billfold and handed it to her. "Take it all," he said. "I don't need anything."

He went into his room and throwing his coat on a chair he flung himself on the bed. He began to sing again very softly.

"In the mill the wheel is turning, tac, tac, tac. . . ."

"It's Mitica's song, God forgive him!" said *doamna* Porumbache. She smiled as she opened the door, and her eyes filled with tears. "Sing it again. . . ."

"And the miller wields his hammer, tac, tac, tac . . ."

Biris continued, raising his voice slightly.

"Tac, tac, tac," *doamna* Porumbache echoed, weeping, her voice low. "Mitica's song. Listen! He sang it like that too, God forgive him! tac, tac, tac!"

"This is a new song," said Biris without lifting his head from the pillow. "We young people sing it: 'In the mill the wheel is turning . . .'" he began again, much louder.

"It's old," *doamna* Porumbache insisted. "It's Mitica's song. Listen, he sang it that way when he was tipsy, 'tac, tac, tac. . . .' It's an old song, from the old days. *Finu** Lica sang it too, 'tac, tac, tac. . . .'"

Then suddenly she began to cry again and sat down on the edge of the bed. Biris stopped singing and lay still, gazing at the ceiling.

"If only I could see you married," she said. "I could go and join them. I dreamed of him again the day before yesterday, my dear departed husband, God forgive him! I thought he spoke to me. It seemed that we were in Ferendari, at the time when he was mixed up with a dressmaker, someone called Marioara. . . ."

"I know," said Biris, "the Zissu woman. Uncle Mitica rather liked the girls and he knew how to pick them!"

"The devil he did!" *doamna* Porumbache said quickly, wiping her eyes

---

*Godson.

with the back of her hand. "A nobody of a dressmaker, a poor girl, who'd lie with first one and then another to get food for her children. I didn't worry about her. *Finu* Lica gave her a dressing down—right in the middle of the street! But I wasn't afraid that someone like Marioara would wreck my home. I wasn't young anymore, but I wouldn't give in to ten like her. . . ."

"And how was he, Mitica, in your dream?" Biris interrupted, sitting up to light a cigarette.

"It seemed we were in Ferendari," *doamna* Porumbache began wistfully, with her eyes fixed on a corner of the room. "And all at once I saw him open the door of that big room, the one that faced the street, and he said to me, 'Are you here, Viorico? Haven't you gone to bed yet?' At first I didn't answer. I pretended to be angry, the way I sulked at that time, when he was mixed up with Marioara and came home late at night. And anyway I don't remember what he said to me, but next it seemed that we climbed into a carriage—no, that's not right—only he climbed in because I changed my mind and I said to him, still sulking, 'You go alone, Mitica. I know good and well where you're going!' May God forgive me!" she said, dropping her voice and crossing herself. "May it not be some sign. He seemed to want to take me with him, but I wasn't thinking about that. I was thinking that he was going to Marioara, to his mistress. . . . But it seemed to me the dream had come true when I heard you singing. Sing it again! Sing, 'tac, tac, tac!' "

"In the mill the wheel is turning . . ."
began Biris, his voice tired, a hint of hoarseness in it.

Doamna Porumbache smiled as she listened, and her eyes were filled again with tears.

"Petrica, honey, I want to see you in your own home with a wife and children. But not with someone like Catalina. I'll find you a good girl, one with wealth. So we can move downtown, so we can see people again, so I can have servants like I used to. Oh, Petrica, if you'd listened to me, you'd have an automobile today. . . ."

Biris raised his voice suddenly. "Tac, tac, tac. . . ."

"That's how Mitica sang it too. I seem to hear him now, God forgive him! 'Tac, tac, tac. . . .' "

It was only after a week had passed that he was allowed to inform Ioana of his arrest. In all that time he had neither washed nor shaved. He slept on the cement floor of a little room in the jail at the police station. The powerful light overhead burned constantly day and night. Gendarmes in three-hour shifts sat on the chair near his door, guarding him. They were not allowed to speak to each other. However, some of the guards who came on duty after

147

midnight talked to keep from falling asleep. One of them, a peasant from Ialomita, even became quite friendly and trustful of his prisoner. When he accompanied Stefan to the toilet he waited outside the door. The other guards, thinking that Stefan might try to hang himself, obeyed their orders precisely and went inside.

During the first three days they did not question him, but finally he was summoned to an interrogation. He was ashamed as he went unshaven and without a tie, followed closely by the guard, through the halls. Everyone, it seemed to him, was watching him suspiciously, almost with hatred.

The inspector asked him how long he had been a Legionnaire* and with whom he had worked.

"I'm not a member of the Iron Guard," Stefan responded calmly.

"All right. We know this, they all say the same thing," the inspector said, appearing bored. He selected a photograph from the stack that was in front of him.

"Do you know this person?"

Stefan shrugged. He had never seen the man.

"What about this one?"

Stefan looked at it and answered without hesitation. "That's Ioachim Teodorescu. Only now he wears a mustache."

"In other words, you know what he looks like!" exclaimed the inspector. "You declared that you met him in Germany. What were you doing in Germany?"

Stefan explained. The inspector looked directly into his eyes and played with a paper cutter. Stefan wanted to speak further about his duties at the Ministry and his mission to Japan but the other interrupted him.

"It's of no interest to us! Everyone says the same things. . . ." He pressed a button and the policeman entered clicking his heels. The inspector signaled with an abrupt movement of his head. After that Stefan was no longer permitted to buy his meals at the canteen. They brought him some cabbage soup that evening, with a piece of stale bread, while from somewhere near in a summer garden the strains of a popular tango, "My Blue Heaven," reached him. The trite, commonplace music seemed unaccountably sweet.

Two days later he was again taken to be questioned, this time by a young commissar who regarded him absently. "You have influential protectors!" was his greeting. "Who has intervened for you? I have orders to let you go. Sign this declaration and you're free."

He held out a piece of paper which Stefan accepted with a smile. The inevitable administrative complications, he said to himself. But as he began to read it his face suddenly grew red. "I can't sign this!" he said firmly. "It's a declaration of my separation from the Legion of the Archangel Michael. I can't be separated from it if I never belonged to it!"

*A member of the Legion of the Archangel Michael (the "Iron Guard").

"It's just a formality," the inspector said wearily.

"It's more than that. Why should I lie, saying I am no longer something I never was? Something, besides, that I could not be, because it opposes my fundamental ideas, both ethical and political. . . ."

"So much the better. This is precisely what we ask you to declare."

"Then let me write my own declaration. I'm ready to sign a criticism any time, because these are my views. But I can't confess that I regret having been a member of the Legion and that from now on will have nothing more to do with it."

"This is a standard declaration," explained the inspector, visibly irritated. "If I had to let everyone summarize his political convictions where would I be?"

"And there's even more to it than that," Stefan insisted. "I'm an employee of the Ministry. I've been given a foreign assignment. I'll represent the Romanian government as I have represented it before, many times. I've been given this assignment just now when the government's engaged in a struggle with the Iron Guard. I can't allow my superiors to consider me a dishonest person who camouflages his political views until he's caught and then with an even less honorable recklessness renounces them. . . ."

"That's your business," said the inspector, pressing the button. "If you change your mind tell the orderly on duty and he'll bring you back again to sign."

After that he was not summoned anymore. Eight days after his arrest Ioana was allowed to visit him. She was permitted to bring a change of clothing and a cold meal. In the presence of the guard she remained calm, although she was embarrassed and started using French. The guard approached, separated them abruptly, and commanded, "Speak Romanian!"

Ioana told Stefan everything that she had found out. In his dossier were two grave accusations. He had met Teodorescu in Germany and he possessed two residences.

"Well, but no law forbids you to have as many residences as you please!" cried Stefan in exasperation.

"They're going to pass one soon," Ioana informed him.

"Retroactive?"

Ioana shrugged. The five minutes had passed quickly. The guard stood up. Only then did Ioana become frightened, throwing her arms around Stefan hopelessly, on the point of crying. She demanded heedlessly, "Who should I speak to? What must I do?"

Vadastra had visualized the scene in its most minute details. "I regret, *doamna*," he would say, "that I was forced to proceed in this way. Life does not recognize the law of honor. Since your husband has preferred to work with incompetents instead of calling upon capable, efficient collaborators like me, men of personality, I've simply been compelled to ask for my rights. Because, my dear *doamna*, no one today has more right than I do to control two million lei. What are two million out of your husband's fortune? Not a thing! But it means everything to me. Why does a man like me work from morning till night? Why does he waste his energy and genius on unimportant tasks? And all the while Bucharest groans because of rascals and racketeers who don't know what to do with money! So, please, *doamna*, don't speak to me of blackmail!" (Here he would raise his voice.) "I'm not a blackmailer but I've been blackmailed from the moment I, a country lad, set foot in this Bucharest of yours. And I do not scruple, *doamna*, to confess that I am a son of peasants, that I'm proud of my origin, just like anyone else in my place. . . ."

He awakened from this daydream as he reached home and broke off the thread of his thoughts. Summoning the elevator he surveyed the lobby for a moment with a curious attentiveness, as though he were seeing it for the first time. As soon as he entered his room he hastened to the desk. Unlocking the drawer, he felt around at the back of it with a trembling hand. The box was still there, no one had tampered with it. He sighed with relief and prepared to wait. Tonight she has to come, he told himself. She just has to come!

He took off his monocle, placing it with great care on the little table beside the bed, and stretched out in the easy chair. He felt the monotony of the slow-moving flow of time, languid, sullen. At intervals he heard a clock striking in the distance. But as the night advanced each moment seemed longer than the last. At first he had made up his mind to watch all night, but after a few hours he concluded that this precaution was pointless. If the mystery woman had not gone by now she would not leave before morning. And with a sigh of pleasant weariness he settled more comfortably in his chair, took off his tie, and went to sleep.

He woke up several times. At about six in the morning he felt a strange uneasiness begin to envelope him. Because he was afraid the floor would squeak he got up from the chair very carefully and began to straighten his clothes in haste. He moistened his lips continually and ran his hand through his hair. His excitement was increasing.

The lieutenant's door opened and Vadastra leaned back on the edge of his desk, his face pale. Now! If she leaves with him I'm lost! But it was clear to him that Baleanu's footsteps were going in the direction of the bathroom. A few minutes later he heard the orderly preparing the milk in the kitchen. Then, as usual, at twenty minutes to eight the lieutenant left. Spiridon remained motionless for a long time, leaning on the desk. He was breathing with his lips parted as if he were laboring to remember something, something that was hard to locate in his disorganized mind. After a while he sighed deeply and pulled out the desk drawer. He removed the box that he had hidden with so much care and checked once more the mechanism of the camera. Then he put it on the desk where he could reach it easily, retied his tie, ran his hand again through his hair, and set his monocle in place. He went to the door and listened. There was not a sound in the hall. The orderly, in obedience to his orders, never left the kitchen before eleven in the morning. Spiridon went back and sat down in the chair beside the desk, waiting. His eyes were on the camera, which he had tried to operate only a few times. He was sure, however, that he knew how to use it. As he stared at it blankly he thought with a trace of fear, "If only there's a good light in the entry!"

The bedroom door opened again and he sprang to his feet, seized the camera from the desk, and grasped the doorknob. The next moment he was standing in the doorway of his room taking picture after picture, holding the camera in his trembling hands. In front of him stood a young woman, dumbfounded. She was rather modestly dressed, bareheaded, and she was staring at him in fright, without the courage even to hide her face.

"Don't be angry, *doamna*," Vadastra began in a voice that his excitement had rendered dry and rough. "Please come for a few moments into my office, my law office. I shall inform you of things of the greatest importance to you. Please, *doamna*, please come in."

The woman listened to him spellbound, unable to take her eyes from the camera. As she entered Spiridon pressed the shutter release several more times, photographing her in the doorway.

"But what is this?" she finally managed to utter, upon finding herself in the middle of his office.

Vadastra stared at her with a morbid curiosity. She was quite good-looking. Her eyes were very large and black. Her skin was dark, and she had a large mouth with full lips. Over her forehead she let her hair fall in disorder, probably in an effort to make her look younger. But what disturbed Vadastra most was her body—a body whose vitality could be guessed from the slightest movement, whose curves were unimaginably soft and yielding.

"What does this mean?" she asked again, fear still in her voice, as Vadastra's dark monocle held her fascinated gaze.

"One moment, *doamna*, one moment," he said going back to close the door.

"What is the meaning of this behavior, *domnule?*" the woman demanded with more courage. "Exactly who do you think I am?"

Vadastra shot a greedy glance at her, a look full of hatred. He smiled. He cradled the camera in his right hand for a moment, enchanted by it, and then walked up to her triumphantly with the words, "I don't know what you think about me, dear lady, I don't know and I don't care. I asked you to come in here, as you see, into this law office, in order to avoid a scandal. . . ."

The woman blushed and inquired, "What do you mean?"

"This camera has recorded a dozen photographs of you in the entry of this apartment in which I reside with my friend, Lieutenant Baleanu, the seducer—a dozen photographs which show you leaving this apartment at a certain hour in the morning."

"You're indecent, sir, and I'm going to complain," protested the woman, making a move toward the door.

"One moment, dear lady, before you complain," cried Vadastra, blocking her way. "I could show these photographs to your husband. . . ."

She stopped and turned pale, one hand at her breast. She stared at him.

"Besides, I took these pictures with the intention of showing them to your husband," Spiridon continued. "Unless, of course, you should decide to redeem them. . . ."

"What are you trying to tell me?" she whispered, agitated.

"Have a seat!" He hastened to draw up the armchair. She sat down, bringing both hands to her face. Instead of tempering Spiridon's anger the gesture of weakness made him even more furious.

"I regret, *doamna*, that I have been forced to proceed in this manner,' he began in a dramatic voice, "but I am not to blame. The fault is with our society, which does not know how to appreciate values, which leaves a capability like mine to vegetate in a sordid post instead of putting at my disposal the means for bringing to a successful conclusion a work that would be useful not only to our own country but to all mankind. The fault is also yours and your husband's. You do not request the services of a man like me instead of a dandy from *calea* Victoriei. . . ."

The woman raised her head and looked at him in bewilderment. He knew by the expression on her face that she had understood nothing.

"Yes, *doamna*, dandies and nobodies, good-for-nothings, idiots, these are your husband's collaborators! A personality like me, a man with an ideal in life, is not encouraged. You scatter millions among loafers and flunkies, while I'm obliged to kill myself with work. But why prolong this conversation? I only wanted to explain the reason why I feel constrained to proceed this way with you and your husband. . . ."

"But I don't understand anything you're saying!" With an effort the woman stood up.

"I shall try to make myself clearer. I have here twelve photographs, as you can see. If you do not bring me a million lei by a certain time tomorrow, a time fixed by you, I'll present these photographs to your husband."

"My God!" cried the woman sinking weakly back in the chair. "My God! God in Heaven!" she repeated, her voice hushed.

"I said a million in condescension to you," added Vadastra uneasily, "although I had planned to ask for two million, since that's the amount I need."

"But, my God, where would I find millions?" She regarded him fearfully and began all at once to cry, trembling, burying her head in her hands.

"Stop, *doamna*, don't cry! Your husband commands an amount a hundred times greater than that. What's a million in a fortune like yours?"

The woman continued to cry. She did not seem to hear.

"I'll give you five minutes to make up your mind." Spiridon was getting nervous.

"Where, *domnule?* Where would I get it? We hardly make ends meet. . . . My husband . . ."

"Stop! Stop!" interrupted Spiridon. "Sell some jewelry, or if you prefer sell some of your husband's oil stock."

"What stock?" asked the woman raising her head again, stunned. "We've never had any stock. . . ."

"But what about Campina? The refineries? Your husband's companies?"

"My husband is an employee of the railroad," declared the woman, her courage returning. "Hasn't Aurica told you? He's a poor clerk . . . and a scoundrel besides. It's because of him that I've made a life for myself. I've had enough of wasting my days. . . ."

Vadastra felt that he was hearing all this in a dream. He had the sensation of watching a strange dream in which he had no role to play, of being present only by some peculiar accident. He remained motionless, the camera hanging from his inert hand, his eyes red from lack of sleep, staring foolishly at the woman.

"I have a right to do this," she went on, "and if I haven't separated from him before now, it's because of what people would say. He's away from home for weeks. He says he has night duty, inspections in Moldavia. . . ."

"Then he lied to me!" Spiridon spoke chiefly to himself, but he added, "Your husband doesn't have refineries at Campina? He's not an oil man? Baleanu told me he was an oil magnate, that he had a hundred million if not more. . . ."

"Ah!" exclaimed the woman, her face brightening suddenly. "I know who you're thinking about. I know about her from Aurica. You thought I was Lucia. Lucia Fintesteanu. Her husband is rich, all right! He's rolling in money. . . ."

"And then?"

"But do you think that she would get involved with Aurica, a poor lieutenant? That girl has her lovers, she's finicky, she's something special. . . . You thought I was Lucia Fintesteanu? That's good!" She was almost laughing.

"And he spoke about a pure love!" muttered Spiridon, his voice barely audible.

"Love, hell!" the woman said looking him boldly in the eye. "She let

153

him think that. She led him on with her sweet talk. She's nothing if not wanton! She came here one night when her husband was at Campina. Aurica told me. We were at odds then but don't think that it was because of her! We had an argument over my coming here at night. I didn't like it. He said he didn't live alone, and I didn't want anyone to know. . . . And I was right! At the time she came I was in the country, but we made up later. Aurica came to me and asked my forgiveness. . . . That was when he told me Lucia had been here once. But I knew it wasn't anything serious. . . . So you thought I was Lucia?" she asked after a pause, gazing at him with curiosity, contemptuous. "But you're a fine one to talk! Who told you about Lucia?"

"He did, Baleanu," responded Spiridon exhausted. "He told me."

"Yes. And what else did he tell you?" she demanded, standing up again.

"He said that she's the most beautiful woman in Bucharest, and that between them there was a pure love."

He felt his cheeks burn anew in his humiliation, in his fury, and he clutched the camera in his right hand as though obsessed with a desire to shatter it. "But don't think for a minute, *doamna*, that you have to do with a man devoid of manners," he began, his temper rising. "I am somebody, a man who has succeeded by his own efforts, not a master of millions like the others, you understand. I also have the right to have my say in Romania. And someday I'll say it, you can be sure of that! I don't know if Baleanu has spoken to you about me," he added lowering his voice.

"You're *domnul* Vasilescu Vadastra, aren't you? I know a lot about you from Aurica. . . . But I didn't expect something like this from you after all the good things Aurica said."

"I'm not to blame, *doamna*, I'm not to blame! You don't know what I've gone through to get where I am today. I'm an honest man, *doamna*, I have an ideal in life, dear lady, and in order to realize this ideal, I'm prepared to do anything, even to commit a crime! I was perfectly justified in proceeding as I did toward the wife of a millionaire, a woman who lets her husband tend to his business at Campina while she spends the night in a lieutenant's room! I'm not talking about you. You're case is entirely different. You have your reasons for not keeping faith with your husband. . . . That's your affair. I won't interfere in the matter and I give you my word of honor that I'll destroy all the negatives of the pictures I took a little while ago."

He regarded her again as she stood before him in all her aggressive femininity. She did not seem to be the same person who had recently covered her face with her hands, frightened and in tears. Spiridon was reminded of his hopes, his nights of waiting, his dreams that had been nurtured by the camera, and all at once he felt exhausted. This conversation, which had been prolonged meaninglessly, seemed vain and humiliating. He strode to the desk, opened the drawer, and tossed the camera in it, shoving it well to the back.

154

The woman looked at him inquisitively.

"We have nothing more to say to each other, dear lady," he continued, starting for the door. "This secret, I hope, will die between us. Meanwhile, a thousand pardons for the grave confusion which my friend Baleanu provoked."

"Thank you, *domnul* Vasilescu," said the woman with a smile, extending her hand provocatively. "I'm pleased to have met you. I hope we'll see each other again."

Spiridon felt a painful shiver of sensuality sweep over him. Prudently he opened the door first to check the hall. He thought that he heard footsteps hurrying toward the kitchen, but this detail seemed insignificant. When he was finally alone he went to the window, crushed, and looked out at the colorless sky that spread over the city. It heralded a torrid day.

For three days after the death of Queen Marie, during the period of national mourning, visits to the prison were suspended. Ioana could not see Stefan. On the evening of August 2, an agent instructed him to collect his things. They would be leaving in the middle of the night.

"Where are we going?" asked Stefan, astonished.

"You'll find out."

"But I have almost nothing with me—no money, no clothes. . . ."

"You'll receive them later."

At five minutes before midnight the door opened again. Two gendarmes carrying automatic rifles stood on the threshold in the company of several agents in plain clothes. The corridors were brightly lighted. In the interior courtyard of the building two floodlights concentrated their beams on a group of closed trucks. Stefan saw the inspector talking with one of the drivers. He thought for a moment that he should go to him and protest, but then he realized how futile such a move would be.

The glare of the floodlights hurt his eyes. Because he had not known the refreshing coolness of the dark for twenty days, he anticipated the shadowy interior of the truck with pleasure. "My Blue Heaven"—the orchestra in the adjacent garden was playing the song again as he climbed into the van. An agent directed Stefan with the beam of his flashlight to a seat near a small window. Other prisoners were already seated inside. When the agent left, someone behind Stefan whispered, "Long live the Legion and the Captain!"

He turned and replied politely, "Good evening."

The vehicle left suddenly and the floodlights went out. Aware of the beating of his heart, Stefan prepared to look out of the window. On each bench an agent in civilian clothes sat with the prisoners. One of them was

155

sitting next to Stefan. At the front and back of the van the gendarmes, holding their automatic rifles, were stationed.

They crossed *calea* Victoriei at high speed and Stefan caught a glimpse of the street that seemed momentarily endowed with magic, but the van soon veered into the back streets. Once they reached the highway they sped along rapidly. Stefan stared at the trees that appeared in dizzying succession in the beams of the headlights and as quickly vanished. A little distance beyond Snagov they saw a shadow loom ahead of them in the middle of the road. The inspector, who was seated beside the driver, whispered something that made the guards grip their rifles tightly, while the agents drew their revolvers. This turn of events puzzled Stefan. Someone behind him was trying to whisper.

"Shut up!" one of the agents shouted in a voice that was unexpectedly sharp.

The van accelerated, and then with a sudden metallic squeal the brakes were applied in an effort to avoid running into the ditch. An automobile had turned over on the highway and lay against a wagon that had been partially demolished. The neighing of an injured horse came from beside the road. The inspector leapt out of the truck, his revolver in his hand. Two gendarmes accompanied him.

"Police officers!" he shouted. A woman appeared out of the darkness, her blouse torn, her face smeared with dirt. She was followed by a peasant who was limping and wailing hysterically.

"An accident... My fiancé..." Stefan could just make out the words.

When the woman passed in front of the headlights again he saw that there was blood on her neck. And then all at once he recognized her. It was Ileana! He started to get up. The agent encircled Stefan's neck with his left arm and thrust the revolver between his ribs.

"She—she's a friend of mine," stammered Stefan. "I've got to find out what's happened...."

"An accident. Her fiancé's been killed.... That's all."

Two more agents got out of the van and helped to push the overturned vehicle aside.

"Pardon us, *doamna*, Stefan heard the inspector say. "We're on an assignment. We can't take anyone. We'll inform the police in Ploiesti and a car and an ambulance should be here in an hour at the most."

"... Maybe he's still alive," Ileana murmured.

"Not a chance! He died instantly!... Don't delude yourself."

The van took off with a long, grinding roar. Stefan closed his eyes. A bitterness without limit suddenly suffused his soul. Everything seemed to be stripped of meaning, deprived of importance. He was almost indifferent now to what was happening around him. The chill of the Carpathians was not sufficient to arouse him, nor was he moved by this road to Predeal, so dear to him, so linked with memories of many years past. It seemed strange to hear someone behind him whisper, "Miercurea Ciuc."

Still indifferent, he recalled reading in the newspaper that there was a concentration camp for members of the Iron Guard at Miercurea Ciuc. He was not sleepy, although his body felt crushed with fatigue. As they entered the forests of the Ciuc at sunrise a deer fled into the woods, frightened by the van, and almost unconsciously Stefan smiled.

Baleanu knocked briefly on the door and entered. "Vadastra," he said. "You and I have something to talk about."

"Come in!" Spiridon got up from his armchair and greeted him. "At your service!"

The lieutenant regarded him steadily from the middle of the room, incapable of proceeding. He was pale. A furrow deepened between his brows. Spiridon felt his own breathing quicken. His lips became dry and his throat hot. For a long moment he returned Baleanu's gaze. The lieutenant seemed to him to be larger, stronger than usual, and Vadastra began to shiver slightly as if he felt cold.

"How are you?" he asked finally, trying to smile. "I haven't seen you for a long while. Don't you want to sit down?" Quaking with excitement, biting his lips and licking them furiously he uttered the final phrase. The lieutenant continued to stare at him, appearing to grow a little more pale.

"It's beginning to turn cool," whispered Spiridon. He found it difficult to swallow. "Fall came overnight."

As though he had been waiting for these words to help him make up his mind, Baleanu advanced two more steps, coming face to face with Spiridon. "Vadastra!" he cried, aroused. "Take off your monocle!"

"Why?" Spiridon exclaimed sharply, recoiling against the desk. "Why must I take it off?"

"I have to slap you and I can't when you're wearing it! I can't!" repeated Baleanu in a voice that was choked with emotion. "I can't hit you when you're wearing your monocle!" His agitation astounded Spiridon. He thought he must be dreaming, but after a pause that seemed endless he heard the lieutenant thunder again, "Take off your monocle!"

"Don't hit me!" Spiridon cried hoarsely. "Don't do it! I'll cripple you! Don't do it or I'll kill you! You know I'll kill you!"

Frowning and sad at heart Baleanu stepped closer to Vadastra.

"Don't hit me!" Spiridon's voice faltered as he felt his strength ebb. He maneuvered to get the desk between them but in a few rapid strides the lieutenant had seized him. Baleanu's hand communicated its excited trembling to the wretched Spiridon, who was already quaking with fear.

"What have I done to you?" murmured Vadastra. He lacked the courage to raise his hands and try to free himself from the other man's grasp.

"This is the code in our army," said Baleanu, the words issuing from his lips with considerable effort. "I must slap you! After that do whatever you want! Challenge me to a duel, kill me—whatever you want!" Reluctantly he snatched off the monocle, and placing it on the desk, he raised his hand to strike Vadastra. But in the act of seizing the monocle he had also turned the glass eye in its socket, and this gave to Spiridon a most peculiar appearance. His healthy eye was closed in terror, while the lid of the other—red, sunken, ugly—revealed only the white of the glass orb, which was now unusually conspicuous. Added to the general appearance of his face, very pale, with his hair standing up like a brush on the top of his head, his mouth half-open and his lips blue and dry—that glass eye, askew, gave his whole countenance a ghastly expression. Baleanu's hand shook. He closed his eyes and touched Spiridon's cheeks with his fingertips in a gesture that resembled a caress. Then in confusion he went to the easy chair, collapsed limply in it, and seized his head in his hands, despairing.

He remained in that position for some time, exhausted by his efforts to talk to Spiridon and to slap him. When Vadastra felt the lieutenant's fingers touch his face briefly he blushed and opened his eye in distress. He had expected to receive an especially hard blow and at first he did not quite understand what had happened. But he saw Baleanu in the chair, spent, his head in his hands, and he realized that he had already been slapped. At once humiliation welled up within, overwhelming him.

"And now that I've insulted you, you must challenge me to a duel!" Baleanu said without lifting his head. "I had to slap you. It's written in the regulations. I have to defend the honor of a soldier. . . . It's been hard. . . . Please forgive me. . . ." He passed his hand across his forehead and raised his eyes to Spiridon. But the white of the inverted glass eye met his glance and he whispered, "Please put back your monocle! Please put it back!"

Vadastra stood for a moment uncomprehending. Then a hot wave of mortification burned his cheeks. "Why should I put it back? Why? Because you don't like my eye? Because I'm blind? Then why did you slap me? Since I'm blind why did you lift your hand against me? Because you're an officer? Because you have two good eyes and you're strong and you know that you can fight a duel? Is that why you slapped me? You knew that I was blind and can't fire a gun or fight with a sword. You're a coward, you are! Look closely at me and slap me again! Slap me again, you coward!"

Baleanu's face reddened and he lifted his eyes. He bit his lips, hesitating.

"You may consider yourself insulted as much as you like!" screamed Spiridon. "You can get up and slap me again. You know you're stronger than I am, and you're a coward!"

"Vadastra, take that back, or . . ."

"*Ei*, what can you do to me?" Spiridon burst out in exasperation. "Will you hit me again? Or ten more times? And then what? You're stronger—and

158

I'm an invalid. That's why I've never been in the army. I was rejected. It's easy for you to slap me! But don't suppose that I'll forgive you. The wheel turns and my day will come too! I'm also going to be somebody in Romania. Then I'll destroy you! I'll teach you to slap defenseless people! Coward! And you wear the uniform of an army officer! It does you no good, you're still a coward!"

Baleanu approached him frowning and put his hand on Vadastra's chest but the lawyer continued to scream insults and threats. Spiridon felt the lieutenant's hand fall heavily against his cheek. He clamped his jaws together, his lower lip trembling. With a tear in the corner, the eye that looked at Baleanu blazed in a dark ring. He swallowed several times but did not manage to speak.

"I asked you to take back your words," said Baleanu in a voice altered by emotion, "but you wouldn't do it! I'm sorry. . . ."

"I'll kill you!" Spiridon hissed, staring at him, breathing laboriously.

"You have the right," responded the lieutenant with great weariness. "If you can't fight a duel you have the right to kill me. Here, shoot!" And without further warning, without giving Spiridon the least hint of his intentions, Baleanu pulled a revolver from the pocket of his tunic and held it out to him.

"It's loaded," he said very quietly, trembling. "Here! Take it! Shoot!"

Vadastra looked at the revolver without making any move to grasp it. I'll kill him! a voice in his mind was saying. It's loaded. I'll shoot it and I'll kill him! I'll kill him!

"You have the right," added Baleanu, his voice hardly audible. "Don't say that I'm a coward. Here! Shoot!"

But Spiridon did not dare to take the gun. After several seconds the lieutenant went to the desk and laid it on the corner with the grip toward Vadastra. Baleanu's hand was shaking and he had become even whiter.

"You can see it's loaded," he repeated, lowering his eyes and walking away from the desk. "Shoot! You have the right!"

Vadastra licked his lips and with a bound he picked up the gun. It seemed extraordinarily hard in his hand. Fearing to put his finger on the trigger he held the handle tightly with the barrel pointing down. He shook so violently that he was soon forced to grasp it with both hands. The weight of the revolver seemed to increase. He shivered when he touched the metal. I'll kill him! I'll kill him! He heard the voice crying.

The lieutenant drew back and stood still, his head bent, his hands behind his back like a condemned man, waiting. Vadastra wanted to raise the gun and fire, but his right arm was paralyzed from the shoulder and in spite of all his efforts he could not move it. A great and terrible fury filled him anew—a fury directed against Baleanu, against himself, against the revolver that trembled in his hand.

"Get out!" he commanded suddenly. "Get out of here!"

159

Baleanu raised his eyes. He was so pale that Spiridon recoiled, shaking the revolver nervously.

"Get out before I shoot!" Vadastra shouted in a voice choked with terror. "I'll shoot you like a dog!"

He bit his lip in an effort to rouse himself. His right arm was completely numb. The gun would have slipped to the carpet if he had not also supported it with his other hand. Baleanu appraised the situation in one fleeting glance and a smile of astonishing kindness lighted his face. He breathed more easily and started toward the door.

"Get out!" Spiridon shouted again.

When he heard the door close behind the lieutenant, Vadastra suddenly felt his right arm come to life and he raised the revolver with trembling hands. But in the same instant he knew it was too late. Motionless, he stood for some time staring at the revolver and moistening his lips. Drops of sweat began to form on his forehead and his hair felt damp. His heart surrendered to a boundless sadness. The cheek that had been slapped burned increasingly hotter.

"I'll destroy him!" he whispered, staring wildly at one corner of the room. "I'll destroy them all!" His emotion conquered him and he began to cry quietly. The tears slipped from under his eyelids and mingled with the drops of perspiration. "I'll destroy them!" he repeated, swallowing hard in an attempt to control his weeping. "I'll destroy them to the last man!"

Transferring the revolver to his left hand, he used his right to wipe away the hot tears that now flowed copiously from his eyes. "To the last man!" he hissed through his teeth. But he could no longer control himself. He returned the revolver to the corner of the desk and collapsed in the armchair, burying his face in his hands in tearful abandon.

"They'll see later on!" he muttered between sighs. "They'll see! I won't forgive one of them! I'll shoot them all like so many dogs!"

As he wiped the tears from his face he realized his glass eye was turned around. He removed it and held it for a long time in his hand, stroking it half-consciously. It felt cold to his touch, hard, indifferent.

160

5

THEN SHE REALLY WAS ENGAGED, STEFAN TOLD HIMSELF ONCE AGAIN AFTER HE had made the rounds of the camp. An impressive building, formerly a school of agriculture, stood at the foot of a hill. The forest lay behind it while the plain dropped away in front with the Odorhei Mountains outlined on the distant horizon. The space left free for the prisoners to use as a walkway was a rather narrow one, enclosed by a fence of barbed wire ten meters from the walls of the building. Without curiosity Stefan slowly counted the gendarmes who, armed with their automatic rifles, gazed at him through the wire as though they did not see him. There were six guards and a sergeant. She was engaged, he thought again, and had decided to return.

The majority of the Iron Guardists confined—there were about three hundred—were intellectuals. Almost all of them had allowed their beards to grow during the three or four months of camp life, and their clothing was in tatters. Stefan found it difficult to distinguish one from another as they walked about in groups, looking over the fence at the mountains and conversing.

A tall young man with an immense black beard approached Stefan and took his arm. "Are you the one who gave Ioachim a room?" he asked in a whisper.

"I'm not an Iron Guardist," Stefan hastened to tell him with propriety, almost coldly. "There's been an error. I was brought here by mistake. Politically I'm even an opponent of your ideas."

The man with the black beard stared at him for a long time, smiling in embarrassment. He released Stefan's arm but he did not know what to do with his hands and began to rub them together. Then, suddenly ashamed, he hid them in his pockets.

"I regret of course that you're here behind a fence," Stefan continued, troubled. "As a human being I feel compassion for you, but I shouldn't want any ambiguity to exist. I have absolutely no sympathy for your ideas and your

161

political methods. I'm diametrically opposed to you. Of course," he added quickly, "with respect to your struggle with the police I'm neutral. I have the same aversion toward the police that I have toward fascism."

"I understand," said the man with the beard and he smiled again, discomfited.

Stefan felt a sudden pity for him. "Tonight," he said, abruptly changing the subject, his voice expressing more warmth, "on the highway just ahead of us there had been an accident. The fiancé of a friend of mine was killed. . . ."

"I heard about it. The boys told me. He was a captain."

"A captain?" Stefan repeated the word automatically. "A captain? He was my friend's fiancé. . . ."

Somewhat later he realized he was standing near the fence alone. He turned back slowly and climbed the stairs to the small room on the second floor that he shared with six other men. Throwing himself on the bed, he made an effort to keep his eyes open and was not aware that he had fallen asleep until he felt someone shake him. He awoke crying, "I told you I'm neutral, I'm not one of you. . . ."

The pale young man standing near him was dressed in faded overalls. He wore glasses. A few strands of reddish blond hair were scattered thinly over his cheeks. "Dinner is served," he said, "but if you don't feel well I'll bring you something to eat."

It came back to Stefan then: she was engaged. Her fiancé was a captain. Captain Melinte. He remembered the name suddenly and a hopeless sadness pervaded his whole being. He sighed.

"Are you sick?" asked the young man. "I'll send one of the doctors. We've many among us."

"No, I'll go down to dinner."

As he entered the mess hall the smell of hot grease assailed him. The men had finished the soup and were waiting now for the pasta, which two of them had just brought to the table in a steaming kettle. Stefan looked around and hurried to take the vacant place on a bench near the door. All those bearded men seemed to be eyeing him. He felt isolated and embarrassed, and picking up a big piece of bread that lay on the table in front of him he began to eat. The youth with the glasses stopped beside him, accompanied by a man who was almost bald and whose clean-shaven face was covered with blotches.

"Hello," said the man. "Any fever? Dizziness?" He took Stefan's hand and calmly, with detachment, took his pulse.

"He's a doctor," the young man with the glasses said, and he smiled.

"How long did you stay at police headquarters?" the doctor asked.

"Almost twenty days."

"It's nothing. Indigestion, insomnia, lack of fresh air." The doctor's tone changed as he added, "I'm Doctor Stanescu. Aren't you a friend of Bursuc's?"

"Not exactly a friend."

"Wonderful boy," cried the doctor, revealing two gold teeth when he smiled. "And smart as a whip! Have you seen him lately?"

Stefan tried to remember. "The last time I saw him . . ."

"Never mind," the doctor interrupted. "We'll talk again." As he left he raised his hand in a friendly gesture.

Stefan began to eat the pasta. It was almost cold and smelled strongly of grease.

"What's new in Bucharest?" the man opposite Stefan asked abruptly. He was middle-aged. His face was long and dark and bony, and it was lengthened further by his sparse black beard. "How's the atmosphere? What are people saying? Do they know anything about us? What do they say? What's the news?"

The men sitting near him, Stefan noticed, began to smile and make signs to one another. He started to reply but the other man continued to question him, "How's the government doing? Badly, I think! What do you think? What do people say? Discontented, aren't they?"

Stefan felt one of his neighbors step on his foot in warning. The others watched him steadily and intently.

"I don't really know," Stefan ventured. He stopped, and resumed eating his pasta with his eyes on his plate. Then they all stood up while someone whom Stefan could not see recited the "Our Father." The men crossed themselves and started for the door. In the courtyard someone took Stefan's arm. It was the tall man with the black beard who had spoken to him that morning.

"They tell me that Oprea tried to pump you," he whispered. "I must alert you to the fact that he's a security agent. Be careful what you say to him!"

"I . . ." began Stefan. "I already told you. Even if I should want . . . Oh well, it's not important. . . . One of these days they'll realize their mistake and let me go."

The other man gazed at him for some time, irresolute, and started to smile. He looked all around and then asked in a barely audible voice, "But what else do you know about Ioachim? Have you seen him again recently?"

Frowning, Stefan tried to recall the exact day on which they had last met. But the next moment the man squeezed his arm meaningfully as Oprea came toward them.

Stefan found that remembering the endless kiss he had given Ileana was sufficient to enable him to withdraw effortlessly from the life of the camp. He began by turning his thoughts inward, plunging deep within himself into his past. There he soon discovered Ileana standing before him in the rain, hidden under her umbrella. He had only to wait, for he knew that at a given moment he would bend over her and take her in his arms, kissing her lips. Thus he would remain engrossed in her, with no other desire, conscious of nothing but the kiss. Once, on rousing himself, he noticed one of the soldiers standing a few meters in front of him looking through the fence with his habitually blank, unseeing stare, and Stefan resumed his leisurely stroll around the camp. The prisoners continued walking in groups, talking among themselves, but they seldom turned to look at Stefan anymore. They had grown accustomed to his solitary ways.

One morning some of them saw him walk through the gate in the fence in the company of a sergeant, going toward the major's office. Rumors spread quickly throughout the camp.

"He's gone to sign the declaration of dissociation," someone said. "I'm amazed he hasn't signed it before now."

"Perhaps the order to release him has arrived," said the pale youth who wore glasses. He slept in the same room with Stefan and from the first day had shown great sympathy for him.

Stefan was received very courteously by the major, who held out his hand and invited him to be seated. The major was a shy man. Embarrassed, he turned back to his desk and opened a register.

"You've been with us for twenty-three days," he said slowly, taking pains to pronounce the words with a deliberate solemnity. "And you've said ever since you arrived that you're not a Legionnaire. Why, then, won't you sign the declaration? You'd save yourself and me too. Don't you see how the world is today? What does a signature on a scrap of paper matter?"

Stefan looked at him, bewildered. When the sergeant had come to get him he thought the order for his release must have arrived. He had rejoiced. But a few moments later he thought of Ileana. He felt that he loved her more than he loved Ioana, and he planned to telegraph her first, informing her of his return to Bucharest. He would ask her to meet him at the station.

"Twenty-three days?" he repeated slowly, almost whispering. Then, raising his voice, "The order from the Ministry hasn't arrived yet?"

The major began to hunt through a stack of bulletins. "I don't believe it came. You were dismissed from your post. I'll show you the statement of dismissal. It was published in the *Official Monitor*." He continued to search without haste but he was visibly losing his patience.

"Don't look any more," Stefan said helpfully. "I believe you. . . ."

"It's here somewhere," said the other. "I underlined it in red especially to show it to you."

Stefan could think of nothing more to say as he rose from his chair. He did not want to offend the major. "Thank you," he ventured finally. "Thank you for thinking of me and underlining it."

When he stood up he hesitated in front of the desk. A series of thoughts and images passed through his mind suddenly, but he knew they were merely subterfuges. They had come to him so quickly just to prevent him from taking note of the terrible truth—that although he had learned of his dismissal and he

164

knew that Ioana would no longer receive his salary from the Ministry, it was Ileana who was first in his thoughts. His love for Ileana exceeded his love for his wife! Fortunately the major also stood up then and came from behind the desk to escort him to the door.

As he went back through the gate followed by the sergeant he saw the waiting crowd of bearded men devouring him with their eyes, consumed with curiosity.

"What news?" someone asked in a whisper after he had passed beyond the fence.

"Bad," responded Stefan without raising his head. He went directly to his room.

Now—when he understood how much he loved Ileana, when he realized he had loved her thus from the moment he had seen her from afar in the Forest of Baneasa—now he was humiliated most by the thought of the lie he had told her. Why had he felt it necessary to lie? Why had he told her that he had painted a picture of the car and that he would show it to her? He guessed he must have thought that she would agree to come to his secret room only if he told her this. But he ought to have admitted the truth that night when he had taken her home. He should have told her it really was not possible to see the picture because in fact it did not exist. There was nothing but a single canvas on which he was continually dabbing colors without concern for artistic effect, but simply because such play enchanted him. It allowed him to rediscover somewhere very deep within him another sort of Time, another kind of existence.

He flung himself on the bed and contemplated the ceiling. He was aware that someone had opened the door with great care and was approaching him on tiptoe. It was Iroaie, the tall man with the immense black beard who had asked him several times about Ioachim.

"The boys said you received bad news," he began. "What's happened?"

"I was dismissed," said Stefan with effort. "He wanted to show me the order of dismissal, but he couldn't find it. He said it appeared in the *Official Monitor.*"

Embarrassed, Iroaie looked at him for a long time, as he often did, smiling and blinking his eyes. "Didn't you talk about anything else? Didn't he ask you to sign the declaration?"

With a quick gesture of irritation Stefan put the pillow under his head. "He spoke to me about the declaration too, but I acted as though I didn't hear him. I've declared once and for all that I'm not a Legionnaire. Either they accept my word and let me go, or they don't believe me and . . ."

"You're dreaming," interrupted Iroaie. "No one gets out of here. I mean no one leaves without signing the declaration of dissociation."

Stefan smiled and closed his eyes. It seemed as though his whole life depended on the reply he would make to Iroaie. He resolved not to say

165

another word. He sensed that the other man was waiting impatiently beside the bed, but that he did not dare to disturb him. Finally he heard him tiptoe to the door and open it quietly. Stefan took a deep breath, brightening suddenly. He had the impression of just having escaped a great danger. Stirred, he returned quickly to Ileana's long, incomparable kiss.

When he roused himself he noticed immediately that there was an odor of hot grease in the room. The young man with the glasses, the student Petrescu, had brought him his food and was waiting beside him smiling.

"Today we have grapes too," he said, "but they're not ripe yet." .

After that they were given grapes for lunch every day.

"If anything makes me infuriated with the Iron Guardists," said Biris, "it's the restrictions imposed on our civil liberties because of them. In fighting them the government is obliged to use fascist methods and in consequence the Legionnaires are not the only ones to suffer. We all do. Anyone can arrest you on the simple pretext that you're an Iron Guardist, and while you're waiting for them to discover that you're not, they fire you from your job or send you to a concentration camp. That's probably what happened to poor Viziru."

"Now you're starting..." Catalina interrupted.

Biris turned his head in surprise. Catalina's expression was cold, malicious, harsh, but when her eyes met his she began to smile.

"You'll become a maniac too," she added, "just like Dan. He talks to me about nothing but the theater that *conu* Misu is planning to build for him."

"But you know, *duduie** Catalina, I *am* going to build it," said Misu Weissman, his face suddenly red. "Things have been delayed a little because of the international situation, but this is a transaction of over a hundred million lei, and I tell you I'll build it!"

Biris set his glass of cognac on the table and glanced quickly, furtively at his watch.

"Come with me," said Catalina, getting up suddenly. "I can't stay here any longer. I've got a headache."

Misu Weissman watched them leave, and turning to Bibicescu nervously, he said, "*Duduia* Catalina's wrong to be angry. Perhaps she doesn't think I'm serious. Perhaps she thinks there is no transaction...."

"If you want to pacify her," responded Bibicescu absently, "don't send her any more flowers. It would be better if you'd invite us to dinner again. By

*Young lady, mistress.

166

the way," he added, his voice brimming with the excitement of his secret, "do you know that I've begun to inquire about a site?"

They walked close together without speaking. Evening fell. "Autumn in Bucharest is beautiful," Catalina said finally, looking at the sky. Then she was silent again. Biris took her arm gently.

"What was the matter with you today?" he asked. "You seemed bored and on edge."

"You know the reason," she replied softly. "Why do you keep asking me?"

"It's absurd," said Biris, tightening his grip on her arm. "The idea is entirely absurd!"

Catalina shrugged. "We'd better not talk about it anymore." She drew closer to Biris suddenly and asked in a different tone, "What are you doing this evening? Wouldn't you like to go for a walk with me?"

Biris felt the shiver, familiar now, that ran through his body whenever she spoke to him that way. "I had an appointment with a friend, but if you like, I'll leave him a note . . . and we'll go for a walk."

"I'm sorry," said Catalina sadly. "I thought you'd be free. I wanted very much to go walking with you. . . ."

"But I told you I can leave him a note and then we can meet and take a walk," he interrupted, shaken.

"I feel that this is my last autumn, that these are my last weeks," she whispered, growing still more sorrowful.

Biris exploded. "You're talking like a child! These are absurdities! This is what happens to you when you live with a madman. You become mad yourself!"

"You know very well that's not so," said Catalina without looking at him. "You know he's not to blame. He's a poor miserable failure and I pity him. . . ."

"Then," Biris interrupted in exasperation, "it's you who are mad and he's just your victim!"

"It won't do any good to scold me," Catalina continued in the same faint voice. "You know very well it's not so, that this must happen to me. It's stronger than I. It has to happen. Once the decision had been made it had to happen. And again the day is drawing closer. . . ."

"Stop it!" exclaimed Biris, dropping her arm. "If you keep saying such awful things I'll leave you here alone and go home!"

She turned her head and smiled at him. "I'd be bored alone. I'd feel very sad. Abandoned by everyone . . ." Then she seized his arm and put her face close to his ear, murmuring warmly. "Please don't go!"

"I think they're a little better today," someone was saying as Stefan entered the mess hall. The man stepped nearer to one of the baskets of grapes and put a few in his mouth, breaking them open and sucking the juice slowly, thoughtfully. Then he repeated, "They're better today. They've begun to ripen."

Sometimes Stefan would wait in front of the fence to watch the sun go down behind the mountains. On one such evening he remembered about the Conference in Yokohama. It had ended in September. By now he would have been with Ioana and their son in Tokyo. No doubt Vidrighin had been sent in his place. "The Germans are involved somehow." He recalled the words of the Secretary General. "Be very careful. . . ." And yet they had dismissed him.

The cold rain of the past three days had been enough to make the leaves, already pale at the end of September, turn coppery. They fell from the trees at the slightest breath of wind. Autumn had arrived. From the windows on the second floor it was possible now to see a long way down the highway. At rare intervals cars passed by on the way to Odorhei. Breathless with excitement, the men watched them. If a car stopped at the first sentry box and turned to the left it meant that it was coming to the camp. Then sudden anxiety would seize everyone. They would begin to move about in great agitation and to gravitate toward the gate in the fence. Once or twice a month a visitor came. Someone would be summoned by the sergeant to go with him through the gate, between the sentries. A half-hour later the man would return happily. Most of the time he was the bearer of news. It was in this way that Stefan found out about the Munich Accord a month after it had been signed.

On another day as he entered the mess hall Stefan heard someone say, "Today we have muscats. They're ripe." The young man beside him stopped in front of the basket of grapes, nibbling at some of the clusters, savoring them, smacking his lips slightly. "Excellent," he said. "They're muscats." "This is the season for them," Stefan heard another voice, "At home in the vineyard . . ." He picked up the piece of bread in front of him and began to eat. Stefan knew the man, whose name was Ionescu, rather well now. He had listened to him talking many times after finishing his soup. He was an employee of the bank at Campulung. He had a vineyard and was married to a girl from Constanta, but whenever he had the opportunity he liked to recall that his father-in-law had been in business in Brazil. His wife had been born there. "At our vineyard . . ." he said, but Stefan was no longer listening. By now he had attained exceptional mastery of himself. He could pursue his own thoughts regardless of how boisterous the men around him might be. Once he had resolved to do so he heard nothing more. From time to time someone tugged at his arm saying that it was his turn that day to wait on the tables or to wash the dishes. Then he tied the apron of heavy cloth around his waist and carried out his tasks with utmost concentration. He almost always managed to pour the same amount of soup into each bowl and to divide the pasta skillfully into equal portions. The smell of hot grease was insupportable, yet his pride prevented him from showing a sign of disgust as he bent over the kettle.

All his clothing, including his underwear, had worn out completely. Earlier, the student Petrescu had brought him several shirts, which he could not button at the collar because they were too tight. At the end of October Petrescu had also found him a woolen pullover and an overcoat. He had lain ill with a fever for a number of days and Doctor Stanescu came up to see him frequently, taking his temperature with the only thermometer in the camp. The doctor spoke to him about Bursuc and his friends and acquaintances at the coffee shop. It seemed to Stefan that Stanescu took great pleasure in all these recollections, and he let him talk. He smiled whenever their eyes met although he did not always listen. Ioana was often in his mind when the doctor was with him, and he no longer wondered as he had at first if she would manage to come and see him. He was thankful now for the way things had turned out. It would have been dreadful if she had come upon him in the major's office, where all the visits took place. With the very first glance she would have realized that it was Ileana whom he loved.

"The tragedy is," he said suddenly, raising his head from the pillow a little, "that you can never love two people at the same time. First you love one, and then the other. That is, you're just like all the rest of the people who aren't saints. Today you love one person more, tomorrow you love the other. Suppose you could become the lover of the other woman too. But what solution would adultery be? Just between you and me, man to man, I ask you, what will it resolve if I take her to my secret room and go to bed with her? If I didn't love anyone else perhaps this would be an answer, a provisional one until I could get a divorce and marry her. Although I'm not so sure of this now. I think you also heard about that automobile accident. The captain who was killed was her fiancé, Captain Melinte. So... she had become engaged...."

Doctor Stanescu listened to him calmly, almost with indifference. He had noticed several red-violet spots on his patient's face. Like the doctor, Stefan had insisted on shaving every day, using a safety razor that belonged to one of his roommates. But as time passed the task became increasingly difficult because there were so few blades in the camp. He's got an infection too, said the doctor to himself, examining Stefan's cheek attentively. He's in for it like me. It will ruin his face.

"... If I just loved her alone!" Stefan continued, his voice grown dark with sadness. "How simple everything would be! I'd be like other men again,

169

but at least I'd be an honest man. . . . I had dreamed of something else," he added, letting his head fall weakly back on his pillow. "But here I've realized once more that I'm not capable of it. Or maybe I don't deserve such a miracle. It's Ileana I love. I want only her. . . . It's very sad." His voice became fainter. "If all I've accomplished is to replace one love with another, what good were my expectations? I haven't settled anything. I might as well let things take their course. What can I change? We'll all end together in futility. Why resist any more? The major told me that I was dismissed. And so? Do you think that's so serious? Can it have any importance now?"

He stopped, exhausted, and closed his eyes. The doctor packed up the thermometer very carefully, as well as the little bottle of alcohol and the tubes of aspirin. "Try to sleep," he said. "There's nothing wrong with you. You're a little distraught, that's all. Ask Petrescu to make some tea for you this evening."

This had happened at the end of October. A week later when he went downstairs to walk, dressed in the pullover and overcoat that Petrescu had brought him, he did not see Oprea and Iroaie. A number of other familiar faces were missing also. He was surprised. "They were transferred the day before yesterday to Vaslui," the student explained. "I wonder that you didn't hear of it." Actually it's not important, Stefan thought, resuming his walk around the building. Yet he felt a kind of regret. He had become accustomed to these men. He liked to come upon them as they walked in circles around the courtyard, following one another.

In the evening after the prayer that ended the meal the men gathered together in certain of the dormitories. Stefan had often been invited, but he had gone only once. A young man had read a long poem about autumn, but Stefan had not listened.

With the first line he retired into himself. He evoked a great many memories from his adolescence and youth, surprised at the serenity with which he relived them. Then his thoughts turned again to Ileana. This time he chose their meeting on the eve of Palm Sunday, when she was dressed for spring and wore a blouse the color of lilacs. He had regarded her for a long time, unmindful of anything else, and she returned a gaze equally profound. She seemed to sense that it would be a long time before they met again. "I felt a need to pray," she had told him. Stefan was certain now that she had raised herself on tiptoe, waiting to be kissed. After they had left the church they talked about other things. She had questioned him again, teasing him as she always did about her car in the Forest of Baneasa, but she had made no reference to his paintings. I wonder if she didn't understand even then, that evening, Stefan said to himself, and he smiled.

170

All the men around him began to applaud and Stefan joined them. He soon
realized that he had been attending a lecture by a professor's assistant. This
man had let his beard grow too, but he had trimmed it carefully with scissors
and it gave him the air of a painter or a romantic poet. He looks like someone
I know, Stefan thought, but I can't think who. Just then he heard someone
beside him whisper, "He gave a good talk, but he omitted the essential thing.
He didn't say anything about history. . . ."

Stefan smiled again, a knowing smile. It was their great passion to talk
about history, about the historic moment, the historic mission. He heard
them discussing it and sometimes he felt tempted to stop and take part in the
conversation also. But he kept his word. I'm neutral. They believe in something and for that they've been confined behind barbed wire. I believe in
democracy but I don't mingle in politics; therefore I don't participate in their
conflict. The defenders of democracy are the very ones who arrested them and
brought them here. I'm outside their struggle. I have no right to mix in their
discussions. I'm neutral. . . .

That night after the meeting he went out to walk again. Far away in the
midst he could see the lights of Miercurea Ciuc and he stopped near the fence
to gaze at them. He remembered suddenly that the lecturer had not mentioned history. He had forgotten the essential thing. . . .

"Were you at the meeting?" The man approached unexpectedly and
stopped beside him.

"I was," replied Stefan enthusiastically. "But you and your movement
ascribe too great an importance to history, to the events of life as they unfold
around us. Life for the people of the modern world, for us, wouldn't be worth
living if it were reduced only to the *history* that we make. History takes place
exclusively in Time, but man by means of all his higher powers opposes Time.
Remember when you were first in love. Were you living then in Time? . . .
That's why I prefer democracy. It's also antihistorical. It proposes a rather
abstract ideal that resists the historic moment."

The man glanced at Stefan from time to time and stroked his beard. He
was dressed in a long brown peasant's robe of coarsely woven cloth. "Those
soirees in room number six are nice, but I don't understand them very well.
What I like are the meetings in number two, because Caminita sings ballads
there. I'm from a village near his. We're both from Nasaud. . . . But come to
number two on the Night of St. Andrew and listen to Caminita tell stories
about vampires and sorcerers."

One day Stefan was walking rapidly with his hands buried deep in the
pockets of his coat. A few days before, the weather had suddenly turned cold.
The Odorhei Mountains had become white overnight. "Don't forget to come
this evening to hear Caminita," the peasant from Nasaud reminded him.

This is the Night of St. Andrew, Stefan remembered. Anisie had spoken

171

about it too. "On the Night of St. Andrew I read stories about ghosts, or I listen to them."

On the other side of the fence Stefan saw one of the guards fix his automatic rifle in a firing position. Then he discovered that the number of sentries along the fence had increased. There were now about fifteen. He saw the major also armed, hastily cross the courtyard in front of his office accompanied by a sergeant. Little by little gendarmes appeared from all sides. The prisoners came out of their rooms and formed several groups in the court. Whenever one of them tried to approach the fence the soldiers shouted and raised their guns. At last a sergeant went up to the barbed wire with a newspaper in his hand and motioned for someone to approach. A tall thin man whose beard was prematurely gray stepped forward. The sergeant folded up the newspaper, rolled it as tightly as he could, and flung it over the wire. The other man bent over to pick it up, unrolling it as he walked back to the middle of the yard. Opening it, he stopped, then staggered. All the prisoners rushed to him, and Stefan heard a cry, a savage, strangled cry like that of a wounded animal, "They've shot the Captain!"

Nothing more was heard then, not even the sound of breathing, in the whole courtyard. That stony silence seemed to Stefan far more terrible than the cry. The next moment all fell to their knees, weeping and moaning. Some of them beat their heads on the ground. Others howled like whipped dogs. With their rifles in their hands the sentries watched them. Stefan crossed himself and bowed his head, his mind blank.

Now and then Ioana lifted her eyes from the book and glanced at the clock. It was nearly midnight. He should have come, she said to herself. But no matter how late he might come, even if he should not return that night at all, she felt her grief could not be made greater. Nor was this sadness, without limit and without meaning, because of Stefan. She was reading the last novel that Partenie had written. It had appeared around Christmastime, a few days before Stefan's return. She had almost finished it. There were only about sixty more pages, but she progressed slowly, her heart filled with a strange foreboding. Nothing she had ever read was more depressing, nothing more sad and somber.

When she had telephoned him Partenie had told her that he could not come until the next morning. "I'm finishing the last corrections tonight," he said. "It must come out before Christmastime." He was referring to this book, A *Walk in the Dark*.

"I'm finishing the corrections tonight. . . ." "Then come as soon as you can in the morning," she had implored, and she had heard him say after a slight pause, "I'll be there at eight." She had replaced the receiver with an unsteady hand. Exhausted, she had let herself fall into the armchair. He's working tonight, she remembered suddenly and got up again painfully, hardly conscious of what she was doing. She put on her fur coat and went downstairs, gripping the banister.

In front of the tram station all that had happened an hour earlier came back to her: the man reading the newspaper as he leaned against a light post; the car that had passed in front of her, fast and very close to the curb; the large headlines of the newspaper that she had stepped on. It was a special edition. After the man by the lamppost had read it he had let it fall to the ground, where Ioana had walked on it unseeing as she made her way to the tram. But there were too many people and she had gone back to the sidewalk. It was then that the headlines of the special edition had caught her eye, and she had returned to telephone Partenie.

She found them at dinner. "Don't you want to eat with us?" Adela asked her. "I'm not hungry," said Ioana. "What's the news?" Raducu inquired. She realized then that they were dressed to go out. "We've a bridge game at the Olteanu's," Adela explained. "Is everything all right over there?" asked Raducu after a moment, and Ioana answered. "I'm afraid for Stefan. Have you heard what's happened?" "What?" "I saw a special edition. They've shot Codreanu." "Ah, yes," Raducu had said, "now that story's finished too. He's been liquidated." "I'm afraid for Stefan," Ioana whispered. "They'll all be allowed to go home," Raducu said. "Of course, he'll have to sign a declaration like all the rest. I tell you he'll be home by Christmas!" Ioana felt a rush of love for Raducu and she sighed. "We're sorry we have to hurry," Adela said, getting up from the table. "Come to see us again." "Come and eat with us some-day," added Raducu. "Give us a call."

She found herself on the sidewalk, hesitating. She would have gone to Cotroceni, but she was afraid. Old Bologa would meet her at the door. "What news?" he would ask, and seeing that she looked down he would either smile in embarrassment or shrug his shoulders and continue in the same vein as he had on other occasions. "I told you to give him an ultimatum. What, is he mad? Does he want to disgrace us all? Send him a telegram!" "They can't receive telegrams. I've written more than thirty letters and sent them through the mail. I've sent others through the gendarmerie." "Send them through Police Headquarters. They're the ones who arrested him. If you telegraph, order him to sign the declaration. The telegram will get to him." "I can't order him," Ioana said in despair. "I've begged him, I've implored him, but I can't order him." "Then you're both collaborators!" Bologa exclaimed, exasperation smoldering in his voice. "You're both Legionnaire sympathizers!" "And all on account of Ioachim Teodorescu," *doamna* Bologa put in once to divert the course of the argument. "If only you hadn't run into him in Ulm! Why in heaven's name did you go to Ulm anyway?" "Because of a cathedral!" exclaimed Bologa. "What will you do now that he's been fired from the Ministry?" There was a tremor in his voice that was difficult to control "You ought to go to the Gendarmerie Headquarters tomorrow," said *doamna* Bologa. "Maybe your turn to visit has come." "I'll go tomorrow but I know it's not my turn. The colonel told me. About a hundred visits have been approved on the list ahead of me. But they only consent to two or three at the most per month. The colonel told me." "Send him a telegram then," Bologa began again. "Give him an ultimatum. Say he's disgraced the family. Threaten him with divorce. Tell him you'll take his son. . . ."

She returned home on foot in a fine, cold rain that was mixed with flakes of snow. "Of course it's my fault," Ioana repeated to herself. "I should have been more forceful. I should have fallen on my knees to the colonel and pleaded with him. I should have taken the baby with me, and burst into tears, and pulled my hair. I should have told him that I'd kill myself, that my baby would die. . . ." She stopped suddenly in the middle of the street, terrified, and made the sign of the cross. "God forbid!" she whispered. "God forbid!" Quickly she crossed herself several times and hurried on.

It was late when she went to sleep, feeling engulfed in her own emptiness. Her dreams were all of Stefan. She awakened very early while it was still dark and cold in the room, and she stayed in bed until she saw the window become light. Without thinking she began to dress. When she heard the clock striking eight she went into the study to look outdoors. The morning was ashen, the sky low and murky. Ioana put her hands on the radiator, which was beginning to get warm. "It will soon be quite comfortable," she said to herself, and the thought was reassuring. Seeing a car stop at the gate, she drew back, startled.

She opened the door herself for Partenie, who remained irresolute on the threshold.

"Please come in. I wanted to see you. Just to see you." She spoke softly, biting her lips slightly and gazing at him. He seemed more sullen than he had in the past, almost morose.

"I wanted to see you," she repeated. "I'm sorry that I made you come. I only wanted to see you." She did not have the courage to look away from his eyes. When he smiled she added quickly, "It's been a long time since I saw you. I've wanted . . . You haven't changed at all. . . ."

"With your kind permission, I'll sit down," said Partenie, heading

174

for an armchair. He took out his cigarette case, carefully chose a cigarette and began to rub it between his fingers. Ioana stood by the door
and watched him, fascinated. He had done the same thing that day
almost five years before. He had sat down without an invitation and had
selected a cigarette from his case in a leisurely manner. At that time she
had hastened to light it for him. She looked around now in alarm.
There were no matches on the table or the bookcase. She would have to
go to the kitchen.

"Don't bother," said Partenie, searching in a pocket of his vest. "I
have a lighter."

"I'm afraid for Stefan."

"That's exactly what I imagined." Partenie inhaled the first smoke
of the cigarette, taking a deep breath and raising his eyes to hers.

For several minutes Ioana remained mute. She looked at him
again, spellbound. "And you, how have you been?" she asked at last,
seeing that the silence persisted.

He shrugged, "I live."

Ioana felt her heart leap as if those simple words proclaimed a
matter of extreme gravity.

"I heard you went to Ulm," he said, staring at her almost severely.

She sat down in the other easy chair. All at once she felt exhausted.
"Who told you?" she asked, her voice low.

"*Domnul* Bologa."

Because he had not seen an ashtray anywhere near, he shook the
ashes into the palm of his left hand, which he held motionless, resting it
on his knee. It was just what he had done before. Now she was supposed
to get up, go to him and hold out her hand. Partenie would slip the
ashes into her palm. But this time she felt too tired and did not rise.

"I wondered this summer how it happened that you didn't call
me," he continued, smiling. "I don't enjoy playing the role of a sister of
charity, but for you I'd even do this. . . ."

He fell silent and gazed at her. Then he stood up and went to the
buffet, crushing his cigarette in a pot of flowers. He brushed the ashes
from his hand.

"Perhaps you still remember," he began, sitting down again in the
chair, "that I had, and have yet, a horror of getting up in the morning;
especially when I go to bed at dawn, which happens often, and which
happened today. When I heard the clock strike seven and I remembered
that I had to come to see you, I hated you. You destroyed my life.
Maybe you never realized that, but you destroyed it. If I had never met
you I probably should have met someone else like you and I'd have
loved her as I loved you. Like everyone else I'd have known rest and
oblivion. But I met you, and ever since I've stayed the way I was the day

175

we met. Don't imagine that I've been faithful to you in the romantic sense of the word. No. I have loved, as the poets say, countless women, and probably I have also been loved by them. Some were more beautiful than you, others had more charm. Many times I've thought that I was really in love, but I was mistaken; I wasn't. I can't fall in love anymore. This chance for happiness you have killed in me. I stopped loving you long ago, but I can't love anyone else either. Since then my life has been a wasteland. When the alarm woke me at seven I felt the wasteland all around me and all through me. You wanted at any cost to get me out in the morning—in the darkness, in the cold, in the reek of ashes. . . ."

Ioana's face was pale as she murmured, "I wanted to see you. . . . Only to see you."

"And I gave you this pleasure," Partenie said with a smile. "But if you knew how much I hated you this morning. . . . You've been my misfortune. Maybe it wasn't your fault, but I hated you! You've burned up everything inside of me, even the love I felt for you five years ago. When you phoned me last night I said to myself, Maybe they've shot Viziru too, and now she's a widow. She's free again to be my wife. . . . But this thought didn't give me any joy. I no longer love you. Long ago I knew that I didn't love you anymore, but sometimes I still hoped. Maybe I do love her, I told myself. Maybe one of these days I'll love another. But this morning when the alarm sounded I realized once more that I don't love you and that I'll not be able to love again. I can't ever love again."

Ioana stared at him, very pale, uncomprehending. She had wanted to interrupt many times but her strength was gone. She did not know what to say.

At length she whispered, "Forgive me," and she put her hand to her forehead. "Forgive me," she repeated faintly.

Partenie gazed at her for some time in silence, taking another cigarette from his case. "It's not your fault. And if the alarm hadn't wakened me this morning I wouldn't have said anything now." He continued to smoke, looking at her without speaking. Ioana felt the tears slide slowly down her cheeks, but she made no move to wipe them away.

"Did you want to tell me something?" Partenie had finally asked, getting up to throw his cigarette and ashes in the flower pot.

"No. . . . I just wanted to see you."

He remained on his feet. "I can't stay any longer. I have to go to the printer's. . . . Good-bye. . . ." He went to her, patting her gently on the shoulder and bowing over the hand that she had extended to him. He kissed it politely.

"Good-bye," he said once more from the threshold.

"When she heard the door close behind him, she buried her face in her hands, sobbing.

Her eyes dim with mist, she looked at the clock again. Two in the morning! He's not coming now, she said to herself. It was as if she had been waiting for just this confirmation of her fears to be able to abandon herself entirely to despair. She threw herself down on the bed and began to sob, hiding her face in the pillow. She had finished reading A *Walk in the Dark* and now she understood everything.

She understood what Partenie had meant when he told her that morning in December, "You killed my chance for happiness. . . ." Above all she understood how he had felt five years before when she had met him as usual in front of the Faculty of Letters. She had taken his arm and had demanded suddenly, "Do you think that we could be friends? Only friends?" Her voice had throbbed with emotion and fear, when she had intended simply to be confidential. "I should like for us to remain friends," she had added then. "I think I love someone else. . . ." She had not dared to look at him. A flower vendor had stopped in front of them just then with a bouquet of pinks in her hand. Partenie took it and held it out to Ioana without a word. Then he thrust his hand into his pocket in search of change.

She realized that it was not Partenie's sorrow and despair that made her cry. She pitied him but this was not the cause of her tears. The sadness of the book had overwhelmed her, the sadness for things that had once been and now are no more. After a while she felt she could cry no longer and she raised her face from the pillow. Passing her hand over her eyes she sighed deeply. She would have liked to get up from the bed and hide Partenie's book, but she lacked the strength. Her bones felt crushed and all her energy seemed to have been dispersed in her weeping.

This was the way she had felt that evening when the colonel had told her, "Mr. Viziru will come too in a few days. That is, of course, if he also signs the joint declaration." Then he had extended his hand—she was quite unprepared for this gesture—and laid it on her breast. She had taken a step backward, but he had placed the other hand heavily on her shoulder. "It's still not certain," he had continued, lowering his voice. "It's still not certain that he'll be released." Again she had felt his hand on her breast and she had remained motionless a moment as though held fast by her disgust. Then she had withdrawn rapidly to the door. "Thank you," she said with her hand on the doorknob, "thank you for

177

the news you've given me. . . ." At home she had flung herself fully clothed on the bed and buried her head in the pillow.

When Stefan had returned from the camp she had heard the doorbell ring insistently and had run to open it, springing into his arms. She had not even been able to stop and inspect him, but in his embrace she sensed how much he had changed. Then he gave her a long look and smiled. "You're not the same as you were when we last saw each other! You've grown more beautiful!" He had not lost much weight, but there was something different about him. He appeared ill-at-ease, with another way of smiling. His gestures, his movements, were subdued and they held a suggestion of weariness. She became more aware of this as he walked toward the pile of books. "I brought them from the hotel," she said, blushing. "They rented the room and I brought them here." He smiled again and said without looking at her, "The *Sambo* room." "Bluebeard's room," she said, and caught him in her arms once more. "But I didn't see it. They had already brought the books down when I went to get them." "The *Sambo* room," he repeated. "Another time I'll tell you why I call it. . . ." It was not until then that he inquired about the baby and went into his room to see him.

"Did you miss me?" she asked again and again. "How could I help it?" Shaved, his hair trimmed, dressed in clean clothes, he had begun to look like himself again, although something strange and unfamiliar persisted. He had changed. "I've aged," he said, "but I'm not sorry. It's disagreeable to be young. I don't want to waste time any longer. It was a great stroke of luck to be fired from the Ministry. I've become a free man again. Free in my time. . . ."

"Stefan," Ioana interrupted, frightened, "what's the matter? What's wrong with you?" With a smile he had put his arms around her and held her tight, wordlessly imploring her to be silent. After a moment she whispered, "You're sad." "We're all sad," he responded "We don't always see it, but all people are sad. And yet who was it who said that the only great sorrow is that of not being a saint?" Ioana knew what he was thinking about and she said nothing. He had added, "I don't want to see anyone during the holidays. Let's stay here alone, just the two of us."

Then one morning he had demanded, "What did you do with the picture? There was a picture hidden behind the bookcase!" But he had quickly changed the subject. "If we're alone on New Year's Eve I'll tell you the story of the room *Sambo*. . . ."

Ioana sprang from the bed in alarm and approached the little table. Her watch was under Partenie's novel and she could not find it immediately. She leaned over and held it under the shade of the lamp, blinking her eyes several times so that she could see more clearly. Five minutes to three. Where can he be now? He doesn't have the *Sambo* room anymore. The secret room, Bluebeard's room, doesn't exist any longer. It was rented. Where can he be staying until this hour? . . . Going back to the bed she arranged the pillows, and then sat down in the easy chair by the lamp to wait. She was not sleepy. She even had the impression that she did not feel so sad now. Something's happened to him. He's changed. The camp changed him. Something happened to him there, something that he's afraid to remember, that he never will talk about—just like that colonel's heavy, sweaty, dirty hand. She could never speak to Stefan about it—the colonel's hand. If they had humiliated him too she would never find out. "Really, what did you do all the time you were there at the camp?" "Nothing special. I slept as much as I could. I waited for time to pass. I enjoyed not having anything to do, being a free man without a schedule, without duties. . . ."

She heard him open the door into the entry and come groping on tiptoe to the bedroom. He did not turn on the light in the hall, but made his way slowly through the darkness.

"Haven't you gone to bed yet?" he asked from the doorway.

"I wasn't sleepy. I was reading until a little while ago. Where have you been?"

"I was with Biris. He kept me talking until now." In the lamplight Stefan appeared to be even more pale than she had realized. Noticing that she was watching him, he smiled. He hasn't even seen that I've been crying, she said to herself.

"He kept me talking for five hours," continued Stefan, "just to tell me when we broke up that he's getting married."

As soon as the train stopped moving Stefan leaped onto the platform and ran toward the waiting room. His heart was pounding as though it would burst. I've reached Bucharest, a voice deep within him was crying, "I'm going to see her! He had telegraphed Ileana the evening before from the station at Ciuc. With excitement and apprehension he looked around the waiting room, searching for her; and because he expected at any moment to see her come in and run into his arms, he kept turning back to watch the door. He went out on the platform, picked his way among the throngs of passengers, and returned finally to the waiting room. She hasn't come, he realized at last. Probably she didn't get the telegram. He ran to a telephone booth. *Doamna* Cretulescu answered his call. "She's gone to Predeal. She left the day before yesterday to ski at Predeal." Then after a pause, since Stefan did not say

179

anything more, she asked, "Is it you, *domnule* Viziru? She's been expecting you all the while. She kept thinking you'd come. She read in the newspaper that you were to be released, and she was waiting for you to telephone her." "I just arrived," murmured Stefan. "I'm still at the station..." *Doamna* Cretulescu began to laugh. "Well, good luck to you!" she exclaimed. "You're the general all over again. I can hear him now, 'Believe me, my dear young lady, I just arrived!' Good luck!"

Now as he embraced Ioana he felt that he had not ceased to love her for a single moment, but his love was not the same. He no longer loved her as he had loved her before. He would have liked simply to look at her, to be able to hold her tightly in his arms without speaking. It was difficult for him to talk to her. Fortunately his glance fell on the pile of books and he slipped gently out of her arms.

After that moment he repeated his maneuver whenever he had nothing more to say. He moved away from her and turned to some object, any object, letting her continue to talk. Even on New Year's Eve when he told her about the room *Sambo* he felt that it was no longer he who was speaking, that he was alluding to an incident that had taken place long ago and that had not happened to him. He felt that he was not talking of himself or of events that had any relevance to his life.

When he had met Biris it seemed to him that his friend's smile was somewhat cool.

"I envied you all the while you were imprisoned," Biris had said. "What luck you have! What a unique opportunity! To suffer for a cause not your own!" He was suddenly inspired. "To take upon yourself a sin you didn't commit and to atone for that sin by your own innocence! How much I'd give to have had such an experience! To pay for a crime I not only didn't commit, but one that was detestable to me. I'd have suffered with joy in company with the others just because the dictatorship, the political crime, was and is hateful to me. And when I found out that you refused to sign the declaration of dissociation at Police Headquarters, I was almost jealous of your good fortune...."

Stefan had listened to him, puzzled and with irritation. In their friendship something always had to come up to separate them! "I can never be one-hundred-percent friends with Biris," he told Ileana once. "Probably something deep inside of me, or perhaps in him, prevents it. We met and became friends because he too confused me with Partenie."

"I was jealous of your good fortune," repeated Biris, "as I am of Alyosha Karamazov who, in order to atone for his brother's crime, shared his punishment...."

Stefan shrugged his shoulders wearily. "If you'd like to know the truth," he said, managing a smile with effort, "and so that you won't envy me, I must inform you that I stayed in the camp for reasons completely different from those beautiful ones you've imagined. I stayed there because Ileana had become engaged and it was very difficult for me to come home. I told you that I love my wife, Ioana. It was hard for me to come home, terrorized as I was by Ileana's engagement." His voice changed. "Of course I had learned by then that her fiancé had died in an automobile accident. But it was no less true that she *had* been engaged. She had been engaged to a captain."

Biris gave him a penetrating look, paused, and then burst into a coarse, vulgar laugh. "That makes us even!" he said. "I must inform you that I'm engaged too—to the daughter of a merchant. . . ." He lowered his voice and added, "I don't know if you noticed it, but there was a kind of 'official interview' going on when you came in. You made the mistake of saying that you had just come back from the concentration camp and the people quickly left. They thought you'd begin to criticize the government. They're well-situated, in comfortable circumstances, and they don't want any trouble."

"And which one was the girl, your fiancée?" inquired Stefan.

"She didn't come. She's at Severin. She was invited quite a while ago to the home of one of her brothers-in-law. He's also a merchant. She sent only part of the family to make arrangements with us."

"But what's she like? Have you seen her?"

"I've just seen her photograph. According to her picture she looks like a good housewife."

"Now if Biris gets married," Stefan told Ioana that night, "we'll have to invite them here more often. We'll have to go to the wedding and give them a gift. Now of all times, when we don't have any money. You'll have to write to my father again."

Since fall, when he had found out that Ioana was no longer receiving Stefan's salary, the elder Viziru had sent her twenty thousand lei each month.

"You'll have to ask him for more," continued Stefan. "Tell him we need the money to buy a wedding present. Our best friend is getting married and we have to give him a present. . . ."

A little disquieted by his tone, Ioana looked at him and her face became pale.

"Stefan," she asked gently, "what's the matter? What's wrong with you?"

"I forgot to tell you that Ileana was engaged too—that girl I told you about last year, the one I thought I might be in love with. She became engaged too!"

Ioana stared at him for a moment, unseeing, then she sat down slowly on the edge of the bed and began to cry.

"Her name's Ileana," added Stefan, troubled.

181

He remained standing with his head bowed slightly, watching her cry. All at once he remembered about Japan. We would have been in Tokyo now. For several months we all would have been in Tokyo and nothing would have happened. We'd all have been there, far away, very far, in another world, in Tokyo. He rushed to her suddenly and knelt before her, trying to put his arms around her shoulders to draw her to him.

"Forgive me!" he whispered, trembling. "I've always loved you more. Don't go away, don't leave me alone. I love you more. Help me! Don't leave me!"

Ioana gave a start and looked at the door in alarm. "I think the baby's awake," she said, springing to her feet.

Catalina curled up in her customary position at the end of the divan and demanded, "Now, what's the girl like?"

Biris smiled in embarrassment. With the palm of his hand he smoothed the hair on the top of his head. Catalina observed that he was beginning to get bald. Unshaven, with his slight figure and thinning hair, he suddenly looked ten years older. It won't be long before he'll be like that, she said to herself, and aloud she questioned him again, "Is she beautiful?"

"She's much better looking than I expected," admitted Biris, still embarrassed. "At any rate, she's too beautiful for me. I'm a homely man, Catalina."

"Yes, that's so," she said with great compassion.

Biris blushed and began to laugh. He got up from his chair and, still laughing, he approached the divan, studying her face for a few moments.

"Sometimes you're strangely outspoken," he said finally. "If anyone should hear you express yourself so frankly he'd think you might even be dangerous. Perhaps you were once, before you met Bibicescu. But your friendship with him has corrupted you. In a way you've become crazy too. You live in a pseudo-myth that you've constructed piece by piece, and you believe that you're living out a destiny, that you're carried along by a fatal necessity! This fable about suicide ... "

"We'd better talk about the girl," interrupted Catalina.

" ... This fable about suicide on a predetermined date," Biris resumed, sitting on the edge of the divan, "it's in bad taste, it shouts to high heaven. Do you call this a *fatal necessity?*"

He paused. Catalina smiled at him very sweetly. "Why did you say she's too beautiful for you?"

" ... But don't you see that this *fatal necessity* is artificially constructed from beginning to end? How can you project into your future a certain prophesied date on which you will do away with your life? An absolutely arbitrary date, an ordinary October 19, an October 19 in 1939, or 1949?"

Giving him a fond, melancholy look, she lifted a lock of hair that had fallen over her face, then casually tucked it behind her ear.

"You know very well that October 19 is no ordinary date in my life," she said. "It was then that I had a revelation of futility . . ."

"That was the day you met the Buddha!" interrupted Biris with a bitter smile. "On that extraordinary day you read a biography of Buddha and that was enough for you. You didn't even read a scholarly account of his life. You didn't even read an anthology of Buddhist texts in an acceptable translation. You read a mediocre novel based on secondary sources. And this book revealed the futility of life to you! That's all your vocation to sainthood means!"

Catalina pretended not to hear him and asked calmly, "What's her name? What's the name of your fiancée?"

Biris frowned, then rubbed the crown of his head again and smiled. "Her name is Theodora, but she's not my fiancée, and I don't believe she ever will be. She's too beautiful for me. And she has the name of an empress. I don't like it. . . ."

"Theodora is a very lovely name," Catalina said wistfully.

"Bibicescu has stuffed all these things into your head," continued Biris. "All these undigested ideas about futility, Time, illusions, pain, and who knows what."

Unwinding herself with some difficulty, Catalina got up from the divan. She opened a cupboard. "It's getting rather cold. Let's have some tea."

Biris lit a cigarette, watching her as she placed the teapot, the cups, and the sugar bowl on the table. He was reminded of his first visit to this flat many months before. She always went through the same motions. First she set the teapot on the table, then the cups and sugar bowl. Next she went into the adjoining room to put the water on to boil. Coming back to the divan, she pushed the lock of hair behind her ear, and asked him some unimportant question. After a quarter of an hour she remembered the tea and stood up suddenly, exclaiming, "How forgetful I am! With or without lemon?" Each time he responded, "With."

"Actually it's useless for you to try to hide it," said Catalina when she returned from the next room. "It's no use to pretend you don't like the girl. You're beginning to fall in love with her!"

"That's absurd! I don't know if I'll even see her a second time."

"We all say that." Catalina installed herself on the end of the divan near the wall. "We all say that, and in the end we find ourselves in love. We aren't even aware of how it happens. We see each other once, twice, ten times—and then we feel that we have to see each other all the time, that one cannot do without the other. And this is called being in love. And if we go to bed together, we find we can't sleep without each other, we can't sleep alone anymore. And we become so accustomed to each other that if someone

183

should try to separate us, we'd feel that he was taking a knife and cutting into one body, trying to sever the limbs from a single body." With a smile she added, "Something like this always happens to each of us."

"And that's what happened to you," commented Biris. "That's how your passion for Bibicescu began."

"Of course," said Catalina simply. "I saw him first when I was at the Conservatory. He was playing at the Little Theater. He impressed me although I sensed he didn't have any talent. It seemed to me he was a man who was suffering—suffering especially from loneliness. I wasn't mistaken. When I knew him better I found it out from him directly. After that I saw him at Tantzi's one evening, and then we met five or six times. I thought I was in love with him, and I suppose he felt the same way, because he told me he did. Ever since then we've slept together and we say we love each other . . ."

"Fortunately," intervened Biris, "the nineteenth of October came along."

"Fortunately. On the nineteenth day of October I understood the futility of any existence, beginning with ours, beginning with my own."

"Then why didn't you, on that very day, accept the consequences of your discovery?"

"I was afraid," Catalina confessed, speaking more softly. "I'm a coward. I have a terror of death. I've begun to be accustomed to life, but I'm terribly afraid of death, or the act of dying. And I pitied Dan. He's used to me. What would he have done if I'd killed myself on the spot? So I decided to condition him to the idea. I get him upset once, at most twice, a year. The rest of the time he's calm."

"As calm as a madman can be," interrupted Biris brutally.

"It only seems to you that he's crazy. Actually he's a very normal man. He's aware, however, that he has no talent, that he's a failure. And so sometimes he tries to take refuge in madness in order to keep on believing in himself."

"And I," Biris burst forth suddenly, "I—where do I fit into this round of selfishness, madness, and habit?"

Catalina looked at him a long time, her expression one of love without limit. Biris blushed and glanced at the floor.

"You're something entirely different. You're my very best friend, my only friend, really. You help me to go on living. You're my prop. For you I have a feeling that I can't have toward any other human being. But at the same time you're the source of my only doubt. Sometimes I wonder what would have happened if I had known you five or six years ago. What would my life have been like? Could I have been happy?"

Biris felt he could not endure any more. He had heard those words countless times and yet they always hurt him beyond measure.

"I think the water's boiling," he said.

Catalina rewarded him with a glance so warm that he again looked away. "How forgetful I am!" she exclaimed, getting up.

When she had gone out Biris touched his face with his hand momentarily then unconsciously rubbed the top of his head. He went to the window and looked out over the housetops at the murky February sky. Someday I'll have the courage to do it, he found himself thinking. The door is always closed. I'll turn off the light, take her in my arms and throw her on the divan. She loves me. She won't resist me. But I'll need something to drink first. . . .

Catalina returned and poured the boiling water into the teapot, her hand trembling slightly. "Nevertheless," she said, "No matter what you say, you like that girl, Theodora. . . ."

On that clear serene morning in March, Ciru Partenie awakened with an unusual craving to write. He seldom worked in the morning but this time he went directly into his study, where he reread the last paragraphs of his manuscript. Almost without realizing it he picked up the pen and bent over the new sheets of paper. When he had gone to bed at midnight it was raining, but now the sky was fresh and sparkling, washed clean. In front of him on the desk he found indications of the many times he had put down his pen to light another cigarette. This morning he wrote five full pages in one hour. He had not known such a mood for a long time. The book presented itself to him whole, complete, perfect. This seems to be truly inspired! he said to himself with a smile, recalling that Lucia was still at Sinaia and that he was fortunate not to have anything scheduled for a week.

It was nearly noon when he counted the pages he had written. Suddenly he felt troubled. The work had progressed too rapidly. He was afraid he might have been carried away by a false inspiration, by a facility which always threatened after several hours of labor. He started to reread the results of the morning's efforts. They appeared to be excellent. Yet he had the impression that something prevented him from going on. He went to the window where the street, brilliant in the sunlight, met his eyes. How absurd to confine yourself to the house at such a time!

Quickly he put on his coat, checked the pockets for a package of cigarettes, and descended the three flights of stairs almost running. When he reached the garden the fresh smell of earth and air, purified by the rain, intoxicated him. But he seemed to be even more intoxicated by the book he had abandoned a few moments before. That unfinished page beckoned him. On the sidewalk in front of the garden he paused undecided and then sauntered in the direction of *bulevardul* Pake Protopopescu. Like an alien spirit the

185

manuscript called him back to his study, trying to take possession of him, to deprive him of his freedom. He walked faster to free his thoughts of this obsession.

Near the Foisor a stranger accosted him, coming almost at a run from *bulevardul* Ferdinand. The man had not shaved for several days. A thick black mustache almost covered his upper lip. He wore dark glasses. Taking Partenie's arm, he looked at the ground and whispered, "God has put you on my path, *domnule* Viziru. Lengthen your steps a little . . . and don't look back. I think I'm being followed. . . ."

He's confused me with the other one, Partenie thought and his face darkened. All the euphoria of the morning seemed to have vanished. He found himself again in his habitual mood—sullen, out of sorts, worn.

"I've heard about you," continued the young man in a whisper. "I've heard how well you acquitted yourself at Police Headquarters."

Partenie withdrew his arm gently and slackened his pace. "You've confused me with another man, sir," he said. "Probably you've confused me with Stefan Viziru."

The young man stopped, uneasy. At that moment he caught sight of three men in overcoats who were crossing the street in front of him. All three had pulled their hats low over their eyes. Their hands were hidden in their pockets.

"Pardon me, please," the stranger murmured softly and drew the palm of his left hand across his mouth. He slipped his right hand into his pocket slowly, looking furtively behind. He had recognized the men at once. Two of them were agents who had been following him for almost an hour. They hastened forward. The young man drew closer to the wall, keeping the men in his line of vision. "I'm cornered!" he whispered. He felt his lips grow dry and rough.

"What's wrong?" asked Partenie in astonishment.

"Nothing . . . It's too late now!"

"Teodorescu! Ioachim Teodorescu!" cried one of the three without taking his hand from his pocket. "You've given us a lot of trouble for a long time, boy!"

Partenie turned to look at the speaker just as Teodorescu opened fire. A few steps away from him he saw the stout man double up and fall on his knees at the edge of the sidewalk, his hand on his stomach. The next instant he heard the sound of gunfire all around him. "What's going on? What's wrong?" The question ran foolishly through his mind. He felt his knees weaken and he would have fallen but for the sudden sharp twinge, burning and freezing at once, above his heart. It was followed by another, and still another, in a region of his body that he could not accurately define. It doesn't hurt, he thought, it can't be serious.

Suddenly he found himself lying in a pool of blood on the sidewalk near

Ioachim, who was still holding his revolver in his hand, a twisted smile on his lips. He confused me with Viziru! The thought came to Partenie again. He confused me.... Then he noticed the blood that trickled from Ioachim's matted mustache, and all at once he felt very tired. He wanted to close his eyes but he could not.

"He doesn't want to marry her now, honey!" exclaimed *doamna* Porumbache. "He's made us the laughing-stock of the neighborhood! He liked the girl a lot at first. She's a beauty, pretty as a picture, and well-behaved, cultured. She went to the University! He liked her a lot and they saw each other several times. And then one day it struck him that he didn't like her anymore and he broke his word! That slut of a Catalina's to blame! She egged him on! That whore! The devil take her!"

Doamna Porumbache wept, wiping her eyes with her apron, as she spoke of all the houses that Theodora's parents owned.

Several days later Stefan met Biris.

"I can't marry Theodora," the teacher said. "She's young and beautiful and quite intelligent. I don't have the right to make her unhappy. I've had a chest ailment and I'm not completely cured yet. I smoke too much, I stay up all night, I don't take care of myself. How can I condemn a young creature to that kind of life? Someone who's never done me any harm?"

"Then why did you ever agree to marry her?" demanded Stefan.

Biris smiled a long wistful smile. "I didn't expect to meet a girl like her, like Theodora. I didn't imagine that the people with whom my aunt associates would have such offspring. I thought she'd find me an ordinary cook, a woman not so young, someone stout and sturdy who wouldn't be afraid to take a chance with my bacilli. Such a vehemently carnivorous woman I'd have gladly married. She'd have kept my aunt company, we would have been overfed, and everybody would have been satisfied—the ideal wife for a pedagogue. But poor Theodora? She's only twenty-two and she's read Rilke, although she comes from a family of worthy butchers. But I think there's tuberculosis in her family too, as there is in ours. I can't bring disaster upon her."

He stopped and examined Stefan from head to foot, as if he were laboring to comprehend the change in him. "But what's the matter with you? You're so gloomy!"

"They've reinstated me at the Ministry," said Stefan with a gesture of extreme lassitude. "On Monday I go back to work. I'm starting the same life over again. I'd grown used to doing nothing. That is," he added, smiling suddenly, "I was making all sorts of plans, each one more beautiful than the

187

last. I should have liked to settle in the country, like Anisie, and reconcile myself with Time."

He left Biris after about an hour and was returning home, walking slowly, when a newsboy passed him with the evening papers. Stefan whistled and the boy ran back, handing him a copy hastily. The news of Partenie's death was on the first page, and beside it the picture of Ioachim Teodorescu with the revolver in his hand, riddled with bullets, a thick streak of blood spreading down his chin. Stefan stopped in the middle of the sidewalk. As he grasped the import of what had happened he felt his legs grow weak. Ioachim's photograph began to quiver before his eyes and he sat down on the nearest bench. Breathing deeply, he took out his handkerchief and involuntarily wiped his hands. He was perspiring. His hands were wet, limp, sticky.

He sat there for a long time, his mind empty of thoughts. Suddenly he found himself in darkness. A little distance away a lone streetlight was burning. By now we would have been in Tokyo, he said to himself. All at once he got up and went home. Ioana was waiting for him in the hall with the little boy playing on the rug in front of her.

"What is it?" she asked, frightened.

"I'm very tired." He went to the bathroom and began to wash. Mechanically he rubbed his hands with soap and lathered his face. Then changing his mind, he turned on the shower. Ioana tried the door but it was locked. She knocked several times.

"What's the matter with you?" she asked, repeating the question again and again.

"Nothing. I'm all right. Just a minute. I felt tired, but it will go away."

Later, after the boy had gone to sleep, Stefan went to her and put his hand on her shoulder. "I have sad news for you. Ciru Partenie is dead."

"It's not possible!" Ioana whispered, terrified, and she put her hand to her mouth. She might have been stifling a scream.

"He was shot by mistake," Stefan went on, gripping her shoulder with his hand. "He was with Ioachim Teodorescu and they shot him too—Partenie. Look, read the paper."

He watched her as she read, following her staring eyes as their glance moved over those sinister lines. He remembered Japan. He remembered that on Monday he must present himself at the Ministry. "How many days can I stay here?" Ioachim Teodorescu had asked him. "Can I stay until Monday?" . . . Monday he must present himself at the Ministry. "Get ready to leave," the Secretary General had said. "No one knows what may happen by autumn." He sensed that Ioana was about to faint and he helped her to lie down on the sofa. She did not cry—she who was always ready to weep on any pretext.

"Biris has broken his engagement." Stefan spoke abruptly. "He's not going to get married. . . ."

"Please, let me be alone a moment," whispered Ioana. "Just a moment."

"I think you understand what happened," Stefan went on. "Ioachim Teodorescu didn't know him. He confused him with me."

Ioana raised her head and stared at him, horrified, with her hand on her mouth.

"Because of me he was shot," Stefan continued. "He confused him with me. In a sense, I killed him."

6

BIRIS STOOD UP, EXHAUSTED, FROM THE SIMPLE WOODEN TABLE THAT HE HAD
transformed into a desk. He went out on the balcony. It seemed to him that
the sun had halted directly opposite his room, and yet the air was cold. Snow
had fallen a few nights before. For a long time he gazed over the tops of the
firs at the white crests of the mountains. At last he sighed in resignation and
annoyance, and turned back to the room. I'll have to write it, he said to
himself. I can't put it off any longer. Today or tomorrow he'll come again to
get the article. I'll have to write it. His irritation was aroused by the editor of
Our Beacon, who had visited the sanatorium one day to get information for a
report requested and paid for by the Society for the Prevention of Tuberculosis. Biris had discussed Partenie with him. Before they separated he had
been rash enough to promise the journalist an article. Almost a year had
passed since the death of Partenie, and *Our Beacon* had already announced
several times that the appearance of a study was imminent. I'll have to write it!
He repeated the words to himself frequently each day, but when he faced the
blank white sheets of paper he felt paralyzed. If he could light a cigarette
perhaps it would go better. For several weeks it had been almost impossible for
him to find any. Earlier the doctors and nurses would bring him some once in
awhile, but one time he had unfortunately drawn too suddenly and deeply on
a cigarette and the cough that racked him brought on another hemorrhage.
They had confiscated his cigarettes then, and since that evening he had been
positively forbidden to smoke.

"I'm counting on you, *domnule* Biris," the editor had implored him. He
was a zealous young man with a degree in literature, and he wanted, he said,
to transform *Our Beacon* radically. He wanted to make the weekly from
Pietrosita into a focus of culture for the whole country. "Put on paper what
you just told me and it will be an exceptional article," he had added. "I don't
think that anyone has seen these things so clearly before. Put them on paper!"

190

Biris had spoken about Partenie's haste. "He certainly had a premonition long ago that his days were numbered," he had told the journalist. "This explains his rush to write and to publish, and his thirst to live, to enjoy life at the same time." "Put it on paper!" the editor repeated enthusiastically. "I assure you, it will be a sensational article!"

Undoubtedly it would have been less difficult to write it if he were not haunted by Viziru and his insomnia. Whenever he bent over the paper to begin he saw again the scene of a year ago, on that afternoon at the end of March 1939, in Bibicescu's study.

Biris had gone there with his mind made up to ask the actor if he intended to marry Catalina. If so then he'd better do it quickly, very quickly! If not Biris would issue an ultimatum. He must break all ties with her because he, Biris, planned to marry her himself. Bibicescu must quit disgracing her to no purpose. But he had no chance to bring up the subject. A few minutes after his arrival Viziru was announced. "I'll have to receive him," Bibicescu whispered. "Perhaps he's bringing important news."

Biris didn't speculate about the kind of news Stefan might be bringing. He had discovered a long time ago that the actor often blurted out words before thinking what he was saying. When Stefan came in, Biris regarded him with astonishment, almost anxiety. His friend was pale, his skin dry. His eyes were sunk deep in his face.

"I can't sleep anymore," said Stefan, suddenly self-conscious. "For quite a while I've been suffering from terrible insomnia. . . ."

Bibicescu, without saying a word, had seated himself at his desk and fixed Stefan with his customary stare.

"I went by Professor Antim's for a moment," Stefan resumed, forcing a smile. "It was at his house last year that I met Ioachim Teodorescu. I wanted to know what the Professor had to say. He wrung his hands a moment and exclaimed, 'What times we live in! What times we live in!' Then he recalled that last year I brought luck to his house. He had even told me so at the time. 'You, *domnule* Viziru,' he said, 'are a man of luck. You've brought good fortune to my house.' Then he added, 'If God wills, a year from now this affair will be finished. But a man will have to die!' He didn't tell me what he meant by 'this affair.' . . ."

Stefan spoke with restrained fervor and yet his voice betrayed a great weariness. He rubbed his eyes incessantly.

Abruptly Bibicescu rose from his desk and stepped to the other side of the room. "You came here with a precise question in mind," he said in a grave and solemn tone. "What is it?"

"You're right," smiled Stefan. "I came to see you in connection

191

with a play of Partenie's. I heard that shortly before his death he was writing a play, *The Wake*. But it wasn't found among his papers. I thought perhaps you might know something about it. I heard that he had given it to a friend to read."

"I was not his friend," Bibicescu interrupted. "We just knew each other well enough to say good morning."

Stefan looked in silence at the floor.

". . . But I, too, have heard about this play," continued Bibicescu. "I don't know if it was finished. He told me last summer that he was working on it. He told me even more: that he was writing it with me in mind, thinking of how I should play it." He crossed the room with long strides and sat down at the desk again.

"What he didn't tell me was that he had conceived this play following a long conversation with me. I can even affirm that it was I who suggested its theme to him. I had spoken about the time concentrated in the performance, about those few hours in which so many events are compressed and so many destinies fulfilled. Then I explained my new theory about the actor. It's too complex to summarize here, but this is in essence what I told him. By virtue of the fact that the actor personifies in turn innumerable characters, he lives a considerable number of existences. Therefore he consumes his own karma in a much shorter time than the rest of humanity. . . ."

"But where did you hear about karma?" demanded Biris with a smile.

"From Catalina, naturally," replied Bibicescu, annoyed. "Catalina has an extraordinary intuition. I heard her talking one evening about karma, and I understood in a sort of revelation the true destiny of the actor. For he—the actor—identifies himself in turn with innumerable human existences, and he suffers, if he is a good actor, just as the character he represents on the stage suffers in his life. This means that he knows in a single lifetime the passions, the hopes, the suffering, and the revelations of fifty or a hundred lives."

"Very interesting!" commented Stefan, unable to remove his eyes from the other man's face.

He's wondering where Bibicescu heard this theory of the actor, assumed Biris, and he smiled again.

"Very interesting!" Stefan repeated.

"Ciru Partenie told me the same thing after listening to me," Bibicescu continued. "I met him again several weeks later, and he confided to me that he was writing a play, and that he was writing it with me in mind, that I should stage it for him and also play the principal role. . . . From what he told me I understood that the problem was precisely this: the performance, the actor, Time . . ."

192

"Then why did he entitle it *The Wake?*" Stefan inquired timidly.

Bibicescu shrugged. "All his titles have hidden meanings. They're camouflages." he said. "He was a very singular individual."

All three were silent for a few moments.

"I wonder where the play could be!" remarked Stefan. "Who could the friend be to whom he gave it to read?"

"Surely you don't think that the play is here?" Bibicescu asked, tipping his head back a little as though he wished to see Stefan better.

"I had hoped so for a moment," Stefan admitted. "But now I'm at a loss. I don't know where else to look."

Getting up again from the desk Bibicescu went to Stefan and stood before him. "But, after all, why are you so interested in this play of Partenie's? He wrote other plays, too. He published about fifteen books. Read them again and you'll fathom his works better than you will by running around after a manuscript whose very existence is doubtful."

Stefan remained silent, embarrassed. Then slowly he lifted his head and gazed directly into Bibicescu's eyes. "There's more than a literary curiosity at the heart of this matter," he said. "Ever since Partenie was shot I haven't been able to sleep. From time to time an intern comes and gives me an injection and then I sleep for twenty-four hours at a stretch. But this isn't sleep. It's an anesthetizing, a faint. . . . A week ago I heard about Partenie's play. The title, *The Wake,* caught my attention. This is what I've been doing ever since his death—holding a wake! But why? And for how long? I don't understand it. . . ."

He dropped his eyes again and passed his hand over his face. The light in the room was fading and his face began to take on a dull, ashen sheen.

"I said to myself that perhaps I would find the solution when I read the play," he continued, seeing that the others said nothing. "You know that our lives were interwoven in a rather curious manner. The same mysterious interdependency may be continuing even after his death."

That evening Biris had given up his plan of confronting Bibicescu with the problem of Catalina, and he had left at the same time as Stefan. Bibicescu accompanied them to the threshold as he always did, then closed the door without a word.

"I'm sorry for you," Biris told Stefan when they reached the sidewalk, "but I have the feeling that you want to mystify yourself. You've had a shock because Partenie was shot on your account. You ought to rest a few days. It will go away."

Stefan did not answer immediately. He rubbed his eyes a long time with the back of his hand, then turned up the collar of his overcoat although the evening was rather warm. "There's something else at the heart of this," he said. "I feel that it's a mystery and I don't understand

193

it. I've been given a sign, a portent, and I don't know how to interpret it. . . ."

The room *Sambo*, Biris recalled. He felt a sudden irritation toward his companion. The painting that could not be seen, and the other things. . . . False credulity and naive superstitions. What bad luck that he had chosen just that time to visit Bibicescu! Still, this evening in Catalina's flat I can try it anyway. After that she can make the decision to tell him and to leave him.

"You ought to get yourself admitted to a clinic," he counseled Stefan absently. "An insomnia like yours calls for radical treatment."

"There's something else that escapes me," said Stefan as though he had not been listening. "Why did he call his last play *The Wake?*"

How could he have known that this would be his last play? Biris wanted to shout sarcastically, but he said nothing. He remembered that this evening he would not be able to see Catalina. After the theater she and Bibicescu would stay in town as guests of Misu Weissman. Perhaps I'll try it tomorrow night. Suddenly he found himself depressed, weary, ill-humored. When he had shaken hands with Stefan at their parting, he had noticed how eagerly the other man's eyes, burning from lack of sleep, sought his and held them for a long time.

"He has a guilt complex," he told Ioana a few days later. "He ought to go into a clinic." It was the third time that Biris had seen her. She too appeared to be ill, and her mind wandered.

"I know what I ought to say," she murmured with a sad smile, full of mystery. "Still, I don't have the courage. But someday I'll make up my mind. I have to tell him."

Had she really loved Partenie? Biris wondered as he went down the stairs. She no longer resembled the woman whom he had met a few months before when he rang at her door one morning to ask for news of Stefan. "He ought to arrive any day now!" she had exclaimed from the sill. "I'm expecting him any day—he'll surely come! At this very moment he might be on the train or even at the station, already here. . . ." Her movements were soft and graceful, undisturbed by any amount of agitation. Pride and dignity shone in her face. She had a strange and rather uncommon beauty arising from imperceptible asymmetries. She doesn't look like a married woman, he had reflected then. That's why Partenie liked her so much he became engaged to her—he, whose heroines become interesting characters only to the extent that they fail in marriage. . . .

Now she no longer seemed to be the same woman. Although she did not dress in black, her face had taken on the expression of the women in mourning you sometimes glimpse on the street. Their cheeks are pale, their eyes lustreless, the lids slightly swollen. A baffling abstraction suffuses their glances and their gestures. They seem to be unable to move as they once did, or perhaps they no longer dare to do so. Biris had wondered many times if all this were because of Partenie. Or is it because she's uneasy about Stefan? he asked himself. Is she afraid of losing him?

Two days later Viziru entered the clinic and Biris went to see him.

"I'm very frightened," Ioana had whispered when he met her in the corridor. "I don't know what will become of us. You tell him too that it disappeared—that the manuscript disappeared without a trace. . . ."

When they entered the room Stefan seemed to be trying to smile, and Biris felt sorry for him. In the last few days he had suddenly aged. He found it difficult to hold his reddened eyelids partially open over eyes that had become even more deep-set. His temples were emaciated and shadowy. His face had the pallor of gray smoke, as if it were smeared with cigarette ashes.

"You know, it's serious," Biris had told the others that evening at dinner. Bibicescu had shrugged his shoulders indifferently, but Catalina looked at the teacher and smiled. "Why the smile?" he inquired. "Ask Dan," Catalina replied evasively. "Perhaps if he finds out that Viziru is dying, he'll tell you." Biris turned abruptly to Bibicescu. "What's the use of being so mysterious? It's in bad taste. If you know something about the manuscript, say so!" "It's not about the manuscript," interrupted Catalina. "It's something else entirely. . . ."

The next day Ioana was waiting for him on a bench in the garden of the clinic. She waved to him from a distance. She seemed more calm, almost serene, although her voice and eyes still betrayed a great weariness.

"I made up my mind, and I told him," she began very softly as soon as Biris sat down beside her on the bench. "I lied to him. I told him I knew what Partenie wrote in *The Wake*—that Ciru himself had told me when he came to call. But it's not true. He didn't tell me anything. I lied to Stefan. But now he's sleeping."

She turned to him and smiled. Biris noticed that her eyes were again full of tears and he looked away in embarrassment.

"I'll tell you what I told him," continued Ioana warmly. "I must tell you. But not here. It's getting cold. . . ."

They went out on the boulevard to look for a *cofetarie*.

"Not this one," Ioana said. "I was here once with him, with Ciru. . . ."

The shop that they entered was a modest one, dark and deserted. Biris remembered that he didn't have enough money with him, and after hesitating slightly he confessed this to Ioana.

"I have some," she reassured him and smiled again so warmly that Biris smiled too. Then, closing her eyes for a moment, she became serious. "Don't laugh at me, but I had to tell him this. I told him that Ciru came to see me once when Stefan was in the camp, and that he spoke to me about the play he wanted to write. I didn't tell him the plot. I told him that I didn't know what it was, that Ciru hadn't told me, that he had only spoken about the play in general terms. . . ."

She stopped, looking at him briefly with unexpected intensity, then lowered her eyes and blushed. "I haven't confessed everything to you yet," she resumed. "I told him something else. I lied to him. I said that I had continued to love Ciru. I knew this would please him. He's maintained for a long time that I had loved Ciru and was still in love with him. That wasn't true. I didn't love him anymore. I don't think that one can love two men at the same time, but Stefan believes it's possible. That's why I told him. I knew it would make him happy. He looked at me a long time and he smiled. He squeezed my hand. I knew what he was thinking about, but I let him squeeze my hand. I knew it would make him happy. . . ."

A girl from the *liceu* came into the *cofetarie* and sat down timidly at a little table. "I'm waiting for someone," she said to the waitress, and she blushed.

"I feel terrible that I had to lie to him," continued Ioana. "But someday, after he gets well, I'll tell him the truth. I ask you to tell him then, too."

"What shall I tell him?" Biris inquired, embarrassed.

"Tell him that I lied to him," Ioana murmured quickly, looking down. "I told him I loved them both equally and that in my love they were inseparable, they were one. And I explained that Ciru wanted to write *The Wake* because he didn't know this. He didn't know that I still loved him. Ciru believed that he was dead to me, the way he had felt when I broke our engagement."

"I don't quite understand," said Biris, his embarrassment increasing.

Ioana's voice was hushed. "I told him all that had followed since then was nothing but a deathwatch, that it was for that reason he had called his play *The Wake* . . . that we two, Stefan and I, had held a wake for him for five years. . . . I didn't know what else to tell him!" she exclaimed suddenly, shaking her head in despair. "I have no imagination. I don't know how to imagine a play. I've read a great deal in my lifetime, but I don't know how to make up a play. . . ."

"Have you been here long?" A cadet from the military school approached the young girl's table and spoke to her.

Ioana turned her head in fright and brought her hand to her

forehead. The girl blushed again as the boy kissed her hand and sat down noisily. He looked around impudently at the deserted shop.

"And he believed you?" asked Biris suddenly. "He could believe that?"

"He smiled all the time while I was telling him. He believed me. Then he closed his eyes and fell asleep."

"He has a great weakness for melodrama," said Biris, smiling.

"I didn't know what else to tell him. But perhaps you don't know everything. You don't know that he's in love with a girl, Ileana. He told me himself. He's in love with Ileana. . . ."

She could control herself no longer and burst into tears, hiding her face in her hands. The young couple looked at her, their eyes reflecting their astonishment. The girl gave Biris a glance that was hostile, almost fearful, and it made him feel ridiculous. He sat there, unable to move, an unlighted cigarette in the corner of his mouth.

Three days later he had seen Catalina again. "Do you know that Stefan's recovered?" he told her. "He's sleeping. He's freed of his insomnia."

Catalina was trying to find the outlet in order to plug in the small lamp with the Japanese shade that stood near the divan. She did not like the bright light of the bulb on the ceiling.

"Who did you say is free of his insomnia?" she asked as she seated herself again on the sofa, moving back toward the wall with little pushes and bounces.

Lighting a cigarette, Biris began to tell her the story. "Stefan Viziru. He's been sleeping for three days. That is, he's sleeping normally, without sedation, for about fourteen or fifteen hours a day. He's cured." He hesitated a moment, touching the top of his head on the spot where he seemed to feel the hair becoming relentlessly thinner with each passing day. Then he told her about his meeting with Ioana. "I'm telling you too so you'll also be a witness," he said in conclusion.

"Be a witness to what?" inquired Catalina with a sympathetic smile that was also provocative.

". . . So we'll have an extra witness," repeated Biris. He began to have misgivings. "Perhaps I ought not to have told you, but I wanted you to know too that Ioana lied to him. Viziru is probably suffering from a rare form of masochism. He insists on believing at any price that his wife continued to love Partenie up to the last moment."

Catalina began to laugh in a way that was sensual and brutal,

197

almost obscene. Fascinated, Biris watched her. His hand trembled a little and he gripped the arm of the chair. Suddenly a perfume, warm, complex, exciting, invaded his nostrils and his lips, even the roof of his mouth: the fragrance of a woman partially undressed.

"How naive you are, you intelligent men!" Catalina said, looking into his eyes. There was that laugh again, still in her glance, still obscene, still tantalizing.

Biris clutched the arm of the chair more fiercely. Now's the time! The thought ran through his mind. One swift move to disconnect the cord, maybe with my foot, and I'll throw myself on her in the dark!

"When it's no longer a matter of a female character, a woman in a book or in a play," continued Catalina, "you men don't understand anything. Dan's like that. . . . Viziru probably is too," she added, her tone shadowed with seriousness.

Now! cried the voice in his mind, but all at once he felt as though the blood had left his body and his strength with it. He began to tremble.

Catalina seemed to be talking to herself as she went on. "That woman loved them both. Do you think this is so difficult? To love two men?"

She smiled as she said the last word, but the next moment she saw Biris bound out of the chair, as though impelled by a spring, and enter the circle of light under the shade of the lamp. His eyes had become very small, his mouth was open and dry. She smelled the odor of tobacco that clung to his clothes. She smelled his panting breath. She heard words she could not comprehend, words that were swallowed as soon as uttered, drawn back into his throat like sighs. With her arms across her breast she struggled, pulling her head back and twisting it first one way, then the other. She did not dare to cry out.

"Petre!" she whispered. "What are you doing? Petre!"

He managed to bring his lips to her throat in a wild, awkward kiss. She could feel it burning moistly.

"Please!" she cried, her voice choked. "Please don't, Petre! Don't do that! I'll kill myself!" Once again she tried to slip out of his embrace, and as she bent her knee he caught a glimpse of her thigh, with its almost unearthly whiteness beyond the top of her stocking. "Please don't!" she whispered instinctively.

"I love you!" His voice was low. "I want you! I want you to belong to me, to be my wife! I love you!"

"Let me alone! Oh, how awful!"

Biris hesitated. His mouth was still close to her throat. An overwhelming sense of shame seized him suddenly, a tremendous self-pity. He got up from the divan. The lamp cord was wound around his foot,

198

but he reached the chair and rested his hand on its back, his breathing labored and noisy. He ran his fingers through his hair and straightened his tie.

"Please forgive me," whispered Catalina. "I can't! I love you too much. I love you like a brother!"

He turned his head to look at her and saw that she was crouching in the middle of the divan, her head bent, her hands covering her face. Her hair, almost golden in the lamplight, fell across her forehead and over her arms. He started to the door.

"What are you doing?" asked Catalina, raising her head. "Where are you going?"

"To the prostitutes!" said Biris at the door, without turning around. "It's my fate, the fate of a common teacher, to go to the prostitutes."

"Petre!" Catalina cried, frightened. "Petre!"

He halted and moved his hand over his head once more, letting it rest for a moment on top. His shame and self-pity gave way to a burst of hatred within. He felt it climb hotly and settle in his breast, a nameless hate, a burning fire.

"Please don't go!" he heard her implore again. "I won't think of it anymore! It will be as if nothing has happened. Don't go!"

With a smile of exhaustion on his face he returned, unhurried, looking over his shoulder as he passed by. He sat down in the easy chair and began to search for his cigarettes. Catalina remained seated in the middle of the divan, her head bent.

"To the prostitutes," repeated Biris, opening the package with nervous, trembling hands. "Because I'm a philosophy teacher. A distinguished, intellectual. If *coana* Viorica had had a young servant girl, I'd have gone to bed with her. That's what intellectuals have to do—go to bed with servant girls. But I have to go to the prostitutes. The woman I love . . ."

"You platonist," Bursuc had said to him one evening in his coarse, vulgar voice, as they stood at the entrance to the Cafenea. "You idealist, haven't you realized yet that all women are whores?" "That tart Catalina, she's destroyed your mind, honey," wailed *coana* Viorica. "That idiot sleeps with all the men." "So what," he kept telling himself. "So what? She's the woman I love. . . ."

". . . goes to bed with other men, with imbeciles, with men who have money," he went on in an abnormally low voice that threatened to burst its restraints at any moment. "The woman I love is an intellectual too, a prostitute deluxe. She sleeps only with the one she snared—a blockhead

199

who pretends to be mad in order to seem interesting—and with anyone else who pays well!"

"Petre!" cried Catalina, raising her head. His name burst from her lips in a short, desperate scream, as though he had struck her, injured her.

"That's what they say downtown." He spoke in a matter-of-fact tone, but his mouth was dry and he swallowed with difficulty. "That's what everybody says—that you go to bed for pay!"

She covered her face with her hands.

"I, who love you, have to go to the prostitutes. You love me too, but unfortunately you love me too much. You ask me to respect you. . . ." He broke off suddenly, as if he had choked on the cigarette smoke, and he began to laugh raucously, a laugh soon stifled in a fit of coughing. It lasted so long that his eyes filled with tears. He took out his handkerchief and spat in it several times with a noisy flourish.

". . . To respect you!" he repeated, and laughed again. "Like Stefanescu did! Or haven't you heard about Stefanescu and the woman he respected?" He paused expectantly, waiting for Catalina's comment, but she remained silent, still resting her head on her hands, her face concealed.

"It happened four years ago, when I was at Brasov," Biris began in high spirits. "I was living in a hotel. Once late at night I heard voices in the next room. Another couple has come! I said to myself. This occurred rather rarely in Brasov, but it happened nonetheless. Couples came from Bucharest and Cluj. But this time all was quiet next door. Whispers, kisses, more whispers, and that was all. I went to sleep. And all at once I was awakened by a woman's scream. It was sharp, exasperated, the scream of a hysterical female. 'Rape me, Stefanescule,' she said, 'Don't respect me any more, rape me!'"

Biris laughed uncontrollably, and his body shook with hiccoughs that would not stop. He saw Catalina raise her head from her hands. Her eyes were dry, indifferent, and she looked at him as though she wondered what was the matter with him.

"In my case things occur exactly in reverse," he resumed after his laughter had subsided. "You should have cried, 'Respect me, Petrache, and don't rape me! Respect me because I'm not an ordinary whore. I'm the woman you love, the person you think of first when you wake up in the morning, the person you think of when you struggle to sleep at night. Respect me! And when desire for me seizes you, go to the prostitutes! I have to sleep with that sterile genius Bibicescu, the man I thought I loved because I understood that he was a perfect nonentity, the one I keep going to bed with because one October 19 I met the Buddha!' What hogwash!" exclaimed Biris, suddenly rising from the armchair. "What dismal hogwash!"

200

He started toward the door again with firm, heavy steps, but at that moment Catalina got up quickly from the divan and cried out in fright. "Don't go!" she said. "Please stay!"

He turned his head and saw her beginning to undress hurriedly, trembling, not knowing what to remove first—her blouse, her stockings, her skirt. She unbuttoned the blouse, then she began to unfasten her skirt but gave that up. She was too impatient. Raising her skirt, she started to pull off her stockings. With brief boyish motions she kicked off one shoe and then the other. Biris stared at her.

"Stay," she said quickly. "Stay and sleep with me. Look, I'm undressing. Don't say I didn't want to give you this pleasure. Come to bed with me."

He saw her standing there in her slip, turning aside to look at him, trembling, with one hand on her breast. "Never mind. Don't bother," he said finally. "Get in bed before you catch cold. Good night!"

"Petre!" she cried. "Don't leave me! I'm afraid alone!"

"Maybe I'll come to sleep with you tomorrow," Biris said, opening the door. "We'll see! Who knows what might happen by tomorrow?"

He closed the door behind him and hurried down the stairs, as if he were afraid she might run after him. He still saw her as he had left her standing in the middle of the room, almost naked, imploring him to stay, to go to bed with her. He still saw that unbelievable scene, so improbable that he would not have dared to conjure it in his most absurd imaginings.

A few days after Stefan had left the clinic, Biris saw him again and was struck immediately by the glow in his eyes. He looked rested. His complexion was almost ruddy and his face had regained its smooth and childlike freshness. In his eyes the pale blue light gleamed with unusual intensity. He was standing by the window as he waited for Biris. From there he could see the towers of nearby churches among the roofs of sheet metal and slate that shimmered slightly in the gentle breeze of the May morning.

"Do you know that I've come out of the labyrinth?" Stefan began suddenly, still gazing out of the window. "And because I've managed to escape this ordeal, I want to entrust you with a message. It's a very delicate matter. I have to tell you now while I still seem able to understand something of it, while I still remember it."

He broke off and turned his head abruptly, looking at Biris. His whole face smiled. It seemed to reflect the glow of an unseen fire blazing near him. He left the window and, passing in front of the

201

bookcase, sat down in the armchair under the painting that Biris liked so much—the one depicting a few flowers flung hastily on the corner of a table beside a woman's black glove.

"I'm always waiting for her to come back from the telephone," Stefan had said once. "I imagine that I've entered the home of someone who, a few minutes before I came, had just returned from a long walk outside the city. She scarcely had time to drop these wild flowers, with their long stems cut so carelessly, on the little table in the entry and to pull off a glove when she heard the telephone ringing. She has run to answer it. I sit here looking first at the flowers, then at the glove, and I wait for her. She hasn't returned yet, but I'm not tired and I'm not bored. I just wait."

Biris watched as Stefan sat down in the chair, smiling silently. "I'm going to ask you to do something that requires great delicacy, but maybe I should explain several other things so you'll understand what it's all about."

"Get to the point," Biris interrupted. "Is it about Partenie and *The Wake?*"

"No," Stefan replied very gravely. "It has to do with a message that I want to entrust to you now while there's still time, while I still understand. I know well enough that I won't understand it very long. These things are quickly forgotten. Probably I'll soon be the same as I was before, I'll be myself again. But the message will remain. I'll be able to get it from you at any time. . . ."

"Why not write it down then?" interposed Biris with an ironic smile that betrayed boredom. "Revelations are better preserved when they're committed to writing."

"I can't write," explained Stefan quietly, fervently. "I have to tell it to you. Above all I ask you to convey it to someone else. I'm sorry that Ioana isn't here to listen too, because it's of interest to all three of us. I beg you to deliver this message to Ileana. It concerns her especially."

He stopped and sat there for some time, his eyes fixed on the carpet. Slowly and deliberately Biris lit a cigarette. He had felt dismay from the beginning, from the moment he heard Stefan mention the labyrinth.

For a long time he had been telling himself the same thing—I seem to be lost in a labyrinth. He had repeated this observation one day long ago when he realized that he was thinking constantly of Catalina. I shouldn't see her again for a week, two weeks, three, and then three months, six months, nine months—until I come

202

out of the labyrinth. But he had continued to visit her. And while he listened to Stefan he envisioned her again as he had last seen her, almost naked, with one hand on her breast, imploring him, "Don't leave me! I'm afraid alone!" Since that evening he had not returned to her flat. And yet he would have gone at any time. He would have gone back that very night if her words had not continued to sound in his ears: "I'll kill myself! *I love you like a brother!*"

I disgust her, Biris had realized. She has a real aversion toward me. But she pitied me and she undressed in front of me.... From pity.

"It's about the automobile," Stefan began suddenly. "Everything I told you two years ago in my secret room was invented. I told you what I did in order to make you come. I never painted a picture of the car. I couldn't have painted it even if I had wanted to. As I told you then, I don't know how to paint. But that car *exists.* I'm asking you to tell this to Ileana."

"Why don't you tell her yourself?" inquired Biris. "Have you quarreled?"

"We haven't seen each other for a long time. She calls me at the Ministry often. I've spoken with her frequently since March 16—you know, the day Partenie was shot. Since then she's called many times. I'm asking you to tell her not to telephone me any more. I'll return to my office tomorrow. Ask her not to call me again. I'm going to see her soon. Tell her to expect me. Someday very soon I'll go to see her." He was silent again.

I suppose I ought to go to see her, said Biris to himself, his thoughts with Catalina. For a long while he contemplated her through the smoke of his cigarette, standing there in front of him scantily clothed, her hand at her breast. He gave a deep and inadvertent sigh, choking on the smoke. He started to cough, and his friend stared at him with curiosity as long as the attack lasted.

"You know," Stefan resumed abruptly, "when I was there in the labyrinth I felt closed in on all sides. I was like a captive in a huge metal sphere. I didn't feel anymore that I was in the belly of the whale. I was inside an immense metal sphere. I didn't see the limits anywhere, but I felt I was locked hopelessly in it. I felt that no matter how much I might struggle, no matter how far I might go forward—the farthest distance possible from the center, the farthest possible from my point of departure—toward the edges, I couldn't reach those iron walls. They were always inaccessible to me. I felt condemned for the rest of my life to whirl blindly, vainly, inside that sphere which was like a dark labyrinth. And yet one day, almost without realizing it, I broke through the wall and came out as if I had emerged from an enormous egg, an egg with an impregnable shell, invulnerable as stone. But it was a shell that broke at a mere touch and I came out again into the light. I came out of the labyrinth. . . ."

Stefan's animation increased as he spoke. He dropped his voice at intervals as though he were afraid that someone else might hear, but the fresh clear light in his eyes remained undiminished. Biris swallowed several times, giving all his strength to mastering another attack of coughing that threatened him. He noticed at that moment a vague odor of kerosene that hung about him, emanating from his clothing, from his body. Timorously he raised his hand to his nose and sniffed it. His fingers smelled strongly of tobacco.

"This is the message I'm asking you to tell Ileana," continued Stefan. "She's not to give up hope. That car in the Forest of Baneasa *exists*. I've seen it several times. She hasn't seen it yet, but one day she will. She may not recognize it, but it's her car. . . ."

Biris was only half listening to what Stefan was saying. There was a salty taste in the back of his mouth and at once he thought: I choked, I've coughed too much. He swallowed again with effort. Probably a little blood, he told himself. But it's not a hemoptysis. It's not like it was that time. He smiled suddenly, reassured. He understood where the smell of kerosene came from.

It came from far away, from his adolescence. He had caught a cold that winter, the first winter after the war, and he had stayed in bed a week. It was in Ferendari, in *coana* Viorica's house, where electric lights had not yet been installed. In his room, with its flowered wallpaper the color of young wheat, stood a large kerosene lamp. That evening *coana* Viorica had stayed late in the city. He was alone. It had become dark, and he began to get bored. He got out of bed and, groping about for the matches, he removed the lamp chimney and turned up the wick. An odor of kerosene engulfed him, so strong that it made him dizzy. At the same time he felt a gurgling, soft, warm, and a little salty, somewhere in his throat, at the back of his mouth. He wanted to spit but he didn't know where. Finally he spat in one hand, and with the other, half asleep, exhausted, he struck a match and lit the wick. A reddish-yellow flame blinded him. It was shrouded in a cloud of thick smoke that trembled menacingly in front of his face. He tried to set the chimney over the flame, but he glanced at his other hand, still closed in a fist, and he stopped, petrified. Between his fingers a reddish foam with blood was dripping.

"Do you remember who said that miracles are unrecognizable, in the sense that they are camouflaged among the events of every day, that they are accomplished apparently by people who look like everyone else, ordinary people?"

Stefan leaned a little toward Biris as he questioned him, as if he wanted to shorten the distance between them. He did not give Biris time to answer but went on in the same clear, impassioned voice.

"It's very true. It's precisely so. Everything that doesn't belong to our world still resembles our world. I read once that Fat Frumos* had to choose an apple of gold out of a hundred apples that were only gilded. If he didn't guess right, his head would be cut off. Exactly the same thing happens with us. In order to get out of the belly of the whale we have to guess, among the billions of things of our world, that unique example which doesn't belong to our world. But in appearance it differs in no way from the billions of other things of its type. If we don't guess it we're lost, they cut off our heads. Fortunately we're given a whole lifetime to make the choice, but if we haven't guessed it before we die, we're lost."

He stopped again and looked at Biris, who said nothing and didn't even try to hide his indifference. It's not the same as then, he told himself. It's not a hemoptysis. I've been smoking too much. This has happened to me before.

Countless times since then, during his adolescence, he had felt this same salty taste in the back of his throat, even after he had been sent to Calarasi. *Doamna* Porumbache did not believe in doctors or in sanatoriums. In order to cure him she had entrusted him to a brother-in-law in Calarasi, a butcher. When Stere came to get Petre he was an old man, but he had ruddy cheeks and he was bursting with health. "Give him to me, Viorico," he had said, "and by summer I'll mend his lungs." Stere's butcher shop was situated at the edge of town near the slaughterhouse. At four in the morning he awakened the boy and gave him a rare filet of beef, almost raw, and a big glass of red wine. "Get up, nephew," he said. He was wearing his butcher's apron, which was stained with fresh blood. The odor of blood never left him. Still sleepy, Biris began to eat reluctantly, and he shuddered when he had to down the glass of red wine. "It's from *finu* Lica's vineyard," Stere said, but to Biris the wine seemed to be mixed with blood. Then the uncle went back to the slaughterhouse and the nephew fell asleep immediately. Three hours later, awakened again, he ate another rare filet and drank another glass of wine, and once more

*Romanian folk hero, "Prince Charming."

it put him to sleep. He slept until ten o'clock, when his uncle brought him the third filet and two raw eggs, which he gulped down with his eyes closed. This treatment lasted until May, when Stere discovered him in the room of a niece, who had been recently orphaned and whom he had brought from a village on the Danube to assume the place of a wife and servant. Stere calmly took his heavy belt from under his blood-stained apron. "Don't beat me, *Nene!* I'm sick!" cried Biris. But Stere headed for his niece and began to lash her across the back methodically and without haste, yet thoroughly. The girl set up a wail, pulling at her hair with both hands. "Why should I bother with you, nephew?" said Stere. "I have nothing to fear from someone like you. It's she who's responsible, since now she knows the passion of a young man. . . ."

"Now that I've come out of the labyrinth," Stefan began again, his voice somewhat less fervent. "I understand that the sphere which seemed infinite and whose unseen shell seemed inaccessible was in fact cracked in different places. But of course I didn't know that it was cracked, that I could go out through any of those breaks, that each crack was a window. You can jump outside any time through a window. . . ."

"All these things are part of your message for Ileana?" interrupted Biris seriously.

"All," Stefan replied firmly. "I've spoken to Ioana about them, but I want Ileana to know too. And because I can't go to see her yet, I'm asking you to tell her. Tell her that all that happens to her now is of no great importance. She knows that I love her, too; she learned it from me, in fact. That was something I couldn't hide. I see that you're not saying anything. This means that you've understood, that you agree. Where could such a love lead? Anna Karenina? Tristan and Isolde? That would be too sad. One love that takes the place of another, a common adultery, born in Time, ground down by Time, fated to die like any ordinary creature born of death and returning to death? No. If I cannot succeed in loving one just as I love the other, what meaning can this new love have? Why have I met Ileana and why have I fallen in love with her? I've always loved Ioana. From the moment I saw her I knew I'd always loved her, knew this love was my destiny. Then why have I fallen in love with the other one? Only so I can go to bed with her? If this new and unexpected, unsolicited love leads only to replacing Ioana with Ileana it wouldn't have any meaning. . . . Tell her everything I've told you now. I'll repeat it to her too, when I meet her again, but I'd like her to know it now. Tell her that the car exists, that windows exist, that this sphere which encloses us is only apparently made of steel, that in

206

reality it's broken in innumerable places. It's like an eggshell that's cracked all over. Tell her all these things now while I still understand them. Tomorrow or the day after I'll forget them and I'll return to my ordinary self again."

Biris stood up suddenly and held out his hand. He was again aware of the moistness in his throat, the same salty taste of warm blood in his mouth. He had to spit. Stefan looked at him anxiously as the teacher gripped his hand and left. On the stairs Biris pulled out his handkerchief and spat in it. There was no blood however, just a little reddish-colored foam. Nothing's wrong with me, he said to himself. I'll have to smoke less.

A few steps farther down he encountered Ioana, who was climbing slowly, resting her hand on the stair rail.

"I lied to him for nothing," she said. "He doesn't believe a thing I told him at the clinic. He said so himself the next day."

Her smile was sad and preoccupied. Biris realized he still was holding the bloody handkerchief in his hand and he hid it hastily in his pocket. Blushing, he felt drops of sweat suddenly cover his forehead. He wanted to wipe it, but he did not dare to take out his handkerchief again.

"He's not interested in *The Wake* any longer," she said.

Finally he had to get out his handkerchief and hold it to his mouth to spit. "I've got to stop smoking," he said with difficulty, forcing himself to smile.

He felt his whole body wet with sweat. His shirt stuck to his back and to his chest. He especially felt the perspiration streaming from his forehead and his face. Ashamed to wipe with it in front of Ioana, he squeezed the wet handkerchief tightly in his fist.

That evening he went to see Catalina. "I've waited for you every night since then," she told him.

He looked at her and found that she was still the same. Her large green eyes were full of questions, her blond hair framed her temples and fell upon her shoulders. Her face seemed young and at the same time ageless, though weary of the cheap makeup applied in the tawdry theaters where she played now and then. (She performed only a few times a month, substituting for some second-rate actress.) Yes, she was still the same, with her round cheeks, approaching plumpness, like those of a sad, wicked puppet. He could never look at her mouth without feeling his own breath grow hot. She was still the same.

He sat down in the armchair and took out his package of cigarettes. The window was opened wide and a fragrance of distant lilacs drifted into the room.

"I thought you'd come the next evening and I waited for you."

With deliberate calm Biris selected a cigarette, turned it in his fingers and smelled it, taking a deep breath. Then he raised his eyes with a smile of secret satisfactoin. "I'm the bearer of a very important message from the labyrinth," he said suddenly.

Disconcerted, Catalina returned his smile. "I should have made the sacrifice long ago," she said. "You were the being I loved and admired most in the world. I should have given you up too. Please forgive me for delaying so long."

"Aren't you at all curious to hear the message I've been entrusted with?" interrupted Biris, still playing with the cigarette.

"There was just one thing left to me that was pure and undefiled," Catalina went on in the same flat monotone. "I've had to renounce this too. I haven't been lucky. But maybe its better like this. . . ."

At that moment the door opened suddenly and Bibicescu entered. They had not heard anyone knock.

"You're here?" exclaimed Dan, surprised, looking at both of them intently, almost sternly. He turned to Catalina. "Have you forgotten that *conu* Misu expects us at the Modern?"

"I'm not hungry," Catalina declared. "You go alone. If you wish, come back with him afterward. I'll wait for you here with Petrache. I'll make you some coffee."

Biris had the impression that he was listening for the second time to the dialogue begun one evening long ago in the entrance to the Cafenea, when he had made the acquaintance of Bibicescu. "Enchanted," the actor told him as they shook hands. He looked deep into Biris's eyes. "Wouldn't you like to dine with us?" Bibicescu was alone. Biris turned his head to look in the Cafenea, wondering if someone else were there. "No," Bibicescu had added, "she hasn't arrived yet. She ought to be here any minute. *Conu* Misu has invited us, Catalina and me, to the Modern. Do you know Catalina Palade? She's a remarkable woman. But I'll ask one thing of you—don't bring up the subject of Buddhism."

Just then Biris saw her approaching. Her head was bare and her hair fell across her forehead. He surmised that she wanted to look like Greta Garbo. With her hands in the pockets of her beige topcoat she walked indolently and somewhat absently, looking vaguely ahead of her. She's trying to create a style, thought Biris. "No, I'm not hungry," said Catalina. "You go alone. I'll join you for coffee. I want to walk." That evening they walked together for the first time. Although Biris was hungry he had agreed to go with her, and they started out along *bulevardul* Lascar Catargiu, going toward Sosea. He stopped before a vender of cracknels and bought some of the crisp biscuits. "Give me one too," said Catalina. "I seem to be getting hungry." Then, taking his arm, she added, "I like you. I believe that we might be friends. . . ."

Bibicescu turned to Biris and inquired, "Aren't you hungry either?"

For a long time Biris had been sitting with the cigarette between his lips, unlighted. He was satisfied with chewing and sucking it, taking it out of his mouth now and then to smell it.

"I've eaten," he answered finally. "I came here on a mission. I've been entrusted with a message from the labyrinth."

"A message from his friend Stefanescu of Brasov," said Catalina suddenly, and she began to laugh.

Biris turned slightly pale but he bit hard on the cigarette and said nothing. Bibicescu looked at each of them in turn with a long face.

"*Conu* Misu's expecting us," he said again, beginning to pace about the room with great strides.

"We can't go," stated Catalina after her laughter had subsided. "Biris and I have to decipher the message of Stefanescu of Brasov."

Bibicescu stopped in front of her, his hands in his pockets. Again it seemed to Biris that he had witnessed this scene innumerable times; these sudden deliberate halts were part of the action in the play Dan had rehearsed for so many years, the play that never would see the footlights and so would never end. Biris would witness his nervous pacing, his abrupt halts, his penetrating glances until the end of his life. If I don't quarrel with him someday, I'll have to endure him as long as I live. He took the cigarette out of his mouth, and biting off the wet end, put the remaining piece back in his mouth with great care.

"Light your cigarette, damn it!" Bibicescu burst out. "You're getting on my nerves! Light it!"

"I don't smoke anymore," Biris explained calmly. "I think I had a slight hemoptysis this morning, so I'm not smoking anymore. If I have an attack of coughing I'll spit blood again."

The silence that followed this statement frightened him, yet it also gave him pleasure. It was like the countless silences that he had been provoking constantly since his youth. Although he feared the abyss that would yawn suddenly between himself and others, the isolation those silences imposed also attracted him.

At the University he had courted another student, Marietta Postavaru, a redheaded girl with a freckled face and a youthful, robust, exciting figure. She liked George Sand. He had kissed her the first time on a night during the Easter vigils in the garden of the Church of the Holy Icons. A half-hour later Marietta had mentioned Musset and George Sand, and Biris confided to her, "Do you know that I have tuberculosis too?" The girl did not seem very disturbed. A warm but detached look of compassion appeared in her eyes. "Just today I had a hemoptysis. I spat blood." Only then did he feel the silence grow stony around him.

"Why do you look at me like that?" he asked very casually. "I've never concealed the fact that I have a chest ailment."

"You ought to take care of yourself," said Bibicescu. "This is no joke." He addressed Catalina: "You're not going? Then we'll be back in an hour or two. . . ."

He left without telling them good-bye. Catalina raised her head and looked directly into Biris's eyes. "Light your cigarette and don't torment yourself anymore," she said, and she added thoughtfully, "Now I understand everything. I understand what happened to you that night. I've forgiven you since, but now I understand. And that's why you broke off with Theodora, too. I understand now."

He lit the cigarette and inhaled the first smoke greedily, taking a deep breath. "Aren't you at all curious to find out what the message is about?" he asked her presently.

"I understand very well," continued Catalina in a low monotone that was like a lament. "When you want me, tell me. I'll be your woman. I'll be Stefanescu's woman. I'll wait for you every day, at any hour you tell me. I too will be one of those women. I don't think I have the right to be anything else now. . . ."

She stopped abruptly and they were both silent for some time. He remembered the scenes that his imagination had constructed before he had been moved to action. They seemed far more true than the words Catalina had just uttered. He felt that she was speaking to some other man. He listened to her as he had listened so many times at the theater, deeply regretting that she did not have more talent.

"Actually you're still in love with Theodora," resumed Catalina, smiling sadly. "Your attraction to me is only physical. You really love the other girl. That's why you could give her up. For you I'm Stefanescu's woman. But I can't help it. This is my fate. I'll wait for you and when you want me, come."

In his mind Biris saw Theodora again—small, fragile, with a face of such exceptional purity that it might have been sketched by one of the old masters. Her eyes looked dark because of her myopia. She wore her glasses only at the theater and for reading, and he

210

enjoyed this trace of coquetry in a young scholarly woman. Undoubtedly she too knew why they had been introduced. She knew that *doamna* Porumbache had asked for her in marriage to her nephew, yet this did not seem to intimidate the girl. She had dressed modestly, and her clothes were youthful and in perfect taste. He saw her again as she looked when she rose to accompany him, fresh, clean, wholesome, and he had a moment of sorrow. If Catalina had not existed that gracious and cultured young woman would have been his fiancée. From that evening on, he might truly have been in love. It was inconceivable that such a girl could have accepted him, and yet in spite of everything the miracle had happened and she had. Probably it was because that evening they had talked of Rilke, he thought later when he was trying to convince himself that Theodora could not love him, that she would quickly regret her action, that they could not be happy together. But there was Catalina. It was all in vain because on a certain evening someone who was coming out of the Cafenea in a hurry had introduced him to Bibicescu while the actor was waiting for her. Another time, another evening he realized that happiness for him meant only to drink of the deep green waters of Catalina's eyes, and when he once touched her breast with his arm he knew that only Catalina's could disclose what no woman's breast had revealed to him before.

"I see that you're not curious to learn the contents of the message," he said at last, getting up from the chair. He put out his cigarette and started to the door. Catalina watched him leave, still seated on the divan, resting her chin on her fist absently. She did not speak again.

He put it off for a long time but finally he made up his mind and telephoned Ileana. Each morning when he awakened his strength seemed to have diminished, and it was only with much effort that he managed to get out of bed. He had requested a medical leave of absence from the *liceu* and he could have rested all morning but he feared yielding to his fatigue. He was afraid to remain in bed. Nevertheless he postponed calling Ileana from one day to the next. He no longer remembered clearly what he was supposed to tell her.

"I've been expecting you for a long time," she declared over the phone. "Stefan said you were coming to see me. When can you come?"

He went to her house the next afternoon. It had been an exceptionally hot morning, but toward midday the sky had begun to lose its brilliance. The whole city seemed to be buried in dust. When he reached *strada* Batistei he was already tired and perspiring heavily. He longed to take a deep breath, a great breath, and exhale it quickly like a sigh, but he did not dare.

"I bring a message," he said with a tense smile, as soon as Ileana had opened the door. For the first time he looked at her closely. Whom did she resemble? He was sure he had seen those unusual green eyes somewhere before, eyes that assumed a golden light with every smile. He was certain that he had encountered somewhere the same bronzed face, the same mouth, very red, with its bright, white, gleaming teeth. Probably in a film, he said to himself in an attempt to banish the thought, but it persisted and again he searched his mind. It was not her face nor the color of her eyes and hair that plagued him, but something in the nature of her presence. There was something in her expression that made him think not so much of a woman as of a state of being that he had experienced in a time long gone, a time that he could not determine precisely. She reminded him of a certain epoch, a certain life lost in the distant past. All at once he felt less tired and he began to breathe without anxiety, fully, to the bottom of his lungs. But a few moments later he caught himself in a sigh and he blushed. He took out his handkerchief and started to wipe his forehead, his face. Yes, she resembled someone. . . .

"Stefan asked me to deliver a message to you," he began after he had relaxed for a moment in the easy chair.

Ileana offered him the box of cigarettes, but he lifted his right hand quickly, almost in alarm, as if to protect himself.

"I'm not smoking anymore! I haven't felt very well for some time. That's why I delayed my visit. I should have come long ago." He was silent, watching her avidly as she lit her cigarette.

"Does it have something to do with the dead bone, with the tooth already arrived in the land of the dead?" Ileana asked abruptly.

Suddenly the room seemed to grow dark. Biris started. "How did you know about that?"

"From Stefan," said Ileana, smiling diffidently. "Stefan tells me all sorts of things that I don't understand. I like to listen to him speaking of things I don't understand, talking about the belly of the whale, the room *Sambo*, and the car that should have disappeared on the Night of St. John, and the car that he painted. . . ."

"Now, I remember," Biris interrupted. "He asked me to tell you that he didn't paint it."

Ileana raised her head and looked directly in his eyes.

"The car exists, he assured me, but he didn't paint a picture of it.

Besides," he added smiling, "he couldn't have painted it. Just between you and me, I don't think he ever painted anything!"

Ileana stood up and, going to the window, pushed aside the curtains. It had become quite dark outside. The clouds hung low and leaden. They seemed motionless. The branch of a tree, old and bushy, waited unmoving in front of the window. Not a leaf stirred.

"Is it true that you have a tooth already in the land of the dead?" Ileana asked, sitting down again opposite him. "Tell me about it."

"I lost it." He searched for his handkerchief again and wiped his forehead. "It was extracted last year."

"Too bad," murmured Ileana absently. "But why did you say that it had already reached the land of the dead?"

"It doesn't matter now," Biris responded with a great weariness in his voice. "It's a long story. It's a story about Time. . . ." He was silent, breathing deeply. He felt that he was suffocating. The room seemed to be collapsing under the weight of the oppressive, humid heat.

"The story of youth without old age and life without death?" Ileana said very softly, making another effort to smile.

"Will you please open a window a little?" whispered Biris. "I don't know what's the matter. . . . I'm suffocating."

Ileana sprang to her feet, glancing at him in alarm. Then she rushed to the windows and opened them wide. He thanked her with a smile.

"Don't you feel well?" she asked returning to her chair.

"It's passed now. I didn't have enough air."

The fragrance of wild roses penetrated the darkened room. Outside the clouds sank menacingly lower.

"It's because of the storm," said Ileana, as she sat down again. "It's always like this before a storm."

He saw her put her hands to her temples, but she seemed to remember suddenly that he was with her and she dropped them quickly. She tossed her head, looked at him, tried to smile. She loves him, he realized. Nothing can be done. There's no way out. She loves him.

"Stefan asked me to bring you a message," he began again. "It will be difficult for me to repeat it exactly because I was rather tired when he told me and I didn't understand it very well. Stefan asks you to wait for him. . . ."

She got up then and went to throw the cigarette out of the window. Something could be felt now in the air. The leaves seemed to rouse from their inertia. Biris breathed deeply and wiped his forehead with his handkerchief. What I'm doing is absurd! I shouldn't have taken him seriously. He was hardly out of the clinic. . . ."

"I'm sorry. But he insisted I come to see you."

213

Ileana returned to the middle of the room and stood there docilely, her hands behind her back.

"You're a philosophy teacher, aren't you? Stefan thinks a lot of you. He admires you very much. You're his only friend, he told me once, the only person with whom he can discuss things. Do you understand him? Do you always understand what he says? Especially now, after . . . Partenie. . . . Do you understand anything? Tell me, what goes on inside him?"

They heard a distant peal of thunder and the branch in front of the window shook as if suddenly frightened. Ileana did not look at Biris while she was speaking.

"He suffered a nervous shock, that's all," Biris replied casually, and he added, smiling, "History has taken revenge on him. He has a phobia against History. He has a horror of events. He'd like things to stand still the way they seemed to do in the paradise of his childhood. So History takes its revenge and buries him as often as it can. It throws him into the detention camp by mistake. It kills men in his place, always by mistake, and so on. Look at me. I live in History, and I'm reconciled with History, and nothing ever happens to me!"

His strength spent, he stopped and searched again for his handkerchief. It was almost dark in the room. The branch began to quiver violently, beating against the glass with great force and whistling shrilly as though animated.

"Please don't close it!" begged Biris when he saw Ileana go to the window. She leaned on the sill and put her head outside.

"It's beginning to storm," she said without turning around.

The thunder sounded closer. At intervals the sky was laced with reddish flashes. The branch struggled and moaned.

"I didn't ask you that—about what happened to Partenie." She returned to the middle of the room. "I'd like to know if you always understand when he talks to you about Time, and the belly of the whale, and the Night of St. John. Or maybe he talks to you about other things," she added quickly, approaching him. "I don't understand him. I know he loves his wife very much. He's told me so himself. But I don't understand what goes on inside him. I just don't understand!"

She stopped and closed her eyes, frowning, a smile of suffering on her lips. The glare of the lightning, green tinged with red, flickered at the windows, and thunder shook the building a few moments later. The rain seemed to have been waiting for just this signal to begin falling suddenly—heavy, leaden, tumultuous—coming down solidly with a roar. Ileana jumped up to close the windows. She searched nervously for a cigarette and lit it. Biris gave her a penetrating glance and sighed.

"He's very dear to me," she began without looking at him, "and I

214

should like for us to be friends. I should like to know his wife, Ioana, too. He told me he loves her very much. I'd like to know both of them better, to be friends with them. Only I can't seem to understand him. Sometimes three whole months go by without a sign of life from him. Then he telephones me in the middle of the night, comes to see me at dawn and stays all day with me. He doesn't go to the Ministry, he doesn't go home. . . . And he talks to me about all kinds of strange things that I don't understand. I like to listen to him talking about all these things. I like to listen to him. But I wish I understood what's going on inside him, what he intends, what he wants to do. I wonder what he wants to happen. . . ."

She stopped to wait for the thunder. In the room the lightning flashed again like moonlight and the windows vibrated for some time. Biris closed his eyes. All at once he felt his body covered with perspiration again and instinctively he put his hands to his throat. I haven't smoked yet! I haven't smoked a cigarette today. It can't begin again. . . . I haven't smoked yet. . . .

"He told me to tell you to wait for him," he said suddenly. "That's all I understood, that he asks you to wait for him. . . ."

It was raining now with unrestrained fury. The branch struggled in terror and beat desperately on the windowpane. The flashes of lightning were almost continuous. Now and then the whole house seemed to rock on its foundations. Ileana looked at Biris but her glance faltered somewhere in front of her, searching, unseeing.

"He told me a lot," Biris continued in a muffled voice, "but I didn't understand him very well. I was sick . . . I'd been smoking too much without realizing it and I was dizzy. I couldn't follow him very well but I understood one thing—he asks you to wait for him. . . ."

Ileana held her head in her hands and sat listening to the storm without speaking. Again Biris felt that he was suffocating and he took another deep breath. I've got to leave, he said to himself. His throat was burning more than ever and he expected momentarily to taste the blood in the back of his mouth. I've got to go. I'm suffocating. . . .

"I met one of the directors of the Ministry," said Ileana. She did not raise her eyes. "He told me that Stefan is the best negotiator they have, that he has a better sense of economic realities than anyone else. In the field of economic agreements he's a genius, the man told me. Then he must be like other men. . . . And yet, in spite of that, I don't understand what he wants!"

"He said that he'd been wandering in a labyrinth." Biris began to speak again with great effort, but he thought he heard the doorbell ring and he stopped. "I think someone's at the door," he said.

Ileana listened to the metallic sound continue for a long time and did not move. "I'm not expecting anyone. Maybe it's some friend of *Tante* Alice's who got caught in the rain somewhere in the neighborhood."

She sprang from her seat and ran headlong down the hall. Quickly Biris took out his handkerchief and spat. He looked in fright at the reddish foam, then he spat several more times and wiped his lips carefully. He started. He thought that he heard Stefan's voice, and then Ileana's. "He's here!" he seemed to hear her whisper. "Biris! He's here!"

When the rain stops I'm leaving. I'll hide in an archway and spit. I have to spit. Then I'll take a cab and go home. *Coana* Viorica will make me some tea.

He saw Stefan come in dripping wet, trying to push back the hair that stuck to his forehead. There was a bouquet of lilies of the valley in his hand.

"I ran all the way through the rain."

Ileana, smiling, stared at him a long time with her hands clasped behind her back. At last she took the little bouquet of lilies.

"Did you bring them for me?"

Stefan was breathing hard and deeply. With a guilty smile he looked at the streams of water that ran down on the carpet. He did not dare to move again.

"Go to the bathroom and dry yourself off," Ileana commanded. "Come with me. . . ."

They left the room together. I've got to go, Biris said to himself, and with great exertion he stood up. He leaned on the back of the chair with his eyes half closed, waiting for the clap of thunder. The windows rattled for a long time. I could go to the bathroom after him. . . . To spit. . . .

"What are you doing?" Returning alone, Ileana questioned him in surprise.

"I have to go," he said, managing a smile. "I have business. . . . I think I'll get a cab."

"Don't go!" whispered Ileana, suddenly troubled. "You saw the state he was in when he arrived! Don't leave!"

He leaned weakly on the back of the chair and took out his handkerchief again. If only it would stop raining. . . .

"Are you ill?" demanded Ileana with a frightened glance. "Let me get you something. What would you like?"

"What's the matter?" Stefan asked as he reentered the room and approached them.

"I'd like to go home," said Biris. "I don't feel well. Where's the bathroom?" he asked, turning crimson.

He went out quickly, followed by Stefan. Once inside he bolted

216

the door, trembling, and bent over the sink. He spat many times, coughing, gagging. He turned on both faucets and began to wash his hands and face, breathing deeply, frightened. After a moment's hesitation he pulled out his handkerchief and began to rinse it out, looking absently at the water that gurgled in the sink. And all at once he remembered.

He was little. They had gone to the Fair in the carriage. *Nea**
Mitica held his hand. *Coana* Viorica was walking a step ahead of them carrying a small umbrella of pink silk. It was very hot. "I'm thirsty!" he whimpered. "Hold on, we'll soon be there," said *nea* Mitica. "When we get to the garden, I'll buy you a lemonade." He let himself be led by the hand through the deafening crowd, through the dust that rose high above them, even higher than the colorful balloons. "I'm thirsty!" he repeated. All those unfamiliar odors seemed to burn his lips. Everywhere smoke was rising— from the kettles filled with frying doughnuts, from the grills, from the buckets of red hot coals holding popcorn that jumped about with sharp little snapping noises. "I'm thirsty!" he kept repeating, and he felt the salty tears flow down both dusty cheeks.
    "Give him a lemonade, Mitica!" said *coana* Viorica, brandishing the pink umbrella furiously. "If I'd known he'd act this way, I wouldn't have brought him with us!" *Nea* Mitica jerked him along, walking faster, making his way with difficulty through the crowd. He stopped in front of a stand. Someone handed Petre a big glass of pink lemonade. He seized it with both hands and put his head back, staring fascinated at the girl. She was inconceivably beautiful with her blue-green eyes and pearl-white teeth. And her smile! Never had anyone smiled at him with so much love. "There, little boy!" she said, "There, little monkey!" He heard the lemonade gurgle, he felt it trickle down from the corner of his mouth, and he heard her repeat, "There, little monkey. . . . Little monkey. . . ."

"Let me go and get you a cab," said Stefan when Biris returned to the salon.
    "It's not necessary. I feel better now. Much better. . . ."
    All three were silent, listening to the storm.
    "I know now who Ileana looks like," Biris said abruptly, leaning on the back of the chair and trying to smile.
    "Why don't you want to stay?" She looked at him in desperation,

*Uncle.

217

pleading with him. "I'll give you a drink, or if you'd rather I'll make you some tea."

"I know who she looks like," he repeated with the same exhausted smile. "I'm awfully glad I remembered who she resembles. I was four years old. She was my only requited love. I looked at her, I think, for about half a minute. I thought I'd always remember her, but I forgot. . . ."

Ileana glanced at him again with the same strange look in her eyes as if she did not see him. Stefan had remained standing in the middle of the room, embarrassed. "It's better that you didn't tell her anything," he said suddenly.

"I only told her that you'd been lost in the labyrinth," interrupted Biris with a gesture of impatience. Once more he felt that he was suffocating, that he needed air, and he extended his hand to Ileana.

"I'm sorry," she murmured.

"You were my great love in childhood. The only soul I felt had truly loved me."

He smiled at her sheepishly. Not until he reached the street did he dare to take a deep breath again, one that went to the bottom of his lungs. But it had begun to hail and he quickly found refuge in an archway. He wanted to spit, but he was ashamed to, since already several people had gathered under the vault. He took the wet handkerchief from his pocket and automatically pressed it to his mouth.

That summer he went to spend a month at the rest house for secondary school teachers at Comarnic. He had been there twice before, but this time he followed rigorously the regimen prescribed by the doctor. The problem is simple, he said to himself. I'll have to return for a certain length of time to the condition of a larva, forego the activities and the expenditure of energy that devolve upon adults, overeat and sleep as much as I can. Nevertheless the picture of Catalina kept returning to his mind. He saw her in her slip, without stockings, with a hand on her breast, saying, "Please stay! . . . Whenever you want it, come; I'll be waiting for you!"

He had managed to visit her less frequently, but every evening brought a struggle with the temptation to go to her place. In order to be sure that he would not surrender he undressed as soon as the sun had set and went to bed. *Doamna* Porumbache came in to entertain him, bringing with her the coffee pot, or, when the

218

weather was very hot, a bucket of ice in which she had put a bottle of wine and another of soda. While she sipped her coffee and talked to him he watched her, staring intently as she puffed on her cigarette, sighing. Sometimes he asked her to let him light one for her and he inhaled the first smoke avidly but with great care. There's nothing wrong with me, he was constantly reminding himself. I just smoked too much. The problem is simple— regression to the state of a larva. *Doamna* Porumbache recounted until late in the night all her long-remembered tales and he listened fascinated. She reported to him in the most minute detail things that had happened to people whom he had never met or to others whom he had barely glimpsed at a time when they were only poor shadows of their former selves.

"You didn't know my godson Lica and Fanel, his brother, when they had the Gradina Veseliei,"* she began. Biris knew everything that would follow—how Mita Biciclista came there once with the girls from the cabaret. He asked the customers, who were all people from the poorer neighborhoods, to get up so that the girls could dance on the tables between the meat platters and glasses of wine. He made a bet that they wouldn't tip over a single glass. *Doamna* Porumbache stopped and poured herself more wine and sighed again as she put the bottle back in the bucket. Biris waited impatiently for the rest of the story, although he well knew what came next. One of the girls slipped, someone jumped to catch her in his arms, and all the men rushed to the others and began kissing them. An unforgettable scuffle ensued, because the girls had brought army officers with them. One of the officers, a Lieutenant Sideri, fired a shot in the air with his revolver, but the people thought the men were firing on them and the women began to scream. They tried to jump over the garden wall, but their long dresses held them back. It was just at that moment that they heard *finu* Lica roar, "Who fired that pistol, hey?"

But Biris did not always have enough strength of will to undress, climb into bed, and call *coana* Viorica to keep him company. Impatience gripped him like a fever as soon as the sun went down. He shaved, changed his shirt, and started out with a scowl of despair, hastening to Catalina's flat. Sometimes he did not find her at home and then he waited for her, smoking one cigarette after another, pacing the sidewalk or leaning against a wall. He waited until he saw her coming, walking a step behind Bibicescu, her head bent, her hair falling over her face. "How are

*Garden of Gaiety.

219

you, Stefanescule?" she called when she saw him. Deliberately he lied to her, "I was on my way home and I came by to see how you are."

Sometimes she was there alone, apparently waiting for him, and he found it very difficult to endure her presence, especially when she inspected him slowly, patiently. In his exasperation he began to talk, confiding in a low, excited voice how often he had thought about her *before*, how he had desired her for a long time, what plans he had made for their life together, the way he had imagined their love. He talked until he was exhausted, until he felt as though the blood had been drained from his body. Then he rose from the chair and started to the door. Catalina followed him silently with her eyes. "Whenever you wish," she told him as he put his hand on the doorknob, "Whenever you want that pleasure, come. I'm always waiting for you. Instead of going . . . you know where . . . it's better you come to me. At least you can be sure you won't get a disease. . . ."

The problem is simple, he told himself stubbornly again and again at Comarnic. He did not make friends with any of the other patients but spent most of his time stretched out asleep on a chaise longue in the park, or pretending to be asleep. He had brought several books with him, but he seemed to be afraid to read them. He did not want to repeat what had happened five years before, in 1934, when he had come to the rest house for the first time. As he was reclining on his chaise longue reading, a young woman, a teacher from Moldavia, approached him. "What are you perusing with so much interest, *domnule* Biris?" she had asked. They became friends and loaned books to each other. At night they strolled together. He neglected the prescribed routine that year and failed entirely to keep to his course of treatment. He had gone home quite as thin as when he had left and even more tired. This time he stubbornly persisted in his decision to return to the state of a larva.

One day he received an envelope forwarded by *doamna* Porumbache from Bucharest. It contained a summons to military duty. He sent the paper back to the regiment enclosing a medical certificate, but a few days later he received another order. He was instructed to present himself at the military hospital at Brasov. The very next day he left wearily, irritated that his month of rest had been cut short. He thought he was going to be examined immediately, but the commission would not meet for three days, so he was admitted to the hospital. They gave him a dismal room smelling of creoline and carbolic acid, its windows black with filth. The handles of the doors were wrapped in rags soaked in a chemical solution—"to disinfect it," explained the orderly. Biris did not know why he felt so certain that in that room, in the same bed in which he lay, a soldier had recently died—one of those peasants who were mustered from every corner of the country, who slept at night in railway stations with their heads on their laps, waiting for the train that would take them to their regiments. Almost no one came to see Biris. Undoubtedly, he said to himself, people are still haunted by the painful memory of the corpse they discovered one morning in my bed.

Finally he was summoned for the X-ray examination. He took off his shirt and waited in the darkened room with several soldiers who trembled now and then as if they were shaken by fever.

"Biris Petre!" he heard someone shout through the darkness. Groping, he approached the army doctor and allowed himself to be placed in front of the X-ray machine. He knew what he would be required to do: "Breathe! Take a deep breath! Cough!"

"Your occupation?" inquired the doctor.

"Secondary school teacher," Biris replied dutifully.

"You ought to be more careful of your health," the doctor muttered. Then he turned to the orderly who sat near him writing by the feeble light of a red bulb. "Exempted from duty for six months! . . . Next!"

Biris felt his way back to the bench where he had left his clothes. He hunted for his shirt. Several sharp raps resounded on the door. It opened and a man entered hurriedly, but he hesitated in the obscurity of the room.

"The major," he whispered, "I want to speak with the major!" He made his way almost to the orderly, and then he approached the doctor.

"The colonel wants you, sir," he said. "It's urgent!"

The doctor muttered something and continued his work. The messenger stepped closer and added, "Von Ribbentrop's in Moscow. They're negotiating a Russo-German nonaggression treaty!"

They were all silent. Biris felt the cold grip him and he put on his coat quickly. The doctor stepped away from the X-ray equipment. "I'll be back in five minutes," he told the orderly.

After that day Biris found himself living a different life—a life that was still his but one that in no way resembled the life he had led until that moment. He returned to Comarnic to finish the treatment, but he did not have the patience to sleep on a chaise longue isolated from everyone else in the depths of the park. He bought all the newspapers and spent most of his time in the coffee shops where he knew he would meet acquaintances. He went to the station and waited for the train to Bucharest to go by, and he contemplated one after another the faces of the people—worried, jolly, or indifferent—who leaned out of the windows to talk or to buy fruit in little wicker baskets, or to ask if the

221

newspapers from the capital had arrived. At daybreak on the first day of September he also left. On his arrival in Bucharest he found that the special editions were just announcing the invasion of Poland. He hurried out of the station, carrying his own luggage with some difficulty, and went along *bulevardul* Dinicu Golescu, looking for a taxi. The people walked in silence, anxious and solemn. Few eyes were lifted to the fresh, unsullied morning sky. In the tram stations people grouped themselves by twos and threes in order to read the same newspaper. Now and then from the sidewalk across the street came the cry, "Taxi! Taxi!" Biris, too, shouted several times but without much hope. Nevertheless a cab drew up and stopped beside him.

"Which way?" asked the driver, grumbling. Biris gave him his address and the man nodded, motioning for him to get in.

"This is my last run," he said. "Tonight I have to leave. I got my order for active duty." He waited a few moments, and when he noticed that Biris did not answer, he continued.

"The earth can't stand him any more, he's never satisfied! I've done five month's conscription already this year, and all on account of him! He'll never be satisfied! All he does is grab, grab, grab. . . ."

That afternoon Biris went to the Cafenea. Bursuc was seated at a table by the window, talking. At regular intervals he closed his eyes for a fraction of a second and they seemed to disappear in a layer of fat. From time to time he burst out with his gross, vulgar laugh that made his great belly heave.

"The war is coming," said Bursuc. "I've taken shelter. I'm ordained. I've found a parish, too, near Deva. You'll go to the front and leave your bones there. I, a priest of the parish, will tend to my sheep near Deva on the estate of Patru Fruncea."

He went every day after that to the Cafenea. Bursuc was always there, seated at the table by the window, talking about Patru Fruncea, who had the estate near Deva.

"It was hard to find my man," he said. "He had to be stupid, rich, and ambitious, because only this kind knows how to play politics. Now that I've found him, I can wait. Let the war come. . . ."

Again Biris was consuming two packages of cigarettes a day. During the time when they were waiting for the battle of the Vistula to begin he started smoking heavily. There was a great anticipation concerning this battle which surely would change the course of the war. Bibicescu alone appeared to be skeptical, indifferent, hiding with difficulty his boredom and disappointment. Now he knew that Misu Weissman would not be able to build the theater very soon. His great project had been postponed again. When the three of them met for the first time after Biris's return—he did not want to go to Catalina's house

222

and he had arranged with Bibicescu to meet them at the restaurant—they talked only about the theater that Misu could not build and about the battle of the Vistula, which might annihilate the German armored divisions and save everyone. Catalina no longer called Biris Stefanescu, as she had done that summer in front of Dan. Now she called him by the name that she had always used, Petrache. She was preoccupied and melancholy, and when their eyes met she smiled wistfully. "Autumn is coming," she would say now and then. "This year I felt it coming far in advance." But the nights were still warm and each morning Bucharest found the sky the same, blue and shining. "What a catastrophe!" he heard the people exclaim in the Cafenea. "This drought! What a tragedy! If it would rain the German tanks couldn't advance. They'd bog down in the swamps of the Vistula and the great battle would begin!"

On the first evening after he returned, he had gone to see Stefan. "He was called to duty in northern Ardeal," Ioana told him. Standing in the doorway, she asked, "Do you believe war is coming? Do you think it will happen to us too?" He went to see her again two weeks later but did not find her at home. He rang the bell several times, leaning against the door frame, listening to it echo far away in the empty house. He left with a great sadness in his heart. Why he had gone to see her or what he would have said if she had been there, he did not know, but he descended the stairs feeling dejected and tired. Warsaw had fallen, the Germans had occupied more than half of Poland, and what was left was beginning to be taken over by the Soviets. Thousands of thousands of Poles sought refuge in Romania daily. Some of them had arrived in Bucharest and at times Biris saw them at the Cafenea. They would come up to the table with strained smiles on their faces, revealing in half-closed fists pieces of jewelry, perhaps a few rings; or one of them, thrusting a hand into a vest pocket and looking around carefully, would pull out a gold cigarette case.

Then one day at noon the Prime Minister was assassinated by a team of Iron Guardists. That morning Biris had a hemoptysis. Pale and giddy, unshaven, he had gone to see Catalina as soon as he had heard the news. She had just come home and had not yet had time to take off her coat. "What's the matter with you?" she asked, frightened. "Are you sick?" "I spat blood again," said Biris. He lay down on the divan, and Catalina rolled up some pillows and placed them under his head. "Do you want me to call a doctor?" she asked, stroking his forehead. "No, there's no need for a doctor. Make me some tea. . . ." He listened to her as she opened the door and went to put the water on to boil. The he heard her rummaging around in the cupboard for the teacups and the little sugar bowl. And it seemed to him that he was returning to his true time, the only time that belonged entirely to him and to him alone, a time that could not be diminished by events. He smiled, letting himself be sustained by that intimate, incommunicable happiness. Then he closed his eyes and went to sleep.

When he awoke he saw Catalina seated beside him on the divan. The lamp with the Japanese shade was burning but the light was obscured by several silk shawls. "I'm thirsty," he said, trying to raise his head. But he was dizzy and he fell back again on the pillows. Catalina gave him a drink from the cup in which the tea had cooled. He started to say something else, but she stopped him with an upraised hand. A little while later Bibicescu arrived with a doctor, who gave Biris an injection, and then the two men took him downstairs, supporting him under his arms. They went in a taxi to *strada* Macelari. "Don't say anything," whispered Biris. "Don't say anything to *coana* Viorica."

The doctor came back to see him the next day and gave him another shot. He slept all night, perspiring copiously. On awakening he felt somewhat rested and asked at once for the newspapers. In direct retaliation for the murder of the Prime Minister, several hundred Legionnaires throughout the country had been shot and their corpses displayed in public squares. In Bucharest the bodies had been thrown on vacant land near Cotroceni, and people had been invited to come there to look at them. Without saying anything to Biris, *doamna* Porumbache had gone that very afternoon. She returned in the evening, tired, disappointed.

"There were too many people," she began, taking off her dusty shoes, "and they pushed and shoved each other. I couldn't begin to see—just the feet of some of them. . . ."

Then, in the middle of October, Biris left for Moroeni. He arrived at Pietrosita shortly before sunset. As the car started to ascend through the forest around the sanatorium, he felt suddenly a lust for life such as he had never known before, a happiness without name, simply because he was alive. They advanced slowly through the firs, under the beech trees and the birches with their yellow leaves. From everywhere the fragrance of the mountains assailed them, pungent and intoxicating. In the heights they came unexpectedly upon the sanatorium. It was an immense building in the form of a semicircle with concrete balconies facing south, overlooking the forest. Biris's room was on the fifth floor in the center section. From the balcony he could see the tops of the mountains very far away, blue-violet in the dusk of evening.

That night he awakened several times. In his sleep he remembered that the nineteenth of October was approaching and he woke up, uneasy, thinking about Catalina.

He had not seen her recently at all. He had stayed in bed the whole time. *Doamna* Porumbache had threatened to throw Catalina out of the house if she came there. "That slut's ruined you. She's consumed your youth. Don't bring her around here! I'll throw her out!" "Speak more softly," he told her. "Maybe Bibicescu will come, and you know she's his girl. She's lived with him for several years. . . ." *Doamna* Porumbache gazed at him a long time and then she began to cry. With a weak, exhausted gesture she lifted her apron to her eyes. He listened to her choking sobs, her muffled sighs, and he smiled, gently closing his eyes. "He's always thinking of her, Aneto," *doamna* Porumbache exclaimed suddenly, "always thinking of that hussy, little sister! That boy you left to me, look what's become of him! He spits blood, but he can't forget that whore!" Opening his eyes, he fixed his gaze on the same damp gray spot on the ceiling. "Speak more softly," he said. "Bibicescu may come. She's Bibicescu's girl. . . ."

But Bibicescu rarely came, and then only briefly at nightfall. He was always bored, preoccupied, and he paced the room incessantly with an absent air, his hands in his pockets. "What's new?" he asked from time to time, halting in front of the window, as far as possible from the bed. "How're you feeling?" "Fine," responded Biris. "And what are you two doing?" "We're dining with *conu* Misu this evening. By the way," Bibicescu recalled suddenly, "*conu* Misu asked about you, If you need anything . . . maybe some money. . . ." "No, I don't need anything. I'm going to the sanatorium. Perhaps *coana* Viorica needs something. Ask her. . . ." Bibicescu began again to pace back and forth, looking at his watch occasionally. "But why doesn't he come himself—*conu* Misu?" "Oh, didn't I tell you?" said Bibicescu, pausing in the middle of the room and turning to look at the sick man. "He guards her all the time. He took charge of her this morning and he doesn't leave her side. He waits for her in a car at her gate, and he doesn't let her out of his sight all day."

The nineteenth of October is approaching, Biris realized. That's why he's guarding her. . . .

The nineteenth of October is approaching, he remembered as he woke up in the night, that first night, at the sanatorium. He was covered with perspiration, but he did not want to call the nurse. Using the sleeve of his pajamas he wiped the drops of sweat from his forehead. When he awoke the next day he was filled with wonder to discover, through the open window, the mountains and the forest there before his eyes, and it

225

seemed to him that he had been wandering aimlessly through a strange dream. Lying motionless he breathed deeply of the brisk mountain air and began to feel more cheerful. In his room he noticed two other beds, both empty, and he said to himself, probably they died before I came.

When he heard the bell ring for lunch Biris breathed a sigh of relief. He assembled the papers that lay on the table, stowed them in a portfolio, and stepped out again on the balcony. The sun was high in the sky. Several gray clouds floated lazily over the mountains. I'll write to him this very day, he said to himself. I'll write him that I've been forbidden to make any intellectual effort, that I have to have another operation. But he knew that the editor of *Our Beacon* had already found out about his thoracotomy of that winter when two of his ribs were removed. The man would never believe him. I'll tell him I'm tired, or perhaps that I'll write about something else. I'll write about *The Wake.* . . .

One damp rainy Sunday in February Stefan had borrowed a car from a friend and had come to see him. He had hesitated a moment on the threshold, looking with curiosity at Biris as he lay stretched out on the bed. He doesn't recognize me anymore, Biris realized, and he smiled. "You've put on weight," said Stefan. "You look well, very well." He knew how he looked. He gazed at himself many times a day in the mirror and followed closely the least change in his appearance. His cheeks seemed to have swollen suddenly, somewhat artificially, and when he laughed a roll of fat appeared beneath his chin like a crop. He also knew he had lost a great deal of hair in the past month. "You've put on weight," repeated Stefan. Then after a moment he added, "Catalina's with me. She stayed downstairs in the hall. She wants to know if you're up to seeing her too."

A few minutes later Catalina came in. "I didn't have the patience to wait. I knew you'd see me." She too seemed to have changed. She looked younger. "How beautiful it is here!" she exclaimed as she approached the balcony. A fine rain had begun to fall and the mountains were hidden in mist. Catalina looked out over the forest, inhaling slowly, deeply.

She's with Stefanescu, Biris said to himself, and he began to laugh. Stefan smiled, somewhat puzzled.

"I was thinking of Catalina," Biris explained. "I was wondering if she's met Stefanescu. . . ."

"I've met him," Catalina said, turning away from the window and

226

sitting down on the edge of the bed. "But he wasn't you. He doesn't look like you."

"The mountains are always beautiful," Stefan interposed awkwardly. "They're beautiful in the rain and mist. I spent five months in the Maramures Mountains."

Biris thrust his hand under the mattress and drew out a cheap tin cigarette case, the kind that soldiers carry.

"It'll make you sick," Catalina warned, looking into his eyes.

". . . I was on military duty there, in the Maramures Mountains," continued Stefan.

When Biris lit his cigarette he noticed that his hand trembled a little and he was annoyed. Catalina kept looking at him. She seemed not to be listening to Stefan, who continued speaking, quietly at times and then with animation, about the Maramures Mountains. She was there beside him and he could scarcely believe it was she. She looked younger. She had changed. Because of Stefanescu, surmised Biris, and he began all at once to laugh again. Stefan stopped talking and turned a bewildered gaze on him.

"Why are you laughing?"

Biris ran his hand over his face and covered his mouth in an attempt to check his laughter. Catalina took the cigarette from his fingers. Rising, she walked to the balcony and crushed it on the concrete. *I wasn't even curious to find out what happened on the nineteenth of October, it suddenly occurred to him. I don't love her anymore, I don't desire her. She can do whatever she pleases, go to bed with anyone who takes her fancy. I'm cured. She's here beside me and it's as though she doesn't exist.*

"I think he looks more like Partenie now," said Catalina unexpectedly, sitting down again on the edge of the bed.

Biris inspected Stefan. He did not appear to be troubled as he stood there in the center of the room, waiting to continue.

"He was not so handsome as Stefan, but he was more vain," she resumed, distantly, as if she were speaking to someone else, someone other than her two companions. "He was very vain. He was never reconciled to the fact his fiancée left him."

"But when did you meet him?" Biris asked her in a subdued voice. He felt the blood rush suddenly to his cheeks. He tried to slip his hand under the mattress again to pull out the cigarette case, but Catalina leaned over and caught his arm, lifting it gently and laying it across her lap. . . . *When you need that pleasure, come. I'll be waiting for you every evening. . . .*

"When did you meet him?" he repeated with restraint. "You never spoke of him to me. You never told me that you knew him."

227

Catalina regarded Biris with great tenderness. She smiled.

"I knew him well for only a few months before his death," she said in the same distant tone. "I thought we were going to have a great love for each other. He had even begun to write a play for me. . . ."

"Bibicescu claims he wrote it for him," interrupted Stefan, "that he wrote the play so Dan could act in it."

Catalina turned to look at him as though she wondered who was speaking. She shrugged her shoulders. "He wrote it for me," she repeated with tempered eloquence. "He confided it to me himself. He told me, 'I thought of you this evening when I began to write my play and I've found a beautiful title for it—one that says everything: *The Wake.*' "

"Do you know anything else?" asked Stefan eagerly, drawing a chair to the bedside and sitting down in front of her. "Do you know if he finished it?"

"No, I don't," Catalina replied. "I don't think he did. . . . I'd like to have played a role in it," she added dreamily a moment later.

"But you never said anything to me about him!" Biris exploded, and he pulled his arm away, trying again to thrust his hand under the mattress after the cigarette case. "You knew how much I was interested in Partenie and you never mentioned him to me!"

Catalina smiled, studying him. She watched as he pulled out the case, opened it and selected a cigarette, turning it nervously between his fingers. This is absurd! My hand's trembling, he said to himself. She's noticed it too, that my hand's trembling.

"We were on the point of creating a great romance," Catalina went on in the same detached voice that seemed to come from somewhere far away. "We met like two students in love, going to art galleries, to parks, in the evenings. There was snow. It snowed all the time."

"It was in January," Stefan said. "It snowed a lot that January."

"He said that he had a great need for me," continued Catalina absently. "He said that only I could reconcile him to life again. I believe he was very vain." She stopped. Suddenly she seemed tired, older. "And yet he was afraid of something. He said he had great need of me . . . that he was happy that he met me. . . ."

"I'm sorry he didn't meet Bursuc!" Biris exclaimed, with a twisted smile, raising his head from the pillow. "Not Anisie, not Stefanescu. . . . They weren't characters for him. But Bursuc he really should have met!" . . . *You platonist, you idealist, haven't you realized yet that all women are whores?* . . . "Bursuc was his kind of man!" he repeated in a thick, muffled voice. "Bursuc he ought to have met!"

Catalina looked at him again for a long time, smiling, and Stefan drew his chair closer to the bed in anticipation.

228

"Then one day it happened. . . ."

"Bursuc would have been the man for him!" Biris said again, resting his head on the pillow. He extinguished the half-smoked cigarette on the lid of the case. He felt exhausted to his very marrow and tried to close his eyes, but he quickly reopened them almost in terror, looking at the ceiling. There was no gray, smoky stain there. The ceiling was white, spotless.

"What did you say happened?" asked Stefan.

"What you know very well," Catalina explained in a quiet, indifferent tone. "They shot him. . . ."

I might write an article about *The Wake*, Biris said to himself, returning to his room and stopping in front of the mirror in order to inspect his appearance. He ran his hand over the top of his head, then he straightened his tie. I might write about the enigma of *The Wake*. I could tell what I know, what I've heard. ". . . But somehow I don't believe that my insomnia of that time . . ." Viziru had started to say once long ago. It was after his visit to Ileana. But Biris had not been listening to him. He did not know what else he had said in the long sentence, full of reservations and half-veiled revelations. "He didn't believe me," Ioana had said. "I lied for nothing."

Slowly he made his way downstairs to the dining hall. Beside his place his mail was waiting—the last issue of *Our Beacon* and a letter from Viziru. Stefan said that he would try to see him early in April, before he left for London. (There's a war on! Biris suddenly remembered. Why is he going to London?) In any case, he asked Biris to write to him if he wanted something from London. "I'll be staying there several weeks, but on my return in May, I'll come to see you at Moroeni with Ioana." He had first written "Ileana," then he had crossed out her name and had added above it, very distinctly, "Ioana."

229

7

ON THE TENTH OF MAY THERE WAS A RECEPTION AT THE ROMANIAN LEGATION in London. After the service at the Greek church Stefan went on foot to Belgrave Square with several of his colleagues from the Commission. A half-hour earlier he had learned that the Germans had launched an air attack over France, Belgium, and the Netherlands. Now, as the men crossed Hyde Park, Stefan listened without a word to the comments of his companions. The Minister was receiving the guests in the entrance to the salon and he did not appear to be preoccupied. Stefan saw the military attaché with a group of people and he started in that direction, but as he made his way across the salon he caught sight of Antim and Vadastra standing near the window with glasses of champagne in their hands. They seemed very solemn.

One afternoon several weeks after he had left the clinic, Stefan had gone to visit Antim and had noticed Vadastra hurrying down the steps. Although they had not met for about three years, Stefan recognized the lawyer by his determined walk and the way he held his head. Vadastra passed by without seeing him.

"How did you meet him?" Stefan asked Antim.

"On the train, just as I met you. I was pleased that he knew Latin. It's a rare thing today to know Latin." And then Antim had glanced at Stefan mysteriously with a smile of complicity. "For many people it's still a secret," he added, "but you're a part of our house now, so I can tell you. You know that I have a niece, Irina, the daughter of my sister Gherghina, whom you met here one day. This Irina is a strange girl. She spends most of her time at the church and at homes for the aged. She's even had the idea of entering a convent, but her mother wouldn't allow it. She's her only child. What's to be done? The rest of us in the family are so sinful that God has taken pity on us and sent us a pure soul

230

to pray for our transgressions." He paused in his monologue to chuckle quietly.

"To make a long story short, one day Vadastra saw her, and he was infatuated. It's true the girl has a dowry and she's rather pretty, but of all the young men she has met he's the only one she's liked. She says he's an unhappy person who needs her help. And since her mother liked him too, because he's a boy of culture with a good position, I believe things are just about arranged. As you see, it's a marriage of love and sacrifice. . . ."

Stefan made his way through the crowd, smiling at the two men from across the room. Vadastra waited motionless, his glass in his hand, standing rigid and solemn with a vacant stare. When Stefan approached them Antim tried to turn away, pretending not to see him.

"When did you arrive?" asked Stefan.

Antim extended his hand coolly. "The day before yesterday. May I present *domnul* Vasilescu-Vadastra? A lawyer," he added.

"We've known each other on sight for a long time," said Stefan.

Vadastra adjusted his black monocle and inspected him. "I believe so," he said and turned his head to look at the door. A group of British officers were coming in at that moment.

"And . . . the matter that you were concerned about. . .?" inquired Stefan, speaking more softly.

Antim did not seem to have heard him. He too turned his attention to the door. "They're officers from the General Staff," Vadastra whispered. "The other man, the one with the gray hair, is the military attaché. I recognized him by the way he saluted."

A few days before he left for England, Ioana had entered his study. "Professor Antim has come. He wants to talk with you. He says it's something important and urgent."

It was the first time the professor had come to his house. "I'm in a hurry," he said, sitting down wearily on a chair. "I've come to ask you a great—a very great— favor. Don't say no. Only you can do it."

He was breathing with difficulty and seemed to be anxious. "I told you a long time ago about the secret, so to speak, of my life," he began confidentially. "I told you that I was waiting for a certain masterpiece to complete my collection. I didn't tell you, however, what kind of masterpiece I meant. I didn't even give you a hint, and I've done the same with all my friends. I was forced to proceed in this way in order not to be discovered. Everyone thinks it's a painting from the French impressionists school or the work of a great Romanian painter because they know my preferences. The truth is something else and it is tremendous!

231

The pearl that I've been waiting for, that I acquired a few weeks ago, is a Rubens! A genuine Rubens and not a studio copy, as the heirs who sold it to me believe. Because—I forgot to tell you—I've been lying in wait for this canvas for twenty-eight years. It belonged to an acquaintance of mine, who inherited it through his wife's family from an Austrian baron. For a hundred years this painting has been considered a copy or the work of a pupil. I became convinced a long time ago that it is a true Rubens. I studied the problem for years without anyone's being aware of it. I became the greatest Rubens expert in eastern Europe and I didn't even dare to reveal my knowledge to anyone. I'm very proud of this skillful piece of deceit perpetrated over a period of twenty-eight years!"

He broke into a brief sardonic laugh and his entire face became suddenly animated. His fatigue seemed to have vanished, as if by magic.

"Finally, to continue," he went on, "on March 9 I laid my hands on the painting, paying a nominal price for it. And from this point on another secret begins. I'm asking you to keep this to yourself. You'll understand why immediately. I don't want a rumor to be spread in Romania that I own a genuine Rubens. I'm afraid I wouldn't be able to keep it. The Palace would ask for it, or perhaps I should even feel obligated to surrender it to a museum for a ridiculous sum—because I consider myself a patriot too! On the other hand I have no use for a Rubens. It's not for me. It doesn't fit in any of the categories of my collection. I want to sell it, not here but abroad. A true Rubens will sell for a fantastic sum today—tens of thousands of pounds sterling. Do you realize what that means in our poor lei? What it means for the future of my collection? But in order to sell it I have to get the endorsement of a European art expert. I've heard of a renowned English authority at the National Gallery. . . . And now I come to the great favor I'm asking you to do for me. . . ."

He was silent a moment, looking at Stefan with a pleading glance that was full of significance. "I've heard that you're leaving for London. Is that so?"

"I'm going next week. We're negotiating a loan. But I don't see how I can be of use to you," Stefan hastened to add in embarrassment.

"Wait a bit," interrupted Antim. "I'll tell you directly. I can't send the painting to London and I can't take it with me now in wartime. Besides I don't have a British visa yet. I'm expecting it however from one day to the next. But the delicate thing is transporting the painting. And here's what I thought. You'll have diplomatic courier privileges because you're going on an official mission. I'll wrap up the picture very carefully and you can slip it into one of your valises. And when I arrive in London I'll manage the rest. . . . I have my means. . . ."

232

"I'm terribly sorry, Professor Antim . . ." Stefan began.

Antim looked at him, surprised and fearful, and stopped him with a motion of his hand. "You didn't understand me correctly. I didn't say you yourself necessarily will have to carry it. You could put it in the diplomatic courier portfolio. I believe this is possible. And of course I'll see that the one who carries it is properly rewarded."

Embarrassed, Stefan was silent for some moments, then he said softly, "Impossible! At least for me. It's impossible for me to do it."

"But why, may I ask?" demanded Antim, irritated.

"I'm an employee of the Ministry of National Economy. A valuable painting represents a state asset. What you're asking me to do is equivalent to supporting a smuggling operation on a grand scale."

"*Ei!* Just a minute!" Antim cried, shocked. "You know well that it's not smuggling. I'm just asking you to do me a friendly favor, something that civilized people are accustomed to doing for one another."

"It's impossible for me!" said Stefan, smiling.

Antim began to rub his hands nervously. "I came to you because things are happening so fast. They've landed now in Norway. This very day the fighting on the French front may start. I have to go and return while there's still time. Right now is the ideal moment. You have your mission, I my visa promised. . . ."

He was silent again, looking at Stefan long and inquisitively. "I'm sorry that I bothered you," he said, suddenly rising. When he reached the door he added, "However, I'm counting on you to be discreet."

Vadastra adjusted his black monocle again and turned to Antim. "That woman who just came in is the greatest American woman correspondent. I know her."

"I'm glad you've arrived," Stefan tried once more. "And I suppose that the matter you were concerned about . . ."

"Everything's been arranged," Antim said without looking at him.

"It was arranged under the most favorable conditions possible," said Vadastra, suddenly raising his head. "Thanks to connections which I had with the Ministry of Foreign Affairs. . . ."

But at that moment someone in the front row gave a signal and all the conversations were abruptly hushed. Stefan heard the Minister say "Long live the King!"

"Long live the King!" the audience repeated in a chorus.

". . . Thanks to connections I have with important personages in the Ministry of Foreign Affairs," continued Vadastra, "I managed this *tour de force* in less than two weeks. Both of us were sent to London on official business!"

He looked at Stefan in triumph, then solemnly sipped again from his champagne glass.

"It's true," Antim said, and a smile of pride lighted his face for a moment. "We're here on an official assignment!"

"I was even offered a diplomatic courier portfolio," Vadastra continued, "but I refused it. What would I need of a diplomatic courier? It would have been imprudent. Too great a responsibility. But please don't ask me any more, because I should not be able to answer. All I can reveal is that it is a question of a mission of the greatest delicacy. I shall ask you, even, to be very discreet. I informed the Minister in a long secret audience on the very evening of our arrival. But I haven't yet received detailed orders. I can't tell you anything else."

Everyone began to move toward the dining room.

"A hundred German planes have been shot down already," Stefan heard someone near him say. "It was announced just now on the radio. . . ."

"Where are you staying?" inquired Stefan.

"For the present at the Rembrandt Hotel, next to the Legation," said Vadastra, speaking more quietly. "But this is only temporary. We have big plans. I can't tell you any more . . . you understand why. . . ."

The very next day Stefan went to see them. At the Rembrandt Hotel he was told that they had left without giving any address.

"Besides, they're no longer in London," the military attaché told him in the course of the week, smiling significantly. "They're on a mission."

The economic agreement was signed at the height of the campaign in France, but the members of the Commission could still take the plane to Paris and return to Bucharest. However, the expert who had to check the first shipments was delayed, and Stefan was directed to take his place. For the next several weeks he was always on the move, although he did not forget to inquire about Vadastra at the Legation when he was in London. Once the military attaché said, with the same mysterious smile, "I saw him the day before yesterday, but I don't think he stayed more than a few hours. They aren't living in London."

In the middle of June the Ministry of the Economy announced that the expert would not be coming. Stefan was given instructions to expedite the shipments of trucks and medical supplies, the only goods that had any chance of reaching Constanta. For ten days he remained in Birmingham. On his return to London he was summoned to the office of the Minister.

"I have good news for you. You're not going back to Romania. You're staying with us. You've been appointed Economic Secretary in place of Magheru, who was transferred to Berne."

He saw Stefan hesitate and he added, "I know what you're thinking, but

234

don't worry. We'll bring your family here by plane. We'll bring them in a few days by way of Ankara. Telegraph home and tell them to get ready for the trip."

"Do you know anything about Vadastra and Professor Antim?" Stefan asked suddenly.

The Minister did not reply immediately. He just gazed at Stefan and played with a letter opener, turning slowly in his chair. Finally he inquired, "Do you know them well?"

"Just Professor Antim. He's an art collector. And I know that they've come here on a mission."

"I can't quite figure them out. They both came with official passports. At first they received a sum of money also, but I've had no precise directive on their assignment. Vadastra led me to understand that he was sent by the Secret Service, but I find this hard to believe. He gives the impression of being a fanatic. But in any case, be careful. . . ."

After that Stefan went every day to the Legation. Sometimes when he saw the military attaché he was told, "There's no news. They haven't come back." And the man would smile mysteriously, so that Stefan wondered if he were concealing a secret or simply joking.

"Have a little more patience," the Minister advised. "There are some difficulties. The flight schedules have not yet been fully reestablished. They can still find seats to Cairo, but between Cairo and Barcelona, and especially on the Lisbon-London planes, it's impossible at the moment to get places."

One morning he bought a paper and when he opened it he stopped, aghast, in the middle of the sidewalk. In an ultimatum the Soviets demanded the surrender of Bessarabia. Someone grasped his arm and Stefan raised his eyes from the paper, startled. It was Vadastra. He seemed unusually excited. He brought his face close to Stefan's and asked, "Have you heard?" Raising his voice he continued, "Tomorrow it will be our turn—all of us! That's what will happen if no one takes care of us, if we're abandoned in the middle of the war without the most elementary protection!"

"But what's happened?"

"Last night they arrested Professor Antim! But I'm going to raise a row!" he added, shaking his forefinger in a threatening gesture. "I'll telegraph the Prime Minister. I'll protest through the newspapers! I'll demand the recall of the Minister if he doesn't intervene immediately on behalf of my uncle!"

"This is wartime," said Stefan. "They may have made a mistake. Perhaps this very hour the professor has already been released. . . ."

"Anyway, I'm going to protest!" Vadastra interrupted. "We came here on official business. I'll ask the Minister to protest in the most energetic terms!"

"I don't know if he'll receive you," remarked Stefan. "I don't even know if he's at the Legation. After the Soviet ultimatum . . ."

"What ultimatum?" Vadastra asked with a scowl.

"They demand that we withdraw from Bessarabia in three days."

"Ah!" said Vadastra. "It was expected. I foresaw this a long time ago." He was silent, rubbing his hands in some embarrassment. "Do you think he'll be released?" he asked after a long pause and in a more subdued voice. "Do you believe it's just a mistake?"

"Probably. Speak with the Consul General. He'll intervene personally. But," he added, "do you know of any motive for his arrest?"

"On my word of honor, I have no idea," said Vadastra solemnly. "We arrived in London several days ago and we've been away all the time."

"Perhaps that's the very reason. . . ."

"But why?" Vadastra was indignant. "Just because England is at war are we then no longer free to travel around on the trains? We haven't been on a joyride! We've been on business!"

After looking around carefully he approached Stefan again and took his arm. "I know you're in on the secret too," he said very quietly. "It's a question of our Rubens. We've been looking for an expert. The one from the National Gallery is in America. And we have to be very careful, very discreet, as you understand. Fortunately," he added, wiping his forehead, "the matter is about to be concluded. The painting was authenticated and we've also found a purchaser. We won't receive the sum that we had anticipated at first, but we made an excellent bargain anyway. The problem now is what to do with the money? That's why we haven't yet closed the sale. We're waiting. We have no reason to hurry. The longer we wait, the higher the prices of classic paintings will climb. . . ."

> Stefan did not manage to listen until the end. Suddenly he had remembered one of his former classmates from the University, Chelariu, who was now a professor at Chisinau in Bessarabia. His wife, Stefan had learned the year before, had given birth to another baby, their fifth. Chelariu had bought a small vineyard near Chisinau and had set up a part of his library there. He had told Stefan once that he was still occupied with the same subject he had selected for his degree thesis, old Romanian law. . . . In three days, specified the ultimatum, the troops will withdraw from Bessarabia, leaving all the military, industrial, and administrative facilities intact. . . .

". . . And now," Vadastra continued, "I'll give you some good news. I received it a long time ago, but I've kept it secret. I'm going to become a father very soon."

"My congratulations!"

"Thank you. You know, I was informed long ago about this happy event. I wanted to wait and surprise you, all of you, the Romanians in London. But now that I don't have any chance of leaving soon, I've decided I can tell

236

you. I hope it will be a boy," he added, frowning slightly.

"We'll cede it," the people around Stefan were saying. "What else can we do? We're a little country." Chelariu was working on old Romanian law. Romanian law. . . . "I don't think they'll hold him long," someone said. It's just a mistake. They'll let him go. . . ." "But what about your wife?" Stefan was asked. He shrugged his shoulders. The airline service had not yet been restored. Ioana had telegraphed him in the ministry code: "Impossible through Cairo. They are trying to get seats through Lisbon." "I went to the Foreign Office," the Minister said. "They promised to reserve places on the plane from Lisbon." Then, the next evening, Stefan was summoned by the Minister. He was pale but appeared to be calm. "I've been recalled," he said. "I was expecting it. Of course I won't return. I believe the democracies will win; there's no question about it!"

"This evening Antim was released," he heard someone say. "It was a mistake." "They've settled in London," announced the military attaché. He was no longer smiling. He seemed to be worried. "Transylvania will be next. We'll cede it too. We've held fifteen divisions on the frontier for almost two years—all for nothing." "You who are interested in contemporary history . . ." said the Minister. . . .

"With you it's different," Biris had said. "You're married, and you're probably happy in your marriage. *History* doesn't interest you. You'd like everything to stand still, to become fixed just as it is now, because you're happy, you're at peace, and you wish time would stop flowing."

"You who are interested in contemporary history," the Minister said, "read this." It was a little notice in a paper, underlined in red, and it announced that the wolves in the Zoological Gardens had begun to dig holes. They were digging their burrows very deep in the earth. "They're preparing too for the siege!" Then the Minister asked Stefan, "What's happening at the Legation? How do you get along with your new chief, the chargé d'affaires?"

"I've asked him to intercede again at the Foreign Office to get seats for my wife. . . ."

". . . For you, of course, all these things are of no interest. You're married, and probably happily married. . . ." "I am happy," he had said. "But I don't believe that's the reason. I don't think it's simply because I'm happily married that I try not to let myself be confiscated by history, that I try to emerge from Time. . . ." "What do you mean?" Biris interrupted him. "What does this monstrous proposition mean: to emerge from Time?" "Once when I was little, I rode home in a wagon full of hay. This happened at our vineyard near Ramnicul Sarat. I had gone to sleep and suddenly I woke up alone in the wagonload of hay, and there

237

above me were only the stars. Only the stars. And it seemed as though everything had stopped there, in its place. It seemed as though time no longer flowed. Only the stars were there." "All this means nothing," Biris said. "Naive, infantile emotions with absolutely no significance. . . ." This conversation had taken place long ago on *strada* Macelari. They were not yet friends, they didn't call each other *tu*. That was before Biris had found out about the room *Sambo*. Otherwise he would have said, "You're trying to recover an Edenic, infantile state. *To emerge from time.* This for you means the return to the hay ride of your childhood, or to the forbidden room on the second floor." "I've told you this," Stefan continued, "to prove to you that even when I was a child I *knew* that time can stand still. It wasn't necessary for me to wait until I was happily married to discover this fact." "Stefan, what's happened to you?" demanded Biris, wondering, last year. "What's happening to you and Ileana? You're a lucky man. You had the great good fortune of loving your wife. . . ." "I still love her," Stefan said. "I love my wife very much. . . ."

"We could come through Switzerland," Ioana wired. "Hold the places on the plane from Lisbon." "I'm deeply sorry, my dear Viziru," said the chargé d'affaires, "but you must have patience. Tomorrow I'll go to the Foreign Office again." "We're coming via Switzerland," Ioana telegraphed again.

"I'm going to Switzerland," Ileana had said that morning in March. "The Valkyrie has invited me to Lausanne. She's inherited the estate of a very wealthy aunt. I'm going to live with her. Anyway, I've heard that you're leaving for London." "Just for a few weeks to conclude some economic agreements. I'll be back by the end of May at the latest. You won't leave before I come back, will you? Please. . . . I want very much for you not to leave. . . ." Ileana looked at him for a long time and then she smiled. "It's impossible for me to understand you," she said. "Sometimes I seem to be dreaming, talking with you in a dream." She was dressed in a gray tailored suit and she wore a little bunch of violets in the buttonhole.

The twenty-third of March—he remembered the day very well. It was cloudy and a cold wind was blowing. Spring seemed far away. "*Drôle de guerre*," Ileana had said, surprising Stefan in a furtive glance at the news kiosk, where a boy, arriving on a bicycle, had just unloaded the afternoon edition. "Nothing happens." "I'd like to ask you something," he began finally, as they neared her home. "Probably you've guessed already what I want to ask you." Ileana had released his arm suddenly and turned her head. "Stefan, please!" She spoke in a voice that was unexpectedly harsh, and she regarded him coldly, severely. "Please, if you want us still to be friends. . . ."

238

One day Antim entered Viziru's office meekly, carrying a portfolio under his arm. In the three months since Stefan had last seen him he had aged incredibly. He appeared to be terrified.

"I'm very sorry that I didn't come before," he said, closing the door carefully. "I have complete confidence in you. You're an honest man." He looked around him suspiciously as if he were afraid that someone might hear him.

"I was glad to learn that the police didn't hold you," commented Stefan. "Probably it was a routine error."

Antim sat down in the armchair in front of the desk. "An error!" he cried, searching for his handkerchief in order to wipe his forehead. "Do you think the English ever arrest people by error? They don't exactly make a game of it! I was arrested for espionage! They never said it openly, but they intimated it. I was fortunate enough to be examined by a fine man who had an appreciation of French culture and who also had a great weakness for old things. . . . There was an informer."

He took the portfolio, which he had placed on the desk, and laid it in his lap. "I wonder who would be interested in denouncing me as a spy," he added, raising his eyes suddenly as if he wished to surprise some facial movement of Stefan's. "A spy!" he repeated, and he lowered his voice meaningfully.

Probably that's the reason why they don't find space on the plane from Lisbon. We're all under suspicion. Romania has renounced the Allies and gone over to the side of the Axis. From now on it's Hitler who guarantees us. That's why we abandoned Bessarabia. . . . Chelariu studied old Romanian law. Romanian law. . . .

"Don't you have anything to say?" demanded Antim.

"I'm waiting for my wife," Stefan said promptly, spiritedly. "For a month she's been expecting to get places on the plane from Lisbon."

"You can't get them anymore," said Antim. "We wanted to leave a long while ago too, but we can't find seats. Or they won't give them to us. We're caught here like mice in a trap. Just like mice," he added, dropping his voice again.

He looked around, apparently searching for something. "I really wonder who might have had an interest in denouncing me. The inspector who interrogated me . . ."

At that moment they heard the air raid alert and Antim sprang to his feet. "Do you have a good strong shelter in the Legation?" he asked, holding the portfolio tightly under his arm.

"There is one, but it's not too strong. Although so far we haven't gone down very often when the alert sounds. You've noticed that there hasn't been so much bombing."

"You shouldn't play with fate!" exclaimed Antim. "Where did you say the shelter is? Or maybe you'll go down with me . . ."

239

"I suggest we wait a little longer, *domnule* Professor," Stefan proposed. "Perhaps the planes won't come our way. If we hear the guns in Hyde Park we'll go down."

Antim sat down again, but he did not seem to be entirely reassured.

"*Domnul* Vadastra told me that you found a buyer for the painting. I was glad to hear it."

"When did you see Spiridon?" asked Antim, his astonishment not unmixed with fear.

"On the day you were arrested he came to the Legation to protest."

"Hmm. . . . So he's a busybody too. . . ." Antim paused, listening attentively. "Was I just imagining it or did I hear the guns?"

"You just imagined it. But if you have a premonition you'd better go down to the shelter. In these matters each one ought to follow his own intuition."

Antim took out his handkerchief again and wiped his forehead. "I've been nervous for some time," he said. "I don't recognize myself anymore."

"Why don't you leave London? Go somewhere in the country. There you wouldn't have anything to worry about."

"I've been considering that, but I'm afraid," replied Antim, speaking more softly. "I'm afraid to bury myself in a village with this treasure of mine." He pointed to the portfolio. "And I don't want to sell it yet. What would I do with the money? I can't keep it at my house and if I put it in the bank, there it will stay! Any time now they'll be freezing the accounts. Everyone says so. At least here in London I feel more secure. . . . I might put the picture in a bank, in a safe," he added after a short pause, "but suppose they don't want to give it back? It's better to carry it with me."

They began to hear the batteries in Hyde Park quite distinctly. Antim turned pale and got to his feet. "See how your hunches play tricks on you!" he said in a whisper. "Let's hurry. . . ."

Stefan went downstairs with him to show him the way to the shelter. "Don't tell Spiridon I saw you! Pretend you know nothing about me."

He was silent, absorbed in thought. They no longer heard the guns.

"That boy's a bit crazy," added Antim. "I don't know what's got into his head. He says he's had premonitions of disaster, that we'll leave our bones here. He says we ought to make our wills."

"As a lawyer he thinks of every possibility," said Stefan.

Antim halted abruptly in the middle of the stairway. "But I won't do it! It would be a bad omen!"

I should have asked him about *doamna* Zissu, Stefan remembered after he had parted from Antim.

"If you wish we can talk about something else," Ileana had said. "Several years ago when I first met you, you spoke to me about Vasilescu-Vadastra and his great love, *doamna* Zissu." "I don't know that she was his great love," he interrupted. "I don't know who she was. . . ." "Tell me about her, or about Vadastra," continued Ileana. "It doesn't matter what you tell me, but if you want us to remain friends don't ask me anything!" She had cried out almost in desperation, "Don't ask me anything!" He could see again the glimmer of fear in her eyes, in her pleading glance.

I should have asked him about *doamna* Zissu.

A few days later they met in front of the Legation. "I came especially to get you," said Antim. "We'd like you to give us the pleasure of dining with us this evening. I hope we won't have an alert." He looked at the sky. "It seems to be getting cloudy. . . . A bad sign." He seemed to have aged even more since Stefan had last seen him. His vandyke had grown out unrestrained, his cheeks were gaunt, his hair was white. He was clutching the portfolio tightly under his arm. "But what's the matter?" he asked Stefan. "Have you received bad news from home?"

"Yes and no. My wife can't come now. They can't get seats on the plane for several months. However I wasn't thinking of that. Perhaps it's better for her to stay in Romania, at least for the time being. But I've been thinking of what's happening to us, to Romania. You've heard that Hitler has summoned us to an urgent meeting in Vienna."

"Unfortunately for us," murmured Antim. "When you're a little country, what else can you expect?"

They walked along in silence. Stefan stopped to buy the final editions of the evening papers and he gradually mastered his uneasiness as he glanced over them. "Nothing serious for the moment, thank God!" he whispered, relieved.

He had arrived at nightfall in that hamlet lost in the mountains. The soldier had taken his pack and led him toward the outskirts of the village. "It's a good home," he said. "Well-to-do people . . ." The rain had intensified by the time they reached the yard. A woman came out on the porch to meet them with a rushlight in her hand. "Are you the lieutenant?" she asked. "Welcome! If you please, come in! Please!" The table was ready and they had set a place for him too. The husband took Stefan's hand in both of his and held it fast for some time, repeating several times, "We thank you for this honor. Thank you for coming to us. . . ." Then showing him to his children he had stated solemnly, "Do you see him? The good lieutenant has come here to protect us. He is a leader in the Romanian Army. He defends our frontiers."

241

"But you *will* eat with us this evening?" Antim broke the silence suddenly. "I don't know what the meal will be because Spiridon has planned it. He understands English and takes care of the housekeeping." He tried to laugh but the mirth was forced and it faded quickly from his face.

"We live in Hampstead," he continued. "I don't know very well how to pronounce it. Spiridon found the apartment, too. The owner has gone to New Zealand and we rented it very cheaply. . . ."

In the Underground Antim was silent almost the whole time, clasping his portfolio tightly on his lap. He seemed plunged in deep thought. Stefan unfolded the newspapers. "We've been summoned to an urgent meeting in Vienna. . . ."

He had come to the edge of a village once in a fall of fine dry snow. A group of peasants was coming down the side of the mountain and he had stopped to wait for them. "Good evening," he said. The men approached and one after another they raised their fur caps. "What's the news, officer?" one of them asked. "What do you hear about the war?" "It's still going on," responded Stefan. "That's the way war is," said an older man. "It goes on and on. It's God's punishment. . . ." "Perhaps God will help us to escape," Stefan said. "Everything comes from God," the old man added. "It is all as he wills. . . ." He was silent.

They stood there in the snow without speaking, gazing at Stefan, occasionally pulling their *saricas** up around their shoulders. "And you," Stefan began again, "are you from the mountain?" "From the mountain," said one of them. "From Saraceni." "And how is it there?" "Fine," the old man said. "It's fine. Soldiers are there too. They're everywhere. But if there's a war, that's the way it should be." Then he was silent again, watching Stefan. "But what do you have to say? How do you adjust yourselves to the hardships?" The old man spat to one side and pulled his cap down on his forehead. The snow had begun to fall more thickly. "We have enough troubles," the man said. "The devil take them! Since our sons have gone to the army only a few are left, and all of us old, to do the work! But the times are like that. . . ." "So they are," spoke up another man. "These are hard times." "Hard," the old man echoed. Stefan, troubled, looked at him. "And besides that?" he asked. "What else do you hear?" "They say there will be war in our land too," one man replied, and the old man said, "As God Wills. . . ." "But you, what do you say?" "What can a man say? As God wills!" "But if war comes?" insisted Stefan. "If it comes there's nothing to be done. All men go to war. It's a man's destiny. When there's war, he must fight."

Stefan said nothing. Night had fallen. Lighted rush-candles ap-

*Peasant's fluffy woolen mantle.

242

peared at several of the windows. "Am I not perhaps delaying you? It's late and maybe you have far to walk. . . ." "Ah!" said the old man, "we were just resting a moment. As for walking we've just now hit the road. We'll be walking all night. . . ." "Don't let me detain you longer then . . . A safe journey!" "God help you!" said the old man, raising his cap.

They departed, each one close upon the heels of the man ahead, silent, swallowed quickly by the darkness. A cold, biting wind began to blow. It sent the snow swirling high in the air. Stefan stood there following them with his eyes as they vanished in the obscurity. He was filled with a great calm that rose spontaneously from the depths of his being, impelling him to silence. Nothing can ever happen to them. They are from the mountains and they are like the mountains. They're men from another age. Everything will continue to be as it is now, unchanged, undisturbed—the people, the rocks, the seasons. When they die other men like them will be born in the mountains. These are men to whom nothing will ever happen.

"I was called to active duty too, last year, for about five months," Stefan began, seeing that Antim was staring at him impatiently, blinking frequently as if he were trying to stay awake. "I was in the Maramures Mountains."

"I'm rather tired," said Antim, "and I'm tired because I don't sleep well. When I hear the alert I go to the shelter. The day before yesterday I didn't close my eyes all night."

"And even so, as you've seen, strictly speaking they aren't air raids. They're only observation flights. You don't have to pay any attention to them. Maybe the Germans are doing this just to keep us from sleeping."

"But how do you know that someday they won't give us a massive bombing as they did Rotterdam?" the professor inquired.

"It's not the same thing at all. London is well defended," replied Stefan, and again Antim was silent, lost in thought.

"Talk to me about something else. . . . Tell me about Vadastra and his love, *doamna* Zissu. . . ."

It was dark when they came out of the subway station. Nothing was visible but the pale flashes of the traffic signals.

"I'd like to ask you something." Stefan broke the silence suddenly. "Maybe it will seem rather strange . . ."

"Speak," said Antim, seeing that his companion hesitated.

"You'll think my curiosity is ridiculous," commenced Stefan with a sheepish smile.

243

Antim halted and looked at him for a long time knowingly. "I rather suspect what it may be," he said. "You want to ask me about Spiridon."

"Something to do with him," Stefan began briskly. "We lived in the same hotel and my room was next door to his. I often heard him talking with his friends. And he spoke all the time about a certain *doamna* Zissu, an acquaintance of his from early youth. I wanted to ask you if you know anything about this *doamna* Zissu, if he's ever spoken to you about her."

Antim continued to stare at Stefan, perplexed. "She may have been a sweetheart of his when he was young."

"But has he never spoken about her?" insisted Stefan. "Hasn't he ever mentioned her name?"

Shaking his head Antim replied, "I don't remember that I ever heard it. . . . I thought you were going to ask me something else," he added after a pause. "But we'll talk about it another time. Now, we just cross the street and we're there. . . ."

They found Spiridon setting the table. He had removed his jacket and had put on the coat to his lounging pajamas. When he saw Stefan come in he stopped in surprise. He searched hastily for his black monocle and set it in place. Then, forcing a smile, he went to shake the visitor's hand.

"I met him on the street by chance," declared Antim, embarrassed, "and I invited him to eat with us."

"We should like it very much," said Spiridon. "Let me set a place for you. This evening we're having canned smoked tongue and fried potatoes." He hurried out of the room. Stefan looked at Antim in astonishment.

"Forgive me, please," the professor whispered. "I wanted to have you with me. Maybe we can get him to talk. I have the impression that he's somewhat mad. . . ."

Vadastra returned from the kitchen with a plate, some silverware, and a clean napkin. "What marvelous organization!" he cried. "You find everything you want. In England you have no need of servants." Arranging Stefan's place at the table, he stepped back and surveyed it from a distance, his eye slightly closed. Then he picked up the entire place setting and moved it to the other side of the table.

"Do you speak English well?" Vadastra asked Stefan. "I speak it perfectly. Each day I get compliments from everyone. Only *nenea** Iancu doesn't believe me."

He looked at Antim with an affectionate grin, which the professor re-

* Uncle (approximately).

turned, shaking his head. "Of course I believe you," he said. "I believe you."

A few moments later Antim rose from his chair in haste and headed for the bathroom with the portfolio under his arm. "Excuse me a minute," he said in embarrassment. "Old age, you know. . . ."

As soon as the door was shut, Vadastra approached Stefan and took his arm, drawing him to the other side of the room. "You've noticed too, I think, how much the professor has changed," he said very softly. "He's afraid of death. He talks constantly about death. He says that we'll leave our bones here. Is he losing his mind, perhaps? And then, what will we do with the painting? You saw him, he even carries it with him to the bathroom. I could take offense at that. Can it be he's afraid I'll steal it? But who brought him to London? Who got an official passport for him? If it hadn't been for me with my connections . . ."

"I'm sure you were talking about me," said Antim, who had returned to the dining room unobserved. He looked at each of them suspiciously.

"*Domnul* Vadastra was telling me about his connections with the Ministry of Foreign Affairs," remarked Stefan.

Spiridon went back to the table and reset the places absent-mindedly. He did not appear to be listening to what the others were saying. He addressed Antim, "Shall we fry some potatoes or just get along with the smoked tongue? We have a bottle of beer too."

The professor looked eloquently at Stefan. "I say to fry some potatoes too. Smoked tongue by itself isn't enough. Maybe *domnul* Viziru's hungry."

"On the contrary," said Stefan, distressed. "I eat almost nothing in the evening."

"That's better for your health," Vadastra declared. "So, we won't fry any potatoes?"

Antim sat down at the table without answering. A few moments later he rested his head on his hands and began to doze. Vadastra went about on tiptoe, bringing the food from the kitchen. He carried one article at a time: the plate of smoked tongue first, then the bread, then the beer. Whenever he passed Stefan he put his finger to his lips and pointed to Antim. "Shhh!" he hissed very quietly. "Shhh!"

The professor had fallen asleep. But he shifted his position in order to cradle his head more comfortably on the table, and his portfolio slipped to the floor. He woke up, frightened. "Has it stopped?" he asked. "Have they sounded the 'all clear'?"

The last words were spoken sleepily in English, to Stefan's surprise. He smiled, and just at that moment Vadastra came in with three glasses. "Were you frightened, *domnule* Professor?" he asked sarcastically.

Antim looked around in chagrin, rubbing his temple with his left hand. The other hand had already reached for the portfolio, which rested again in his lap.

"There hasn't been any alert tonight," continued Vadastra, setting the

245

glasses on the table. "If there had been we would have awakened you, don't worry."

"I don't believe I was asleep very long," said Antim, looking for his watch. He studied it carefully, with great feeling. "Not quite nine twenty-five," he said sadly. "How will this night ever pass?"

Turning to Stefan he added, "Time seems to stand still as soon as it gets dark. The nights are becoming increasingly longer, and the alerts make them seem endless to me."

"Come to the table," Spiridon announced solemnly, looking once more at the places, the platter of smoked tongue, the bottle of beer and the glasses. "Dinner is ready!" He spoke in English, pronouncing each word slowly. "The beer is fresh! The tongue is good!"

"Too bad you didn't fry some potatoes!" said Antim ruefully as he helped himself to the meat. "We're going to be hungry later. . . . Hold it!" he exclaimed after a short silence. "I thought I heard something!"

Everyone listened attentively. Vadastra took off his monocle and bent his head as if he expected to hear a noice coming from under the ground. "Nothing!" he declared, replacing his glass.

"Praise God!" said Antim, and he crossed himself. He started to eat, intent, absorbed in himself. Insofar as it was possible Stefan refrained from looking at him. He no longer recognized in the professor the man he once knew.

Vadastra poured the beer and lifted his drink ceremoniously. "Let's toast the health of our guest," he proposed, nodding to Stefan. They touched glasses without speaking. Stefan put his to his lips but set it down again quickly. The beer was warm, flat.

"Let us also drink to the independence, integrity, and autonomy of our country, Romania," Vadastra intoned solemnly, "and to the Romanian woman, or better, to the Romanian wife. To our wives, I mean, to our wives who are also mothers!"

He emptied his glass. Stefan tried to do the same but he could swallow only a small amount of the beer, and he set it down on the table again. He began to eat without looking up. Antim stared at him.

"What's wrong? Why don't you drink?" he asked suspiciously. "Have you noticed some unusual taste in your beer?" Antim had not yet touched his.

"It's the best beer in the neighborhood," said Spiridon. "It's guaranteed. Only I opened the bottle a little too long ago. You know," he turned to Stefan, "in this house where you find everything you need I still haven't found that simple tool for opening bottles of beer."

"Let the man speak!" Antim cut in. "What's wrong with the beer? Does it have an odd taste?"

"It's very good," answered Stefan. "It's just that I was not especially thirsty. But since we toasted the health of our wives and our children's mothers, I'll drink it to the bottom of the glass!" And so he did, but with considerable effort and trepidation because Antim was looking at him with fear in his face. Suddenly Vadastra got up from the table and went to the kitchen.

"Take a taste of mine, too, please," the professor implored, and without waiting for a reply he poured a little of his beer into the guest's empty glass. Stefan swallowed it with a smile.

"Don't leave soon," whispered Antim, bringing his head close to Stefan's. "Stay longer and talk with Spiridon. Maybe he'll tell you something about *doamna* Zissu. You can stay as long as you want. We have an extra bed for guests."

The alert surprised them far from home and they took refuge in the first shelter they could find. There was no one in it. Antim took out his watch, looked at it closely and sighed, preparing to wait.

"Do you think it will last long?" he asked presently. "Can we still catch the train?"

At that moment two old men entered the shelter, saying politely, "Good evening."

"Let's not talk any more, so they won't notice we're foreigners," whispered Vadastra.

Antim nodded his head, and leaning against the wall, he began to doze. Soon the firing of the antiaircraft artillery began and he awoke with a start. But Vadastra signaled him with a finger on his lips that he should say nothing. The two old men began to regard them with some suspicion. They heard another series of shots and a group of people noisily sought refuge in the shelter. A woman entered carrying a sleepy child in her arms. Giving her a smile, her husband stroked the baby's forehead with his finger, then pulled a newspaper from his pocket and began to read. The girls who had entered so boisterously watched the intimate family scene and leaned against the wall, beginning to talk in whispers among themselves. Antim was about to fall asleep again when the whole shelter was shaken violently, rocked by a muffled explosion somewhere nearby.

"Did you hear that?" he cried, his face pale. "That one fell right beside us!"

"Yes, yes!" Spiridon spoke in English, embarrassed, and again he motioned to Antim to be silent.

Just then a second explosion was heard, even nearer. Antim drooped limply. He seemed to be trying to make himself as small as possible, to occupy as little space as he could.

247

"Now! Now!" he declared softly. "The next one! You know it will fall on us!"

The shelter rocked heavily again and they heard several explosions simultaneously, coming from different directions. Placing her hand on the baby's face, the mother bowed her head. Her husband dropped his newspaper and waited. Anxious now, the old men looked at each other, and the girls were suddenly silent, holding their breath.

"God help us!" cried Antim with a terrified glance at Vadastra.

"Yes! Yes!" Vadastra continued to repeat the English words as he looked in vain for a place by the wall.

Then for several long moments it was quiet. They heard some distant explosions and another round of antiaircraft fire. Taking up his newspaper the man started reading again, while the rest of the group looked curiously at Antim and Vadastra.

"Do you think they've gone on?" asked the professor a little later.

The father interrupted his reading and listened to them. Then turning to Vadastra he asked, "Romanians?"

"Yes!" responded Spiridon in English, wiping his forehead with his handkerchief.

"Read here!" With a smile the man showed him an article in the paper. Vadastra took it, thanking him politely.

"What does it say?" Antim inquired interested. Spiridon ran his eye over the article without answering. A few minutes later he said, "It's about us. The withdrawal from Transylvania has started, and General Antonescu has asked the King to abdicate!"

His words were interrupted by a new explosion. The shelter reeled and the lights went out. Everyone was quiet.

"Where are you?" Antim was breathing heavily. "Take my arm! I can't feel my feet! Great Lord God! Lord God!" He stopped all at once and demanded of Spiridon, his voice hoarse, "But where's the portfolio?"

"I have it," the other whispered.

"Give it to me, I'll hold it! . . . So those people won't notice it," he added softly. Vadastra did not answer.

"Give me my portfolio, sir!" Antim cried in a sudden outburst, reaching out in the darkness. He found the case and thrust it under his arm, shaking with excitement.

"You frightened me!" he said and heaved a long sigh.

On the evening of the ninth of September, Fotescu, the secretary for the press, invited Stefan to dinner. Stefan found him playing poker with several other Romanians.

"We've been playing since five," the secretary said, "in order to forget our troubles. If we let every catastrophe engulf us we'd lose our minds. . . . Three times the pot!" he added addressing the other players. They examined their cards attentively.

"Count me out!" said a lady.

"Distraction from the war!" Fotescu exclaimed in good spirits, turning to Stefan. "I read somewhere that a game of cards is the best defense against panic."

"It's too bad that I don't know how to play," remarked Stefan, drawing a chair close to Fotescu. "But perhaps I'll learn too, before long."

"But what do you do all the time?" the woman next to him asked. "What do you do to forget—to forget the war and everything that's happening?" She was still young but her face was wasted and weary. Her fingers bore the telltale yellow stains of a chain smoker. When she spoke her upper lip trembled slightly.

"Especially since you're alone," she continued, "separated from your family. . . ."

"What are you doing? How have you organized yourself?" the Minister had asked him the last time they had met. "I defend my essential freedoms," he replied, smiling. "I keep a part of my time for myself alone." "No," interrupted the Minister. "I was asking something else: How have you organized yourself—your affairs—in the event of an invasion, or of massive bombardments? Will you stay in London?" "I was trying to respond to that question too. Whatever the eventuality, I have arranged my program to preserve a few hours a day for myself alone. In those hours I have no contact with events. I don't listen to the radio, I don't read the papers. No matter what happens, no event can reach me in the fragment of Time that I snatch from history and keep only for myself." The Minister had looked at him in his habitual way, a kind of vacant stare. "I envy you," he said finally.

". . . It must be very difficult for you," continued the woman.

"Difficult, naturally. And it will become harder and harder as time goes on. God only knows how many more catastrophes lie ahead."

"So, what do you do then?"

"I try to defend my essential freedoms." He observed that the others were looking at him in some annoyance because he had interrupted their game, and he stopped talking. If at such a time, he thought, Romania should be invaded or, God forbid, some other catastrophe of a different order should occur, I should be among the last to find out about that tragedy. These ahistoric hours permit me to tolerate the terror of history the rest of the time. Eventually that terror catches up with me, but at least for a few hours I have the satisfaction of remaining *free*. I have the satisfaction of not being automat-

249

ically integrated into events, like a slave who moves or stands still at the command of his master. . . .

"You mean. . . ?" Fotescu asked, his fingers playing over the cards. "How do you defend your freedoms?"

"Today the master of all of us is the war," Stefan began again. "It has confiscated the whole of contemporary history, the time in which we are fated to live. All Europe's behaving like a monstrous robot set in motion by the news being released every minute from hundreds of radio stations, from special editions of the newspapers, from conversations among friends. Even when we're alone we think about the war all the time. That is, we're slaves of History. The terror of events is not only humiliating to each of us as human beings, but in the long run it's sterile. Nothing good comes of this constant contact with History. It enriches no one; we discover nothing really worth being discovered."

The woman stared at him with intense concentration, as though trying to find some other meaning in his words, while smoking constantly, drawing deeply on her cigarette.

"History is invigorating and fertile only for those who make it, not for those who endure it. Take the British aviator who defends the English sky and risks his life every moment. For him, naturally, contemporary history is productive, because the history he makes aids him in self-revelation. But for us, for all the others who watch passively from the ground his struggle against the German aviators—what does this struggle reveal to us? Only terror. . . ."

He was somewhat uneasy, since he felt he was boring everyone, but he continued. "Against the terror of History there are only two possibilities of defense: action or contemplation. The airman who defends the English sky acts. Our only solution is to contemplate, that is, to escape from historic Time, to find again another Time. . . ."

One of the players, a young man almost bald and the son of a grain merchant, found it difficult to hide his irritation that the game had been interrupted. He examined his cards once more. "How much did you say?" he asked, raising his eyes.

"I think I said three times the pot," Fotescu replied.

"I'm out," repeated the woman next to Stefan.

"Me too," said the fourth player.

The woman turned to Stefan. "Please continue. You were saying some interesting things . . ."

"Actually," commenced Stefan, becoming agitated and speaking with increasing rapidity, "any of us could die at any moment and we could die without glory like ants trod underfoot, like mice caught in a trap, doused with gasoline and burned alive. We cannot escape this destiny. However, we have an obligation to protest against it. And as for me I have no other means of protesting except to refuse to let it grip me, torture me, and terrorize me. If

250

I'm going to die today, tomorrow, or a month from now, I'll die. But at least I shall die proud that I have not renounced my human dignity or my freedom. History will kill me, but it will not kill a slave. It will kill a free man who knows he has snatched some small fragment of his life from that terror!"

"You said three times the pot?" Scowling, the bald young man repeated his question after examining his cards once again.

"Three times!"

The young man paused thoughtfully, then without hurry he began to count his chips.

"Very well," said the woman, "but I still don't understand what you do."

"Here's what I do," said Stefan, smiling. "During the hours when I tear myself away from the war, I read things that have absolutely no relation to current events. I read, for instance, poets, philosophers, mystics, or books about prehistory. In those hours I reject the vaguest allusions to contemporary circumstances. I forbid myself even the least stray thought about the war. Above all I don't want to remember my wife and my child, or the misfortunes of my country. More precisely, I don't want to think of my wife, my child, my country as they are *at the present moment*. When I think about them I project them into another Time, a moment in the past or an imaginary Time. I remember, for example, certain journeys I made with my wife. Or I try to imagine Romania fifteen or a hundred or five hundred years ago. There were historic tragedies then too and I'm not averse to remembering them, to meditating upon them, but I do this of my own free will and not because I'm obliged to do it. I am free to decide upon what historic tragedy of the past I shall focus my attention. My decision is free, and not dictated by information I've heard on the radio or read in a special edition of the newspaper."

"Actually," the press secretary interrupted him, "it's a kind of ivory tower. . . ."

"It's not exactly an ivory tower, because I don't shun historic reality. I just defend my freedom to break away periodically from that reality in order to recover a more essential one, the reality of poetry, mysticism, philosophy, love. . . ."

The bald young man counted his chips painstakingly. Fotescu stole a glance at him and a sly smile lit his face momentarily.

"But what's the good of it," the fourth player asked, "if you still can't change anything?"

"For the present my duty is not to change something but to prevent myself from being transformed into a larva by the circumstances of History. That is, I preserve for myself a minimum of freedom for later on. . . ."

"But how?" exclaimed the woman with a hint of exasperation in her voice. "How?"

"Look, *doamna*," Stefan said kindly, "today, for instance, I've brought a poet with me." He produced from the pocket of his coat a small volume,

251

bound in leather, and showed it to her. "The *Sonnets* of Shakespeare. If there is an alert and I find myself in a subway or a shelter, I begin to read. I *refuse* in this way to be present at a very small historic event. While I'm reading Shakespeare I escape from the present moment, from the moment that was intended to grip me and terrorize me. And if at that moment a bomb falls and kills me, it kills, as I told you, a free man and not a slave! Because it kills a man whose mind is entranced by the genius of a poet, and not one who is wondering whether or not the airplanes have left the vicinity of his shelter. . . ."

He was interrupted by the prolonged wail of the siren and he put the volume back in his pocket with a smile. The others looked around the table in confusion. Each one seemed to be waiting for his neighbor to make a decision.

"I don't believe it will last long," said Fotescu. "Let's finish this hand and then have dinner. What are you going to do, *domnule* Gherghel?" he asked the balding young man.

"Three times the pot," Gherghel began in a confident voice, pushing a stack of chips toward the middle of the table, "plus—nine times the pot!"

Suddenly they were all excited. *Doamna* Fotescu, curious, approached the table.

"Paid!" Fotescu said, counting his chips hurriedly. "How many cards?"

"I'm satisfied!" stated Gherghel.

"I'll take one," and Fotescu picked a card from the pack with a rapid gesture, preparing to pay it out. Suddenly they heard several explosions surprisingly close by. Again they raised their heads and looked at each other with questioning glances.

"It's the antiaircraft guns," said *doamna* Fotescu. "We have a battery in the neighborhood."

"What are you doing?" Fotescu demanded with an uncertain smile.

Another explosion, muffled, shook the house from top to bottom. The woman got up from the table.

"Do you have a good shelter?" she inquired, nervously puffing at her cigarette.

"There's a sort of cave in the basement," *doamna* Fotescu said.

"What are you doing?" asked Fotescu again, getting up.

"I'm counting the pot," Gherghel replied. "I want five pounds more."

"Five to you," cried Fotescu triumphantly, "and give ten more to me!"

The windows began to rattle. A few moments later the whole house seemed to be jarred from its foundations and a deafening explosion brought them to their feet. The card table overturned, spilling the chips all over the carpet. No one moved to right it.

"That was an aerial torpedo!" exclaimed the fourth player. "And it struck with full force!"

252

"What shall we do?" asked *doamna* Fotescu, who was very pale. "Shall we go down to the shelter or eat first?"

"Either in the shelter," Gherghel observed, "or here—we have two more stories above us."

The antiaircraft fire increased.

"I say to go down," said Fotescu, and he addressed his wife, "Have you turned off the gas in the kitchen?"

A new series of explosions flung everyone against the wall. "Quick, let's go down! They're right over us!"

They exited hastily through the hall and began to descend the stairs to the basement. There was no more talking. Stefan heard a voice calling, "Wait for me!" It was the young woman, who had lagged behind. He paused, his flashlight in his hand, until she joined him. She clung to his arm.

"I can't go on!" she murmured, in tears. "I think I'm going to be sick. . . ."

Somberly Fotescu greeted them in the entrance to the shelter. "Come on, gentlemen!" he exclaimed nervously. "Hurry up, for God's sake!"

The cave in the basement was almost full. Heard from the shelter, the explosions and artillery fire sounded even more violent. No one spoke. Fotescu clenched his teeth and looked at the floor, almost with fury.

"I think they've gone away," someone said after a while. "Perhaps we've been spared once more. . . ."

The others remained silent.

"They gave us a terrible fright," the fourth player remarked presently.

"What a shame!" said Fotescu, turning to Gherghel. "Do you know what I had? A royal flush of queens!"

Gherghel looked at him, irritated, but not without admiration. "You played it badly then. I had four aces. It wasn't necessary to raise me ten pounds. You should have asked for one or two to see what I'd do."

"Maybe you're right," Fotescu admitted thoughtfully. But the explosions began again, and he scowled in silence, forcing himself to breathe as deeply as he could.

That evening they ate no dinner. During a moment of calm someone went out on the street and returned with the report: "London's burning!" Stefan and Fotescu also went to look. In the direction of the city the sky was ablaze. From the area that glowed red, the color of blood, flames surged to dizzy heights, faded, and sprang to life again. An odor of soot and tar hung in the air. They could hear the constant boom and rumble of distant explosions.

When they returned to the shelter they found everyone looking very pale. No one seemed bold enough to ask about what they had seen.

"This time the serious bombing has started!" someone said. "It's the beginning of the battle of London."

No one spoke.

A middle-aged Englishman, who had also gone outside and returned, explained, "They're attacking in waves. . . . There they are again. They're over us now. . . ."

Indeed, a few moments later the house shook once more and the explosions became more frequent. In the shelter there was no sound except the labored asthmatic breathing of an old woman.

"They're coming," whispered the young woman, looking fearfully at Stefan. "This time we won't escape!" Stefan bowed his head, waiting.

"A man lives authentically only a few hours in every ten or fifteen years," he had once told Ioana. They had gone out together on the balcony. It was at Predeal, a clear August morning at Predeal, long ago, in another time, *before*. Was it 1934? It was *before*. A summer morning. They had visited the mountains many times, and this time they were at Predeal. Summer vacation. Nothing happened. "A man lives authentically. . . . A believer has no more than two or three religious experiences in his whole lifetime," he had added. "The rest is routine. Just like our lives—an endless series of reflex actions. Just a few authentic hours out of ten or fifteen years. And when you try to get out of the routine, you make history. . . ."

"What are you thinking about?" inquired the woman. The sound of the explosions receded. "What were you thinking about just now?" she insisted.

Smiling, Stefan shrugged his shoulders.

"I'm getting hungry," said *doamna* Fotescu, "but I don't have the courage to go upstairs. What if they come back again? I'd be terrified to stay up there alone."

"I'll go up and get some biscuits and maybe a few sandwiches," Fotescu proposed. But as he neared the door, the house quaked again. The explosion they heard a moment later frightened everyone.

"Do you suppose it fell on our house?" someone asked.

The middle-aged man went outside to check. When he came back he was accompanied by the home guard for the neighborhood, a tall, vigorous old gentleman wearing a steel helmet.

"The bomb fell at the street corner," said the guard in a cheerful voice. "It only damaged a wing of Dr. Elwin's house. But incendiary bombs have fallen too, several right here on the sidewalk. I put them out. Now I have to inspect the roof. Who'll come with me?"

254

Several men stepped toward the door. The home guard turned to Stefan. "Are you married? Have you any children?"

"No."

"Do you know the stairs well? Do you know where to get out on the roof?"

"Approximately."

"I know the way better," said the middle-aged man. "I live on the fourth floor. You," he said to Stefan, "check the sidewalk again. Do you know how to put out an incendiary bomb?"

"Yes," replied Stefan.

Suddenly he felt himself begin to tremble with excitement—or was it fear?—and he started toward the door, humiliated and furious. He heard timid footsteps behind him, yet he did not turn to look back. When he reached the street he saw that it was Gherghel who had followed him.

"I've neither wife nor child," he said, trying to joke, "but I don't know how to put out incendiary bombs."

"I don't think it's hard. You smother them with sand. There's a bag of sand near the door. As far as I can see," Stefan added, looking all around, "there aren't any more bombs. And I don't believe any more will fall for awhile. The planes have passed over us. They've gone to the city, over there where you see the big fire."

He would have liked to continue to talk. He felt more secure when he was speaking. *"Talk to me about Vadastra, talk to me about his love, doamna Zissu, talk to me about anything else...."* A few minutes after they had reached the street panic seized him again. The fire seemed to have spread. The flames had multiplied and the whole sky was red. *"What are you thinking about?" "Look, doamna, the Sonnets of Shakespeare...."*

At the end of the street, in front of the house that had been hit, a group of men had gathered. They looked like shadows as they moved about in the light of the fire. At the other end of the street the roof of a cottage was ablaze. The yellow flames issuing from the eaves like so many pointed tongues seemed to be trying to lick out as far as possible. In a window Stefan saw an old woman flourishing a feather duster, perhaps making signals to the people in the street. *"A man lives authentically only a few hours in every ten or fifteen years...."* The next moment the woman was lost in the darkness of the room. *"How have you arranged your affairs?" "I defend myself...."*

"I say let's go back," Gherghel said. "With our heads uncovered like this we might get hurt by shell fragments." It was only when he approached that Stefan realized the young man's teeth were chattering.

"Lets-s-s go ins-s-side!" Gherghel whispered in a strangely sibilant voice. A new series of explosions and antiaircraft volleys accompanied them back to the shelter. Inside everyone was nervous and restless.

"But, my God, how much longer will it last?" the woman's eyes searched

255

Stefan's. "It's been two hours since the alert sounded. They just seem to be circling around overhead, dropping bombs all the time."

Why are you afraid? You won't escape. It could . . . He closed his eyes suddenly, almost crushing them in his fury. *"Talk to me about whatever you like, but something else, something else!" "He kills a free man, not a slave. . . ."*

The home guard entered again with the same cheerful smile. "There was only one poor incendiary bomb, half burned out," he said speaking quite loudly. "I got the better of it with my hand." And he showed them his hands, blackened with oil. One finger was bleeding. Without haste the man took out his handkerchief, poured a little whiskey from a metal canteen on a corner of it and washed the wound. Then he put the canteen to his lips.

"Who else wants a swallow?" he asked, beginning to laugh. "It's a jolly good defense against Hitler's pigeons!"

The group brightened up immediately. An old man, two women, and the man who lived on the fourth floor passed the canteen from hand to hand.

"What shall we do?" asked the young woman. "Stay here all night? If only it were a good shelter! Do you think it can stand a direct hit?"

"Few shelters can withstand a direct hit," said Gherghel. "You won't find absolute security anywhere except at the hotel where Neagu and Paun live. There are ten floors and the shelter is five meters underground. And there's a bar in the hotel lobby. We can give ourselves a chance to recover. What do you say? Does the idea tempt you? Well, I'm going anyhow!"

"If we wait a little longer maybe it will stop," said Fotescu.

"I say it would be better to take advantage of the first lull and go," his wife declared. "This could last all night."

"I'm afraid to go out," said the woman, trying to catch Stefan's eye again. "I'm terrified to go out on the street and see the fire. It's better to stay here. What will you do?" she asked Stefan.

"I'll leave with them. I'm going home."

A half-hour later they left. The woman followed them with her eyes as they disappeared one after the other into the darkness of the corridor.

"Don't go!" she called to them once again. "I have a strange premonition. Don't go!"

A strong odor of smoke, soot, and petroleum hit them. The fires on the street had been extinguished, but on the sidewalk about ten meters away some remnants of bombs were burning low, like bonfires about to go out. The sky, however, was everywhere red as blood. Now and then the searchlights would illumine a barrage balloon. In front of them a fire truck passed at full speed.

256

They set out hurriedly, almost running toward the Underground station.

"But I don't think the trains operate during the alert," the fourth guest recalled.

"Anyway the entrance is open. We can take shelter there if we don't find something else better. . . ."

When they reached Cromwell Road they saw small fires scattered along the entire length of the street. Squads of men ran in and out of the shadows. Two policemen stretched a rope across the street, fastening it at each end to wooden sawhorses.

"Diversion!" said one of the men, and when he saw them hastening toward the subway he called out, "There's a good shelter at number 37, a few houses up on the left!" They hesitated.

"Don't stay on the street!" shouted a home guard who appeared unexpectedly in a doorway. "Fragments keep falling all the time. Get to the shelter fast! Number 37. . . ."

"I'm going to the hotel, no matter what!" said Gherghel.

"So are we," whispered *doamna* Fotescu, frightened.

They took off again staying close to the houses, hunching their backs as if they were afraid something would drop on their heads. As the rumblings began to increase they ceased to talk. Someone stopped them near a pile of debris. "Look out! This is a wrecked house!"

They heard a shrill whistle and threw themselves on the ground. In front of them a reddish-green light flashed, followed immediately by an explosion. Stefan closed his eyes. He felt that all the blood in his body had rushed to his heart. For a moment he thought he would suffocate. He began to count: one, two, three. . . .

"All Biris said was that you sent me a message from the labyrinth," Ileana had insisted. "But I didn't understand at all. I don't understand what you want to tell me!" At that moment he closed his eyes. The thunder shook the house and the windows rattled for a long time. "I wonder where that boy's going in this rain?" Ileana asked suddenly, getting up from the sofa and bringing her hands to her temples. Then she turned and looked at Stefan, exasperated, despairing. "Why did you ask him to come?" She demanded in a voice choked with emotion. "Why did you tell him too? I didn't understand at all." "I told him I had come out of the labyrinth. But I asked him to tell you something else. Now I can't remember it very well myself. . . ." He was silent, exhausted, and he listened to the hail beating against the window. It was almost dark. Then he raised his head abruptly and questioned her. "What about your fiancé, Captain Melinte?" Ileana stopped in the middle of the room, startled, and turned to face him. "Did you love him?" he asked anxiously, almost in a whisper.

257

Raising his head slowly, Stefan saw the whole vault of the sky crossed by wandering searchlight beams that broke away, white and sparkling, from the dark red circle of the night. Antiaircraft guns rattled intermittently, booming in fitful volleys that were suddenly hushed, as though someone had stopped to listen, and then resumed again. A searchlight rested a moment on a captive balloon, but went off at once, reappearing in a neighboring area.

"Now! Quick!" said Stefan getting to his feet. "We'll have to run!"

Silently they all rose and set off after him, but they had not gone far when they came upon a taxi.

"It's empty!" cried Fotescu.

"But there's no driver!" Gherghel said, disappointed.

With difficulty a man crawled out from under the car. "What a piece of luck!" he exclaimed. "I got underneath it in time. It's riddled with shell fragments." But he did not want to give up his shelter. And anyway, almost all the streets in the neighborhood were blocked, he said.

"We're going to the Park Hotel," explained Gherghel enthusiastically. "It has the best shelter in London. We'll pay double your fare and you'll be safer there. Bombs have been falling here all night."

"I'd have to take you over there," and the driver pointed toward the reddest part of the sky. "It'll be hard. And there's too many of you."

"I'm not going," said Stefan. "But you should leave now, before another wave of planes arrives."

Finally the driver allowed himself to be persuaded. They climbed into the taxi silently and did not look in the direction of the city, where the flames appeared to be mounting higher.

"Good luck!" said Stefan.

His heart contracted as he followed the car with his eyes until it was lost in the curtain of red smoke.

Toward midnight it appeared that the attack had ceased. Stefan left the Underground station where he had found shelter an hour earlier. He started to walk home. Some of the searchlights had been turned off and the sky over the areas that were in flames now seemed more gory than ever. The air was full of the heavy smell of fuel oil, smoke, and concrete. As he came out into the gloomy darkness of the night he had the impression of awakening from sleep.

In the station someone near him had said, "They're getting ready for an invasion. This is their strategy—to draw attention to the capital and attack somewhere on the coast to assure the successful landing of the first units. . . ." Stefan had turned his head to look at the speaker, a man

258

with an unusually long, thin neck and a habit of blinking in constant accompaniment to his slow speech. From time to time he moistened his upper lip, almost sucking it. "These days are decisive," he had added. "Now let's see them!" a woman cried. "Now, here, on our soil!" And all at once they no longer seemed so tired. They looked at each other and smiled with a sudden stubbornness in their eyes. "It's a good thing it's begun," someone at the back of the shelter exclaimed. He had started to hum a tune, but he stopped for a moment and added, "The invasion, I mean. It's good that it's begun. . . ." *"How have you arranged your affairs? In case of invasion, I mean."* Stefan had taken the volume of poems from his pocket and opened it at random. A moment later he noticed that he had read the same lines several times without comprehending them. *"With my mind entranced by the genius of a poet. . . ."* The truth is that I was afraid. . . . *"Talk to me about* anything else. . . ." He had turned the page, continuing to feign attention. The people were talking quietly among themselves, their conversation interrupted by long intervals of silence. "It's lasted four hours," a woman remarked, and she went outside. "Everything out there seems to be whirling around," she said when she returned about ten minutes later. "I'm glad I didn't decide to leave. A bomb fell at the end of the street." "We heard it down here," said the young man with the long neck. "No, you only thought so. That was the firing of the antiaircraft guns."

When he had gone a little distance beyond the entrance to the Underground, the darkness encompassed him and he felt alone again, and lost. He was fully aroused now. The neighborhood was an unfamiliar one. In the station somebody—a man who had almost fallen asleep crouched beside the ticket booth—had told him that it was about an hour's walk to his house. He had to pay careful attention to the streets that he took or he would get lost. He walked as fast as he could, but at the first corner he stopped. The street was blocked by a rope. A policeman shouted to him to get away quickly. Several unexploded bombs had landed there and he was waiting for a demolition team to examine them. When the policeman told him what streets to follow, Stefan began to run. After a while he thought he heard the roar of planes returning. He stopped and leaned against a wall. *"A message from the labyrinth. I didn't understand at all. Talk to me about* anything else. . . ." He began to run again, keeping as close as possible to the walls. The sound of the planes seemed to be growing increasingly distinct.

For a long time he had waited, listening to the hail pelt the window in sporadic onslaughts, thick and gray. Then he raised his head suddenly and asked her, "Did you love him? Was it he you loved? Did you love your fiancé?" Ileana looked at him fearfully. She gazed at him as though she did not dare to believe he was still there near her, still talking to her, his words coming faster, his voice choked with emotion. He demanded again, "Did you love him? Do you think you really loved him?... In the camp I thought about this all the time. I wondered: Does she truly love him? Can she love him, too, her fiancé? Why don't you answer me? Did you love him too?..."

Occasionally he passed policemen on the street or home guards leaning against gates or standing in the entrances to concrete shelters, men who wished him "good evening". Overhead, invisible and far away, he could hear the sound of engines circling. Yet they haven't dropped....

"Why don't you answer me? When I was in the clinic I had the feeling of being lost in a labyrinth. I knew that somewhere there was an exit, but I had lost my way. I kept asking myself, Did she love him? Was it he she loved? If I'd known the answer I could have gone out of the labyrinth.... Why don't you answer me?" Ileana continued to look at him, terrified. "You don't realize what this means to me—to *know* if you loved him too." "He died beside me," she said abruptly. "He died in my arms. Don't ask me anything more." "But did you love him? Do you believe you loved him?" She went to the window. The hail had stopped. Rain was pouring down now, rain that fell like a curtain of foam. "I became engaged to him in despair," Ileana said without turning her head. "It was an engagement of despair, if you can understand what that means." Then all at once she opened the window. The rain, the storm, the smell of fresh leaves and wet earth, the fragrance of shattered roses, rushed suddenly into the room. "If you want us to remain friends, please don't ever speak to me about this again. If you had a little imagination.... If you had a little love for me..." He realized then that she was crying, that she had allowed the rain to fall on her face to cover her tears. But he remained motionless in the middle of the room, watching her. He did not dare go near.

Exhausted, he stopped to check the name of a street. Here the city seemed deserted, sinister and dark, but there were areas where he had seen streets bright with the light of fires, areas where fire trucks and police cars were heading in a continual stream. Now and then he heard the sudden report, solitary and somewhat muffled, of a delayed-action bomb. He deciphered the street name with difficulty and realized he had lost his way. He started on again, spent, hugging the walls, searching the darkness for a home guard. The street on which he walked did not seem to belong to the London that was bombed and burning, but to an entirely different city. Each house had its garden or at least its trees. He thought that the smell of smoke and tar was not

260

so strong here. Viewed from this place even the sky looked less bloody. He leaned against a wall to rest, and a sweet weariness diffused his troubled body. body.

"No, I'm not angry," Ileana said. "I don't understand why, but I can't be cross with you. You're not like anyone else, like us. You live in a dream, a world of your own. I pity myself, I lament my luck, Why did you meet me? Why did I have to meet you of all people? At Zinca, *Baba** kept foretelling good fortune for me, luck in love, luck. . . . And even after I met you she repeated, luck in love, luck. . . . I'll have to ask you to leave now, please. The rain's stopped. . . ."

Later, at the end of an alley, it seemed to him that he saw a shadow and he went toward it. However, after a few steps he halted, thinking he heard someone talking in Romanian. The voice sounded familiar to him at first but he could not identify it. Only when he drew nearer did he recognize with a start that the speaker was Vadastra.

"Poor *doamna* Zissu!" he was saying over and over. "Poor *doamna* Zissu! She came all the way here to help me!"

Disturbed, Stefan approached him. He said, "Good evening," and Vadastra wheeled sharply. He was bareheaded and his black monocle was missing.

"You speak Romanian?" he demanded, frightened. "Are you Romanian?"

"I'm Viziru." He held out his hand, but in the darkness Vadastra did not see it, and Stefan quickly drew it back.

"How do you come to be here at this hour? Where's the professor?"

Vadastra did not answer. He ran his hand through his hair. Stefan noticed that he was hugging Antim's portfolio tightly under his left arm.

"What's happened?"

"I received a telegram." Vadastra spoke with difficulty. "I have it with me. . . . Wait, I'll show it to you," he added, and began to rummage in his pocket. He held out an envelope.

"I can't read it. You tell me what's in it."

"It's from Irina. She informs me in a very special way that I'm a father. The baby was born at dawn yesterday morning. It's a boy."

"My congratulations!"

"Thanks! This news, although expected, thrilled me very much! We opened a bottle of champagne and drank it, *nenea* Iancu and I. And then the air raid began."

"But where's the professor?"

*Old woman.

261

"I don't know what happened to him. He stayed behind. He's lost!"

"That's impossible!"

"He got lost from me at about nine," Spiridon stated wearily. "I searched for him for half an hour. I'm afraid something's happened to him."

"But weren't you in a shelter? Why did you leave it?"

Vadastra said nothing. He still clutched the portfolio under his arm.

"You were very foolish," insisted Stefan. "You shouldn't have left the shelter during the attack. Especially since the professor is afraid of air raids."

"It's a delicate question. I can't tell you . . . a question that concerns us, the family. . . ."

"We'll have to search for him," Stefan said, suddenly troubled. "We must go immediately!"

Vadastra did not reply, but continued to run his hand mechanically through his hair.

"What happened to the professor?" Stefan demanded again, almost shouting.

"I don't know. . . . He wandered away. . . . We'll find out tomorrow morning what happened to him."

They began to hear the noise of airplane motors, followed by massive volleys of artillery fire. In his fright Vadastra gripped Stefan's arm. "They're coming again!" he murmured. "They're coming back! And this time they're upon us!" He began to tremble, clinging desperately to Stefan. "What's to become of us?" he asked. "This time I won't escape it! You know I won't escape now!"

Dozens of searchlight beams, etched at that instant on the sky, crossed directly over their heads.

"Let's find a shelter," said Stefan glancing around. "Come with me!"

He began to run up the street toward the place where he thought he could distinguish the outline of a large building. But a few moments later he heard the shrill whistle of a bomb and he threw himself to the ground. He felt sand and debris strike the back of his neck and his hair.

It was just like that other time when he would have screamed but found he could not. His throat felt strangled, caught by an invisible rope. And yet he had seen Ionel's head bob up for a moment on the surface of the water, in the foam. "Mia!" he had called. Stefan was sure he had heard Ionel cry out. Then it seemed to him that the whole sky had fallen on the lake and crushed it like a tremendous tent collapsing with a deafening noise. He could no longer hear anything.

He tried to rise, to look for Spiridon, but he stumbled on a slab blown out of the sidewalk and fell down. At the same time he felt a sharp pain in both knees. He lay there motionless for several seconds, his eyes closed, clenching his teeth. Somewhere behind him he heard Vadastra calling.

"Where are you?" Spiridon shouted in alarm. "Where are you?"

Stefan had difficulty rising but he started toward the building with Vadastra after him. As they neared their goal the noise of the motors was so loud that they both fell to the ground again, holding their breath. Stefan realized then that some kind of excitement had begun behind them, several houses down the street. He heard voices and an automobile horn, and he turned to see what had happened. Small fires had broken out on the rooftops, in a garden, at the edge of the sidewalk. Incendiary bombs again, he said to himself. He was preparing to get up when he felt Vadastra crawling beside him, and he heard him whisper, "Don't move! I know what's coming. More bombs will fall now! *Doamna* Zissu told me."

The conflagration spread and illuminated the entire street. The buildings all around were in flames. In the distance sounded the siren of a fire engine, and again Stefan started to get up but Vadastra seized his arm.

"Listen to me! Don't move! That's what happened to *nenea* Iancu. He left too soon. . . ."

Another series of blasts resounded not far from them. Spiridon moaned. "Didn't I tell you?" he whispered, his voice rattling in his throat, his head bent. "Now others will come . . . and others . . . and others. . . . That's how they killed *nenea* Iancu. . . ."

Stefan clenched his fists, trying to rouse himself.

"He'd gone out of the shelter because of his infirmity," continued Vadastra with difficulty, as though he were suffocating. "He sat down on a curb, the way we're sitting now. I told him to hurry, not to stay long, because the bombing would begin again. But he didn't pay attention. The picture fell down in the dark and he couldn't find it. . . . But it was right there under him. I found it. It was a little wet. . . . What do you think? Is it ruined? Has it decreased in value because it was wet? What do you think? Such a precious painting, if it were a little wet on the corners would it lose value? What do you think?" he repeated the question several times in desperation.

"I don't think so."

"My opinion too. What could it matter if it was a little damp? By tomorrow morning it will be dry."

"But what happened to the professor?"

"There was a stone stairway there and he was tending to his needs on the sidewalk at the top of the stairs," Vadastra began anxiously.

A woman's scream stopped him, ringing out from somewhere very near, compelling them to raise their heads. Several meters up the street the roof of a house was burning furiously. The woman, shrouded in smoke, holding a child in her arms, shouted desperately from a window. Vadastra trembled and gripped Stefan's arm.

"It sounded like Irina's voice," he said.

Once more they tried to get up and again a series of explosions pinned them to the ground.

"Do you believe in angels?" demanded Vadastra, moved. *"Doamna* Zissu said that angels do exist. She saw them several times. She said every man has his guardian angel."

"What happened to the Professor?" cried Stefan. "What happened to him?"

"He's dead," Vadastra said with considerable coolness. "He slipped on the stairs and he died. I told you that he was relieving himself. . . . He slipped, like that, and he died. . . . Bombs were falling around us all the time."

Stefan struggled to rise but Vadastra held him down, leaning on his arm with all his weight.

". . . And *doamna* Zissu came. I scarcely recognized her. Poor *doamna* Zissu! How different she was from the way I left her! It's true, many years have passed since then. . . ."

The woman's screams had become even more desperate. Gritting his teeth, Vadastra rose to his feet with great effort. He held out the portfolio to Stefan. "Hold it, please, for a moment," he said in a flat voice. "I have to go rescue that woman. . . ."

When Stefan tried to stand up Spiridon shouted at him in alarm. "Don't move! Guard that portfolio well! It's our only wealth!"

He took a step but turned back, running his hand through his hair, and added, "You know, the truth is I killed him! . . . I pushed him down the stairs when he was tending to his needs, and he fell to the bottom, dead. It was useless for *doamna* Zissu to tell me I didn't kill him. I know very well I pushed him. I saw him roll over and over all the way down. I took the portfolio and I left. So many bombs were falling that I wonder how I survived. . . . But this is a secret between us, you know. You must be very discreet, please. . . ."

He turned around and with surprising agility began running toward the burning house. Stefan's knee felt paralyzed. He tried several times to move, without success. He saw Vadastra enter the house after shouting something to the woman at the window. But a few moments later he saw him on the street again among the other men, appearing and disappearing in the light of the flames. Stefan made another attempt to rise, but the pain in his knee was so intense that he lost consciousness. He kept gripping the portfolio tightly in his hand, as if he were in desperate need of something to cling to.

He woke up in a strange bed and realized immediately that he was in a hospital. the bright light in the room and the distinctive odor of medicine stirred his memories, but he was unable to place them with precision anywhere in his past.

"Where am I injured?" he asked the nurse.

"Nowhere. You're perfectly well. We'll even ask you to get dressed. We don't have any more beds. . . ."

Stefan blushed. He sat up and felt an immense fatigue sweep over him. "And yet I fainted. I wanted to get up but I felt a terrible pain in my knee."

"Probably you hit it falling," said the nurse. She smiled and went away.

Stefan dropped his eyes quickly. The ward was full of the injured. At intervals he heard their moans and sighs. He moved his legs and although the feeling of exhaustion persisted the pain was gone. He found his clothes lying on the edge of the bed and he began to dress hurriedly under the covers. Vadastra's portfolio was there too, reminding him of the events of the night before. He was troubled. He wanted to ask for news of Vadastra, but he realized that the nurse had no way of knowing. Another nurse took him to an office where he signed several papers.

"You were uncommonly lucky," the clerk said, looking at him in astonishment. "Everything around you was burning. When the ambulance picked you up they thought you were seriously injured. It was impossible to rouse you. And you were holding fast to that portfolio. . . ."

Stefan blushed again, thanked him, and started to leave, but after a few steps he turned around. "Did you find a fellow countryman of mine, Vasilescu-Vadastra, among the injured on that same street?"

Methodically the clerk consulted the file. "No," he said. "But you know," he added without raising his eyes, "they only brought the injured here, and not even all of them. . . ."

Near the hospital he found a taxi to take him to the Legation. Many bombs had fallen in the neighborhood and some of the windows of the building were broken. On Cromwell Road several houses had been burned and the top story of the Museum of Natural Science was still smoking. However the doorman at the Legation seemed cheerful. He had spent the night extinguishing bombs and his hands were covered with scratches and burns. He said that the chargé d'affaires had come that morning and made arrangements for part of the services to be transferred to the Embassy in Belgrave Square. They had a strong shelter there and it was spacious enough to accomodate all the members of the Legation. Stefan went up to his office in order to file his documents, but after a few minutes he abandoned this task and telephoned Belgrave Square. Fotescu answered the call himself, happy to hear Stefan's voice. They had all been worried about him, he said, when they saw that he had not shown up at the Legation that morning. Stefan asked if he knew anything about Vadastra and Antim. Fotescu said no, that up to that time the Legation had not been informed of any loss among the members of the Romanian colony.

265

With Antim's portfolio under his arm he went downstairs and set out for a nearby restaurant to get something to eat. He stopped to buy a newspaper in front of the Underground station.

"That was a real blitz, sir!" the newsboy said to him, and he smiled.

But it seemed to Stefan that his smile was somewhat forced. He went on, looking at the faces of the people around him. All bore traces of the sleepless night. Their skin seemed sallow, their lips were compressed. A look of deep resignation had appeared in their eyes. The restaurant was half demolished, and Stefan noticed all at once that he was no longer hungry. He entered a neighboring pub and asked for a sandwich and a glass of beer.

He sat for a long time without thinking of anything, holding the portfolio that contained Antim's painting and mechanically eating his sandwich. Then he roused himself and began to read the paper. He felt fatigue overtake him and got up with an effort, paid the waiter, and started back to the Legation. He remembered that he must telegraph Ioana to put her mind at rest.

At four o'clock, after he had finished packing the records that were to be transferred to Belgrave Square, he could no longer resist the temptation to take a nap. Bending over the desk, he rested his head on his right arm. He dreamed of Ioana. It seemed that she came to look for him at the Legation and could not get inside. The doorman told her through the door, "No one's here anymore! They've all moved to Belgrave Square!" Ioana persisted, beating harder than ever on the door with her fists. "It's urgent!" she cried. "I came with *doamna* Zissu. I came to search for Vadastra. . . ." "In Belgrave Square! In Belgrave Square!" shouted the doorman.

He felt someone shake him and he awakened with a start. In front of him in the gray dusk of the twilight stood Iancu Antim. Stefan, wide-eyed, remained motionless for a moment. Then he sprang to his feet in alarm.

"I knew I'd find you still here!" said the professor. He sat down wearily in the armchair in front of the desk and Stefan noticed the black sling that held his right arm. It was only when he saw Antim seated in the chair that the rapid beating of his heart subsided. The next instant he felt a great weakness throughout his body and he too sat down. Antim took his handkerchief and wiped his forehead with great care. Stefan saw then that Antim's face was covered with bruises. A large gash under his right eye extended far into his beard.

"Colonel Chabert! Dear *domnule* Viziru," Antim began, trying to smile. But it probably irritated one of his cuts because he quickly put his handkerchief to the corner of his mouth and pressed it, holding it there for a long time.

266

"What happened?"

"Colonel Chabert! Didn't I tell you?" asked Antim without lifting the handkerchief from his mouth. "They thought that I had died. They found me half dead with my head broken! And now there's nothing wrong with me! Absolutely nothing!" He stopped and wiped his forehead carefully again.

"That thief Spiridon pushed me! I'd felt for a long time he was lying in wait for me. And then at the top of the stairs I saw him getting ready to shove me. I made myself limp and I fell. I never thought I'd survive. But God is good . . . and when a man has vitality. . . . Well, here I am safe and sound! The punishment of God! Because Spiridon won't escape me now! I have proof! Prison'll get him! And he won't be able to sell the painting. I've informed the police that he stole it from me. And I came here to tell you too. And to put myself under your protection. That criminal is capable of trying to kill me again!"

"I ran across him last night," said Stefan.

Antim raised his head suddenly and looked at the other with intense fear in his eyes. "Did he have the painting?" he asked quickly.

"Yes," replied Stefan. He left the desk and went to the corner of the room where he had deposited some of the files that had to be evacuated. "He gave it to me to keep. That is, to put it more precisely, he gave it to me to deliver to you."

Antim jumped to his feet and took the portfolio in both hands. He was trembling. He made a large sign of the cross. "May God and the Holy Mother protect you!" He said with strong feeling. "May God protect you!" He was unable to continue and he began to weep, shaking with sobs, covering his face with his handkerchief.

"But I don't have any news about *domnul* Vadastra," Stefan said quietly. "I don't know what became of him. He ran to help a woman in a burning house. I'm afraid something may have happened to him. . . ."

"God protect you!" Antim continued to repeat between his sighs. "God and the Holy Mother protect you! God and the Holy Mother! . . . Colonel Chabert! . . ."

8

HE ARRIVED AT BRISTOL AT TEN O'CLOCK AT NIGHT. THE STATION HAD BEEN bombed and he had trouble finding a taxi to carry him with his two suitcases to the hotel where he had reserved a room. In the darkness the city seemed ominous. On both sides of the street he saw the gutted houses outlined against the sky, which could be glimpsed through the ruins in some places. At the hotel, the only large one that had been left intact, few voices could be heard although the lobby was filled with people. They spoke to each other in whispers or dozed wearily in the armchairs.

"Did you hear the nine o'clock news broadcast tonight?" he asked the man at the desk as he presented his passport. "What's the news from Romania?"

The rather elderly clerk wore a short gray mustache and gold-rimmed spectacles. He raised his eyes from the register and looked at Stefan politely, deliberately, in the manner of someone trying to recall something. "Romania?... Oh, yes. There's a revolution. The Iron Guardists have risen against General Antonescu."

Although Stefan had found out about the rebellion that morning in London when he bought the newspapers at the station, he was not aware of what had been happening.

"Nothing else?" he demanded insistently. "Are there any more details about the situation?"

"The situation seems confused. It's a revolution. . . . You have room 84 on the third floor," the clerk added quickly, as if he were sorry he had spoken, and he looked down again at the register.

Absently Stefan went up to room 84. A vague sadness hovered between the walls, the sadness of a deserted house or of one that is in mourning. The heavy curtains that covered the window were somber and old-fashioned, left there from another age. He lit a cigarette and began to undress. He was cold.

Laying the sealed diplomatic portfolio beside him on the bed, he turned out the light, but he could not sleep. He rested his head on the pillow and smoked, as he had started to do when he was with Antim that night.

As they were going down to the basement of the Embassy Stefan had tried to take the professor by the arm. "Don't touch me, please!" Antim had said, drawing back. "Wherever you put your hand it hurts. I feel as though all my bones were crushed."

Two long narrow rooms in the basement had been converted into a shelter by setting up army cots and several small tables. Stefan went directly to the darkest corner. Removing his tie and jacket he put on a dressing gown and went to bed. He fell asleep immediately.

Late in the night he had awakened and looked around him in astonishment. He did not realize where he was. Some of the lights had been turned off, and the room was cold. He saw Antim sleeping beside him with the portfolio under his head. After a few moments a captain entered, bringing coffee on a tray.

"What time is it?" Stefan asked.

"Two-thirty," answered the captain, setting the tray on a table. "Wouldn't you like some coffee?"

"Yes, I think so."

The captain brought a cup to him and held out a package of cigarettes. "You must have been really tired if you could sleep," he remarked. "I couldn't close my eyes. Not so much because of the bombs as the antiaircraft guns. . . . There's a battery near here. They're quiet now but they'll be starting again. . . ."

Stefan lit his cigarette and pulled the cover up under his chin. It seemed to be getting colder. Antim whispered in his sleep and began to sneeze. Stefan reached out to adjust the blanket over him, but Antim jerked suddenly and seized the portfolio with both hands.

"Was that you?" he asked in fright. He peered around suspiciously. Stefan smiled at him and curled up under his blanket. He felt almost frozen. He wanted to go to back to sleep and he closed his eyes, but he opened them again immediately. Antim was still sitting up watching Stefan's movements intently. Their eyes met for a moment. Embarrassed, Stefan turned his face to the wall.

That week the air raids had kept up continuously night after night. Antim seldom left the Embassy basement. During the day, when there were no alerts, he went up to the large salon, which had been made into a waiting room. He sat down in an armchair, holding the portfolio on his lap, and dozed. If an alert sounded at lunchtime, or if the sky were too cloudy, he did not dare go out to the restaurant but contented himself with a sandwich. In the evening the cook at the Embassy gave him something to eat. He did not want to go home, not even in the company of Stefan. The captain brought him some underwear in a small valise, and an overcoat.

"No one has seen him dead!" Antim murmured from time to time.

He had quarreled with the chargé d'affaires because he had wished to inform Bucharest of Vadastra's disappearance and Antim had been opposed to this. "You'll alarm the girl for nothing," he said. "You'll bring grief to two poor women! No one's seen him dead!"

The house Vadastra had entered had burned to the ground. A number of people had perished there, but Antim still did not want to believe that Spiridon was dead. "You don't know who he is," he murmured to himself, fidgeting in his chair. "I can't talk about it further, but you'd cross yourselves if you knew!"

He had taken on the tics of old age, nodding his head when he spoke and constantly sucking his lips. He slept fully clothed with the portfolio under his pillow. His beard had grown unkempt, and in order to hide the frayed, dirty collar of his shirt, he always wore a scarf around his neck.

Then one morning toward the end of September he had come to Stefan, his face distorted with fear. "I'm going with you to Oxford," he said in a whisper. "I can't stay here any longer!"

It had been decided to evacuate all employees who were not regular members of the Embassy staff, and Stefan had gone to Oxford to look for lodgings. He had just returned. The city was overcrowded and he had located two rooms with great difficulty in a modest pension, Oxoniensis.

"I'm going with you! I can't stay here! There's a madman with us in the shelter. He went insane during the air raid. I haven't slept a wink all night. He terrifies me. . . ."

Toward midnight someone had begun to wail. Nobody had dared to get out of bed to see what was the matter. They all waited, stunned. Then the wailing had stopped suddenly, and the man had gone back to sleep. But Antim could not close his eyes again. "He's mad!" he murmured. "He's a raving lunatic!"

They arranged to meet at the station at five o'clock. Stefan waited for him there on the platform for half an hour. In the meantime the alert had sounded and since Antim did not arrive Stefan imagined that he had been afraid to cross the city when it was under bombardment. Perhaps he had abandoned his plan to leave that evening. Stefan got on the next train. It was the first time he had traveled during an aerial attack, and he did not feel entirely at ease until they had passed Uxbridge.

The next day he had found out that Antim had taken a taxi from Belgrave Square around four o'clock. A few hours later someone had telephoned the Embassy that the professor had been found dead in a waiting room at Paddington Station. He had suffered a heart attack. The next evening he was buried.

Stefan put out his cigarette. He wasn't meant to go to Oxford, he whispered to himself in order to banish his sad thoughts. He closed his eyes. "There's a revolution. The Iron Guardists have risen." Antim had predicted it. "These men will make a revolution," he had said. "These men will kill the General."

When they were burying him it had begun to rain. Four mourners had come to the cemetery—the captain, the cook, Fotescu, and Stefan. The chargé d'affaires had sent a wreath. "In memory of our dear compatriot." He would have liked to have come also, he said, but he was called to the Foreign Office. When they were returning from the cemetery in Fotescu's car the rain had begun to fall more heavily, so they left Stefan at the station. All the way to Oxford he had watched the fine, cold drops beat gently against the train windows, and during the days that followed the rain accompanied him everywhere. Harsh and gray, the sky seemed to come closer to the ground. There was a smell of withered leaves and everything was wet. October.

He awoke at six o'clock. The airport van was waiting in front of the hotel, and at seven it left. When they started it was still dark outside. Two women and several men had climbed into the car with Stefan. An officer sat beside him with an absent air, smoking constantly and looking at no one. The car passed along streets watched over by ruins through which the murky light of dawn appeared, and when it was full daylight the rain began again. The car veered sharply, stopping in front of a gate of barbed wire as a guard came out of the concrete sentry box. Dodging the puddles, he drew the gate aside and the vehicle entered the airport.

Two soldiers in raincoats unloaded the luggage while the passengers were led into a gray building. The officer followed them silently. The inspection of the baggage and the collection of fees were handled rapidly, and they went on then to have their passports checked. Stefan, waiting with the sealed portfolio, was the last to be called. A soldier directed him to enter a room in which he found the officer from the car as well as a civilian clerk. They asked for his papers and examined them one by one with great care. Then without raising his eyes the officer asked Stefan what his mission in London was.

"Your name is not on the list of the diplomatic corps," he said, holding it out. Stefan glanced over the names of the employees of the Romanian Legation. His was not there.

"Your billfold, please," said the officer. He opened it, took out all the papers, counted the bills, then passed everything to the clerk beside him. Stefan watched it all with growing apprehension. He was reminded fleetingly of the Police Headquarters in Bucharest. He wondered if there might perhaps be a note or a name in his wallet that would appear suspicious.

"Have you anything else in your pockets?" demanded the officer. Stefan began searching through them and removed everything. He took out his handkerchief too, but started to put it back quickly.

"Leave it out, please," said the officer. "Which are the keys to your valises? Your baggage will be inspected in the next room."

The Minister had been right. The thought, It's because of Duma! flashed through Stefan's mind. The officer put all the objects in a little basket with the exception of a package of cigarettes that had already been opened. This he left on the desk. He pressed a button. A soldier entered, approached the desk and took the basket. The civilian clerk checked every scrap of paper in the billfold carefully. He set to one side a number of visiting cards with notes on them.

"A search of your person will be made," said the officer, rising.

Stefan blushed. It was true, just as the Minister had foreseen. He was under suspicion.

"I should think the fact that I possess a diplomatic passport and was on an assignment . . ."

The officer did not let him finish. "Your government is behaving badly," he said, going to the door. "Our correspondents were arrested by Legionnaire police, beaten and tortured. The Gestapo in Ploesti pulled out the teeth of one of our newspaper men."

"But that was the Gestapo!" Stefan interrupted, suddenly raising his voice.

"It's all the same," said the officer, closing the door behind him.

The civilian employee asked for Stefan's coat. He pushed the button and a young man with small gray eyes entered. Taking the coat, he went to the window and began to inspect it slowly, running his fingers skillfully over every seam. At the same time the clerk examined his vest. A third man came in, asked for his shoes, and withdrew with them into a corner. In a few minutes Stefan was naked. He sat down on a chair, trying to ignore his humiliation. I should have expected this. It's because of Duma. The Minister foresaw this. He stretched out his hand to take a cigarette from the package lying on the desk.

"What do you want?" the civilian asked sternly.

"A cigarette." The Englishman picked up the package and pulled one out for him. Then he held up a lighted match.

"Thanks."

The man nodded his head and returned to his work.

On that Sunday in November a name had kept coming into his mind. Mihai Duma. He was sure he had heard it somewhere, but he couldn't manage to remember the circumstances. After about an hour of effort he had given it up and had gone downstairs. It was dark. Rain had begun to fall. He pulled the collar of his coat tight around his neck and started walking quickly toward the river. He knew of a spot that he liked very much where the river passed through a wood. A little antiquated steamboat floated motionless and empty near the bank. It was like a relic of a time that was gone, of England before May 10, 1940—evidence of a life that he had known only in books, but one that he had loved. It began to rain harder as he walked on, and since he was bareheaded he looked for a place to take shelter. He skirted a park where he noticed that tents had been erected. There were also a number of camouflaged trucks. He knew that they belonged to the troops whose duty it was to defend the region from the first waves of parachutists, and he hurried past. Any Romanian is suspect. He walked faster. Finally he reached a house with a kind of canopy over the door facing the street. Here he could protect himself from the rain. The iron fence that surrounded the yard had been removed and donated to the war industry, a fate that had befallen all the ornamental iron in Oxford. Mihai Duma, he recalled suddenly, is someone Biris spoke about. But he couldn't remember anything more and he turned homeward, annoyed, head bent, pelted by the rain.

At the pension, Oxoniensis, his supper awaited him: a sardine on a leaf of lettuce, a slice of smoked tongue, a piece of bread, two biscuits, a cup of stewed fruit. He ate rapidly and climbed the stairs to his room as soon as he had finished. Dropping a shilling into the electric heater, he pulled it close to the desk to warm his feet. Then taking up a book, he opened it and began to read at random. He looked at the title later and found that he was reading a volume of literary criticism by Virginia Woolf. Biris had spoken about Mihai Duma one night. "I went to see someone, a Mihai Duma," he had said, "at Cotroceni . . . all the way to Cotroceni. . . ."

He was beginning to feel cold. "But I had an official assignment," he protested suddenly. "I don't see much difference between the Gestapo and you, the great democracy!"

One of the policemen, the one who was examining the shirt in front of the window, turned his head slowly and smiled. Naked, with the stub of a cigarette in his fingers, Stefan felt that he appeared even more ridiculous as he tried awkwardly to rise from his chair in indignation.

"We won't pull out your teeth," the man said placidly.

"I met an interesting man!" Biris had told him that night. "A Mihai Duma."

The next morning when he was at the Legation, Stefan had decided impulsively to telegraph his friend. He knew that it was unwise, but he felt he would not rest until he had received a reply from Biris.

273

"Please wire precise details about Mihai Duma stop Interested to highest degree in this man stop Cordially Stefan." He had begun to put the telegram into the code of the Ministry of the Economy, but then he remembered that this code had been obsolete for several months. He would have to ask Fotescu or the counsel for the Legation to give him the new code. He hesitated for some time, then went downstairs and sent the message himself, without transcribing it. Three days later a response arrived from Biris: "Man lacks interest stop Broke off any connection with him long ago stop Happy nevertheless for sign of life from you stop Cordially Petre."

The policeman held out the shirt to Stefan, who took it without thanks and quickly drew it over his head. He was a little less cold and a little less ashamed, but he continued to feel ridiculous.

That evening the chargé d'affaires had invited him to dinner at the cottage near Oxford which he had rented some time before. He took Stefan home with him in his car, but soon after they had passed Uxbridge the fog began to descend upon them and it was necessary to drive more slowly. Stefan brought up the subject of Antim's Rubens, which had disappeared in Paddington Station after having survived so many mishaps.

"This is the first time I've heard about that! Why didn't you inform me earlier? There may be more to the matter than we imagined. We'll have to notify the police, the chargé d'affaires had added absently as he tried to find a place where he could pull the car off the road, "to begin investigations. . . ."

The highway was totally engulfed in fog, thick, white, stifling. Stefan began to feel it weigh on his chest like a heavy stone. This is the first fog I've experienced in England, he intended to say, but the other man continued, "Although with all that's happening in the world, and especially here, this story will seem ridiculous. In any case we must make an inquiry. . . ."

Three days after that an inspector had come to see Stefan at Belgrave Square. He asked him to relate all he knew about Vadastra and Antim, listening without showing any interest, almost indifferently. He seemed tired. From time to time he passed his left hand over his eyes in a gesture that was brief, automatic. A week later he came again and this time he was more affable and more attentive, keeping his eyes fixed on Stefan. He asked for a list of all the people whom he had met on the day of Antim's death and even, approximately, the duration of the encounters.

"You don't suspect me, do you?" Stefan had asked.

The inspector gave him a faint, courteous smile.

274

Shortly before Christmas there was a discussion with the Minister. . . .

"You can get dressed," said the clerk, giving the other two men an expressionless glance. Stefan began to put on his clothes in silence. After a few minutes the officer returned.

"The examination of your baggage will take a little longer," he said, sitting down at the desk.

Stefan did not reply. Passively, he sat and looked out the window. The other two men left the room without speaking.

"The plane will arrive in Lisbon at least an hour late," said the officer. "And all an your account." He smiled, wearily extinguishing his cigarette. Then he opened the newspaper and began to read.

He remembered that day very clearly, the twenty-second of December. Near Holton Hills there were great trees, trees that were very old, very wise. He had rediscovered them bare of leaves but serene. They're waiting! he realized, and a nameless joy swept over him all of a sudden. They know well that everything will begin again from the beginning in spring, that nothing anywhere is final. What happens has happened before and will happen again. The death of the leaves does not mean the death of the trees, because winter is a favorable time for them and sweet like a sleep, like a long rest. As they stand now, stripped and rigid, displaying only their hard, somber bark, they deceive us. They lead us to believe that they have returned to the state of a mineral, that they have re-established a mineralogical condition of existence. But this regression to dead matter is only apparent. It is simply an *imitation of death*, for the purpose of a better rest. Life only apes this condition— puts on the disguise of a mineral in order to be left in peace, to recreate itself from within. . . .

After about ten minutes a soldier brought back the basket that contained Stefan's papers, handkerchief, keys, and billfold.

"You know that you can't take the diplomatic courier portfolio," said the officer without lifting his eyes from the newspaper. "We don't recognize you in the capacity of courier."

Undecided, Stefan paused a moment and then rose quickly to his feet. "Let me speak to the Embassy by telephone."

"The line is disconnected. There's an aerial alert in London just now. . . . And there won't be time. In fifteen minutes you leave."

"And what if I refuse to leave?"

The officer shrugged. It could be seen, however, that he was upset. "In that case you'll have to reimburse the airline company for the two-hour delay you've caused. A thousand pounds, that is," he added.

Maybe they think that I've hidden the painting in the courier

275

portfolio—or even military secrets. Stefan knew what it contained—letters to families in Romania, delayed consular reports, several expense account vouchers. He had gone over them himself with the chargé d'affaires.

"Since we're alone," the Minister had said to him that day, the twenty-second of December, "I'm going to ask you something. What connection do you have with a man called Mihai Duma?" Stefan looked at him, suddenly disturbed. "None," he said. "I don't know him, but a friend of mine did, and one day . . ." He stopped abruptly, embarrassed. He was ashamed to admit frankly that once he had telegraphed Biris just to put an end to an obsession. "You can tell me the truth," the Minister encouraged him. "Everything you say will remain strictly between the two of us." "Unfortunately, I have hardly anything to tell," Stefan exclaimed almost hopelessly. "Actually, it's rather childish. . . ." And he told him about it while they walked together under the trees in Holton Hills. He was careful to withhold nothing. "If I didn't know you," the Minister said, "it would be hard for me to believe you. And undoubtedly no one else will. I understand this obsession of yours very well, but what I don't understand is your imprudence in telegraphing your friend openly. You seem to have forgotten that England is at war, and every one of us could be suspected of espionage. The mere mention of a name was suspicious. But when it was a question of Mihai Duma! . . ." "Well, what was so serious about that name?" Stefan asked, interested all at once. The Minister hesitated a moment, then he laid his hand on Stefan's arm. "It so happens that this man is very questionable. He's in the Secret Service and he works for the Germans." Stefan stood still, dumfounded. "But how should I have guessed that he was someone like that?" he exclaimed almost naively. "I heard this name from my best friend, who's a philosophy teacher and has nothing to do with politics." "I'll try to patch things up," the Minister added, "but it's going to be hard. Meanwhile you're in great disfavor at the Foreign Office. Don't mention this at the Legation, but the British government wants to ask for your recall." Stefan blushed. "Then I'd better ask for it myself. I've stayed here in a spirit of loyalty to my colleagues and because I didn't want them to say that I was afraid of the siege of the island. It's better for me to go back home voluntarily as I wanted to do long ago. Tomorrow I'll ask to be recalled by telegram." "This too would appear suspicious," the Minister said. "Wait a few more days, or even a week. We'll see later what's to be done.

"I think that it's time," said the officer, looking at his watch and getting up from his desk. "Your luggage is probably in the plane. We'll give you an affidavit to certify that the sealed portfolio will be handed over to the Romanian Legation in London."

Of course they'll open it and go over it piece by piece. He thought about the personal letters and the expense vouchers inside and he smiled, shrugging his shoulders.

"What do the newspapers say today about Romania?" he asked calmly.

"The rebellion is spreading throughout the country. There's fighting in the streets in Bucharest between the army and the Iron Guardists."

The officer accompanied him to the airplane, an immense Dutch craft that had flown between Amsterdam and Batavia before the invasion of the Netherlands. A pilot saw him coming and climbed on board cheerfully.

"Have a good trip!" the officer said, holding out his hand. But Stefan saw himself at that moment naked, cowering on the chair, waiting for them to bring him his shirt, and he climbed the ramp without turning around again, as though he had heard nothing.

The plane was nearly empty and the few passengeres looked at him crossly, but one of the pilots put a hand on his shoulder as he passed. The windows were covered with sheets of cardboard. He could feel the plane take off and gain altitude, but because he could not see anything he experienced an uneasy sensation of misgiving. After about half an hour he heard the noise of the motors decrease, and their speed slackened. Then he felt the plane touch the ground. The pilot who had put his hand on Stefan's shoulder came out of the cockpit.

"We're loading fuel," he said.

Stefan looked at each of the passengers in turn. One woman was crocheting: another, younger, was reading an illustrated magazine. An Egyptian dozed in the seat in front of him. There were two other men in the back who were talking quietly to each other. He lit a cigarette. He had nothing to read. The books and magazines that he had brought from London had been confiscated. They had even taken away the newspaper that he had purchased in the hotel lobby on his departure. He closed his eyes. There was nothing to do. No refuge. The rebellion is spreading throughout the country. Fighting between the army and the Iron Guardists. . . .

On that evening of January 22, Misu Weissman rang Catalina's doorbell for a long time but no one answered. He leaned against the wall and lit a cigarette, resolving to wait. His hand shook as he lifted the match. Nervously he stroked his face, which looked pale and dirty, and pulling his handkerchief from his pocket, he wiped his forehead, his chin, his cheeks. Despite the freezing weather he was perspiring. He opened his overcoat and removed the muffler from around his neck. Exhausted, he hesitated a few moments and then sat down on the top step of the stairs in front of Catalina's door. Whenever he heard the elevator coming he rose to his feet with great effort.

He was beginning to doze when he thought he heard shots. He leaped up, flattening himself against the wall. Straining to listen, he detected in the distance sounds of shouts and cheers, the muffled drone of people singing. More shots rang out. Weissman turned up the collar of his coat and approached the door to Catalina's apartment, his hand raised to ring the bell. When he heard the elevator coming he pushed the button, trying to make his movements as normal as possible. After a moment he caught his breath, sighing with weariness, and leaned on the wall again, listening. He no longer heard shooting, but far away in the frozen evening there was the subdued roar of many voices shouting in unison, cheering, booing. Tensely he lit another cigarette and paced back and forth in front of the door. Again he looked at his watch. It was five minutes past nine. It occurred to him suddenly that she might have gone to the theater, and he closed his eyes as if he wished to drive away an apparition that terrified him.

A few minutes later Catalina arrived with Biris. Weissman put his arms around her.

"I've been looking for you!" Catalina told him excitedly. "I've been looking all day, since morning. If you only knew what I've been through!"

"Let's go in, let's go in!" said Weissman in a whisper. It was only when they went into the bright light of the room that they noticed his wretched state. "I didn't sleep all night," he said, taking off his overcoat. "Luckily I was warned. Otherwise you never would have seen me again! They've devastated all the shops in the district."

"But where were you?" demanded Catalina. "This morning when I learned what had happened, I went to your place immediately. . . ."

"You'll find out later where I was," Misu said, and he smiled for the first time. "All I can tell you is that I haven't slept, and I've had almost nothing to eat."

"Let me make you a cup of tea." Catalina went into the next room as Misu collapsed on the sofa.

"Now we've seen this too, *coane* Petrica!" He turned to Biris. "People murdered in the streets! Jews fleeing like wild beasts, stabbed and cut to pieces like in a slaughterhouse. We've seen this too, now!" he repeated, sick at heart.

Biris went to the sofa and put his hand on the other man's shoulder. "Thank God you escaped! The worst is over—it's the beginning of the end. General Antonescu has control of the situation now, and the army's on his side. They're shooting the Iron Guardists. Any day now the revolt will be liquidated. . . ."

"Do you think so?" asked Weissman. "But the Germans? What will the Germans say?"

Resting his hand again on Weissman's shoulder Biris smiled. "The Germans support Antonescu. They've given him a free hand to liquidate the Legionnaires. Do you think Hitler is a sentimentalist? That he would con-

278

tinue to encourage even a fascist movement if for any reason it confuses his calculations? The Fuhrer is interested in just one thing: to have peace in this country so he can harvest grain and transport oil. Without oil he couldn't keep up the war for more than six months."

"May God hear you!" said Misu. "But what I've seen! I'll never forget it!" He lit a cigarette and settled himself more comfortably on the divan. Biris sat down near him, absorbed in thought. The door opened and Catalina returned carrying the teapot and cups on a tray.

"Why are you two so quiet?" she inquired.

"*Conu* Misu is tired," said Biris, and after a moment he asked, "Where are we going to hide him? Do you think he can stay here with you?"

"Of course." Catalina approached the divan with the tray. "Where else?"

"Thank you, *duduie* Catalina," said Misu. "But don't think that I'll be safe here at your place! A large number of Jews still live on this block. If the disturbance breaks out again tonight the well-to-do areas will be attacked. When I came they'd already begun to gather at the end of the street in the Garden. And I heard shooting all the time."

"This neighborhood is well guarded," Biris observed. "I met cordons of military police on all the streets. They've even brought out tanks too. Don't be afraid. Nothing will happen here. I told you that all the Legionnaire positions are occupied by the army or else under siege. In a day or two order will be restored."

"What do you know about it?" Misu asked. "While the army is fighting the Legionnaires, the rabble rises and begins to plunder. I saw several bands when I got out of the taxi. They were common tramps and rogues. They take advantage of the rebellion to loot and murder. I tell you I saw them! Here, in this neighborhood, it's not safe! We'd better go to Dan's."

Biris glanced up at Catalina, who was staring at the floor as she listened. They both remained silent. All at once a volley of shots was heard. Misu jumped up from the sofa. "Do you hear it?" he cried. Isolated shots continued to sound, and then, after a long interval of silence, there was the rattle of a machine gun.

Putting on his overcoat, Biris said, "Ill go see what's happening."

"Petre, you're crazy!" exclaimed Catalina.

"Don't worry. I have the feeling they're shooting in the air." And he went out quickly before Catalina could stop him.

When they were alone Weissman looked at the young woman questioningly. "Am I mistaken or do you want to break up with Dan?"

Catalina did not answer but continued to prepare the ham sandwiches.

279

"You're wrong," he went on. "Dan is a remarkable man."

"How can you say that, *coane* Misu?" cried Catalina with a smile. "After all he's done! Of the two of us, I should have thought that you had the greater right to be angry. . . ."

"But what has he done?" interrupted Misu. "He's donned the green shirt of the Legionnaires. And is he the only one? But I know what he thinks about those people. He's told me many times. He put on the green shirt in order to be made director of the Theater. And they did well to give him the job. At least he's an able man. You've seen what bold plans he has. . . ."

Catalina approached him and stroked his cheek. "You're a remarkable man, *coane* Misu," she said. "Even after all that's happened to you, you don't want to change!"

Weissman blushed. "What does that have to do with it?" he said. "They're two different things. I've known Dan for ten years. He told me he's not a Legionnaire and I believe him. . . . But that's not what we were talking about," he added quickly. "What's happened between you two? As soon as I went away something happened. I hardly ever see you together anymore."

"Nothing's happened, *coane* Misu," said Catalina in a tone of sad indifference. "You know that if I haven't separated from Dan before this, it's because I believed he couldn't live without me. Actually, this is about all that's left of a love affair after a few years—the fear that if you separate the other will suffer more than you. . . . But I've noticed that ever since he became director of the Theater he can live very well without me. Now he can fulfill his dream of producing and playing Shakespeare as he believes he should be played. . . ."

They heard more shots followed by cheers, screams, boos. Quickly Catalina went to the window, and opening it she leaned out for a moment to look.

"It's not on our street," she said. "It must still be at the Garden. . . . But what could Petre be doing? Why hasn't he come back yet?"

Misu finished eating the last sandwich and lit a cigarette. Catalina closed the window and sat down, sad at heart, on the divan beside him.

"And yet, as far as I can see, you haven't made the break."

"Not yet, but almost," she said with a tired smile. "Absorbed as he's been for the past few months with his Theater, he hasn't even noticed that I'm no longer staying close to him. And each of us lives his life as his heart advises. . . ."

Biris returned a half-hour later. "I don't quite understand what's happening," he said, wearily removing his overcoat. "The radio station is still in the hands of the Legionnaires. They're announcing all sorts of absurdities. Behind the Garden there were several incidents, with shooting on both sides, but no one could tell me exactly what had happened or who started it. All I could find out was that they shot from inside the houses right into the crowd. If this is true it means that there are a number of *agents provocateurs*. This complicates things. . . ."

"Didn't I tell you?" cried Misu, getting up and beginning to walk about the room with quick, nervous steps. "Tonight the rabble from the outskirts will turn to the center of the city and then you'll see an uprising!"

He stopped in the middle of the room and looked at them both with an uneasy smile. "Why couldn't we all sleep at Dan's tonight?"

"If we decide to do that," Biris said, "I'll go hunt for a taxi, but I don't think we can find one easily. I could telephone someone to come and take us in his car. I'll leave it to you to decide," he added, looking at Catalina.

"All right," she said softly. "Let's go."

They arrived at Bibicescu's place a little before midnight because it took Biris about an hour to locate a car. Several times they encountered cordons of soldiers who inspected their papers and searched for arms. At one corner a barrage of bullets whistled over the car, and a short, nervous laugh broke from Catalina's lips. Biris was quiet, his muffler pulled up over his chin, but now and then he trembled as if he were shaking with fever. They found the actor at home, wearing his overcoat. Inside it was cold because the fire in the stove had gone out and he didn't have the energy to go down to the cellar for wood. He seemed tired.

"I sent someone to your house, *coane* Misu, to look for you!" he said. "But you had disappeared. I've had a fright. . . ."

Weissman blushed happily. "I knew you'd worry about me. But what I've been through!" He began to tell them everything, interrupting himself to ask questions, smoking, coughing, continually wiping his face with his handkerchief. They comprehended little because Misu did not mention names, nor did he give specific details. He just spoke about "a person who is indebted to me," about "a very luxurious house where they offered me an apartment," about the man "with whom I must transact the business I told you about." After about ten minutes, seeing that his guests were cold, Bibicescu looked for his flashlight and went out and got wood. Catalina helped him make the fire, while Biris watched, still wearing his overcoat and smoking dejectedly. Misu lay down on the sofa. He seemed on the point of falling asleep.

"Do you think we ought to put a green shirt on him?" asked Catalina, smiling. "Or is he safe like this because he's in your house?"

Bibicescu frowned and looked at her as though he had not understood. Then he shrugged and continued to blow on the fire.

"How have you been?" he asked presently, addressing Biris and Catalina. "I haven't seen very much of you at the Theater."

Catalina looked at Misu and motioned to Bibicescu. "Where's he going to sleep?"

"In the next room."

"I'll go see if the fire's still burning," said Catalina.

Weissman rubbed his eyes, yawned, and again lit a cigarette. "Was there any trouble here?" he asked.

"No. This is a quiet neighborhood."

"I like the way you put that," began Biris all at once in a good humor. "Do you think that the other neighborhoods—Misu's for instance—are essentially not quiet? I have the impression that you don't know what's been going on the past two days. Let me tell you. It's a sort of revolution, not the kind that Bursuc expected and predicted, but an uprising. The Legionnaires have risen against General Antonescue, after governing the country with him for almost five months. Now they want to overthrow him. The army is on General Antonescu's side and for two days they've been shooting at Legionnaires. But the Legionnaires shoot at anyone who's there—at Misu, at me, even at you."

"I thought it was something more serious!" Bibicescu said with a wry smile.

Biris did not answer. Picking up an armful of wood, Catalina went into the next room followed by Bibicescu.

"Why do you tease him?" whispered Misu, moving closer to Biris. "Don't you see how nervous he is? I think he's had bad news. . . ."

"I'll tell you the news he's received," Biris responded calmly. "He's been fired from the Theater. He was nominated to the post by the Legionnaires and now all appointments made by them will be canceled. Someone like him was destined to be among the first to go."

"How do you know?"

"You have only to look at him. Does he still look like a director of a theater? Remember how he was two or three weeks ago . . ."

Just then the actor returned and took off his overcoat. He opened a cupboard, searching for something in it. "If you're sleepy you may go to bed, *coane* Misu," he said, coming toward them with a bottle of cognac and some glasses. "But first drink a little of this to warm yourself. It's rather cold in there."

Weissman emptied the glass, shivered, and began to rub his hands. "And how is it, my friend, that you don't know anything about what's happening? Don't you have a neighbor to inform you? Whether it's over or not?"

"Whether what's over?" Bibicescu asked in surprise.

"The rebellion."

"Be serious, *coane* Misu." Bibicescu smiled. "There wasn't and there won't ever be a rebellion. A rebellion is an organized action led in a unified fashion. Where have you seen organization and leadership? There's only a series of incidents, provoked by a handful of criminals and madmen. Plus several thousand loafers who take advantage of darkness to destroy and plunder."

"That's what I said too. . . ." began Misu timidly.

282

Biris laughed again. "You'd better go to bed, *coane* Misu," he said, "before you drop from exhaustion."

Misu gripped their hands with deep feeling and went into the next room. Slowly Biris sipped his cognac. Bibicescu leaned over the stove.

"Apart from that, what's new?" asked Biris finally.

"I'm rather tired. I've worked terribly hard the last few days."

Catalina came in and poured a glass of cognac for herself. She sat down on a chair near Biris.

"I've arranged the program for the whole season," continued Bibicescu, "done away with a lot of clichés I inherited from the former director, and managed finally to persuade them to perform *The Wake*. I shall direct it myself and also play the principal role. Moreover, this will be the only role I'll be playing this season."

Catalina raised her head, tossed aside the lock of hair which had fallen over her eyes, and looked at him in astonishment.

"It was very hard," the actor went on, "but I finally succeeded. Next week the rehearsals begin."

"Dan," Catalina interrupted, "how can you commit such a sacrilege?"

Frowning, Bibicescu lifted his head and looked at her. "What do you mean?" he asked with resignation in his tone.

"You know very well what I mean. When we discussed it the last time, before Christmas, I thought we were agreed. In any case you can't present *The Wake*. It would be perpetrating a fraud!"

"But why?"

"Because your *Wake* is not the work of Partenie. You have no right to take an author's sketch and construct a play that he didn't have time to finish. His conception was altogether different from the way you imagine it. . . ."

Bibicescu shrugged and began to pace the floor with his hands in his pockets. "What you say is absurd! It's not the first time a director ever staged an incomplete text."

"But it's not an incomplete text," Catalina broke in. "It's only an outline and a few fragments."

"Other manuscripts were found. The first two acts were nearly finished."

"How is it that no one has seen these famous manuscripts?" demanded Catalina, smiling. "How did precisely the notes that were missing happen to fall into your hands? And how did it happen that just these two acts were delivered to you already typed?"

"I have my reasons for believing they're authentic."

"Quite so. If you wrote them!"

Bibicescu stopped in the middle of the room and gave her a look that was unusually severe, almost furious. "Who put that notion into your head?"

"It was very simple," she answered with composure. "You didn't have the courage to take the responsibility for the play that you wrote using the fragments that were found among Partenie's papers. Nevertheless, the problem fascinated you because, as you yourself said, you had suggested the theme and the problem of *The Wake* to Partenie in a conversation you had with him. So you've written the play according to your own ideas and you'll perform it under the name of a great author. But your play is bad and what you're doing is a fraud and a sacrilege—if it's not, in fact, an act of supreme jealousy intended to disgrace an author posthumously. You always were a little jealous of Ciru Partenie. Why don't you admit it?"

"You're talking nonsense!" said Bibicescu, pacing the room again.

"But actually," Biris interjected, "what makes you think that *The Wake* Dan wants to present isn't authentic?"

Catalina hesitated a moment and lowered her eyes. Then she suddenly made up her mind. "Because Ciru told me the story of his play before he died, and it was not at all like Dan's text. . . ."

The actor stopped abruptly. "I didn't know that you were such a good friend of Partenie! You never said anything to me about this."

"What was the use?" Catalina asked with a shrug. She went to the desk and poured herself another cognac. No one spoke. Biris drained his glass. Bibicescu filled the stove again with wood. All at once a burst of machine-gun fire pierced the silence. Perplexed, they stood looking at each other as if they had just been awakened from sleep. Biris got up and hastened to Bibicescu, taking his hand and shaking it vigorously several times.

"My congratulations, Dan! You're a great man. You're simply extraordinary! You've managed to make us discuss your theater even on a night like this. You beat us all! A fixed idea always triumphs! And soon you'll triumph too!"

The rattle of machine-gun fire increased. Misu opened the door slightly. He was wrapped in a blanket but his feet were bare.

"What's happening?" he asked sleepily. "Am I mistaken or did I hear something?"

"You're mistaken," said Biris jovially. "This is a quiet neighborhood. It's inhabited by peace-loving, God-fearing people."

Bibicescu, morose, fell silent, staring at a corner of the rug. "If only those imbeciles don't do something stupid!" he said softly. "If they do, all my plans will go to the devil. . . ."

Ioana read and reread the telegram, trying to quiet the pounding of her heart. "Razvan! The Emperor is coming!" she cried.

From the adjoining room a little blond boy entered carrying a big cardboard box. Ioana caught him in her arms and lifted him high in the air until she felt his feet touch her shoulders.

"The Emperor's coming!" she kept repeating. "He's in Lisbon! He's escaped from the war! He's in Lisbon!"

"The Emperor!" declared Razvan solemnly, almost in alarm. "The Emperor's coming!"

"Why do you let him talk like that?" Mrs. Bologa always reprimanded her. "What kind of fad is this to say 'The Emperor'? Why doesn't he call him 'Father' like other children?" "Stefan taught him," Ioana responded in defense of herself. "He says that this is more beautiful and that it's good for him to learn from the beginning how to pronounce difficult words."

"Now you'll see!" Smiling, Ioana threatened him. "Now you'll see what it means to have the Emperor with us! You'll see!" She brought him down quickly and released him. Continuing to laugh, she began to wipe away the tears that gathered in her eyes. Razvan watched her with excitement, somewhat fearfully.

"The Emperor's coming!" he whispered. "What will Irina say? She never saw him. What will she say?"

"The Emperor isn't at war with Irina," said Ioana promptly. "The Emperor is at war with the Black Airplanes. Irina is on our side. We and Irina and *Tata Mosu** are on the side of the White Airplanes."

"The Emperor is at the war," Razvan murmured gravely.

"He's not anymore. Now he's escaped from the war. He's in Lisbon. In Lisbon where the oranges are! And one of these days he'll be here! He'll come with the White Airplanes!"

I'll have to let Irina know, Ioana said to herself, but immediately she remembered the revolt and her face grew somber. If I can find a taxi I'll go. She came here that time. . . .

In fact on the afternoon of November 30, Ioana was trying to get an English station on the radio when Maria had come in and announced the visit of *doamna* Vadastra, "the niece of Professor Antim," she had explained. Ioana was startled. She knew that both Antim and Vadastra had died in the bombing. Stefan had written to her about it in great detail, sending the letter by means of the courier of a neutral legation. She went quickly to welcome her guest. Irina's youthfulness and her pallor, emphasized by her mourning clothes, struck Ioana at once. She had the appearance of a *liceu* girl recently orphaned. Her hair was very

---

*Grandfather (for Vasile, Irina's father-in-law).

285

blond, braided and wound around her head, and she had a high forehead that curved gently. Her face would have been wan and expressionless had it not been illuminated by a radiance from an unknown source. Only when she smiled, revealing her beautiful teeth, did a shadowy sweetness transfigure her features momentarily.

"Call me Irina," she murmured in a voice of exceptional warmth, after Ioana, finding her waiting modestly in the middle of the salon with her hands behind her back, had invited her to be seated. "Call me Irina. We're going to be friends. . . ."

She sat down in an armchair and continued to smile, but her gaze was so penetrating that Ioana lowered her eyes in embarrassment.

"I'm sorry about your great misfortune," Ioana began. "Stefan wrote me about how it happened. . . ."

Irina stopped her with a shy, sad glance. "They both died without confession or communion, like pagans," she said very softly. "On the night when I felt my first pains I seemed to foresee and understand what was going to happen. I thought then that the spirit of poor *doamna* Zissu appeared and quieted me. 'Calm yourself, *fetito,*' she seemed to say. 'God has taken pity on you and the calamity will strike far away from you!' Poor *doamna* Zissu, God forgive her!"

She made a large sign of the cross slowly and with respect. Ioana listened, troubled and a little afraid. She had not understood her and was at a loss for something to say.

"I didn't know that she was dead . . ."

"She died long ago, long before I ever suspected I would be Spiridon's wife."

"And who was she?"

"I don't know. Spiridon only talked to me about her once. But I gathered that he had somehow done her a service when she was in great need. And God repays you tenfold for good deeds done for the needy, just when you least expect it. . . ."

She got up quickly and went to Ioana, laying her hand on her shoulder. Then with the same secret smile she sat down on the sofa. "Don't think I'm a lunatic. I say whatever enters my head."

She rested her hands on her knees like a schoolgirl. "As long as I can remember I've wanted to be a nun. But I was unworthy. I had to think of marriage. For years and years I resisted it, but finally I met Spiridon and I understood that God had predestined him for me. He had a great need for a helpmeet. He was unhappy. I'd waited for him ten years. And from the moment I saw him I sensed he was my predestined mate. . . . I'd like to see your son," she added, getting up suddenly. "I can't stay long. I have to go back to nurse my baby."

Ioana started to ring for the maid. "No." Placing a hand on her

286

arm Irina stopped her. "I want to see the room where he sleeps, where he will sleep tonight."

Ioana led her to the bedroom. "He sleeps here with me," she said, pointing to the child's bed.

Irina went in, walking with gentle steps, examining every detail of the room. At the head of Ioana's bed was a shelf that held some books and several photographs of Stefan. Smiling, she looked at them and hesitated.

"That's the Emperor," Ioana said softly. "That's Stefan."

Irina nodded and went to Razvan's bed. Over it hung an icon.

"Listen to me," she said, blushing all at once. "I'm going to ask you to do something and I want you to do it regardless of what you may think of me. Tonight take down the icon and lay it on the table. Or if you'd rather, pull the bed out a little into the middle of the room, closer to your bed."

Puzzled, Ioana stared at her.

"Listen to me," Irina pleaded again. "Do as I tell you. . . ."

"But why?"

Irina paused, embarrassed. "I don't exactly know why," she said finally. "But last night I had a bad dream. . . . God protect you. . . ."

She glanced around the room once more and brightened. "Now I must leave. But I'll come to see you again!"

That night Ioana was awakened by a roar that seemed to erupt from the depths of the earth. As she opened her eyes she thought she was slipping out of her bed and she screamed, seizing the sheets with both hands. I was frightened, she said to herself. I had a bad dream. Immediately the bed began to shake and the windows rattled. She sprang up, terrified, searching in the darkness for her slippers while the floor quivered under her feet. She knew then that it was an earthquake, and almost instinctively she hurried to Razvan, jerking him from his bed. She held him tightly in her arms. The roaring grew louder. The windows vibrated. From the next room came muffled noises that culminated in a tremendous crash. Stefan's bookcase, thought Ioana, and she hugged the child closer as if she were trying to bury his cries in her body. The house began to rock on its foundations. Ioana stood near the door, trying to stay on her feet. She trembled, and the sound of her teeth chattering frightened her still more. Later she noticed that she was praying continuously, without stopping, without knowing when she had begun or what she had said. By this time she had abandoned hope. Her eyes had become accustomed to the semi-darkness and she saw the chandelier that hung from the ceiling swing violently. Helpless, she waited for it to plunge to the floor. If she could have done so she would have fled, but now she felt that there was no time for flight. At any

287

moment the house would surely collapse. Involuntarily she screamed, all the time continuing to pray. She closed her eyes. Razvan struggled in her arms. Although she wanted to comfort him she seemed to have forgotten how. She only pressed him closer to her breast. Finally she bent her head over the child and crushed him against her body, waiting. It seemed to her that time had stopped. The earthquake must have started with the beginning of the world. . . .

It was later, after she had gone downstairs in her bare feet and the landlord had advised her to go back lest she catch cold, that she remembered Irina's visit and the advice the girl had given them just that afternoon. A great fear seized her and she crossed herself quickly. She returned to her room and tried to get Razvan to go to sleep, but she could no longer control her tears and began to cry, crossing herself again and again. And yet as she cried she felt her entire being dissolve in blissful tranquility.

The very next day she searched for Irina's address, but a week passed before she managed to find it. One morning she went to see the young woman.

"I came to thank you," Ioana said, embracing her.

Irina blushed. Ioana caught her by the hand and drew her closer. "It's hard for me to believe. How did you know there was going to be an earthquake?"

"I didn't know. I had a terrible dream the night before."

"But how did you guess it was an earthquake and not some other kind of misfortune?"

"God and the Holy Mother enlightened me." Irina smiled.

Ioana looked at her self-consciously. She thought that she could see in her eyes the weariness of weeping. They were troubled and looked tearful, and her eyelids slightly swollen.

"Let me show you Gheorghita," exclaimed Irina. "You'll see how healthy he is!"

"Wait," begged Ioana. "Stay with me a little longer. I feel more calm here with you. . . . You're probably a saint," she added in a lower tone.

"Don't say that! It's a sin!" whispered Irina, frightened. "Don't say that!"

"Maybe you can tell me something else," Ioana implored. "Tell me something good. . . ."

"Shall I tell you about the Emperor?" Irina asked suddenly, her face alight. "Don't be anxious on his account, because he'll come back. The Emperor will return!"

After that Irina had come to see her often. "Long live the Emperor!" she would say as she came in.

Once she looked all around the room with a radiant smile, and sat down on the sofa waiting for Razvan to appear. "What news is there from the Emperor?" she asked, taking the child in her arms.

The little boy declared solemnly, "The Emperor is at the war!"

"Let me tell you how it is with the Emperor," began Irina. "There where he is, across seven seas and seven countries, is the land of the White Airplanes. The Emperor lives in a house with many stories above him and from his window he sees a tree. Now he gets up from the table and goes to the window. He pulls the curtain aside and looks at the sky. The sky is not blue like ours. There the sky is like lead. He looks, and he thinks of you. He remembers you and he smiles. . . . Now he's no longer smiling. Now he's sad. He thinks about your mother and he counts in his mind. . . . He adds up the days. . . ."

"Is that true?" Ioana asked, blushing.

Irina smiled and shrugged her shoulders. "That's the story of the White Airplanes. . . ."

Once as she was entering she stopped in the doorway, troubled. Then she went quickly to Ioana and put an arm around her waist. "Why are you so sad? Give it to me to read. Give me that book that made you so sad. I want to read it."

Ioana started and looked at her in fright, her face pale. "How did you know?"

"Give it to me to read too," insisted Irina.

Ioana went to the bookcase and took down the copy of A *Walk in the Dark*. "It was his last book," she said, lowering her eyes. "It's very sad. As though he had a premonition. . . ."

"Did you love him so much?" Irina asked her abruptly.

"Yes, I think I loved him very much. If Stefan had not appeared in my life . . ."

"You only think you loved him," Irina interrupted. "It was the Emperor you loved from the beginning. It was Stefan who was destined for you. . . ."

Irina's words seemed to fill Ioana with great peace. She put her arms around the girl and whispered, "It's true! It's true, "He's the only one I've loved!"

Irina returned a few days later. "The poor man," she said. "He too perished without candles, unconfessed and without communion, like a dog killed with a stone in the street. Do you pray for him? For Partenie? He loved you very much. Do you pray for him?"

Standing in front of the girl, Ioana avoided her glance. "I don't know how," she whispered. "I don't know how to pray! Teach me! Teach me to pray!" she exclaimed, moved, suddenly raising her eyes.

"I can't teach you because I don't have the gift. I only know the 'Our Father'. Say the 'Our Father'. . . ."

Although he realized that he was dreaming he could not arouse himself. The airplane had taken off again. On the lap of each passenger the steward had set a tray containing a sandwich, an orange, and a cup of tea. Next he returned to take away the pieces of cardboard from the windows. At once the whole arch of the sky surrounded Stefan. Beneath him was the ocean, seen through clouds that looked like puffs of dusty cotton floating lazily by without direction. He could not hear the noise of the motors. Instead, indistinct and all but forgotten melodies began to sound in his ears, coming from a segment of Time no longer within recall. Gradually those disturbing, unresolved measures were transformed into a distant chorus that grew stronger and stronger. Sometimes the voices were lost, drowned by the violent crashing of breakers; then they rose anew, triumphant, dominating even the roar of the turbulent unseen sea. He listened, captivated, trying to remember, and slowly in his mind, fragment by fragment, the Forest of Baneasa emerged.

He gave a start and woke up with the sun on his face. For a few moments he didn't know where he was. Then a rush of blissful happiness overwhelmed him and he sprang from the bed, opening the windows wide. The trees of the Avenida were bare of foliage, but the sky was clear and a fragrance of spring hovered in the air. With a metallic rumble, an electric tram glided past. He regarded it with excitement. Already he seemed to see the trams of Bucharest. He began to dress hurriedly. . . . News reports are confused. The rebellion is spreading throughout the country. . . .

> From the bus as it passed along the street he had gazed at every lighted window with a joy difficult to contain. The ride from the airport at Sintra to Lisbon had taken three-quarters of an hour. He was enchanted by everything—the wooded hills, the eucalyptus and cork trees, the lights, the country houses surrounded by stone walls—but above all by the lighted windows. His weariness had vanished as soon as the bus entered the shining Avenida. It smelled like spring and the evening was so warm that Stefan took off his overcoat and laid it on his lap. "We've reserved a room for you at the Hotel Tivoli," Filimon had told him, welcoming him to the Legation. "I'm sorry I can't stay with you this evening, but I have an invitation. I have to be home in half an hour to change. . . . The news reports are confused," he added a few minutes later. "Some informants maintain that the rebellion is spreading throughout the country. Others, that General Antonescu has the situation under control. . . ."

Stefan went downstairs and started toward the desk to leave his key. As he approached he heard the porter, who was at the telephone, say, "*Non,*

Madame, M-elle Zissu n'est pas encore rentrée. . . . Non, Madame, elle n'est pas à Lisbonne. . . ."

The taxi left Stefan in front of the Legation, whose offices occupied a modest, rather shabby apartment in a building on Avenida Antonio Augusto Aguiar.

"I notified Bucharest last night of your arrival," Filimon told him. "I added that they searched you. . . . But what's the matter?" he asked.

"I'm still light-headed from the flight." Stefan smiled ashamedly. "What's happening in Romania?"

"It seems that the rebellion has been suppressed. . . . It seems that. . . ."

After a few minutes Stefan was aware that Filimon had stopped talking again and was looking at him, puzzled.

"By the way," Stefan remarked with an attempt at casualness, "are there other Romanians at my hotel? A little while ago I heard the name of a *domnisoara* Zissu mentioned."

"A *domnisoara* Zissu?" said Filimon in astonishment. "This is the first time I've heard of her. She's never been to the Legation. . . ."

The revolt was snuffed out on the following day. Then the reprisals began— massive arrests of Legionnaires, summary court-martials, raids and searches. Cordons of military police blocked the streets, and the pedestrians, especially the women, were searched for arms. Catalina was stopped on *bulevardul* Domnita and subjected to a prolonged search by a sergeant. When she realized that it was for him something more than a search for weapons, she slapped his arm.

"You're under arrest!" the sergeant shouted, showing his gold teeth in a grin. Catalina cast around her a frightened glance that begged for help. Several men smiled in embarrassment and looked away.

"But I haven't done anything!"

"Keep moving! Keep moving!" commanded an inspector, and those who had already been searched went on their way with sighs of relief.

"I haven't done anything!" Catalina repeated.

An officer crossed the street and spoke to the sergeant. "What's the woman guilty of?" Catalina thought she detected genuine kindness in his voice and she ventured a timid smile, which the officer returned.

"Insult to the armed forces," the sergeant said. "She struck me. . ."

"Because you were too free with your hands!" exclaimed Catalina. "Under the pretext of searching me for weapons he reached up under my skirt!"

Several people who were awaiting their turns to be examined began to laugh. The officer went to Catalina and bowed politely. "May I escort you?" he asked. "I am Captain Baleanu Aurelian."

291

Catalina took his arm quickly and the two moved away, followed by the glances of the military police. "She has protection!" said someone behind them.

In front of the Rossetti statue Catalina stopped. "Thank you for accompanying me," she said, extending her hand. "I'm out of danger now."

The captain gazed at her. She noticed now that he had very blue eyes with a violet tint. And as he stood before her—tall, broad of shoulder, with his calm, full-lipped mouth and serene face—he seemed very handsome, though his comeliness was at once somewhat distant and somnolent. "Perhaps I'll have the pleasure of meeting you again. . . ."

At home she found Bibicescu waiting for her. She frowned when she saw him sprawled on the divan smoking. "The woman came to do the rooms and I took advantage of the opportunity to come in too. I didn't think you'd mind."

Catalina did not reply. She took off her coat and went into the next room. When she came back Bibicescu caught her in his arms. "What's the matter with you?" he demanded. "Don't you love me anymore?"

"No," Catalina responded with a smile, and she sat down on the divan. Joining her hands behind her head she leaned back and gazed blankly at the ceiling.

"I can't believe you," murmured Dan. He paused, waiting for her to speak. "You know they fired me from the position of director," he continued after a while. "The same old story. Whenever I'm ready to do something a catastrophe strikes. When Misu lines up a deal, a war breaks out in Europe; when I'm appointed director, an earthquake damages the Theater, or a rebellion erupts. . . ."

Smiling sadly, Catalina watched him begin to pace about the room.

"And now of all times! Just when I'm at the height of my powers! When I've solved all the problems . . ."

"What problems have you solved?"

"All the problems! All the problems with respect to the theater, I mean. If only you knew how clearly I see things now! If you knew how much I have in mind! I'm going to start writing again. I've thought of an extraordinary play done with masks. *Time Is Money*, it's called, with a single principal character—Time. And maybe fifty secondary characters, the people. . . . Would you like me to tell you about it?"

Catalina nodded absently. Bibicescu crossed the floor to the sofa and began to narrate the plot. "In Act I, Time will be a child of eleven or twelve. In the second act he will be a man of thirty-five or forty. . . ." She raised her hands to her forehead. Her sorrow was beginning to make her head ache. After five minutes she could restrain herself no longer. "But it's false!" she cried. "It's false, it's artificial, it's pretentious! Why can't you see it? And this whole story with masks is copied from O'Neill!"

292

"I haven't read it!" declared Dan, offended. "You know very well I haven't read it!"

She shrugged and looked at the ceiling again. He frowned, hesitated, then finally sat down on the divan and took her hand. "Do you honestly think I'm a failure?" he inquired, his voice very low. "That I'll never be in a position to do something significant? In the theater, I mean. . . . Do you truly believe this?"

Catalina felt tears come into her eyes and she turned her face to the wall. But she took his right hand in hers and caressed it, holding it to her breast.

". . . Sometimes I wonder, too, and I even doubt myself. But when I compare myself with others, I immediately realize my worth. . . . And then there's you. You're the only one who understands me and gives me courage. If it weren't for you with your intelligence, your power of divination. Really, your love has meant a very great deal to me, and it still does. . . ."

"Wouldn't you like some tea?" she asked, getting up quickly.

Bibicescu pulled her to him and kissed her cheek. "It's a good idea," he agreed.

Catalina went into the adjoining room. Dan lit a cigarette and began to walk about, preoccupied. When he saw her come in with the tea he brightened.

"Maybe you're right," he said more cheerfully. "The masks complicate the staging too much, and besides, my colleagues would be delighted to claim that I'd plagiarized O'Neill!"

Seeing that she did not answer, he stopped suddenly and went up to her. "What's the matter?" he asked again.

"Nothing." Catalina did not raise her eyes, and he watched her set the cups on the saucers beside the little silver teaspoons that were so old and fragile. She cut a piece of lemon into fine thin slices.

"And yet," he went on, his voice hushed. "I can't believe it! I can't believe that you don't love me anymore. . . ."

Catalina remained with her head bent, while a lock of hair that had fallen over her temple swung gently in the air. It seemed to be straining to touch her arm.

"So many things bind us together," he continued emotionally. "So many years. And to lose all these things suddenly. . . ." Without realizing it he began to weep. "To lose them all, suddenly, with nothing left—absolutely nothing. . . ." Choked with feeling, he stopped and took out his handkerchief, wiping his eyes. Standing with the handkerchief in his hand, he waited, disconcerted.

"Don't you have anything to say?" he asked presently, his voice troubled, almost despairing.

293

She looked at him, standing there very close to her, and she sighed. "Let's drink the tea first," she said and reached up to stroke his face.

From then on they kept asking Ioana, "When is he coming?" "He ought to arrive any day," she replied. "Another telegram came this evening. He still has a few little things to clear up, then he'll come. . . ."

After the rebellion had been suppressed and the inspections on the streets had become less frequent, Ioana went every morning with Razvan to Cotroceni. They went on tram number fourteen and *domnul* Bologa met them at the station. Although it was early in February and the snow was still deep, the severe cold had begun to moderate. While he waited *domnul* Bologa paced back and forth on the sidewalk, occasionally striking his gloved hands together. "What's the news?" he asked as he bent to kiss Razvan on the cheek. "Surely he'll come soon," answered Ioana. "I expect a telegram today or tomorrow. For three days I haven't received anything." "He ought to hurry," observed *domnul* Bologa, "because look, it's been two weeks since he arrived in Lisbon." "I've heard that in some places flights have been canceled." "He could come by train!" *domnul* Bologa exclaimed. "It's the war!" cried Razvan. "The Emperor is at the war!" "No, I told you he's not at the war anymore," Ioana interrupted. "The Emperor is coming home. He's staying in a palace now, among the oranges, and he's waiting for a White Airplane to bring him home."

"What can be the matter with him, *maica?*" *doamna* Bologa asked in a low voice so her husband in the next room would not hear. "What can have happened to him?" "Nothing's happened," said Ioana, cheerfully. "I had a long letter the day before yesterday. They've given him some sort of additional duties, but I don't know what. And he was in Spain for a few days. I'm not at all uneasy," she added brightly, forcing herself to keep the smile on her lips.

At home alone, however, she often found herself crying in despair. Stefan's letters were so impersonal, almost cold. He mentioned a number of technical things, commodities that could be purchased in Portugal, and especially something that Ioana had never heard of—sisal. He said that Romania would be able to import sisal and tungsten and other strategic materials. Or he wrote about his surroundings in Lisbon, or about the brilliant style of Manuel de Mello. His telegrams alone seemed to have warmth, especially the shorter ones in which he sent her a "thousand hugs."

"Do you know what sisal is?" she inquired once of Raducu. "No. Why do you ask?" "It's on account of it that Stefan is delayed." Ioana smiled. "He wants to buy sisal for Romania—sisal and tungsten. But I don't know what these things are and I haven't met anyone who can explain them to me." "As

294

scatterbrained as he is," submitted Adela, "he may have become involved with some Portugese woman. He was always like that as a student. Any girl could lead him around by the nose. In his position he could have flirted with fine girls from good families, but instead you'd see him prowling around with anyone he happened to pick up! Maybe some street-walker's got her hands on him. . . ." "I don't believe it!" "I know him better," Adela continued. "He has a talent for getting mixed up with just about anybody." "Razvan," commanded Ioana, turning to the child, "go play in the salon!" "I'm waiting for the Emperor!" whispered Razvan docilely. "Irina told me the Emperor's coming and she said I have to wait for him!" "Haven't you ever broken him of the habit of calling Stefan 'the Emperor'?" cried Adela, shocked.

One night there was a blizzard and by morning the streets were blocked with snow. Ioana had awakened several times to find that the heat had been turned off long since and the room had become cold. As she lay listening to the storm she began to be assailed by fears and she quickly murmured the "Our Father." I had a bad dream, she told herself, but she did not succeed in remembering what she had dreamed. She only knew that it was about the *Doctorita*.

Shortly before, the *Doctorita* had paid her a call one evening. "Hasn't he come back yet, *draga?* I've stayed here especially for him. But I can't wait much longer. Papa begged me to spend this winter with him. I don't think he gets along too well with Eleonora." Her tone became confidential. "He's aware that she's living with the pharmacist's son. I told her, 'I'm not meddling in your affairs. You're young. Father's old and sick. I understand. But see to it that he doesn't find out. He hasn't long to live. Don't make his last days bitter ones. . . .'"

The old man may have died! Ioana thought, and crossed herself rapidly a number of times. Maybe that's why I dreamed about the *Doctorita*. . . .

Several months earlier Adela had learned about Sofioara's decision to move to the country, to the villa of the elder Viziru near Ploiesti. She had laughed in her short shrill way and looked at each of them in turn with a scornful glance. "She's pulled the wool over your eyes, all of you! What's come over her to show Father all this love so suddenly? How many times I begged her at first to stay with him and take care of him so Eleonora wouldn't get her hands on him! But there was nothing to be done! The *Doctorita* was going back and forth then between Resita and Bucharest—yes, she's leaving him—no, she's not leaving him. . . . Until finally her husband walked out on her without any warning. And now suddenly she's seized with love for Father and she'll go to stay with him in that isolated villa of his. She went there when she found out Eleonora was involved with the pharmacist's son. As if we didn't know that good-looking Bolintin boy's turned the heads of all the girls in the neighborhood! As if we didn't know about how he comes to the villa every evening, presumably to bring medicine, and stays until late at night talking with the *Doctorita*, while Eleonora stalks from room to room like a madwoman, slamming doors and cursing! And as for Father, no one gives a thought to him!"

That morning Ioana stayed home, watching out the window, seemingly waiting to learn the news. But nothing had happened to old *domnul* Viziru. Several days later she received a letter from Sofioara. The old man was still ill with gout, but his condition had not become worse despite all the snow and cold weather. He had been frightened, however, when the rebellion was going on, since he had heard shooting all around the villa.

The next day Ioana went to see Irina.

Not long after the earthquake Antim's niece had moved into her uncle's house, along with her mother, Gherghina Ivascu, whom Ioana had met several times. She was a short woman, rather stout, who wore heavy makeup and bleached her hair to hide the gray. Every smile revealed the gleam of a few gold teeth. She was dressed in mourning.

"So you're *doamna* Viziru," she had said when she met Ioana for the first time and had looked her over from head to foot. "Irina has told me so much about you and your little son. A sad event binds us to you," she continued, searching for her handkerchief to wipe away the tears. "Two sad events," she added, and began to cry without restraint.

Irina was not at home but the housekeeper invited Ioana into the salon to wait. A few moments later *doamna* Ivascu came storming in with a wooden stirring stick in her hand. "Are you hiding in here, you little beast?" She cried from the doorway.

Her eyes fell on Ioana and she halted, bringing her left hand quickly to her breast.

"You frightened me! I thought you were with Irina. I was looking for my kitten. He's wet again in the dining room. Ever since I had him neutered he wets all the time, wherever he pleases!" Her eyes swept the room, then she stepped softly to the sofa and leaned over to look behind it. Ioana was suddenly fearful.

"I don't think he's here," *doamna* Ivascu said with a faint smile. "I don't think he's hiding here." She knelt and struck the floor here and there under the sofa with the stirring stick. "It's no good for him to hide. He won't get away from me." With a sigh she got up. "When is *domnul* Viziru coming back?" she inquired, and finding a chair, she sat down.

296

"He ought to return any day now. I'm expecting him from one day to the next. The airplane flights have been canceled. . . ."

Suddenly she heard herself repeating almost exactly the same phrases she had used eight months earlier, in June and July of 1940, when she was waiting to go to London. She had packed and unpacked her luggage countless times. "I'm leaving any day now," she said at first. "I'm expecting to leave from one day to the next. The flights from Cairo to London have been canceled. . . ." Then she said, "I'm going through Lisbon. I'm waiting from one day to the next. I'm waiting for them to find me a place on the plane from Lisbon. . . ." Finally she became so tired that she just replied, "They've canceled the flights . . ."

She put her hand to her forehead, all at once feeling completely drained of strength, filled with despair.

"We're all waiting for him impatiently," said *doamna* Ivascu. We'll find out from him how our misfortune came about." She sat a moment, brooding, twirling the stick between her fingers. Then the door opened and an old man came in. His hair was gray and rather sparse in front, but it fell thickly over the nape of his neck. He was curiously dressed in striped pants and a yellow-green pullover the color of an unripe lemon. Over it all he wore a black tunic that he had not closed completely.

"*Domnul* Vasilescu, Spiridon's father," *doamna* Ivascu said, presenting him to Ioana. "This lady is *doamna* Viziru. You know who her husband is, I believe."

The teacher hastily buttoned his tunic, leaving only the collar of the pullover showing. He approached Ioana, bowing politely and kissing her hand.

"I know. How could I not know!" he said, taking a chair that faced the sofa. "Your husband was witness to our tragedy," he added in a trembling voice. "He, *domnul counsilier* Viziru, shared in the heroism of our dear departed ones, fallen valiantly in the mightiest air raid of the century!"

He sighed deeply and looked at Ioana as though waiting for a word of consolation from her.

"I'm very sorry," she began, dropping her eyes in embarrassment. "What a tragedy . . ."

"My dear lady," the teacher interrupted gravely, "it is more than a tragedy. For us, the family, it was a catastrophe. My son's father-in-law, Professor Iancu Antim, was a glory to Romanian scholarship. . . ."

"I knew him," Ioana acknowledged quickly, looking up. "I met the Professor about four years ago. He was a great scholar."

"He was a second Nicolae Iorga, my dear lady. Since I have had the honor to live in this house, a veritable museum . . ."

297

"He lives here with us," explained *doamna* Ivascu. "He's lived with us since Christmas. We thought... but you tell her! You tell her!" she added hastily. "Pardon me for interrupting you! He doesn't like to be interrupted." She turned to Ioana with a smile.

"This house is a veritable museum," the teacher continued. "It is, I can say, a center of culture, a focal point for the whole country. We have the duty—we, the successors of the great Professor Iancu Antim—we have the duty, I say, to carry on this center, this national museum. It's a sacred obligation for us, the family." Exhausted, he stopped and took out his handkerchief, wiping his forehead and running it over his lips.

"And this gentleman himself is a man of culture," said *doamna* Ivascu. "He reads constantly...."

"I'm a poor country schoolteacher, a humble disciple of the great Spiru Haret. But in my youth I also was in my own way a person of importance. However, I did not have the privilege of being near this center of culture that Professor Iancu Antim established. Only now since I've been living in this museum have I had the honor of drinking directly from the spring."

"He reads constantly," repeated *doamna* Ivascu. "He stays by himself until long after midnight and reads. He sleeps in poor Iancu's room, alone among the books."

"It's a magnificent library," the teacher said with feeling. "It's a center of culture." He got up suddenly and strode out of the room. *Doamna* Ivascu began to sniff the air, bending her head toward the rug.

"Don't you smell something?" she asked in a low, confidential tone. I can't stand cat *pipi*. I had Viteazu neutered to keep him off the street, so we could sleep in peace. It was a complete bedlam here before. All the cats gathered in our yard and we couldn't close our eyes all night. But since then, since I've had him altered he's driven me crazy. He wets all the time. He's spoiled all the rugs...." She stopped abruptly, frowning. Irina had entered, walking softly, and was coming toward them with a smile.

"Well, girl, I asked you to let the devil take the church—God forgive me—at least now, as long as there's this flu epidemic. And Gheorghita began to cry as soon as you left."

"I wasn't at the church," said Irina. She went to Ioana and kissed her on both cheeks.

"You weren't by chance at the asylum again, were you?" *doamna* Ivascu asked, afraid.

"No, *maicuta*, I just went to the corner. I had a little business...."

"And you went out again without powder or paint! As though you weren't a settled matron! You're worse than Lina, the washerwomen."

"I forgot, *maicuta*, forgive me!" Irina bent to kiss her.

"Go on, you'll muss my hair!" protested *doamna* Ivascu with a gesture of

298

defense. "And tell me, just what are these mysteries? What business did you have at the corner?"

"I'll tell you after I nurse the baby." Turning to Ioana she took her friend's hand. "Let's go see Gheorghita."

They found him asleep in his cradle. Irina opened her blouse and brought him to her breast. With her eyes on the baby she asked Ioana, "What's the trouble?"

"I felt the need to see you," murmured Ioana as she sat down beside Irina on the bed. "All at once my heart contracted. I had a nightmare and I'm afraid something terrible may have happened."

"Nothing's happened," Irina interrupted her. "The Emperor is returning."

"I wasn't thinking about him. I was thinking of the old man, Stefan's father."

Irina looked up and smiled. "Nothing's happened. Don't be afraid."

Ioana breathed a long sigh of relief. "I kept waking up last night. I was afraid. I said the 'Our Father' and still I was afraid. . . ."

Irina played gently with a ringlet on the baby's head as she listened to Ioana talking. "Don't ever be afraid," she said, animated, suddenly raising her eyes and seeking Ioana's. "When you feel yourself becoming frightened, pray to God. . . ."

"Maybe I don't know how to pray," Ioana whispered very softly. "Teach me."

Musing, Irina remained for a moment lost in thought. "When you say the 'Our Father,'" she began, "don't think about anything. Say over and over, 'Father! Father!' until everything becomes dark. Then say more loudly, 'Father! Father! Our Father!' And then listen. But don't be afraid. Perhaps he will speak to you, perhaps he will call you. Don't be frightened if he calls you. . . ." She stopped abruptly, almost fearfully, and crossed herself at once.

"Listen to me." She took Ioana's hand. "When you're afraid take Razvan in your arms and just say these words, 'Father! Our Father! Our Father who art in Heaven!' Hold him tight in your arms and say over and over, 'Father!' Don't be frightened if you hear him call you. He is our Father. Hug Razvan in your arms and make him say 'Father! Our Father!' too."

"If Stefan would come home, if the Emperor would come, I wouldn't be afraid anymore. . . ."

Irina averted her eyes. "I wasn't speaking of how it will be when the Emperor is here," she said quietly. "I was speaking about. . . if you should ever be afraid when you're alone. . ." She was overcome by emotion then and began to cry. She grasped Ioana's hand again and pressed it to her cheek, then held it to her lips in a long kiss.

"Irina, what's wrong?" asked Ioana, frightened.

Irina sighed softly and without raising her eyes she said in a voice full of weariness, "I went to the asylum today, the home for old people. I didn't want mother to know." Gently, silently, she wept with Ioana's hand held tight against her cheek.

"Don't ever be afraid," she continued to whisper. "Whatever happens, don't be afraid. Just say, 'Our Father who art in Heaven'. . . ."

A few days after this Biris came to visit her. She had not seen him since summer, when she was expecting to leave for London. He seemed thinner, more neglected, his baldness more pronounced. A few locks of hair of an indefinite color still remained and he was always searching for them, flattening them against the top of his head with his hand. "I supposed he'd be back by now," he said as he came in.

"He ought to come any day," Ioana began. She showed him the long telegram she had received that morning, and she read several sentences aloud. Biris glanced up from time to time, regarding her without expression.

"Maybe he's put off coming in order to wait for the members of the London Legation," he said. "Now that Britain has broken off diplomatic relations with us, the whole Legation is being evacuated from London. Perhaps he's waiting so they can return together." But he spoke without conviction and stopped abruptly, dropping his eyes.

"He *should* come home, though," he began again, raising his voice suddenly. "Telegraph him please, on my behalf, to take the first plane or the first train, and come! It's not necessary to tell him this, too," he added resolutely, "but all sorts of rumors have begun to circulate on his account. Bursuc told me that . . . but never mind, it's not important."

"Please tell me. I won't write anything, but I'd like to know what people are saying."

"I don't know where Bursuc found it out," Biris said, averting his eyes again, "but there's a rumor that Stefan had some difficulty at the airport in England. He was searched to the skin and they confiscated his courier portfolio. No one knows exactly what was in the bag, but it seems there were things of value. It's because of this, they say, he hasn't come back. He might be afraid of the consequences. . . . But that's absurd! He's very highly regarded at the Ministry and he has no reason to be afraid. But he should come immediately! So as not to encourage all these ridiculous rumors by his silence and passivity . . ."

"Stefan's been staying in Lisbon in order to buy sisal and tungsten for the Romanian government," said Ioana in a voice that was quickly confident, "to buy strategic materials. Maybe this is a secret matter, so I'll ask you not to talk about it. But this is the truth. . . ."

Biris, interested, looked at her for a long time, then he smiled. "I'm relieved. Now I understand. But I know that Stefan's a little naive, and it

300

crossed my mind . . ." He burst out laughing all at once and passed one hand and then the other over the top of his head.

"This fall," he said, in much better spirits, "it happened that he telegraphed me to ask about an acquaintance of mine, Mihai Duma. I was dumfounded to get the wire. At first I thought it was misaddressed, or else he was joking. I only saw Duma two or three times in my life. I hadn't seen him or thought of him in ages. I didn't know what he was doing or where he was. Then out of a clear sky he telegraphs me to ask about him. I told Bursuc about it. He made great sport of it. 'I'll have to meet this Duma too!' Bursuc said. . . ." Biris got up all of a sudden. "I'm going. Ask him to let me know as soon as he comes."

Near the door Ioana caught his arm. "I want to ask you something," she said, blushing. "You remember that I told you once at the *cofetarie* about a girl who . . . a girl, Ileana, whom Stefan liked. I want to ask you, do you know anything about her? Do you ever hear about her?"

Biris looked at her a moment, blinking rapidly. He seemed to be struggling to remember. "No, I haven't heard anything. There's nobody who could tell me anything. But I don't believe she's important. I think Stefan only imagined . . . He's strange, that boy!" he added, smiling. "When I got that telegram about Mihai Duma, I was dumfounded. . . ."

Ioana began to laugh, encouraged, and patted him on the shoulder.

"You're a pig!" Her voice kept sounding in his ears. "You're a pig!"

Smiling he lit his cigarette and leaned on the bench, letting his gaze wander far away to the hill opposite, to the Hospital dos Capuchos. "What an idea! To make a date with me here in the Botanical Garden," she had exclaimed, and he had replied, "It's one of the most beautiful spots in Lisbon. . . . And I want to show you several trees and a certain species of cactus of the genus *Cereus*. When we go near them I think I'll know who you are—Calypso or Circe." He heard her say again, "You're a pig!"

Every evening for a week he had questioned the doorman, who always replied, "No news. She's still in the north." Then one evening the answer was, "She's notified us to hold her mail. Probably she'll be back any day now." But she did not return until the beginning of February. He recognized her from the way she was dressed, and by her firm and nimble step as she entered the hotel lobby. She was a young woman, tall of stature, with red hair and frosty green eyes. Her mouth was large and moist and scornful. Her teeth were very white but irregular, and

301

you couldn't take your eyes away from them. You expected to see them bite her fleshy lips until they were torn and bleeding. Stefan rose from the easy chair and approached her.

"*Domnisoara* Zissu?" he asked in Romanian.

"Yes." She looked at him, surprised, aloof.

"My name is Viziru. I arrived about ten days ago from London. I heard about you, and if I may I'd like to ask you something. Won't you come into the bar with me a minute? I wouldn't presume to detain you very long."

"That depends," declared *domnisoara* Zissu, and her smile exposed her glistening white teeth. "It depends on how long I'll want to stay with you. . . ."

After they had taken their places at the table she supported her chin in her hand for a moment and looked at him attentively, appraising him. "What were you doing in London?" she asked.

"That's just what I wanted to talk to you about. I had a friend there who often mentioned a *doamna* Zissu in Bucharest."

"My family is from Focsani," she broke in.

Stefan looked at her regretfully. "Then probably it's a case of another *doamna* Zissu . . ."

"Probably. But what about her?" she inquired, observing that he was still deep in thought. "Why were you so interested in her?"

"My friend died in an air raid. And shortly before he died, he mentioned this *doamna* Zissu again. I'd like to know who she is, so I can inform her about these things . . . and others. . . . I've many things to tell her. . . ." He was silent again, finding it difficult to conceal his disappointment.

"His name was Vasilescu-Vadastra," Stefan continued after a while. "Spiridon Vasilescu-Vadastra. He was a lawyer."

"I haven't heard of him. You say he died?"

"He died in an air raid."

"God have mercy on him!" She picked up her glass of whiskey and began to drink greedily. Again Stefan caught a glimpse of those shining, irregular teeth framed by gums and lips that were so very red, blood red. They troubled him. He was unable to turn his gaze away from her mouth.

"And so. . . . What were you doing in London?" she asked, setting her empty glass on the table.

"I was on an economic mission . . ."

"Pardon me for interrupting you," she said, smiling. "Order me another whiskey, please. Don't you drink?"

Annoyed, Stefan turned his head and signaled the waiter at the bar.

302

"Tell me what you were doing in London."

"Please excuse me for bothering you," apologized Stefan.

"You're not bothering me. On the contrary, I'm enjoying it. I wanted to meet you, too. I heard about you at Porto. I heard that they stripped you to the skin, and I wanted to meet you. . . ."

"You heard about that?" cried Stefan in amazement.

"There were some Romanians at Porto. We had a big party one evening and found out all the news. What a laugh I had over your affair! I said to myself that you must be a *consilier* of a certain age, bald, with a pot-belly—and I enjoyed imagining you naked in front of the inspection commission! How I laughed that night! . . . But now I don't think you were ashamed. I see you're a handsome man. You're tall, well-built, you're still rather young. . . . I like you! And you have a nice name, Viziru! What are you doing this evening? Won't you take me to a movie?"

As they were leaving the cinema she asked him about *doamna* Zissu. "What about her? Why are you so interested in her?"

"Frankly I don't understand myself why she interests me. But I feel that *doamna* Zissu represents something essential in my life, although I can't say precisely how. Sometimes I have the feeling that a true mystery, in the theological sense of the word, is hidden behind that name, behind that person. I tell myself sometimes that maybe this interest I feel for a woman I know absolutely nothing about *for certain* was aroused in me to make me discover my intellectual passion for theological mysteries and problems of metaphysics . . ."

"Oh, now, really! You're boring me!" interrupted *domnisoara* Zissu. "Better take me to the bar. I have an urge to dance with you."

After the orchestra had stopped and they had returned to their table, Stefan resumed his confidences over the glasses of whiskey.

"I'm very much in love," he said. "I'm in love with my wife Ioana, but at the same time I love another girl, Ileana. . . ."

"You're a big pig!" interjected *domnisoara* Zissu.

"I only kissed her once, but that kiss helped me to live through several months. If I hadn't kissed her, and if I hadn't remembered her kiss later, I think I'd have gone mad. That was when I found out that she had become engaged. . . ."

"The same old story!" declared *domnisoara* Zissu, draining her glass. "Come on, it's better we dance!"

"It's a question of a mystery," Stefan began again when they had returned to the table. "That is, I don't understand intellectually how it would be possible to achieve such a thing: to love two women at the same time. And this is precisely what gives me hope—the fact that on a *rational plane* I don't understand what's happening to me. I tell myself

303

that probably what happens is of a different order from the rational, and so it no longer belongs to human experience, realized in time, but to another order of experiences, ecstatic so to speak, that take place outside of Time. . . ."

"The same old story!" *domnisoara* Zissu commented. "You get all worked up over someone, you think you've lost your mind when you kiss her, and the next thing you know she's engaged."

"For many years I've wondered if there really doesn't exist some way of escaping from Time, some way of living, at least intermittently, in eternity too . . ."

"What's got into you?" demanded *domnisoara* Zissu, a little frightened.

". . . Because I don't want to die!" he said passionately, with a catch in his voice. He seized her hand. "I don't want to grow old, to turn into a mineral spiritually, and then one day to die. I want to live eternally young, as in our folk tale 'Youth without Age and Life without Death.' I believe I have this right: to ask for my share of immortality . . ."

"The immortality of the soul!" exclaimed *domnisoara* Zissu somewhat sadly. "We're all immortal. But we have to die first!"

". . . All the other rights that history struggles to gain definitively—liberty, for instance, or respect for the individual—are just a preamble to the only right that is truly inviolable, the right to immortality. . . ."

"We have to die first," *domnisoara* Zissu repeated gloomily.

"That's not enough! In a certain sense the immortality of the soul is only a palliative, a right that has been retained for us, beyond death, as a consolation because Adam lost the right to be immortal *here* on earth, in life. . . ."

His companion leaned her chin on her hand, watching him sadly.

Troubled, he continued. "The immortality of the soul is only a consolation. But we mustn't abuse it. . . ."

"No," she said, shaking her head firmly. "No, we mustn't. Let's dance."

"Wait just a moment, let me finish. We must not abuse it. We must not place ourselves, here on earth, alive, in bondage to Time and therefore to Death. We have to hope that someday, here, we shall recover the primordial Adamic condition, that we shall live not only in Time but also in Eternity."

"Come on," she said, taking his hand. "Come on and dance!"

When he woke up the next morning and his glance fell on her flaming hair spread out on the pillow very close to his cheek, he smiled dubiously. Suddenly he remembered. "You like the immortality of the soul, do you? You like immortality! You're a big pig!" Then he saw

304

again her red, red mouth and those gleaming teeth approaching him menacingly. I've got to leave! he told himself. I've got to leave as quickly as possible! At that moment the woman awoke and turned her head, frowning. Then she smiled a long smile and stretched.

"What are you thinking about?" she demanded absently.

But she did not wait for him to answer. She threw the cover to one side and sprang out of bed naked, her hair falling over her shoulders, redder than ever. She went to the bathroom and stepped under the shower. Still naked she returned a few minutes later, and stopping in front of the mirror, she lifted her hair in both hands, spreading it out with movements that were gentle and full of grace. Stefan watched her. She met his glance in the mirror and smiled at him.

"I like you," she said without turning around. "As a man you're good. . . ." Then she broke into a laugh and went to him. "You like the immortality of the soul, do you? You're a big pig!"

There before him again he saw her full lips, redder and more insatiable than ever, slightly parted, menacing. From then on he was with her constantly.

"Come to the immortality of the soul!" she murmured laughing.

Usually she paraded nude before him, her red hair bouncing on her shoulders. "And you say that you only kissed that girl once? Tough luck for her!"

It was not often that she left him alone, since she had changed her room and now occupied the one next to his, with a connecting door. She stayed near him all the time, naked, smoking continuously, speaking very little but following him around with her profound, searching gaze.

"The immortality of the soul!" she exclaimed once unexpectedly. "You're a big pig! I like you. . . ."

When she caught him looking at her she rose suddenly and stood directly in front of him. "What are you thinking about?"

"I'm wondering about what's happened," he began, troubled. "I still don't understand what's happened. . . ."

"I'll tell you what's happened. You like me."

"Maybe you've cast a spell over me," he said with a smile.

"Of course I have! I do it to everyone. All the men are crazy about me."

"You could be a witch," he added thoughtfully. "You could have given me some magic potion to drink. . . ."

"I think so too," she said, putting her arms around him and seeking his mouth. "And I'll give you more. I'll give you more. . . ."

He knew nothing about her. She did not tell him anything concerning her life. On the first evening she had said only that she had a

305

visa for the United States and that she had been in Portugal almost two months waiting to get a seat on the Clipper. Occasionally she awoke early in the morning and approached the mirror with an uncertain, preoccupied expression.

"I'm going to the Consulate," she said once. "I hope my turn hasn't come yet. . . ."

"I hope it *has* come," he began, smiling. "I even hope you'll have to leave tomorrow. You know that they notify you at the last minute on the Clipper. I'll wait for you here. I won't get dressed. I'll wait for you, to find out the big news. I can see you coming in . . ."

Suddenly she turned away from the mirror and looked at him wildly, almost with hatred, her lips opened slightly. "All you men are pigs and criminals!" she exclaimed in fury. "Criminals! I hate all of you!"

"I told you that I'm in love. I told you the first evening. I love Ioana and I love Ileana. I don't love you. Did I ever tell you I loved you?"

"You're all criminals! Brutes! If you knew how I hate you!"

"I don't know what you have against me," he continued, looking up at the ceiling. "I told you that I was in love, that I can hardly wait to go home again. . . ."

"How I hate you!" She went to him, treading lightly, trembling. "I hate you more than all the others. I'll never forgive myself for getting worked up over you. You're a brute! You talked to me about the immortality of the soul. You devoted yourself to me. You liked me! As soon as I saw you I could tell you liked me. And you like me now," she added, approaching him with a smile on her lips. "You've never met anyone like me before! Have you? Tell me, have you? And you'll never meet another like me! You'll never find another immortality. I'm your soul's immortality. It's I who give you immortality of the soul!"

Somehow he managed to go to the Legation every day to find out the news and to send a telegram to Ioana or write her a letter.

"Why don't you try to get appointed Economic Adviser here, the post you held in London?" Filimon asked him. "There are good business deals to be made with Portugal. We can buy cork, textiles, and sisal—especially sisal and tungsten."

One day after Filimon had studied Stefan for awhile, hesitating, he said, "I've heard that you've been seen rather often with *domnisoara* Zissu. What you're doing is not very wise. She claims she's going to the United States, but I was told at the American Embassy that she has no visa. It seems rather suspicious to me. . . ."

"And to me. But I don't think there's any great risk involved. We don't do anything together except make love and sometimes go for walks

306

around Lisbon. Yesterday we went to Arrabida. . . ."

"I'm glad," said Filimon with a smile. "But how old are you?"

"Almost forty. I'll be forty in February."

"You don't look it. On the contrary you seem much younger—in your appearance, and especially in your spirit. You're awfully indiscreet. . . ."

"I'm in love," admitted Stefan gravely. "I adore my wife. I often tell *domnisoara* Zissu about my wife . . ."

"After all," Filimon interrupted him, "I don't want to meddle in your personal affairs, but I feel it's my duty to alert you."

Sometimes when he told her he had been to the Legation she asked him, "Hasn't someone spoken to you about me? Probably they've found out I'm a spy."

"And aren't you?"

"Yes, indeed! But they don't need to know it. I've been too careless. I shouldn't have gone out so often with you."

At times she disappeared for a whole afternoon without telling him where she was going. She returned late, distracted, an oppressive shadow in her glance.

"The same old story!" she began, but she interrupted herself abruptly and stared at him with veiled eyes. "Probably you've found out—you too, now," she went on, her smile malicious and scornful. "You've found out too that they've canceled my visa." She turned toward him, her steps as soft as a cat's.

"On account of you and the Legation!" she exploded. "The men at the Legation! The men! You're all criminals!" Pausing, she searched with nervous fingers for a cigarette, lit it, and inhaled the smoke in silence. Then she smiled again, provocatively.

"But don't think I won't get it back! Tell *domnul* Filimon that no matter how many charges he makes against me I'll recover my visa and I'll fly to America! I haven't canceled my place on the Clipper," she added with a flash of triumph in her glance.

She was silent again for a long time, smoking, musing. "I like America!" she said all at once and her face brightened. "There we're not at your beck and call—you men! We're not your slaves. I'll be free! I'll be rich! All the men will go crazy over me, but I won't fall for one of them! All men are brutes. You don't have any souls at all. You're evil, selfish. . . . I hate you!" Her last words were spoken softly, almost in a whisper through her clenched teeth. "I hate all of you!"

One morning she vanished immediately after finishing her coffee. "Good-bye till tonight," she said. "I have business today. I have to repair what the cyclone wrecked!"

Two days earlier a cyclone had devastated Portugal. It had begun

307

suddenly at lunch time, tearing up trees by their roots and knocking down telegraph poles. In the Praça do Comércio, rows of mounted policemen held back the crowds at ten meters from the dock. The Tejo was unrecognizable. Its yellow waters had turned livid and they broke against the dikes like ocean surf. Washed by the waves the steamships had taken refuge in the middle of the river, their anchors torn loose. After several hours the wind had stopped and the clouds dispersed. A strange peace had settled over the desolation.

"Till tonight!" she called once more.

The morning was clear but cold. Stefan went to the Legation.

"I looked for you the day before yesterday," Filimon said. "I wanted to take you with me to see the cyclone. I thought I'd go as far as Estoril. . . . But if you knew what I went through!" he exclaimed suddenly. "I barely escaped! Right in front of me, *mon cher, a car turned over!* The waves broke over the dike and flooded the highway. I barely escaped! It was a miracle I wasn't crushed by a tree! *And that car was overturned right in front of me*—overturned, *mon cher*, by the storm, and struck by the waves in the middle of the road. . . ."

When he came out of the Legation and found himself again under the open sky, he stopped, deeply moved. *"That car was overturned. . . ."* A peculiar feeling of bliss swept through him. It seemed especially to be in the light that surrounded him, in the blue of the sky, in the trees that lined the Avenida. He breathed very slowly and gently, afraid that he would awake. The quality of Time had changed. It was no longer the same time in which his morning had begun, but a former Time, a Time that he had lost long ago and had found again now, all at once, unaltered.

He set off at a fast pace, feeling so light that he had to check himself to keep from running. That glorious noontime glow seemed to come not only from beyond him, but from within as well. He was not blinded when he lifted his glance to the sky, when he opened his eyes wide, unblinking, and let the sunshine bathe them. The city disclosed itself to him as it had never done before. Every house, every window, every stone on the sidewalk seemed to come to meet him, displaying itself, revealing itself. He walked faster, feeling no want, no desire for anything. Suddenly all things around him seemed to be proffered in abundance. He was aware of traversing a *full* universe, one with no empty spaces, no voids or deficiencies. Seemingly all things were in their places, and all had been provided eternally.

When he reached the Praça do Comércio and saw the uncommonly blue water of the Tejo, he stopped and breathed deeply. A tern flew directly over him. He followed it with his eyes and he thought that it rose very high, flying straight into the sun. He was mute with bliss.

308

Almost in fright he dropped his eyes and started in the direction of the wharf. A ferryboat was ready to leave. He scarcely had time to buy the ticket and run up the gangplank. Far away in the middle of the river a school of dolphins played. He could see their backs arching through the waves.

He had been here on the other bank several times, but now the once familiar scenes were unrecognizable. With new eyes he saw the same houses—white, blue, the color of brick—in the park of umbrella pines that ascended the gentle slope toward the Naval Academy in Alfeita. He came upon a eucalyptus grove with trees uprooted by the storm, their great branches torn and dangling. The road climbed steadily. Then suddenly there at his feet lay the Tejo, immeasurably wide, an immense gulf with invisible shores. He sat down on a rock. In the distance, across the water, loomed the hills of Lisbon, directly opposite him, shimmering in a golden haze.

"What an idea! To make a date with me here in the Botanical Garden!" she repeated.

"You'll understand why directly," he began with a mysterious smile, "when I show you a certain species of cactus. . . ."

"And that idiotic ticket you sent me this morning!" she interrupted. "Why didn't you come yourself?"

"At that hour you were sleeping." He continued to smile under her furious, blazing stare. He sat down on the bench. *Domnisoara* Zissu lit a cigarette.

"I waited for you two hours last night in the bar. If you knew how I hated you! I was bound to imagine . . . You're a man. You're a coward too, like all men. Why didn't you come?"

"I missed the boat."

"But where were you?" she asked with a trace of fright in her voice. "Where were you last night?"

"Where wasn't I?" he exclaimed, stretching his arms along the back of the bench. "I didn't sleep all night. I was walking the whole time. I went to Setúbal, Caparica, Arrabida—everywhere. And of course I couldn't get a boat that would bring me back. I spent the night on the other side of the Tejo. But I didn't sleep. I just went on walking, dreaming. . . ."

"How stupid you men are!" Her smile was malicious. "You don't even know how to concoct a good lie!"

". . . And once more I regretted—how many times in my life I have regretted it!—that I don't know Greek, that I was not able to quote from memory those famous passages from the *Odyssey* about the nymph Calypso and the sorceress Circe . . ."

"Probably you think that I've lost my mind over you," she interrupted

309

him again, "that I'll believe anything you tell me. Probably you think I'll listen to you now, the way I did before when you talked about eternity. . . ."

He looked at her innocently and smiled. "I'm sorry." His voice altered. "I don't know if you've realized it, but I've discovered who you are."

Domnisoara Zissu broke into a laugh. "You found out, no doubt, from Filimon."

"You're one or the other of those two semi-divine beings, Calypso or Circe. While I, at this moment, am one of the innumerable variants of Ulysses, one of those millions of heroes who have repeated, since Homer, a more or less dramatic Odyssey on their way home. . . ."

"You're a lunatic!" cried *domnisoara* Zissu suddenly, flinging away her cigarette only half-smoked. "You believed all the stupid things Filimon told you. That criminal has put it in your head that I'm a spy. . . ."

"I've never believed that. Probably you're Calypso. The nymph Calypso, you remember, held poor Ulysses captive on that island of hers with the four springs and innumerable species of trees. Probably this is your island." With a sweep of his arm he indicated the garden.

Domnisoara Zissu stared at him. Her eyes narrowed threateningly. "I think I'm beginning to forgive you, and I'm sorry. I should keep hating you all the time, like last evening, like last night. But I made a mistake—I liked you, I fell for you. I'm sorry!" she added, lighting another cigarette.

"Come and let me show you a certain species of cactus of the genus *Cereus*," he began enthusiastically. "When we get close to it I think I can tell who you are, Calypso or Circe. . . ."

"What's got into you?" *Domnisoara* Zissu interrupted with a gesture of impatience.

"I'll always remember you with much love and gratitude. The way Ulysses remembered Calypso when he returned to Ithaca. Even the way he remembered Circe, probably, although she wanted to change him into a little pig like his companions. Have you forgotten?"

Domnisoara Zissu looked at him once more, searchingly. "Where *were* you last night?"

"I can't be angry with you," he continued wistfully. "You've helped me too, in your way, although you held me prisoner in your cave on this magnificent island with its four springs, this island which we don't see, but which is located somewhere around us. . . ."

"What's the matter?" she asked, frightened. "Tell me quickly, what's the matter with you?"

"I asked you to come here so I could tell you good-bye. I'm going back to Romania. By an exceptional stroke of luck. . . ."

"You're crazy!" she whispered, taking his hand.

"By an exceptional stroke of luck I've found a seat on a plane to Madrid. I'm leaving in a few hours."

310

"Stefan!" she cried in fear. "I'm not a spy. Don't believe I'm a spy!"

"I'm leaving in a few hours," he continued kindly, musing. "And tomorrow morning I'll fly home."

"But I love you!" she said all at once. "I'm mad about you. I can't live without you! I love you!"

"Calypso also loved Ulysses," he said, smiling.

"I was crazy," she interrupted, seizing both his hands. "I made a false accusation against myself at the Consulate so they'd cancel my visa and I could stay here with you. I'm not a spy! I swear to you I'm not. I'll show you the accusation. I wrote it myself! My turn on the Clipper had come and I would have had to leave. . . ."

"Tomorrow morning I'll fly to Romania. If I have the same luck from here on, in two or three days I'll be in Bucharest—or in Ithaca, to call it by its true name. . . ."

"You're crazy!" *domnisoara* Zissu whispered softly. "And now what happens to me? How can I stay here alone?"

Just then the sun slipped under a small cloud which floated lazily and alone in the immaculate sky.

"Don't you want me to show you the cactus?" asked Stefan a moment later in a gentle voice.

"You're a pig!" she exclaimed, crushing her cigarette under her shoe. "You're a brute! You're a big pig!" All at once she got up and started toward the exit. A few steps brought him to her side. He took her arm.

"Then you're Circe, the sorceress Circe!" he murmured.

"Leave me alone!" protested *domnisoara* Zissu, jerking her arm away. "Do you want me to call the police?"

She looked at him with such hatred that Stefan stopped, his smile frozen on his lips.

"Pig!" she cried once more. "Pig!"

"I'm terribly sorry," he said softly. "I thought you were fond of mythology, too, as I am."

But *domnisoara* Zissu was already far away. She could not hear him now.

9

ON THAT AFTERNOON IN MAY STEFAN WAS STUDYING HIS SON WITH UNUSUAL concentration, following him attentively with his eyes as he moved about on the carpet. Razvan had made a column of boxes, stacking one upon the other, and now he hesitated: Should he knock them down with his foot as he had done the last time, or simply reach out his hand and pull away the large one that formed the foundation?

"Come, let me tell you a story about the Emperor Anisie," said Stefan suddenly. Bending over he lifted the boy in his arms, setting him on his lap. Razvan was silent, excited. Ioana waited indecisively in the middle of the room. Her dress was the color of ripe apricots and her hair seemed darker, with a hint of red, just as Stefan had observed on that day in February when she had met him at the airport.

"Over mountains, over forests," began Stefan, "the country of the Emperor Anisie extends. It's like ours, and yet not exactly the same. And there, as here, are gardens and orchards of fruit trees, but there's something else. Listen carefully so you can understand the story of the Emperor Anisie. There, over the mountains, stands a white house which no one can go near. It's not possible to go near it because it's so white that no one can see it. It's the house of the Emperor Anisie. . . ."

He had recognized the farm from a distance. Everything looked the same, just as it had looked four years earlier—the house freshly whitewashed, the same shining May sky, trees clad in the same young green leaves. Only the road had changed. Stefan kept meeting military trucks and units of soldiers dressed in combat uniform.

"No one can see it because it's enchanted. The Emperor Anisie lives there. He has lived there since the beginning of the world. This emperor does not die. . . ."

312

Troubled, he had regarded Anisie. The man looked younger although his emaciated face shone with a splendor that made him seem ageless. The mild morning sun illuminated the entry. Stefan heard blackbirds and, very near, the hum of bees. While Anisie was pouring water so Stefan could wash, he asked his guest if he prefered to have milk, honey in the comb, or coffee. "I think I can find a little coffee," he remarked. "The farm was requisitioned until a few months ago, and I don't know how many things were left in the pantry. . . ."

"But emperors can go into the land of the Emperor Anisie whenever they wish."

"Was my Emperor there?" demanded Razvan.

"He was. He came from there, from the Emperor Anisie's country. There at his place you draw milk straight from the well, and if you reach out your hand you find a honeycomb. In the land of the Emperor Anisie there has never been a war and there never will be one."

"Eventually the whole world will enter the war," Anisie had said serenely. "This ordeal will spare no one. The old world has begun to fall apart. And the process of disintegration accelerates with the passing of time. Another war will follow this one, and then another, until nothing of all that has been will remain, not even the ruins! All that will be left in the very end will be a few survivors—to begin things from the beginning and to try to make them better. . . ."

Stefan had listened to him, much distressed. "You're not at all encouraging!" he murmured, forcing himself to smile. "That depends on your perspective," Anisie replied calmly. "If for you the glory and worth of man is bound up with his history, that is, exclusively to his recent activities—because history has existed for only a few thousand years!—if this is so, then truly the immediate future does not seem encouraging. For this future promises a devastating series of wars and catastrophes destined to reduce to dust everything that history has built in the last several thousand years. And for historic man, for that man who wants to be and declares himself to be exclusively a creator of history, the prospect of an almost total annihilation of his historic creations is undoubtedly catastrophic. But there exists another kind of humanity besides the humanity that creates history. There exists, for instance, the humanity that has inhabited the ahistoric paradises: the primitive world, if you wish, or the world of prehistoric times. This is the world that we encounter at the beginning of any cycle, the world which creates myths. It is a world for whom our human existence represents a specific mode of being in the universe, and as such it poses other problems and pursues a perfection different from that of modern man, who is obsessed by *history*. I have every reason to hope that the annihilation of our civilization, the beginning of which we are witnessing already, will definitively close the present cycle. We have been an integral part of this cycle for several thousand years. Perhaps such annihilation will allow the other type of humanity to reappear, a humanity that does not live as we do in historic time but dwells only in the moment—that is, in eternity. . . ." He stopped abruptly and smiled.

"I too dream of escaping from time, from history, someday," Stefan had replied. "But not at the price of the catastrophe you forecast. Human existence would seem vain to me if it were reduced solely to mythical categories. Even that ahistoric paradise of which you speak would be hard for me to endure if it didn't have the hell of history accompanying it. I believe—I even hope—that an exit from time is possible even in our historic world. Eternity is always accessible to us. The Kingdom of God is realizable at any time on earth, *hic et nunc*. . . ."

Anisie had listened patiently. "You're still a sentimentalist!" he had said.

"And what next?" asked Razvan. "What next?"

"The Emperor Anisie said that there won't be a war," Stefan continued with a heavy heart. "There won't be a war. . . ."

Seeing Anisie's distant, detached smile he had felt a sadness descend on him as if the light outside had suddenly faded.

"Then what is going to happen to us?" he asked diffidently. "Will we perish without a trace? Will we be burned alive? Will we die in a gas chamber, like mice in a trap?"

Anisie gave him a kindly smile. "I'm no prophet," he declared. "And in a certain sense it doesn't matter much what happens to us. It seems to me that only what comes after is important. And I believe that later the few who survive will recover the true dignity of man. Then man will become again a decisive factor in the cosmos. To me this is the only thing that truly matters. As for our disappearance by fire or water, it shouldn't upset you any more than the disappearance every year of billions of fish, birds, or mammals. And this destruction is one willed to a large extent by our contemporaries, by human beings. Actually it's almost the same thing, the slaughter of a zoological species. Our contemporaries, striving to make as much history as possible, have themselves met with the fate of the other zoological species. Contemporary history is, as you yourself saw in London, the quintessence of zoological cruelty. And this new cruelty, this historic cruelty, doesn't even have the excuse that animal cruelty has—that of being committed by instinct. So if you would be objective you wouldn't be too saddened by the fate awaiting humanity. Because it is 'humanity' only in name. In

314

reality it's a zoological species driven mad by its so-called freedom to fashion its own destiny."

"And can we expect deliverance from no quarter?" inquired Stefan anxiously. "Can't God do anything for us? We are, after all, his creatures! Will he let us kill ourselves, burn ourselves alive, drown ourselves, to the last man? And all this just so we can exit from history and return to a new era of myth?"

Anisie gazed at him a long time, still smiling, still silent.

"Are we doomed to death," continued Stefan with more ardor, "because the world is guided today by a handful of ambitious madmen?"

"The flaw is more ancient," Anisie interrupted. "Our downfall began long ago, very long ago in fact. Hitler, Stalin, and the others are just agents through whom the disintegration hastens its own process. If it were not they, there would be others. . . ."

"And then?" asked Stefan with a hint of terror in his voice. "Then what? Is there nothing to be done?"

"There's always something to be done. There is no historic moment in which man is not free to do what he wishes or what pleases him. But he cannot any longer aid another. He can only do for himself. In Christian terms, a man can save no one but himself. He can no longer help another to salvation. He doesn't have time! Time has stepped up its pace. Our days are numbered. Our energy is limited. We can scarcely manage to deliver ourselves. We can no longer extend a helping hand to another. . . ."

"But God, what about God?" Stefan inquired again. "Can't he do anything? . . ."

"And what next?" demanded Razvan impatiently. "What next?"

"He'll tell you tonight," Ioana said, approaching them. "When you're in your little bed the Emperor will tell you."

"What next?" pleaded Razvan.

"The Emperor Anisie sees God all the time," Stefan responded. "He sees him in the evenings when God comes down to earth and goes to the sheepfold. Other people see him too but they don't know that he is God and they pass him by as though they don't realize he's there. But Anisie knows him and he goes straight to him. 'Good evening, *Mosule*,'* says he, because God is old, very old. 'Is it far to the sheepfold?' he asks. 'It is very far,' God answers."

Holding his breath Stefan gazed at Anisie. Then he asked abruptly, "What is God like? The only reason I came was to ask you this question. All I've said up to now is unimportant. If you will—if you can—I beg

*Grandfather, old man.

315

you to answer this one question: What is God like? Probably you've reached him by roads other than those of reason or holiness. In a certain sense you found yourself face to face with him in the moment when for you Time ceased to exist, in that moment when you recovered eternity. So I ask you: What is God like? From the lofty height you have attained, how does God appear to you? How do you see him? How do you understand him?"

"The Emperor Anisie asks him once more, 'Is it far to the fold?' and God answers, 'It is very far. . . .' "

Anisie smiled silently. Stefan implored him with his rapt gaze. After a time Stefan spoke again. "If there is some question that is truly the right question . . . If there's any question that *must* be asked it's this one: How does God look to you? I'm not asking you to describe his qualities or attributes. I'm only asking you this: Tell me what you see. . . ."

Neither spoke for a long while. They looked at each other. Anisie continued to smile.

" 'I'll go with you to the fold,' says Emperor Anisie. 'I'll accompany you all the way to the fold. You'll be less bored along the way.' 'Come,' God says. 'But you know the fold is far away, it is very far!' "

". . . And yet," Stefan went on after a time, "I believe this was the right question, the question it's been necessary for me to ask since I stepped a second time across the threshold of your house. But maybe I was wrong. Quite long ago I read an article commenting upon a detail from the legend of Perceval. I've thought that the same thing would happen to me, but probably I don't have anything in common with Perceval. . . ."

"And then what?" Razvan asked. "Then what?"

"Emperor Anisie accompanies God to the sheepfold. But God is old. He walks slowly, he stumbles all the time, because it's night and he's cold. 'What's the matter, Lord?' Emperor Anisie asks. 'I'm getting old, Emperor,' God says. 'Help me climb to the fold.' But he stumbles again. 'What's wrong, Lord?' asks Emperor Anisie. 'I'm ill, Emperor, I'm ill,' says God."

"You remember the illness of the Fisher King," began Stefan, suddenly animated. "It was a rather mysterious illness—impotence, old age, total exhaustion. And concurrent with his infirmity the life of the whole region wasted away in the same mysterious manner. The waters dried up in their channels, the earth was no longer fruitful, trees no longer put out green leaves in spring, flowers ceased to bloom. The castle itself was overgrown. The walls crumbled slowly, crushed by an unseen

316

force, the wooden floors rotted, the stones broke loose from the parapet and turned to dust as if centuries had rolled by like moments. . . ."

" 'I'm, Emperor, I'm ill,' God sighs, and then Emperor Anisie tells him, 'We're approaching the fold, Lord. The fold is in sight!' "

"Knights kept coming from all corners of the world," Stefan continued with fervor, "attracted by the fame of the Fisher King. But they were so amazed by the ruin of the castle and the mysterious illness of the king that they forgot why they had come—to ask about the nature of the chalice of the Holy Grail, and where it might be found. But in their perplexity they came before the sick man and asked about his illness, pitying him or consoling him. And after the visit of each knight the king's sickness became worse and the entire land suffered a more frightful devastation. . . ."

"God asks him, 'Is the fold in sight? I'm old and I can't see anymore. 'It's in sight, Lord, it's in sight!' the Emperor Anisie says."

"Until one day Perceval arrived. He didn't let himself to be impressed by the ruin of the castle or the illness of the Fisher King, but came before him and asked the right question, the question that *had* to be asked, the only one—where can the chalice of the Grail be found? At that moment the king recovers, the whole region regenerates, the waters begin to flow again in their channels, and all the forests become green. . . ."

"And then what?" asked Razvan. "Then what?"
"In the entrance to the sheepfold, God begins all at once to laugh. 'And how is it, Emperor,' he asks, 'that you actually believed I was ill, that I was tired and couldn't see the fold?' 'I believed it, Lord,' responded the Emperor Anisie. 'I was pretending, just pretending, to put you to the test,' God answers. 'But my powers are infinite. Behold!' And with his little finger God lifts the sheepfold and flings it into the heights of heaven. 'Behold, Emperor!' God says once again. The Emperor Anisie raises his eyes to the sky. 'I don't see it anymore, Lord,' says he. 'I don't see the fold anymore . . .' "

"Even before the knight had received a satisfactory reply," Stefan continued, "and simply because he had uttered the 'right question,' all was regenerated and made fertile—not only the human being, the ailing king, but also the entire Cosmos. I discern in that symbolism the solidarity of man with the whole of Nature. All of cosmic life suffers and withers because of the indifference of man toward the essential problems. By forgetting to ask the right question, by wasting our time on

317

futilities or frivolous questions, we not only kill ourselves, we also sterilize a portion of the Cosmos and cause it to die a slow death. I might even go further. I might presume that men continue to live *in good health* and that the Cosmos continues its rhythms solely because of the questions asked by a few chosen ones—men like Perceval, who suffer for our spiritual sloth. Perhaps overnight we would become listless and ill if there did not exist in every land and in every historic moment certain resolute and enlightened men who ask the right question. . . . And this would not at all exclude the possibility that the chaos and catastrophe into which we now are about to enter are due in the last analysis to the disappearance of those resolute and enlightened men; or if they have not disappeared perhaps the right question is no longer being asked by them. . . ."

"And then what?" Razvan asked. "Then what?"

"'I don't see the fold anymore,' says Emperor Anisie. 'I don't see it anymore. . . .'"

Anisie had been listening to him quietly with his face still lit by the same placid smile. Stefan was silent for a moment, then he passed his hand over his face and continued. "Now I ask you once again: What is God like? And if you won't answer me this time I'll be forced to conclude that my question has no meaning or that it's poorly phrased, or at any rate that this is not the 'right question.'"

"I don't think I'd be able to answer it," said Anisie. "No matter how I might respond you wouldn't understand me. There's also a problem with language in all this. . . ."

Tensely Stefan looked at him again. Once more he implored in a whisper, "Then tell me something! Tell me anything! Tell me what you wish, what you believe will be useful for my salvation. . . ."

"'I don't see it anymore,' the Emperor Anisie repeated. 'I don't see it anymore. . . .'"

"And then what?"

"Enough for now. He'll tell you tonight, in your little bed," said Ioana, taking the child in her arms. "The Emperor is tired."

"What did Emperor Anisie say?" Razvan implored.

"Nothing more, but God patted him on the shoulder and said to him, 'Tomorrow you will find the fold still here on the top of the mountain. It will only stay in the sky overnight. I put it there to protect it from men. . . .'"

"Come, Razvan," said Ioana. "He'll tell you more this evening. . . ."

Together they went out on the porch. The sun was now behind the tall poplars that were standing guard in front of the gate. They could hear the murmur of bees and in the air hovered a sweet scent of wild roses.

"You still grant an exaggerated importance to language," Anisie told him a moment later. "You speak of your salvation in terms of questions and answers. As though salvation depended on the pronunciation of several more or less mysterious words! Don't forget that history was made possible by and owes its existence to an excess of words. To escape from history, to break away from it, try to recover that lost phase of the life of humanity in which the word was only the bearer of a sacred reality. You'll see that at the same time you'll regain a number of other instruments of expression. . . ."

Several minutes later Ioana returned, and kneeling on the rug, she began to collect the boxes with which Razvan had been playing.

"What was that story about Anisie?" she asked without raising her head. "When did you see him?"

"Last week when I was at Brasov."

Ioana put the boxes in a corner of the room and went to the window. The sun had gone down and the towers of the churches began to gleam in the twilight.

"You might have told me about it," she remarked after a while without turning around.

"I hadn't much to tell. I asked him what God is like and he told me to come back in four years. . . ."

"When was it you came to see me the first time?" Anisie had inquired as he walked with Stefan the length of the row of poplars near the gate. "Exactly four years ago, in May 1937." Anisie seized his hand and held it in his firm grip, looking deep into Stefan's eyes. "Come back again after four years. We'll speak then about God's appearance."

"I believed that he was going to tell me something," Stefan went on with a vague sadness in his voice. "I begged him, I implored him to tell me something. I felt I was going astray, that I was lost again. I was tortured by despair and I begged him to tell me something. . . ."

Letting her gaze rove over the distant, shining church towers Ioana blinked rapidly to clear the tears from her eyes. He had spoken again of despair.

"What's the matter with you?" she had asked him one evening soon after his return. "What's wrong? Are you tired?" As usual he encircled her shoulders with his arm, but it was no longer the warm embrace of former times. He seemed withdrawn, listless. "Has something happened?" she continued. "Is it because of the courier? Because of Duma?" "How did you know about Mihai Duma?" he asked, startled.

319

"From Biris." She told him what Biris had said. "No, nothing's wrong," Stefan replied after a moment. "From time to time I feel threatened by despair. I don't understand why. I'm afraid I'm losing my way."

"If you only knew how I begged him to tell me something! But people of his sort aren't generous. They're not like saints. They don't know how to help you, or they don't want to. They aren't like Irina. . . ."

Ioana blinked again, and almost in fury she shut her eyes tight. A cold tear began to slide down her cheek.

"Didn't I tell you that the Emperor would return?" Irina had cried as she opened the door. On seeing Ioana's expression, she frowned and went to her swiftly. "Why are you sad? What's happened? The Emperor loves you!"

"But after all," exclaimed Stefan suddenly. "None of this matters! I'm neither the first nor the last man condemned to die in the belly of the whale!" He was silent for some time, and then he rose from the sofa and went to the window. "Tell me honestly," he began, and his tone changed, "why don't you want to go to Lisbon? Doesn't the life of the Legation appeal to you?"

Ioana did not answer. Gently, timidly, he took her arm.

"I'm thinking mostly of you. I want to know that you're safe. It's highly improbable the war will spread as far as Portugal. . . ."

"You know very well why I don't want to go," Ioana said in a flat, toneless voice. "You know that Ileana is going to Lisbon too. She was appointed to a position at the Legation. I think you found that out long ago. . . ."

"I had no idea!" cried Stefan, withdrawing his hand. "But you. . . . How do you know?"

"Raducu told me. He met her a few weeks ago by chance and they talked about you. She told him that she had been appointed to Lisbon, that she was waiting to leave with the new minister. Didn't you know about it?" She turned her head to look at him. "Haven't you seen her again?"

"I saw her once in March, but she didn't say anything about this."

"At that time she probably hadn't been appointed." Ioana found it difficult to speak. She went to the sofa, but Stefan, embarrassed, remained standing in the middle of the room.

"Of course," he said after a while, "in that case we won't go. If I'd known, I wouldn't have mentioned it. . . ."

Her mind vacant, Ileana sat watching the waves as they broke on the shore at Guincho. Repeatedly she had started to go in the water, but each time she had demurred at the last moment. No one ventured into the ocean here. It was raging furiously, the immense breakers crashing heavily on the beach, propelling the foam and spray across the sand far beyond their reach.

But the intense heat became oppressive and Ileana, slightly dizzy, stood up and headed for the water. Someone behind her called her name. Smiling she turned and signaled with her hand in order to reassure him. Then she knelt down and allowed the foam to encompass her. Moistening her forehead she stroked her cheeks with her wet hands. The water felt cool and refreshing.

She heard one of the Minister's boys shouting at her, calling to her to come to their tent. Ileana rose and hurried across the burning sand with light, rapid steps, almost running. From a distance she recognized Filimon, who was holding a newspaper over his face to protect it from the glare and the heat of the sun. He stood in conversation with the Minister, who was wearing a bathing suit and an improvised helmet made of paper set squarely on the top of his head. He seemed confused and nervous.

"War has been declared!" Filimon called out to Ileana. "Since this morning we have been at war with the Soviet Union!"

She felt her legs grow weak under her and she gave him a frightened look.

"The telegram came an hour ago!" he continued. "I deciphered it and hurried over here. Fortunately, I knew where you were!"

He was paler than usual and seemed distressed. Spotting a group of his acquaintances gathered around a beach umbrella, he excused himself and approached them, still holding the newspaper to shield his face.

"War has been declared against the Soviets!" He spoke in French to a Portugese youth who had just held out his cigarette case to the girl who was with him.

The words had been uttered with a certain solemnity. The young man, seeming not to have heard very clearly, lit his companion's cigarette and raised his eyes to Filimon, who repeated the news and gave the particulars. Since morning Finland, Germany, and Romania were at war with the Soviets. Romania declared as her objective the recovery of the province of Bessarabia, which had been expropriated the year before by Russia.

"What do you say?" he asked, seeing that the youth was silent. "As a Portugese, Catholic and anti-Communist, certainly you are pleased. . . ."

"Certainly, certainly," replied the other. "Let's talk about it later. . . . Perhaps we'll meet at the Palace this evening. Now I must say that I'm rather tired. It's so hot and the ocean's so beautiful and it's so isolated here. It would be too bad to spoil it by discussing politics. . . ."

Embarrassed, Filimon returned to the tent. He found the Minister already dressed, preparing to leave.

"I have more bad news to give you," said Filimon to Ileana, who had continued to sit silent and thoughtful in the shade of the tent, her knees drawn up to her chin. "Bad news for me. I've been appointed to Stockholm. I leave

321

next week. I'm sorry—especially now since you've come," he added gallantly. Ileana thanked him with an absent smile.

"You're getting away in time," Stefan had told her. "We'll be entering the war soon too." He had called her on the telephone one evening in the latter part of May. "I've just packed my baggage," she informed him. "I leave the day after tomorrow in the morning." "I'll get a cab and come to see you. I'll be with you in five minutes!" "No, don't come," she whispered. "It's better to meet in town. . . ."

That morning it had rained but toward evening the sky had cleared, disclosing an unexpected moon, nearly full. Ileana found Stefan sitting on a bench, resting his head against the back. The scent of the beginning of summer pervaded the garden.

"All the same I'm sorry you're leaving," he said. "I like to know that you're here, not far from me. . . ."

Smiling, Ileana placed her hand on his shoulder. "You're the most extraordinary man I've ever known," she began, astonished that she spoke so calmly. "We were separated for almost a year and after you came back from London you saw me only once. And on that happy day of our reunion you were in a terribly bad humor. . . ."

"I was annoyed," he interrupted. "I'd seen Biris and he had told me that Bibicescu tried to perform a play of his own, claiming it was Partenie's *The Wake*. But the lie wasn't successful. No one would believe it. The play was too bad. And I remembered how much I suffered two years ago. . . . Forgive me! I'm afraid I was rather peevish that afternoon."

"Terribly so! I thought you'd come the next day or the day after to ask my pardon. But I still didn't know you well. Even now I'm just beginning to know you. You tell me that you're sorry I'm leaving, although for some time now we've been meeting only once or twice a year. . . ."

"I was away for ten months," interposed Stefan with a sheepish grin.

"You could have at least written me a postcard and dispatched it by diplomatic courier. Or you might have sent me a simple telegram with greetings for the New Year. . . ."

"Yes, that's true!" he murmured. "And yet I was thinking of you all the time. . . ."

Ileana smiled again and ran her hand through her hair, shaking her head several times. "I don't think there's anything to be done," she stated after a long pause. "I pity you. I pity your wife. Probably you make her suffer constantly."

"Constantly," whispered Stefan without raising his eyes. "And still

I love her very much. Possibly I love her even more than I love you!"

"Please! Hush!" Ileana said, closing her eyes. "Hush!"

It had become dark. Along the lane from time to time young couples passed, walking with their arms around each other. The fragrance of lilies and roses was heavy in the air.

"You might at least have asked me why I decided to leave," Ileana resumed after a while, "and why I didn't want to receive you at home. I'll tell you why. I've quarreled with *Tante* Alice. It was the worst quarrel we ever had. For several weeks we haven't spoken to each other. But of course the day after tomorrow, before leaving, I'll go to her and I'll kiss her and beg her forgiveness. . . ."

"Why did you quarrel?" He turned suddenly to look at her.

"Because she has fixed ideas. Regardless of anything, she wants me to get married before I'm thirty. And I haven't long to wait." She smiled. "And then, since I don't have a fortune, I took the examination at the Ministry of Propaganda and I was successful. I could have gone to Rome or Stockholm. I don't know why I chose Lisbon. . . ."

"Lisbon's a beautiful place," he said absently.

"What irks me is the fact that I'm not going alone. My chief is going with me and I don't like the man. I met him last week and he made a most unfavorable impression on me. He's not stupid but he's rather boorish. At any rate he knows how to manage things. Overnight he was appointed press secretary and he speaks very little French! I don't believe he knows any foreign language well. That's why he insisted on having me with him."

"But who is your chief?" inquired Stefan idly.

"You wouldn't know him. A very ordinary fellow. . . . Mihai Duma."

Stefan bounded to his feet, frightened, with a stare that was almost hostile.

"What's the matter with you?" she asked, troubled. "Do you know him?"

He raised both hands and began to rub his temples nervously as though he were trying to wake himself. Then he burst into laughter— dry, strident, insupportable laughter.

"What's happened?" she questioned him again. "Do you know him? Do you know something about him?"

"Yes and no," responded Stefan after a moment, sitting down again beside her on the bench. "But it's a long story. . . ." And he began to laugh once more, but quietly this time as if he were alone.

"Why don't you tell me what's happened?" she persisted. "Or is it another story about Vadastra and the room *Sambo?*"

"By the way," he interrupted her in a more normal tone, "I don't know if you've heard that Vadastra died in an air raid in London. I was there when he died. He disappeared before my eyes. That was why I stayed so long in Lisbon. I wanted to find out something about him, or more exactly, something about *doamna* Zissu. For a while I thought I was going to learn something definite about *doamna* Zissu."

That week in July seemed interminable. After the first German communique on the twenty-ninth of June she waited with so many others for the special dispatch that would announce the final defeat of the Soviet armies. Cities fell one after another. The Panzer divisions advanced at an incredible rate, yet the Russian front did not collapse. The war threatened to run on into autumn. Gradually time began to flow more slowly.

Then Ileana found that she had begun to anticipate something other than the special communiques from the Russian front. She was waiting for the first of September, the day when she could move. One afternoon she had taken a boat ride on the Bay of Cascais and from the water she had selected her new home. She had seen in the distance several fishermen's houses that had been built just above the rocks. She gazed at them wistfully. There was one in particular that she liked, with its arbor painted white and blue, and with wild morning-glory vines full of flowers climbing all the way to the roof. That evening she had gone to look at it, ringing the bell in great excitement. An old woman opened the door and invited her to the terrace, where she could see the many yachts and sailboats that floated at anchor a few dozen meters off shore. She heard the gentle murmur of the waves washing among the rocks. The old woman talked continuously, but Ileana scarcely heard her. Moreover, it was only with difficulty that she understood anything the woman said. One fact, however, she had comprehended clearly. The cottage would not be available before September 1. Inquiring about the rent, she found it was almost half her salary, but she said to herself, I'll take it!

On the night of the first of September it was late when she went to sleep. The sound of the waves kept intruding on her consciousness as they broke against the rocks below the terrace. It was a night without a moon, and far out on the sea she saw the lanterns of the fishermen's boats. She kept imagining that she heard muffled noises, footsteps on the wooden stairs leading to her bedroom, a confused and obscure whispering that seemed to come from below, from among the rocks. She had been told that all fishermen's houses on the coast were infested with rats, but that night it was not rats that frightened her. She had the feeling that she was surrounded by unknown spirits of the dead. "Tony!" she cried suddenly, lighting the lamp, and immediately she thought, This is absurd; he's too far away to come here. . . .

324

Then she seemed to hear him again, saying as he had that night, "It's a wagon! What in God's name is that imbecile doing?" When she regained consciousness she felt Tony's body under her and she began to scream. Someone helped her get out by pulling her feet. The muffled sound of the motor reached her ears. "Tony!" she cried involuntarily. "He's dead, *cocoana*, he's dead! And you've smashed my wagon and killed my horse!" She heard the groans of the horse, a neighing that was strangled in blood, and then again the noise of the motor still running in the wreckage of the overturned car. It was a sound that seemed to come from another time.

She lit a cigarette. The waves broke dully, dispassionately, at the base of the rocks.

"But why don't you want to attend too?" the Valkyrie had demanded the year before. "He's a remarkable medium." "I don't believe in it. And even if I did, I don't want to go." The Valkyrie's schoolgirl interest in spiritualism was still flourishing; and Ileana had found her fatter than ever, just as blond, with the same enthusiasm for singing. Since she had become wealthy she had taken special lessons with the most renowned masters and she attended all the premiers at La Scala. She was always flying to Germany for concerts. "If it weren't for this absurd war, I could go to all of them!"

"Ileana," the Valkyrie had said once, "I don't recognize you any-more. You're in love!" Most of the time she had managed to change the subject, but finally she told her friend about Stefan. "He's in London now," she confided one evening. "I'm sorry you don't know him too. He's an interesting man. You'd like him...." "You're in love with him!" the Valkyrie exclaimed. "No, I don't think so. I've seen him only ten or twelve times in my life. What exasperates me is that I can't forget him. I don't think about him all the time, but whenever I meet a man I might be able to like I remember Stefan. It's exasperating!"

When they strolled on the shore of the lake they recalled their school years. "Look, on that bench . . ." the Valkyrie had begun.

Ileana saw herself again as she sat with the Valkyrie on the same bench in the late autumn twilight, a few weeks after *Tante* Alice had brought her there. That was in 1921. She was eight years old at the time and dressed in black. "She's an orphan! She's an orphan!" one of the girls had whispered in the school yard. Sitting down beside her on the bench the Valkyrie had taken her hand. "I'm an orphan too!" she murmured, leaning close to Ileana. "My mother died when I was three. My father married again so I have a different mother now, but she's not really my mother." "My mother died this summer in the sanatorium," Ileana had said, averting her eyes. "We stayed at Davos too, but we didn't live in the sanatorium. Children aren't allowed to live in the sanatorium if they aren't sick. I stayed with *Tante* Alice in the village." "And your father?" the Valkyrie had asked. "He died a long time ago. I don't remember him." She had continued to gaze at the leaves as now and then one fell, singly, quivering, at their feet. At that time, when she was eight, she did not know that her father, Major Sideri, had committed suicide under mysterious circumstances without even leaving a note.

Shortly after her eighteenth birthday *Tante* Alice had questioned her one day. "Didn't you receive anything?" she asked. "No letter? No sealed envelope?" Her aunt had regarded the girl with unusual intensity, looking deep in her eyes. "I thought that the Major left you something." "That only happens in novels, *Tante* Alice!" Ileana had replied, speaking in French as she had done for so many years. "Please speak Romanian!" *Tante* Alice interrupted sharply. "You've forgotten how to speak Romanian. . . ."

Sometimes during summer vacations *Tante* Alice came to get her at Lausanne and took her to Zinca, to the country estate of her aunt Cecilia, Alice's sister. "You mustn't forget Romanian," she said. "Talk with the peasants." At the station the manager of the estate waited for them in a yellow carriage. They climbed in with only a few packages in their arms, since the cart would bring their suitcases to the manor house that evening. "Look," *Tante* Alice said, lifting her parasol and pointing about her. "All this land was ours. It was your mother's dowry. The Major squandered it on his sins and follies." She stopped and regarded her niece furtively, already regretting she had said so much. Ileana stared straight in front of her at the road, which wound in a leisurely fashion through the fields of grain. Cecilia had never spoken to her of the Major's follies nor about the lands and houses that had once been theirs. Ever since she had known her, *Tante* Cecilia's hair had been white and she had always been a little deaf. She lived all year at Zinca and took care of Alice's land also. Until Cecilia died, *Tante* Alice never stayed more than a few weeks in the country, returning in September to get Ileana and take her to Lausanne. On her departure *Tante* Cecilia always kissed Ileana in the doorway and said, "It's good that I've seen you again this year. Who knows if I'll live to see another?"

She said this every year until one winter she died. The telegram had come from *Tante* Alice a few days after Ileana's fifteenth birthday. It informed her that *Tante* Cecilia had died and that Ileana would receive a package on her behalf. Then that same week *Tante* Alice had written her a long letter. Cecilia had passed away without suffering, in

326

her easy chair beside the stove in the large room where guests were received. The package that she had left Ileana could not be sent because it was sealed and the post office would not accept it.

That year Ileana had come home to Romania for Easter and had gone directly to Zinca. The armchair was still there beside the stove in front of the picture of *duduca** Ralu. On that day, the housekeeper had told her, Cecilia was expecting a visitor, although it was a Sunday in January and all the roads were blocked with snow. Around the house it was piled as high as the windows. "I'm expecting a visitor," Cecilia had said that morning. "Make a fire in the salon." After the holidays the room had not been heated again and the walls were frozen. "Fill the stove well," Cecilia had said, and she kept going into the salon to inspect it. "Bring more wood," she said, "I'm expecting a visitor." She had put on a velvet dress, dark violet in color, one she had not worn for many, many years. And as soon as she had drunk her coffee she had gone into the salon and sat down in the chair beside the stove. "I'll take a little nap," she said. "The fire makes me drowsy. But keep bringing the wood. I'm expecting a visitor." Later when it became dark the housekeeper realized that she had died.

In the sealed package that her aunt had left her Ileana found fifteen Napoleons and a number of photographs of Major Sideri. "Whatever you hear about him later," Cecilia had written, "don't forget that he was your father." Until then, when she had gazed, troubled, at the photographs in the April twilight, all that Ileana had heard about him was that he had shot himself in their house at Jassy. It was in 1914, the year of his promotion to the rank of major. Ileana was a year old. Despite her efforts to remember him later she had never been successful in doing so. It had been a long time since she had even seen a picture of him.

In 1916 she and her mother had gone to Davos accompanied by *Tante* Alice and her husband, Manole Cretulescu. Manole was the magistrate at Jassy. "We'll come to see you at Christmas," they had called from the train window. "We'll come at Christmas!" She remembered the scene very well—*Tante* Alice beside Manole, both leaning out of the window, she with a handkerchief to her eyes and Manole waving his hand. "We'll come at Christmas!..." After they could see the train no longer her mother had begun to cry. That year she had not yet become so very ill and they lived in a cottage with many balconies. Sometimes the doctor came to see her mother. He was a tall man with gold-rimmed spectacles and a short beard that was turning gray. Sometimes she

*Mistress.

327

heard him tell her mother, "Don't think about the past anymore, dear lady. Think of your child. She must not find out. . . ." Then one evening she heard him speaking with unusual harshness, "It's your own fault! There's nothing seriously wrong with you. It's purely and simply a matter of will power, of courage. Think of your child! Today you ought to be completely cured and at home in Romania. . . ."

Ileana had never seen Manole Cretulescu again. That fall Romania entered the war and at Christmas they only received a telegram, which her mother showed her with a laugh. "They're all at Jassy!" she said. "Manole is with them. He's home on leave from the front!" But when Ileana saw *Tante* Alice again in 1919, her aunt was in mourning. Manole had died several months before of typhus. That year they took her mother to the sanatorium. "It's only a question of courage," the doctor said. "*Doamna* Sideri does not want to live, she does not want to be reconciled to life." Mother smiled. "I'm tired, Doctor. I feel very tired." She said this constantly after that. "I feel tired, Alice." Sometimes her daughter found her crying. "Run away, Ileana, leave me alone!" Then one night before they had taken her to the sanatorium, Ileana heard *Tante* Alice whispering, "Have you told the child anything? Has she found out anything?" "Don't say anything to her," Mother had answered in a whisper. "Do you think if she goes back to Romania now she'll find out something?" "Why should she go back?" *Tante* Alice had inquired. "Let her finish school here first. . . ."

"What did Cecilia write to you?" *Tante* Alice had asked suspiciously. "What's in the package?" Ileana showed her the pictures and the bag of gold coins. "Photographs of Father," she whispered, and suddenly the word 'father' sounded strange, unnatural, as it fell from her lips. *Tante* Alice, Cecilia, the housekeeper—they all called him "the Major." "I don't want to see them," protested *Tante* Alice, lifting her hand. "I know them well enough. . . ." Ileana selected one of them—one which showed him as a young lieutenant with a short moustache, very deep-set eyes, and thick hair falling in a great shock over his forehead—and she framed it. When she returned to school the Valkyrie exclaimed, "What a romantic face! I'm sure . . ." Then she had stopped suddenly and smiled a guilty smile. "He committed suicide at thirty-five," Ileana said. "No one knows the reason. . . ."

On that Easter vacation she walked back and forth, back and forth, in the salon in front of the painting of *duduca* Ralu and the armchair in which *Tante* Cecilia had died. She did not understand why but it

328

seemed to her that they were one and the same person, that the picture of *duduca* Ralu represented *Tante* Cecilia when she was young. That spring at Lausanne, when the girls held séances, she prayed in her mind for *duduca* Ralu to come, because she had not known her and was not afraid of her; but she was sure that it would be *Tante* Cecilia. "What a romantic face!" was the Valkyrie's exclamation whenever her eyes fell on the photograph of Lieutenant Sideri. "I'm sorry to tell you this," she confided once, many years later, "but I'm sure that your father took his life on account of a woman. Probably she was a princess or a queen and he received an order from his superior to kill himself. . . ."

She saw the Valkyrie again during the first part of June, when she was on her way to Lisbon, and she spent two days with her at Lausanne. "I think I'm in love too," the Valkyrie had told her. "This time I believe it's serious. He's a great artist. . . ." Ileana thought that she looked even more overweight than before as she spoke of her love for this artist. She had not wanted to reveal his name. "He's too famous a man. Undoubtedly you know him too. . . . But what about you? Do you still love that man?" "I've never loved him," said Ileana. "But this time anything there was between us is finished. He's an egotist. I'm sorry I quarreled with *Tante* Alice because of him. . . ."

"I know very well why you don't want to get married!" *Tante* Alice had said when they quarreled. "You're still in love with Viziru and probably you've been his mistress for a long time. . . ." "*Tante* Alice!" Ileana cried suddenly. "But you're committing a sin if you want to break up his home. He's a married man and he has a child. God won't help you if you break up his home!" All at once Ileana began to cry. "If you love him and he loves you," *Tante* Alice went on, "there's nothing to be done. It's up to God to join together and to separate. But if only you were married, at least in the eyes of the world . . ." "I've seen him just once since he came back from London," she said, wiping her eyes furiously. "And last year I saw him only twice." *Tante* Alice stared at her, frowning. "Then you're both fools! And you're the greater one. You must get married without fail. This year you must get married!"

Every afternoon she was happy as soon as she boarded the electric train that took her to Cascais. She forgot, then, about the war. She forgot the monotony of the work at the Legation. Alone, she prepared her evening meal, but not before she had gone for a swim. She made a detour around the boats moored in front of the house and soon gained the open sea, returning when lights began to appear in the windows of the houses.

Although she had met a number of people, she received very few callers at her house. Just once, on a Sunday, a week after she had moved, she had invited the Minister and their co-workers at the Legation. One of these was a young Portuguese woman with whom she was on friendly terms and who sometimes came to spend a Sunday with her. Others she was content to meet on the beach. This desire for solitude soon gave her a questionable reputation, which she learned about from her Portuguese friend. Rumors concerning her adventures were beginning to circulate around the Legation.

"You're too beautiful! And you smile too readily. Then, too, you're indiscreet. You live alone in an isolated house, you go to bars, you dance too much, you go home late. . . ."

Ileana shrugged. "The Valkyrie will be coming," she replied. "An old friend of mine, a Swiss girl, is coming to stay with me. I won't be alone much longer. . . ."

But the Valkyrie kept postponing her trip. "Maybe I can come this winter," she wrote. "Just now it's out of the question. I'll tell you why when we get together. . . ." And then, unexpectedly, one day at the end of October, in a letter from *Tante* Alice, she learned that for some time Stefan had been at the front as a volunteer. Her face became pale, and since she felt Duma's eyes riveted upon her, she left the office at once.

"The brute!" she muttered furiously between clenched teeth, crushing the letter in her fist. "The brute! Now he hits me with this! The beast! That merciless egotist! He doesn't think of anyone but himself. A volunteer! In a regiment on the front line! And no one knows anything more about him. . . . No one knows anything more about him!" From that date she felt she had begun to hate him.

One Sunday afternoon when she was alone she heard someone knock insistently. She was not expecting guests. Arranging her hair hastily she extinguished her cigarette and opened the door. It was Mihai Duma. Ileana did not try to hide her annoyance. Until that time she had managed to maintain only an impersonal, official relationship with her chief.

"I'm not disturbing you?" he inquired, smiling. Ileana led him to the terrace without a reply.

"I was in the neighborhood," continued Duma, sitting down on the chaise longue, "and I came by to see how you are." He stopped and looked at the bay. A boat was preparing to put out to sea. The wind billowed the red sail suddenly, tilting it far to one side, all but overturning it.

"You have a beautiful place," he said. "You can forget your troubles here, forget the war. . . ."

Ileana's attention was claimed by the maneuvering sailboat. Caught by the wind, it glided over the surface of the water at an extraordinary speed, inclining steeply.

"By the way," began Duma, changing his tone. "You know a lot of people. Have you met a compatriot of ours, a certain *domnisoara* Zissu?"

330

"I've heard of her," said Ileana, "but I haven't met her."

Duma gave her a quick reproachful glance, then he smiled. Ileana found the smile especially repugnant, for it seemed to her to betray a cruelty that was ordinarily concealed by his placid face.

"You made a mistake not to meet her before this," he went on. "She's a woman who interests us. She says she has a visa for the United States, that she's waiting for a seat on the Clipper, but she's been waiting for ten months and we're very suspicious of her. But she's also quite intriguing. . . ."

"I don't see how she would be of interest to me," commented Ileana.

Somewhat severely Duma looked straight into her eyes. "To you directly, perhaps not. But that's not the point. It's a question of what interests us. And we're concerned with any Romanian who's bound for other parts of the world. Remember, we're at war. And we're fighting on the side of the Germans against the Russians—a fact that many Romanians tend to forget. I know about your pro-American and pro-British sentiments. You're free to cultivate them as much as you wish. We're not intolerant of the feelings of our employees. We shut our eyes! On the condition, though, that each one does his duty. . . ."

"Is that a graceful way of criticizing me?" asked Ileana, blushing.

"Yes and no. I'm satisfied with your work at the Legation. You're a very conscientious secretary, but that's not enough. You move in so many circles, you see so many people. You ought to keep your ears open and tell us what you hear, what is said, what's being planned. Aside from the great secrets of state, none exist which don't eventually become known—at least in certain circles. Such secrets interest us. Therefore it would be well if you would meet this *domnisoara* Zissu, make friends with her and talk with her about your Anglo-American sympathies. . . ."

Ileana felt her face grow redder.

"You can invite her here to your house," he continued in a jerky monotone. "And you can even invite certain gentlemen, distinguished men. . . . It's not necessary that your guests always be on the side of the Axis," he added with a smile.

He stopped in front of the door as he was leaving. "One thing more. Vidrighin, our new economic adviser, arrives tomorrow. He was in Tokyo and Chile—he's coming here from Chile. He's a very good man. Costescu and I are going to meet him at the dock and I'd like you to come with us. His wife is Norwegian and doesn't know Romanian. . . ."

Several weeks later, toward the end of November, she learned by chance about the impending arrival of an economic mission to arrange for the purchase of sisal, tungsten, and, secretly, of rubber. On that same afternoon Duma handed her a list of names.

"Do you know any of them?" he asked without raising his eyes. She began to examine the list and suddenly her face grew white. "Do you know anyone?" he demanded again.

"Stefan Viziru," she said, moistening her lips. "But I thought he was at the front in Russia."

"He might have found it bad at the front," said Duma, standing up. "Especially now that it's turning cold."

"He might have been wounded," murmured Ileana absently.

". . . Add that here in Lisbon, besides the lordly salary, there's also the possibility of a nice commission. You yourself know the system. . . ."

She blushed and her glance challenged his. "But you don't know Stefan Viziru. If you knew him you wouldn't make such an insinuation."

Duma laughed silently as he opened the safe. "So this is the only one you know?" he asked, replacing the dossiers with care. "So much the better. I place him in your hands. Follow him everywhere. Show him the city. Take him to the bars. . . ."

"Viziru already knows Lisbon quite well," interrupted Ileana.

"I know. He was here last winter. He stayed a long time—a little too long, in fact. He couldn't bear to leave. . . . And I keep wondering—why, indeed? Only on account of Stella Zissu?"

Ileana felt the blood rush to her cheeks, and she began to open a package of cigarettes with trembling fingers. Duma closed the safe and turned to her.

"Or perhaps you didn't know this?" he inquired, smiling with exaggerated surprise. "Then you're not curious to hear what is being said around you?" He was silent a moment and then went on, "And it's just this relationship that seems interesting to me. Interesting, even suspicious. It wasn't just on account of *domnisoara* Zissu's beautiful eyes that he stayed here nearly a month. This young woman saw all sorts of people. She was really a woman of the world. But not like you. . . . I say 'was' because unfortunately she left the day before yesterday. She found a seat on the Clipper at last and she's gone to America. . . .'

One morning during the Christmas season she came to the Legation and saw several suitcases and courier bags standing in a corner of the corridor. She realized that the economic mission had arrived. Stopping a moment to quiet the rapid beating of her heart she proceeded to Duma's office with feigned

332

indifference. The sound of men's voices came from the Secretary's room. She walked more slowly and her heart began to pound again. The door on her left opened suddenly and Stefan appeared on the threshold.

"Good morning," he said casually. "How are you?"

"Fine. And you?"

"I'm fine. A little tired. . . . But when did the Legation move here to San Mamede?"

"A few months ago. The old building had become too crowded."

"I believe it. You've expanded since I left. You're beginning to look like an Embassy. . . ."

Something's happened to him, she said suddenly to herself. He had aged, he was thinner, his whole face seemed altered. The hair at his temples was streaked with gray. He held his eyes half shut as if the light hurt them. Even his voice seemed no longer the same.

"I hope we'll see more of each other around here," he added, giving her a pat on the shoulder. "Maybe we can have dinner together some day. . . ."

"As you wish," agreed Ileana, smiling.

On Christmas Day she telephoned him several times at the hotel without locating him. She left her number but it was after midnight when he returned her call. Anxiously she lifted the receiver.

"Merry Christmas!" he said.

"Merry Christmas!" Her voice was low. "I waited for you all day. I thought perhaps you'd remember me. . . ."

"When would you like to get together?" he asked.

"Come the day after tomorrow at lunch time and eat with me. There'll be just the two of us. . . ."

"Good."

Thinking that he would continue Ileana waited a few moments, then she cried, "Hello! "Hello!"

"Yes," said Stefan, "what is it?"

"I thought we'd been cut off."

"No, we weren't cut off. . . . Until the day after tomorrow. . . . Good night!"

"Good night," she said very softly.

A copious but fine rain began to fall on the morning of the third day after Christmas. Stefan was mistaken about the address and arrived a half-hour late, bareheaded, with the collar of his overcoat turned up. The flowers he carried were so wet from the rain that he took them out of the paper while he

333

was waiting in front of the house. He shook the water from them and sheltered them under his coat until Ileana opened the door.

"Happy holidays!" he said as he stood smiling on the doorstep.

She raised herself slightly on the tips of her toes and kissed him on both cheeks. "Many happy returns of the day! I don't suppose you've forgotten this is your saint's day."

As he entered the room Stefan took out his handkerchief and began to wipe his face and hair. "It's very beautiful here," he remarked, approaching the terrace.

Nothing could be seen but the rain falling gently on the dark blue waves. A tern struggled up from the rocks, hovered a few moments, then fell back upon the water.

"Today it's not as beautiful as it usually is," said Ileana, "but I like it this way too. . . ." She started. For a moment she seemed to see the Stefan of former times, to recognize the light in his eyes and his special way of running his hand through his hair. But he only fingered the back of his neck and his collar.

"I think I'm soaked." He smiled.

"Come close to the fire." The small cast iron stove was glowing and Stefan sat down beside it on the rug. Ileana brought the tray of aperitifs, installing herself next to him. "It's my first house and I'm very fond of it. . . . Cinzano or gin?" she asked after a moment, raising her eyes.

Stefan looked at her suddenly almost in astonishment, as if he were seeing her for the first time. Ileana smiled, embarrassed, waiting for his reply. Finally she poured a glass of vermouth and held it out to him.

"*Noroc!*"* she said, as they touched glasses. "May all your dreams come true!"

"And yours too!"

She got up quickly and went to the kitchen to see if the woman were ready to serve the lunch. When she came back she found Stefan standing on the terrace in the rain gazing down at the waves that broke on the rocks.

"You're crazy!" she cried from the doorway. "Come back in the house! You'll catch cold!"

"There's something down there," he said without turning his head. "It looks like a book. . . ."

Ileana went out on the terrace after him. "Please come in the house!" she begged, taking his arm. "The woman's waiting for us with the lunch."

"Just a minute." And before Ileana realized what he had in mind he had disengaged his arm, mounted the parapet, and climbed quickly down among the rocks to the water's edge. Clinging to a large stone with his left hand he leaned far out and grasped the book. He glanced quickly at the title and

*Luck!

334

scrambled up the rocks, tearing his trousers on the way, vaulting over the little wall to the terrace. Ileana was waiting for him by the stove.

"I thought I could guess the title," he said as he approached her, wiping away the seaweed that clung to the book. "And I wasn't mistaken. Look— *Encore un instant de bonheur*. . . . If only you knew what that title calls to mind!"

Ileana noticed his torn trousers and she smiled. Laying the book on a footstool to dry beside the stove, Stefan proceeded to shake the water from his hair.

"What a lucky man you are." Ileana spoke suddenly. "I bought that book for you. I wanted to give it to you for Christmas, but I was afraid you'd see some allusion in it so I didn't. I was even provoked with you because you were so ill-bred that you waited for me to call you on the phone. And by evening I was so furious I threw the book off the terrace. I never imagined you'd find it." With an abrupt toss of her head she added, "I believe it's time we thought about eating."

Under his napkin Stefan found a little date book bound in leather. On the page for January 1, 1942, Ileana had inscribed in English the word "Remember." She had underscored it several times.

The rain continued to fall all afternoon. At about four o'clock a fine mist descended over the ocean and the entire bay was gradually obscured. Only a portion of the bank of the Estoril remained in view. Smoking, they sat side by side on the carpet near the stove, looking straight ahead.

". . . And I told Biris too: ever since then I've had a great loathing for myself."

"I believe it's a normal thing," interrupted Ileana. "Probably everyone feels the same way. . . ."

". . . Not only because I was afraid. Everybody's afraid in the presence of death. But I felt how much I'm bound to this everyday life. I'd have been ready to commit any act of cowardice to be able to enjoy life once again—but not what I'd regarded as beautiful and worthwhile. Instead I wanted to live to scratch the back of my neck where a vicious horsefly had bit me a little earlier, or to stretch out my feet once more because they'd gone to sleep, or to be able to wipe the sweat from my forehead with a handkerchief. . . . This was why I prayed to God in my mind that the mortar shells wouldn't touch me in that half-dug trench where I crouched when the Russians discovered us. . . . I felt then how *good* it is to be alive. . . ."

"This seems very normal to me," Ileana commented.

"Probably that's how we're made—all of us. But to me it seemed that all my illusions were shattered in that moment. I'd thought I was different. I'd believed that for me, at least, death also has a positive aspect, since every death is a leap beyond into the unknown. No matter how much I love life there still remains this fascinating component of death—that by it we *resolve* something, we learn something. At least we find out if *something* exists on the other side or if we return to nothingness. Biris laughed at this, but I told him that even this nothingness is in a certain way an answer we've waited for, an answer to a question that we've asked ourselves for such a long time here on earth. And so, however we look at it, death still remains an essential fact that totally engages us. . . . But at that moment death seemed absurd, absolutely meaningless. A single thought possessed me—that I was a fool or an imbecile to let myself be drawn into such an adventure, volunteering to be sent to the front. On the contrary, I ought to have tried by any means to escape, to run away, to seek safety . . . Ever since the day the mortars found us I haven't been able to forget this. Sometimes I wake up from sleep and feel humiliated, slapped, spat upon. Since then I seem to have lost faith in myself. . . ."

"That's absurd!" declared Ileana. "You've suffered a shock, like all the others in the first days of the war. But it will pass . . ."

"I hope so. But even though I stayed at the front almost two months after that it didn't go away. I became ill. I despised myself. If I see—and surely I will—that it doesn't leave me, I'm going back . . . especially now when the situation is growing steadily worse and there's so great a need for men. . . ."

Abruptly Ileana turned and regarded him with alarm. "You're mad!"

Just at that instant the bell rang and there were several raps on the door. She stood up quickly and lit the lamp, leaning slightly toward Stefan. "Tell me, please, is it true that you had an affair here with a certain *domnisoara* Zissu?"

"Yes, it's true. But why do you ask?"

"I'll tell you another time. . . ." Insistently, the bell rang again. "Now I have guests," she added hastily in a whisper and ran to open the door. A few moments later Vidrighin came in, accompanied by his wife and Mihai Duma.

Climbing continuously they walked for almost an hour through the woods. It became quite cold. Sometimes the wind shook the topmost branches of the trees momentarily and then all was still. The cedars were left behind, lifting their limbs high above the forest, dominating it. But the trees became more dense as the two approached the top of the mountain. Then at a bend in the path they caught sight of the cross—*Cruz alta*.

From this point they could see the whole region, a vast panorama. In the twilight the contours of the mountains on the horizon were beginning to merge. Close at hand they discerned valleys and meadows, innumerable roads and ploughed fields that were red, brown, the color of bark.

"Let's climb to the top," suggested Stefan.

An old man who was waiting on the stone steps that led to the cross greeted them and stepped aside. They began to ascend the stairs. When they reached the top they leaned against the parapet and looked toward Coimbra. White, somber, the Monastery of Santa Clara stood in lonely isolation above the green ocean of the hills. The Mondego gleamed, very far away, as it meandered among the weeping willows, the poplars and plane trees. A large bird flew overhead, circled a moment almost without moving its wings, then glided down into the valley.

"Sometimes in my dreams," mused Ileana, "I find myself somewhere beside you on a very high mountain, looking down at the land below as we're doing now. . . . And now I feel I'm in a dream and I don't know what to do to keep from waking up too soon. Maybe I shouldn't say anything. . . ."

She drew closer to him and pressed her cheek against his. The sun went down. A bluish haze began to spread over the meadows and fields beneath them.

"I'm cold," she said all at once, shivering.

At the foot of the stairs the old man took off his hat politely and then held it out. Stefan stopped and began to search in his wallet. *"He said he came back from the Bratianu Statue especially to bring them to you. I gave him a hundred lei. . . ."* As soon as they entered the forest he caught Ileana in his arms and pressed his lips to hers in a long, long kiss.

"Shall we spend New Year's Eve with the others, or will it be just the two of us alone?"

"Just the two of us."

She sat down at the table and looked around at the brightly lighted room with its heavy chandeliers, too ornate, hanging from the ceiling.

"I was almost afraid when I climbed the stairs the first time," she said. "All those men with their fierce, bearded faces and all kinds of weapons in their hands, the sailing vessels everywhere crushing against each other. . . ."

"I like them," declared Stefan. "I like the *azulejos*."

Ileana caught his hand quickly in hers under the table. "I still can't believe it," she said.

The other places filled rapidly as the orchestra began to play. Stefan and Ileana ate in silence, glancing mutely at each other from time to time. When the music stopped they could overhear conversations around them in English, while at intervals a German word found its way from a more distant table.

"Why are you suddenly so serious?" she demanded.

Stefan smiled and took her hand. "Forgive me. It was involuntary. I found myself all of a sudden in history. I remembered that we're at war. . . ."

"Stefan!" she murmured in dismay. "You promised! At least this evening . . ."

"Forgive me. . . . But I remembered that our men are dying at the front in Russia—dying by thousands from the cold and the bullets . . . and I'm a party to an economic mission in which Vidrighin gets a cut of hundreds of thousands of escudos and there's nothing I can do, nothing!"

"Stefan!" she implored.

"I can't do anything! If I withdraw from the mission Vidrighin will take a cut ten times as large, and in the end no goods will ever arrive in Romania. . . . And there's nothing I can do, nothing!" He passed his hand over his face, distraught, and then he added, trying to smile, "But I'm talking nonsense!"

Ileana gazed at him. "I was afraid all the time that I'd wake up. I wondered what could happen that would wake me this time. I didn't think about the war. We speak of it every day—we're accustomed to it. In a sense I'd forgotten it. . . . But you had to remember it on the last night of the year . . . on our first night together, the night I thought you'd spend with me. . . ."

"We never escape from history!" he said in an attempt to joke. "It's even reached us here at the Palace Hotel in Bussaco, here in this ancient royal castle built on a hill, hidden in the forest, protected by the neutrality of the whole Iberian peninsula. . . ."

Ileana felt his tenseness and dropped her eyes. Again the orchestra paused. A tall dark man in evening clothes announced from the dais the program for the New Year's Eve celebration. He stepped down and the scattered applause was quickly lost in the music as the band started to play "When they begin the beguine. . . ."

"In London," said Stefan, smiling suddenly, "the orchestras in all the restaurants would strike up this song whenever the air raid alert sounded. . . ."

By the time they had descended to the last terrace they found themselves in darkness.

"Because we have only an hour until midnight," Ileana began, "I have to tell you the truth. We didn't meet by chance as I've let you believe. I wanted us to meet. I made up my mind a long time ago not to go to Madrid, but of course I didn't tell anyone. Everybody thinks I'm in Madrid. I went down to Entroncamento and took a train for Coimbra. I knew you were coming here

338

too, although I didn't know when. But I imagined where I could find you and I let you think that it was you who had found me. I imagined you'd come to the fountain of Inés de Castro and I waited for you there every day. I came in the morning and I didn't leave until night. I told people I wanted to write something about Inés, and a young man offered to explain the legend to me in detail: how Ines sat on a rock waiting for a letter from Don Pedro, and how Don Pedro sent her letters in a little box that floated on the water from the spring. And so forth. . . . I asked him to leave me alone so I could be inspired. I think I offended him, but he left me in peace. I was sure you'd come. I waited under that old tree by the spring. Oh, that scent of old, wet, decaying leaves! I recognized you from a distance. My heart was pounding so hard I was afraid you'd hear it. But I pretended that I hadn't seen you—that I was lost in my thoughts. . . ."

As he kissed her, he felt her lips were moist and hot, but her face was like ice. "We must go in," he said. "You're cold."

"I'm afraid," she said quickly. "I'm afraid when you're in the light, in the midst of people. I lose you. You wake up and you forget me. I like to be here in the dark under the trees, just the two of us alone. In the forest I feel that you can belong to me. Here I have found you again, in the darkness, among the trees."

Now and again, borne on the wind, the sound of the orchestra and the tumult from the ballroom reached them.

"How beautiful you are!" His voice was low. "How beautiful you are!" Gently his hand stroked her body, warm and bare. "How much I've wanted you! And for how long! I've wanted your body, your warmth. I dreamed of you and I woke up telling myself that no one can have such beauty. . . . I felt how beautiful you were when I first held you in my arms—and after that I couldn't forget you. I've wished for your lips, wished that I could kiss you once more, just once, for a long time . . . that I could cling to your mouth so you couldn't breathe . . . until you would fall . . . you'd fall. . . ."

He was awakened by the sound of heavy blows on a door somewhere. They grew increasingly stronger. *It's not for us!* he remembered. *He's an Adventist. He's selling Bibles. . . .*

"Who's knocking?" cried Ileana, waking suddenly, afraid.

"It's not for us," said Stefan, extending his hand to caress her in the darkness.

At once she nestled against him. "It frightened me!" she whispered. "I was afraid! Please . . . turn on the lamp."

The knocking began again. It sounded far away but seemed to be more

339

violent. Stefan turned on the lamp that stood on the night table. He looked at his watch. "It's almost four. I don't understand what's going on." He was interrupted by the music of the orchestra and a few indistinct, weary voices trying to sing in chorus "For he's a jolly good fellow. . . ."

"I was afraid," repeated Ileana. "Give me a cigarette, please."

The sound of the orchestra grew louder and more voices were raised in song.

"Stefan!" Ileana whispered, taking his hand and kissing it. "Stefan!" she repeated softly with a smile. "Stefan!"

Now the blows resounded again, frantically, betraying panic. Then just as suddenly they ceased.

"I ought to go and see what it is," Stefan said, frowning. "Maybe something's wrong, and all the people are probably downstairs watching the festivities."

"Don't go!" said Ileana, throwing her arms around his shoulders. "Don't leave me alone! I'm afraid!"

Stefan leaned over and kissed her. Then they sat side by side with their arms around each other, smoking silently, listening to the music. "For he's a jolly good fellow. . . ." Again they were startled by the knocking, which was faster this time and more desperate. Someone seemed to be kicking a door. *It's an Adventist. . . .* Stefan suddenly jumped from the bed.

"I suppose what's happened is that someone's locked himself in the bathroom and can't open the door. I'll go call the porter."

He put his coat over his shoulders and went out into the corridor. Only a few dim lights were burning. He listened for a long time but he heard nothing and went back into the room. "Now it's stopped!" he said with a shrug.

"Come here to me! You'll catch cold."

Stefan hung up his coat and put his hand briefly on the radiator. "There's no heat. That's why the room's so chilly." He returned to the bed and she clung to him, encompassing him with her warmth.

"Happy New Year!" he said, kissing her on the temple. "It's the New Year, and may it be a happy one!"

The orchestra stopped, its music drowned in a remote din of voices and applause. A few moments later they heard it start to play "It's a long way. . . ."

"I was very jealous," whispered Ileana. "I was jealous of Stella Zissu. I didn't want to believe it when they told me. If you hadn't confirmed it yourself I couldn't have believed it. . . ."

Embarrassed, Stefan smiled.

"I was very jealous," Ileana repeated.

Stefan leaned toward her to kiss her but the sound of renewed pounding made him pause. Three deliberate blows seemed to thunder from the depths of the earth.

340

"This is exasperating!" Ileana exclaimed. "You'd better call . . ."

Stefan picked up the receiver beside the bed and waited. Ileana lit a cigarette. "Hello! Hello!" he said after a moment. "There's no answer." He got out of bed again and put on his coat. After he had left the room the telephone rang and Ileana raised it anxiously.

"Yes . . . I called. There was some knocking. . . . I heard knocking in the hall, as though someone's locked in the bathroom. . . ."

She replaced the receiver and began to smoke again, listening absently to the melody that drifted up from the ballroom.

Sometime later Stefan returned. "It was just the opposite of what I thought," he said, smiling. "Someone was locked in his room and wanted to get out and couldn't. I didn't quite understand what happened because he spoke in Portuguese. But now the porter's come."

As he passed the radiator he placed his hand on it again. "It's completely cold. They haven't fired the furnace yet."

Ileana drew him again into the circle of her warmth. "I was jealous," she said again. "I didn't want to believe. . . . But I like the way you were honest and didn't lie. Don't ever lie to me."

"I was jealous too and I still am," Stefan began. "You know why. . . ."

Ileana promptly threw her cigarette in the ashtray and kissed him. "Please, don't talk," she said very softly. "Don't talk to me about that. . . ."

"There's just one thing I'd like to know . . ." Stefan tried to speak but Ileana cut short his words, her lips on his, holding him with a long kiss.

"Please!" She released him at last.

"I'd like to know if you loved him. . . ."

Bewildered, Ileana ran her hand through her hair. "I thought you already knew," she murmured after a pause, without looking at him. "I never loved him. I gave in to him in despair. I gave in to him in order to forget you. . . ."

"For he's a jolly good fellow. . . ." The orchestra began to play with vigor. They could distinguish a number of loud, hoarse voices attempting to sing, and then shouts, cheers, applause. They listened in silence.

Turning her head and seeing his face, Ileana was suddenly frightened. "What's wrong?" she asked. Stefan remained silent, drawing deeply, angrily on his cigarette.

"Stefan! Stefan! What are you thinking of?"

"Just the same, I thought . . ." Again he took a long deep breath, inhaling the smoke absently.

"Please!" she whispered. "Stefan! My darling. . . ."

"I imagined that if you loved me . . . what happened before wouldn't mean anything to me. . . ."

"Stefan!" Desperately she tried to kiss him.

341

"... But after you knew that you loved me, that you were in love with me—after I told you that I loved you ... I thought...."

"You're crazy!" she murmured, alarmed. "Stefan, I beg you, don't say anything more! I implore you!"

"I imagined..." he repeated mechanically. "But probably I deceived myself in this, too...."

"Stop!" she cried, trembling. "You humiliate me!"

He was silent, smoking and gazing vacantly in front of him. The music of the orchestra had ceased. Now only the muffled, obscure clamor of the ballroom could be heard. Suddenly Stefan got out of bed and went to the chair where he had left his clothes. Ileana followed him with frightened eyes as he began to search for his shirt.

"What are you doing?"

"I'm going upstairs to my room," he said, continuing to dress.

"Stefan!" she cried, appalled.

He glanced at her and smiled.

"If you leave now," whispered Ileana, leaning toward him over the bed, "we'll never see each other again!"

Without replying he dressed quickly. He felt as though he were in a dream. He knew his hands were trembling and he tried to hide them. He kept his face averted.

"Never!" cried Ileana. "Look at me! I'm not joking! You'll never see me again!"

Stefan looked up, smiling at her with great effort. Her hair was falling over her face and across her bare shoulders. Her eyes blazed with dismay and consternation.

"Stefan!" she exclaimed again. "Listen to me! Don't do this! You'll never see me again!"

Trembling, he finished dressing but he did not put on his tie or button his vest.

Suddenly Ileana's voice became remarkably calm. "You'll search for me to the end of the earth and you won't find me again! You'll crawl on your knees to the end of the earth looking for me but you'll never find me!"

"Forgive me," he whispered, approaching the bed. "I'll tell you about it tomorrow..."

Ileana stared at him, biting her lips so hard that they bled.

"... I'm only going up to my room," he added, exhausted.

"Don't go!" She held out her arms. "I forgive you.... Stay here!"

He kissed her cheeks and reached out to stroke her shoulder. "I'll explain tomorrow.... Good night."

"Stefan!"

In front of the door he turned around again. He was without his tie, his coat was over his arm. He smiled. The orchestra was playing again, and the music sounded surprisingly near.

"Good night!" He opened the door quickly and disappeared.

Ileana grasped her head with both hands and sat motionless for a long time, listening. Then she sprang quickly from the bed and went to the door. After she had turned the key in the lock she began to dress, shivering.

PART TWO

1

FOR SOME TIME HE STOOD HIDDEN BEHIND THE CURTAINS AND WATCHED THE man from the window. When he saw him open the little gate, he drew back quickly and sat down in the yellow leather armchair. This was where it pleased him to be found, surrounded by the massive glass-fronted bookcases in which Iancu Antim had once kept his volumes of old Romanian literature. Putting on his glasses, he picked up a book at random from the desk and opened it, but he did not attempt to read. A few moments later he recognized the familiar three short raps on the door and called out eagerly, "Come in!"

"I've found them!" said the man, pausing an instant in the doorway, catching his breath. "I've found almost all of them!"

He was getting along in years and carelessly dressed, his trousers spattered with mud. His face, covered by a beard of several days growth, looked dirty. He had very narrow hunched shoulders, and he breathed with difficulty like an asthmatic. Under his arm he held an enormous cardboard portfolio, very old and crammed with books.

"It was difficult," he added, approaching the desk. "Things are going badly at the front. No one wants to sell anymore."

The teacher, Gheorghe Vasile, took a school notebook out of the drawer. Opening it, he adjusted his glasses on his nose, waiting, watching the other as he placed the pile of books on the edge of the desk with a hand that trembled slightly. There were about thirty volumes from the Library for Everyone, their covers faded, some of them tattered and soiled.

"Number 61!" cried Gheorghe Vasile suddenly, impatiently.

The dealer in secondhand books found it quickly and held it out to him. "It was very difficult," he repeated. "I searched high and low to find it. Where didn't I look! . . . Things are going badly at the front," he said again in a low voice. He seemed to be talking to himself. "The Russians have crossed the Prut and invaded Moldavia."

347

Gheorghe Vasile examined the little book carefully, verifying the number and checking the name of the author and title in his notebook. It was a translation into Romanian of a book by Camille Flammarion.

"What a treasure!" he exclaimed softly, laying the book down beside him with care. "This is the richest library of practical knowledge in the world. It's a veritable treasure." With a red pencil he made a mark opposite the title in the notebook. Then, looking over the top of his glasses, he called out, "Number 73!"

"That one I didn't find. I even looked for it in Jassy. . . ."

"*On the Lives of the Insects*, by J. H. Fabre," Gheorghe Vasile read from the notebook. "Translated by Victor Anestin."

"I know, I know. It's unobtainable."

"But what about our agreement?" demanded the teacher, raising his head. "I engaged you to complete my collection to the last number. I still lack more than a hundred volumes. I myself collected twelve hundred. . ."

"I'll find that one for you too," the book dealer interrupted. "I looked for it in Jassy. Don't ask me how I got to Jassy. I came within an ace of being caught there and detained by the Russians. I told you, didn't I, that they've invaded Moldavia?"

At once chagrined and pensive, Gheorghe Vasile looked sadly into his eyes. He did not seem to understand clearly what the other had said. "Well, this was precisely why I made an agreement with you to complete my collection. We don't have any more time to waste. The Russians are invading Romania."

The dealer dropped his eyes and began to search nervously through the pile of books. His fingers seemed to tremble even more violently. "I found this one for you instead," he said, suddenly triumphant, holding out an old volume without a cover. "You could offer a hundred thousand lei and still not find another copy in the whole country. . . ."

Scarcely able to control his excitement, Gheorghe Vasile seized the book and held it a little distance away in order to see the title more clearly. He pronounced it solemnly: "Number 74, *The Theory of Universal Undulation*, by Vasile Conta. . . . What a treasure!" he added quickly in a muted voice. "Too bad it has no cover. I'll have to have it bound. . . ."

As he bent over the notebook and made a mark with the red pencil, he heard a knock at the door. Before he could respond Irina appeared on the threshold. She seemed very pale.

"No news from the Emperor," she said. "I went to see Ioana. . . . No news. She's afraid he's been taken prisoner in the Crimea. . . ."

It was not until then that she seemed to notice the old bookseller. She smiled at him. The man greeted her, inclining his head several times.

"Alas for our misfortunes!" he said softly. "The Russians have broken our front."

Irina stared at the stack of little books from the Library for Everyone. She was silent, waiting.

"*Domnul* Ghedem has found several more for me," the teacher said somewhat timidly. "Perhaps God will help us to complete the collection."

"It's very hard," said Ghedem, shaking his head. "They were out of print before the war."

"What will you pay him with? We haven't any more money."

Gheorghe Vasile removed his glasses in embarrassed silence, staring straight before him at the wall at the end of the room.

"We have an arrangement," Ghedem explained. "We give credit. I knew *domnul* Antim . . ." He stopped abruptly, and to indicate that he was without responsibility in this affair, he fixed his gaze on the large photograph on the desk. It was a picture of Spiridon's wedding, framed like a painting. It showed Irina on the steps of the church in her wedding gown, standing between Iancu Antim and Spiridon Vadastra. She looked frightened and tearful. Beside them, holding *doamna* Ivascu's arm and staring unflinchingly at the photographer, stood Gheorghe Vasile. He was dressed in a new suit. His shirt was clean and white, his trousers were pressed, and on his chest he wore an immense gold rosette.

"We give credit," Ghedem repeated, observing that the silence persisted.

Irina turned to face him and smiled again. Then she opened the door slowly and withdrew without a sound, as though she were walking on tiptoe. Vexed, Gheorghe Vasile got up from the chair, went to the door and locked it.

"How many items are there in all?" he asked.

"Thirty-six."

"How much do you think they're worth?"

Ghedem shrugged his shoulders and shook his head. A sound that resembled a laugh burst from his lips, stifled, ironic, somewhat forced. His gold teeth gleamed. "These have no price in lei," he said. "We'll continue as before. Maybe we'll still find collectors. . . . Although with the Russians in Moldavia our chances are slim."

Gheorghe Vasile motioned to him to approach the glass-fronted bookcase. The most valuable books had been taken out and sold long since. A few old volumes still remained, in the bindings of the era, some with marginal notes. The book dealer leafed through them, shaking his head, and set them on the desk.

"If only you had some manuscripts, some old registers, or letters of Eminescu. For those I could perhaps find buyers."

But all the charters, the monastery registers, all the dossiers of manuscripts and letters which Antim had collected over a period of thirty years had been sold long ago for a trifling amount or exchanged for a few dozen volumes of the Library for Everyone. Ghedem continued to thumb through the remaining books, setting them aside on the desk, his face still registering the severity of his disappointment.

349

"They're of no value," he said at length, rubbing his face with his handkerchief. "I can't get anything for them. Perhaps you can find an icon, an old snuff box, or a painting, so I can at least recover my loss. I went all the way to Jassy just to look for these."

The teacher pulled out the desk drawer in which he had for some time been depositing a number of valuable objects that he had withdrawn stealthily, one at a time, from the various showcases and cabinets in the parlor. Grasping them in his trembling fingers, the dealer began to examine them individually. He brought each one close to his eyes, then he held it at arm's length, turning it over and over in the dreary light of the March afternoon. There were Turkish and Phanariote trinkets, strings of beads from the past century, boxes made of mother-of-pearl, snuff boxes, shells with inscriptions that had been partly worn away. He shook his head repeatedly and set the articles down on the desk beside him.

"They don't amount to very much," he said. "People don't collect them nowadays. If you just had a painting to give me."

Embarrassed, Gheorghe Vasile began to scratch the top of his head. "I'd rather owe you the money," he said, trying to smile. "The walls are almost bare now and it would be noticed. *Coana* Gherghina counts the pictures every morning when she cleans the room. . . ."

"You're already in debt for the last time," Ghedem said, beginning to place the old books and baubles in his portfolio. "But we trust you. We give credit."

After the man had left, Gheorghe Vasile locked the door again. Then, excitedly but without haste, he gathered up in one arm the little books that the dealer had brought, took the notebook and the red pencil in his free hand, and went to the opposite side of the room. There in a simple cabinet with wooden doors he had made an orderly arrangement of the small volumes—more than twelve hundred of them—of the Library for Everyone, as well as other popular Romanian books and pamphlets. He began to place the newly acquired items on the shelves according to their respective numbers, first checking the titles in the notebook and marking them in red. When he had completed the task he left both doors of the cabinet standing wide open and sat down in front of it, gazing at the well-filled shelves for a long time, musing. Approximately seventy volumes remained to be found in order to complete his collection. After a few minutes he sighed deeply, and getting up from his chair to close the cabinet, he locked it with a padlock. Then he returned to the yellow leather armchair quite exhausted. Here he liked to sit and dream for hours at a time, holding in his hands a book that he did not read. He settled himself comfortably in the chair and declared softly, solemnly, as if he were reading an inscription engraved in letters of gold on a marble plaque: "The Cultural Foundations of Professors Iancu Antim and Gheorghe Vasile."

350

He had begun to be preoccupied with the thought about a year earlier on a winter evening in 1943. Returning home a little drunk from the wine, he wished for something to read and realized that among all the thousands of books and pamphlets that Antim had collected there was nothing for him. The library was composed for the most part of French books, rare editions, or scholarly works of history, archeology, the history of art—all subjects that Gheorghe Vasile could not understand. What he especially liked were the popular editions and above all the Library for Everyone. In that series, the authors of which were many and various, he found works more suited to his taste and comprehension. The idea occurred to him then that by selling some of the paintings and valuable objects in the salon he could buy scores of the little volumes in the popular Library.

Already he had sold several paintings to obtain pocket money for himself. He never would have imagined how easy it was to pick up large sums of money, sums even greater than he found necessary. One morning he had selected one of the pictures that covered the parlor walls, hid it under his coat and appeared with it at a shop on *strada* Academiei. The painting was by Luchian and the merchant gave him eighty thousand lei, but at that time, in 1942, it was worth ten times as much. Even so, Gheorghe Vasile could not believe his eyes. Since then whenever he needed money he went back to *strada* Academiei. He brought paintings, icons, and antique costumes of boyars and high Phanariote officials.

For a long time he had been greatly annoyed by Viziru because Stefan had noticed the disappearance of the paintings from the beginning, and whenever he learned from Irina that Stefan was coming home on leave from the front he became morose. He left home early and returned long after midnight, staggering and in tears. One night he could not manage to find the keyhole, and Irina came to open the door. She found him leaning against the wall with his face buried in his hands, weeping silently, shaken by sobs. "Our men are dying at Stalingrad," he began without raising his head. "Our poor men, dying of cold and hunger! They've all been captured at Stalingrad!"

This had occurred during the first days of January 1943. Stefan had observed six months earlier that the painting by Luchian had disappeared. That was the first time he had returned from the front and he and Ioana had come to see them. He wore the uniform of a captain, and despite his sunburnt countenance, he appeared to have aged. He smiled with some effort but he smiled constantly, giving the impression that he had acquired a tic. Ioana's eyes never left his face. She was absorbed, engrossed in him, as if she could not believe that he was really there near her in Antim's vast salon. The odor of mothballs hung on the air and the blinds were half-closed to shut out some of the glare of the July afternoon, but there was still enough light to distinguish the paintings that hung crowded together on all the walls.

"He was in the Crimea," began Ioana. "He'll tell you what happened to him with the camels. . . ." But they were not able to hear the story until half an hour later when *doamna* Ivascu came back with the tray of coffee and begged him again, insistently, to tell it. "It happened like this," Stefan began with an embarrassed smile. "After a march of several days, I arrived with my unit at sunset on the shore of the Sea of Azov. Suddenly a line of camels appeared, coming toward us from the direction of the sea. When the men caught sight of them they stopped in their tracks. One of them turned to me, and I saw the tears stream down his cheeks. 'We'll never go home again, *domnule* Captain,' he whispered. 'We'll leave our bones here in this God-forsaken place.'"

"They were terrified," said Ioana with spirit. "It was only when they set eyes on those camels that they realized how far from home they were."

"I remember very well that there used to be a painting by Luchian," Stefan broke in, looking toward the far end of the salon. "It was of some flowers, some purple iris on a gray-white background." He got up from his chair and began to examine the pictures again, one by one, as he had already done several times that day, stopping at each step. "Iancu must have sold it before he went away," said *doamna* Ivascu. "Or he may have put it in some cabinet for safekeeping. . . ."

"Haven't you made an inventory?" Stefan had asked Irina when he had returned on a leave of a few days toward the end of autumn. At that time two Romanian divisions were surrounded at Stalingrad. "What are we going to do, *domnule* Captain? What are we going to do?" Gheorghe Vasile exclaimed abruptly. "Our boys are being massacred at Stalingrad. . . ." Stefan stared at him with the same smile lingering in the corner of his lips, a smile that had begun to grow weary, making him appear old before his time. Then his eyes lit suddenly, as though he had decided to say something very important, perhaps a great military secret, but at once he changed his mind and shook his head, resuming his smile. "You ought to make an inventory," he insisted, speaking to Irina. "Business affairs are the death of us," *doamna* Ivascu said.

"You, *domnule consilier* Viziru . . ." Gheorghe Vasile began then in a grave tone, full of emotion. Stefan turned his head abruptly and regarded the old man again. This time he looked at him as though he did not clearly understand to whom the other had addressed his words. "I wanted to ask you," continued the teacher, a little intimidated, "how you view the military and international situation. . . ." After a prolonged silence Stefan passed his hand over his face. "I'm no expert," he said.

"You know I'm no longer a combatant. I'm in charge of supplying the troops in the Crimea." "Don't question him any more," Irina told Vasile after the two of them had escorted Stefan to the street. "He doesn't like to talk about the war. . . ."

That winter Stefan had flown home several times for short visits and left by air again after one or two days. These were missions having to do with supplies for the front, Irina told her father-in-law. There was not always time for Stefan to go to see them, but Gheorghe Vasile did not regain his peace of mind until he knew that Viziru had returned to Russia. Then, after the fall of Stalingrad, he heard nothing of Stefan for a long time. Once in a while Ioana came, and he would see her making her way through the drifts of snow in the courtyard, holding Razvan by the hand. He observed her from behind the curtains. His glance followed the blank face which betrayed nothing, not even her preoccupation, and he tried to catch a glimpse of the eyes that stared unwaveringly ahead. He went quickly to lock his door and then seated himself in the yellow leather chair, preparing to wait. He knew that Ioana never stayed long and that after her departure Irina would come knocking at his door. "No news from Stefan," she would say.

That same winter he had decided to create "The Cultural Foundations of Professors Iancu Antim and Gheorghe Vasile." Those thousands of books that could not be read, the paintings and portraits from the eighteenth and early nineteenth centuries that seemed so frightful to him, those anomalous objects amassed in the cabinets and showcases, ought to be transformed into a popular library of several thousand useful books that would be of interest to everyone. He would be the custodian. He began then to sell without scruple books, manuscripts, paintings, icons. He hid part of the money under the mattress and the rest in the bottom drawer of his desk, always marveling at the abundance of it. At night he locked the door and counted it, and then with renewed vigor he returned to his desk to complete the list of books he had yet to buy. His dream was to possess the entire collection of the Library for Everyone, approximately fifteen hundred little volumes. He searched through all the bookstores and secondhand shops but many of the titles he was not able to find. Then panic began to seize him. Because of a mere trifle—fewer than two hundred were now out of print—his dream might not be realized. His "Cultural Foundations" might not be established. He could not imagine it without a complete set of the Library for Everyone. Sometimes, to escape from his obsession, he went to the taverns in despair and drank alone, retreating to the most secluded table. But his spirit could not endure it, and soon he took from the pocket of his jacket the notebook in which he had inscribed the numbers and titles of the volumes that were unavailable. He added them again and made innumerable calculations until the wine softened his heart. Remembering Stalingrad and all that had followed, he began to cry. "Alas, our men are dying, poor souls! They're dying by the thousands!" he repeated, choked with emotion.

Then that summer he had met Ghedem, the dealer in old books, and he was reassured. Ghedem promised that he would complete the Library for Everyone, and the next time they met he brought a large number of volumes. He did not want money. Instead he requested in exchange the books and art objects from Antim's collections. In a few months all the rare imprints and first editions of the Muntenian poets had passed into Ghedem's hands. Vasile, delivered from the nightmare of the Library for Everyone, was now engaged in gathering together all kinds of useful works, which he classified in his catalog of the future "Foundations" under various rubrics: theoretical knowledge, practical knowledge, urgent knowledge, knowledge for fathers with wealth, etc. Sometimes Irina surprised him seated at his desk, facing the pile of books and pamphlets that he had bought that day, copying their titles in his notebook. She stood a long while in the doorway gazing at him. With his glasses slipped down a little on his nose, pen in hand, Gheorghe Vasile waited without lifting his eyes. "You've bought some books again," Irina said finally. "Don't let mother find out! We don't have any money left. . . ." When he heard the door close behind her, he rose quickly and turned the key in the lock.

Stefan had come unexpectedly one rainy evening in November when the Russians had retaken Kiev and the whole front seemed to totter again. He had come to see them alone, without Ioana, and Irina called through the door, "Stefan's here—in the salon. He wants to talk with you." Gheorghe Vasile had found him walking around in front of the paintings with his hands in the pockets of his uniform. The salon was still cold and it smelled of smoke, since the fire had been kindled just a few hours before. Stefan shook the teacher's hand with unexpected warmth. "Bad news, *domnule consilier* Viziru?" "He's a major now," Irina had interrupted. "He's been promoted to major." "I'm glad to find you all well," Stefan remarked. He seemed changed, but Gheorghe Vasile was not able to understand in what way his face differed. Perhaps the gleam in his eyes was no longer the same. His smile betrayed less fear.

"My congratulations!" the teacher said, grasping Stefan's hand again and shaking it vigorously. "We can say that we also rejoice in the heroism of our friends! And we're proud of these heroes. . . ." "I'd like to speak with you about a delicate matter," interrupted Stefan. "That's why I came to see you alone, without Ioana." Embarrassed, Gheorghe Vasile grew pale and brought his hand to his collar. Irina started to the door but Stefan stopped her. "You may stay. This will be of interest to you, too. It's about Vadastra. . . ." Gheorghe Vasile sat down on a chair and sought his handkerchief, intending to wipe his forehead, but he changed his mind and pressed it for an instant to his eyes without speaking.

"Do you know a Major Aurel Baleanu? He told me he had lived with Vadastra. They occupied the same apartment about five or six years ago. Do you know him?" Stefan had taken a chair beside Gheorghe Vasile, who now regarded him impatiently, his eyes shadowed with troubled curiosity. He sponged his face several times with his handkerchief. "I've heard of him, but I haven't met him," the teacher said finally without lifting his eyes. Irina stood with her hands held behind her back, quietly following their conversation. "Too bad!" declared Stefan. "I thought you also knew him. Too bad. . . ." He took out a package of cigarettes and absently lit one.

"But what happened to this Major Baleanu?" demanded Gheorghe Vasile. "He was wounded. That's how I met him—in the hospital. We were in the same room. I forgot to tell you that I was wounded also about two months ago. Don't be alarmed—it was nothing serious. One of the buildings in which I worked in Odessa was blown up. Some guerillas threw a bomb at it. Nothing serious. . . . I was more frightened than hurt. I was in the hospital for only a week. Baleanu had been wounded too, but his injuries were more grave. . . ." Suddenly Stefan rose from his chair and began to walk about. He stopped with an appearance of casualness in front of a showcase that was almost empty, and bending over, he looked very attentively at the articles that remained—a few snuff boxes, chibouks, strings of beads. "A past without heirs!" he exclaimed suddenly, forcing a laugh. "The happy times when the country mourned under the heel of the Turk. . . ."

Irina walked to the door without a word and left the room, followed by Stefan's reflective gaze. "You were wrong to mention Spiridon," said Vasile, putting his handkerchief to his eyes once more. Stefan sat down again, embarrassed. He took out the package of cigarettes and offered them to the teacher, who remarked, "I don't smoke much. Just now and then like this, to please my friends. . . ." Holding the lighted match for Vasile, Stefan watched him draw on the cigarette in the manner of a peasant. "Forgive me if I'm intruding in a matter that doesn't concern me," he said, laying the match still burning on the edge of the ashtray, "but what are you doing with the money you get for the things you've been selling?"

Gheorghe Vasile paused in consternation with the cigarette protruding from his lips. With difficulty he extinguished it and began to twist it nervously between his fingers. "You're not obliged to answer me," continued Stefan. "But you know, I just want to say this—do quickly whatever you feel you must do. We've lost the war. In a year or two the Russians will be here among us in Bucharest." He rose again

355

from his chair and snuffed out his cigarette with a quick gesture. "It's too bad you didn't know Baleanu," he added, beginning to pace the room.

"We've lost the war?" demanded Gheorghe Vasile. He seemed suddenly to have awakened. "You say we've lost the war?" Shocked and fearful, he buried his face in his hands and began to sob. Stefan continued from the other end of the room. ". . . We might have been able to understand many mysterious things."

From that day Gheorghe Vasile had no more peace. He waited behind the curtains, sometimes for hours at a time, for Ghedem to arrive; and when his patience was exhausted he went out on the street to meet him. It had begun to snow during the first days of December. Very soon the drifts were piled high, filling the courtyard. The days grew shorter and every evening the city was plunged into darkness at an earlier hour, since the blackout had been recently reimposed. Gheorghe Vasile went out immediately after dinner, unnoticed by anyone, swallowed by the shadows. He always locked his door when he left because once when he had come home unexpectedly, he had found Gherghina and Irina there, in his room. He realized immediately that Gherghina had opened all the cabinets one after another, apparently searching for some particular thing, which in the end she had not found. Once outdoors he walked for a long time to find a free taxi. Then he went to the secondhand book dealer's shop on *strada* Academiei. Under his coat he carried a sort of knapsack, held in place by a strap that he slipped over his shoulder. It was loaded with things to sell. After leaving the shop he stopped in the darkness to conceal the bundle of bills, and then he sought out a tavern where he spent several hours before going home.

Once when he returned earlier than usual he found Gherghina, Irina, and Ioana in the salon. All three had pulled their chairs close to the stove and sat listening to the man who was standing before them—a thin man, nearly bald. "This gentleman is a philosophy teacher," said Gherghina. "He's a friend of Ioana and Viziru."

"Biris," said the man, introducing himself and holding out his hand. To Vasile his smile seemed ironic. "I'm honored to see at last the collections of Professor Antim. *Doamna* Vadastra was kind enough to invite me a long time ago, but I didn't have much leisure then. Now I'm on vacation." This was during the week of Christmas. Vasile sat down nervously and looked at each in turn, expectantly, as if he thought they had in important message for him.

A timid knocking on the windowpane created a diversion. "It's the children with the Christmas Star,*" said *doamna* Ivascu. "They've been driving

---

*A translucent box on the end of a pole, bearing a picture of the Nativity within a star, lighted by a candle.

356

me mad! They all seem to aim for our house. I don't have anything more to give them." She got up and started toward the door, but Gheorghe Vasile held out his hand in a gesture of quiet assurance and stopped her with a smile.

"Will you receive the Star?" came the voices of the children at the window.

"Of course, of course!" the teacher replied, suddenly in a good humor. He stood up quickly, and going to the window, he invited them, "Come in, boys!" Then turning to the group by the stove, he added, "The festivals are the inspiration of our people! Gherghino, give them some wine. I'll treat them. I have money. . . ."

One by one the boys came timidly into the hall. *Doamna* Ivascu brushed the snow from their clothes with a whisk broom and made them wipe their shoes well on the mat, inspecting each one carefully. They carried a large star, which they had just then lit, since they did not dare to walk with it lighted during the blackout. They grouped themselves in front of the door and began to sing, "The Star rises high, a great mystery in the sky. . . ." Irina had gone to get her little boy, leading him by the hand. Biris listened, still holding a cigarette in the corner of his mouth, although it was no longer burning. He kept both hands in his pockets.

Gheorghe Vasile shook his head, struggling hard against his melancholy. "Our national festivals!" he exclaimed when the boys had finished the carol. "Who knows what the next year may bring?" Ioana stood up, preparing to leave. "Wait, *doamna consilier*, and drink a glass of wine with us. God knows what will happen to us next year. . . ." He went out quickly into the hallway in the direction of the kitchen.

The boys began another carol. "Alas for our poor men!" exclaimed Vasile, returning with two bottles of wine and beginning to fill the glasses. "Dying by the thousands at the front. . ." He sensed Irina's penetrating stare and raised his head in astonishment. The girl motioned to him. Ioana was gazing blankly over the heads of the carolers, playing shyly with her wedding ring, turning it round and round on her finger. She wore a pearl-gray dress, and to Gheorghe Vasile she seemed very elegant and very beautiful as she stood in the lamplight. Her red-blond hair was done up without regard to the fashion of that year, pulled back a little over the temples and falling on the nape of her neck. Her large hazel eyes, washed with gold, turned fleetingly about her, seeing nothing. The pale oval of her face revealed a faint touch of rouge on her cheekbones. The teacher studied her for a moment, embarrassed, with the bottle in his hand; but the boys had finished their song, and he lifted his own full glass high, crying gravely, "Long live Romania! Long live the heroic Romanian Army!"

A few days later Biris returned in the company of a tall thin man with very white hair. He was wrapped in an enormous fur-lined coat that he did not want to take off. He even kept his scarf around his neck. He looked at the paintings, stopping in front of each one, stepping back in order to view it better, then bringing his face close to the frame to examine the corners of the canvas. "Happy New Year, *domnule* Professor!" Gheorghe Vasile cried from the doorway. "May the New Year, 1944. . . ." Disconcerted, he broke off when he caught sight of the old man.

"*Domnul* Goanga, from the National Museum," Biris introduced him. "Irina asked me to bring him to evaluate the collection."

"It is no longer what it was," said the expert. "Many things have been lost." He continued his examination, leaning over the showcases, shaking his head, moving on with the same disappointed air. "I knew about some old manuscripts and a collection of letters," he said later, when he came back from the far end of the salon.

"Some of the things are in my study," said Gheorghe Vasile with difficulty because his mouth felt dry. He led the men to his room and opened the glass-fronted bookcase with a hand that shook with increasing violence. Biris followed his movements without comment. Seating himself in an easy chair, the specialist began to examine the books one by one.

Irina entered the room unobtrusively and approached Biris. "No news," she whispered. "I don't know what to do. I'm afraid something will happen to Ioana. . . ."

The expert got up from time to time and went to the other bookcases in silence. "But I don't find the collection of letters," he said at length, going to the padlocked cabinet in which Gheorghe Vasile had assembled the little volumes of the Library for Everyone.

"This is my personal library," the teacher said, laboring to unlock it. Glancing casually over the titles the expert shrugged his shoulders and went out of the room followed by Biris. "What does this devilment mean?" Gheorghe Vasile demanded angrily of Irina.

"We don't have any more money," she said, "and mother wants to sell some of the things. We don't have any money at all. . . ."

He often observed during the course of the winter, not without a mixture of sadness and indignation, that the paintings were gradually disappearing from the parlor. "I sold them," said *doamna* Ivascu. "There are twenty-seven left. I've counted them." And one day he saw that each painting had a number on a card attached to the bottom of the frame with a tack. One evening he surprised Irina on her way to her room, weighed down with a large number of objects from the showcases, piled one upon the other in a clothes basket. "They're for Gheorghita when he grows up. Mother told me to put them aside. The rest we're going to sell. . . ." Whenever he went into the parlor he always encountered someone. *Doamna* Ivascu spent the greater part of her time there seated on the sofa, playing solitaire at a low table or crocheting. When she was not in the room he found Irina with her forehead pressed against the windowpane looking at the snow, or seated on the carpet beside the stove, playing with her little boy. Sometimes he saw Ioana there—a Ioana who was always silent except on the day when Irina cried, "Stefan has written!"

"He wrote to Razvan too," Ioana added, smiling at him, and the brilliant intensity, the fullness, the serenity, of her eyes astonished him.

"That girl will go mad," he had heard Gherghina saying to Irina a few nights before. "When he comes again, take Viziru aside and tell him to get some sense in his head. Tell him to forget the front and stay here with his wife and child. Did you ever hear of such a thing? A genuine high official from the Ministry, a volunteer on the Russian front for two years?"

One night Vasile opened the door of his room as softly as possible and started toward the salon, walking on tiptoe. But he found Irina in the doorway, as though she were waiting for him. "I wasn't sleepy," she told him. "Let's go inside... maybe it's warmer." They went into the room and sat down near the stove. There were still some live coals under a thick layer of ashes and Irina turned them up with the tongs. Gheorghe Vasile watched her in silence. He didn't know what to say, how to begin.

"What do you suppose Viziru wanted to find out about Major Baleanu?" he asked all of a sudden.

"He's been made colonel now," said Irina. "They brought him to the military hospital here in Bucharest and they made him a colonel. I learned it from Ioana. They telephoned from the hospital to inquire if Stefan had returned. They told her they were calling on behalf of Lieutenant-Colonel Baleanu."

"So, then they've promoted him in rank," Gheorghe Vasile remarked thoughtfully. "He must be a great hero. . . ."

"He's still in the hospital," continued Irina. "Probably he's seriously wounded. They didn't know that Stefan had left the front. . . . Now he's in the Crimea," she added very softly. "And yet he hasn't written for quite a long while. . . ."

She stooped down to look for a piece of wood, and after turning over the ashes again, she laid it on top of the coals, watching the flames as the bark began to burn. "Stefan asked me what you did with the money," she resumed without raising her eyes. "I didn't know then how to answer him, but I saw you'd collected a whole cabinet full of books. It's very nice. . . ."

"I'm going to establish a Foundation," Gheorghe Vasile began firmly, lifting his head. "A Foundation for the people in order to bring light to the villages. . . . To immortalize the name of the great scholar of our land, Iancu Antim."

"It's a shame we don't have any more money," Irina said in a low voice. "And we're in arrears with the taxes. Mother thinks we'll have to rent part of the house. . . ."

Gheorghe Vasile was silent for a long time. He seemed to be waiting for

359

Irina to add something more. At last, seeing that she said nothing, he sighed deeply, stood up, and ambled toward the door. The piece of wood had caught fire now and was burning with lively red and blue flames. "I'm afraid for Ioana," Irina began suddenly. "Stefan doesn't write anymore. I told her, 'The Emperor's well, don't worry. . . .'" Gheorghe Vasile stopped in the middle of the room. "That's what I told her," repeated Irina with a note of hopelessness in her voice. She did not lift her glance from the flames. "That's what I told her. . . ."

He encountered her after that whenever he tried to enter the salon at night—no matter how late it was, even toward morning—in order to collect more things from the showcases. She seemed to be aware of his intentions well in advance, before he could get out of bed, put his overcoat across his shoulders, and open the door noiselessly, holding a small pocket flashlight in his left hand to light his way. At the end of the hallway or in front of the salon he would come upon her, pale as a wraith, moving slowly through the darkness with her hands behind her back. "I'm not sleepy," she would whisper. "I can't go to sleep." Embarrassed, he would turn off the flashlight, leaving them standing there together without speaking, face to face in the dark. Each would try to guess what the other had in mind, until in his anxiety Gheorghe Vasile would switch on the light again and examine her from head to foot. She would be wearing an old housedress, sometimes with a faded woolen shawl thrown over her shoulders. "It's getting cold," she would say, making an effort to smile as the beam of the flashlight fell across her face. She would add in a whisper, "Walk softly. . . . Don't wake the baby," and noticing that her father-in-law had nothing but slippers on his feet, she would continue, "Go back to bed quickly. . . ." Then she would resume her walk through the hallway or open the salon door and disappear in the shadows.

More than once after retreating to his room in humiliation, Gheorghe Vasile had waited an hour or two, dozing in the yellow leather armchair, and then returned to the salon. He always took the same exaggerated precautions, but lacking the courage to use the flashlight, he would grope his way forward, clinging to the walls. Invariably he found her somewhere in the corridor. She would whisper to him from a distance, "Father. . ." and he would stop at once. His blood seemed to freeze in his veins, because her voice came to him unexpectedly out of the night. He never knew where she was. Ahead of him and on each side he could see nothing, not even a shadow. Then he would hear her whisper again several times, "Father. . . Father . . ." and as the words grew clearer he knew that she was approaching him through the darkness. Trembling, he would wait until her outstretched hand touched his face. "Haven't you gone to bed yet?" she would ask.

Toward the end of March it was suddenly spring. Easter fell on the fourth of April and every evening Irina went to get Ioana and Razvan and take them to the services. The teacher watched her from behind the curtains, and as soon as he saw her going out of the gate he went downstairs to the salon, full of excitement, trying to quiet the pounding of his heart. He knew that Gherghina had left too, to attend the vigils in the church down the street. But now, for the first time, he found the door of the salon locked. Astounded, he paused with his hand on the latch. Until that moment it had not occurred to him that such a thing was possible. The door had never been locked before. He realized in a flash of humiliation and fury that Gherghina must have sent for a locksmith sometime during his absence and had the mechanism repaired. He hastened to his room and came back with the key to his own door, which he tried several times without success. Cursing through his teeth he went to the kitchen in search of other old keys that had been left lying about in the drawers. None of them fit.

He repeated the same procedure the next day and the next. After he saw Irina leave he went downstairs, taking with him all the keys that he had been able to find in the meantime. He tried each one obstinately, shaking the door, struggling until he felt he would break the lock.

When he tested the latch on the fourth day he found to his great surprise that the door was unlocked, and he burst suddenly into the room. Biris was there, seated on a sofa before a low table laden with objects from the showcases. He was examining the articles one at a time and searching through a voluminous leatherbound notebook lying open on his lap.

"Irina asked me to check the catalog of the collection," he said without getting up from the sofa.

Stunned, Gheorghe Vasile stood in the middle of the room, an empty bag over his shoulder and a ring of old keys in his hand.

"They just found it," continued Biris, "but not much is left. The better things have been lost. . . ." He paused, then added, "They've disappeared."

"Our poor country!" Gheorghe Vasile murmured, approaching and taking a chair beside the little table. "Our poor country! The war is going badly. . . ."

Slowly Biris raised his eyes from the notebook and looked at the teacher. "Now and then we also receive a piece of good news. Viziru telegraphed. Everyone escaped from the Crimea. It was possible to evacuate them by sea. . . . They're at Constanta now," he added. "They'll arrive on Sunday, Easter Day."

He scarcely spoke at all during the days that followed, and to show them how angry he was, he refused to go with Gherghina on the Night of the Resurrection to the church on their street but set off alone for the Metropolitan Cathedral. He had gone only half the distance when he changed his mind and entered the first church he found along the way.

It was after midnight when he returned, because he walked slowly in order to reach home with his Resurrection candle burning. He climbed directly to his room, blew out the flame and placed the taper carefully in a drawer of the desk. Then he dropped into the armchair and dozed. When the cold in the room awakened him, he realized that he had fallen asleep. He rubbed his eyes and took out his watch. It was nearly three. If Irina remained to hear the entire service, as she usually did, she would not be back until four o'clock. He felt excitement mount within him and pulled out the drawer quickly. Picking up the candle again, he lit it, found his bag and put it over his shoulder. With shaking hands he crossed himself several times and made his way downstairs to the salon.

The door was not locked, and Gheorghe Vasile hesitated a few moments on the threshold to quiet his rapid breathing. Then he went in cautiously, walking on tiptoe. Placing the lighted candle in an ashtray, he approached the first glass case. On close inspection he noticed that very few objects remained, and he did not dare to touch them. He turned to another case and, trembling, raised the glass lid, exposing some old snuff boxes and Turkish water pipes. He selected a few at random, stuffed them in his bag, and moving on, he paused in front of the paintings. He was sure that if he took a picture—just a small one—its absence would not be noted. He was still standing there deep in thought when the room suddenly filled with light and he heard Irina's voice crying out to him, "Christ is risen!" Vasile turned his head and saw her in the doorway with one hand on the light switch and in the other an Easter candle.

"He is risen indeed!" the teacher murmured.

Irina went to him at once and kissed him on both cheeks. She seemed transported. Her face was pale, her eyes misty and abnormally dark. Gheorghe Vasile walked slowly to the sofa and sank wearily upon it, grasping his head in his hands. Without a word Irina laid her hand gently on his shoulder and held it there for a time, but then, suddenly remembering something, she left the room in haste. When she returned carrying a tray of eggs dyed red, poundcake, and a bottle of wine, she found him talking to himself.

"A worthless man, that's what I was. The dregs of human society. . . ."

Irina set the tray on the little table, poured a glass of wine and handed it to him. Then she offered him an egg. Gheorghe Vasile wiped away his tears with the sleeve of his coat, sighed deeply and sat waiting for several moments, the red egg resting in his hand. Irina approached him and struck her egg against his.

"Christ is risen!"

"He is risen indeed!" replied Gheorghe Vasile. "He is truly risen!" he reiterated, choking. "And don't think . . ." But immediately his weeping overcame him and he could not continue. Irina took the glass of wine from his hand and set it on the tray.

"Think what?" she asked suddenly in a voice that was unexpectedly clear. "Didn't you tell me yourself that everything is for the 'Cultural Foundations'?"

"For the Foundations. Nothing for me. I was among the dregs of human society when I met Professor Antim. . . ."

Irina held out the glass to him again and then began to walk about with bowed head, her hands behind her back.

The teacher downed the contents of his glass in a gulp. "I met him," he resumed, "and I understood that I too have a mission: to bring to a successful conclusion the work of the great apostle to our country, Iancu Antim—to create the 'Cultural Foundations.' . . ."

Irina was not listening to him as she walked back and forth in the room.

"A center of culture for the whole Romanian nation. . . . To become somebody myself, an apostle. . . . To bring the light to the villages. . . ." He wanted to pour himself a second glass of wine, but he was hindered by the strap of his bag, which was about to fall from his shoulder. He pulled it off in disgust and seized the bottle.

"Come drink a glass too," he called to Irina. "What's the matter? What are you thinking about?" he asked, seeing that she came toward him in silence.

"My heart is heavy," she said softly. "I can't rest. . . ."

Gheorghe Vasile poured the wine and lifted his glass, touching it to Irina's. "The Lord help us and forgive us," he said, closing his eyes as he drank. "We ought to get Gherghina up too," he added. "It's Holy Easter."

"Let her sleep," said Irina. "She's very tired." With a vacant stare she sat down beside him on the sofa. Sighing, Gheorghe Vasile helped himself to a piece of cake and began to eat it.

"I don't know what's the matter with me, why I can't sleep," began Irina suddenly. "I keep thinking . . ."

She turned her head, and seeing him with the empty glass in one hand and the piece of poundcake in the other, she picked up the bottle and poured some wine for him. "It's Ioana. She thinks Stefan doesn't love her anymore. She found out about a girl he met in Portugal when he was there the second time. . . ."

She turned and looked at him again. The teacher dipped his cake in the glass of wine and sipped the wine slowly, thoughtfully.

"Her brother-in-law Raducu told Ioana about her. And he told her other people knew about it too, because Stefan suddenly decided to come back to Bucharest, although he was supposed to stay there all winter."

Gheorghe Vasile listened intently, holding his glass very close to his lips. His hand trembled slightly. "Where was he supposed to stay?" he asked suddenly.

"There, in Portugal. . . . But he came home and then left for the front."

"There was the war," said Vasile, and he sipped from the glass with some uneasiness.

"But nobody knew that Stefan himself had asked to be sent to the front. His petition even went to the Minister of War. Raducu learned about it later, when he intervened to get Stefan discharged. Then they showed him all those requests to be sent to the front, to the first line. . . ."

She got up abruptly from the sofa and began to pace the floor. "I'm not at all sleepy. My heart is heavy. I took communion but God did not find me worthy. . . ." She turned anxiously to Vasile and added, "Don't say anything to Mother about these things. . . ."

"What things?"

"What I told you about Ioana. She's committing a great sin not to believe him. Stefan loves her. What happened between him and that girl is something else."

Gheorghe Vasile listened to her now with considerable difficulty. He had begun to feel drowsy, and there was a pleasant weariness in his bones. The salon seemed to have become suddenly cold, and he poured more wine into his glass.

"But how do you know this?" he asked, blinking his eyes rapidly in an effort to stay awake.

Irina shrugged her shoulders. "Ioana told me. And Stefan told me too. They're both unhappy and it's such a pity. It's a pity, because they love each other very much. . . . But perhaps this was God's decision," she added softly, beginning to walk about again.

Half-asleep, Gheorghe Vasile tried to peel the red egg, but it slipped from his fingers. He watched it roll over and over on the rug. Irina picked it up and began to peel it for him.

"I'm very sleepy," he said, trying to rouse himself by rubbing his face.

Irina refilled his glass and held out the peeled egg. "I wanted to tell you something else. You know that Spiridon and I are joined for eternity. Mother would like to see me get married again, but I won't do it. She doesn't talk about it in order not to grieve you, but I wanted you to know that everything that belongs to me and my son is yours too. If God should take me before you, I'd like you to know that there are some things at Biris's house for safekeeping. Take good care of them. They're to get money for Gheorghita's education. . . ."

In the morning Irina set off early, walking fast, as if she were late for an appointment. With eyes cast down, half-closed, she did not look where she was going but turned from one street into the next at random, apparently struggling to remain awake. She kept meeting groups of people chatting almost lightheartedly, since the spring day was so clear and the blue sky uncommonly serene. Occasionally she found herself in front of a church, and she slowed her pace for a few moments to watch the children playing on the steps in their Easter clothes. Then she hurried on.

When she heard the siren she stopped and looked around anxiously. At first she did not recognize the quarter. Leaning against a fence, she breathed deeply and bowed her head in weariness. A man came out of a courtyard then and spoke to her as he passed by, "Don't be frightened. It's just a drill to test our antiaircraft defenses. It was announced on the radio. . . . "

He smiled and went on, turning his head now and then to see what she was doing. For some time she remained leaning on the fence, until with sudden decision she set off in the opposite direction. Policemen whistled continually and children ran noisily along the sidewalk. People appeared at the windows. Uncertain, they closed the blinds, then raised them and leaned out over the street, peering all about. "It's a drill!" Irina heard someone say. "With the water shut off?" inquired an old woman from behind a wooden fence. "It was announced on the radio," repeated the other stubbornly.

Then all of a sudden the sound of antiaircraft guns burst out, seemingly from everywhere at once. "Get in the house!" shouted a man's voice. "They're using real shells and you could be hit on the head with a frag-ment. . . ." "I just want to watch a little," said a woman. Irina raised her head and looked at the sky. It was still the same serene blue, although tiny white clouds had begun to dot it like a rash. They appeared suddenly and as quickly dispersed. Peering intently she saw a metallic gleam very, very high, and while she was blinking frequently to clear her eyes, she saw another and then another until the entire squadron was revealed flying in formation leisurely, as though on parade. The noise of the motors became increasingly distinct, and soon they could be heard over the salvos of the antiaircraft artillery. Irina covered her face with both hands, remaining motionless for several moments. When she roused herself she no longer heard people talking around her. Brushing her hand across her face, she began to run.

She saw a church in the distance. A number of people ran up the steps and disappeared inside. When Irina reached the building she was exhausted and breathless, and she fell limply on her knees in the shadowy doorway. The church was almost empty, but candles were still burning and the smell of fresh, leafy greenery and incense was strong. "It's not a drill! It's real!" a woman cried. "The Americans are bombing us. Now the Americans have come upon us too. . . ." Pale and fearful, the people kept coming in. They knelt before the icons, hiding their faces in their hands, murmuring to them-selves. All the women had gathered near the altar. The priest appeared, and casting a haggard glance over the assemblage, he quickly entered the chancel and donned his ecclesiastical robes.

"Give us your blessing!" cried a woman.

The priest opened the great gate of the iconostasis and stood unmoving, as if awaiting a sign.

"Give us your blessing!" Many voices echoed the appeal.

There were more explosions then, very near, and the church was so shaken it seemed moved from its foundations. Several pieces of stained glass from the windows in the tower burst out with a muffled crack, and fell in fragments on the flagstones. The next instant a flock of sparrows rushed in through the opening and began to fly around in the vault of the church, twittering.

"Blessed be the name of the Lord!" the priest began, raising his eyes. His voice sounded choked.

The explosions that followed seemed farther away and more muffled, and the screams of the children were lost in a prolonged subterranean rumble that again shook the foundations. Irina moaned and promptly brought her hand to her mouth. "Give me strength, Holy Mother!" Her whisper was barely audible, and she felt despair sweep over her. She rose abruptly and ran toward the altar without looking down, pushing her way through the group of women to the priest, where she flung herself on her knees before him.

"Give me strength, Father," she murmured.

All at once a strange quiet filled the church. Nothing was heard for a few moments except the chirping of the sparrows as they circled in fright under the tower.

"Give me strength, Father!" begged Irina softly. The priest gazed at her in wonder.

"She's afraid!" said a woman, extending a hand to pat Irina on the shoulder.

"May God give you strength!" The priest spoke slowly.

Then the salvos of antiaircraft artillery began again and the children started to cry. The priest looked at Irina, who was crouching at his feet with her hand over her mouth. Suddenly he became very pale, and bending over with difficulty because of his vestments, he caught her under the arms and lifted her. Irina seized his hand and kissed it. Just then a whole series of explosions was heard coming from every direction. All the windowpanes shattered and the candles went out. They seemed to have been extinguished by one great puff from an invisible mouth. The priest joined his trembling hands and raised them toward the altar screen.

"Christ is risen!" he cried in a voice that was unexpectedly strong. "He is risen indeed! Christ our Lord has risen and triumphed over death! Our Heavenly King has risen! . . . Lord, Great God," he added, lowering his voice suddenly and kneeling in front of the altar.

The sparrows began to fly lower above the bowed and silent women as they pressed their foreheads to the flagstone floor.

• • •

Later, when the raid had ceased and the church was empty, Irina hid several candles under her coat and went outside. The steps of the church were covered with debris and bits of splintered glass. A cloud of black smoke rising in the north darkened the sky, and the air was laden with soot and dust. The sun seemed very close, pale red in the smoky haze that hung over the city. From every direction came a confused murmur of frightened voices punctuated by muffled screams. As she descended the church steps and reached the street, Irina saw a woman with disheveled hair hurrying toward her, crying, "There's no water!"

The woman seemed not to see Irina as she went by, running with difficulty and continuing to shout, "There's no water! There's no water!" Down the street several houses were burning, the flames leaping to great heights. Smoke of a peculiar yellow color formed a cloud over them that drifted lazily, hesitantly, in the dust-laden air. "There's no water!" The words were repeated again and again. Bewildered people came and went over the littered sidewalks, dirty with soot and debris; they appeared and disappeared in the courtyards and at broken windows, calling to one another and looking at the sky, wondering what had happened. Only after she had turned her back to the fire and reached a nearby street, walking rapidly, mechanically, her eyes on the pavement, did Irina begin to understand the meaning of the words that kept feebly buffeting her ears.

"They've destroyed the North Station!" "They bombed the railroad yards!" "They've destroyed..." "They've bombed..." "*Calea* Victoriei is burning." "They've destroyed..." "The Americans..." "They've bombed..."

Without realizing what she was doing she started to run.

"On Easter Day!" The words followed her relentlessly. "They've bombed..." "They've destroyed..."

After she passed the Public Garden the people she met seemed less frightened. No bombs had fallen here, but there was smoke and dust everywhere. "They bombed the reservoirs." "We won't have any more water...."

She kept meeting automobiles, taxis, and trucks that were trying to avoid the bombed streets, all headed for the boulevards, dodging about as though the smoke had made the drivers dizzy. She noticed that she had set out in the wrong direction, and she turned back, her steps faltering wearily. When she found herself opposite the Garden again, she went in, sat down on a bench and waited for a long time, staring blankly, her hands lying in her lap. Some sparrows had regained their courage and begun to play close beside her in the gravel. After a while she hid her face in her hands and started to cry.

About a half-hour later she got up again and set off toward Ioana's house,

367

her head bent in an attitude of great fatigue. Her legs gave way as she approached, and she leaned against a wall. Here too the people were rushing about distractedly. They seemed not to know where to go or what to do, and they passed by without seeing her. Here there was a dense haze of smoke and dust which the sun's rays penetrated with difficulty. The sounds of automobile horns and the screeching brakes reached her through the murky twilight, but she didn't know where the noises came from, since the street in front of her appeared deserted. With great effort she pushed herself away from the wall and went on, clenching her fists in despair. When she came to the corner she suddenly understood. On the spot where Ioana's house and several neighboring homes had stood, bricks and rubble lay in smoking heaps strewn out into the middle of the street. People were climbing up and down on the ruins, staggering, blinded by the dust, stumbling over joists and girders. Involuntarily they would cry aloud, then quickly cover their mouths with their hands, and from time to time they lifted bloodied arms toward the sky.

She didn't know how long she stayed there on her knees among the bricks in the middle of the street, seeing nothing, hearing nothing. She only felt at times that her mouth was very dry and she found it hard to swallow. Then she seemed to rouse for a few moments and the tumult overwhelmed her once more. The same shadows were still moving to and fro in the dust. When she discovered that the candles before her were no longer burning, she lit them both again, shielding them for a moment with her hands. But they did not burn long, and she was unaware when they went out a second time.

After awhile she felt someone pull her by the arm. It was a soldier whose face was covered with dust. Struggling to her feet, Irina gathered up the candles from the pile of bricks and went with him to a spot on the other side of the street, in front of a house that was still standing. She heard someone behind her exclaim, "There's no water!" She wanted to sit down on the sidewalk, but it was littered everywhere with broken glass and debris. The soldier had disappeared, and Irina started back toward the ruins. It seemed to her that night was beginning to fall. On an improvised litter made of planks lay several bodies, half-covered with a blanket. She crossed herself as she went by. A truckload of soldiers had stopped at the intersection, but she continued on her way, intent, as though she were searching for someone. Then she returned to the place of her earlier vigil and knelt again among the bricks and relit the candles. For a long time after that she was again oblivious to the sights and sounds around her.

Later, upon opening her eyes, she noticed that the candles had gone out again, that one was almost completely burned. She took another from her pocket, lit it and the one that remained, and held them in her cupped hands until she felt the heat of the flames. Then, raising her eyes suddenly, she saw him in the distance. He was coming toward her unsteadily, dressed in his uniform minus the cap, his face dirty, a bleeding cut on his cheek, his eyes half-closed. As he drew nearer she saw him try to bring his hand to his face, but he hesitated and stood with his open palm close to his head, bewildered, until his arm began to tremble and he let it fall limply. The next moment he ran toward the ruins, stumbling and falling. Getting up quickly, he started to run again. He clambered up the pile of bricks, reached the top and fell, only to advance on his knees, tearing at the bricks with his bare hands. Finally one of the soldiers climbed up after him, seized him around the waist and pulled him back into the street. Irina ran to him and took his hand, covering it with kisses.

"Emperor!" she whispered.

Stefan looked at her a long time. He did not seem to recognize her. "They're here, both of them," he said at last, brushing his bloodstained hand across his mouth.

"Emperor!"

"They're here!" He turned his head to the ruins, where several soldiers had picked up the litter and started toward the truck. Irina caught his arm, but he jerked away and ran to them, making his way through the groups of people crowded around the vehicle. A moment later she saw him go back to the ruins, fall quickly to his knees, and begin to throw the bricks aside, clearing away the rubble by hand, trying to pull out a beam. She went to him and tapped his shoulder, but he kept on working breathlessly, as if he had not felt the touch of her hand.

"They're not here," she said. "It's not this house. . . ."

Stefan raised his head and looked around frantically. Irina pointed to the house that stood in front of them, only partially demolished. He stared steadily at it, then he looked to the right and left, and again to the right toward the end of the street. He seemed to be making a supreme effort to orient himself.

"Where are they?" he demanded.

"They're no longer here. They've gone. . . ."

"Tell me where they are," he whispered in a voice that sounded strangled. "Irina, tell me where they are!" He gripped her arm. "Irina!" he implored, squeezing her arm with greater force. "Irina!"

"They've gone," she said finally, without lifting her eyes. "They received the sacrament last night and this morning they've gone. . . ."

Stefan let her arm drop and gazed at her, struggling to understand. "What happened?" he asked. "What?"

"It's Easter," said Irina, her voice very low. "It's the week of light. . . ."

2

SHE RANG A NUMBER OF TIMES, TOUCHING THE BUTTON BRIEFLY, REPEATEDLY.
Adela opened the door.

"He isn't seeing anyone. He's been shut up in his room since yesterday
and he isn't seeing anyone. He hasn't eaten anything."

Irina entered. On a chair in the hallway Biris was waiting, an unlit
cigarette between his lips. Smiling, she shook his hand and followed Adela to
the door at the end of the hall. For a moment she stood unmoving, holding
her breath.

"It's me, Irina," she murmured, and she waited with her face close to the
door.

"It's Irina," she said again in a louder voice.

She heard the key turn in the lock and she went in. Stefan was standing
in the middle of the room in civilian clothes. He was not wearing a tie, and he
had a beard of several days' growth. The cut along his cheek had begun to
heal. Irina went to him and kissed him. Stefan looked at her a long time, his
face expressionless, then he turned to the window. Outside the sky was cloudy
but there was no rain. The trees, which had recently put out leaves, bent their
branches before the brisk wind.

"Biris is here too. He's just outside," said Irina. She waited a few
moments, but seeing he did not reply she sat down. This was the little boy's
room. The child's bed had been removed and a couch brought in for Stefan.
She sat on a chair beside it and waited. After a while Stefan turned his head
suddenly away from the window and looked at her in alarm.

"What are you doing?" he demanded. "You're not praying, are you?"

"No, I can't pray," said Irina softly.

"I thought you were praying," he continued more calmly. "I thought
you were praying to God. . . ."

"No. I can't," she repeated, her voice very low.

370

They were both silent again for a long time. Stefan pressed his face against the windowpane.

"Why don't you smoke?" Irina asked him abruptly. He turned around, astonished.

"I brought you some cigarettes," she went on, and going to him quickly, she held them out, along with a box of matches.

"Oh . . . yes, so I see . . ." he began, but he cut himself short and returned to the middle of the room, lighting a cigarette. He sat down on the couch and smoked silently. After some time he went to the window again and, opening it, flung the butt into the garden.

"Strange," he said, "I'd forgotten about cigarettes. . . ."

After that whenever she came she found him smoking. The room would be filled with a thick, stifling haze, and Irina would go directly to the window and open it. Then there would come a timid rapping at the door she had just closed, and retracing her steps, she would take the tray from Adela's hand.

"He hasn't eaten anything," Adela said each time Irina came to the house. "He smokes all the time, but he doesn't eat. We're desperate. He won't see us, his own family. He doesn't open to anyone. Luckily on that very day . . . you know . . . he was discharged. . . . They took him back at the Ministry, but Raducu got him a leave of absence. . . ."

She talked incessantly as she prepared the sandwiches and placed them on the tray. When Irina saw that everything was ready she went to knock at Stefan's door. Adela waited outside with the tray until Irina returned. Stefan's sister had gone into the room only once when she had found the door open. He had not turned away from the window nor uttered a word, and he had not touched the food. After a quarter of an hour Adela had left and she had not tried again to enter.

Stefan remained beside the open window, watching the constant, gentle trembling of the branches. Sometimes, but rarely, they stopped shaking and everything was motionless for a single, infinite moment. Then they began to quiver again, as if something had surprised them, leaving them restless and suspicious.

"Biris was here to see you," said Irina. "He waited several hours, then he left. He'll come again tomorrow."

She set the tray on the little table beside the couch. Then she went to the window, took him by the arm and drew him gently after her. Stefan sat down on the edge of the bed and brought his hand to his face, rubbing his eyes.

Irina offered him a sandwich in one hand and in the other a glass of milk.

"I'm not hungry."

She put the sandwich back on the plate but continued to hold out the glass of milk. Finally Stefan took it and began to drink, but not without difficulty. It seemed to make him choke.

The wound on his cheek had healed completely. On the morning of the bombardment, Adela had told her, the train from Constanta had stopped about thirty kilometers from Bucharest. After walking a long time along the highway, Stefan had been overtaken by a military truck which brought him as far as the toll house, but there the truck had overturned. It was not clear to her how this had happened. She had not found out these details from Stefan but from one of his fellow-soldiers whom Raducu had met at the Ministry.

For several days he had allowed his beard to grow. Then one morning when Irina entered his room she thought he looked different. He appeared much thinner and more pale, and the scar on his face seemed deeper. She realized that he had shaved.

"Today is the requiem of the ninth day," she told him. "You'll have to dress. . . ."

She watched him run his hand mechanically through his hair, and went to him with the black tie that Adela had given her.

"Where are we going?"

"To the church." She took his arm and led him unprotesting down the stairs. Below on the street a taxi was waiting for them.

Then later, over a certain period, she saw his face change from day to day. Lightly shadowed at first, it looked dirty, then it became darker, stern, almost vicious. But one morning she found that he had shaved again and the cut on his cheek seemed once more to have deepened.

"I'm not hungry," he said.

Irina set the sandwich on the plate and held out the glass of milk again until she felt her arm ache. Then she transferred it to her other hand. Stefan stroked his face and rubbed his eyes, and at last he took the glass, drinking slowly, with effort. All at once he got up and strode to the window. The branches were full of leaves now and the foliage a darker green.

"He won't open the door," complained Adela to Irina one day as she placed the sandwiches on the tray. "He doesn't listen to anyone. It's as though he had no family. Anyway, it's a good thing his parents-in-law aren't in Bucharest. Old Bologa has heart trouble and couldn't come. Stefan hasn't answered the telegram he sent, or any of the letters. He doesn't answer anyone. . . ."

Sometimes the sky was very blue, and white fleecy clouds sped dizzily by, while on other days it was almost night in the room, the somber heavens threatening rain. The branches in front of the window shook suddenly with a frightened sigh.

"He's received hundreds of telegrams and letters of condolence," said Adela once, "from the front, from the Ministry, from everywhere. He hasn't even opened them. Some—the more important ones—we read to him through the door, but I'm sure he didn't listen. There were telegrams from the ministers too, and Raducu replied to them. I also asked Biris to answer in his name. . . ."

Then there was the second and the third air raid, and although Adela and Raducu pounded on his door and begged him, implored him, to go down to the shelter, Stefan remained immobile before the window, watching the sky. After the alert was over they knocked at his door again and called to him: "Stefan! Stefan!" He never answered. He continued to smoke, contemplating the sky or the branches that trembled without ceasing except in those rare moments when they seemed suddenly turned to stone, causing Stefan to recoil apprehensively.

"Raducu went to the Ministry again," said Adela another day. "They extended his leave of absence. But how much longer will he be able to keep this up? He ought to write the Minister. The Secretary General came here to offer his condolences, but Stefan didn't want to see him. We did what we could to make excuses for him, but in times like these with so much misfortune all around, so many dead, it's not easy for someone to come personally and offer condolence. He ought to consider that. . . ."

Irina took the tray, tapped on the door, calling, "It's me, Irina . . ." and waited until she heard him turn the key. She went in. He returned immediately to the window and stared at the sky.

Once Adela greeted her with considerable anxiety. "He's vanished! He's gone! I went out to do some shopping, and when I came back I found his door wide open and the room empty. . . . I telephoned Raducu to take a cab and go to look for him at the cemetery, because I hate to go there alone. But he wasn't there. Anyway I don't know if he'd be able to find the graves. You know how they were buried, poor things. . . . So little was found. . . ."

Irina hurried downstairs to the street. The heady fragrance of wild lilacs poured from the neighboring courtyards into the mild May morning. Very few bombs had fallen here, but the street was almost deserted and the houses with their closed blinds seemed to have been abandoned. Irina walked rapidly, almost running, in search of a taxi.

She saw him in the distance, seated on the curb. The street was just as she had left it, pitted with bomb craters and half-blocked by wreckage. The heaps of bricks, debris, and girders could not be shaken and remained an aggravating presence even after the many rains had packed them down and rendered them more solid, more indifferent. Irina sat down beside him in silence.

"It was in a village in Moldavia," Stefan began abruptly without turning around, "in January of 1943, after Stalingrad. The people went out one night, the whole village went out, and they knelt in the snow with torches and candles in their hands, with the priest in his robes in their midst, and they began to pray. They said that the dead were returning from Stalingrad, that whole regiments were returning to their homes, and that they passed by there along the highway at the edge of the village. . . ."

He stopped and for a long time sat there staring vacantly. Then he searched for his package of cigarettes and lit one.

"How did they know the dead would pass along the edge of the village?" he asked without looking at her.

"God revealed it to them," said Irina softly.

Stefan smoked, his eyes wide, seeing nothing. Suddenly he turned his head and fixed his stern, menacing gaze on her face. *"How did you know?"* he demanded. Irina bent her head quickly. "How did you know?" he repeated, seizing her arm, increasing the pressure of his grip.

Irina raised her hand to her eyes and began to cry gently, silently. Stefan continued to stare at her, and then he released her arm.

"If you knew you could have told her," he resumed after awhile, looking away, "the way you warned her about the earthquake. . . ."

"I did tell her," she whispered. Startled, Stefan turned his head. "I told her about myself. I thought it would happen to me. I told her how to pray, how I would pray. I told her to light candles and to stay with me all that day. I told her that if I should die without the sacrament or confession . . ."

Stefan got up all at once and strode quickly away without looking back, his steps determined and firm. He was soon lost to sight among the ruins at the end of the street. Irina stared after him for a long while and her eyes were blurred with tears.

"Forgive me, Lord, if I have done wrong," she whispered at last and exhausted, rose painfully to her feet.

When she knocked on his door the next day Stefan did not open it. She stood before it for a long time and tapped at intervals, saying, "It's me, Irina!" Adela waited wearily beside her with the tray in her hands. After a quarter of an hour Irina abandoned her efforts and went back to the front hall just as Biris came in.

"I wanted to ask you something," he began, somewhat embarrassed.

374

"Catalina told me that one of the wounded men at her hospital, a Colonel Baleanu, asked to see Stefan. She says he wants to see him without fail. . . ."

They were sitting on the sofa. Adela had gone to do some shopping. Irina had taken the tray from her and was holding it on her lap when Stefan appeared unexpectedly. The cut on his face was oozing blood again, and it looked raw, as though he might have scraped it purposely as he was shaving.

"Colonel Baleanu would like to see you," said Biris.

Stefan sat down in a chair that faced them. "He can't see me. He's blind. . . ." He plunged his hand into his coat pocket, and pulling out his package of cigarettes, he offered it to Biris.

"He wants to talk to you," insisted Biris, taking a cigarette. "He begged Catalina to tell you. He's on her floor. . . . No, I won't light it yet," he added quickly, seeing that Stefan had held out a match. "I smoke too much. . . ."

"I know what he wants, but I won't go. Tell Catalina to make an excuse for me."

"But he insists."

"I know. But I can't." He got up suddenly from the chair. "I'd planned to go to the Ministry today," he added, "but I'll go tomorrow. There's nothing to do anyway. . . . What's happening at the front?" He turned to Biris.

"It seems somewhat stabilized in northern Moldavia."

"There's nothing to do," repeated Stefan. He took out his handkerchief and pressed it to the bleeding cut.

"Come to my room," he said suddenly, and he preceded them down the hall.

Irina carried the tray into the room. Both windows were open and they felt the gentle breeze of the May noon as they entered. The branches, now covered with leaves, quivered lightly in the sunshine. Stefan sat down on the couch.

"It's been thirty-three days," he said. "What should I do, Irina?" Silently she set the tray on the little table. Biris brought the cigarette to his nostrils once more, then decided to light it and hunted nervously for the box of matches.

"I know what Baleanu wants," continued Stefan. "He wants to tell me that I'm to blame, that it happened because of me. . . . And he's right," he added quickly, choked with emotion. He rose and went to the window.

Breathing deeply, Biris drew in the smoke of his cigarette and expelled it with a long sigh. Irina placed her hands in her lap and waited. The sunlight played across the branches and fell on the carpet in large golden patches that were constantly shifting.

"Of course, he's right," resumed Stefan, coming back to the middle of the room. "It happened to him like that. It was many years later, but it happened. . . ."

He sat down on the couch again and appeared to be more calm. He looked at Irina. "It's on account of Vadastra. He told me so himself. Anyhow, he's a fine man. He has a lot of courage. . . ."

He was silent. Irina ran her hand over her face and then returned it to its position beside the other in her lap. Biris got up to look for an ashtray.

"He's Catalina's great love," he said, agitated, shaking the ashes from his cigarette. He went back to the couch, continuing to smoke without looking at either of the others.

"He said that it's on account of Vadastra," repeated Stefan. "He told me they quarreled once long ago, when they were living together, and when he slapped Vadastra he knocked out his glass eye. 'And now God has punished me,' he told me, 'God has taken away the light of my eyes. . . .'"

"It's not true!" Irina interrupted, horrified. "Don't say that again. It's a sin!"

"This is what he believes. And he knew it would happen to him. He knew it for a long time, ever since the war began."

"It's not true!" Irina said again, her alarm increasing. "I'll have to go see him . . ."

"He was always volunteering. He led squads against the partisans hidden in the underground tunnels of Odessa. He knew what was going to happen. He was walking through the dark, hugging the walls, and then suddenly they blinded him with their flamethrowers. The partisans didn't have much ammunition and they used flamethrowers a lot. Baleanu knew what was in store for him."

"I must go to see him without fail," Irina repeated in a tone of desperation.

Biris stood up to put out his cigarette. The patches of sunlight flickered on the rug and shifted slowly toward the mirror. A few moments later Adela came to the door and hesitated anxiously on the threshold.

"It was announced on the BBC that we'll be bombed again," she said hurriedly. "They said if we don't surrender we'll be bombed day and night. We'll be bombed till not a house is left standing in all Romania."

She stopped in embarrassment and tried to smile, looking at each of them, one after another. "It was announced just now on the BBC," she repeated.

The next day Stefan resumed his work at the Ministry, and after that Irina came to see him only in the evening. She didn't always find him at home and when this happened she stayed awhile to talk with Adela. They sat together on the sofa in the hall and waited for him.

"Ioana's mother was here," Adela said one day in a tone of mystery. "She

376

spent a long time with him in his room. She told me that he cried like a child. . . . I've never heard him. Perhaps he only cries at night. . . ."

She looked insistently at Irina, expecting some comment from her, but a moment later the younger woman stood up abruptly.

"I can't wait any longer," she said. "It's getting dark."

She left, wrapping her woolen scarf around her neck, and her shoulders quivered, although the May night was not cold. She walked rapidly through the darkness as though she were afraid. Far ahead of her she saw the burning tip of a cigarette and slackened her pace, approaching him with caution so as not to startle him. Hidden in the night she hesitated briefly before whispering, "Stefan! It's me, Irina. . . ."

Sometimes she came upon him seated on a bench under one of the old chestnut trees that stood guard over the boulevard, and she sat down beside him without speaking. For some time he continued to smoke in silence. He did not seem to be aware of her presence at his side.

"We had a photograph," he began once. "It was our first photograph together, when we were engaged. It was taken in May, 1933. I always told her it was our best picture. A young boy took it for us. I'm sorry I never knew his name. He was with his mother and a cousin, a girl from the *liceu*. He had taken their picture several times together, but he wanted to be included in the group at least once. We were passing by just then and he asked me to take the picture for him. Then he came toward us smiling timidly and said to me, 'If you will permit me. . . .' Ioana began to laugh and turned her face toward me, catching my arm quickly. And at that moment he snapped the shutter. . . . Afterward he asked for our address, but I didn't think he'd send us the picture. And yet he did. It was mailed in Brasov, but it didn't have his name on it, or his address. . . . That was in May, 1933. She was wearing a blouse with red polka dots. It's strange. . . . After that she never made another blouse with red polka dots. . . ."

He was silent again for a long interval, smoking and gazing straight before him into the blackness. Occasionally cars passed along the boulevard with their headlights dimmed, advancing slowly, cautiously. Irina wrapped the shawl more tightly around her neck and waited. At last, Stefan turned and faced her.

"Aren't you going home?" he demanded.

She arose slowly and held out her hand, but Stefan did not see her gesture. Irina remained standing with her hand extended, but after a few moments she withdrew it in confusion, hiding it in the pocket of her coat.

"Good night," she said as she left him and vanished quickly in the night.

She persisted in returning every evening. One time Adela told her, "He wants to move. A fellow-worker at the Ministry who was evacuated to Timisoara has offered him his apartment. . . . Besides, it's likely that we'll leave too," she added, lowering her voice. "We'll also be evacuated. . . ."

377

"It's me, Irina," she whispered as she knocked on his door and waited. She heard the sound of the light switch and then that of the key turning in the lock. She found Stefan in the middle of the room and she put out the light quickly, since he always left the windows open.

"Blackout!" she murmured. "They'll send you straight to the concentration camp!"

Stefan went to the window and Irina sat down on the chair near the couch. The moon had disappeared and the night had recovered its solitude, its plenitude. The stars twinkled timidly, hazily, so far away that they seemed powerless to penetrate the shadows rising from the earth filled with the pungent odors of fresh leaves and sap. Outside, the black branches, dozing, nodded from time to time, almost without a sound.

"She said she would be afraid alone," Stefan began without turning his head, "but she liked to walk with me in the mountains at night. When we stayed at the Cabana we always strolled at night in the direction of Bulboci. I'd let her go ahead of me on the path, but when we had to cross the bridge I went first and held her by the hand. That was in July 1933. After that we went to the mountains often. . . . It's strange I don't remember what she said to me. I talked all the time. Now and then she managed to say something, but I don't remember now. Nothing remains except images. But they're very precise images, even to the last small detail. I can see now every stone we sat on when we wanted to rest or look at the moon. . . ."

He turned away from the window and began to walk slowly through the darkened room. After a while Irina got up suddenly, as though she had just remembered something urgent. "Good night, Stefan," she said.

On the following day there was another massive air raid, and toward evening the sky over the city became stained with red. When she went to see Stefan, Irina had to make long detours around several streets that had been ploughed up and made impassable by the bombs.

"We're leaving tomorrow," Adela confided to her at the door in a whisper. "Raducu says the government's acting stupidly and we ought to surrender. He says the Anglo-American forces will give us guarantees. . . ."

He was standing in the dark in front of the open window. Above the trees the sky could be seen glowing in the light of distant fires. Irina went to him and put her hand on his arm.

"Tomorrow will be forty days," she said. "I'll wait for you at the church at eleven o'clock."

"What for?" Stefan asked without looking at her.

"It's the requiem of forty days."

Automatically he took the package of cigarettes from his coat pocket and lit one, but after the first puff he threw it into the garden. "I can't do it! I can't smoke anymore. I think I'm poisoned."

378

From time to time they heard the far-off, prolonged rumble of explosions that shook the building from top to bottom.

"I'll expect you tomorrow at eleven," said Irina again and she started to leave.

Stefan spoke abruptly. "I dreamed about her last night. She was wearing the dress she had on when she met me at the airport three years ago. She seemed very happy and she smiled at me. I thought she wanted to tell me something, but she didn't say anything."

He left the window and began to walk about, but after a few moments he sat down on the edge of the couch. The room brightened in the reflection of the red glow that lit the sky.

"I dreamed about *doamna* Zissu," said Irina.

"But how did you know that it was she?"

"I dreamed about her once before. I knew it was *doamna* Zissu. . . ."

The branches beyond the window began to quiver again, as if the wind had awakened them. Stefan put his hand in his pocket and pulled out his cigarettes, but immediately he remembered his distaste for them. After turning one around in his fingers for awhile, undecided, he set it on the table.

"Poor *doamna* Zissu," he said. "How much Ioana suffered because of her. . . ." He sprang to his feet and resumed his walk around the room.

"I thought we had our whole lives ahead of us, that I'd have plenty of time to love her, to be hers alone. I was in no hurry. I had my secret room and I had personal problems to solve. I wanted to learn, above all, who *doamna* Zissu was. This became the whole purpose of my existence. I would devote it to unraveling the mystery of *doamna* Zissu! I think I must have been crazy!" he exclaimed in a dry voice. "Raving mad!"

He hesitated an instant by the door and then opened it resolutely and strode down the hall. Irina quickly drew the blinds at the window and turned on the light. Soon Stefan came back with a bottle of wine and two glasses. With a frightened glance Irina took his hand.

"Stefan!" she implored. "Stefan! Don't drink!"

"I can't smoke anymore." He filled the glasses. Irina watched him fearfully. In the glare of the exposed globe his face seemed withered and aged, with cheekbones that protruded under his skin, lips that were blanched and dry, eyes veiled with mist. His hair had shown signs of turning gray a few years earlier, but recently his temples had taken on the pale tone of cigarette ash. The scar on his cheek showed very clear and deep.

"Stefan! It's wrong!" whispered Irina.

He looked up suddenly and his eyes met hers for a few moments, then he smiled. "Don't be afraid. . . . Just this evening, since I can't smoke. . . ."

That week he moved to a bachelor apartment on *strada* Bucovinei, turned over to him by the man who had been evacuated to Timisoara. The

379

section of the Ministry in which Stefan worked had been transferred in part to Snagov, but he had asked to be allowed to remain in Bucharest. Recently he had been put in charge of coordinating the services that had been evacuated to various regions of the country. He went to his office very early, took his lunch and often the evening meal at the canteen, returning to *strada* Bucovinei rather late. Every evening he saw Irina in the distance walking along the sidewalk, her head bent. She always wore her coat, although the nights were getting warmer. All the cars crept by with their headlights dimmed, and now at nightfall there were very few pedestrians on the streets.

One evening, the first time that Stefan had seen her approaching, Irina had just been accosted by two drunken men. One of them laid his hand on her shoulder and started to talk to her with a certain amount of difficulty, while the other watched the scene and laughed in great amusement. Irina leaned against the wall, smiling, embarrassed. Stefan hurried to her and took her arm, pulling her after him. That evening they walked as far as *bulevardul* Elisabeta, where they sat down on a bench.

"When I passed by here this morning," Stefan began, "all of a sudden I saw her in front of me. She was dressed exactly like Ioana, and her figure was the same. And yet when I came closer I saw that she didn't resemble Ioana at all. But from a distance..."

He stopped to allow a convoy of loaded army trucks, going toward the head of the bridge, to move past.

"I'm always trying to figure it out. What did we have? A few years together. And after I left for the front the second time I saw her just a few weeks in all.... I don't know why it seemed to me that we had our whole lives ahead of us—that we would grow old together.... And of course I didn't stay with her then...."

He stopped and turned a moment to face Irina, then he looked for his package of cigarettes. He took one out and lit it.

"I often wonder," he continued a little later, "and just now I was wondering, why I only tell you lies. Why do I lie to you all the time?"

"You don't lie to me!" Irina protested at once.

"Yes, I do. You have no way of knowing. When I left for the front I believed that I'd never come back. It was a sort of suicide. I was sure I'd remain there forever, like so many others—hundreds of thousands of innocent men—not guilty, like me. I wanted to make an end of everything. It seemed to me I had failed completely. I laughed at my luck. It's hard to explain. I'd believed in something, hoped for something, and it had turned to ashes in my fingers. I had nothing more to cling to. I felt I didn't love Ioana anymore...."

"That's not true!" said Irina in a frightened whisper. "You love her and you've always loved her. You only thought that you didn't love her...."

Stefan turned his head and looked into her eyes, suddenly shining in the dim light.

"I know," he said, "but I didn't realize it then. It seemed to me that I didn't love her anymore as I had loved her at first. Actually it's the same thing. It's just as serious. . . ."

"That's not true," Irina repeated. "That's not true. . . ."

The following evening she was waiting in front of his house in the entryway. A fine drizzle had begun to fall, and she had gone in seeking a shelter from the rain. They climbed the stairs to the fourth floor. His room was pretentiously but tastelessly furnished with so-called "modern" pieces which already seemed shabby and out-of-date. Irina sat on a chair near the desk with its display of several glasses and two bottles of wine.

"I feel better here," said Stefan. "It's very ugly but I like it."

He stopped in the middle of the room and followed Irina's glance with his eyes. "Don't be alarmed. I drink only when I can't smoke." He sat down on the edge of the divan. "I dreamed about her last night, but a strange thing happened. She didn't look like herself any longer. It's as though she's beginning to become someone else. . . ." He stopped, his gaze wandering.

"What exasperates me most is that I can't remember what she said to me. . . ."

"What she said to you in the dream?"

"No. Her real words. What she told me when we were together. . . . The images are very clear in my mind. . . ." He was silent for a long while.

"I remember," he began again in a low, deep voice, "I remember the day when I first told her about my secret room. She was wearing . . ."

He was still and after a moment he smiled. She had been wearing the same blouse with the red polka dots. They had recently become engaged, and they were walking together under the linden trees in Cotroceni. Ioana kept looking at him with her large eyes, so extraordinarily limpid. He could see them now. He stood up abruptly, uncorked a bottle of wine and filled two glasses. Irina watched him, absorbed. Stefan held out a glass to her. Then he sat down on the edge of the divan again and began to drink, but soon he shook his head and set the drink on the table.

"I can't do it," he said. "I can't drink anymore. . . ."

"What was she like in your dream?" asked Irina quickly, faintly.

"I don't know now if it was she. She didn't resemble . . . I often have the impression that she's no longer the same, no longer herself, that she has become a different person. . . . When I saw her in her wedding dress . . ." He stopped and stared blankly before him. "Ah yes, I remember. She told me a lot of things then."

He seized the glass again, sipped a little from it and held it awhile in his hand.

381

"She pitied Partenie," he went on. "She was sorry for him. . . ."

He set the glass down on the corner of the table and reached for a cigarette but delayed lighting it. He turned and twisted it about in his fingers, brought it to his nostrils, and recalling then that these were Biris's gestures, he replaced the cigarette in the package.

"I feel as though I'm losing my mind!" He sprang to his feet suddenly. "There's nothing left anymore. I can't smoke. I can't drink. I've tried—many, many times. I can't drink. I can't!"

Irina watched him walk about the room.

"I have only one photograph, the one I carried in my billfold. There's nothing else left. When I saw her the last time she was reading a book. I remember very well. She kept it in a leather jacket so she wouldn't spoil the covers. I didn't see the title. I should like at least to be able to read that book, but I don't know the title. I didn't have the curiosity to leaf through it, to see what she was reading. . . ."

He sat on the edge of the divan and buried his face in his hands for a moment; then ashamed, he turned to Irina and smiled at her as though asking her pardon.

"If only I could dream of her every night. I once saw a film . . ." He stopped and put his hand to his forehead. "Yes, but in the film it was different. It was something else. . . ."

Biris went as usual to the same bench in the hospital garden and sat down. Unfolding his newspaper he began to read. It was a few days after the landing of the Allies in Normandy, and since that morning of the sixth of June the Bucharestians had become discouraged. Until the last moment many had hoped the invasion would take place in the Balkans, while some people had even believed it would be attempted on the shore of the Black Sea, along the Romanian coast. Biris, however, had not entertained any such illusions. When he opened the newspaper he read the telegraphed reports without hurry, almost without curiosity. He still had to wait a half hour. Catalina always came down at the lunch hour, a few minutes after the hospital clock struck twelve. Every time she crossed the courtyard in her nurse's uniform Biris regarded her with the same mixture of admiration and hatred he had felt six months earlier when he had seen her dressed in white for the first time.

After meeting Baleanu she had decided to become a nurse. Until that time she had never thought of being of service to the wounded in any other capacity than that of a dramatic artist. From the beginning of the war she had been working with a number of impromptu theatrical

382

troupes that toured the hospitals in Bessarabia, and later in Odessa and the Crimea, giving performances for the injured men. She went first in the autumn of 1941 with a group organized by Dan Bibicescu. Exasperated, Biris had accompanied her to the station. He seemed to have a presentiment of all that was going to ensue. Catalina had been separated from Bibicescu for a long time, but when she returned from Bessarabia they resumed their life together. She herself told Biris about it. Again she seemed to have changed. She was preoccupied, and she would repeat frequently, "It doesn't matter. . . ." Then at Christmas time, several months later, she and Dan had broken up again. He quit arranging entertainment for the wounded soldiers and went back to the Regina Maria Theater. Catalina brought Biris this piece of news on Christmas Eve.

"It's finished, finally and forever," she told him. And because she saw that Biris was blushing and avoiding her eyes, she added quickly, "Anyway, it doesn't matter. We never loved each other. It was just a habit. Now I have somebody else. . . ." Biris looked up suddenly. "He's a handsome boy. I met him at Jassy when he was on a furlough from the front. He says he loves me. I don't quite believe it but I enjoy it." Biris felt the blood rush to his temples and he drew deeply on his cigarette. "And what's become of the nineteenth of October?" he demanded in a thick voice that was muffled by the smoke. She smiled with surprising sweetness, then shrugged and said, "It doesn't matter. . . ."

A few weeks later she went away again. He escorted her to the platform in the North Station. It was bitterly cold and the group of actors and actresses had crowded close together in a poorly heated coach, wrapped in long coats and capes made of cheap furs, with blankets over their legs. They smoked bad cigarettes and drank from canteens of rum. Biris had made his way through them with a vague feeling of pity. Most of them were unsuccessful actors who had played a season or two in the provincial theaters in insignificant roles and then sought the haven of a prefect's office or a town hall, occupying themselves with presenting cultural programs, organizing charity fetes, and reciting poetry at celebrations on January 24 and May 10.* There were young people prematurely aged and women whose years could not be guessed through their heavy makeup. Several students from the Conservatory were also in the group—young girls who looked about them excitedly. Biris glanced at Catalina and saw that she appeared much older with her faded puppet's face and her time-dusted hair, which fell across her face. It occurred to him that here she had found her true

*National patriotic anniversaries. May 10 commemorates independence gained in 1877.

family; but he quickly ran his hand over his face in an attempt to banish his despair and drew her to one side in the corridor of the coach. "Why must you go with these people?" he asked in a whisper. Catalina shrugged. "We all do our duty in the best way we can," she said. "Yes, but . . ." The signal for departure sounded and Catalina pushed him toward the door, where she stopped and, clasping his head in her hands, kissed him on both cheeks.

She never forgot to write to him. Simple postcards they were, without any indication of origin, and they came through the military mail service. She always informed him by telegram whenever she was returning to Bucharest. "I met Viziru at Odessa," she told him once, in the spring of 1942. "I didn't know that he was at the front too." "I hope he won't stay there," Biris said. "It's one of his crazy ideas." "He came to the theater and I had a chat with him. What's happened to him? He looks like a different man." "Love," said Biris with a smile. "Probably," she observed. "I like men who believe in love." Biris puffed furiously at his cigarette. "But you, how's your love-life?" he asked. "What's become of your friend?" Catalina shrugged her shoulders. "I'm not with him anymore. We separated a long time ago and I haven't heard from him since. I hope he's all right. He was in the Crimea too. . . ."

There was a long period when he did not know exactly what had happened to her—whether she had remained in Odessa as a member of the theatrical troupe there, or if she were still touring the military hospitals with a group of roving actors. She had written him often from Odessa and described the plays in which she acted, the roles that she was preparing. Then one day he received a telegram, and he went to meet her at the station. He noticed that she looked even older than when he had seen her last. Her face was more ravaged, her forehead slightly wrinkled, her eyes tired. But as soon as he had seen her at the window of the coach he felt his heart leap and he began to anticipate that wonderful, incomparable moment when, after descending from the last step, Catalina would embrace him and kiss both of his cheeks. That was the one moment when he felt that she was truly close to him.

Sometimes she looked at him severely. "You're thinner again! And you have a fever. You're cheeks are flushed. What's happened?" Biris shrugged. "Nothing serious. I had an X-ray and they told me it's nothing serious. . . ." The truth was, however, that he had not had an X-ray for a long time, not since the autumn of 1941, when he had spent several months in a military sanatorium. "You're almost completely bald!" Catalina exclaimed another time when he met her on the station platform. "You ought to shave your head. Take advantage of the warm weather. It's summer and you're on vacation. . . ."

Suddenly, without any warning, she had notified him that she was taking a course in nursing. He had received the letter in the fall of 1943 from Odessa, and a week later she telegraphed that she was arriving in Bucharest. She was unrecognizable. Her hair was styled in an entirely different way: it no longer tumbled over her ears and cheeks, but was cut short in a boyish bob. Now, all at once, she looked much younger. Her lips had regained their bright color and her eyes had lost the mist that recently veiled them. "I've met a saint," she said in the taxi which took them from the North Station to her apartment. "He's blind. I've fallen in love with him. . . ."

It was one of those unusual days that sometimes come at the beginning of November, warm and summery. The chestnut trees along the boulevards had long since dropped their leaves, but their branches appeared about to bud again in the moist, gentle, golden light. Something in the air smelled like an old, neglected graveyard or a forest.

"I met him three years ago. He was a captain then and he had the most beautiful blue eyes. . . ."

The taxi stopped. Biris roused suddenly, and picking up Catalina's two small valises, he carried them to the elevator. Then he held out his hand in an involuntarily pathetic gesture, as if he were saying good-bye to her forever. "Aren't you going up with me for a moment to have a cup of tea?" she asked. As he settled himself in the familiar armchair, Catalina silently removed some of her things from the valises and went into the next room to put the water on to boil. Although he was well acquainted with her ritual, it seemed to him that someone else was performing it—someone who had not yet had time to learn it well. "Now I know too what it means to be in love," she said later.

After a few days she had gone away again. She wrote infrequently, informing him that she had finished her nurse's training, that she was working at the hospital where Baleanu was a patient. In February the injured officer was transferred to Bucharest and assigned to a wing of the hospital where badly mutilated men were awaiting plastic surgery. He had had one operation at Odessa, but whenever Catalina remembered it she covered her face with her hands. "Half of his face is burned," she said. "Not only his eyes but half his face. . . ."

Biris learned a little later how they had met. "I was going from ward to ward reciting verses. In one room there was a wounded man with his face entirely covered with bandages. He called me, 'Miss, miss. . . .' I stopped in surprise. It was a gentle, manly voice, and I felt sure that I'd heard it before. 'Miss!' he called again and again. I went to him and took his hand and then I remembered. We both remembered. . . ."

At noon he heard the hospital clock strike the hour. Very methodically he folded up the newspaper and waited. She descended the dreary concrete stairs and turned in his direction. He stood up to kiss her hand and they sat down on the bench together.

"How's he doing?" asked Biris.

"Just the same. Next week they're going to try another operation."

Biris selected a cigarette and lit it.

"What else has happened?" asked Catalina.

"It's bad. The end is coming. . . ."

"I didn't mean about the war," she interrupted. "I want to know what's happened to Viziru. Aurel keeps waiting for him. He wants to talk with him."

Biris continued to smoke, gazing directly ahead of him, across the flower beds, at the immense and sinister wall of the hospital. "It's a long time since I saw Viziru. I told you how he answered me the last time—that he knows what Baleanu wants to say to him. . . ."

"He doesn't know anything!" exclaimed Catalina, silencing him. "Aurel wants to talk to him about something else. He wants to encourage him, to console him. . . ."

Biris threw down his cigarette, crushing it on the gravel with his foot. "Are you eating with me today or will you stay at the hospital?" he asked.

"I think I'll eat with you. Wait a minute while I go and change."

His eyes followed her as she walked away, her hands in the pockets of her hospital jacket, skirting the plots of flowers in the bright sunlight. He smiled resignedly.

On the morning of August the twenty-fifth, Gheorghe Vasile, aided by Irina, began to carry the packages of books to the wagon that was waiting in front of the house. They constituted his collection of pamphlets and popular editions, all wrapped in newspapers and tied with twine.

> For a long time the teacher had hoped to be able to transport the library of the Cultural Foundations by train, and the crates full of books had stood for weeks in the salon, while he searched the city for a means of sending them to Giurgiu. But it had become rather difficult to ship freight, and in addition the teacher didn't know where to go or whom to ask. At last, in mid-July, he had decided to move them in a wagon.
>
> The idea of evacuation had begun to tempt him after the third air raid. Several bombs had fallen on a neighboring street and many of the windows in Antim's house had been broken. That afternoon *doamna* Ivascu had gone out in search of a glazier, leaving Vasile in the salon

386

reluctantly sticking paper tape on the cracked pane of one of the windows. He heard the little gate to the courtyard open and saw a woman enter. She was elderly but still strong and energetic, and in her hand she carried an old suitcase made of cardboard. It must have been rather heavy because she stopped in the middle of the courtyard to set it down, wiped both hands on her skirt and looked around her in wonder and admiration.

"I'm looking for Madame Irina," she said. "I'm Madame Porumbache, Petrica Biris's aunt. I've brought some things for Madame Irina. . . ." In the salon she sat down and peered at everything, marveling. "What a beautiful house!" she exclaimed several times. "We lived like this, too, in Ferendari. Maybe you know the neighborhood. . . ." She began to describe the house, relating the whole story of her days of abundance before the other war. Her eyes filled with tears and she looked around the room again, deeply moved. Then suddenly she changed the subject.

"Petrica, my nephew, is sick again. Maybe it's because he was frightened. A bomb fell on a house right at the end of the street and smashed it to bits! And he asked me to bring these things for Madame Irina. He says that they're things of great value and that if—God forbid!—a bomb should happen to fall. . . ."

At that moment Gherghina Ivascu returned with the glazier. They opened the suitcase and found in it three paintings and, wrapped with great care in tissue paper, a number of the articles from the glass cases.

Gherghina demanded angrily, "Hasn't Irina come back yet? Ever since Ioana was killed that girl's lost her mind. She's forgotten everything, even her child!"

Gheorghe Vasile left her complaining to *doamna* Porumbache and retired to his room. He was worried and fearful, and he contemplated the cabinet in which his collection was stored. He had almost completed his Library for Everyone. Only eleven volumes were lacking. And all these treasures might be destroyed someday in an air raid. In despair he collapsed in his yellow leather chair. Then all at once he realized how naive he was. The Cultural Foundations made no sense located in the capital of Romania. They had been conceived to bring enlightenment to the villages, and above all to the village where he had been a teacher, namely to Dobresti in the district of Vlasca.

He had begun to wait for the wagon since the first of August, after having written to his sister, to the new teacher, to the mayor, and to the priest. He had even sent a postal money order for the traveling expenses of the driver. A cousin of his, Cojocaru, was coming. He had been a drayman at Giurgiu before the war and had just received a medical discharge from the army. One arm was paralyzed from the shoulder.

Every morning Gheorghe Vasile would go out to the street to wait for him. He walked back and forth in front of the house and as far as the end of the street. Sometimes he ventured to go all the way to the tram station on the boulevard, but then he would return, feeling nervous, dejected, and discouraged. In the last few days, since the Russian offensive had begun along the entire Moldavian front, bringing fierce fighting to the gates of Jassy, he had become desperate. "The Russians are upon us!" he said. "They'll catch us here like mice in a trap. . . ."

Cojocaru arrived late at night on August 23, tapping on the windowpane with his whip handle and awakening Irina, who opened the door for him. The horses were exhausted and famished. It was too late to take them to the stable that Vasile had found for them in Obor. The men unfastened the harness and brought them into the courtyard, leaving the wagon on the street with the brakes set. The next day, after Cojocaru had left for Obor with the team, they heard a news bulletin on the radio announcing the *coup d'état* of King Mihai and the cessation of hostilities with the Soviets. Gheorghe Vasile stood in the middle of the floor, for a moment unable to move. After awhile he rubbed the back of his hand across his mouth and turned to Cojocaru.

"Let's go tonight, cousin, before the Russians overtake us."

Cojocaru shook his head. "The horses can't do it. They've got to rest at least a night and a day. Otherwise they'll drop on the road. . ."

The following morning Irina and Gheorghe Vasile began to load the boxes of books on the wagon before Cojocaru had brought the horses back from Obor. Several German planes passed overhead. They flew very low, at an altitude of less than fifty meters, heading toward the center of the city. Cojocaru returned just at that moment.

"It's bad on the boulevard," he told them.

Gheorghe Vasile did not seem to have heard this remark. He had climbed up on the wagon and was placing the packages in the crates with great care. Irina brought him two blankets, a basket of food and another basket containing bottles of wine, as well as a large jug of water. *Doamna* Ivascu came out on the sidewalk to wish them a safe journey. Gheorghe Vasile kissed her hand, and then he kissed Irina on the cheeks.

"I'll go with you as far as the boulevard," said Irina, climbing quickly into the wagon. *Doamna* Ivascu started to say something but her voice was drowned in the deafening roar of the planes as they erupted over the housetops. Tossing their heads the horses jerked the wagon sharply and took off with a sudden burst of speed. When they reached the boulevard, Cojocaru tugged on the reins and brought the team to a halt. He turned to Irina and waited for her to get down.

"I'll go a little farther, to Obor," she said, "just to see you past the tollgate. . . ."

Some pedestrians glanced at the wagon in passing, showing no interest. They appeared tired and disheartened, but their movements were restless and agitated, as though they were waiting for something—what, they did not know. A young man with glasses and a very pale face kept looking up at the sky. As the wagon set out again Irina made a sign of the cross.

"If only they don't catch up with us," said Gheorghe Vasile. "Because if there's an armistice and no one stops them, they'll be here in a day or two. . . ."

Irina got up and tried to find a more comfortable spot for herself among the crates. But the jolting was just as bad in the new position and after a few moments she returned to her original seat behind Cojocaru. Two policemen were watching as she bounced around among the boxes, and they smiled at her. A siren sounded behind them. Cojocaru looked around with a scowl and saw a fire engine coming toward them at top speed, swarming with men. Several of them were aging army reservists but many were civilians wearing wild expressions on their faces and waving their arms in the air, shouting something no one could distinguish. In their midst sat a police chief with a solemn, impassive face. Cojocaru pulled on the reins with all the strength of his good arm and the weight of his body as he leaned back precariously. He managed to bring the wagon to a halt just as the truck grazed them and disappeared like an apparition, trailing a cloud of blue smoke. A strong smell of gasoline surrounded the wagon. A youngster emerged from a courtyard with a bicycle, climbed on it and with a few turns of the pedals came toward them. As he drew up beside Gheorghe Vasile he cried, "The Germans keep bombing the Palace, but they don't have any bombers. They just come over with fighters and drop the bombs from them! If we can only hold out another day or two we'll be safe. . . ."

They passed a number of houses that had been leveled by the bombs. Two children sprawled in the sunshine on top of the ruins, following the wagon for a long time with their eyes. After leaving the boulevard they stopped suddenly and Cojocaru began to crack the whip over the horses, swearing. Someone stepped down from the sidewalk to help, but the horses strained, the wagon jerked suddenly, and the man waved at them with a laugh. Gheorghe Vasile tipped his hat in salute as he jogged along, shaking and bouncing.

"Now I have to find a site," he said, leaning toward Irina, "where I can build the Foundations. . . ." He wished to continue, but he stopped suddenly and raised his eyes in fright. There was a sound of airplanes again and they saw the people scatter, shouting, disappearing into the courtyards or throwing themselves to the ground. The horses broke into a gallop, and Gheorghe

Vasile shrank down in the wagon, trying to hide among the boxes. Irina covered her eyes. Three German planes went past like lightning directly overhead, accompanied by the short sharp whine of bullets and flying chips of asphalt. Cojocaru pulled on the reins to check the flight of the horses and turned to look at the others, exhilarated, his eyes sparkling.

"Those are fighters!" he shouted. "Did you see that? Did you see how they shot at us?"

People reappeared on the sidewalks again, noisy, restless, looking all about them, crossing the streets to meet each other, gesticulating vehemently.

"Maybe it would be better if you didn't go on," Irina suggested. "Maybe you should wait a day or two. . . ."

The sun shone directly in their faces now, blinding them, and Gheorghe Vasile pulled his hat over his eyes. He seemed not to have heard her. Cojocaru began to whistle. The street was pitted with holes here and there, and the horses advanced at a walk with their heads held close to the pavement as though they were sniffing at it. The teacher took out his handkerchief and wiped his face.

"Now that we've started I won't give in," he said after awhile, with determination and a kind of restrained fury. "I won't give in until I've built something the likes of which has never been seen before in Dobresti!"

It was not long before they turned into a paved street lined with new little houses that appeared to be unoccupied. Cojocaru, whistling all the while, calmly urged the horses forward, but at the end of the street they were stopped by two soldiers wearing combat uniforms and helmets and carrying machine guns.

"We're going to Obor," Cojocaru told them. "We have some books with us. . . ."

Gheorghe Vasile got to his feet in the wagon. "They're useful books, books of culture for the entire Romanian nation!"

The soldiers approached the wagon, perplexed, their sunburnt faces covered with sweat and dust. "You can't go there," said one of them. "They're fighting with the Germans at Obor. Haven't you seen the planes?"

"The whole city's surrounded by Germans," the other added. "Haven't you heard the radio?"

"I know how to get out of Bucharest," said Cojocaru. "We don't have to go through Obor. I know other ways. . . ."

"These are books of great value," Gheorghe Vasile began again. "I have to find a safe place for them. The Russians are coming. . . ."

The soldiers stepped aside and signaled to them to pass. Cojocaru brought two fingers to his temple in a military salute and the wagon started off again, creaking brassily.

As they neared the railway station at Obor they began to hear the sound of rifle fire and now and then the brief rattle of a machine gun. The wagon drew up in front of a courtyard filled with tall hollyhocks, where two old women rested on low stools in the garden beyond the fence.

"What's going on at the tollgate, auntie?" asked Cojocaru.

The women looked at him inquisitively and in silence. Gheorghe Vasile doffed his hat to them. "Is it possible to go past the tollgate?" he asked.

One of the women left her stool and approached the fence timidly. She scrutinized them for some time through the hollyhocks. "You can't go," she said finally. "I hear that the Germans are there, waiting for the Russians. . . ."

Cojocaru turned his attention abruptly back to the horses, circling the whip angrily above them, and the wagon lunged forward with a sudden jerk. Soon they reached a crossroad where an army truck was parked in the shade of a locust tree. It was occupied by only one soldier, who sat dozing behind the wheel, his helmet thrust far back on his head. Cojocaru sprang down from the wagon and went up to him.

"Can we go to Obor?" he demanded.

"If you'll wait a little longer you might," the soldier replied, subjecting the other to a lengthy inspection. "This morning there were only two machine-gun nests left. But you know there's an airplane that keeps circling around here. . . ."

"There're three of them," said Cojocaru, spitting to one side. "We saw them just a little while ago."

"I don't mean those. They're planes from Baneasa, from the airfield. They're strafing the downtown area and the boulevards. I mean the one that's guarding the station and the railway."

Several other people had gathered about them while they were speaking. "You might not get by," said one of the newcomers, a man who had not shaved for many days and whose misty eyes betrayed a lack of sleep. "The plane will spot you. It's flying just above the housetops."

Gheorghe Vasile climbed out of the wagon too, leaving the reins in Irina's hands. "We don't have time," he said. "There's an armistice. The Russians are coming. . . ."

The people stared at him quizzically but made no further comment.

"You can try," said the soldier, removing his helmet in order to wipe the sweat from his face. "But don't go by way of the station."

Cojocaru and Gheorghe Vasile returned to the wagon where Irina waited, quietly holding the reins.

"I know a way," remarked Cojocaru, "but it's a big detour. We'll barely make it to the highway by evening." He stopped and looked at Irina, then turned his questioning gaze upon the teacher.

"I'm going with you as far as the highway," Irina declared.

Cojocaru jumped up on the wagon, whistled to the horses, and turned back down the street in the direction from which they had come. They heard the sound of the rifles again, somewhat muffled this time, and after an interval came the brief response of the machine gun. The horses started to gallop and a dusty, frightened puppy ran along beside the wagon, which was making an ear-splitting racket. It was difficult for Irina to keep her balance among the boxes that were bouncing and bumping together almost constantly. The horses stumbled wearily after a few hundred meters and Cojocaru relaxed the reins, letting them walk ahead slowly.

"I know a way," he said again, turning his head and smiling.

They were passing along a street of shabby little houses hidden in the shade of old mulberry trees. The lane seemed to be deserted but women and children kept appearing behind the fences, watching them with quiet curiosity.

"Folks are scared," said Cojocaru and he whirled the whip once more, high in the air.

At the end of that street they had to stop again. Two military trucks loaded with soldiers came pell-mell from the direction of the center of the city, blowing their horns steadily. People rushed from their houses and courtyards, and in a few moments the street had come to life.

"The Russians have come, you know," Irina heard a woman say as she drew her kerchief over her mouth.

"They've barely reached Buzau," commented someone else. "They won't be here for two or three days yet."

"If only the Germans don't occupy us first," said another. "I heard they've crossed the Danube and are coming toward us from Bulgaria."

They went on several hundred meters and Cojocaru stopped the wagon beside a fountain, climbed down with a bucket, and gave the horses a drink.

"What are we going to do, cousin?" demanded Gheorghe Vasile.

"Don't worry. I know the way," Cojocaru declared calmly. "But it makes a big detour. . . ."

He let the horses rest and rolled a cigarette for himself. The teacher rummaged in his pockets and found a package. Half of the tobacco had been shaken out of the cigarettes, but he selected one and lit it. Staring vacantly ahead, Irina grasped the reins.

"We have to hurry!" Gheorghe Vasile muttered, mostly to himself.

They set out again over poor unpaved streets, thick with dust as deep as the breadth of a man's hand. The tiny, dilapidated houses were really no more than hovels, and in the uncultivated gardens with their broken fences, corn and sunflowers mingled with hollyhocks and morning glories. Cojocaru halted the wagon at another crossroad and looked around with a frown. He seemed to be trying to recall which way he should go. Finally he urged the horses down the most wretched of the lanes, one that was rutted and full of holes. Several large shepherd dogs dashed out of the yards and began to bark at them. People with sleepy, frightened faces appeared on the other side of the fences and followed their progress until the wagon was lost in a cloud of dust.

About a hundred meters farther one of the wheels became stuck in a hole, and all the straining of the horses could not budge it. Cojocaru handed the reins to Irina and leapt down from his seat, followed a few moments later by the teacher. Surrounded by the dogs, they put their shoulders to the back of the wagon and began to push. After several fruitless attempts Cojocaru gave up, muttering curses as two men emerged from a nearby yard. They shouted threats at the howling dogs to drive them away, and all four leaned on the wagon, while Irina brandished the whip above the horses. The vehicle bounded out of the hole.

"But where are you going?" asked one of the newcomers.

"To Giurgiu," the teacher replied. "We have a valuable library with us. The Russians are coming. . . ."

The man kept staring at him with his eyes half-closed, squinting in the bright sunlight. He did not appear to have heard Vasile.

"We have many precious things, books for the Cultural Foundations. . . . We're taking them to a safe place. . . ."

The man began to scratch the top of his head. "You can see the road's no good," he said. "Back of the tavern are the Davidoglu Pits. Don't go that way. When you get to the streetlight go to the left."

Gheorghe Vasile thanked him, lifting his hat, and they started off once again, harrassed by the dogs, but now Irina was driving while the two men walked beside the wagon in the dust, which became thicker as they continued on their way. The sun was directly overhead. Finally they came to a spot where the lane seemed to disappear, swallowed by a tract of vacant land. The last of the shanties had been left behind.

Irina pulled on the reins and stopped the horses. "I think we've passed the streetlight," she said. "There aren't any more houses in sight. . . ."

An old woman was coming toward them across the open field with a basket in her hand. Cojocaru stepped out to meet her. "Is there a streetlight somewhere around here?"

She set her basket down in the grass and observed them suspiciously from the corners of her eyes. "Who're you looking for?"

"We want to go to Giurgiu," said Gheorghe Vasile. "We're looking for a tavern at the Davidoglu Pits. . . ."

The old woman raised her head and skeptically turned upon them a rapid sidelong glance. "It's on the right," she said finally, "after you cross the field."

They set out again with Irina still holding the reins. The blazing heat of the noon sun had become oppressive, and she covered her head with a kerchief. The horses advanced with difficulty because the wagon road had been supplanted by a number of dusty paths that crossed and recrossed at random, appearing and disappearing aimlessly among the wild camomile and other weeds that grew there in profusion. Here and there they came upon mounds of dung and rubbish. But they continued on their way, and after a hundred meters or so they saw the streetlight and then a little farther on they noticed a tavern. Beyond it on the left a new row of shanties began.

"I say let's stop at the tavern to give the horses a rest," suggested Cojocaru.

At sunset they had not yet reached the highway. They had stayed more than an hour at the tavern, where they had eaten while the horses rested in the meager shade of the locusts. Because the innkeeper had a radio, people were constantly coming in to find out the news. It was announced that the Russians were moving toward the capital in a forced march. Although Bucharest was surrounded and under continual aerial attack, the city was resisting. The German forces had not succeeded in breaking through at any point.

The travelers left at two in the full heat of the afternoon, intending to go through the field in order to avoid the Davidoglu Pits. The road was difficult from the start. It was necessary to climb a knoll that towered above an abandoned brickyard, and a number of people went with them to help the wagon up the incline. In addition to the teacher and Cojocaru, there were five husky men who put their shoulders to the wagon. Irina drove, cracking the whip awkwardly over the horses. When they came to the summit of the knoll, they were startled by an airplane that seemed to be flying directly toward them, very low over the gardens, with its motor shut off. The men flattened themselves against the ground. Irina gripped the reins with all her strength, tilted her head and looked squarely into the pilot's eyes. She thought that she saw a smile of astonishment on his face, but then she caught a distinct glimpse of the machine gun. She waited. The plane passed over her noiselessly, and she turned her head at the same moment that the pilot turned his. He was still smiling at her. She heard the motor start again and watched as the plane gained altitude, dipped a wing and headed toward the tavern. After a few seconds that seemed endless, they heard the sound of the machine gun. The men jumped up, looked back at the tavern and quickly dispersed. Two of them slid down the steep clay slope that descended on the abandoned brick kilns. The others returned by the route they had taken to the top.

The wagon traversed the crest of the hill for half an hour, with Cojocaru leading the horses by the bridle, while Irina and Gheorghe Vasile followed behind, watching the wheels. Finally they came down from the knoll at a truck farm and were greeted from afar by the barking of dogs. An elderly man came out of a hovel and walked toward them. He was pointing to something out beyond the shacks and the fields of corn, gesticulating and uttering incoherent sounds.

"He's mute, poor fellow!" said Cojocaru. "Tough luck!"

All three climbed into the wagon, and the horses moved forward slowly because the road was poor. After they had gone a few hundred meters a soldier appeared suddenly out of a ditch, waving them to a stop. "Where are you going?" he shouted. "There are German patrols ahead. They've attacked three times since morning. . . ." More soldiers, dirty, with blood on their hands, rose out of the ditch. Others came from the cornfield. A sergeant-major approached the horses and began to pat their heads. . . .

Returning to the truck farm, the three found the mute waiting for them, surrounded by his dogs, muttering constantly and motioning to them to follow him. They went around the beds of cucumbers and tomatoes until they came to an uncultivated area that was covered with weeds. Gesturing awkwardly, the mute pointed across the field to a shabby little house hidden under some cherry trees that had been blighted by the heat. They thanked him and set off in that direction, but it took them almost an hour to cross the field. There was no sign of a road. Irina went ahead and pulled the horses by the bridle, while Cojocaru and Gheorghe Vasile walked behind the wagon, pushing and swearing. When they reached the rear of the house Cojocaru began to shout, but the only reply was the distant barking of a dog. Cojocaru leapt over the fence into the garden and called again. The house was deserted. He tried the door several times and then returned to the wagon. With great difficulty he brought it around to the front of the house. Bending over, he examined the wheels one by one, swore again, and spat to one side angrily. Presently they saw a woman coming toward them.

"Who're you looking for?" she asked when she was still some distance away.

The teacher raised his hat politely. "We're going to Giurgiu," he began. "We have with us . . ."

"Then you're on the wrong road," interrupted the woman. "This one will take you to Bucharest."

Cojocaru stopped her. "I know the way," he insisted.

The woman stared at him and shook her head. "The only other road goes to the Davidoglu Pits." She pointed across the field to the truck farm.

Cojocaru spat again several times, and then, without another word, he climbed back into the wagon and applied the whip to the team. The woman stepped back, frightened. As they passed, the teacher tipped his hat to her and bowed.

Now the horses advanced rapidly. They were on a wagon road, a rather good one that passed between vacant fields, with here and there a hut, and then proceeded toward a group of houses. The heat had diminished, but they were blinded by dust. When they reached the houses, people began to come outdoors to stare over the fences at them.

Obviously annoyed, the teacher exclaimed, "We're back in Bucharest!"

Cojocaru yelled and cracked the whip. They passed the houses at top speed and a half-hour later they had left the last shanty behind, emerging in an open area with a factory on the other side. Cojocaru turned to Gheorghe Vasile and smiled, pointing with his whip.

"That's what I was looking for! I told you I knew the way!"

As they drew near, however, they heard the clatter of a machine gun, coming, they thought, from the wall of the factory. The horses reared and started to run again. Someone in the field called to them, but his words were incomprehensible. The machine gun rattled again, and when Cojocaru heard the bullets whistling overhead, he stopped the horses.

"You fools!" shouted a voice from the field. "Go back!" cried another. "The Germans are in the factory!"

They noticed then that several soldiers and armed civilians, who were scattered about the field, hidden in the grass and hugging the ground, were motioning to them. With a curse Cojocaru tugged on the reins and turned the wagon around. A red sun was setting in a sky darkened with dust and smoke as they halted beside a well to water the horses. That was when Irina showed them the bullet hole in her kerchief. "I felt it go through my hair," she said.

As midnight was approaching Cojocaru realized that he had lost his way. He turned the wagon around again and headed back toward the abandoned brickyard near the Davidoglu Pits. They had passed this way the second time about an hour before, after a circuitous route through the fields and among the truck farms. They reached the kilns at one o'clock in the morning.

"We'll leave at dawn," said Cojocaru as he freed the horses and led them, hobbled, into the field to graze. Then he climbed into the wagon, yawned several times, and wrapping a fur coat around him, he promptly fell asleep. Gheorghe Vasile and Irina made pallets of straw for themselves at the mouth of a ruined oven and lay down under the blankets. A little later Irina got up.

"I can't sleep," she said, and picking her way lightly, carefully, around the wagon, she went toward the horses in the field and began stroking them on the neck while whispering in their ears. She could imagine the distant city keeping watch, sleepless. Here and there ruddy flares flickered in the sky, and sometimes the muffled rumble of cannon reached her ears. She put her cheek against the horse's neck and waited. Finally she returned slowly to the ruins. The teacher had awakened and was smoking, his cigarette hidden in his fist.

"We ought to leave," he whispered, "if we don't want to be caught by the Russians!"

Irina sat down on the straw and pointed to the wagon. "He's sleeping. Give him at least another hour. . . ."

"Sleep escapes me," declared the teacher, wrapping himself more snugly in the blanket.

They were both silent for a time, listening. The chirping of the crickets had died away. They could hear the short, hobbled steps of the horses and Cojocaru's breathing, deep and muffled.

"I told him," Irina began suddenly, "I told him that drinking and smoking will do him no good. These things don't help very long. They're of some benefit at first, for a day or two perhaps. Now he has to come to his senses and pray. He said, 'To whom do I pray if I don't believe? To what God do I pray if he doesn't exist?' But I told him to pray for her, Ioana. She needs his prayers . . . to pray to the God she believed in. Ioana believed in God . . ."

"Did he say that God doesn't exist?" Gheorghe Vasile interrupted, his tone unexpectedly solemn. "A great mistake. Science and learning have demonstrated that God exists. I have a number of books on the subject. I'll give them to him to read. . . ."

"I told him," continued Irina, "he has to pray. This is true love—to believe in what she believed in, Ioana. But he, the Emperor, has something on his conscience. . . ."

She stopped abruptly and ran her hand across her face. She felt that the teacher was scrutinizing her intently, peering at her through the darkness.

"Science has demonstrated the existence of God," he said. "The laws of nature are laws made by God. That's why man is mortal. Science has proved that if we were immortal the earth would become too small in two or three generations. . . ."

"He told me about Ioana," Irina went on, lowering her voice. "I said to him, 'If you want to find out about Ioana, go and talk with the colonel.' He listened to me, but he looked at me as though he thought I was crazy. He had drunk a lot that evening, and he had made me drink too. My face was burning. 'What can Baleanu tell me about Ioana?' he asked. 'He didn't know her. He never met her. . . .' 'I know,' I said, 'but Colonel Baleanu is a man with a kind heart. He's received consolation from God. He would know how to talk to you and console you. He's very close to Ioana.' 'You're talking nonsense!' he said to me. 'It's useless to get angry,' I told him. 'There's only one thing you can do for her now—pray. And until you pray for her, you won't rest!'"

"Well said!" declared the teacher. "You were right. Science and faith are the consolation of man. . . ."

"The first time I saw the colonel," Irina continued, her voice hardly audible, "I was afraid. Stefan had told me something he had said, but he hadn't understood him properly. The colonel didn't say that God punished him because he slapped Spiridon. . . ."

"He slapped him? When?"

"Once, a long time ago, when they quarreled for a reason I don't know. He slapped him, but then he also asked his forgiveness. . . ."

"He shouldn't have slapped him," said the teacher gravely.

"He begged his pardon and they were reconciled. It wasn't on account of this that he lost his sight. The colonel didn't mean to say that. He has realized that everything comes from God and he's content. He has found consolation. This is what he wants to tell Stefan. That's what Catalina told me, too."

"Is Catalina his wife?"

"No. She'd like to be his fiancée, but he's not willing. He says she's too young and too beautiful to be tied down to an invalid for the rest of her life."

"The colonel's right. It's a manly decision and a wise one."

"But she loves him. He keeps telling her, 'Let's wait a year or two and we'll see then if you still feel the same.' And she answers, 'In a year or two I may be dead or maybe I'll be old!'"

"Listen!" whispered the teacher, sitting up in alarm.

The horses seemed to sense something too, for the sounds of their hesitant steps and their breathing ceased suddenly. A group of men emerged from the darkness and came toward them, walking softly and in silence, careful not to make a noise. Irina sprang to her feet and went to the wagon. She watched them approach and gradually she saw that it was a military patrol guided by a few civilians. Cojocaru woke up. A soldier stepped forward and asked in a whisper, "Have you been here long?"

"Only a few hours."

"Then he couldn't have seen him," said one of the civilians. "He dropped down early in the evening. It was still light. . . ."

"Did you happen to see the airplane?" asked the soldier. "It made a forced landing somewhere near here. He might have run out of gas or had an accident. People saw him come down last evening in the field."

"We haven't seen him," Cojocaru replied. Gheorghe Vasile had joined them and was listening to the conversation. It had turned cold and he was still wrapped in his blanket.

"Then let's go," the soldier said to the group, and they departed as silently as they had come. The others watched them make their way in the direction of the truck farms. A few of them turned aside in back of the kilns and began to clamber up the steep, slippery slope of the hill.

"I'd sure like to go with them!" exclaimed Cojocaru. "To see how they capture the plane."

"I say it would be better for us to leave," the teacher answered. "So we can get to the highway early."

Cojocaru stifled a yawn, covering his mouth with his hand. He jumped down from the wagon and strolled toward the horses.

• • •

398

Nevertheless, the day was breaking when they left. It was difficult to get the wagon moving, and Cojocaru shouted at the horses, describing numerous circles in the air with his whip. For awhile the teacher and Irina walked beside the wagon in order to warm themselves. It was still rather cool. Light mists were hovering over the fields and above the vegetable gardens. All around them they could hear the sparrows chirping, while now and then a larger bird would dart from the bushes, flying very low, almost getting caught between the legs of the horses. Ahead in the distance stretched field upon field of corn. After they had gone a little more than a kilometer across the open country, they came to a road, and Cojocaru halted the wagon so the others could climb in. Whistling, he began to drive the horses at a trot. Soon the sun appeared. They watched it as it rose above the horizon in the shadowy, hazy sky. Suddenly they heard the noise of a motor. There was the plane taking off directly in front of them, almost touching the tips of the corn tassels. It came straight toward them, as if it intended to strike them down. The horses reared, jerking the wagon. Irina raised her head and smiled. It seemed that the pilot recognized her because he returned her smile and saluted, bringing his hand to his forehead. A few moments later the plane had gained sufficient altitude to wheel smoothly on one wing and head again in their direction.

"He's going to shoot us!" cried the teacher, cowering among the crates.

Irina sprang from the wagon and began to wave her kerchief, signaling to the aviator, who looked at her in amusement and smiled again.

"Leave us alone!" she shouted at the top of her voice. "Mind your own business. We're not going to war!"

The plane disappeared over the cornfields. Cojocaru had jumped down too and was holding the horses by the bridle.

"Let's wait and see what he's going to do," he said. "If he keeps circling over us he'll scare the horses and they'll pitch us into the ditch. . . . I wonder why they didn't find him last night?" he added, furious. "He landed here behind a cornfield and nobody noticed him."

They waited a few minutes, lost in thought, almost hypnotized, as though the twittering of the birds had charmed them. The sound of the airplane was fainter now and more distant, but they saw it once more, rather high, and they watched it point its nose at the tavern. Soon they heard the machine gun. All three climbed into the wagon then and they set out again.

The field was deserted. Here and there they saw signs of plowing that had scarcely been started when it was abandoned in great haste. Once they met a youth coming out of a field with an armful of corn.

"Is this the road to Giurgiu?" Cojocaru asked, stopping the team.

The boy approached them silently. "This way you'll come out on the Ciulnita road, going to Baragan."

"That's all right, too," said Cojocaru, and he whistled to the horses.

At ten o'clock they halted the wagon beside a ditch in which a trickle of water was still flowing, protected by the tall, fresh grass. They alighted and lunched at the edge of the ditch. Cojocaru's hand was numb and he rubbed it for a long time to revive it. Then he rolled himself a cigarette and began to smoke slowly and with relish.

"But what are we going to do at Ciulnita?" demanded the teacher a while later. "We're getting farther away. . . ."

"I know the way, don't worry. First we have to get to the highway. After that we take a right turn and go down to the Danube."

Silently he finished his cigarette and gave a bucket of water to the horses. Then they all climbed into the wagon again. They had not gone far when they discerned in the distance a convoy of military vehicles coming toward them. Cojocaru pulled the wagon to the edge of the ditch and stopped. The first truck passed them at top speed in a cloud of dust, its driver motioning to them to stay where they were. Ambulances, automobiles, a number of tank trucks, and trucks full of soldiers followed. Then came an immense trailer with eight wheels, pulled by a huge tractor. Each vehicle carried machine guns in firing position, except the trailer, which was equipped with antiaircraft cannon. After the last truck was lost to sight in the thick, rolling dust, the three removed their hands from their mouths and began to cough.

"They were Germans," said the teacher. "They came from Ciulnita. This means that the Russians are coming behind them. You'll see—we'll meet the Russians . . ."

"Don't worry," Cojocaru soothed him. "Before the Russians come we'll reach the Danube."

It was hard to move the wagon through the dust. They had left the corn behind now and were surrounded by stubble. Cojocaru spat constantly. They met an old gray-haired man driving an oxcart, and when he was opposite them, Gheorghe Vasile could not refrain from asking, "How do we get to Giurgiu?"

The old man raised his whip handle and pointed. "You go to the right. But, you know, it's a bad road. . . ."

"We'll manage," said Cojocaru.

The old man smiled and shook his head. "Don't take the national highway. The Germans are coming that way. I've heard they've crossed the Danube from Bulgaria and are on their way to Bucharest. . . ."

Gheorghe Vasile lifted his hat and saluted him gratefully. Cojocaru urged the horses forward with a whistle. The sun beat down steadily now, and Irina tied her kerchief on her head.

"I want to see you reach the main highway and then I'll go back," she said.

• • •

400

After proceeding only a few hundred meters on the first road that they encountered on the right, Cojocaru had to admit that the old man had not been
mistaken. Perhaps at one time the road had been a fairly good one, but the
rains had eroded it, washing out deep ditches that ran along its length and
across it as well. Then the drought had come and cracks had opened, breaking
it into pieces. Now nothing remained but a succession of holes and ruts
winding in and out between the ploughed ground and the fields of stubble. It
became more and more difficult to make any progress. The horses stopped
frequently, their necks tense with exertion, their muzzles almost touching the
dust. Irina jumped down from the wagon, following it on foot, and it was not
long before the teacher climbed down too.

"I think we took the wrong road," he said.

"This is the one the old man mentioned. It's pretty bad. . . ."

In the distance a few little peasants' houses could be seen, but here in the
fields around them, whether stubble or ploughed, there was no sign of human
life. Toward noon they heard the roar of airplanes and all three looked up at
the sky. At an altitude of about a thousand meters an entire squadron was
flying in the shape of a **V**, like a flight of storks.

"Those are Americans," explained Cojocaru.

While they were watching the planes, the horses hung their heads low in
the dust and rested, their flanks quivering in a continuous effort to drive away
the flies. Then Cojocaru brandished the whip once more and the wagon
started forward with a long drawn-out groan, creaking in every joint. But they
had not gone far when a rear wheel slid into a hole and the vehicle lurched to
one side, crushing the wheel under its weight. The crates collided in shifting
and two fell out on the road, spilling the bundles of books, which rolled to the
edge of the field. Cojocaru whistled with rage and vexation, and he leaped to
release the horses from the shafts. Aghast, the teacher stared at the tilted
wagon. Irina alone maintained her composure. Without saying a word she
began to gather up the books.

"Now, what a mess!" said Cojocaru, scratching his head thoughtfully.

He seized the horses by the bridle and pulled them after him to the side
of the road a few steps away, where he hobbled them. Returning to the wagon
he bent over to examine the wheel. The teacher approached apprehensively,
wiping his forehead with an automatic gesture. Irina continued to collect the
books, brushing the dust from each one and setting it beside the road on a
patch of dry grass.

"First of all we've got to unload those crates," stated Cojocaru. "Then
we'll raise the wagon and repair the axle. . . . If it's possible with the tools we
have," he added, smiling, and turning around he spat vigorously all the way
across the ditch.

The crates could not be lifted until they had been partially emptied, so

401

Cojocaru began to hand the bundles of books to Irina and the teacher, who deposited them at the edge of the road. Within an hour they were dripping with perspiration and covered with dust, but they had managed to unload the crates, push them to the roadside, and raise the wagon. Cojocaru then got out his tools and set them beside him in the dust.

"It's easy enough to fix it," he said after a while, "but we won't be able to carry the books on this road. Maybe on the Giurgiu highway. . . ."

"Then what are we going to do?" asked the teacher in alarm.

"Don't worry, we'll figure it out."

He rolled a cigarette with a thoughtful air and smoked it slowly, studying the broken axle, fingering it, whistling now and then. The teacher sat down, exhausted, on the edge of the ditch beside the packages of books. When Cojocaru had finished his cigarette, he set to work. After half an hour he rose out of the dust, picked up the tools and tossed them into the wagon. Then he harnessed the horses.

"I'm going to the village to hunt for an oxcart," he told them. But he was afraid to climb into the wagon, and taking up the bridle in his good hand he started out. Irina accompanied him silently part of the way, then returned and sat down beside her father-in-law.

"I suggest that you don't establish the Foundations yet," she said. "Wait and see first what the Russians do."

The teacher threw her a quick glance. "Now that I've begun, I'm not going to give up."

It had become very warm and there was not a scrap of shade to be seen anywhere. They changed their positions many times, finally sitting on the ground with their backs against the crates. The cloud of dust left in the wake of the wagon was still visible in the distance. After awhile Gheorghe Vasile stood up. Selecting a little book at random from a bundle that had broken open, he put on his glasses and began to read. Irina rested her chin on her hand and watched him.

Shortly before sunset Cojocaru returned, riding on one horse and leading the other by the bridle. He seemed discouraged.

"The people say we took the wrong road," he began, dismounting slowly and setting the horses free. "They say that the road to the Giurgiu highway is a little farther on. We were misled by that old graybeard. . . ."

"And what do we do now?" asked the teacher, looking at him over his spectacles.

"Later this evening some men are coming with an oxcart to get the books. . . ." He stretched out on the ground beside the road. Rolling up his coat, he placed it under his head and fell asleep.

Irina and the teacher spent that night at the priest's house, while Cojocaru slept on straw in the barn at the farm of the peasant who had rented them the cart. The only inhabitants of the village who slept well were the children. The constable had read the government proclamation that evening. All were instructed to receive the Soviet troops with trust and friendship, because they were coming to help with the liberation of the territory. In addition it was announced on the radio that the Russians were advancing at extraordinary speed and were now a little less than a hundred kilometers from the capital. It was announced further that the last of the German units which had besieged and attacked Bucharest for three days had been disarmed and the capital was now awaiting the victorious entry of the liberating armies. The people listened in silence to the proclamation, then dispersed to their homes. But as soon as it was dark enough, they resumed the work begun on the evening they had learned about the *coup d'état* of the King and the entrance of the Russians into the country. Each buried whatever he had of value and prepared hiding places for the cattle and the women.

The three travelers rose at dawn without having rested. For an amount proposed by the teacher, the peasant agreed to haul the crates of books in his cart to the Giurgiu highway, a distance of about fifteen kilometers. The whole village was up before them, but almost no one ventured out of his house. The people watched them set out with mixed feelings of fear and astonishment. Irina and the teacher went on foot in front, followed by the oxcart, while behind, in the empty wagon, rode Cojocaru, shouting.

The morning was cold. One could feel a foretaste of autumn in it. The road was not bad, and they went ahead rather swiftly because the driver did not spare the oxen. About a kilometer from the village they came upon two mounted men standing motionless on a rise at the edge of the road. They were sentries who had watched all night and were now awaiting their replacements. With the exception of these two, there was nobody in sight. On both sides of the road the plain extended endlessly, completely deserted.

After about five kilometers they passed along the outskirts of a village. On the highway the constable and the magistrate were on guard, waiting. They also had had no sleep and they regarded the strangers with anxious eyes as they passed. Irina and the teacher had climbed into the wagon. No longer shouting, Cojocaru drove dejectedly, rubbing his numbed hand from time to time. Two youths on horseback were standing watch a few hundred meters farther down the road, their eyes fixed on the hazy horizon of Baragan.

For a long time no one spoke. They were approaching a hamlet when several scrawny curs came up to them, barking a greeting. But the dogs slunk away quickly and with much whining disappeared into the courtyards. The houses seemed abandoned. They found the priest alone on the other side of the village, mounted on a blue-black horse with the skirt of his surplice raised high, revealing his boots. He too was waiting.

"They say they're close!" he called.

The peasant began to beat the oxen in desperation. Then after a few hundred meters he leapt from the cart, and seizing the yoke, he began to pull on it, urging the animals forward. Before long Irina and the teacher also climbed down, put their hands to the yoke and pushed.

They came to another village. "It's Izvoarele!" exclaimed the driver. "Not much farther!"

Here the magistrate, the priest, and the constable were waiting in the company of a boy dressed in the uniform of the normal school. He was very pale and seemed frightened. He kept looking nervously first one way and then the other.

"We brought him along because he knows a little Russian," explained the constable, trying to smile.

Once they had passed the village the peasant grasped the yoke again with both hands and began to push with all his strength, his head bent, gritting his teeth. On the other side Irina and the teacher pressed on in silence, puffing. Now and then Cojocaru got down and whipped the oxen lustily, with much cursing.

"Not much farther!" encouraged the driver, lifting his head and wiping the sweat with the back of his hand. "The highway's over there where you see the locust tree. . . ."

He stopped with his mouth agape, staring off into the distance as he stood by the oxen. Far away on the horizon they could see a cloud of dust rising. The peasant turned to the teacher in distress.

"There they are!" he said, swallowing with difficulty. "What'll we do with the woman?" They were silent, watching the dust.

"Maybe there's time to go back to the village," suggested Cojocaru finally.

The peasant shook his head and wiped his face again with his hand. "Better to go right over this ploughed ground and hide in the field."

The next moment they saw two men on horseback galloping toward them, and the peasant stepped out into the middle of the road, signaling to them with his arms held high. One of the horsemen shouted to them from a distance, "The Russians are coming!" and passed by without stopping.

"Take the woman!" the three cried in unison, pointing to Irina, who was standing beside the oxen, smiling calmly.

The second rider managed to rein in his horse and turn back. Sweat ran down in streams over his face. "Put her on behind me!" he commanded.

Irina ran to the teacher and embraced him, then shook hands with the other two men.

"Don't worry!" she called back to them as she mounted the horse. "You've made it to the highway!"

Cojocaru helped her to climb up at the rider's back. Clinging to his shoulder with her right hand, she turned her head and watched the wagons for

404

a long time. She saw them move forward slowly. They left the road and made their way with difficulty over the ploughed fields, jolting and shaking. All three men were pushing on the yoke now.

On the skyline the cloud of dust grew larger. Mounting upward, it spread over the field and gradually blotted out the horizon, darkening the sky.

3

BIBICESCU HAD ENROLLED IN THE COMMUNIST PARTY A FEW MONTHS AFTER
the Soviet occupation of Romania. As he confessed to his friends, it had not
taken very much time for him to realize that the Russians would be the real
masters. He had observed that the actors and other artists who frequented the
Anglo-American legations and establishments were regarded with suspicion.
He saw how several dozen armed Communists, transported in Soviet trucks,
terrorized the factory unions and other political parties without anything ever
happening to them. Divisions of Romanian soldiers were fighting far away in
Hungary and Czechoslovakia by the side of the Russians and against the
Germans. They were always being forced into the front ranks, where they
were then decimated. In spite of the armistice all the troops who had been
found on the front in Moldavia had been captured and sent to Russia.
Scarcely any armed units were left in the country. Gradually the constabu-
lary, the police, and the Security Services passed into the hands of the Communists. "We must draw the obvious conclusions," said Bibicescu. "These
people are our masters.

"And then there's something else. There's the Soviet theater. The
Russians have solved a number of problems, preeminently the problem of
man. That's what I'm trying to do myself. . . ." He lectured them thus on
strada Macelari one rainy afternoon in late November.

"I thought it was the problem of Time that interested you," Biris cut in.
"The concentrated Time of the performance, and so on. . . ."

"It's almost the same thing. The Soviet theater goes back to Shakespeare.
But they introduced this novelty—the consciousness of a historic mission."

Biris looked at him in surprise. "But where did you learn all these things?
Who's been talking to you about History?"

"We discuss it at our meetings. We have a very interesting circle. . . .
You ought to join us," he added after a pause. "Come now, at the beginning,
while there are still openings. In a year or two all the intellectuals will be

flocking to the Party, but the important positions will have been long since occupied. . . ."

"I'm curious to hear what you have to say about History," said Biris, interrupting him. "Tell me more. Tell me about the 'historic mission.'"

In his customary manner Bibicescu was pacing from one end of the room to the other. He stopped abruptly, thrust his hands into the pockets of his jacket and shrugged. "I see that you don't want to be serious."

"On the contrary, I couldn't be more so. The problem of History has engaged me for about fifteen years, and I should like to know how you have discovered it too, just three months after the Russian invasion of our country. . . ."

"I should call your attention to the fact that you express yourself improperly. What does that mean— 'the Russian invasion of our country'? We signed an armistice and now we're fighting together against Hitler. . . ."

"We're fighting beside our 'natural allies,'" Biris checked him, "principally by the side of 'our great ally, Soviet Russia.' These are the formulae employed everywhere in the press and official pronouncements. It's a matter of semantics and political expediency. But now we're speaking candidly between friends. You yourself said that the Russians are our real masters. We are agreed. But I'd like to know how, starting out from the problem of the Master, you arrived at that of History . . ."

Bibicescu stopped by the window and glared at him almost crossly. "It seems to me that it shouldn't be hard to figure out. The Soviets are on the point of winning the war. The Russian Revolution will become the *avant-garde* of universal history. We're entering a new phase of the evolution of mankind. Man is becoming free to fulfill his historic destiny. Therefore . . ."

"I understand," Biris broke in. "The rest I know. I just wanted to find out from what philosophical premise you set out. Now I'm enlightened. . . . But I'd like to ask you something in a different category. What are you going to do, then, with your *Return from Stalingrad?*"

In the course of the summer Bibicescu had learned about the religious processions of the Moldavian villagers to the rendezvous with the dead from Stalingrad. He had thought of writing a drama on that theme. In a few days he had outlined the scenario. He was interested, however, in certain particulars, and he had wanted to question Stefan. On an oppressive evening early in August he had gone to see Biris. A presentiment of the coming catastrophe seemed to be in the air. The starless sky hung low, heavy with menace, as though ready to crash down upon the city. It had been many years since Bibicescu had visited *strada* Macelari, and Biris was startled to see him at the door. "It's an extraordinary theme!" the actor had exclaimed. "How long I've been searching for something of this caliber! Current, rooted in history, having nevertheless a mythical dimension! A myth of the dead, half pagan, in the

407

middle of the twentieth century! Other dramatic creations on the motifs of folklore have been attempted, but they were done in a narrow, provincial spirit. You have to suggest the myth through modern devices. . . . Let's invite Viziru to dinner some evening and get him to talk about it. . . ." Biris listened with an almost contemptuous disinterest. "I don't believe he'll accept. The man's lost his wife and child. He's lost everything. I doubt that he's concerned about the destiny of myths in the twentieth century." Bibicescu had looked at Biris in astonishment, and then he had remarked, "He gave me the impression of being an intelligent man."

Biris was insistent. "What point of correspondence have you found between a myth of the dead and the acquisition of a historic consciousness?"

"I abandoned that project long ago," responded Bibicescu, and he resumed his pacing. "It was an escape into folklore. Like a great many other people, I also passed through a period of crisis. I didn't see where reality could be found. Now I understand. Art can only be regenerated through a frank and total return to reality, and above all to historic reality. . . ."

That evening Biris went to the Cafenea. He had recently returned to his prewar habits, and now he could be found there almost every day. At first the atmosphere had seemed different to him because a great many new faces had appeared, but, even so, he encountered many of his old acquaintances. At certain tables Anglo-Saxon and Soviet authors were being discussed. The people spoke of books and magazines from the West. They had not been found in Romania for four years but had begun to reappear. At the table by the window he was fairly certain to find Bursuc, who seemed to be still the same. When he laughed his eyes vanished as before in the layers of fat, but one could now distinguish innumerable very fine wrinkles around his temples. He had been enrolled for some time in the party of Patru Fruncea, and he criticized the government for not being sufficiently Sovietophile.

"All who want to get set for the future, come now, come quickly!" he cried, looking all around him. "Come to the Revolution! We're making it now! We have the tanks. . . ." He saw Biris enter and he motioned for him to come to his table.

"I can't stay. I'm looking for *conu* Misu. . . ."

Misu Weissman was also coming again to the Cafenea, cheerful, enthusiastic, well-informed as ever. He had begun to mention his great enterprise again and hinted at an impending trip to London.

"What do you have to do with the Anglo-American plutocracy?" demanded Bursuc. "Stay here with us and make the revolution . . ."

Biris smiled absently and went to another table, where there was talk about the situation at the fronts. He stopped for a few moments and then continued his circuit of the Cafenea, moving slowly, watching for Weissman. Finally, somewhat disappointed, he left. The rain had ceased and a cold wind had begun to blow. Biris turned up the collar of his overcoat and started for Catalina's apartment. Probably he would find her at home at this hour, and she would detain him to drink a cup of tea. Entering, he would say to her, "I have a lot of news for you about Bibicescu. He's discovered the historic mission of the proletariat, and he's abolished the myth of the return from Stalingrad. . . ." She would smile at him and say, "You know what he's like. He's interested in just one thing—to be able to direct a theater. He doesn't care who gives him money or what political views he's compelled to share. . . ." "Only now he'll quarrel with *conu* Misu," Biris would respond. "Misu is on the side of the Anglo-Americans. . . ." "You don't know *conu* Misu," Catalina would answer. "They'll always be the best of friends. *Conu* Misu is a remarkable man. . . ." Then she would pour the tea and ask him for news of the war. He would shrug and say, "All day long we talk of nothing else—how the war's going. . . ." Then with little bounces she would settle herself against the back of the divan and begin to speak about Baleanu. "He's a remarkable man," she would say. "He's a saint. . . ." Biris would light another cigarette. "When you get to know him too . . ." Catalina would continue, and she would go on like this for an hour, a year, a century. She could talk to him this way until the end of time, eternally going over the same refrain, repeating the same gestures. Seeing that he remained silent, Catalina would cease to discourse on the sanctity of the colonel, and she would say, "Am I mistaken or are you thinner?" He would shrug again and smile and hold out his empty cup, which Catalina would refill with tea. Then after another long silence she would ask him, "What's become of Viziru?" "I haven't seen him for a long time," he would reply. "He'll be reconciled someday too," she would continue pensively. "Everyone is. We are all alike. We suffer what we suffer, and one day we feel that we can suffer no more, and we love life again, and we go back to the place where we left off. . . ."

Biris stopped in the middle of the street. He threw away his cigarette almost untouched, sighed deeply and turned around, hurrying back to the Cafenea. Bursuc was the first to see him and he beckoned, but Biris passed by without stopping. At the back of the room Misu Weissman was having a lively discussion with a group of strangers. When Weissman saw Biris, he took his arm and drew him aside.

"I've found out some extraordinary things," he said in a mysterious voice. "We'll have to meet, without fail. I'd take you to dinner with me this evening, but I'm not free. I'm invited out myself. It's a very important matter—someone in the American Military Mission. . . ."

When he went to see her one evening in January, the fall of snow was becoming increasingly dense, and as soon as he entered Catalina's apartment he took his customary position by the radiator in order to warm himself. On the low table she had placed a few sandwiches and cups for the tea. They began to talk about the war and about the typhus which was spreading in Moldavia. Catalina was telling him that Baleanu had been moved to the Home for the War Handicapped when without any warning the blizzard began. They heard a long moan that sounded much like the wail of a wounded animal, and the storm pounced suddenly upon the houses. Glancing at each other in alarm, they pushed aside the curtains and looked out. The snow was so thick in the air that the street could no longer be seen. Catalina went into the next room to get the teapot and the boiling water. They drank several cups of tea, which was not unusual, and they talked, pausing from time to time to listen to the tempest. But when Catalina went to the window again she said to him, "You can't leave at a time like this. Stay here tonight."

Biris lit a cigarette. It was beginning to get cold in the room. They tore up a newspaper and plugged the cracks around the window as the blizzard continued to grow in strength. The noise became deafening. Biris compelled himself to talk without stopping so that he would not have to think, but his mouth felt dry and he had to swallow constantly. At two o'clock Catalina pulled the cover from the divan and made the bed. Biris watched her, fascinated, uncomprehending. She went into the bathroom, and about ten minutes later she came back wearing her pajamas. Quickly she slipped under the covers.

"I don't know what to give you to wear," she said. "Try a pair of my pajamas. . . ."

She put out the light and Biris undressed without being aware of his actions. He seemed to be in a dream. The jacket to Catalina's pajamas was rather small for him, but he put it on and climbed into the bed, trembling with nervousness.

"We'll behave ourselves!" promised Catalina.

Biris extended his arm and found her there very close to him, very warm.

By morning the city was shrouded in snow. They awoke at the same time and Catalina smiled at him. Then she jumped out of bed and went to prepare the tea. Biris ran his hand over his face, and it seemed to him that his beard was rougher than usual. He raised both hands to the top of his head, taking pains to arrange the few remaining strands of hair, smoothing them, pressing them flat. He felt old and very ugly, and he was seized suddenly by despair. Reaching for Catalina's package of cigarettes, he took one, lit it quickly and smoked it with caution, careful not to inhale the smoke lest he choke and induce an attack of coughing. Soon Catalina returned, and drawing the little table to the side of the bed, she placed upon it the teapot and two cups. Their eyes met and she smiled—a smile that he could not decipher, that he did not know how to interpret. She crept into the bed beside him and they drank their tea together with little comment.

It was almost noon when he went home. *Doamna* Porumbache waited anxiously for him at the window. Her fear had kept her awake all night.

"A patrol arrested me," Biris told her. "They took me to the police station. I didn't have any identification with me."

He strode into his room and closed the door, and flinging himself on the bed, he lay there for a long time, staring at the ceiling. He tried to understand what had happened to him. But he did not understand even after spending another evening in Catalina's apartment, coming home late, almost at midnight. Nor did he comprehend in the days that followed. He would take her in his arms as soon as she opened the door, and she would return his kisses with a smile. Then he would begin to undress her, trembling in his haste. They seldom spoke. When they were not in bed together, they did not know what to do. Once, seeing that he was pensive, Catalina took his hand and whispered, "Don't think about it. . . . It was bound to happen. . . ."

But Biris was not thinking about it. He wasn't thinking of anything. He simply stared before him blankly, his mind empty.

"Don't be sorry," Catalina told him another time. "We haven't done anything wrong. . . ."

She still talked to him about Baleanu, but her voice was different, as if she were speaking of the honored dead or of a saint. She told Biris that Baleanu was the only man at the Home for the Handicapped who had accommodated himself to the new way of life. He never complained, she said.

"Of course he guessed from the first day," she added with a smile. "When I gave him my hand he asked me, 'Biris slept with you last night, didn't he?' 'Yes,' I told him. 'I kept him because of the storm. . . .'"

"You should tell him the truth," interrupted Biris.

"He understood. And then he quickly changed the subject and spoke about other things. . . ."

When he came to his senses in the middle of February and began to realize that for several weeks he had been living the life that he had longed for so many years ago, he had already become accustomed to the bliss. It all seemed quite natural. One day he sought *doamna* Porumbache in order to warn her.

"If I should ever stay away from home at night don't be alarmed. You'll know that I'm sleeping at Catalina's."

"Petrica, *maica!*" cried *doamna* Porumbache, wringing her hands.

"Don't be alarmed. Nothing will happen. Catalina loves her fiancé, Colonel Baleanu. She sleeps with me for friendship's sake. She doesn't love me. Maybe she even goes to bed with me out of pity. What do you think?" He raised his glance to her suddenly.

"Petrica!" exclaimed *doamna* Porumbache with dramatic emphasis.

"It was bound to happen," he continued sadly. "It's not our fault. We're sinners. Irina, Baleanu, and others like them are saints. We live in sin. That

411

is, more precisely, I live in sin. Catalina sleeps with me from pity, from Christian charity. Probably she told herself, 'I'll have to give in someday to that poor unfortunate whose life's a failure on account of me.' She's taken the sin upon herself in order to save me. Don't you agree?"

"Petrica, she's bewitched you again!" cried his aunt, rubbing her hands together. "That whore'll finish you! She'll send you to your grave!"

"Don't worry," Biris interrupted. "Now that I've known this too, I want to live. I want to see what else can happen. Or as Bibicescu would say, I want to see what direction History will take!"

"What can she have charmed you with, *maiculita*?"

Biris shrugged his shoulders and strolled calmly to the door. "But I tell you, she did it out of Christian charity! She loves Baleanu. Catalina's destiny was to meet and fall in love with great men. For years on end she was with Bibicescu, the unappreciated genius. Now she loves a saint, a blind man, a war hero. . . . It's I who am the true sinner. Probably someday I'll have to pay for all these transgressions," he added from the threshold as he closed the door behind him.

Soon after that Catalina began an engagement at the Little Theater and Biris changed his schedule again. They began to meet in the afternoon. Sometimes he came to get her at the Theater and they spent the night together, although Catalina continued to visit Baleanu every morning.

"He told me he'll consent now to our getting married. He said that we need each other now. . . . I don't know what to do," she added, embarrassed.

Standing by the radiator with a cigarette between his lips, Biris listened to her. "And you—what did you say to him?"

"I haven't given him an answer yet. I told him I'm playing in the theater now and can't think. . . ."

"Did he ask you if you still love him?"

"He knows I love him," said Catalina with sudden weariness in her voice. "He's known that for a long time. . . ."

Biris shivered and drew closer to the radiator. "Then it's true," he murmured. "Everything I said to *coana* Viorica is true! I thought it was just something I made up—an excuse—but actually I guessed the truth . . ."

"Don't think about it," interrupted Catalina. "It's not our fault. . . ."

"It's true!" Biris repeated in exasperation. "It's beyond my power to comprehend and yet it's true! I hold you tight in my arms and you like it and you cry, 'Petre!' And yet . . . it's true!"

"Don't think anymore," whispered Catalina.

Biris extinguished his cigarette and sat down in the armchair near the radiator.

"You're right," he began after awhile. "It's better to talk about something else. I've had the good fortune to see a page of world history being turned in front of me, as Bibicescu would put it, while I, like an idiot, let myself get all wrapped up in personal problems!"

He started to add something more but reconsidered and shrugged. Presently he burst into laughter, a dry laugh and a bitter one, and he put his hand to his mouth as if he were ashamed of his mirth and wanted to retract it.

"Say something!" cried Catalina suddenly. "Talk! Don't leave me like this!"

Biris regarded her with distress. "I ought to talk to you about History and the historic moment in which we are living, about the typhus in Moldavia, the destruction of the Romanian divisions in Czechoslovakia, the imminent downfall of Hitler. But then I'd be doing nothing but repeating what Bibicescu told us."

Catalina bent her head and covered her face with her hands. She had allowed her hair to grow, and now it was as long as it used to be, tumbling again over her ears and cheeks.

"Petre," she said in a calm voice without looking up at him, "what do you require of me? What do you want to do, how do you want me to behave, so you won't be upset this way? So you'll just be an ordinary man living your life the way the rest of us do?"

Biris continued to look at her, perplexed, struggling to smile.

"We'd better stick to the problem of History," he began after a moment of silence. "I met the teacher again. I found out how he buried his library. . . ."

One evening during the Christmas season, on returning home he had heard a thick masculine voice in his aunt's room. Gheorghe Vasile was there, and he was in a mellow mood. He had brought three bottles of wine, and he was just opening the third bottle when Biris made his appearance. "To your health, *domnule* Professor!" he had cried on seeing Biris. "We've returned from our mission and we've come to see our friends. Won't you drink a glass of wine with us? It's good wine from a reputable vineyard. . . ." Raising his glass solemnly the teacher approached Biris with a mysterious air and whispered, "I've hidden them! I buried them! The Bolsheviks won't lay their hands on them if they search for a hundred years! *Coana* Viorica will tell you how much I've gone through and what perils I've been delivered from! But I found a hiding place for them and I buried them!"

"He buried it in a sort of underground cave in the chapel of the cemetery. Just as in the days of the barbarian attacks. Just as our ancestors buried their crops when the barbarians invaded us. . . ."

He stopped and put his hand to his forehead for an instant, then ran it

413

over the top of his head, carefully fingering the thin strands of hair. Momentarily he became very serious, intent, and then he suddenly started to laugh again. Catalina looked up quickly.

"I'm an idiot!" he declared, musing, after his laughter had subsided. "I don't understand anything. A country schoolteacher has to come here—a half-drunk maniac—to open my eyes and show me what's happening around us, to reveal the meaning of History to me!"

He left the chair and moved closer to the radiator. The room suddenly seemed chilly to him. He lit a cigarette and began to smoke absently. Catalina went to the little table and turned on the lamp with the Japanese shade. Taking Biris's hand, she caressed it.

"Don't think so much! You don't know how I love you. I'll do anything you ask me to. Just tell me what to do. Tell me what I must do. . . ."

Mollified, he looked at her and smiled. "I was thinking about the teacher. I was wondering how he guessed that we Romanians are about to return to the Middle Ages. . . ."

"And I told you," insisted Catalina, "for you I'll do anything, anything you ask of me. Just tell me what I must do. . . ." Abruptly she pulled away from him, and glancing at the clock on the table, she began to dress. She was playing that evening in *The Cherry Orchard*.

Some time later Stefan came again to see Biris. It was an unexpected visit one evening in the autumn of that year. *Doamna* Porumbache opened the door, and when she saw him she hesitated in embarrassment on the threshold, at a loss for something to say. All at once she started to weep. Bowing, Stefan kissed her hand and went quickly into Biris's room.

"You can tell Catalina that I've done what she wished," he began, sitting down on a chair. "I've seen Baleanu."

"I know. Catalina told me."

"I'm glad I saw him," continued Stefan. "He's a fine man. We talked a long time about Ioana. . . ." He paused in confusion.

Biris was aware that *doamna* Porumbache was listening at the door. Picking up the filled ashtray, he went into the hall, where he found her pressed close against the wall. He took her by the hand and drew her into the kitchen.

"Please leave us alone," he whispered after he had closed the door. "I think he wants to tell me something and he'll be embarrassed if he suspects you're listening. Stay in your room. I'll tell you about it later, after he leaves. . . ."

He rejoined Stefan, who was standing before the yellowed photograph of

414

Biris's mother. He walked about the room briefly and then sat down again.

"It's odd how some people have the gift of being able to comfort you, to cheer you. I don't understand where this power comes from. After I saw Baleanu I felt more at peace, almost happy, as though I had regained a state of mind that I had lost a long time ago. How do you explain these things?"

Biris found it difficult to control his irritation. "I don't explain them. Catalina says that Baleanu has something of the saint in him."

"You ought to meet him. It might be to your advantage. But I don't understand how he knows so many things about Ioana. That is, to be more precise, he doesn't know them. He surmises them. He feels them. I talked about Ioana with him as I would have talked with an old friend who had known us both for many years. I just talked. . . ."

He stopped and smiled, and all at once his whole face brightened, as it had done so many years ago when Biris first met him.

"I told him about an absurd event. . . ." Again he stopped and gazed at Biris, and with a sigh he searched for his cigarettes.

"Actually it's of no great importance what I told him. But his intuition astonished me. It was as though he'd been there when it happened. Sometimes I had the impression I was dreaming. Baleanu seemed to remember certain details better than I did. . . . It's strange," he added after a pause.

A cold rain had begun to fall, and they sat for some time listening to it.

"I have to leave. From here to my place it's a half hour by tram. I've moved a long way off. I found a room at the home of a friend. Old Bologa invited me to stay with them in Cotroceni, but I can't. . . ."

After that Stefan came to see him often, but he did not always find him at home. "He's at Catalina's," *doamna* Porumbache lamented.

At nightfall the streets were nearly deserted. People no longer ventured out of their houses to wade through the snowdrifts in the dark. A few Russian soldiers, proceeding unsteadily, were all that could be seen and after midnight bands of robbers roamed the streets. The Romanian patrols had received orders to shoot without warning. From time to time a distant scream would be heard, followed by gunshots. Then the silence would descend again, more ominous than before.

When Stefan found Biris at home they would pull their chairs close to the stove and talk.

"There are so many things I don't understand," Stefan commented once. "I think that I loved her as few men have loved their wives. And yet I hid myself from her. I not only had a secret room but a large part of my true life was secret. I talked to her all the time about superficial, inconsequential things. The real, essential part of myself I concealed. How do you explain this madness?"

"Maybe you made the mistake of thinking they were things that wouldn't interest her."

415

For an instant Stefan gave him a profound look, and then he lowered his eyes. "And yet I told Ileana about some of them. . . ."

An embarrassed silence ensued. For years Stefan had not mentioned Ileana's name.

"What became of her?" Biris asked after awhile.

"I don't know. I haven't seen her. Probably she stayed in Portugal."

One evening a week later *doamna* Porumbache begged Biris to stay at home nights, since there had been several burglaries in the neighborhood. Otherwise, she threatened, she would go to Irina's house to sleep. Biris had just shut himself in his room when he heard Stefan's voice. He was talking with *doamna* Porumbache.

"I wondered if I could eat with you tonight," he said as he entered. "I brought some things. But I see that you've already eaten. . . ."

He sat down beside the stove. "I saw Bursuc this evening," he said. "He was making propaganda for the Communist Party and he said he's going to become a monk. Do you still think he's a demoniac?" he asked with a smile.

Biris shrugged with a gesture of annoyance. On that evening it was especially distasteful to him to discuss Bursuc. Because of him, Biris visited the coffeehouse less frequently now. Regardless of what table Biris would head for, Bursuc would beckon to him as soon as he saw him enter. "*Conquistador!*" he would shout loudly. "*Conquistador!*" And his gross, vulgar, insupportable laugh would burst forth. He would call Biris to the attention of all the others at the table, pointing to him with a flourish of his outstretched arm, without the least embarrassment. Then, bending his head a little, he would begin a whispered conversation, interrupted only by his own paroxysms of hilarity or the guffaws of his audience.

"He said that among all the Romanian intelligentsia, only Bibicescu has understood the direction History is taking. And he also said that Bibicescu's going to get the post of director of the National Theater."

Again Biris shrugged. Happily *doamna* Porumbache came in just then with a tray of several kinds of meat—ham and salami and sausage—and a bottle of wine. She set it on a little table.

"I've hated eating alone," Stefan said, apologizing once more.

But he ate alone that evening too, listening to *doamna* Porumbache tell about the teacher's adventures, the burglaries in the area, and the people who had been found frozen to death in the snow. She was the only one who talked, and she talked most of the time. After she went out, taking the tray with her, Biris got up quickly and followed her to ask her again not to listen at the door.

"When I return from seeing Baleanu," began Stefan abruptly, "I seem to come to my senses and for awhile I realize what's going on. But this lasts a very short time. In ten or twenty minutes I'm lost again. It's hard to explain. Something's wrong with me. I have the impression that I went astray at a

416

certain moment. Until a certain date I lived a life I felt was my own, and after that I took a different road. I got lost. Since then, I've lived an existence foreign to me, the life of another person. . . ."

Biris listened to him sullenly and without enthusiasm. He was thinking again of Bursuc, when the priest had once slapped him on the shoulder within sight of everyone, as if he were congratulating him for some extraordinary act. "You're a man of probity!" he had exclaimed. "You've joined the ranks of the righteous!"

"I don't know how to explain it to you," continued Stefan. "It seems to me that everything goes back to a summer evening nine years ago, the Night of St. John in 1936. It's absurd, but sometimes I have the impression that ever since that moment I've been lost, that ever since then I haven't been living my own life. . . ."

"Everybody feels like that," Biris broke in. "After a certain age a man imagines that he's been shipwrecked, that his life has miscarried, that he's led an idiotic, absurd existence—a life that just *couldn't be his own*, that could only be the life of someone else. It's because we have too high an opinion of ourselves and we can't believe that if we had truly lived *our* life it could have turned out to be so idiotic. . . ."

As he watched Stefan, who was listening to him with his head inclined slightly forward, his eyes gleaming, an almost imperceptible smile illuminating his face, it seemed to Biris that he had returned to a time many years in the past when they had had their discussions about Partenie and Time. He felt at once a curious melange of tenderness and sadness.

"You're right. But I wasn't referring to that general human sentiment of failure. With me I think something else has occurred. . . ." He drew his chair closer to the stove, closer to Biris. "I was at the Ministry, attending to my work. It was a clear summer day. I don't know what prompted me to look at the calendar on my desk, but I saw it was June 23. The summer solstice, I thought, and all at once I felt my heart begin to beat faster and I was seized with a desire to see again the places where I spent my childhood at Baneasa. I ought to tell you that I had never before felt tempted to leave the Ministry to go for a walk in the forest. This happened to me only one time—on the Night of St. John in 1936. And then in the forest I met Ileana. It was as though she had drawn me there, or perhaps I had drawn her. Why would a beautiful young girl go walking so far away, alone, in the Forest of Baneasa?"

Biris recalled her then, and suddenly he found that he longed to see her, to hear her voice again. It seemed to him that very many years had passed since their last meeting—he was not sure how many, but it was not a definite number like four or five. He seemed to be separated from that blissful time before the war by something other than a span of measurable duration. There had been a rupture, and now an immense abyss stretched between his present

417

life and those years when Ileana had stood before him, her hands behind her back, tossing her head from time to time, her green eyes gazing at him and smiling.

"Sometimes," continued Stefan, "I seem to wake up and realize that since then my life has lost its meaning. It's as though it's no longer my life. I don't know how to explain it to you. Since then everything has been false and artificial. My life has not been lived by me, but by events. I've only been carried along by a life that wasn't mine. . . ."

Without understanding why, Biris felt suddenly ill at ease and he looked around quickly for something to do. He knelt intently in front of the stove and began without haste to stir the coals. At last he carefully set a thick log on top of them.

". . . And yet things aren't so simple. This feeling of losing track of my life, of being lost and living the life of someone else, is accompanied by another feeling, one of guilt. Often I feel responsible for the deaths of Partenie and Ioana. I tell myself that if I hadn't interfered in their lives perhaps they'd still be alive and happy. At any rate they'd be living the life they were destined to live. But unintentionally I intruded upon their lives. Ioana mistook me for Partenie on the street one day and soon afterwards broke her engagement to him. If she had met me a few weeks later, very probably she wouldn't have made the mistake. At most she would have said, 'I met a man today who bears an amazing resemblance to you. . . .' And he would have answered, 'Yes, I know him. I've seen him too a few times.' And that's as far as it would have gone. They would have lived their lives, while I, three years later, would have met Ileana and I'd have lived my life. . . ."

"But how can you be sure you would have met her?" Biris spoke as though he had just awakened.

"I believe I'd have met her. What I felt on that Night of St. John can't be explained otherwise. Probably Ileana was the woman who was destined for me, but I was no longer free. I had rushed things and taken the woman destined for someone else. I spoiled their lives and I spoiled Ileana's life. Ultimately I killed Partenie and Ioana, and I lost Ileana. I don't know what's become of her now. . . ."

Biris recalled her again, and that vague fragrance of the years before the war seemed even more appealing. Unconsciously he smiled.

"In any event this would explain what's happened to me, why I've had this feeling for a long time that I'm no longer living my life, that I'm living in a sort of dream, an absurd dream in which I can't participate. For a long while I thought that my meeting with Ileana might have had another purpose, that it would teach me how to love two human beings at the same time, how to discover a new and truer kind of love—one that was closer to that of the saints, who can love an infinity of persons at the same time. But it's more likely that I told myself these things to ease my conscience. It was probably just a desperate attempt to understand my situation, to find a reason for a love I didn't know what to do with. . . ."

A few moments of embarrassed silence followed. Then Stefan jumped to his feet and held out his hand. "Forgive me," he murmured. "I'm really a fool. I shouldn't have told you all this. It's an absurd, criminal thought which has obsessed me for some time. It's tortured me until I'm almost crazy. But please believe me that it was Ioana I loved, only Ioana. If I were sure that by committing suicide I'd find her again I'd have killed myself long ago. But I'm afraid that I'd only lose her. I'd lose her forever. I'm afraid Christianity's right in condemning suicide as the sin *par excellence* of despair. I'm afraid especially for Razvan's sake. I have a great longing for Razvan. Many times I've felt them near me, particularly the child. I don't know how to tell you, but I was afraid I'd lose him if I killed myself. It makes no difference to me if people say that suicide is a coward's way out, and so forth. . . . It's not these precepts that deter me. It's the fear of losing Ioana and Razvan. . . ."

For several days they awaited the denouement. Berlin had been taken by Soviet troops, the death of Hitler had been announced, and that evening all sorts of fantastic rumors were circulating about Himmler and Admiral Dönitz. The city had recovered the feverish excitement of better times. People began to hope again. If the war ended, the Russians would withdraw from Romania, and the Groza government, imposed on them on the sixth of March by Vishinsky, would fall automatically.

"You're wrong!" shouted Bursuc at the Cafenea. "You'll be liquidated—you Anglophiles and American sympathizers! We'll never consent to your robbing us of the fruits of victory this time!"

Biris heard Bursuc as he was entering the Cafenea, and he left precipitately. He felt exhilarated. On the way to Catalina's apartment he bought all the special editions. He rang the bell several times but finally resigned himself to waiting for her on the stair. When he saw that it was almost eight o'clock, he left to look for her at the theater. She was not there, and since she did not have a part in the play that evening, she was not expected. Returning to her apartment, he rang again, but after a quarter of an hour he gave up and started home.

The next day he had classes at the *liceu* until lunchtime. *Doamna* Porumbache informed him on his arrival at home that Misu Weissmann was looking for him. He had come in a taxi and had left a note on Biris's desk. The envelope was sealed, an astute precaution on the part of Weissmann. "Come immediately to the Coltea Hospital," he had written. "Catalina has had an accident, but it isn't serious."

419

It was not without difficulty that he finally located her. She had spent the night in a ward, and just a short time before he arrived a double room had been found for her. She was very pale.

"Don't be alarmed," she whispered. "It's not so bad. A truck struck me and threw me to the sidewalk, and some vertebrae were displaced. It's annoying that I have to be in a cast just now.... I've a terrible headache," she added, trying to smile. "I fell...." She raised her arm to show him the spot that hurt, over the fontanel.

"Have you seen Dan?" she asked. "Who told you?"

"*Conu* Misu left a note for me this morning."

"It's better that you haven't seen Dan," she said and closed her eyes; then she added with a smile, "Give me your hand."

"You know Germany's surrendered. Thank God it's over."

She opened her eyes and looked at him, pressing his hand in both of hers. "Probably it was because of that..." she began, but she broke off abruptly. "The truck, I mean. The driver was drunk."

The nurse entered.

"Please give me something. My head aches dreadfully."

"The doctor's coming now. We're going to make another X-ray."

Catalina closed her eyes again. Biris observed two small tears glistening among her lashes and he was disturbed. "Have they already put you in a cast?"

Catalina's hand moved almost imperceptibly. "Temporarily," she whispered. "I think they're going to operate...."

Biris felt as though his heart had been drained suddenly of its blood, and for a few moments his mind went blank with fear. Before he had recovered he was asked to leave. In the courtyard of the hospital he met Misu Weissmann.

"You can't go in now," he said. "The doctors have come. They're having a consultation.... Just what happened?" he inquired a moment later, lighting a cigarette with trembling hands.

Embarrassed, Misu Weissmann began to hunt for his handkerchief, and finding it, he wiped his face and hands. "A Russian truck knocked her down," he said finally. "It was extremely lucky that she didn't fall under the wheels. She was thrown against the curb."

Some of the buildings in the city were flying the flags of the Allies and the street showed a certain amount of animation, but one could already sense a suggestion of weariness as well as disappointment. The people had had to wait too long. It was too late when the capitulation had been finally announced.

"They telephoned me from the hospital this morning," continued Weissmann. "They called Dan first, last night, but he wasn't home...." Abashed, he stopped and took out his handkerchief again. "Have you seen Dan?" he demanded hastily, without looking at Biris. "Don't you want to go and see him for a moment now?"

"I'm going home. I'm tired."

"It would be well if you would go," Weissmann persisted. "Dan was with her last evening before the accident. She went to see him. . . ." He continued to avoid glancing at Biris, who restrained his impatience and smoked his cigarette in silence. They found a taxi and set off to visit Bibicescu. He was lying on the sofa when they arrived and he looked very pale.

"Something's not quite right with my heart," he stated without rising. "I don't know what it is. I have to have an electrocardiogram. A doctor was here a little while ago."

"We've come from the hospital," broke in Weissmann. "I got there too late, but he saw her."

Biris sat down, selecting a chair as far as possible from the sofa. "Just what happened?" he questioned the actor, taking out his package of cigarettes.

"I must request you, please, not to smoke," Bibicescu said. "I believe I have heart trouble. This morning I had an attack. . . ."

"Don't exaggerate," interrupted Weissmann. "Probably it was a simple muscle spasm. You just imagine you have a heart ailment."

"This is the third time it's happened," Bibicescu continued, gravely regarding the ceiling. "But this morning it was terrible. I think it's angina pectoris. . . . If that's so," he added, "the devil with the theater! And just now, when . . ."

"Who filled your head with this tale of angina pectoris?" Weissmann cut in again. "The doctor said it can't possibly be a case of angina."

With great effort Bibicescu smiled. Biris stood up and approached him. "I have a right too to know how the accident happened to Catalina!"

Bibicescu continued to stare silently at the ceiling. "She came here last evening," he said at length, slowly and deliberately in order to spare himself further fatigue. "She stayed a very short time. I was busy. . . ."

"But what did she want with you?" Biris interrupted, unable to keep silent any longer. "We had a date last night. I waited an hour for her!"

"She wanted to talk to me. She had something important to tell me."

"What?" demanded Biris, raising his voice.

"Please don't shout," Bibicescu continued calmly. "Don't you see that I'm a sick man? She had something important to tell me, but she didn't say what. I was busy. . . . I was not alone," he added after a moment's hesitation. "Someone else was with me. . . ."

"But how did the accident happen?" insisted Biris. "How did you find out about it?"

"*Conu* Misu telephoned me this morning. It was after my attack. The doctor had left not long before."

"Let me explain," Misu Weissmann intervened. "It happened not very far from here. Catalina wanted to cross the street and had just stepped off the sidewalk when a truck went speeding by and knocked her down. She fainted from pain and shock. It was a miracle she wasn't killed. When she came to again at the hospital she asked them to telephone Dan, but he wasn't home. . . ."

"She might have informed me."

"She knew you didn't have a phone and she supposed that one of us would notify you immediately."

"Please ask her to forgive me for not coming to see her," Bibicescu said, his eyes still fixed on the ceiling. "I'm waiting for the result of the cardiogram. They'll make it this afternoon or tomorrow morning."

"I doubt if they'll do it today," remarked Weissmann. "No one's working. It's the end of the war. . . ."

The next time he went to the hospital he was told he could not see her. The operation had been performed. He was not allowed to see her the next day either, but he managed to talk with one of the doctors, who reassured him. It was not serious—a few displaced vertebrae and a small fracture. The operation had taken care of everything, but she would have to stay in the cast for about forty days. It was not until the fourth day that he gained admittance to her room. She was much thinner and her paleness made her appear younger.

"Have you seen Dan?" she inquired. "What did he say to you?"

"He complained of his heart—which is why he asks you to excuse him. He's waiting to see the result of the cardiogram."

"There's nothing wrong with him," Catalina said, smiling. "He's always imagining he's seriously ill. This time he has a reason. . . . But I'd rather he didn't come to visit me."

"I don't understand why you went to see him before the accident."

Catalina closed her eyes. "I went to his house. . . . I remembered that I had something to tell him in connection with the Theater."

"He said it was something important," interrupted Biris.

"Perhaps it was. I don't know now. . . ." Her voice changed and she added, "I've a longing for home. Not the one that I have here—for my parents' home at Botosani. It must be very beautiful there now in May. It's been a long time since I've seen my family. I'd like to go home. . . ."

She had kept her eyes closed most of the time while she was speaking. Biris thought that she wanted to go to sleep.

"How are you feeling?" he asked after awhile.

"Well. Except for this headache that doesn't go away. . . . What time is it?" she demanded suddenly.

"Almost three."

"Aurel should be coming. I'm glad you'll meet him. . . ."

"I ought to leave. . . ." said Biris, embarrassed.

"When I woke up after the operation," continued Catalina as if she had not heard him, "I said to myself, 'It's the nineteenth of October.' I don't know why, but all at once I felt happy. I remembered a little bookshop in Botosani. When I was in the *liceu* I went every Saturday afternoon to look in the window. Once I saw a book about India, but it was in French and I felt I didn't know the language well enough to read it. But I looked at it all the time because the cover attracted me. At last one day it wasn't there. They'd sold it. . . . I want very much to go back to Botosani," she added after an interval of silence. "I don't know how I've let so many years pass."

At that point the nurse came in, holding the door open wide so that Baleanu and the elderly nun who was leading him could pass. Biris withdrew in embarrassment to the window. The colonel was dressed in civilian clothes. His large dark glasses did not succeed in hiding the red patches on his cheeks. The nurse led him to the bed, and he held out his hand, which Catalina grasped quickly.

"I was telling Petre about Botosani," she began. "I've a longing for home. . . ."

Baleanu turned his head toward the window and smiled, bowed a slight greeting, and extended his hand. Biris stepped forward and gripped it.

"Please excuse me." He was ill at ease. "I have an appointment."

The next day when he returned, he found not only Baleanu there but also Weissmann and Irina. He did not try to hide his displeasure as he stepped to the bedside.

"I dreamed about you last night," Catalina said to him with a strained smile. "We were walking together on *strada* Unire in Botosani. It seemed that all the gardens were full of flowers and I pointed them out to you and you said, 'I don't know that one, or that one. . . .' They were very beautiful flowers—flowers that we've never seen here. When I woke up I felt happy. . . . If only my head wouldn't ache!" she added, closing her eyes.

They listened to her in silence. Then Weissmann looked at his watch and started. Approaching Biris, he whispered as though he had a great secret to impart, "They made the cardiogram. There's absolutely nothing wrong."

"If it aches like this for the forty days that I have to wear the cast I'll go out of my mind!" exclaimed Catalina.

"The doctor said that it's nothing serious," Biris began. "It's because of the fall."

"Forty days. . . . I'll go out of my mind!" Catalina repeated softly.

Misu Weissmann told her good-bye. He was leaving the next day for Brasov and did not know when he would return. "Dan will come tomorrow."

Catalina held his hand in hers and smiled. "If he's afraid, he won't come. He'll wait until it's completely gone. Is it true that he wants to perform Partenie?"

Weissmann was suddenly disconcerted, and he flushed. "Everyone wants to perform Partenie. He'll tell you. . . ."

Soon after that Irina also left. She had not spoken since Biris came in. She leaned over and kissed Catalina on the cheek. "I'll come back," she said.

The end of the visiting hour was approaching and Baleanu gave no sign of leaving. Biris was becoming impatient. He wanted to be left alone with Catalina in order to talk to her without embarrassment, but Baleanu sat waiting silently in his chair.

"Please ring for the nurse," Catalina said suddenly. "I can't stand it anymore. . . . She'll give me something. . . ."

The doctor came and everyone had to leave. "It's fatigue that makes her suffer," he said. "No visitors for a few days."

In the corridor Biris did not know how to take leave of Baleanu. He walked for awhile beside him, and then he held out his hand abruptly and said, "Good-bye, *domnule* Colonel."

Biris went to the hospital daily, but his visits were fruitless. "She sleeps all the time," the nurse told him. "She's resting." On the fourth day he demanded to see the doctor, who received him in a small office near the emergency room. The surgeon appeared to be preoccupied and irritable.

"Complications have arisen. She had an internal hemorrhage which we couldn't locate at first. . . . It's not serious," the doctor added quickly when he saw Biris blanch. "Only, you won't be able to visit her soon."

After that he came for news of her twice a day. Once he was permitted to enter her room for just a few minutes. Catalina was in a deep sleep. She was very pale and appeared changed. They had cut the hair from half of her head when they performed the trephining. Mastering his emotion with difficulty, Biris tiptoed to the bedside and gazed at her. Then he leaned over and kissed her hand, which lay inert beside her body.

One evening two weeks after the accident Biris was at dinner with *doamna* Porumbache, who was complaining to him of the high cost of living, when someone knocked on the door. With a stab of apprehension he hurried to open it and found Misu Weissmann standing before him.

"Come! Hurry! They phoned me from the hospital that Catalina's died!" The next moment he stepped across the threshold just in time to catch Biris in his arms. Petre had stared at him, wavering, and then collapsed weakly, as if he had snapped in two at the waist.

• • •

424

When he awoke he saw everyone around him and closed his eyes quickly. Then he heard them whispering and recognized each of the voices. He opened his eyes and motioned to Stefan to come to him.

"Send them outside," he whispered. "Ask them to leave."

"Ask whom to leave?"

"I'd like to be alone."

Stefan stared at him. "There's no one here. *Coana* Viorica's in the kitchen. There are just the two of us. We're alone."

Biris closed his eyes again. A fly landed on his forehead. He shook his head and felt a dull pain. It felt as though someone had been crushing his brain, and he moaned.

"Where did the others go?"

Perplexed, Stefan hesitated for a few moments before answering. "They haven't been here today. Irina will come this evening."

"Actually it was to be expected," Biris began suddenly in a surprisingly calm voice. "I was sure it would turn out this way. Ever since I saw her at the hospital I realized that this time she wouldn't escape. She was wearing her nineteenth of October expression, her eyes of October 19. . . ."

She wears them only once a year, Stefan remembered, *on October nineteenth*. He felt that he had dropped suddenly into a mythical, fabled time that had been rendered almost inconceivable by the bliss that it captured. He made a desperate effort to return to the surface, to the present moment.

"I'd like to see her once more," continued Biris. "I'll take her some wild flowers. She told me she was homesick for the country. I think I still have enough strength to go to the hospital, especially if you'll go with me. We'll take a cab. . . ."

Stefan continued to look at him as he talked, lying there with his eyes closed, motionless, afraid to shake his head.

"We'll go one of these days. . . ."

"Have you notified Baleanu?" demanded Biris, interrupting him.

"He was there too. Everyone was there except you and Bibicescu."

Biris opened his eyes and searched Stefan's gaze. "Everyone was where?"

Stefan hesitated, but then, hearing *doamna* Porumbache come out of the kitchen, he said quickly, "She was buried this morning."

"Oh, yes . . . of course. I should have known," whispered Biris.

Doamna Porumbache opened the door carefully and entered on tiptoe. But when her eyes met those of her nephew she lost her self-control and burst into tears. "Petrisor, *maica*," she began to mourn. "Catalina, poor thing, poor little thing! You lay here and they put her in the ground! Everyone was weeping for her, and you were raving and laughing in your sleep and calling her, 'Catalina! Catalina!' You said you'd walk with her in the garden and cover her with flowers, and all the while they were lowering her into her grave and covering her with earth! Catalina, the poor little thing! Poor thing!"

425

Thereafter whenever Stefan came, *doamna* Porumbache would talk about Catalina, weeping, when she greeted him. Resigned, Stefan would listen without looking at her and make his way slowly to Biris's room. He always found his friend absorbed in a book. In the last few days Biris had been getting out of bed and reading as he sat in a chair by the window. In the strong light of early June his face acquired the pale freshness of a youthful convalescent.

"I have a request to make," Biris said one day. "Ask Irina not to come anymore. Or, if she wants so much to see me, ask her not to try to console me. I don't feel the need of consolation. I'm a teacher of philosophy and I have at my disposal a considerable number of formulae which can perform that service." He paused and got up to put the book on the desk. Then he returned to the chair and sat down.

"I'd like to say the same thing to you," he continued. "I always enjoy it when you come to visit, but I don't want you to think you're obliged to talk about Catalina. As somebody said—I don't know who—life goes on. I've opted for Life, and that's why I'd prefer to discuss something else."

"Everyone opts for Life," said Stefan. "I don't quite understand why, but that's how it is. . . ."

"I know why. Speaking for myself, I want to live to see what will happen in the end. Now that the war in Europe is over, we'll watch the offensive against Japan. In a year or two she'll be liquidated too. I want to see what will happen after that. I shouldn't want to die before I find out where the world's heading—toward socialism or toward dictatorship. That's why I'm interested in everything that goes on around me, from the decision that Stalin will make to Bibicescu's political career. . . ."

Bibicescu had been made assistant director of the National Theater, but he hoped to become director soon. He had succeeded in introducing into the program of the coming season two plays by Partenie. The Communist Party had appropriated the writer, and his books had been reprinted. The newspapers were full of allusions to him. The rumor had begun to circulate that the police had shot him intentionally in order to liquidate, together with a leading Legionnaire, the most gifted of the progressive writers. Bibicescu spoke more and more insistently now about his friendship with Partenie, and he acknowledged in an interview that the great writer was sympathetic toward the Russian Revolution.

It was the middle of June, and no rain had fallen since April. The city was dusty, and everything was dry and withered. It seemed like the end of summer. Bibicescu came to see Biris in the car that belonged to the director of the Theater.

". . . In order not to tire myself," he explained. "They don't know exactly what's wrong with me, but I have to be careful not to tire my heart. . . ."

Suddenly, in the middle of their conversation, he asked, "Did Catalina tell you anything about me?"

Biris was about to light a cigarette, but he felt his hand tremble, and he quickly thrust the package into his pocket. "She just said that she had gone to see you. She didn't tell me why...."

It was not Bibicescu's habit to sit down, but this time he accepted a chair. "I'm sorry. I was busy. I had someone with me.... I wish I knew why she came to see me," he added in a different tone and stood up again. But he no longer ventured to pace from one end of the room to the other. He stopped near the window and glanced at the sky, which was white with heat. "It's terrible, this drought. We won't be able to pay our war debts."

Before he left, he remarked, "You know, a lot of Partenie's papers have been found. Whole notebooks...."

Biris smiled derisively and shrugged.

"I don't suppose you believe me, but you'll be convinced when you see the manuscripts. He left them in a suitcase in the country, at the home of a friend...."

He took long walks through the city in the mornings or after sunset, when the heat had abated. Very often he went to the cemetery early in the morning, when the cool freshness of the night still lingered under the trees and among the graves adorned with drooping bouquets. He brought wild flowers for Catalina that he had gathered from the edges of the vacant lots and from the fallow fields behind the cemetery. They were small and dusty with faded colors, almost dry. Once as he was entering the cemetery with a larger nosegay—on his way he had met a gypsy selling flowers—he suddenly remembered the painting in Stefan's study: the black glove and the long-stemmed wild flowers thrown down in haste on a little table. "She had just returned from a long walk... when she heard the telephone ringing," Stefan's words came back to him, "She has run to answer it.... I'm still waiting for her...."

He would have liked to take some flowers to Ioana's grave, but it was in the Belu Cemetery in another part of the city. He remembered too what had been said at her burial. The bodies had not been recognizable and many families were not sure that they had buried their own dead. However, after he left Catalina's grave he started out for *bulevardul* Domnitei. On the tram people were already complaining of the heat, although it was not yet ten o'clock. Biris felt immersed in an atmosphere of unreality. He seemed to move in a dream. He was not suffering now from sadness or from loneliness. The entire city with all its people, agitated and noisy, was already lost among his memories. Sometime long ago he must have traveled this same route in this same overloaded tram during a time that had long since vanished. And now he was traversing it again in his mind, with the single purpose of returning to the past.

The bomb craters had been filled in and the street repaired, but the sidewalks were still broken. The ruins were there yet, but they seemed smaller now, more compressed, and among the bricks a few weeds and tufts of grass were growing. Biris walked slowly, trying to find the exact spot where the house had stood. He thought he saw it. There on the pile of rubble some faded blue flowers had survived the drought and heat. With a little difficulty he scrambled up and picked them.

That summer they met rather infrequently. Stefan was away on vacation and did not return until after the fifteenth of August, during the week that followed the dropping of the atomic bomb and the capitulation of Japan. It had been a week of general euphoria. The strength of America reawakened the hope that Romania would not be abandoned ultimately to the Soviets. Their joy at the promise of imminent liberation had helped the Romanian people to forget even the drought that had ravaged the land all summer, as they had forgotten the typhus, the hundreds of thousands of people who had died during the past year, and the hundreds of thousands of prisoners who had not returned from Russia.

On the way to see Biris, Stefan met Mihai Duma. He saw him in the distance, and at first he did not recognize him. Duma's skin was tanned and he had let his moustache grow. He held out his hand gravely.

"My condolences. All of us at the Legation were grieved. I hope our telegram reached you. . . ." He said that he had recently returned on one of the first Romanian liners to cross the Mediterranean again. Vidrighin and almost all the others had remained in Lisbon.

Biris was seated at his deak, reading, when Stefan arrived. He was thinner and seemed to have aged a great deal since they had last met.

"I saw Duma today. He sends regards. . . ." Stefan smiled and stopped abruptly, as though he had recalled something important. "It's curious. I just remembered. The first time you told me about Duma was when I'd returned from Sighisoara. And now today I ran into him."

Biris rummaged around on the desk for a piece of paper, which he folded carefully and placed over the page that he was reading. As he closed the book, the title caught Stefan's attention. It was a collection of myths and legends from India.

"Catalina gave it to me a long time ago, but I'd never read it. I had a horror of her notions about Buddhism and her myth of October 19. . . . But I don't understand what seems so mysterious to you about your meeting Duma."

"It's a strange coincidence that I met him today, when I've just returned from Sighisoara again. I went there to see Anisie. I think you still remember him. . . ."

"Listening to you is an uncommon pleasure," interrupted Biris. "You're the first man who hasn't asked me what I think about the atomic bomb. But let's return to Anisie and the problem of Time. Tell me about him. I've been reading Indian myths and they've prepared me for Anisie. . . ."

"Unfortunately, I haven't very much to relate. I went to see him because he had told me to come back after four years. I'd allowed four and a half years to go by, but it wasn't my fault. I guess I arrived too late. There was fighting last year all over that part of the country when the German troops were withdrawing. The farm was burned and the garden devastated. I didn't find him, and I don't even know what's become of him. Some say the Germans carried him off in the retreat and others think the Russians took him. I even heard that he'd been shot, but no one knew exactly when or by whom."

"Too bad. I'd like to have found out how the story ended—the one about 'Youth without Age. . . .' But before we get started on another topic I want to call your attention to something concerning Duma. If he's come back and hasn't been arrested after working for years for the German Secret Service, it means he's working for the Communists now. You'd better be careful. . . ."

It was difficult for Stefan to hear him out. Mention of Duma's name was a signal for him to abandon himself to his memories, and he saw again the cloud of dust behind the military truck on the road that led to Sighisoara. He had followed it for almost half an hour without being able to overtake it. But when at last the car in which he was riding came abreast of it, he caught a brief glimpse of a Russian soldier sitting beside the driver, jokingly threatening them with his carbine. Beyond, in the background, he saw the smoke-blackened ruins of the farm.

"You and I talk about all kinds of nonsense when we're together but we never discuss things in which I'm most deeply interested. I had gone to ask Anisie . . ."

He broke off again, embarrassed. He had gone to ask Anisie about death, and now it seemed to him absurd that he had made that laborious journey through regions that had been devastated by war and drought just to seek out a stranger—a man he had seen only twice in his life—in order to ask him, as if he were an oracle or a great saint, what happens to a man after death.

". . . I wanted to ask him a lot of things," continued Stefan, forcing a smile. "Although I've never understood what made me think that Anisie knew the answers to my problems. . . . And now that I've seen Duma again, everything seems to have returned to the point of departure. I have the disturbing

429

feeling that events are beginning to repeat themselves. I'd like to find out how Anisie—who claimed not to live in Time—accommodated himself to the History written by the retreating German divisions in the vicinity of Sighisoara. This time I'd really have an example of how you can remain outside of Time, even with tanks and artillery all around you. . . ."

Biris smiled. He picked up the book from the desk and began leafing through it. "Since you speak of Time, I'll tell you an Indian myth I read just this morning. I believe it's like the stories Anisie told. Listen. It's the tale of a renowned ascetic who was called Narada. Impressed by his saintliness, Vishnu promised to grant him any desire. 'Show me your power, your mysterious Māyā,' requested Narada. Vishnu motioned to follow him. After walking for a little while on a deserted road in the full sunlight, they became thirsty, and Vishnu asked Narada to go to the village that he saw not far ahead and bring him some water to drink. Vishnu stayed behind and waited at the edge of the road. Hastening to the village, Narada stopped at the first house he came to, and a young girl opened the door. She was so beautiful that Narada forgot what he had come for. He entered the house and was received by the whole family with the honor befitting a holy man. He stayed in the home as a guest for a long time, and finally he married the beautiful girl. He knew the joys of marriage and all the other pleasures and troubles of the life of a farmer. Twelve years passed in this way. Narada had three children now, and after his father-in-law died, he became master of the household. But in the twelfth year torrential rains flooded the area. In the same night his herds were drowned and his house demolished. Holding onto his wife with one hand and the two older children with the other, he carried the smallest child on his shoulders and made his way with difficulty through the waters. But the load was too great. He slipped and the child fell from his shoulders. He let go of the others and flung himself in the water to catch the little one, but he was too late. The torrent engulfed him in a few moments. At the same time the waves took the other two children and a little later his wife. Narada was exhausted and soon fell, unconscious, swept away by the water like a piece of wood. Cast upon a rock, he woke up and recalled all the misfortunes that had befallen him. He burst into tears. All at once he heard a familiar voice, 'Child, where is the water that you were supposed to bring me? I've been waiting for you more than half an hour!' Narada turned his head. Instead of the waters which had annihilated everything, he saw deserted fields gleaming under the sun of noon. 'Do you understand now the secret of my powers?' Vishnu asked him. 'Do you understand what Māyā is?'"

Biris shut the book and laid it on the desk some distance away from him. Stefan had listened without moving.

"It's a very beautiful story," said Biris, seeing that Stefan remained silent. "I wonder why Catalina never said anything to me about it. . . ."

"But do you think it could be true?" Stefan asked suddenly. "Do you

430

believe that what happens in Time and History is only an immense cosmic illusion, the absurd creation of a demiurge who cares nothing about our beliefs, our passions and sufferings?"

"I didn't say it was true. I just said it's a very beautiful story. It's a story about Time, the kind of story that Anisie told you."

Baffled, Stefan gazed at him. "Narada asks me to believe that Ioana and Razvan and all the others who once were and are no more have never really existed, that they were nothing but shadows born of the cosmic dream of a demiurge. I can't believe it. If this were true, life would be meaningless. If nothing is real, if everything is an idle and absurd creation in the manner of a great dream, an irresponsible game repeating itself *ad infinitum*, our existence would have no significance or value. Then we'd be lost completely!"

"I don't believe that's what the myth means," Biris broke in. "Narada's experience has nothing to do with the meaning or value of human existence. That's a totally different matter. Vishnu probably wants to show him that Māyā, the cosmic illusion, is entirely a function of Time, that Māyā can manifest itself only through temporal duration. If I'm not mistaken, I thought this was your view too. You used to tell me that existence in Time is illusory, without significance, unreal. You said that the only salvation is to go out of historic time. Vishnu agrees with you. He tells you clearly that Time is illusion, that it's Māyā. . . ."

Stefan ran his hand over his face and swallowed with difficulty. "But what am I going to do? And Ioana?" he demanded. "Where will I meet her again? What do I do about all my past, the time which by its passage has made me what I am at this moment?"

"Listen to me!" Biris exclaimed, interrupting him. "I'm sorry, but I have to speak frankly. From the day we met I've heard you say continually that you wanted to go out of Time, to escape from History. Pardon me for pointing this out, but it seems to me your wish has been granted! It's terrible, but that's what's happened. An American bomb put an end to your History. You lost everything. Not only Ioana and Razvan, but even the external evidence of your existence in History—mementos of childhood, books, pictures. You're a man completely removed from History—without a past and therefore without identity. It's what you once told me you tried to achieve when you shut yourself in your secret room. You can start a new life at any moment from the beginning. You've abolished History—something you never really believed in anyway. Narada, so long as he found himself under Vishnu's magical spell, believed in the reality of his life as a farmer, with his herds, wife and children. That's why Vishnu gave him the lesson you heard a little while ago. You were warned, however. Your own intuition revealed to you long ago the unreality of historic Time."

Stefan bowed his head. "I was a fool," he said faintly. "For a long while I've realized what a fool I was. . . ."

431

Biris lit a cigarette. His hand trembled a little as he raised the match, and he hid it as soon as possible, feeling humiliated. But Stefan had not noticed. He was still sitting with his head bent, staring insensibly at the carpet.

"And to speak of folly is to use a vague expression that ultimately says nothing at all," began Biris. "You were and still are a normal man like everyone else. Your longing to go out of Time and to ignore History was probably a desperate effort to recover the bliss of childhood, to reintegrate a lost Paradise."

All at once he realized the cruelty of his remark, and he smoked in silent chagrin.

"Still, I was a fool," repeated Stefan without raising his head. "Not for imagining a man can elude historic Time while remaining alive, and not for thinking he can obtain in this way a full life, one infinitely more precious than our ordinary existence—which consists of nothing but receiving and assimilating History. I still think this is possible. The proof is the life that a saint lives—a life that isn't separated from eternity as ours is. . . . But my folly was something else, and it was ridiculous and absurd. I imagined that I could evade History by following my hunches and hallucinations and by seeking all the time for *signs* around me. Do you know that for years and years I was obsessed by a car? It was one in which it seemed to me that Ileana *ought to have come* and which I sometimes seemed to see in front of me, although I never caught up with it. I was obsessed by that car and by the mystery of Vadastra's life! I spent long hours listening to him talking in the next room. I'd been married only a year or two, but I left Ioana alone in the hope that I'd find out who *doamna* Zissu was. I kept hearing Vadastra talking about this extraordinary woman, *doamna* Zissu. It seemed to me this name concealed a secret which, if I could unravel it, would change my life. I had become obsessed with *doamna* Zissu. I should have had my head examined. . . ."

Biris was embarrassed. He smiled. Getting up from the desk, he went to the window and opened it. "*Doamna* Zissu?" he inquired, deliberately changing the subject. "*Doamna* Zissu? Maybe she's the same person as Uncle Mitica's Zisuleasca. If she is, *coana* Viorica could tell you a lot about her. She doesn't like to admit it, but Zisuleasca caused her some rather anxious days about twenty years ago. She was, so to speak, Uncle Mitica's last great passion. . . . She was a dressmaker. . . ."

He stopped talking and stepped abruptly out of the room. *Doamna* Porumbache was standing with her ear pressed against the wall. "Don't tell him!" she pleaded in a faint whisper.

4

"SHE WAS A DRESSMAKER," BIRIS HAD SAID ON ANOTHER OCCASION. "It seems that she was very beautiful. . . ."

It's hard to believe that she's the same person as Vadastra's *doamna* Zissu, Stefan had thought. At the time of the First World War, when Mitica Porumbache had known her, Zisuleasca would have been almost thirty years old. Vadastra had met *doamna* Zissu in 1925, when he was in the fourth class of the *liceu*. He was about fifteen then, but by that time Zisuleasca, the friend of Mitica Porumbache, would have been over forty. She could not have been Vadastra's first love as Stefan had been tempted to think when he had heard him speak about "the distinguished *doamna* Zissu" or "a distinguished woman who loved me. . . ."

But Stefan was interested in Biris's story. He had listened to it with a suggestion of uneasiness. All those details about things that had occurred thirty years earlier held an incomprehensible attraction for him. He had the feeling that numerous distorted signs were trying to reach him from the past, from somewhere in a region that was inaccessible to him. Biris had not known this woman, but from *doamna* Porumbache he learned that when Mitica had met her she was being supported by a captain who had rented a luxuriously furnished apartment for her on *bulevardul* Pache, and he had even bought her a piano. She had had two children by her former husband, and the captain had fathered a third, a boy who had died shortly after she met Mitica Porumbache at the Garden of Gaiety. That was the cafe *finu* Lica owned. Even before he met Zisuleasca and while he was still a lieutenant, the captain had sought diversion there with his fellow officers and the girls from the cabaret. It was said that the captain was from a good family. He was married, but nothing was known of his wife because they had been separated for many years. When his garrison was transferred from

Bucharest, the captain still came to visit his mistress at least once a week.

At that time Mitica Porumbache was nearing his fiftieth year, but he was handsome and robust and rather well-to-do. He owned houses in Ferendari, a hardware store in Lipscani, and many other properties as well. Zisuleasca was bored being by herself and she began to go in the evenings to the Garden of Gaiety, where she rapidly became involved with Mitica. His neighbors found out that he hardly ever spent a night at home anymore, that he was squandering his money on Zisuleasca. He bought her dresses and jewels, drove her about in a cabriolet in Sosea, and sent her to the baths in summer. Not long afterward the captain disappeared in a mysterious manner, leaving many debts, all of which Mitica paid. When *finu* Lica discovered that the captain had vanished and that Zisuleasca was living with Mitica, he decided to tell *coana* Viorica about it. But she had known for a long time. The neighbors had informed her that Mitica was not at the Garden of Gaiety nights but at the home of his mistress. She feigned indifference, and with a shrug of her shoulders she replied that she would not demean herself to spite a seamstress. When the war began in 1916 and Mitica was called into service, Zisuleasca was expecting a baby. It was born shortly after the Germans occupied Bucharest, when he had gone to Moldavia with his regiment. In those years of the war Zisuleasca's fortunes had declined again, and she had to sell some of her jewels and furniture. But she refused to part with her piano. She gave up the apartment on *bulevardul* Pache and moved into a little house on the outskirts of the city, resuming her work as a seamstress. When Mitica returned from Moldavia in 1918, his child was dead. Earlier that winter it had taken a cold and perished in a few days. This event was decisive for their relationship. Mitica believed that the boy had died because he had not been properly cared for. Since Zisuleasca worked during the day in the homes of other people, she was always away. The baby was left in the care of a neighbor. Mitica Porumbache never recovered from this blow. They renewed their liaison, but it only endured for a year and then he gave her enough money to open a shop downtown. After that he saw no more of her.

But Viorica's triumph was only temporary. A few years later, in 1923, Mitica died, and after his death she discovered that his business affairs were not what she thought them to be. She was forced to sell some of the properties to be able to keep the store in Lipscani, and then she sold the house in Ferendari. But all her efforts were fruitless. Three years after the death of her husband, it was necessary to close the shop. All that was left was the house on *strada* Macelari and a sum of money which was soon reduced to nothing by devaluation and the expenses of Petre's schooling.

"It's too bad *coana* Viorica didn't want to tell you herself," Biris had said later. "Only she knows most of the details. . . ."

Stefan remembered that autumn evening very clearly. The visit had been one of the last that he had made to *strada* Macelari before he left. As he listened to Biris's tale, random recollections of his life as Vadastra's neighbor came into his mind, but he felt he was not reviewing his own memories. They seemed to be concerned with events from some other person's life. These things happened ten years ago, he reminded himself obstinately, as if he were trying to convince himself of their reality. Almost ten years ago—I was in my secret room. . . .

"Do you think she's Vadastra's *doamna* Zissu?" Biris had asked after a long silence.

Stefan did not know what to say in reply. Vadastra would have been fifteen then, he calculated, while *doamna* Zissu . . . "Actually, none of these things matter," he stated finally.

The memories continued to emerge—the piano, the fifteen lei an hour, the workshop, the girls who were employed by *doamna* Zissu and who had prepared tea for Spiridon once at Christmastime when he had tarried late in the evening practicing the *Sonata Pathetique*. That might very well have been the dressmaking establishment of Zisuleasca. . . .

"It doesn't matter," he repeated with a hint of exasperation in his voice. "At that time, ten years ago, it seemed to me that . . ." He stopped again.

Biris rested his elbows on the desk and looked at him, a slight smile of pity hovering in the corner of his lips. Almost ten years had passed since the two had met, and Biris had not changed. He was a strong man. "I've opted for Life," he had said. "I want to live to see how things will turn out in the end." It was already several months since Catalina had died and he was still the same, unaltered. He was a strong man.

"It's not important," Stefan repeated, making an effort to smile. "Let's talk about something else. . . ."

Biris was smoking calmly, with both elbows leaning on the desk. "Look, this desk, as you well know, was formerly inhabited by a death-clock beetle," he had said some years before. "I haven't heard it now for

435

a long time. It died. . . ." He also had a molar which had already arrived in the land of the dead, Stefan recalled then. And now six months have gone by since the death of Catalina and he hasn't changed. He's a teacher of philosophy. I ought to ask him what he believes about death. It's the only problem worth discussing. We waste time talking about so many futile things. . . .

"I wanted to ask you something . . ." he began, but he stopped abruptly and got up from his chair in embarrassment. "It's getting late. I have work to do at home. We'll talk some other time. . . ."

This conversation had taken place one evening early in November, but he felt that it had happened long ago, many years prior to the drought, many years before he had climbed aboard this train that had been waiting—he knew not how long—in this station in Moldavia. Although the blinds were drawn, it was unbearably hot in the compartment. None of the men wore coats, and their shirt sleeves were rolled up to their elbows. Stefan felt the sweat running in streams over his skin, and he stepped back into the corridor. He took out his handkerchief, and slipping it furtively under his shirt, he began to sponge himself.

"What's wrong, *domnule*? Why don't we leave?" he heard someone behind him say.

He remembered very well. He had not seen Biris much after that. Stefan had moved into a bachelor flat on *strada* Campineanu a few days before. He had furnished it with simple, ordinary things that seemed to be without age or style, the kind of furniture that one finds in the waiting room of a second-rate business establishment. A few shelves of technical journals and books on political economy served as a library. On his work table lay only periodicals and assorted documents. There were no pictures on the walls, no art objects, no flowers. When he came home in the evening he liked to enter a neutral room that would not sadden or depress him. He wanted it to be like a box so arranged that he could work and sleep in it. He was always late coming in and he set to work immediately, busy then until two or three in the morning when he fell into an exhausted sleep, dreamless and untroubled. He felt really at ease only when he abandoned himself wholly to the task before him.

All the employees at the Ministry belonged to the Union and Stefan was no exception. He liked to attend the meetings. They talked about serious things that seemed to him foreign and impersonal, allowing him to live a few more hours without thinking. When a course in

436

the Russian language was organized at the Ministry, he was one of the first to enroll, and he pursued it assiduously. He had learned a little Russian at Odessa but only by hearing it spoken by the old woman, Viera, and her nephew. The boy was ten or eleven, with close-cropped hair, so blond that he seemed to have white eyelashes. *"Ia ona nie znaiu,"* Stefan would begin, and the boy would correct him promptly, *"Ia ieio nie znaiu. . . . ."* This time he was studying it methodically, using a grammar and writing the vocabulary and the exercises in a notebook. He devoted an hour to this activity every night. But sometimes he found that his despair broke through in spite of all precautions. Certain words plunged him back into the past to the years that he had spent in Russia.

"Perestanite jalovatsia!" He had heard this once long ago and he had not understood what it meant. That was in the spring of 1942 somewhere near the bend of the Don. He had received a letter from Ioana and he read it as he waited for the car that was to take him to the airport. With a little effort he could have remembered what Ioana had written to him then. *"Perestanite jalovatsia!"* an old man had said to the woman beside him. Stefan had not understood. He had finished reading Ioana's letter and as always he had felt ashamed and despondent. Someday she'll find out that I'm lying to her, he had thought, and I don't even understand why I lie. I don't understand it at all. . . .

Then one day he found out the meaning of *perestanite jalovatsia*. "Stop complaining!" He closed the manual and went outside to walk on the street. He walked for several hours bareheaded in the rain. This was what he did whenever he could not escape his memories. He strode through downpours, through snow, until he was worn out. Then he would return late, spent, and go to sleep quickly, his mind empty of thought.

And yet he would stubbornly take up his work again the next evening. He soon excelled in Russian, a fact that alienated any sympathy that his colleagues at the Ministry still felt for him. Everyone regarded him with suspicion, even the members of his family. Adela and Raducu had been the first to become cool. Raducu had been dismissed from the Ministry of Public Works and had found a position with a private enterprise. He had become more uncompromising than ever and predicted an Anglo-American intervention. He declared that all Communists and collaborators would be hanged in the square in front of the National Theater. Stefan listened to him seriously, without attempting to contradict him. But when Raducu found out that Stefan read Communist newspapers and was taking the course in Russian, he banged his fist indignantly on the table and left the room. After that Stefan had not visited them again.

In spite of himself he had also quarreled with the Bologa family.

437

The old man had been offended when Stefan had refused to live in their house in Cotroceni, which they had finally been forced to put up for lease. Because of his heart trouble Bologa stayed at their vineyard near Targoviste. When Stefan went to see his father-in-law, the old man began to talk about Ioana and Razvan, showing him their photographs. Stefan pretended that he did not see him crying, and from time to time he went into another room or out on the porch to have a cigarette. He had been told that the smoke was bad for the other man's heart. Each time he came back silent and embarrassed, and sat down again beside Bologa. "Look at this picture . . ." the old man said once, pointing it out to him. Stefan nodded his head and tried to smile. He was familiar with it. It was a picture of Ioana in the last class of the *liceu*. He had one like it. He had had copies made of almost all the photographs of Ioana that the family possessed. "Now this photo . . ." Bologa began in a curiously diminished voice. It seemed to have been reduced to a limited number of sounds. Stefan kept nodding his head, but he was not listening. How is it possible for his voice to change so much? he wondered. He has heart trouble. All this has happened because he has heart trouble. . . . After awhile Stefan realized that his father-in-law was no longer talking about Ioana. He had begun to comment on the political situation.

"What's the matter?" Bologa asked suddenly. "Why are you look-ing at me like that? Do you think I'm exaggerating?"

"No. You're right. . . ."

"Allow me to continue!" The old man cut him short and his voice seemed to change again. "We're glad that you're well thought of at the Ministry, although your Minister is a Communist bandit. We're glad that you at least have kept your position, although the majority of honest men and true patriots were purged by those criminals."

"You haven't understood me," Stefan tried to explain.

"Let me speak," interrupted Bologa again. "If what I've heard is true, that you've begun to study Russian and that you've joined the Union . . ."

Stefan permitted him to rant like that for a long time, but he paid no attention to what he was saying and tried to find other things to think about.

"What's wrong, *domnule*? Why don't we leave at once?" Again Stefan heard someone shouting in the compartment behind him. "Have they forgotten we're here?"

When he shaved himself every morning in front of the mirror in the bathroom he left the radio turned on so that he could hear the news and

438

the political commentaries. And yet sometimes he realized that he was no longer listening and was staring at himself with an obscure feeling of hope. He thought that if he made the effort he would be able to recall precisely the day when he had ceased to be young. For a long time he had been obsessed with the idea that he had not been attentive enough to recognize the exact moment when the last trace of his youth had shifted *behind* him, receding wholly *into the past*. He felt that he had been tricked. Someone had teased him into believing that youth is not numbered by years, that when you count them you are not really counting the time of your own life flowing by but something else entirely. . . . He stood close to the mirror and studied his face thoughtfully under the bright light of the naked bulb. Then he ran his hand over his eyes and cheek, and began to dress without further delay.

He tried to avoid thinking about the past, to stop recalling things. But regardless of his efforts, he sometimes found himself making calculations, seeking to convince himself that he was not mistaken, that a definite number of years had actually passed since a certain event. When he thought about the time of his youth, it seemed to have stretched and expanded, to have been crowded with incidents, rich in revelations. His years of study in Paris took on an indefinite duration. They alone attained the dimensions of a lifetime. Then there came a particular moment that he could never quite manage to isolate, and after that the years had begun to fly. Although they went by so fast, they brought him almost nothing that was new. He had been pushed and shoved by events—especially the war—but all of them seemed to have been deprived of duration. He had the impression that his interior time had not been receptive to them. It was as if these events had taken place somewhere outside of him, perhaps on a cinema screen that he had been watching. The action that occurs in a film sometimes spans many years and you understand clearly that time *has also passed* in the picture, but it does not coincide with what you feel in your own being. In this way Stefan felt that he had not really lived the last few years of his life.

"An hour and twenty minutes!" the man in the compartment exclaimed in exasperation. "They've forgotten we're here! And we don't have a drop of water. . . ."

And yet occasionally on the way home he found himself heading for the Cafenea. Some irresistible urge deep inside of him seemed to impel him in that direction. He passed among the tables absently, looking for Biris. He did not always find him, but he met Weissmann, who told him about the trip that he would soon be making to London. He saw, too, seated at the table by the window, Bursuc, who had recently become a monk and now lived at the Metropolitan Cathedral. The priest had grown a short, thin beard which made his face look much fatter and gave him the appearance of a monk in a painting by Fra Lippo Lippi. Bursuc had taken the vows so he would be able to enter into the succession of a former country priest, a Communist sympathizer, whom the government had made a bishop and was preparing to raise to the status of Metropolitan.

Sometimes he saw Bibicescu. After the success which the plays of Partenie had enjoyed, he had expected to be named director of the National Theater, especially since he had introduced a great many works of Soviet authors into the program for the new season. But in February an article that appeared in a Party magazine held him responsible for the bourgeois-reactionary style in which the actors performed. The author analyzed Bibecescu's fascist tendency and recalled his influence when he was the director of the National Theater under the Legionnaire Regime. This seemed to have been a signal for the entire Communist press to take up the campaign, accusing him of betraying the good faith of the authorities and of having introduced himself into the Party through fraud. A few weeks later he had been dismissed from his post as assistant director, although he was permitted to remain in the Union of Dramatic Artists.

One evening as he was threading his way among the tables at the Cafenea, Stefan had seen the actor sitting with Biris and Bursuc. He had seemed extraordinarily pale.

"An individualist would have been hurt at receiving such a severe sanction," Dan said gravely, "but such reactions are out of date."

"If I understand correctly," Biris interposed, "it's a sort of collective psychoanalytic therapy. The Party is helping you to bring your complexes to light and to judge them on an objective level as if they didn't belong to you. Salvation consists in the transcending of subjectivity. . . ."

"That's exactly right," responded Bibicescu. "Subjectivity must be corrected permanently through the consciousness of history, so as not to lose contact with the living realities—that is, with the social . . ."

"You don't understand at all," Bursuc interrupted. "Self-criticism is the revolutionary formula for the confession of sins. By the public confession of our transgressions we return to true Christianity. That's the significance of the revolution. . . ."

That evening he had left the Cafenea in the company of Biris. "What's become of you?" demanded the teacher. "I haven't had a sign of life from you. You don't come to *strada* Macelari anymore . . ."

"I'm extremely busy. I have absolutely no time at all now. . . ."

Biris stopped beside him for a moment, standing on the sidewalk, and gazed at him. "You're a fortunate man," he said. "To have no time means that you've resolved all problems and you're living in a perfect equilibrium. My congratulations. I envy you."

"Then I've expressed myself badly. I meant to say that I no longer have the leisure to be aware of what happens to me. . . ."

"It's the same thing. You're no longer aware of what's happening to you, because you're living exclusively outside yourself. You're living on an objective plane. That is, you're integrating yourself into the historic moment. Although you haven't joined the Party, your reasoning is just like Bibicescu's. I congratulate you—especially since I remember how many years you spent trying to escape from History. Now probably you've persuaded yourself that you were on the wrong road and you're conforming to the Spirit of the Time. . . . You ought to read Hegel," he added with a smile. "If you like, I'll lend you his works and we'll discuss them together. Hegel's a rather difficult author. . . ."

"I've expressed myself badly," repeated Stefan. "It's not that at all. I don't know if what I do is right. It's an extreme kind of solution that I resorted to in desperation. I could have killed myself. It would have amounted to the same thing. Actually I haven't been living—really living—for a long while. I'm just doing my duty when I wake up every morning at the same hour. That's all. That's my whole life."

"But why?" Biris demanded suddenly. "What good does that do? What do you think you've solved by this?" He stopped again and looked at Stefan with an exasperation that he could not control. He was almost raging. Intimidated, Stefan hung his head.

"I don't know myself. I'm not aware of my motives. Maybe it's cowardice. . . ."

"Listen to me," resumed Biris in a quieter voice. "I'd like to have a talk with you sometime. But I'd like to talk frankly, the way we used to talk. I'd have looked for you, but I didn't know your new address. . . . And I don't know it now, either," he added after a pause.

This had happened at the beginning of March. Stefan remembered it very clearly. The evening was cold and foggy. Snow had fallen again a few days before and some of it still lingered on the sidewalk, dirty, trampled under foot. They walked together then for a long time without speaking.

Stefan descended to the platform and placed his wet handkerchief on the top of his head to protect it from the intense heat. The station had been destroyed two years before, during the last months of the war. Sometime since then they

441

had begun to rebuild it, but the work had been interrupted, and the building, only half completed, seemed now to have been abandoned. The offices were lodged in some clapboard warehouses nearby. At each end of the platform a guard from the gendarmes was posted. One of them leaned against the scaffolding in an effort to shield himself from the glare of the sun. The other seemed to have fallen asleep in the sparse shade of a dusty locust tree.

Stefan walked a short distance beside the coaches, with their drawn shades. They appeared deserted, although now and then a passenger in shirt sleeves would raise one of the blinds and show his face at the window, drugged with sleep. For a moment he would glance desperately toward the warehouse and then draw back, pulling the shade down quickly, as though he feared that the stifling heat would invade the compartment. When the train had stopped at the ruined depot an hour and a half earlier, where it should have halted for only a few minutes, the travelers had streamed out of the coaches and run to the well under the locust tree with their bottles and canteens. But they did not find a drop of water. The cistern had been dry for a long time. Momentarily the station had seemed to come alive as if by magic. People ran the length of the platform, there was the sound of voices, and one after another the shades went up. Then, imperceptibly, the activity began to diminish and silence was reestablished. The torrid heat of the July noon alone dominated the scene under the whitened sky, glassy and incandescent.

Stefan paused before the warehouse door, which held a placard with the word "Stationmaster" written on it. He knocked several times and waited. No sound from inside reached his ears. The building seemed to be empty. He knocked again, more loudly, and after a few seconds a rough, sleepy voice growled threateningly, "What d'ya want?"

However, since no one opened the door, Stefan continued to knock.

"What do you want, *domnule?*"

"I came to ask you . . ." Stefan began hesitantly, "to ask if we'll be here much longer—if I can still make the connection for Botosani. . . ."

"You've missed it," responded the same rude voice from behind the door.

"But can you at least tell me why we're standing here? What we're waiting for?"

"It's an order. . . ."

Stefan waited a few seconds and then turned back, holding both hands to his forehead to shade his eyes. The relentless heat of the sun seemed to pour down upon him like a rain of fiery coals. As he walked past the guard, he heard a faint whistle and he raised his eyes. The man motioned for Stefan to approach.

"You won't be leaving very soon," he murmured. "The Americans have to go through first."

Stefan stared at him questioningly.

442

"The American Red Cross train," added the guard almost in a whisper. "It has to pass first. People are dying of hunger."

Behind the station extended the plain, deserted, without a blade of grass, burned by the heat and drought. Here and there thick clouds of dust were moving sluggishly, drifting over the parched earth. The guard noticed that Stefan was watching them and he also turned to look.

"The people are coming," he said. "They've found out. . . . If only they have enough strength to get here!"

Stefan blinked a few times to rest his eyes. The light that rose over the ground, a shimmering sea of incandescence, blinded him.

"Their cattle have died," continued the guard, "and they're coming on foot. Those who fall are left beside the road. . . . It's the punishment of God." He sighed.

"Everything comes from God," said Stefan.

"Everything comes from God," Irina had said. "If God wished you to remain with us . . ."

He had come upon her waiting for him in front of his house one evening.

"How did you find out my address?" he inquired, without taking the trouble to hide his irritation.

"Forgive me," she murmured in embarrassment. "They told me at the Ministry. I wanted to talk to you. . . ."

"I know," he interrupted, opening the door and stepping aside to let her pass. "Tomorrow will be the second anniversary. . . ."

Irina entered the room and glanced timidly around, standing in the middle of the floor. She did not know what to do with her hands and finally thrust them into the pockets of her coat.

"Please sit down," he said, pulling up a chair beside his desk. He paused a moment, then added, "We haven't seen each other for a long time. You've come to remind me that tomorrow is the second anniversary. . . ."

Irina sat down and gazed directly into his eyes. "I didn't come to talk about that."

Very slowly and deliberately he lit a cigarette, allowing the match to burn down until he could feel the heat of the flame against the tips of his fingers.

"I came to remind you of the Emperor," she continued in her calm, grave tone. "It's been two years also since he went away. Now that you're left alone what do you intend to do?"

"I don't understand what you mean. Please be more explicit."

"Ioana and Razvan went away two years ago and the Emperor went with them. You've been left here alone with us, but you don't seem to

443

like any of us. Then what do you intend to do? If God wished you to remain with us you ought to find consolation here and love us."

"Us? Who? Who do you mean by 'us'?"

"We, the living. You don't want to live with us anymore. You've let yourself be carried off somewhere else. But this isn't living. This is only one of your illusions. The Emperor can't be resurrected. He's with Ioana and Razvan now. . . ."

He put out his cigarette in the ashtray and raised his eyes to Irina. His face expressionless, he regarded her for several moments in the way that he would look at some object that was commonplace and familiar to him.

"I'm sorry to have to tell you," he began abruptly, "but for me death is a serious problem. Up to now I haven't even dared to discuss it with Biris, although he doesn't hesitate to remind me all the time that he's a professor of philosophy. Why, then, should I discuss it with you?"

"You're committing a sin," said Irina. "I don't know how to say it any other way, but you're committing a sin."

"Is it so terrible that I still think about Ioana? Is it really such a great sin?"

Irina raised her head slowly and fixed her gaze in his eyes once more, her face alight for a moment.

"I told you there's nothing more you can do now for Ioana except to pray for her. No matter what your future life may be it doesn't concern Ioana. She's gone away and taken with her all the life you had together, so the Emperor has gone too."

"You're very confusing, but I think I understand what you mean. Biris would say that when I lost Ioana I lost the whole 'history' of our life together because I lost the only witness to that history. I agree. But what must I do to annul that fact? If I were to believe Biris . . ."

He stopped suddenly as if he had realized that he had said too much already and he shrugged his shoulders, a tired smile on his lips.

"What you're doing now is not out of love for Ioana," Irina began again in the same quiet voice. "You could have done so much while you were together. . . ."

Stefan stood up sharply from the desk and began to pace about the room. With a vague feeling of uneasiness Irina watched him.

"Now, you must consider us, those who are left," she continued. "You must search for Ileana. . . ."

He stopped in front of her, obviously annoyed. "How do you know about her?"

"From Ioana. She knew you loved her and that on account of her you left for the front. She knew everything."

"Of course she knew. I told you long ago it was I who killed her. You didn't want to believe me. I'm glad that I've convinced you at last!"

444

"You're committing a great sin to talk that way," Irina interrupted him. "You're putting yourself in the place of God and judging yourself in his name. Everything's decided by God. You have no power to change it. How could you change your fate when it was decided by God? It was God who destined you to love two women. Now he's called Ioana to him, and you must search for the other. . . ."

She went to the window and opened it. The coolness of the April evening began to penetrate the room. "There was too much smoke," she said. "A closed smell. The furniture and even the walls smelled closed. . . ."

"So then you ask me to renounce forever a part of my life," Stefan said suddenly, "to say like Job, 'The Lord gave, and the Lord has taken away; blessed be the name of the Lord!'—and then begin another life all over again as if my life before had been just a dream, a hallucination like that of the ascetic Narada in the Indian myth Biris told me!"

"You know that God doesn't ask this of you," replied Irina. "The life you've lived isn't a dream and it isn't a hallucination, but it's gone now to be with God for eternity, and when it's time for you to leave too you'll find it all with him. God knows all these things and remembers them and when you're called to him he gives you back your whole life, everything that's happened to you, down to the very least detail, things you've long since forgotten. But God never forgets. He returns everything. He gives back to you your whole life in a way you could never have known it, because we live our lives piece by piece, and when we're living one year we forget what happened in the years before. But God doesn't forget—not ever. He gives back everything all at one time. He gives you again all the people who were involved with you, the people you loved. That's why only the souls that are at rest know happiness—because they're in Heaven and a soul in Heaven has everything at one time. We living human beings have to take things one after another, and so we don't understand very well what we have. It's only after God calls us to him that we understand. . . ."

Stefan listened to her in wonder and amazement, his eyes fixed on her face. "What you say is very interesting," he declared a moment later. "Then you believe as I do that the one true bliss is possible only when we escape from Time. Through death as well as sainthood, man escapes from Time and contemplates an eternal simultaniety. . . ."

Irina smiled in embarrassment. "I don't understand you," she murmured. "I haven't much book learning . . ."

"Still, it's interesting that you, too, in your way, have been preoccupied with the problem of Time . . ."

"No, I haven't," Irina interrupted. "I'm only telling you the truth. I'm telling you what happens with God. . . ."

A long involuntary sigh slipped from Stefan's lips. He extinguished

445

his cigarette and got up to close the window. As he returned to his desk he glanced at his watch.

"Forgive me for keeping you so long," said Irina. "It's late. I must go home. I just came to tell you that you should search for Ileana. She was destined for you too."

"How do you know that she was destined for me?" Stefan asked in a voice that betrayed his anxiety.

"If you've loved her for so many years and if you love her now, she was destined for you. Only you were mistaken. . . ." Confused, she hesitated and lowered her eyes. "It wasn't your fault," she continued after a moment. "Both were destined for you, since you loved each of them, but you believed that you could love them at the same time, in the same way souls love in Heaven, and this isn't possible. This has been your illusion. In Heaven, after death, all things are given to you at once. God does this and we can't understand it. Everybody we've loved during our lifetime, one after another, we have there together. God gives them back to us and he gives them back all at once. . . . But you thought you could live the heavenly life here on earth. . . ."

"Where did you learn all these things?"

"Your sin is that you want to live death here on earth," Irina went on as though she had not heard him. "But here we can only live life. True death is only to be lived in Heaven. If you try to live death on earth, you sin and you're consumed by despair because you can't do it, and you're neither truly alive nor truly dead. . . . You're just a kind of lost soul, like a *strigoi*."*

"But the saints? How can they love everybody and everything at the same time?" he interrupted nervously.

Irina dropped her eyes and remained silent.

"The saints?" he insisted.

"God takes care of this," she said at last. "We're not saints, and it's a great sin to want to live like the saints if God hasn't given you this honor. God destined you to live as other people live, here, on earth." She stopped suddenly and stood up. "I'm going," she said. "I just came to tell you that you must search for Ileana."

"So you're going to Botosani?" the guard asked. "You've missed your connection with the express but there's another train at midnight . . ."

One Sunday morning he found himself on *strada* Batistei. A scaffold stood in front of number 27. A new building, already half completed, was being erected on the spot formerly occupied by the house and

---

*Ghost, a kind of "vampire."

garden of *doamna* Cretulescu. He could see that a large apartment house with many stories was under construction. For several minutes he walked back and forth before the scaffold, and then with sudden decision he rang the bell of number 23. The door was opened by a kindly old gentleman with silvered hair and a distinguished face.

"Pardon me . . . I've been away from the capital for quite awhile. I know that *doamna* Cretulescu lived at number 27 . . ."

"She died in an air raid," interrupted the old man, "at the time her house was demolished. . . ."

Stefan felt suddenly empty, as though his life had fled from him, slipped outside his body, and yet without apparent strain, he smiled. "I thought this might be so," he said. "I knew her niece, too—*domnisoara* Sideri. . . ."

"She wasn't here. She was abroad. I heard that she returned after it happened, but I haven't seen her." Then he bowed his head slightly and closed the door.

Stefan returned, disturbed, to stand in front of the scaffold. She's at Zinca, he said to himself with a sigh of relief. . . . *You'll search for me on your knees to the ends of the earth and you won't find me!* . . . And yet she had come back to Romania and was now hidden away at Zinca. . . .

He had not been able to sleep that night at Bussaco. Smoking cigarette after cigarette, he had listened to the orchestra playing in the ballroom until morning. At daybreak he had heard a car departing slowly, blowing its horn, and it had startled him. Then, after he had taken a bath and shaved, he lifted the receiver and asked for Ileana's room. He had glanced at his watch while he waited. Nine-thirty—she's awake, he had said to himself. After a moment someone at the desk had responded, "*Domnisoara* Sideri asked not to be disturbed before lunch." He took a walk in the park, but by eleven he could stay away no longer and he went up to her room, only to find the door locked. His repeated knocking failed to rouse her. Returning to the desk, he questioned the clerk, who told him that Ileana had left by cab very early in the morning. He had gone back to Lisbon that night. When he went to the Legation the next day, they informed him that Ileana was with friends in Madrid and was not expected back for several days. A week passed and she still had not returned, and he had heard nothing from her. At that point he had suddenly made up his mind to take a plane for Bucharest.

"She's hiding at Zinca," he kept reminding himself. Since that day was Sunday, the canteen at the Ministry was closed and he had to eat at a restaurant. It seemed to him that the day would never come to an end. He thought that time would not allow itself to be broken down but that he would be compelled to endure it minute by minute, one slow second after another.

"And I'm from near Botosani," the guard added. "Everything's in ruins there, too. . . ."

Stefan blinked again rapidly and repeatedly in order to soothe his eyes, which felt swollen and bloodshot from the heat.

"Then maybe you know how to get to Zinca," he suggested.

"Zinca?" the guard repeated. "Never heard of it. Where is it?"

"I don't know exactly. I was told it might be in the district of Botosani."

In reality no one had told him anything. He had discovered this in the *Geographic Dictionary*. Once he had left Mihai Duma, he began to feel sorry that he had sought him out. Better to have consulted a gazetteer, he kept telling himself, squeezing the wet handkerchief in his hand. It was very warm and his forehead and palms were perspiring. He had had some difficulty locating Duma, who was working then at the Ministry of Internal Affairs. When Stefan had telephoned him, Duma had responded with unexpected affability and arranged immediately to meet him in front of the Ministry the next day. As Stefan approached he saw that Duma was in conversation with a gray-haired man, tall and stalwart, who listened impassively, a cigarette in the corner of his mouth. Duma greeted Stefan with a smile.

"I'd like you to meet my superior, *domnul* Protopopescu," he said.

The man shook Stefan's hand with an excess of warmth. For a few moments his face, cold and unresponsive, seemed illumined by a rush of sympathy. "I'll leave you," he said quickly. "I know that you have something to discuss. . . . Very happy to have met you," he added, gripping Stefan's hand again. "I've heard a lot about you."

As soon as he had gone Stefan began to feel embarrassed. "I came to ask you several things. . . ." He stopped and looked around him. Workers kept coming out of the Ministry. "Wouldn't you like to walk a few steps with me?" he proposed.

They set off slowly in the direction of the boulevard. Although it was scarcely the beginning of May, the noon heat was as intense as that of midsummer.

"I came to ask you about Ileana—*domnisoara* Sideri," he began. "I haven't seen her since I was in Portugal. I'd like to know what's become of her. . . ."

Duma turned to look at Stefan and his face was empty of expression, as though he expected the other to add something that would clarify his statement.

"I thought that you were better informed than we," he said after a moment. "She didn't come back to the Legation. She sent her resignation from Madrid and after that she vanished. I thought she'd gone to America, but it seems that she wasn't able to leave. I thought that you . . ."

"No, I didn't know anything about her. I was at the front for a long time. . . . It's awfully hot," he said suddenly and he stopped, pulled out his handkerchief, wiped his forehead.

"There was much talk about *domnisoara* Sideri," continued Duma. "Now I can tell you that I was in a rather awkward position. She was the secretary for my service. You can imagine. . . . Allusions were made to you too," he added without looking up. "There were some who even wondered . . . Anyway all this isn't important. . . . Things have changed now." He turned his head and smiled at Stefan.

"Yes, I understand," Stefan acquiesced, feeling awkward. "Still I thought you'd know something about her. I'd like to find her. I'd be very pleased if I could meet her again. . . ." He stopped again abruptly and held out his hand, forcing a smile. "Once more, please excuse me," he said, and he walked away with rapid strides, his damp handkerchief in his hand.

Several days after that he had consulted the *Geographic Dictionary*. Under the name of Zinca nineteen villages and estates were listed, scattered all over the country. In Moldavia alone there were seven, and two of these were in the district of Botosani. One was in the valley of the Siret. She's here, he told himself, she's hidden herself here.

"There are two villages called Zinca," Stefan added. "But I was told that the village I'm looking for may be in the valley of the Siret."

The guard frowned slightly, struggling to remember. "It could be, but I haven't heard of it."

Stefan felt disconcerted, but he smiled and turned again to look across the plain, blinking frequently. The clouds of dust continued to creep over the ground. Suddenly the door of the warehouse burst open and the stationmaster came out hastily, trying to put on his tunic as he ran. "It's coming!" he cried. "It's coming!"

The passengers on the waiting train thronged to the windows again to watch the Red Cross express enter the station. It was so long that it seemed endless.

449

There was a hospital car and two sleeping cars, in addition to numerous freight cars carrying armed guards. A group of doctors and nurses got off hurriedly and headed toward the office of the stationmaster, but an officer ran after them and stopped them.

"Give us clearance immediately!" he said to the stationmaster. "We have to get to Jassy. The next train will stop here. It's coming a half hour behind us."

"I got the order," answered the stationmaster. "The people from the other villages found out that you were coming, too." He pointed to the plain, where the clouds of dust, still far away, were creeping slowly toward them. Several guards began to climb down from the freight cars, stamping their feet in order to remove the stiffness from their legs.

It was then that Stefan recognized the man in the dark sunglasses and the white surplice, belted at the waist, who was walking the length of the hospital car. Raising his arm, Bursuc beckoned to him.

"Where you going?" he asked.

"To Botosani. I'm looking for the village of Zinca."

Bursuc frowned at him through his sunglasses.

"I want to remake my life there, at Zinca. . . ." Stefan broke off suddenly and smiled in confusion.

"One life? Why bother?" queried Bursuc, shrugging his shoulders. He looked around to see if anyone was listening to him, then he added in a lower tone, "Life be damned! God damn this———life!"

"I've decided to remake my life," Stefan began again with sudden fervor in his voice. "I'm going to Zinca. There's a girl there. I love her. . . ."

"Listen to me," Bursuc interrupted, placing a hand on Stefan's shoulder. "I like your sincerity. You ought to come with us and see how *we* remake lives!" Taking Stefan's hand he led him to the flat cars that were covered with canvas. "Look. These are Red Cross pickup trucks. We're going to Jassy and from there we'll be going with a caravan through the villages. The people are dying of hunger by the thousands. Haven't you heard?"

"I . . ." began Stefan, embarrassed.

"I know. You told me just now that you want to remake your life. Who do you think cares anything about that?" He was almost scowling as he stared at Stefan. "When are you going to decide to join the human race? To become a Christian like everyone else?"

"I am a Christian," responded Stefan. "I was born a Christian . . ."

"Then look around you. What do you see? What do you comprehend?"

"Drought," began Stefan. "Disaster . . ."

"It's the end of the world, *domnule consilier*! The end of the world is coming. Repent! Your world is breathing it's last. A new world is beginning under the sign of holy justice. Christ, our Savior . . ."

He realized then that a number of the passengers were listening to him

450

from the windows and the platform. He turned toward them suddenly and lifted his arm high in the air. "Repent!" he shouted. "Repent, all of you! Confess your sins! The end of the world is at hand. It will rain fire and brimstone. . . ."

Then he seized Stefan by the arm and pulled him quickly back toward the sleeping car. "Come over here," he whispered. "All those louts are listening to us."

Raising his hand to shade his head from the sun, Stefan inquired, "Do you have any water? I'm awfully thirsty."

"We have water, we have everything. Come with us. We'll take you along. . . . Go get your luggage."

"I've nothing but a briefcase."

"Run and get it! I'll wait for you here."

The sleeping car was far from luxurious, almost shabby, having been built before the war for Boy Scout expeditions. They entered the compartment, and Bursuc closed the door behind him. He removed his surplice, revealing his short pants and sleeveless shirt, open at the throat. After the train started he filled a cracked enamel basin with water and buried his face in it.

"On account of the beard," he said. "It's grown too long and it holds the heat. I'd like to shave it off, but now that I've decided to become a bishop it's impossible to be without a beard."

He plunged his arms into the water up to his elbows and held them there.

"I've made up my mind," he continued, musing. "There's drought and famine. A bishop can do a lot. We must comfort them, the poor people. . . ."

He lifted his arms from the basin and rested them on his lap without drying them. "Poor souls," he continued, his voice dropping. "Worms! We crawl on the earth, but because we have in our minds the image of God, we believe we're his children. We're worms, that's what we are. Children of God! The devil! We're dying of starvation like earthworms in the sun."

"We also have a soul . . ." began Stefan timidly.

"Let me explain to you this matter of a soul," interrupted Bursuc. "You were at the front in Russia. You killed men. You're hands are stained with blood . . ."

"I don't know if I killed anyone," broke in Stefan, distressed.

"Don't worry, you killed them! You all killed, you all have bloody hands. Mine are the only clean hands. I didn't kill anyone. I have clean hands." He held them out to Stefan. They were still wet. "Because it's written in the Holy Book, 'You have washed me with hyssop and all my sins you have . . .' You have what?" he said, frowning. " 'You have washed them away?' No, I don't think that's it. I've forgotten. I used to know the Holy Scripture very well. I got all the prizes at the seminary and graduated *magna cum laude* with a degree in theology. But it's been a long time since then. I've

451

forgotten the dead letter. Only the spirit of the Scripture remains, but the spirit's what counts! We're in a revolution. . . . So, as I said, 'You have washed me with hyssop and all my sins you have . . .' You have cleansed? Anyway, that's the idea—that God has cleansed me from sin. I'm as pure as a newborn babe. I have a right to speak about the soul."

They approached a station and the train slackened its speed as it passed an open grove of scattered trees stripped of leaves.

"The peasants picked them to give to their cattle," Bursuc explained, becoming pensive again. "They just keep the flowers for themselves. They eat locust flowers and die like flies. . . ."

The people had gathered around the station, forming silent compact clusters. Some crouched by the roadside dozing, but most of them huddled together in the shade of the walls. When the train passed all heads were raised and the groups seemed to waken for a moment, to ripple with movement. Several people stood up and went toward the station, but guards were posted at the entrances and on the platforms.

"Understand?" continued Bursuc. "They've heard that there's still cornmeal in Oltenia, so they take knapsacks on their backs and grab a ride on the trains going down to Bucharest. They scramble up on the roofs, they cling to each other on the steps, and they die along the way. They fall beside the railroad tracks, and if the cars don't run over them, they die of starvation. It would be better to order them to be shot, better for a few dozen to die shot by the guards than for thousands to die on the road. . . ."

He sat staring blankly out the window for some time. The train seemed to be slowing down again. As far as the eye could see, the rolling plain extended, burned by the heat to a pale, faded yellow. Once in a while the outlines of deep ravines could be glimpsed, their dry stream beds filled with nothing but rocks.

"And all these things are the fault of you and others like you," Bursuc spoke again suddenly. "You're hands are full of blood and you dare to speak of the soul! It's the punishment of God. . . . Why don't you say something?" he demanded, looking into Stefan's eyes.

Stefan shrugged his shoulders and smiled awkwardly.

"Don't smile," scolded Bursuc. "Answer me—why are you silent? You at least realize it's your fault all this has happened?" He pointed to the calcined plains.

"Yes. . . . You're right."

"You don't need to admit that I'm right immediately. Defend yourself. Try to struggle against me—against God! Be a man! Don't accept everything I say with a bowed head. Maybe I just want to test you, to tempt you. Remember how the Devil tempted the Savior? He raised him to the top of the mountain and said to him, 'Command these stones to become bread and I'll listen to you.' I don't know if he said that exactly, but that's the gist of it. But

452

Jesus answered, 'Man does not live by bread alone. . . .' Defend yourself, too, as he did! Don't let yourself be tempted."

"I try not to, but I really believe you're right. It *is* my fault. . ."

"How could it be your fault?" Bursuc interrupted violently, on the point of shouting. "How could you modify the solar system? Because what else is a drought but a solar phenomenon? So, then! How could it be your fault, man's fault? What can a poor worm do, flung onto an infinitesimal point of the solar system? Defend yourself, because I'm testing you!" He changed his tone and smiled. "I want to test you. I want to see if you, can still save yourself. . . . Who's knocking, *domnule?*" He paused and turned to the door, signaling to Stefan to be quiet.

"Dr. Trandafir. Come have some coffee with us. . . ."

"I'm busy," replied Bursuc sternly. "I'm in conference—a pastoral conference. I can't come." He turned back to Stefan. "Now, where were we? . . . Oh, yes, I was testing you, talking about Jesus and Satan. . . . Do you think he was listening at the door?" he whispered. "They're capable of it. But I'm smarter than they are. I know how to get along with them." Preoccupied, lost in thought, he sat for some time gazing out the window.

"All the same I suppose I ought to go with them," he said presently. He seemed to be speaking to himself. "There's a girl I like, a nurse. We call her *Randunica.** I tease her all the time—and I tempt her, too. . . . I'd better go," he added, making up his mind abruptly.

He put on his robe and began to straighten his beard, smoothing it with both hands. "I can't take you along. I'm afraid it might be difficult for you. Some are American sympathizers, others are Security agents. I alone know how to deal with them and what to say, because I'm 'as wise as a serpent and as innocent as a dove.'"

That night Stefan slept at Jassy in an impoverished and dismal hotel not far from the station. The train, with its carloads of grain and medicines, continued its journey to the north. Only the caravan of trucks, which was to set out the next day for the adjacent district, stopped at Jassy. A half hour after their arrival at the hotel, Bursuc disappeared. He had been invited, with a group of doctors, to dine with the Red Cross representative.

The night was intensely hot and dry. An invisible haze of dust hovered in the motionless air and forced its way into everything, creeping slowly under the eyelids, sticking to the skin, drying the mouth, lodging in the throat. Dense swarms of moths and other flying insects swirled around the street-

*The Swallow.

453

lamp, masking the light like a veil. For a little while they flung themselves
about, striking erratically against the hot, dirty glass, and then they fell to the
sidewalk, while others took their places. Drawn by the light, they advanced
solidly, continuously, out of the shadows, beating their fragile wings to the
point of exhaustion.

Stefan managed to locate a tavern where he was able to get a little dried
salted meat and a piece of cold *mamaliga*.* Flies were everywhere, and he
tried to drive them away while he ate the meager supper reluctantly, accompanying it with frequent sips from the bottle of warm, sour wine. He returned
to the hotel around midnight. It was hot in his room and there was an odor of
dust and creoline. For several minutes he stood before the window looking at
the street. A pharmacy was opposite the hotel and he labored to decipher the
name of the proprietor in the feeble light of the streetlamp. Then he remembered that Voinea had fled to Jassy with the entire subsidy for *The Students'
Progress*. At that time Voinea was a pharmacy student. . . .

Somewhat later he heard a knock at the door and when he turned to
open it he saw that Bursuc had already entered. The priest was sweating and
he wiped his face and beard repeatedly with a large brightly colored handkerchief.

"I drank too much," he said, dropping into a chair. "I wanted to have a
talk with you here, where there's no one to listen to us. . . ."

He pulled his surplice well above his knees and stretched out his bare legs
as far as possible, spreading them wide apart in order to let the air circulate
about them. "You know, you're in great spiritual danger. You said you'd set
out in search of a girl . . ."

"She's at Zinca," said Stefan, sitting down on the edge of the bed. "Her
name is Ileana . . ."

"I'm tempting you," Bursuc interrupted, opening a package of cigarettes
and selecting one. "Consider carefully what you do and what you say."

Stefan went to him and held out a lighted match. "I've loved her for ten
years." He spoke in a low voice, as if he were still afraid that someone else
might be listening. "I loved her, but I didn't want to admit it. I lied to her. I
lied to everyone—to her, to Ioana, I even lied to myself. But now I'm going to
find her. I believe that only she can save me. . . ."

"Consider carefully what you say!" cried Bursuc, threatening him with
the cigarette. "You mentioned salvation. You don't realize what you
said. . . ."

"When I meet her again I'll become another man. This girl was destined
for me and I didn't understand. I let her slip away from me. This was my sin.
Now I have to search for her. She told me this too—that I'd search for her to

*Cornmeal mush.

454

the end of the earth—and she told me I wouldn't find her again. But now I know where she is. She's hiding at Zinca."

Bursuc looked at him searchingly, with a slight frown. He was smoking with gusto. "Why are you silent?" he asked presently. "Speak up! Have courage! Have courage! Confess!"

"I was crazy," Stefan continued, bowing his head. "From the minute I met her I knew that she was my Bride, my destiny, but I didn't want to leave my home and run away with her into the world. I loved Ioana too. . . . I don't know how to explain it." he added anxiously.

"Be a man!" urged Bursuc. "Be bold!"

"I'd have liked to have had her with me all the time, especially when I was painting. I don't know how to explain it. . . . I'd have liked for us to remain there together, just the two of us, in the picture, although I didn't know how to paint . . . although that painting . . ."

"Viziru!" Bursuc broke in. "Don't hide behind words! Tell me the truth!"

"It's hard to explain," murmured Stefan, running his hand over his face. "That painting didn't even exist. It was only a canvas covered with all kinds of colors. But Ileana was in it, and her car, and many other things. . . . I don't know how to explain. . . ." He was silent, embarrassed, and raising his head, he smiled at Bursuc, who returned his gaze and frowned.

"Did you go to bed with her?" he demanded, his voice deepened and muffled by the smoke.

"Yes. This was my sin. I ought not to have loved her like that. She was destined for me in a different way. She was to be my Bride. I shouldn't have loved her like that."

"You went to bed with her," repeated Bursuc, brooding yet severe. "You loved her. And yet you slept with her the way you might have slept with a prostitute."

"Yes. This was my sin. I loved her—I longed for her—but I shouldn't have done that. If I'd had more self-control she'd be with me today, and I'd never have found out! I'd never have found out . . ." He passed his hand over his face again.

"What wouldn't you have found out?"

"I wouldn't have found out that she was unfaithful to me, that she had loved someone else even though she knew I loved her, and she knew that she loved me. Because she did love me! She did love me!" His voice was filled with exasperation.

"She went to bed with someone else?" Bursuc was suddenly bursting with laughter. "Well, what else can you expect? They're all bitches."

At that Stefan raised his head and regarded the priest, who silenced him with a gesture. "I'm tempting you!" he cried. "Keep that in mind. Don't weaken! Defend yourself! Defend yourself! Wrestle with me, wrestle with God!"

"Then, when I found that out, it seemed to kill my very soul," Stefan went on, agitated. "I thought that if she were destined for me, if she were my Bride, she couldn't have loved another after she realized she loved me. I thought she'd have to wait for me—that no matter what happened in her life, she'd have to wait for me. She would have to grow old along with me, even if it ruined her life, but she would not forget me, since I didn't forget her. . . ."

"You were crazy!" murmured Bursuc.

"It was my sin. And if I hadn't fallen into sin, I shouldn't have found out. First of all, I wronged her when we went to bed together. It was important to have faith, to hope—and to wait. I didn't have enough faith. She was like an icon to me, and she should have remained like that—beyond life, beyond time. I dreamed she'd always be that way—exalted, pure, undefiled, like an icon of the Holy Mother."

"How atrocious!" Bursuc exclaimed, squirming in his chair. "What impiety!"

"I wanted to know that *someone* could remain undefiled and inalterable on this earth, that *someone* could live outside of Time, living only for me, sacrificing her earthly life so that I could believe, so that I could be saved. . . ."

"The sin of pride has blinded you," muttered Bursuc. "You've lost your soul because of pride. . . ."

"But there was something else too!" cried Stefan, without restraint. "It wasn't just pride. I wanted to believe that *someone* could remain immaculate on this earth, that the Spirit does not always yield to the body the way it happens to us—the little people, the sinners. I loved the Spirit too much. Is this a sin? Philosophers are always talking about the transcendent. I thirsted for that word, for that thing, for everything that doesn't belong to our world even though it's found here among us. . . . For a long time," he added, lowering his voice again, "I wanted to love the way the saints love. . . ."

"You're lost," Bursuc whispered. "The sin of pride has condemned you. . . ."

His head bowed, Stefan sat staring before him. "I want to do penance," he said in a faint voice. "If you believe in God, forgive my transgressions." Then, more firmly, "Absolve me, Father."

Bursuc sleepily brushed away a moth that kept circling around his head. "I've drunk too much," he said presently. "I'm not fit. . . . But I'll find you a simple country priest and he'll give you absolution. . . ."

Stefan seemed preoccupied and he did not look at Bursuc.

"I'll take you with me to Zinca!" the priest exclaimed, struggling to get up from the chair and shaking his legs in order to arrange his surplice. "And if this girl is waiting for you, I'll unite you in the sight of God. I'll unite you with my own hand, because I have the authority!"

456

"If you have the authority and if you believe in God . . ." Stefan began, becoming suddenly animated. "If you truly believe in God . . ."

"What I believe's another story," interrupted Bursuc. "But I wish you well. You're in great spiritual danger." He started heavily toward the door. On the threshold he turned his head once more and looked at Stefan, who was still sitting on the edge of the bed.

"You've made me terribly sad," murmured Bursuc. "You've made me sorrowful unto death. . . ."

They left at daybreak the next day, riding in a car near the head of the caravan.

"Speak softly," whispered Bursuc. "Very likely the driver is a Security agent and, intentionally or unintentionally, he hears everything. Besides, I'm going to take a little nap," he added, clapping his hand over his mouth to hide a yawn. "I feel very tired."

The sun was rising in the pale haze of the sky as they left the city, and they found themselves again surrounded by the burned and broken, drought-ridden earth. Once in awhile they passed an old tree with its leaves gone and its trunk stripped of bark. The car in front of them, leading the caravan, raised so much dust that it soon obscured their vision. It stood motionless in the air, like a fine-meshed endless net hanging from invisible supports extending from one side of the highway to the other. Stefan pressed his handkerchief to his mouth and closed his eyes in a fruitless attempt to protect himself. Bursuc had scarcely fallen asleep when he began to cough, and he woke up startled.

"Drive slower!" he cried, "or this dust will be the death of us."

"What's the difference?" the driver said without turning around. "It'll be half an hour before it settles down again."

"God damn this whole business!" muttered Bursuc, looking for his handkerchief.

At intervals they saw people sitting on the ground along the edge of the road, shielding their eyes with their hands. They were in small groups, two or three together, with their empty bags slung over their shoulders. Now and then the car passed a man with a cow on a rope. The poor creatures were as thin as skeletons and knelt beside their owners, resting their muzzles in the dust.

"God damn this business!" Bursuc muttered again. "They'll all die of famine. . . ." He faced Stefan abruptly. "Why are you silent, *domnule consilier*? Say something! Talk. Tell me about love and ideals. Tell me about the village of your dreams!"

"I don't know anything about it," confessed Stefan, looking straight

457

ahead over the driver's shoulder. "I don't even know exactly where it's located. . . . Ileana told me that they had a large old cellar there," he added, musing. "I thought about that cellar. It's strange, I didn't think about her—about Ileana. I thought about that cellar at Zinca."

"You're not very entertaining," Bursuc interrupted, yawning again. "I thought you were going to tell me something more dramatic and tender." He was silent a moment and melancholy, and he continued with a shake of his head, "I'm in a mood to recall things that are sad and tender—memories of the village of my childhood. . . . I knew a song once. How the devil does it go? 'In the village where I was born. . . .'" He began to hum, his head nodding a constant beat, his eyes almost closed. Then the car came to an abrupt halt, jerking him upright. A guard approached them.

"Skip this village," he said. "The relief supplies have already been distributed here."

"I know, I know!" snapped the driver, nettled, and he started the vehicle again. He saw some peasants assembled at the edge of the village, and he began to blow the horn, increasing the speed of the car. They watched it go by in the curtain of dust, without hope, and yet one after another they raised their caps politely.

"Beggars!" Bursuc mumbled through the handkerchief that he held to his mouth. "Don't you have anything to say?" He turned and glowered at Stefan. But he was still sleepy and he tried again to doze, his head resting on the back of the seat. It was not long before he was snoring. Stefan drew aside the pane of glass that separated him from the driver and questioned the man in a whisper. "Do you know a village called Zinca in the Botosani district?"

"I know it," was the answer, and the driver did not take his eyes from the road ahead. "It's on our way. We'll be going there . . ."

"What did you say, *domnule?*" cried Bursuc, waking up. "What were you talking about?"

"I asked him where we were going. He told me that . . ."

"I see." Bursuc shook his head sleepily. "And you woke me up for that. . . ."

Stefan roused himself an hour later, realizing that the car had stopped. After a few minutes the ambulance van arrived, followed at short intervals by the other cars and trucks. The caravan regrouped at the outskirts of the village, where at a distance of twenty meters through the dust the teeming mass of the peasants could be seen, held in restraint by several guards. The mayor had stepped up to the ambulance and was talking with the doctors.

Bursuc rubbed his eyes for a long time. Then he got out of the car and strode staunchly toward the villagers. "Repent!" he shouted to them as he approached, lifting his arm high in the air. At once there was silence.

"Repent!" he cried again, and walked faster. "This is the punishment of God for your sins. God has turned his face away from you. The Devil's agents will come and tell you one thing or another, tempting you too to believe that God doesn't exist. But don't you believe them! God does exist! Listen to me! God exists. . . ."

One of the doctors hastened to him. "This is not the time, Father. Speak to the people after the supplies are distributed. . . ."

Bursuc turned his head and looked furiously at the man, but he noticed Dr. Trandafir standing nearby. He shrugged and returned slowly and wearily to the caravan, dragging Stefan along with him by the arm. They circled the trucks and made for the shade of a locust which still retained some of its fragile yellow leaves. There was a smell of dust and gasoline everywhere.

"Do you have a cigarette?" asked Bursuc. "I forgot and left my pack in the car." The combination of dust and smoke soon choked him and he began to cough and spit. "It's a shame," he said softly as if to himself. "I was inspired. I'd have spoken to those people from the depths of my soul. I'd have told them about God and the incomprehensible ways of truth. Because, Viziru, you can take it from me, God does exist. But as for us, we men of the Church, we've become evil and we don't know him anymore. Listen carefully and I'll tell you a secret. For a long time I believed like everyone else that God doesn't exist, that he's an invention of the priests. I went to the seminary. How the devil could I believe anything else? I had eyes to see and a mind to understand. I understood from the seminary that all this story about God and Jesus Christ was invented. I even had evidence. When I went to the services I told myself mentally, 'I affirm loud and clear that all these are just so many invented stories. I affirm that God does not exist, and that Jesus Christ was not born of a virgin. I affirm it! But if I should be mistaken, let him give me a *sign*, send a thunderbolt out of the blue, or let an icon move by itself! Let me feel an unseen hand on my cheek—anything!' Please believe me, nothing ever happened. And so I had proof that God did not exist." He stopped suddenly, spat again, and stood with his eyes fixed on the group of peasants.

"And what then?" asked Stefan timidly. "What happened then?"

"I was given more powerful proofs that God does exist," Bursuc resumed in a hoarse voice. "Real proofs, not the stupidities that priests and theologians speak of. I'll tell you about them. Your soul is troubled. You need faith. . . ." He interrupted himself again and flung the cigarette as far as he could in the dust. Dr. Trandafir was hurrying in his direction, calling to him.

"Father, if you like you may come and talk to the people now."

"I'm not in the mood. . . . I'm no longer inspired. You should have let me speak then, when God willed it, not when you doctors deign to give me permission."

"Then let's go," the doctor said.

In the car Stefan waited for a little while and finally inquired, "What sort of proofs?"

Puzzled, Bursuc turned and looked at him.

"I asked you what sort of proofs you had about the existence of God?"

"I'll tell you about them, but not here. These are very secret things." He looked at Stefan again searchingly, with an enigmatic smile on his lips. Then he exclaimed with an air of satisfaction, "Ah, yes! I see. You're trying to tempt me! You want to find out the proofs that are the foundation of my faith. You're sitting in my place. You're trying to test me, *me*, the way I tested you. . . . But I know how to defend myself, Viziru. I'm prepared. The Devil can't prevail over me! I can sense him from afar. I feel him coming to tempt me and I shout, 'Get thee behind me, Satan!'"

The next day they arrived at Zinca just at sunset. An hour earlier the car in which Bursuc and Stefan were riding had left the caravan and set out alone toward the valley of the Siret. As they drew near they saw that some people had gathered to wait for them where the road entered the village. Bursuc shouted to the driver to stop and he jumped out of the car.

"Who're you waiting for?" he demanded.

For a few moments they gazed at him timidly and in silence. "Our children are dying," a woman murmured at last, but she found it difficult to speak, for she had lost almost all her teeth. Her face was sallow and her cheekbones seemed to pierce her skin. "Our cattle have perished too," she added, and appeared to be trying to smile. Her face wrinkled and in some incomprehensible fashion it lighted up for an instant.

"The Americans . . ." someone said then. "We heard that they're coming through the villages and bringing meal. . . ."

Bursuc glanced around the group and hesitated, perplexed. "Where's your priest?" he asked finally.

"He's dying. He's an old man."

"God has punished you!" cried Bursuc, suddenly becoming animated. "God has struck you for your sins. Repent! You are too sinful! Your hands are stained with blood!"

Lacking the courage to look at him the people knelt quietly, one by one.

"How do you expect God to forgive you if you don't repent?" Bursuc exclaimed, growing more impassioned. "This drought is from God. Some people say that it's a solar phenomenon, as though the sun isn't made by God himself! Doesn't the sun also obey God?"

460

Stefan got out of the car, and detouring around the group of kneeling peasants, he headed for the village. He walked rapidly, his mouth clamped shut in a grim line, looking only straight in front of him. He stopped before the first house and called out, but the only response was the unusually mild, faint barking of a dog that he could not see. He waited a moment and then went to the next dwelling and entered the courtyard.

"Is anyone at home?" he cried.

Presently a little girl appeared at the door. She had very blond hair and large frightened eyes set very deep in her face. She stared at Stefan without a word.

"Hello," he said. "Is there a manor house here at Zinca? Have you heard about two old ladies who have a big house?"

The child continued to stare at him. She seemed to be speechless with fright.

"Some old ladies and a young one, Ileana?" Stefan asked again. "Ileana Sideri? A beautiful young lady with tanned skin and black hair who lived abroad for a long time?" He stopped abruptly and took a step toward the girl. "Do you hear me?" he asked gently. "Do you understand what I'm saying?"

She nodded but retreated inside the doorway fearfully.

"Have you heard of an elderly lady, Alice Cretulescu, and a young one, Ileana Sideri? And do you know of a manor house that has a deep old cellar?"

The little girl nodded her head again and stretched out her arm, pointing through the village. "It's over there," she murmured. Her mouth was dry and sallow, and her single tooth had grown inordinately large.

It seemed to Stefan that the blood suddenly left his heart. He took out his billfold quickly and gave her several banknotes, and leaving the courtyard, he began to run. He had been praying mentally for a long time without realizing what he was doing, mechanically repeating fragments of prayers heard in childhood. It surprised him to find that he still remembered them. The voices of the dogs, whose barking was so faint because they were dying, still reached his ears now and then. He ran on through the village and on the other side he encountered a man sitting with his back against a fence. He looked at Stefan indifferently, as though he did not see him.

"Is it much farther to the manor house?" inquired Stefan.

"It's there," the man replied, raising his arm and pointing. "But there's no one there anymore. The people burned it. . . ." He stood up painfully, clinging to the fence for support, and pointed again. Not far away a few broken walls could be seen among the dead trees that surrounded them.

"Are you from this village?" demanded Stefan. "Do you know *duduca* Ileana?"

The man smiled and nodded. "I know her. She's not been here for a long, long time. She hasn't found out yet about the disaster."

His face white, Stefan gazed at the man. Then he thanked him and went on, but the man set off after him with long strides that he could manage only with great effort.

"How long has it been since you saw Ileana?" Stefan asked him, turning his head.

The man stopped a moment to catch his breath. "A long time," he said. "Before the war. I heard that she went overseas."

They walked sidy by side now without speaking. The sun had gone down long before, but the searing heat still radiated from the cracked and dusty earth. No sound of a living thing could be heard. Even the chirping of the crickets was stilled.

"I heard that the Americans are coming to bring us meal," said the man. "Can it be true?"

Without answering, Stefan began to walk faster, and soon the other was left behind. But the man followed obstinately and in silence. When Stefan reached the entrance to the manor he stopped and looked around. The fence had been torn down long since. There was nothing left of it but the large gate with its two brick pillars, which now showed signs of crumbling. The park had been devastated. The trees which had not been burned had been savagely and recklessly cut. Their thick dried trunks could still be seen with roots emerging from the ground, like serpents twisting around each other. Only a few leafless locusts were left standing, and two pines that were so scorched by the drought that they had the appearance of having been ravaged by fire. It was still possible to distinguish vestiges of flower beds and graveled paths and beyond these stood the high burnt walls with their gaping windows.

Stefan wiped his face with his handkerchief and went through the gate. The man from the village rejoined him. "They set fire to it that winter when it was rumored that the lands were to be divided up," he said quietly. "They divided the land but they didn't know what to do with the boyars' houses. They plundered them and afterward set fire to them."

He followed a step behind Stefan, watching him as he passed by the walls blackened with smoke and stopped in front of the windows. The roof had been completely burned and the rooms were buried under piles of debris. Weeds had been growing among the bricks and in the walls, but they had died long before, dried by the drought.

"There was a large, deep cellar," Stefan said, turning suddenly to look at his companion.

"The people walled it up last summer after they buried Marina, because it was her last wish that they should wall up the cellar. She wasn't in her right mind, poor woman, after *duduca* Alisa died. She kept expecting someone else to come after that. She expected someone even after they burned the houses and divided the estate. She said that surely someone would come. . . ."

"She expected her."

"She said that the Major had a son and that one day he would come. But she just imagined this—she wasn't in her right mind."

462

A horn sounded just then, and they turned their heads simultaneously. The car was approaching them with some difficulty, because the surface of the road was broken and full of ruts. Annoyed, Bursuc beckoned to Stefan, calling to him to hurry.

"Where've you been, *domnule?*"

"She isn't here," said Stefan. "No one's here now."

"Too bad you didn't stay to listen to me preach to them," continued Bursuc, climbing out of the car. "You would have heard the word of God. I was inspired! People wept as they listened, and they repented. I told them about the end of the world. I explained about the Apocalypse. . . . Too bad you weren't there," he added, searching in his pockets and pulling out his package of cigarettes.

"I thought she'd be here." Stefan spoke very softly, as if to himself. "Now I don't know where to look. . . ."

"We have to go to the priest. He's dying," Bursuc went on. "Then I must telephone to Jassy. . . ."

"I don't know where to look for her now," interrupted Stefan. "They've walled up the cellar too." He put his hand to his forehead.

Bursuc tossed his cigarette far from him into the dry brambles, and seizing Stefan's arm, he dragged him back toward the ruins. "If you have the nerve and if you're a man, come with me and curse!" he whispered. "Curse, *domnule consilier*! Raise your fist to heaven and curse! You have something to curse about. Be a man! Defy God and raise your hand against him. Do something! Why are you standing there like a disconsolate female?" he cried, suddenly lifting his voice, exasperated. "Fight heroically! Call the Devil to your aid and wrestle with God! *Do something!*"

Stefan looked at him absently, unheeding.

"You see? You don't have the nerve!" Bursuc whispered, smiling slyly. "You see? You're not a man! You're neither hot nor cold. You're just lukewarm and wishy-washy, and God will spew you out of his mouth in disgust. If only you had the courage to rebel against him and curse him! Then I could pray for you. Why are you silent?" he asked impatiently, raising his voice again. "Say something! Shout! Swear! Pick up a stone and hurl it at God! *Do something!*"

This harangue caused Bursuc to choke and he began to cough. Holding his hand over his mouth he coughed, and then he spat repeatedly and swore through his teeth. In front of him, a step away, Stefan watched with embarrassment. It began to grow dark. At last Bursuc's coughing subsided and he wiped his beard wearily with his handkerchief.

"I wanted to test you," he whispered hoarsely. "I wanted to see if you still have faith. Now let's go to the priest. He's on his deathbed, but we may find him still alive. . . ."

5

BIBICESCU KNOCKED SEVERAL TIMES ON THE DOOR, BUT SEEING THAT NO ONE answered, he went to the window of Biris's room and began to tap nervously on the glass. In a few minutes, however, he lost patience and left, going in the direction of the tram station. He walked rapidly, turning often to look behind him. All at once he stopped, hesitated an instant, and then retraced his steps to the window. He began again to tap on it, louder this time, but when he felt *doamna* Porumbache's hand on his shoulder he sprang aside, pale with fear.

"You're wearing yourself out for nothing," she told him. "He sleeps hard. He's been pretty sick for the last few days. I'm afraid he spat blood again."

It was a hot evening at the end of September, and the dry air was full of dust. Bibicescu took out his handkerchief and began to wipe his face with a shaking hand. The other he held against his heart. *Doamna* Porumbache looked at him in surprise.

"What ails you? Why're you so scared?"

"I'd like to go in for a moment," he whispered. "I have something very important to tell him."

Doamna Porumbache turned to look at him again as she opened the door. "You say it's important? Because otherwise I couldn't bear to wake him up. . . ."

"It's important," reiterated Bibicescu, entering quickly.

Doamna Porumbache went down the hall and put her ear to the door of Biris's room. "He's fast asleep. It breaks my heart to have to get him up . . ." But she decided suddenly and put her hand on the knob. Opening the door, she went in, with Bibicescu directly behind her. On the little table beside the bed a small lamp was burning, its dim light veiled by a shawl that had been draped over the shade. Biris frowned in his sleep and his mouth was open. *Doamna* Porumbache laid her hand on his forehead. "Petrica," she said gently.

He awoke immediately. "I slept too long." He rubbed his eyes. "You shouldn't have let me. I won't be able to sleep all night." When he noticed Bibicescu he gazed at him in astonishment and glanced quickly at his aunt.

"He wanted to talk to you," she said. "It's something important..."

Bibicescu sat down on a chair beside the bed, continuing to hold his hand to his heart. "I don't know that it's so very important," he began, managing an ironic smile. "It's only a matter concerning my humble person. How could anyone be interested in me now that I'm nothing but a poor writer of genius?... You needn't laugh," he said to Biris, who still stared at him, unmoved. "You needn't say to yourself, 'Dan Bibicescu's out of his mind!' Listen—I'm persuaded now that I really do have genius. I've begun to write *The Return from Stalingrad*. When you read it you'll be convinced too. You'll see what Bibicescu can do. O'Neill, Claudel, Partenie? Zero! I tell you and I repeat it: Zero!... Too bad I'm not well," he added with a bitter smile. "But it's nothing. I won't die before I finish *The Return from Stalingrad*! It won't do them any good to sentence me to death. I'm not going to die..."

"What's happened?" inquired Biris.

"I'm being followed," Bibicescu said, making another attempt to smile. "Someone denounced me and they're going to arrest me. They searched my house last night and rummaged through all my drawers. Fortunately my manuscripts weren't there. I took the precaution of putting them in a safe place long ago. I had a presentiment that something was brewing. This morning I was called to Police Headquarters. They questioned me for three hours and they had nothing to hold me for, so they let me go, but I'm afraid they'll come back tonight."

He stopped and looked at Biris and then at *doamna* Porumbache, his right hand still held over his heart. The old woman sat on the edge of the bed and listened to him anxiously without speaking, troubled, her head bent.

"I came to ask you to do a big favor for me—please," resumed Bibicescu. "I came to beg protection and shelter from you for a few nights until *conu* Misu finds me a place to stay." Embarrassed, he was suddenly silent. Biris reached for his package of cigarettes on the night table.

"May I ask you please not to smoke," Bibicescu said. "I'm afraid I'll have another attack...."

Biris regarded him with a smile. "I don't know where I could hide you."

"I could sleep here," said Bibicescu, pointing to a spot under the window. "I'd be satisfied with a pallet—just for a few days until *conu* Misu finds me a safe refuge...."

"But the first thing the police will do will be to look for you at the homes of your friends and acquaintances. Haven't you thought of that?"

"Just for a few days," insisted Bibicescu, clenching his fist and pressing it to his heart. "I have a terrible urge to write. I want to take advantage of it. I need quiet..."

"Where do you think we could hide him?" Biris inquired of *doamna*

Porumbache, as if he had not heard. "I ought to speak to Stefan too. . . ."

"I see you'd rather not," Bibicescu broke in. "Never mind. I'll look elsewhere. *Conu* Misu will find me something."

Biris continued to regard *doamna* Porumbache questioningly. "Take him to Irina's tonight," he suggested. "They won't look for him there."

"I've a terrible urge to write," repeated Bibicescu. "I'll begin this very night. Do you think I'll find paper and ink there—and everything else that I need? I have an extraordinary scene in mind. It came to me just when I was leaving Police Headquarters and I have to write it down tonight. You see. . . ." He struggled to get up, placing his hand on the back of the chair as he stood behind it. "You see," he went on with a cryptic smile, "the action takes place in a blockhouse in Stalingrad. It's nighttime. Only a few people are on stage, and all at once a colonel appears. Parenthetically I can tell you that I was inspired by the life of Colonel Baleanu, but this occurs before the accident. He comes to inspect the advance positions . . ."

"I think you'd better hurry," interrupted Biris, speaking to *doamna* Porumbache, but Bibicescu continued.

"The sound of cannon fire is heard continuously. The colonel . . ." he broke off abruptly and sat down again in the chair, putting his hand to his heart.

"What's the matter? Are you sick?" *doamna* Porumbache asked.

"I'm afraid it's begun," whispered Bibicescu, his face white.

Provoked, Biris watched him and picked up the cigarettes again. "Listen," he said. "Try to cure yourself of that absurd idea that you have heart trouble. *Conu* Misu told me everything. I found out that you've seen I don't know how many doctors and they've made I don't know how many examinations and cardiograms. No one found anything. You're perfectly healthy."

Bibicescu listened with his head bent. He massaged the left side of his chest gently.

"Thank you," he said presently, smiling. "It's gone. There's nothing wrong now. *Conu* Misu will come sometime during the day tomorrow to bring me a pair of pajamas and some shirts. Tonight I'll sleep in my clothes. That is, to be more precise, I'll not sleep at all. I'll be working. It would be even better if I could get some paper from you. . . ."

In the courtyard *doamna* Porumbache motioned to Dan to wait and she went in alone. They were eating dinner. "Petrica sent me," she began, her voice low. "Could we get you to put up a gentleman for a few days? His name's Bibicescu. The police are after him. . . ."

"I know him," Irina declared, getting up from the table. "I know about him from Catalina."

Bibicescu appeared in the doorway then, as if he were on stage. He kissed *doamna* Ivascu's hand and Irina's with great formality, and shook hands with the teacher in a quick firm grasp.

"It is I, Dan Bibicescu." He smiled. "Actor and playwright, former director of the National Theater, and Undersecretary General of Theaters. You may have heard of me. . . ."

"I know about you from Catalina," ventured Irina.

"From Catalina . . ." The actor nodded. "Yes. Of course. I should have thought of that," he added, somewhat daunted. He sat down on a chair and looked around the table slowly and deliberately. One might have gathered that he was rehearsing a scene, trying to find the most effective way to interpret it.

"I've come to beg shelter from you for a few days," he said finally."You can imagine why. I'm being followed. My friend, Misu Weissmann, is occupied at this moment . . . But after all, perhaps it's wiser for me not to go into the details. I just want to say that I only wish to stay a few days. And I'll tell you a secret—I have a terrible urge to write. I want to start this very night. I've even brought some paper. I don't think I'll sleep at all—the whole night. If you'll tell me where I can retire . . ."

Doamna Ivascu was fascinated. She had been unable to take her eyes from his face during the entire time that he was speaking. "In the salon," she said. "We can let him sleep in the salon. We'll make a bed for him there."

"Thank you," said Bibicescu, bowing. "Thank you from the bottom of my heart, my dear lady. But if possible I'd prefer a more secluded room where I can concentrate. . . . I believe I shall write a masterpiece," he added, glancing around the table again.

Irina stepped out of the room discreetly and returned with a tray bearing a bowl of soup and some boiled vegetables. Bibicescu watched her arrange a place and then he began automatically to eat. The teacher poured him some wine and they all clinked glasses.

"If you'll permit me," the actor began, "I'll read you a few scenes at a time around this table in the evenings. I'm writing a piece for the theater. It's not my first, but this time I feel certain that I shall produce a masterpiece. If it were not a great secret I could also tell you what theater I'm writing it for. . . . But maybe I'll tell you later," he added after a moment, musing.

The next day Misu Weissman came in a taxi to *strada* Macelari. He alighted in haste, carrying a heavy valise.

"He didn't sleep here," *doamna* Porumbache told him. "We were afraid... Petrica was afraid the police would be looking for him here, since they're known to be friends. I didn't close my eyes all night. I kept expecting them to come and look for him."

"No one's coming," Weissman said. "I've taken care of that." He left the valise in the hall and went into Biris's room. "You have nothing to fear," he told him cheerfully, wiping his face with his handkerchief. "I've arranged things with the police. He won't be pursued."

"So I imagined," said Biris with a smile. "I thought this business of being followed was about as real as his heart ailment..."

"You're wrong," Weissman interrupted. "The matter of the heart condition is, of course, an obsession with him, but yesterday the police questioned him and he might have been arrested. It's always harder to get someone released after he's been arrested. He did very well to hide. It gave me time to arrange things. I can't tell you more, but his dossier is well-filled...."

He paused and sat down, putting his handkerchief to his face again and wiping it. "Someone informed against him," he went on. "Someday we'll find out who. Probably a co-worker—they're all jealous of him. It's not his fault if he's a genius. Everyone is trying to destroy him."

He pondered for a moment and then inquired with a sudden start, "How long can he stay at Irina's? Ask her for me to keep him at least a week. In the meantime I'll make arrangements to move him somewhere else. When you go to see him tell him I'll be by one evening at the beginning of next week. I won't go now because perhaps I'm being followed too. We must be cautious, at least for a few days. Eventually I'll take care of everything."

"I won't be able to go," Biris informed him. "I'm not feeling very well."

Weissman regarded him with consternation. "You'll have to spend some more time at Moroeni, in the sanatorium. You're getting thin again...."

Biris continued to smoke without comment.

"Send word to him by *doamna* Porumbache," resumed Misu. "Tell him to have patience, that everything will be all right. Tell him not to worry about his papers and manuscripts, because they're in safekeeping. Very soon things will be as he wishes. He'll know what I'm referring to." He smiled. "Just tell him this—don't worry about the papers. Tell him that as soon as he finishes the play to copy it and send it to me. Or no... it would be better to wait for me. I'll come at the beginning of next week and I'll get the play if he's finished it by then. I have a unique opportunity in the coming week—he knows what it is...."

Biris listened carefully, trying to make sense of Weissman's words. He wanted to say something but Misu cut him short.

"Do you ever see Viziru anymore?" His tone dropped slightly.

"I haven't seen him for some time, but I know where he lives now. I intend to pay him a visit when I feel better."

"Tell him to keep in touch with Bursuc," said Weissman, almost whispering. "It's quite important. We need Bursuc. Tell him to keep seeing him, to talk with him, to sound him out. . . . Tell him that it's a matter of vital importance. . . ."

Biris began to smile. "I don't understand any of this, but I'll tell him. I have no idea what this contact might be. . . ."

"Stefan saw him last summer in Moldavia," Weissman explained. "They spent a week together and have remained friends. It's very important. We need Bursuc. . . ."

Since the evening of his arrival Bibicescu had not stopped writing, and all day long no one entered his room. Irina brought him tea in the morning, and she knocked on his door without fail a quarter of an hour before each meal, giving him time to finish the page he had begun.

"A hundred and fifty pages!" cried Bibicescu one evening a week later as he seated himself at the table. "And you must realize that every page has been written and rewritten at least three times. That means 450 pages—an average of more than sixty a day. What do you say to that, *domnu'* Vasile?" He turned to the teacher.

"A second Nicolae Iorga," responded Gheorghe Vasile with respect. "I can scarcely wait to hear you read it to us so we can admire it too!"

With a mysterious smile Bibicescu began to eat, purposely postponing his response. He raised his head suddenly and looked around the table. "The first two acts are already completed. If you agree and if it won't inconvenience you, I'll read them to you this evening after dinner." He smiled and glanced at each of his hosts in turn, conveying the impression that he was improvising a scene whose lines he had forgotten in a sudden lapse of memory. Then, as though he had quite by chance caught sight of his plate, he started to eat again, slowly, intently. He sensed that he was the center of attention, and an extended period of silence ensued.

"Let me put Gheorghita to bed first," said Irina, leaving the table.

"A pity!" the teacher lamented. "I'd have liked for him to listen, too, to become accustomed while he's little to hearing masterpieces. He would have remembered later that at the age of six he listened to the famous play read by the author himself. . . . By the way, what title have you given it?"

"The Return from Stalingrad," declared Bibicescu slowly and with solemnity.

"What a beautiful title!" murmured *doamna* Ivascu. "It's too bad that it can't be performed, since the Russians are here among us."

"Don't worry," said the actor, smiling. "It *will* be performed—and very

469

soon! Of course, not here—it will be performed abroad." He stood up swiftly. "It'll be better if I read it in my room, in the salon. It has more atmosphere. I'll expect you in fifteen minutes!"

When they entered the salon they found him on his feet waiting for them, leaning against the desk, holding in his hand a sheaf of papers covered with writing. At a considerable distance, in the middle of the room, he had placed three chairs side by side. With a slight nod he issued a ceremonious invitation to them to be seated; then he stepped in front of the desk, laying the papers upon it. Thrusting his hand in his pocket, he began a little speech. He addressed them in a theatrical voice, speaking as if he were on a stage in front of a capacity audience.

"Ladies and gentlemen," he announced, "before reading to you the first scenes of my new play I should like to say a few words about the title, the content, and the meaning of this work. The title, *The Return from Stalingrad*, indicates at the outset that we have to do with a drama inspired by a historic event—or more precisely a recent historic catastrophe—quite recent in fact. Aside from the obvious interest aroused by the plot and, as you shall see directly, the importance of the myth that it brings to light, I call your attention to another fact. By utilizing a theme as recent as the seige of Stalingrad I will not be accused, as I have been so often, of being inspired by the unpublished works of another great playwright, nor of having plagiarized him in the sense that I used his manuscripts in my own works. . . . I'm referring to Partenie."

Irina crossed herself quickly and leaned toward *doamna* Ivascu, speaking into her ear. "He was once Ioana's fiancé," she whispered. "He loved her very much."

Bibicescu frowned and glared at her. "I shall ask you not to interrupt me," he said. "Any comments may be made in the pause which will follow this brief introduction. . . . Thus—to continue—I was accused of having been inspired in my last works by Partenie's manuscripts. The truth is exactly the contrary. Those manuscripts that I discovered through a series of extraordinary events and that are today in my possession—those manuscripts were revised and completed by me so that they could be performed. You will recall, I believe, *The Wake*, which I personally produced six years ago when I was director of the National Theater. I can tell you something I never before told anyone—more than half of that play was mine. . . ."

He paused for a long time and looked directly into the eyes of each of his listeners. Although *doamna* Ivascu was uncomfortable in her chair, with its straight back that forced her to sit upright, she did not have the courage to change her position.

"As you know," resumed Bibicescu, "Partenie died in 1939. Hence, it is not possible that he could have left in manuscript form a drama inspired by a historic catastrophe which occurred four years after his death. Consequently no one will be able to accuse me of having plagiarized Partenie's notes. . . . I should like now" he began again after a short pause and in a different tone, picking up the bundle of papers from the desk, ". . . I should like to say a few words to you about the significance of this play. I maintain that I have made a great discovery. I maintain that I have discovered a Romanian myth of the dead that has been hitherto unknown in Europe, or else has disappeared. You shall see directly what it is that constitutes this myth, but I am declaring at the outset that I shall be the first European writer who has the audacity to employ in an entirely unexpected and distinctive fashion a myth of the dead as the theme for a modern drama. . . ."

He stopped again and ran his hand absently through his hair. Then he circled the desk slowly, picked up the pile of written pages and began to go through them, apparently searching for something. Finally he shrugged and, suddenly making a decision, went again to the front of the desk and prepared to read. He cleared his throat, fixed his eyes on each member of his audience in turn, and began.

"This scene represents the ruins of a blockhouse in Stalingrad. As the curtain slowly rises we hear the sound of Soviet artillery. These explosions will continue at regular intervals throughout Act I. It will be understood that this incessant bombardment has lasted from the beginning of the seige and that it will not come to an end until the last resistance is crushed. It is like a *leitmotiv* in a symphony. . . ."

He interrupted himself and looked up from the manuscript. "You will recall the opening measures of Beethoven's Fifth Symphony, the Symphony of Destiny. . . ." He began to hum, beating time on the desk. "Ta-ta-ta-*ta*." He repeated the melody and struck four sharp blows with his fist. "Ta-ta-ta-*ta*. . . . Ta-ta-ta-*ta*. . . . 'Thus Fate knocks at the door!' This is the meaning of the musical motif with which the symphony begins. In the same way here, destiny is signified from the first by the uninterrupted series of explosions of the Soviet artillery. . . . On the stage it is dark," he started to read again, "except in one corner at the right of the scene where a feeble light is gleaming. A wounded man is trying to read a letter by the beam of a pocket flashlight. On the left a passageway, partially buried under rubble, can be distinguished. At the entrance to the passage . . ."

He stopped short, and stepping away from the desk, he began to explain the stage setting. "The passage starts here." He pointed to the left side of the salon. "The ruins, the debris, come to the middle of the stage . . ." and he took a few rapid steps toward the desk to indicate the extent of the destruction. "We are to imagine that a bomb has fallen not long before right on top of the passageway, breaking the arch and killing—probably—the whole group of men who had taken shelter there. In the darkness only the ruins and a few bodies can be seen. A minute after the raising of the curtain we hear the heavy, unsteady steps of a man who is making his way with difficulty through the shadowy piles of debris. . . ." Bibicescu began to step slowly around the desk, stamping his feet noisily, coughing and muttering.

"A few moments later a colonel appears, holding a flashlight in his right

471

hand," the actor read from the manuscript. "He is dressed in a threadbare field uniform. He goes slowly to the middle of the stage and looks around him. The colonel says: 'What's happened here?' "

Dissatisfied with the manner in which he had read this phrase, Bibicescu lifted his eyes from the manuscript, stepped away from the desk, and called out suddenly in a voice that sounded deep and strange, " 'What's happened here? Where are the men? Sergeant!' " Then he returned to the desk slowly, raised the manuscript to the level of his eyes and began to read again.

"The wounded man in the right corner of the stage continues to read his letter as if he has heard nothing. The colonel starts toward him. The colonel: 'What's happened? Where's the sergeant?' The soldier goes on reading. Approaching him, the colonel lays a hand on his shoulder. Colonel: 'Don't you hear me? Where are the others?' But the soldier reads on without raising his head. . . ."

Bibicescu interrupted his reading and addressed the three directly with an enigmatic smile. They remained seated, waiting quietly.

"As you will understand later the soldier was dead, as were all the others around him. The explosion had killed him just as he was reading a letter from his wife and he still did not realize he had died. He wanted above all to finish reading the letter. But, of course, his efforts were in vain because in dying he had gone out of Time and could no longer complete an action which required the passage of Time. Thus in a certain sense he was condemned forever to read the same letter without ever being able to reach the last word. . . . But naturally the colonel does not know the soldier is dead. He sees him there in front of him with the flashlight in one hand, the letter in the other. So he tries again to speak to him and he even loses his temper. The colonel:"—Bibicescu began to read again—" " 'Are you deaf? What's happened here?' "

There was the sound of vigorous knocking on the door. It opened suddenly, and Misu Weissman appeared with *doamna* Porumbache. Misu greeted everyone cordially and went in haste to Bibicescu. "Come quickly— the car can't wait very long."

From the moment he saw Weissman enter, Bibicescu made no attempt to hide his irritation at this interruption. He threw down the papers and, after circling the desk, seated himself in the chair. "What car?" he demanded crossly.

"Didn't Biris tell you I'd found a place for you and was coming to get you one evening this week?"

"No one told me anything."

Misu Weissman turned to *doamna* Porumbache with a questioning glance.

"He only told me to bring the suitcase with his underwear," she explained.

"I was just reading them the first scene from Act I," said Bibicescu. "I'm

472

sorry. If I'd known that I'd be interrupted I'd have postponed it until another time. . . ."

For an instant Misu Weissman seemed baffled, then he asked, "How long do you think it will take you to get ready?"

"Ready for what?" inquired Bibicescu, looking knowingly into the other man's eyes. "Ready for the adventure? For the great adventure?"

Weissman warned him with a sudden frown. "I've found lodging for you," he broke in precipitately. "But the car can't wait very long in front of the house. It belongs to a friend of mine, a man I trust. Only he asked me to hurry. . . ."

"If you good people are in agreement, I think it would be better if I stayed here," stated Bibicescu.

"It's a great honor for us to be hosts to a playwright of such calibre," began Gheorghe Vasile, taking a step in Weissman's direction.

"I like it here—I feel good," continued Bibicescu. "I feel like writing and no one disturbs me. And since my arrival—knock on wood—I haven't had a spell. . . ."

"Then I'll go and tell my friend not to wait any longer," Weissman said, heading for the door.

Bibicescu leaned his elbows on the desk and put his hands to his forehead in a gesture of despair.

"I'm sorry we interrupted you," apologized *doamna* Porumbache. "I didn't know. Petrica must have forgotten to tell me—he's been so sick. *Domnu'* Misu came with the car and asked me to come with him to show him the house and the entrance. He said we had to be careful. . . ."

"It's arranged," Misu said as he came back into the salon. "He'll be available another time. Go on, go on!" he said to Bibicescu. "I'll listen to you too for ten or fifteen minutes, but no longer because I'm expected elsewhere."

By way of reply Bibicescu took the manuscript, thrust it into a folder and opened a drawer of the desk. Misu Weissman hurried to him.

"If you don't want to read any more at least give me the manuscript to forward," he murmured. "I'll have an opportunity next week. . . . I sent you word through Biris," he added, his voice lower.

"I haven't finished. I've written only two acts and I have to copy it again after I've read it. It's only after reading it aloud that I can know if it's dramatic enough. I had just begun when you came in."

Misu Weissman took his arm and led him to the far end of the salon. *Doamna* Porumbache sat down, and all four watched from across the room without venturing to speak, waiting for the announcement that the performance would soon begin again.

"You've made a blunder," whispered Weissman, keeping his hand on the actor's arm and walking back and forth with him at the far end of the room. "I hope you haven't told them anything."

473

"No," replied Bibicescu absently. "They are very reliable people. They're not at all indiscreet."

"I think you realize it's an extremely grave situation," Misu continued in a tone that was hardly audible. "Don't forget that besides our own lives and liberty, the lives of many others are at stake as well."

They turned around then and came back to the group, who still waited and watched expectantly. Weissman was speaking in a loud, casual voice. "Then we're agreed. You'll hear from me one of these days. . . ."

Doamna Porumbache rose from her seat as they approached.

"Stay longer, *coana* Viorico," invited the teacher. "Perhaps he'll begin again and you can listen too. It's like being at the theater. . . ."

"I'll resume the reading tomorrow evening at the same time," Bibicescu announced solemnly.

They stood up, disappointed, as in silence Bibicescu started to return the chairs to their customary places beside the wall and around the sofa.

"It's Sunday," Biris said to himself. "He ought to be home." He stood for a time listening intently and then pressed the button again, letting the bell ring for a long while. This time he heard a little noise in the room and the sound of footsteps approaching the door.

"It's Biris!" he called out.

Stefan promptly opened the door and looked at him in surprise and apprehension, as if he feared bad news.

"I hope I'm not disturbing you," said Biris upon entering. When his glance fell on the easel that had been hastily covered with a soiled white cloth, he remained in the middle of the room, ill at ease.

"I was just getting ready to paint," Stefan explained. "I've taken up painting again. . . . But it's not the same as before," he added, embarrassed, a forced smile on his lips. "I can't accomplish what I did once."

He lifted the cloth from the easel and showed Biris the picture. His brush seemed to have roved at random over the large piece of white cardboard. On either side two shapeless masses of confused color—deep violet—could be distinguished, connected by a spiral figure that was sinuous and wavering. Biris examined the painting carefully.

"It's like a kind of labyrinth," he suggested.

"I can't do it anymore." Apparently Stefan had not heard Biris's comment. "Before, in my secret room, all I had to do was to take the brush in my hand and I felt I'd entered another universe, *a different place*. Now I paint haphazardly. What I mean is, I can't *go out of myself*. . . . I've lost it—I can't recover it. . . ."

"Yes. But all the same it resembles a labyrinth," resumed Biris, outlining with his finger the direction of the spiral. "If you were to add a line or two here..."

"I've tried all sorts of colors," Stefan continued, "but nothing else is right. I keep coming back to this same shade, as though, if I only knew how to use it, I'd find just the right tone. . . . I think you know that it's really Ileana I'm searching for," he added, avoiding Biris's eyes, and, suddenly chagrined, he sat down on a chair. "When I used to paint in my secret room it was enough for me simply to recall the car in order to bring back everything—the forest, the Night of St. John, and her—Ileana. . . . I don't know how to explain it."

"I think I understand," said Biris. "In a certain sense you, like Proust, are trying to recover a lost time..."

"No, it's not that. It was another kind of Time. I haven't lived it yet. It wasn't connected with my past. It was *something else*. It seemed to come from some other place. . . . But it doesn't matter, really." he added quickly, his voice unexpectedly bitter.

He stood up, covered the easel, and went to the window to look out at the street. The sky of that hazy afternoon in October was only partially covered with clouds, but rain threatened to start at any moment.

"I didn't want you to know it before, but I must tell you that I went to Zinca. She isn't there. Her house here on *strada* Batistei was destroyed in an air raid. I thought she was hiding at her estate at Zinca. She told me she liked to spend a good many months every year in the country. But she's not there. She never came back. I can't imagine where she might be. Duma doesn't know either. He assured me that she didn't stay in Portugal, and yet, even so, I know she's hiding somewhere, waiting for me. . . ." He turned his back to the window and smiled at Biris.

"I dream of her constantly. It's strange but sometimes she seems to be playing games with me. One night in a dream I met her on a stretch of lawn. When she saw me she turned and smiled—an ironic and provocative smile, almost sarcastic. 'I warned you that you'd search for me to the end of the earth and you wouldn't find me,' she said. 'And yet here you are, near me,' I replied and started toward her. Only a few meters separated us, but she took one step—only one—and she seemed to move dozens of meters beyond me. I ran after her, but a second step took her so far away I could scarcely see her. Then she tossed her head and looked at me once more with a pitying smile. It's strange, but at that moment in my dream I found myself thinking, I'll never be able to reach her. She's like Ileana Cosinzeana. . . ."* He was embarrassed again and stopped for a moment, returning to his chair.

"It's odd that Bursuc keeps saying this too. 'So you're always looking for Ileana Cosinzeana?' he asks me, and of course he starts to laugh."

*The unattainable princess in Romanian folktales.

475

"Then it's true," said Biris with a trace of bitterness in his voice. "*Conu* Misu was right. You've been seeing Bursuc. . . ."

"I was with him at Zinca. I didn't tell you, and I wonder why. . . . I've begun to acquire some peculiar habits," he commented, trying to grin. "I do a lot of things I don't understand. . . ."

"It was exactly about this that I came to speak to you," Biris interrupted. "*Conu* Misu has sent me with a message. He says you must keep in touch with Bursuc."

Stefan lifted his head and regarded Biris for a long time searchingly. His face gradually brightened. "I go to see him from time to time at the Patriarchate."

The first time he went he had met Bursuc on the street. The priest had just come out of the building, and since he was dressed in street clothes, Stefan almost failed to recognize him. "*Cherchez la femme, cherchez la femme!*" he had said. "They like me this way with my long beard. There's one here—Zoica. She's dying of love for me."

"*Conu* Misu says it's very important," continued Biris.

"We talk about Ileana. It's strange, but I felt a need to see Bursuc, to hear him talk to me about Ileana. . . ."

"So you're always searching for Ileana Cosinzeana?" he asked. Stefan sat down, lit a cigarette, and smiled in confusion. "She's in Spain," he said. "How do you know?" Bursuc demanded at once, curious. "I dreamed about her again. We seemed to be in Spain . . ." Bursuc scowled in anger. "You're like a credulous old woman!" he burst out suddenly. "Heresies and superstitions have gotten the better of you. I ought to excommunicate you. I ought to throw you out of the Holy Church! I have the authority to do it!" Stefan smoked quietly, gazing with vacant eyes through the window at the high wall of the Metropolitan Cathedral. "I'm sure she's in Spain. That's why I've come to ask a favor of you, Reverend Father. I think Duma doesn't trust me. But if Your Grace will speak with him . . ." "You're crazy!" Bursuc exploded again. "You've forgotten what kind of business Duma conducts and with whom he works. . . . You've forgotten Protopopescu!" His voice dropped a little.

". . . I went to see him out of desperation," continued Stefan. "When I didn't know what to do anymore, which way to turn, I went to Bursuc."

That autumn, after he left the Ministry in the evening, he sometimes went to the Forest of Baneasa. "Look, in these places there were once marshes," he recalled. And it seemed to him that he found her there beside him again, or a short distance ahead, walking through the grass with her light boyish step. But then very quickly he would lose her. He went back repeatedly to the place where they had met and he strained to remember, to recapture from somewhere within those singular moments that had been torn out of the time that surrounded them, moments that still lingered although they were not so vivid as before. He wanted to relive the time when he had seen her from afar as she walked through the grass, when his heart had begun to beat so violently, when he had known that she would not be able to go home in the car because it would have vanished at midnight. Now he walked under the trees, under the branches almost bare of leaves, yellowed prematurely by the drought. He repeated to himself, "In these places there were once marshes!" But it was all fruitless because the sound of his steps, the noise made by his feet as they shattered the carpet of dry, withered leaves, kept rousing him. He would emerge from the forest then to walk in the field to avoid the rustle underfoot that constantly assailed his ears. He would remain there well into the night, skirting the forest, returning inevitably to the place where they had sat and watched the stars rise over the wood, the spot where he had told her about the hedgehog that had befriended him during his *liceu* days. "I don't understand you," Ileana had told him then. "I'm sorry. Probably you're saying some very interesting things, but I don't understand you. . . ."

"I don't understand myself why I go to see him," Stefan went on, "or what I could expect from him. Once I remembered what you said to me long ago when we were barely acquainted—that I ought to be afraid of Bursuc because he's a demoniac."

This he had recalled on the first rainy day that autumn. After leaving the Ministry he had gone to *strada* Batistei, where he found that the apartment house at number 27 was almost finished. The windows were being installed on the first floor, and he had stood there bareheaded in the rain watching them put the sashes in place. Here on this spot there had been a bed of flowers and an iron grill between two walls, he recollected. On that long ago night in August when he had come in the cab, fearing that Ileana would have already left for the station, a cat had jumped down from the wall into the garden and had disappeared in the darkness. He had had those black gloves—dry, dusty, moth-eaten—in his pocket, and he kept touching them with his hand. Suddenly he remembered that he no longer knew what he had done with them. He was not even sure if they had belonged to her or not. "You went to all that trouble for nothing," she had said to him that day on the street in the rain, the time they were standing under the shelter of her huge umbrella. "They aren't mine. . . ."

"I told you that?" asked Biris with a smile. "I don't remember . . ."

"I was coming from *strada* Batistei," Stefan explained, "and I was walking through the rain, just like the day I met Ileana when I kissed her under the umbrella. . . ."

Biris extinguished his cigarette and looked at him uneasily, then quickly glanced away.

"Yes," continued Stefan, reflecting. "I kissed her then, just once, in the rain, under the umbrella. Everything that came after that shouldn't have happened. I made a great blunder. Time should have stopped the moment I kissed her on the lips. I kissed her on the lips!" he repeated with sudden fervor, and rising, he went to the window again. "I've never been able to understand how such a thing was possible—that I could kiss her on the lips! Everything should have stopped at that moment. Nothing should have moved anymore, the whole world should have been transfixed . . . for the two of us, of course," he added quickly, "only for the two of us. The Cosmos and History would have continued for the rest of mortal men, but for us it ought to have stood still *at that moment*. No kind of duration had any meaning after that. Once we had kissed what else *could* happen that would equal that irrevocable moment?"

He was silent and gazed out of the window for a long time. The clouds were higher now and a fine rain had started, a tenuous spray that gradually misted the pane.

"You spoke of Bursuc," Biris said finally, breaking the silence. "You said you remembered that I told you he was a demoniac?"

"Yes," said Stefan, rousing himself. "I was walking through the rain and I remembered. It's odd that I remembered it just then. When I was with him in Moldavia, and especially at Zinca, it never once entered my head that he might be possessed. I'd forgotten what you told me. And yet at Zinca I ought to have seen that he *might* be a devil. Especially that time when I suddenly felt myself starting toward him with my hands trembling . . ." He hesitated for a long time and then continued, "I was determined . . ." He was silent again. He rubbed his face with his hand, and going to the easel, he pulled the cloth to one side.

"Actually, I still think that it's here I'll find her. When I dreamed of her at night and woke up with her image before my eyes I said to myself that if I'd begin to paint again . . ." But apparently he reconsidered and covered the picture once more.

"You said that you remembered what I said about Bursuc," Biris reminded him in an effort to reopen the conversation.

"Yes, but I went to see him anyway. I was a little afraid. I don't know why. When I found myself in front of his cell I was ready to turn back.

Nevertheless I knocked—three times. 'Who is it?' he asked me. 'It's I, Viziru,' I said, and then I went in. He was washing his feet. 'I don't like to be dirty like the other monks,' he said. Then he turned and looked at me. 'Why are you standing there by the door like a stone?' he demanded. 'I'm afraid I'm bothering you,' I said. 'You're not bothering me at all,' he replied. 'On the contrary. . . . I've just realized I don't have a towel. Look around for one, will you? There must be one here in the cell someplace.' I began to hunt but I seemed to hit on only the drawers where they were not kept. 'Hunt, man! Faster! The water's getting cold,' he cried, and then I found the towel and brought it to him. I remembered again what you said, that he was a demoniac, and I began to laugh. He looked at me in surprise and began to laugh too. We both laughed like that for quite some time. Then I remembered and was serious again. . . ."

"What did you remember?" Biris asked, when Stefan did not continue.

"I remembered it all—Ioana and Ileana, all I had had before that was taken away from me, all those things that were and are no more. I seemed to recall everything in a single moment. Bursuc looked at me, put on his stockings and shoes, and went outside to dispose of the water in the basin. When he came back he said, 'Still unconsolable?' and he asked me for a cigarette. 'It seems to get more and more difficult for me,' I told him. 'And yet I know she's somewhere here on earth not far from me.' 'Have faith!' he exclaimed suddenly. 'Be a man!' 'She might be in Switzerland,' I said. 'She used to have a friend there—the Valkyrie, she called her. She might be hiding with her. I ought to look for her there.' Bursuc seemed thoughtful. 'What do you intend to do?' he asked me. 'Flee the country?' 'No,' I answered, 'I won't run away, but a team of experts will soon be going to Switzerland. I may be sent too.' 'Listen to me,' he interrupted. 'My opinion is that she doesn't love you any longer. She hasn't loved you for a long time. She's forgotten you. She's a married woman now with children, with a purpose in life. Forget her!' It's strange what an effect his words had on me. For the first time I felt a stab of doubt and I said, 'You may be right.' But he came up and slapped me on the shoulder. 'Look out,' he cried, 'that I don't tempt you!' And that calmed me. I remembered Zinca. He said the same thing there. . . . He is indeed a strange man," Stefan added after a pause.

Biris got up from the armchair and began to walk slowly about the room. He started to inspect the shelf of books, but with the first glance he saw there was nothing but Marxist literature and some volumes on political economy, and he returned to the middle of the room.

"I've been listening to you for half an hour and I still don't get the idea. But after all it's none of my business. I just came to deliver *conu* Misu's message. Did you know Bibicescu is under surveillance and that he's been in hiding for a whole month?"

"Yes, I heard it at the Ministry. And I was reminded of Ileana, of a detail that I'd forgotten. When they took me to Police Headquarters . . ." He inter-

479

rupted himself suddenly and put his hand to his forehead in exasperation, then brought it slowly to rest against his cheek.

"Sometimes I get the feeling that it's all in vain, that it's *too late*. I'm closed in on all sides—not by walls as in a jail, because in that case I'd at least have the absurd hope that the walls might be shattered and I could *imagine* a way out. But I have the feeling that I'm surrounded by an intangible barrier built by Time, erected out of everything I can no longer call back, everything that's happened and is irreversible. . . . I wonder then . . ."

He ceased speaking and shrugged his shoulders. Biris stopped in front of the easel, pulled aside the covering and repeated his examination of the painting.

"Just a few lines," he said, "and it would look like a labyrinth. Do you still remember the message you sent to Ileana by me? I'm sorry I can't reproduce it for you now. I was sick then. I had a fever. But I do recall that you spoke about a labyrinth, a metal sphere whose walls are cracked."

Stefan stared thoughtfully at the canvas. "I remember especially the storm then," he said presently. "I'd gone into a flower shop to buy a bouquet of lilies of the valley and when I came out it had begun to rain in torrents. . . . It was beautiful." he added after a pause. Rising, he went to the painting. "Of course the very fact that you see a labyrinth proves to me that I'm painting and struggling in vain. I can't recapture anything of all that once was. I might as well give up."

He looked again at the picture and drew the cloth over it. The rain became heavier. He searched on the table for his cigarettes and held out the package to Biris. "Aside from all this, what other news is there?"

"Nuisances," responded Biris, lighting his cigarette. "I've been fired from the *liceu*—they purged me. A socially unhealthy element, they call me." He tried to laugh, but he choked on the smoke and began to cough. Pressing his handkerchief to his mouth in exasperation, he motioned for Stefan to bring him a glass of water.

"Socially unhealthy I believe is an exaggeration," he said after drinking all the water at a gulp and wiping his lips with his handkerchief. "Just plain unhealthy is closer to the truth! I've tried without success to get myself admitted to a sanatorium and if I haven't been able to get in yet, from now on it will be impossible. It's a strange feeling to know you're condemned to death and not to be told when you'll be executed. Each day I live seems like a stolen day, a day that I've filched from destiny. It gives me a feeling of euphoria. . . ."

Usually it was after lunch when Bibicescu made his announcement. "This evening at the same hour we shall continue. . . ."

480

The reading took place about twice a week and never lasted more than an hour, because Bibicescu presented only one or two scenes at a time, repeatedly interrupting the dialogue in order to explain the decor and the details of staging, especially the play of lights. Sometimes he did away with all illumination in the salon except for the desk lamp, with which he attempted to create the atmosphere of the ruins of Stalingrad, covering it with colored papers or even veiling it completely with file folders arranged like a tent over the shade.

When the three spectators entered the room at a quarter to nine they always found their chairs placed one beside the other at the same distance— more than five meters—from the desk. They sat down in silence—somewhat timidly—under the stern gaze of Bibicescu, who leaned against the desk with the manuscript in his hand. Scarcely daring to move or breathe, they awaited the moment when he would raise his copy of the play solemnly and prepare to read, announcing, "Scene ____, the same setting," after which he would break off, lay the manuscript on the desk and quickly remind them of the scenery. No one ventured to speak, for they knew the slightest whisper would upset him. They ruffled his composure only once: when he made the statement toward the end of Act I, "From the corridor two soldiers go to the middle of the stage, supporting around the waist the colonel, who is gravely wounded, his eyes bandaged. . . ." Instantly all three exclaimed, "It's Colonel Baleanu!"

Bibicescu paused, frowned, and regarded them fixedly for several seconds without comment. "Yes," he responded tardily, "I was inspired by Colonel Baleanu's accident, but you didn't have to interrupt me for that! You could have communicated your impressions to me at the conclusion of the reading. Not everyone knows Baleanu. The audience sees only that the principal character appears on the stage gravely wounded—and that's all. At most they'll say, 'The colonel has lost his sight.' In no event will they shout, 'It's Colonel Baleanu!' " He resumed the reading, but it could be seen that he was vexed.

As the month of October drew to a close, cold rains commenced unexpectedly. Each evening the salon was more frigid. Bibicescu wore a pullover while he worked, and sometimes he put his topcoat over his shoulders, but he did not discontinue the reading of his play. At a quarter to nine when the three members of the audience gathered in the salon they invariably found him leaning on the desk, waiting for them. After he saw them seated— *doamna* Ivascu and Irina with woolen shawl wrapped around their backs, the teacher wearing an old overcoat—Bibicescu removed his coat, hung it on the back of the armchair, and began. Sometimes it happened that Misu Weissman would come, but those evenings were wasted because Weissman could never stay until the end and it was difficult for Bibicescu to proceed with the reading after the disruption his departure caused.

481

"When do you plan to come with me?" Misu would ask, and once he took the actor by the arm and led him to the far end of the room. "Everything you gave me has reached its destination," he whispered. "It's in a safe place. We'll make our getaway soon too. Be ready with the manuscript!"

Misu always came in a cab. He was pressed for time and nervous, and the first thing he wanted to know was if Bibicescu had done anything imprudent—had he received visitors or had he by any chance gone for a walk in the daytime? But the actor almost never went out of the house and his only visitor had been Biris, who came to see him one Sunday afternoon. On certain evenings, when no reading session had been announced, Irina came to take him for a walk on the street, but he had to be persuaded. He would claim that he was tired or that he was afraid he might have a spell with his heart, but in the end he would set off beside Irina, under cover of the darkness, and they would walk like that for an hour, almost without exchanging a word. One evening, however, on the boulevard he declared suddenly, "When I become famous in Paris after the premiere, I'll go back to my room at night and I'll remember these walks. I'll remember how we strolled furtively in the dark so that no one would recognize me, while those scoundrels from the Theater—whom I created and whom I cast in leading roles when I was director—while those scoundrels were walking at liberty, unhindered, continuing to bring charges against me. . . . *Conu* Misu told me that they've received denunciations at Police Headquarters again," he added, dropping his voice. But then he shrugged contemptuously and continued on his way without further word.

Several days later when they entered the salon, the three spectators halted in the doorway, astonished. It was almost dark in the room. The desk had been set against the wall and the lamp was covered with folders. On the spot where the desk had stood there were two chairs over which Bibicescu had arranged a sheet. Other chairs had been placed nearby and draped with clothing in such a way as to give the impression of people kneeling. Taking his flashlight the actor conducted his hosts to their places. Because of the extreme cold in the salon they were all wearing overcoats.

"You'll understand immediately what's happened," Bibicescu told them. "This is the principal scene. Now the myth of the dead begins to become explicit!"

He went to the desk, picked up the manuscript, and holding it in the circle of light from the lamp, he started to read.

"A road at the edge of a village in Moldavia. On both sides the snow is piled high." He pointed to the sheet. "At nightfall one can distinguish shadowy forms, indistinct—the forms of people on their knees in the snow. For a few minutes after the rising of the curtain all is quiet. Suddenly we hear a muffled voice from the back of the theater: 'They're coming! I know it! I see them!' Then on all sides a confused murmur ascends and fragments of prayers

482

are heard. The priest—who has remained on his feet in the middle of the road—the priest..." Bibicescu turned off the lamp on the desk and with surprising dexterity lit a candle that he had concealed under the papers. "The priest," he continued, his voice somber, "lights his candle, and one after another the kneeling people light theirs. . . ."

As he spoke Bibicescu lit the other candles. He had fastened them beforehand with great care to the backs of the chairs that had been draped with clothing. "In a few minutes," he explained, "the entire stage fills with the glow of hundreds of lighted candles shining far into the distance. The priest kneels in the snow then too and bows his head."

The actor knelt in front of the chairs while he talked, his lighted candle in his hand. He had left the manuscript on the desk and played the scene now from memory, altering his tone to suit each character he impersonated, giving the necessary explanations of the narration in his normal voice.

"We see coming from the depths of the stage a long procession of shades—soldiers in ragged uniforms, some of them wounded, dragging their feet and supporting themselves on crutches or rifles. They lean on one another and do not look around, but stare straight ahead over the snow. They all seem to be blind. They do not turn to look at the people kneeling beside them—apparently they do not see them. Now and then a shade passes too near to a candle and it goes out." Bibicescu blew out one of the candles attached to the chairs.

"Nevertheless these flames light the way. The meaning of the scene is this—that the dead do not even realize how much we do for them—we, the living. The dead continue their existence thanks to us, but they do not know it. They think the new life that begins for them at their death belongs entirely to them."

Irina had been on her knees for a long time there in the darkness, and now she could no longer control her emotion. She buried her face in her hands and began to sob. *Doamna* Ivascu seized her arm and whispered to her crossly, bending to speak into her ear. "Be quiet, you ninny! Be quiet! He'll hear you!"

But Bibicescu went on speaking, grasping the candle, addressing himself to the shadowy room. "Here I believe I've introduced something new and unprecedented in the modern theater, something which only a Shakespeare would have ventured: this idea—that the dead are completely separated from us because they cannot realize that they owe their existence as shades to us, the living. . . ."

Suddenly Irina got up and hurriedly left the room. Exasperated, Bibicescu turned to look at the door and rose to his feet.

"I asked you not to interrupt me—especially during such an important scene as this!"

"She doesn't feel well," murmured *doamna* Ivascu, embarrassed.

"This scene will be talked about for centuries." Bibicescu was inspired. "Only Shakespeare would have had such courage. They'll realize later what Dan Bibicescu meant to the European theater, because—and I'm going to tell you a secret—this play will be performed in Paris! The first two acts are in the process of being translated, and I myself will produce it. They'll see then that I've had genius, but that intrigue and calumnies here in my own country stifled it. Only abroad have I been recognized!" He was becoming increasingly overwrought, but he went on speaking directly to the two remaining spectators, his hand still gripping the burning candle.

"I'm sorry that you interrupted me, and I played it badly, but it's a truly extraordinary scene. The candles go out one by one until only a few remain, and the dead continue to pass, but they move more slowly now because they can no longer see the road clearly and they seem to be groping through the darkness. During this time we hear on the stage the wind of the January night and the murmur of the prayers, and the shades all seem to waver with each gust. The candles go out one by one, except for the priest's candle, and then from the back of the stage the colonel appears. . . ." He paused, confused. Going to the desk, he set his candle in an empty glass.

"But for some time the audience doesn't know if the colonel is dead— part of the procession—or if he has lost his way there among the shades. . . ." He stopped again and turned on the desk lamp. "But this scene is too important for me to summarize. I'll read it to you in its entirety at the next session. . . ."

That evening Stefan found the monk drinking. He was sitting with his elbows resting on the table and staring blankly over the top of the bottles. He cried, "Come in!" because he had heard someone stop in front of his door, but he did not turn his head to see who it was.

"I've been expecting you," he said. "I knew you'd come. Take a chair and sit here next to me. I'm sick at heart. Find yourself a glass. . . . I'm sick at heart on account of you, and on account of your friends. . . ."

Stefan sat down across the table from Bursuc, who raised his eyes suddenly and looked at him with a frown. "Tell Bibicescu to hold his tongue," he snapped, "to thank God that he escaped and to mind his own business. Tell him to lay off Stalingrad!"

"I don't understand what you mean," protested Stefan.

"Don't be coy!" Bursuc interrupted. "I have reliable information. Just tell him this: Lay off Stalingrad!"

Stefan smiled and picked up a bottle, filling his glass with wine. "That's precisely why I came," he said after he had emptied the glass with one swallow. "Biris paid me a visit . . ."

484

"Don't tell me anything!" exclaimed Bursuc, lifting his hand in alarm. "Don't tell me anything! I'll betray you. That's my profession—to betray all of you, one after another," he added in a voice that sounded distant and bemused. Then he broke into a short, strangled laugh that subsided when he put his hand on his glass.

"You'd do better to tell me about Ileana Cosinzeana." He sipped his wine. "What else have you dreamed about her?"

Still smiling, Stefan took the bottle of wine and refilled both glasses in silence.

"I'm involved with a girl—Zoica," Bursuc stated pensively. "I go to see her every night. . . . But they really take me for a fool!" he exploded after a pause. "As though I didn't know what she's up to and who sent her here, close to the Holy Patriarchate, to lie in wait for me on the street and give me the eye." He began to laugh again, amused. "It's a trick of Protopopescu's!" he muttered.

"I know him," volunteered Stefan. "I met him once when I was with Duma."

Bursuc scowled and tried to hide his agitation. "I don't want to hear about it!" He raised his arm in a defensive gesture and silenced Stefan. "I've been honest with you! I told you I'll betray you. . . . I said to hold your tongue. . . ."

Stefan said nothing, but he began to scrutinize him intently. Bursuc ran his hand over his face several times, then let it slip slowly to his cheek and come to rest in his beard. He seemed to be drowsy, struggling with sleep.

"I think you felt it too, then, at Jassy, when we came back." Stefan spoke abruptly. "You guessed what I had in mind. . . ."

"Felt what?" Bursuc asked sleepily.

"I said to myself, Actually, my life has no purpose now that I've been to Zinca and didn't find her. Except to save the world from you! . . . I think you felt it. You noticed how I held my hands. . . ."

"Felt what, man?" demanded Bursuc, raising his voice.

"Because of you, Father, people have lost faith. They see you dressed in monk's clothing and they believe in your words . . ."

"I have a mission," Bursuc interrupted him, passing his hand over his face again. "I've been sent into the world to tempt you. . . ."

"Nevertheless I believe you sensed something when I approached you then."

Bursuc frowned and reached for his glass. He brought it to his lips, but he did not drink. Stefan's smiling gaze remained fixed upon him, unwavering.

"You wanted to kill me?" The priest's voice sounded uncertain, but he pretended to be joking. "To strangle me?"

"I believe you guessed it a long time ago and that's why you've concerned yourself so much with me. You wanted to save my soul. You wanted to help

485

me repent so I could be saved. And that's why I come so often to see you here at the Metropolia. . . ."

Suddenly Bursuc thrust his hand across the table. His voice was hoarse. "Give me a cigarette!"

Stefan opened the package and offered it to him, then held out a lighted match.

"How could I be afraid of someone like you?" Bursuc exclaimed, greedily inhaling the first puff. "I've known for a long time who you are and what you can do. It's hard to kill a man with your bare hands. . . ."

Stefan continued to watch him. "Just the same I think you felt it and were afraid," he said presently.

"And so, pray tell, why didn't you try it?" interrupted Bursuc, provokingly. "Maybe I'd have enjoyed seeing you try. Maybe I had my fists ready. . . ."

"It was *doamna* Zissu who saved you," Stefan said coolly. "When I approached you I suddenly remembered Vadastra and *doamna* Zissu, and I became calm. I became calm as if by magic. . . ."

"Who is this *doamna* Zissu?" Bursuc asked, disturbed.

"I don't know. I never met her. I think she died a long while ago. Vadastra knew her, but after he died too . . ." He stopped speaking and smiled into Bursuc's eyes.

"You're crazy," cried Bursuc. "Don't come here in the evenings anymore. I won't let you in."

"Don't worry," replied Stefan. "That impulse lasted only a few moments and since then I pray constantly that I'll be forgiven that sin. I was tempted—I'm sure I was tempted by the Devil himself. Who were you to me? What did it matter to me if you were or were not worthy of the clothes you wore? I wasn't called upon to judge you, and yet I felt something in the depths of my soul, something that told me I had to save the world from you. That was the Devil's temptation. You'd humiliated me and offended me innumerable times, talking as you did about Ileana, and yet I didn't hate you. I wasn't tempted then to kill you. But all of a sudden, without any motive, I felt I had to save the world from you. . . . I think you realized what had taken place in my soul and you were afraid!" He smiled.

Bursuc too made an effort to smile, but he was unable to hide his agitation. He smoked his cigarette in silence.

"I don't believe you!" he said at last. "You weren't in any condition to kill a man. That requires force and resolve. I know you well. I'm not afraid of you."

"I know," agreed Stefan. "But I didn't kill you. I hadn't anything against you. I'm sure the Devil was tempting me then. And if it was he who tempted me, he would have given me the strength and the resolve I needed to strangle you."

Scowling, Bursuc did not shift his gaze from the other man's eyes. He crushed his cigarette directly on the wooden table with a curt gesture, blowing the ashes onto the floor.

"I'm sorry you didn't try," he said finally. "Perhaps you'd have had a surprise and been cured forever of the desire to kill people!"

Stefan's smile faded slowly, as if an unseen hand had wiped it away. He lit a cigarette and watched his fingers tremble, holding the match for a long time—long enough for Bursuc to see how badly his hand shook. "Were you armed?" he asked abruptly.

"I'm always armed," replied Bursuc, "and if you guess which pocket it's in, I'll show it to you."

"The right one."

"No—but I'll show you anyway." Nervously Bursuc thrust his hand into the inner pocket of his surplice and pulled out a small revolver. He showed it to Stefan with a triumphant flourish, holding it as far away from him as he was able.

"Now I understand," said Stefan, a great calm suffusing his voice. "It was surely the Devil. I don't know why I've never dared to commit suicide. I'm a coward, I suppose. But several times I've courted death—on the front and in other circumstances. . . . But that temptation was sent by the Devil. He wanted *me* to be killed, not you. Actually, it was really a sort of suicide. . . . Now I understand." He bowed his head and smiled.

"And what if I should tell you I bought the revolver last week and I was unarmed back there in Moldavia?"

Stefan began to laugh.

"Don't laugh!" exclaimed Bursuc. "I'm tempting you all the time. Watch out!"

Stefan rose suddenly and held out his hand. "Tell Bibicescu to be reasonable," Bursuc muttered as he replaced the revolver cautiously under his surplice. "Lay off of Stalingrad. . . ."

Passing the salon, Irina heard a low, suppressed moan and stopped to listen. When she approached the door she heard it again. Bibicescu seemed to be moaning in his sleep. She hesitated a few moments before making up her mind, but at last she knocked briefly and went in. She saw him across the room, bent double on the sofa, rubbing his chest with his hand and groaning.

"It seized me all at once," he whispered. "I think it will go away . . ." Gritting his teeth, he closed his eyes and tried not to cry out again. "Ordinarily it passes quickly," he added after a moment. "This time it's lasted longer."

"Let me call a doctor."

487

Bibicescu shook his head with all the strength he could muster. "It's unwise," he said, straining to open his clenched teeth. *"Conu* Misu . . ." He stopped, turned to the other side and pressed his chin against his chest with a groan. ". . . implored me," he continued, "to be careful." He closed his eyes and took a single deep breath that seemed to reach to the very bottom of his lungs.

"Irina," he whispered again, his eyes still closed, "I want to tell you something. It's a secret. I have the life of a human being on my conscience. You knew her—it's Catalina. . . . Come closer. . . ."

Irina knelt beside the sofa and put her head as close to his as she could. Bibicescu had bent over again and was rubbing his chest violently, as if he wanted to tear the skin. "It's never lasted so long," he murmured, burying his head in the pillow to stifle his cries.

"Don't be afraid to cry," Irina told him. "Scream! Wail! Maybe it will do you good."

Suddenly he gave vent to a long groan. He raised himself on his knees in exasperation and slipped off the couch, stretching out on the carpet, rolling over slowly, digging his nails deeply into his flesh. "I don't know what's wrong. It was never like this before . . ."

"I'll go call a doctor," Irina said, standing up resolutely.

"Wait!" shouted Bibicescu, doubling up again on the rug. "They told me it's nothing, it's not serious. . . . They told me it's functional."

For several moments he lay there expectantly, eyes closed, one hand pressed to his heart. "Catalina . . ." He spoke suddenly. "I have her on my conscience. . . . I think it's beginning to go away," he whispered.

"Pray!" pleaded Irina, kneeling beside him again. "Say the 'Our Father.' . . ."

"I have to confess to you. It was because of me. Otherwise she wouldn't have had the accident. *Conu* Misu knows. He says it's not my fault, that it was her fate. . . ."

"Confess to a monk," advised Irina, noting that again he had stopped speaking. "But don't conceal anything. God will forgive all your sins."

He was silent and his eyes remained closed, his hand resting over his heart. He did not move.

"That night she had come to my house because she'd been accosted by a drunken Russian soldier. He forced her into a passageway, struggled with her, tore her clothes, raped her. Her dress was ripped. She came to my place and begged me to find some other clothes for her, no matter what—pajamas, a dress, one of my suits. She wanted to go into the bathroom and throw away her dress. She said that she felt dirty, that she must discard everything she had on and burn it. . . . She wanted to bathe. . . . She said she absolutely had to get into water. . . ." He stopped and slowly straightened his legs. "It seems to have gone," he whispered. "I'm cold. . . ."

488

Irina started to help him up but he prevented her, holding up his hand fearfully. "I'm afraid to move. It might start again."

She pulled the cover from the couch and placed it over him.

"I was with the Theater then," he continued, his voice more calm. "I was afraid of a scandal. I was afraid Catalina would say something—that she'd complain to the police and call me as a witness. I was afraid the Russian would come after her. I didn't know where it had happened. I thought he'd followed her and might break in at any minute. I was afraid. I hated her for coming there, for compromising me, for jeopardizing my career at the Theater—and she realized this. I lied to her, told her I was expecting a guest, a woman, at any moment and so I couldn't let her take a bath, that I didn't want a scandal, having my friend find her in the bathroom. She knew I was lying. She looked in my eyes and smiled. I hated her because she knew I was lying. 'I'm very rushed,' I told her. 'I'm expecting a guest.' 'I'm sorry,' she said. She didn't say why. 'I'm very sorry.' Then she wrapped herself in her coat as best she could to hide her torn dress, and she left. I started to go downstairs with her. 'Don't bother,' she said. 'I know the way.'"

He said no more. The room had become completely dark. Irina stayed on her knees beside him, but she did not speak.

At last Bibicescu said, "I'm still cold."

"Go and make confession to a monk..." began Irina, but Bibicescu interrupted her.

"I'd like you to leave now. Don't tell anyone anything. Just leave me alone.... I'll call you later."

When she opened the door for him Irina thought she discerned a vague disquiet in Stefan's glance.

"It's good that you've come," she murmured. "I wanted to talk to you. I'll walk down the street a little way with you when you leave."

"I have to see Bibicescu," said Stefan.

"Don't scold him," she begged. She seemed disturbed. "I put some postcards in the mailbox for him. I didn't read them, but he told me what he had written. He's not involved in politics—he's not attacking the government. He told me he was discussing the philosophy of the theater."

She spoke in a whisper as she led him slowly toward the salon and tapped three times on the door. Bibicescu was seated at his desk, writing, with his overcoat thrown over his shoulders. He looked up from the manuscript, and astonished at the sight of Stefan, he leaned slowly against the back of the chair.

"I have to speak with you," Stefan began.

"Have you heard about it too?" the actor demanded, getting up sud-

489

denly. "Have they informed you of the agony of the *Nibelungen?* Because I can assure you that it will be quite as magnificent as the final conflagration of the *Nibelungen*. They'll all die, to the last man, fighting, burned alive—but they'll die in the fire with their weapons in their hands. . . ."

He stepped in front of the desk and addressed them rhetorically in a voice that included the unseen audience that might have filled the salon.

"I was slandered all my life for plagiarizing Partenie." His animation was increasing. "But now everyone will see what a gulf exists between Partenie's plays and the theater of Dan Bibicescu! Only Shakespeare, perhaps, surpasses me. Put them side by side—Partenie, Claudel, Bernard Shaw, O'Neill—and altogether they'll still be a hundred leagues behind me! Because now I've solved all the problems: the problem of Time, the problem of Death, the problem of the Theater. I've understood everything. I've rediscovered Myth. I've rediscovered the living roots of the Theater, lost in Europe since Shakespeare. . . . Only I don't have time now to finish all the things I've started. I have two other plays in progress, and the plots of about fifteen more. . . ."

Stefan sat down on a chair near the desk and listened to him absently. "They've learned in town that you wrote a play about Stalingrad. You were unwise."

"I haven't done anything in the least unwise," interrupted Bibicescu. "During the more than two months that I've been hiding here I've received no visitors except Biris and *conu* Misu. No one's come to see me. I've gone out only rarely in the evenings after dark. . . . But, of course, I wrote several letters. I wanted those who denounced and attacked me to know they hadn't destroyed me as they had hoped—that on the contrary I find myself in full possession of my creative powers and that this time they will no longer be able to say I've plagiarized Partenie!"

He circled the desk and seated himself in the armchair, pulling the coat over his back. Stefan stared thoughtfully at the bare walls.

"Don't you have any paintings at all now?" he asked Irina. "Have you sold them all?"

"Irina's gone. She went out a little while ago when I was talking to you."

Stefan turned to look at the door and sighed involuntarily. "I don't suppose you ever imagined you were living in a museum," he said with a smile. "Until about six or seven years ago this house was a sort of museum—especially this room."

"So I heard. That's nothing. Someday it will become a museum again! I have in mind to leave all my manuscripts to the Ivascu and Vadastra families. Here in this room a masterpiece was written and several others begun. The manuscripts will be displayed in glass cases. I've kept all the versions. There were scenes I wrote and rewrote five or six times—and I've kept them all. . . . Of course," Bibicescu added, smiling mysteriously, "all the definitive forms were sent abroad. . . ." He realized suddenly that he had said too much and he shut his mouth tightly, nervously. Stefan hastened to reassure him.

490

"Don't be afraid. I'm on the same side of the fence as you are. You'll find that out later. Perhaps we'll meet again . . ."

Bibicescu gave him a look that was profound and severe, then he rose from the desk, preoccupied, and took a few steps around the room, one hand in his pocket. Finally he inquired, "Have you been in contact with *conu* Misu all the time? Is your connection the same as his?"

"No, I haven't any contact with him and I don't know anything about him."

Bibicescu stopped before Stefan and studied him again. "I'm a little uneasy because I don't know whom *conu* Misu will send to contact me. I'm expecting him from one day to the next, but I don't know him and I don't even know what his name is."

"You must be careful. You shouldn't write any more postcards."

"They thought they could destroy me." Bibicescu smiled and sat down in the armchair again. "I had to inform them that *The Return from Stalingrad* is already finished. In reality it's not quite completed. The last scenes are not in their final form. I'll have to rewrite them several more times. But now I've started something else of the character of the *Nibelungen*. I want to evoke the catastrophes of History." He sprang suddenly to his feet. "I want to teach my contemporaries to live again the true spirit of the catastrophe, to reveal to them the religious emotion of the twilight. Faced with the catastrophe people are only aware of fear and cowardice. I'll make them turn back to the *Nibelungen*. I'll make them realize that they are condemned by History, that they will perish! But I'll teach them to perish heroically, with glory. . . . I've written a number of scenes already. I don't know yet what the title will be, but I assure you that this has none of the pretentious and intellectual style of Partenie. It's pure drama, such as Shakespeare wrote. Maybe I'll call it *The Transfiguration*. I don't know yet. It's about a great fire in which all my heroes finally perish. There are about twenty men and one woman." He paused and then began again, his voice hushed, "I thought of Catalina. This was a role for her. Catalina Palade—I believe you knew her. She was a remarkable woman. She's the only woman I ever loved in my whole life." He raised his eyes to Stefan's. "Why then, you'll ask me, did we separate? I don't know that I could answer that. Destiny. Have you ever reflected upon this mystery, Destiny? It's just a dramatic aspect of Time. Listen to me—I'll tell you something I've never told anyone. Destiny is, in reality, the fragment of Time that History allows us. It is therefore something very limited—ten years, thirty, or seventy—it doesn't matter. It's always very limited. . . ." He ceased to speak and for a moment seemed perplexed.

"Yes. . . . But I didn't intend to tell you that. Those are things that you certainly know. I meant to speak of something else. Listen well—Destiny is that part of Time in which History impresses its will upon us. That's why we must resist it, we must flee from it, we must take refuge in the Theater. I have a whole theory of the Theater which I sum up thus: Concentrated Time. In brief, the Theater forces Time to manifest itself in the form of Destiny so it can be—how shall I put it?—it can be 'exorcised.' Does the verb 'to exorcise' exist in Romanian?"

"I don't think so,"

"We'll have to invent it then," Bibicescu continued, his fervor undiminished. "To exorcise Destiny—this is the function of the Theater. To force it to manifest itself *in your presence, on the stage,* in a concentrated time, so that *you escape, you remain a spectator, you go out of Time....*"

Stefan's eyes widened and he stared excitedly at the actor, who interrupted his monolog abruptly.

"Why do you look at me that way? Does this interest you too? But you know that this is my discovery, this is a *private* idea of mine.... I hold the copyright," he added with a tense smile. "In any case even if you wanted to steal it from me it's too late. I've already written several scenes. They're here," and he slapped the pile of papers. "Whatever happens to me, *scripta manent*! As soon as I perfect them I'll send them abroad...."

He stopped for a moment and looked at Stefan again sternly, scrutinizing him. "Now that you're in on the secret I can tell you that my manuscripts are sent through *conu* Misu's connection to Paris. I'll be leaving soon too, myself. I'm just waiting for a signal—it's a conventional one, a congratulatory telegram addressed to Irina—and I shall quit Bucharest. *Conu* Misu has arranged everything...."

"You're being unwise," Stefan interrupted. "You shouldn't have told me all these things...."

"I trust you. You're a loyal man. In the bottom of your heart you hate the Communists too, just as I do. Once I reach Paris I'll look for a good translator and we'll set to work. I've even decided at what theater we'll be presented.... That's why I work without stopping," he added nervously. "I don't have very much time. Any day now it may be my turn to cross the border. And if I don't have peace and quiet I can't write. Here it's perfect. There's a child in the house, but I don't know where they keep him or how they keep him—I never hear him. That's why I can write so well. I write day and night. And now I must even ask you to leave. I have a terrific urge to write. Every hour is precious!"

"I'd like to see *domnul* Weissman," Stefan said, rising. "Where do you think I could find him? Does he come to the coffee shop anymore?"

Bibicescu regarded him with a troubled expression as he replied, "*Conu* Misu has gone. I think he's already arrived in Paris. Didn't you know?"

Irina, dressed to go outside, was waiting for him in the hall. "Let's leave quickly so Mama won't hear us," she whispered.

A light snow, just a few scattered flakes, had fallen and then ceased, but the night had begun to have the smell of winter.

"What are we going to do with Bibicescu?" Irina asked, taking his arm and drawing close to him. "He doesn't sleep at all anymore. He writes all the time. I'd like to have a doctor come, but *conu* Misu has forbidden it. He said that it's unwise."

"Why didn't he leave with Misu?" demanded Stefan. "Shouldn't they have escaped together?"

They passed a streetlight and Irina searched his eyes, trying to fathom how much he knew. "*Conu* Misu came to get him one night when he was ill." She glanced around her to see if anyone might be listening and began to relate the story in a whisper. "He came rather late, near midnight, and we were afraid. At first we didn't want to open the door because we thought it was the police. He had a car and had come to get him, but Bibicescu was still lying on the rug where I left him after his attack. He didn't dare to get up, although he said the attack had passed long before. Even when Misu came in, he didn't want to get up. He said he was afraid to make the least movement. They talked to each other a long time alone, and then Misu told me that Bibicescu would be leaving a few weeks later with another group. He said it was all arranged, just to have a little patience. . . . But since then Bibicescu seems like another man. He doesn't sleep and hardly touches his food. He writes incessantly and doesn't want to read us what he's written anymore. He says that it's not ready, that he has to make more corrections, that he isn't satisfied with it yet. . . . What should we do?" she asked him after a moment, a trace of despair in her voice.

"I don't know. Perhaps a doctor ought to see him anyway—to give him a sedative so he can at least sleep. . . ."

"He's always waiting for the telegram and yet he's afraid to receive it. He says that after that he won't be able to write, that the telegram is his signal to leave. . . ."

"Maybe it will arrive one of these days and then he'll get away," said Stefan. "He'll be excited about crossing the border and he'll be tired. Then he'll be able to sleep."

They walked for awhile without speaking. Irina's head was bent and Stefan stared vaguely before him.

"But what are you waiting for?" she demanded suddenly. "Why don't you escape? This country will become a cemetery. We'll all die. Don't you feel it?"

"Yes, indeed. But it's hard to abandon a sinking ship. I haven't the heart for it. It seems to me it would be another act of cowardice on my part and I've committed enough of those in my life! This time I'll do my duty at least. . . . That's my luck!" he added with a smile.

"What more do you expect here?" asked Irina, squeezing his arm impulsively. "What else do you hope for? You have no one here anymore. We who

493

remain—forget us! Take Biris and run away together. *Conu* Misu is waiting for you abroad. You'll live a new life there. You'll start all over again."

"It's hard," Stefan said thoughtfully. "It's hard to break away. . . ."

"Search for Ileana," Irina went on, growing more impassioned. "If she's truly meant for you, you'll find her."

"Since a certain time I've dreamed about her constantly. I'm afraid that it's a bad sign—that something has happened to her."

"Don't think about misfortune," ordered Irina. "Think of her waiting for you. Don't look behind. As for those of us who stay here, forget us."

They were silent again for some time, and Stefan felt her arm begin to quiver.

"One morning I woke up happy," he said. "I only remembered that I had dreamed of her, but I don't know what it was. I just felt happy. It seemed to me that all that had happened had not happened. It seemed that everything was once more the way it had been in the beginning."

Stopping abruptly, Irina held out her hand. "I'll leave you now," she said. "I have to go home. Think over what I've told you."

Stefan kept her hand in his for a long time, aware that it was trembling. "I'll come to see you again," he said.

Biris heard his aunt walking back and forth in the hallway. He realized that she did not dare to come in and he smiled. At last in response to a timid knock he opened the door.

"Tomorrow's Christmas Eve," she said. "We don't have any money left."

> She had come to him once before, a week earlier, with the same message. At that time too she had found him in bed with the blanket pulled up to his chin, since it was so cold in his room that he would not even venture to put a hand out to hold a book. In order to make the wood last all winter they built a fire only in the morning, and by lunchtime the room was cold again. "We don't have any money left," *doamna* Porumbache had said. She seemed more frightened than ever and she looked into his eyes, searching them for some sign of encouragement. "We could sell something," she suggested hesitantly. "I'll see if I can sell some books," said Biris, glancing at the bookcase. All at once he bounded from the bed, seized by a kind of frenzy, and began to put on his clothes over his pajamas. He was trembling and shaking as if he had a fever. "Where are you going, sick like that?" *Doamna* Porumbache had tried to stop him, but he continued to dress, shivering and

494

clenching his teeth tightly to still their chattering. He wrapped himself in his overcoat, but his trembling did not cease. Lifting down the empty valise from the top of the wardrobe, he began to fill it with books selected at random from the shelves. "I'm starting with ethics," he said with a wry smile. "I'm selling all my books on ethics. Look—here's the whole of English ethics, all the British classics!" With this facetious remark he pointed to a pile that actually included works on a great many other subjects: history, biography, philosophy. He returned in the evening drenched with perspiration, bringing with him a small amount of money. "To make sure they'd buy them," he said, "I asked a tenth of their value, and they gave a tenth of what I asked. No one's interested in British ethics anymore." And when he saw her staring at him with fear in her eyes, too timid to speak, he added, "Draw your own conclusions. In this part of Europe the English lost the war. Perhaps they won it elsewhere, but here they lost. The British Empire has turned to dust. . . ."

"Tomorrow is Christmas Eve," she repeated, approaching the bed.

"I wanted to surprise you." Biris thrust his hand under the pillow and pulled out an envelope. "Stefan loaned me some money the day before yesterday. I didn't want to tell you. It's for the holidays. . . . Maybe we can buy some wood too. It's cold as the devil in here."

"And won't you get anything from the *liceu?*"

Biris shrugged his shoulders. "I don't know," he replied testily. "They'll give me a pension of some sort later. We'll see. . . ."

Doamna Porumbache went into the kitchen, and when she had counted the money she began to cry. Covering her face with her hands, she smothered her sobs so that Biris would not hear her. Sometime later she roused herself and wiped her eyes, and after counting the banknotes again, she left at once to make some purchases.

That evening they built a fire in the kitchen and another in Biris's room, while outside the snowfall became increasingly dense. Caught up in her preparations, *doamna* Porumbache's courage revived, and time after time she left the kitchen to tell Biris about the holidays in the past in Ferendari. He still lay with the blanket drawn up to his neck, musing, a book within reach of his hand. She brought him a bowl of soup on a tray, with boiled potatoes and a pat of butter, and when she was returning for the tray she heard a knock at the door. She opened it apprehensively, for the hour was now past nine. There in the entrance stood Gheorghe Vasile, winded, with a little jug under his arm.

"A gift for the holidays!" he said after he had caught his breath, shaking the snow from his clothes. "It's good wine, for friends. But I almost lost it on the way," he added, laughing. "At the corner when I was changing the demijohn from one hand to the other a Russian saw me. He was just getting

495

off the tram and he saw me! I stuck it under my jacket and took to my heels.... Let's drink a glass of wine now with *domnul* Professor..."

At that instant the door opened again and a beaming Russian soldier appeared on the sill. "Pac-pac-pac!" he said raising his hand and moving his finger to imitate the firing of a revolver. "*Kaput! Alles kaput!*"

He began to laugh exuberantly, hopping from one foot to the other to shake off the snow. With the jug beside him the teacher waited, fixed, unmoving, and *doamna* Porumbache backed against the wall.

The Russian went to her and held out his hand. "*Priatin!*" he said and shook Vasile's hand also, squeezing it with great vigor, playfully threatening him again. "Pac-pac-pac!" He pointed to the jug. "*Rachi! Verboten!*"

"It's wine," said the teacher. "Wine for friends."

The Russian nodded his head. "*Ia priatin.*" Leaning over, he seized the jug and started without haste for the kitchen door, which was standing open. He beckoned them to follow him. He looked around for some glasses and uncorked the jug, but when he tipped it up and saw that it contained wine he turned up his nose in a grimace of distaste.

"Pac-pac-pac!" he threatened them again. "*Rachi? Vodka?*"

"*Niet rachi!*" declared the teacher. "Wine. It's all we have."

"*Harascho!*" exclaimed the Russian, promptly draining his glass in a single gulp and filling all three glasses again. He sat down on a chair with the bottle between his knees and began to search his pockets. When he located his tobacco pouch he held it out to the teacher, urging him to roll a cigarette for himself. But Gheorghe Vasile had scarcely touched it when the Russian took it back and exchanged it for a glass of wine, which he placed in the teacher's hand. He clinked his glass with Vasile's and motioned to him to drink, but when they finished the soldier discovered that *doamna* Porumbache was no longer in the kitchen and he frowned. He picked up the jug in his left hand and went down the hall to Biris's room. The door was open and the Russian went in, but when he saw that Biris was in bed he stopped in the doorway and took off his cap.

"*Bolnav!*" he said, shaking his head. Returning to the kitchen in haste, he brought another glass, which he filled with wine and held out to Biris with a smile, indicating by a gesture that he should drink it down. Biris obeyed and the Russian sat down on the edge of the bed to watch him. Then he filled the glass again.

"*Filozof....*" He pointed to the shelves of books. "*Bolnav!*"

"Professor," said *doamna* Porumbache, growing bolder. "Professor of philosophy!"

"*Prafiesor, akademician!*" the Russian exclaimed, shaking his head. "*Niedobre. Bolnav!... Filozof kaput!*"

"*Kaput!*" echoed Biris, downing the second glass.

"*Alles filozof bolnav!*" insisted the Russian, turning to the others, ready to give them more wine, but finding that they had no glasses he pretended to be angry, set the jug down, and threatened them again with his imaginary revolver. "Pac-pac-pac! *Kaput!*"

Doamna Porumbache promptly fled to the kitchen to correct this oversight. "You have to do what he commands," she whispered, "or else there'll be trouble!"

The soldier grinned and filled all the glasses. "*Ia ponimaiu po rumunski!*"

"He says he understands Romanian," the teacher said, disquieted.

"That's what he says, but he doesn't understand anything," Biris calmed him and drained another glass of wine—his third—crying, "*Filozof kaput!*"

"*Harascho!*" said the Russian, approaching Biris and filling his glass. Then he set the jug in the middle of the floor, and placing one hand at the nape of his neck and the other on his hip, he began to dance in an awkward, childlike fashion, singing:

"*Cishnic, cishnic, gdi ti bil?
Na fontanke, vodku pil!*"

He sang and danced around the jug with one hand at the back of his neck and the other on his hip, nodding his head and glancing at each of them in turn—*doamna* Porumbache, the teacher, Biris. From time to time he lifted the jug and filled the glasses, then put it to his mouth to drink, gurgling, until he felt the wine flow over his cheeks, his beard, and his neck. Then he set it again in the middle of the floor, wiped his mouth on his sleeve and laughed, seizing *doamna* Porumbache or the teacher by the arm to dance around with him again as he sang.

"*Vipil riomku, vipil dve,
Zashumelo v golove!*"

But once in the midst of his whirling dance, his hand still behind his neck, he stopped suddenly, his glance falling on the window. He frowned, swiftly drew his revolver, and before the others realized what his intentions were he disappeared from the room.

"What's come over him?" *doamna* Porumbache asked anxiously when she heard him go outside to the street.

The teacher drew aside the curtains and looked out the window, pressing his face against the pane. "It's snowing steadily," he murmured. "I can't see a thing."

A few moments later the Russian came back, leading Irina by the hand. Her face was very pale and wet from the snow that had melted on her forehead and cheeks. Snow still covered her hair. Astonished, the others stood motionless and staring.

497

"I waited at the window for half an hour," she whispered quickly. "I tried to hide, but he found me. . . ."

"*Harascho!*" said the Russian, holding out a glass full of wine. "*Ia priatin!*"

Irina accepted the wine with a hesitant smile. Raising the jug to his lips, the Russian took a long drink and then held it close to his ear, shaking it to determine how much still remained. He set it in the middle of the floor again, caught Irina's arm suddenly, and began to dance with her.

"Cishnic, cishnic, gdi ti bil?"

She tried to pull away, scarcely able to maintain her smile, but the teacher whispered to her, "Do what he tells you! Don't antagonize him!"

". . . Stal nash cishnic tantsovati!"

sang the Russian, tapping his feet continuously on the floor like a child to indicate his impatience. All at once Irina burst into tears.

"Don't lose your head!" hissed *doamna* Porumbache between her teeth. "Dance with him! Maybe he'll leave sooner. Pretend to dance! Humor him!"

"I can't," Irina whispered. "Bibicescu is dead . . ."

Doamna Porumbache stifled a scream, covering her mouth with her hand. The teacher froze with his gaze fixed on Irina. Putting his arm around her waist, the Russian began to whirl her faster and faster around the jug, kicking his left leg high in the air again and again.

". . . Na fontanke vodku pil!"

"He's dead!" cried Irina, trying to tear herself loose from his grasp.

"*Kaput!*" Biris shouted abruptly, and struggled to sit up. He turned very pale and began to tremble, holding his hand to his chin in a futile attempt to keep his teeth from chattering. Irina was crying bitterly.

"He's dead!"

"Pac-pac-pac!" The Russian menaced everyone with the fingers of his left hand simulating a revolver. "*Alles krank!*"

Unexpectedly Irina broke loose and fell to her knees, shaken with sobs. The soldier stood perplexed in the middle of the floor watching her cry and embrace his legs. *Doamna* Porumbache fell to her knees then and began to weep, and the teacher sat down on the edge of the bed, his face buried in his hands.

"Lord Jesus Christ, Great God," implored Irina. "Mother of our Lord, maker of miracles, Jesus Christ our God! . . ."

Scowling and troubled, the Russian looked on, hesitating to move lest he strike her with his foot. Finally he scratched the back of his neck and, leaning over, he tried to raise the women to their feet. But Irina clung to his legs and voiced her prayers with increasing vehemence. *Doamna* Porumbache sobbed convulsively. The snow had melted from Irina's clothes and a puddle was spreading slowly on the floor. Eventually the Russian's patience was exhausted and he broke away from her roughly.

"All right, all right!" he cried in English. "Finish!"

He strode to the bed and questioned Biris, who was still holding his hand to his mouth trying to stop the clattering of his teeth. "*Warum?*"

Biris attempted to explain. "*Sein Mann ist tot,*" he said, and again the Russian's gaze rested upon Irina as she wept and prayed. He lifted the jug and drank until he choked. Stowing it under his arm, he stood at attention and executed a military salute.

"Long live Russo-Romanian friendship!" he shouted in broken Romanian. "*Aufwiedersehen!*" He placed his cap properly on his head and left with the demijohn under his arm.

The teacher turned in alarm to Irina and put his hand on her shoulder.

"I found him dead in the parlor after you left," she began, but the next moment she was interrupted by the Russian, who had returned to set the demijohn meekly on the rug. "*Verboten!*" he declared with an embarrassed grin.

Biris stopped in front of the door. The shaking had begun again and his teeth chattered so that he put both hands to his jaws to hold them shut. "You go in." He spoke with difficulty. "I'll join you presently." He glanced at his watch. Eleven-thirty. It's late, he repeated to himself without thinking. That's good. . . . It's late enough. . . . It's much better that it's late, almost midnight. . . . Inside, *doamna* Porumbache was weeping. He heard whispering, footsteps, and with sudden determination he entered the old parlor. Candles were burning in glasses that had been placed on the floor around the sofa where Bibicescu lay, his hands gripping the blanket, his head against the foot of the couch. Irina was kneeling beside him, weeping softly, her face hidden in her hands. Biris looked at his watch again and stepped forward resolutely. It's past eleven-thirty, he said to himself. This way is best. . . .

"What are we going to do now?" the teacher inquired in a whisper as he watched Biris pause beside the couch and cross himself. But Biris felt his legs crumple and it was with difficulty that he managed to drop to the edge of the sofa. *Doamna* Porumbache sprang to give him support.

"I told him not to come," she whispered. "He's sick. He has a fever. . . ."

Exhausted, Biris remained seated on the edge of the sofa contemplating the candles. *Doamna* Ivascu began to relate in a hushed voice the tale of what had occurred. "At about nine-thirty Irina went to see what he was doing. She listened at the door because when he wrote at night he talked to himself all the time, he read aloud as if he were at the theater. She didn't hear anything, so she supposed he was asleep and came in to see if the fire was still burning. Poor man, he always complained of being cold at night. She found him here. . . ."

Suddenly Biris noticed how cold it was in the room, and although he was wearing two pullovers and had kept his overcoat on, he began to shiver.

"What are we going to do with him?" The teacher repeated his question. "If *conu* Misu were still here he'd take him somewhere in a car. He had friends. He'd come in a car and get him. . . ."

Biris glanced at his watch again. "We've got to move him tonight," he declared. "Tomorrow it will be too late. We're lucky it happened at night, so he can be moved. . . ." He stopped short and blushed. He felt that he should not have mentioned luck, that he ought not to have said, "We're lucky. . . ." He hunted for his cigarettes with a trembling hand, and suddenly embarrassed he asked, "May I smoke?" When there was no reply he lit a cigarette nervously, but as he had no place to lay the match he allowed it to burn a long time before blowing it out and throwing it on the floor.

"We have to do something," insisted *doamna* Porumbache.

"Let's take him somewhere tonight," said the teacher.

"Tomorrow will be too late," Biris repeated more courageously. "We'll have to get him out tonight in the dark." He smoked with short rapid puffs and regarded his watch again.

"We'll take him to the church," said Irina, rising. "We'll leave him there in the entry like a foundling child, and tomorrow morning I'll speak to the priest. . . ."

"That's impossible," *doamna* Ivascu interrupted. "There's a police station next door to it. We'd have to pass in front of the station. There are sergeants . . ."

"It's unwise," observed Biris, and he began to shake again. "We ought to go somewhere not too far away and leave him in the street. . . ."

"We can't do that," Irina said firmly. "It's bad enough that he died like a dog. We can't just throw him out on the street. I'm going to take him to the church. . . ."

"You're crazy!" murmured *doamna* Ivascu, frightened.

"We have to move him now before he stiffens," the teacher advised. "We'll take him in a blanket . . ."

"That's not wise either," objected Biris. "We're likely to meet a patrol."

"We'll take him under the arms, you and I," Irina said quickly to her father-in-law. "We'll put his coat on him, and his hat. We'll wrap him up in his muffler. If anyone asks us we'll say he got sick on the way. . . . But it's understood we're taking him to the church."

"We'll have to hurry," Biris said hastily, his eyes on his watch. "It's

500

almost midnight. Later, it'll look suspicious. If we meet a patrol tell them we're coming home from a party." Still shaking, he crushed his cigarette.

"I don't know if he had a hat," commented *doamna* Ivascu. "I don't remember seeing him in a hat when he came. . . ."

The snow was falling lightly now in large soft flakes that brushed the face gently. On the ground it was thick and spongy, and they moved forward as noiselessly as if they were walking on cotton. Biris and *doamna* Ivascu proceeded at a distance of ten meters ahead of the others in order to reconnoiter the route. Trembling incessantly, Biris kept turning to look back. He could see Bibicescu, supported under his arms by Irina and Gheorghe Vasile, being dragged through the snow. The dead man was clad in an overcoat, with a muffler covering his chin and an old broad-brimmed hat of Antim's pulled down as far as possible on his head. Biris noticed that Bibicescu's legs hung close together and slightly flexed at the knees like those of a man who was letting himself be carried along reluctantly, making his body a dead weight. *Doamna* Porumbache followed a step behind to assist if one of them should slip or become tired.

For some time they met no one, but suddenly as they rounded a corner they caught sight of a couple walking toward them. Biris turned his head quickly to signal Irina and the teacher, and they stopped at once. When the couple came near them Irina put her arm around Bibicescu's shoulders and asked in a loud voice, "Are you ill? Rest here against the wall." The couple walked faster and passed by without looking up.

"I'm tired!" said the teacher after the strangers had disappeared.

"Let me have a turn at it," murmured *doamna* Porumbache, taking Bibicescu's arm.

Shivering, Biris waited with his hands in the pockets of his overcoat, watching as they dragged their burden through the snow, and it seemed to him now that Bibicescu had become smaller. His legs were more bent at the knees, his head had fallen forward a little and his hat seemed much too large. It was white with snow and almost hid his face. They stopped.

"We'll have to cross the street," Biris whispered. "We can't take him to the church. It's too risky."

"He seems to be getting heavier," said *doamna* Porumbache, taking a deep breath. "We can't carry him much farther. . . ."

"I'll take him," murmured Irina. "I'll carry him to the church. . . ."

"You're crazy!" *doamna* Ivascu exclaimed. "You'll get us caught and thrown in jail! You'll make trouble for all of us! Remember, you have a

501

child!" She went to Bibicescu and brushed the snow from his hat and shoulders with her hand. Then they all followed Biris, who had already gone across the street.

"I can't go on!" protested *doamna* Porumbache when they reached the other sidewalk. "Let's rest a moment. . . ."

"There isn't time," whispered the teacher. "Let me carry him now. . . ." He seized Bibicescu's arm and began to drag him along furiously as fast as he could go. Breathing hard, with bowed head and in silence, Irina tried to keep pace with him without stumbling. For several minutes they walked quietly, stopping at last when they were unable to go farther. They leaned Bibicescu against a wall, and Biris hastened back to them.

"Let's take him into the Garden of the Icon," he suggested. "It's not very far. . . . I'll help you. . . ."

He put his shoulder under Bibicescu's arm, but with the first step it seemed to him that the dead man's entire weight was crushing him. He staggered, falling to his knees in the snow and dragging Bibicescu down with him.

"God save us!" exclaimed *doamna* Porumbache in a frightened whisper, crossing herself rapidly and hurrying to lift him up, while *doamna* Ivascu picked up Bibicescu's hat out of the snow and replaced it on his head.

"Don't, *domnule* Professor!" said Gheorghe Vasile. "You're sick. You haven't any strength."

When they reached the Garden of the Icon they leaned Bibicescu against the wall while Biris went ahead to see if anyone happened to be there. The snow had stopped falling, and in the pale light of the streetlamps the trees resembled immense icy flowers. Biris breathed a heavy sigh. He felt the tears slide down his cheeks and began to wipe them away with the back of his hand. Then he returned quickly to the others.

"There's a bench over there," he said, raising his arm and pointing. Again he set off ahead in order to clean the bench of snow. He was unable to stop his tears and kept wiping his eyes with hands that were cold and wet. When the others arrived they found him seated at the end of the bench, lost in thought.

They stretched Bibicescu out and set the hat on his head with care. The teacher sighed deeply and pulled a piece of paper from his pocket. He had printed on it in large block letters, "Dan Bibicescu, great Romanian writer, nationally renowned," and at the bottom he had added in haste, "May the earth rest light upon him." He glanced once more over the page and fastened it to Bibicescu's overcoat with a pin.

"God forgive him!" implored *doamna* Porumbache, crossing herself. "Quick! Let's go!"

Irina took from the pocket of her coat some of the candles that Bibicescu

502

had used when he read his play to them. She lit them one by one and stuck them upright on the bench, kneeling beside him in tears.

Each of the others repeated in turn "God forgive him!" Biris and the teacher uncovered their heads.

"Now we have to go," whispered *doamna* Ivascu, approaching Irina and tapping her on the shoulder. "Think of your child. . . ."

Irina rose and leaned over Bibicescu, kissing his fingers. A candle went out. She lit it again carefully and shielded it for a few moments with her hand. "May God forgive us for what we've done," she murmured and made a sign of the cross. Then she started quickly toward the gate, followed by the others. Biris paused once more to look back. The little lights were still burning. Bibicescu seemed lonely, wrapped as he was in his overcoat, the too-large hat on his head, the piece of paper on his chest like a price tag on a mannequin, lying there in the flickering light of the candles. Biris took off his hat and wiped his eyes again with his hand, trying to check his weeping.

"I'll be seeing you, Dan!" he called. "Soon!"

6

WHEN HE WENT OUT ON THE BALCONY, AS HE DID EVERY MORNING, IT WAS THE cemetery that first met his eyes. From this spot on the second floor it could not possibly be avoided, since it lay before him less than ten meters from the building, surrounded decorously by high walls that gave it the appearance of a park adjoining an estate. On boulevard Murat the leaves of the chestnuts had already turned yellow, but beyond them he could see the dense masses of leaves on trees that were still green. Their branches quivered gently now and then in the golden light of late September.

A few moments later he heard the door open, and he left the balcony. At first he noticed only the black necktie. He's supposed to wear black for a whole year, Stefan caught himself thinking. It was an observation that recurred with absurd regularity every time Misu Weissman came into his room in the morning. A whole year—so he has three more months yet to wear it. . . .

"I didn't disturb you last night, did I?" Weissman inquired, lifting a chair by its back and placing it near the desk so he could sit in the sunlight. "I came in very late. I was with friends of Vidrighin . . ."

He saw a speck of dust on the desk and hastened to wipe it with his coat sleeve. Then he stretched out his hand and pushed the ink bottle to within a centimeter of the pad of blotting paper.

These are his little compulsions, Stefan had realized from the first few days on boulevard Murat. Weissman insisted on keeping the desk in perfect order. Whenever he sat down to write a letter or even simply to address an envelope, he took the most extraordinary precautions not to soil the blotter or change the position of the ink bottle, or to disturb the three marble paperweights, each of which had its appointed place on the immaculate surface. "Look at that desk!" he had said the first evening. "A desk for a writer. If it had not been for Dan I'd have found another apartment closer to the heart of the city. But I was expecting Dan. . . ." As he spoke he lifted his hand to inspect the knot of his tie.

". . . friends of Vidrighin . . . but I was on the point of quarreling with one of them. The same old story with your diplomatic passport. 'What? Now even *domnul* Viziru joins the Resistance?' he said. 'After he's worked with the Communists and traveled on their sleeping cars?' But I set him straight immediately."

Stefan shrugged. "Thanks, but you've put yourself out for nothing. You ought to tell him the truth. You know very well why I've come. . . ."

Misu Weissman gazed at him a long time with admiration, then he smiled and shook his head. "I like you. You're a remarkable man. Everyone ought to take you for an example. I told Vidrighin last night, 'If it's a matter of discretion there's no one better than Viziru. I adopted him as a model long ago.'"

He started to laugh, but stopped abruptly and went to the door. "Here I am talking and I forgot," he said. "The coffee's ready." He entered the kitchen, an enigmatic smile on his lips, and touched the pot to see if the coffee were hot enough. He set the cups, with the teaspoons and sugar bowl, on the tray, but at the last moment he changed his mind and lit the gas burner again, placing the pot over the flame for a minute longer. When he returned to the study, Stefan, who was at the window, said to him, "Don't think I'm trying to mystify myself. Don't think that I intend to evade the drama of History by taking refuge in a personal problem. . . ."

Weissman smiled again as he set the cups of coffee carefully on the little table beside the desk. He knew what would follow. It seemed to him he had heard Stefan talking about the mystification of History once before. Possibly he had spoken about it a number of times, but Weissman had trained himself not always to listen. It was sufficient simply to look at Stefan, feigning attention and nodding his head gravely from time to time.

"The true and tragic mystification happens to *others*," continued Stefan, leaving the window.

"Which *others*?" demanded Weissman. "Why are you always thinking about others?" He had just begun to pour the coffee, but he stopped and raised his head suddenly, the coffeepot still in his hand.

"This seems to me to be the most terrible of all mystifications—to believe that the human being finds supreme fulfillment only when he succeeds in identifying himself with the vanguard of History."

"It's no use changing the subject." Weissman smiled. "I said I was with friends of Vidrighin last night. Listen to me—I haven't finished," he added quickly, as though he expected to be interrupted. "I told you that we spoke

505

about you, but I didn't say with whom. I wanted to surprise you. . . ." He finished pouring the coffee and seated himself in a chair, the same secret smile lingering on his lips. "Aren't you at all curious?"

"Yes, of course. But I too wanted to tell you something and you interrupted me . . ."

"I know what you wanted to say. You wanted to change the subject. I know you. . . . As soon as I pronounce the name of Vidrighin you try to change the subject. But you're mistaken. . . . That man appreciates you—he even admires you—very much. . . . Only this time it wasn't a question of him or his friends. Last evening when I was with them I met someone who knows you—who in fact claims to know you *very well* . . ."

"If you'll let me finish," Stefan went on, "I'll listen to you with the greatest pleasure. Because what I wanted to convey to you is a very important matter for me. And since you like philosophy too, you'll understand me."

Weissman nodded several times to conciliate Stefan, and he lifted the cup to his lips. It had taken him some time to become accustomed to Stefan's obsessions and weaknesses. He knew that Stefan needed the presence of another to listen to him think aloud. A friend in Bucharest may have told him once facetiously that Weissman had a passion for philosophy.

"You, *coane* Misu—you like philosophy!" Stefan had said the very evening of his arrival in Paris. That was when it began, on the evening of August 20. In the morning he had lifted the receiver and heard a voice that seemed familiar calling him by name. "*Domnule* Weissman? Stefan Viziru here!" An hour later he stood before the door with two small valises, ringing the bell.

"I've come from Prague—and straight here from the airport. I don't want to go to a hotel tonight. Can you put me up?" He appeared tired and the lower part of his face trembled slightly as he spoke, as though he were suffering from a nervous tic.

"Of course! You'll use Dan's room. But how did you locate me?" Weissman took one of the valises.

"I'll tell you later. Just now I'd like to change. I have an urgent errand to do. . . ."

He shut himself in the bathroom with both suitcases, and a half-hour later he emerged dressed to go out, a valise in his hand. "I think I can find a taxi," he said, crossing the room to the door.

"I'll come with you and show you . . ."

"Don't bother," Stefan interrupted. "I know Paris well. I took my doctorate here. I believe I saw a taxi stand near the Métro."

He shook Weissman's hand and descended the stairs quickly, carrying the valise. Two hours later he returned. Weissman was waiting for him on the balcony, and when he saw him get out of the taxi without the valise he smiled and tiptoed into the study. Seeing his face in the mirror he broke into a short silent laugh which he suppressed at once with his hand, as if he were afraid he would catch someone's attention. "I like him," he chuckled. "I like his discretion. . . ."

"I learned your address in Bucharest," Stefan confided. "It's no secret. Everybody knows it—all your friends, I mean, and they're numerous. But there are about six telephones in this building, and with a little luck you answered on the third try. I have a lot of news for you."

That afternoon he related to him all kinds of incidents that had taken place in Bucharest, the most important being Dan Bibicescu's death. He repeated all the information that Biris had given him concerning it. But he avoided, apparently very carefully, making any reference to politics. Later Weissman discovered that if he wanted to find out something specific he must question Stefan directly, although the replies were always evasive.

"I was on a mission to Prague," Viziru said finally. "I took advantage of an opportunity and caught a plane." He smiled at Weissman, who smiled back and gave him an understanding wink.

"I don't mean to pry," Misu insisted, "but you've come for a definite purpose . . ."

"I'll tell you about it later. I've a lot to tell you. . . ."

That evening Weissman invited him to go to a restaurant in Passy. During the course of the evening Stefan became unusually agitated and rested his hand on Weissman's shoulder. "Because you've displayed such confidence in me I want to explain why I've run away. I'll ask you, however . . ."

"Don't worry," Weissman interrupted. "Anything you may say to me will remain strictly between the two of us. Buried."

Stefan sighed and stroked his face with his hand. "Dear *domnule* Weissman, you have no way of knowing! No one knows except Biris. For many years I've loved a girl—Ileana. Ileana Sideri. I haven't seen her for almost six years. I know she's living somewhere, hiding, and I've come to look for her." He fell silent when the *garçon* approached, and he waited for him to leave.

"You know so many people," he resumed, speaking more softly. "Perhaps you've heard of her. Her name is Ileana. Ileana Sideri." He began to describe her in a voice that was enthralled and impassioned, lingering over the smallest details—the boyish way she ran her hand through her hair, her manner of looking at him, the colors of her summer dresses. But then, suddenly and apparently without reason, he became troubled and seized Weissman's arm again, gazing at him in an access of warmth.

"*Coane* Misu, you like philosophy and you're interested in the

507

problems of the human soul so I can speak frankly with you. . . ."
Weissman inclined his head slightly toward Stefan, assuming an attitude of close attention.

"You know that one of the most difficult things to comprehend is the fact that a man can forget even those events and revelations on which his happiness and his salvation depend. How such an amnesia can occur I still don't understand, but this capacity for *forgetting the essential* explains in large measure the powerlessness of Christianity to change men—in a word, to save them."

Weissman looked thoughtfully into his eyes. "What are you leading up to?"

"Just this: Christianity has revealed the secret of our salvation to us, and yet almost none of us remembers what the secret is. We've forgotten it just as we forget a lot of other things that aren't worth remembering anyway."

"It's true, we forget," said Weissman. "But I don't understand the point you're trying to make. . . ."

"The same thing has happened to me too. There are important things I've forgotten. For years I remembered down to the smallest particular Ileana's clothes, her gestures, her words. I imagined that, no matter what might happen to me from then on, I'd never be able to forget them. That was an illusion. I did begin to forget them, to confuse them, and one day I realized they were gone. I confounded two conversations that took place at widely separated times—the first in a restaurant in the summer of 1936 and the other at Bussaco on New Year's Eve in 1941. It was only last night on the plane that I remembered them clearly. Maybe because I was excited," he added, dropping his voice a little, "and frightened. Until I was a good five hundred kilometers from Prague I was afraid!"

"I don't doubt it," said Weissman confidentially, drawing closer. "You risked being downed by Russian pursuit planes. . . . Say, what was it like?" Impatiently he peered into Stefan's eyes.

"I realized then that I'd been confused. At the time, this discovery delighted me, as if I'd found something precious that I'd lost long ago, but an hour later I realized how serious this was. It means, you know, that Time can nibble away and consume not only the memory of events that it's created itself—events born of Time and condemned as such to fall into oblivion simply because of its passing—it means that Time can attack even the revelations that come to us from beyond it. It can attack them, macerate them slowly, and finally destroy them in the same way that it destroys the memory of any ordinary event. This is very grave, dear *coane* Misu. If this is true then our adversaries—yours and mine—are right and someday the whole world will be theirs. . . ."

508

"You're wrong! That's impossible! They've lost the game!"

". . . Because for them," continued Stefan, as if he had not heard, "man can't know anything except History. In other words, out of all that's happened in the life of humanity, man can only know what he forgets, recalls, and forgets again. . . ."

"The Communists have lost the game, I tell you!" Weissman insisted, trying to change the course of the discussion.

"But I still believe that *something else* exists, beyond Time and History," Stefan resumed with fervor, "and that we can know this *something else*. But a great spiritual effort on our part is demanded to accomplish it. In my case I was incapable of such effort. That's why all those things happened to me. I lost Ioana because I'd already forgotten her. I'm the guilty one. God took her from me because I no longer possessed her. . . ." These final words were spoken with great seriousness, and then he was silent for several moments, ruminating.

"The will of God . . ." observed Weissman. "But you're still young and now you've escaped. You're here, free. . . . Be thankful for that."

Stefan sighed. "Yes, I ought to be. I shouldn't forget that fact—that *I've escaped*. But as I was saying a little while ago, the tragedy is that we forget even the essential things. . . . Actually perhaps it's a mistake to believe that History is of a piece with memory. History is constantly modifying memories, continually according them new values, negative or positive, until eventually it annuls them. This is what's happened, for instance, with Christianity. If man knew how to remember *completely* certain revelations, he would escape from History. My love for Ileana was such a revelation, but already I've begun to forget. It's been no more than six years since I last saw her and I've started to forget the most important details."

Weissman had been watching Stefan and listening to him intently, rubbing his eyes now and then to banish his weariness. "I understand," he said with sudden decision. "You're a wise man. You have a family in Romania. . . ."

Stefan turned toward him with a look of surprise, as if trying to guess his meaning. "My family?" he asked after a pause. "Yes, it's true. There are still a few of them left. My father died two years ago. The house was confiscated long before that. My sister, Sofioara, the *Doctorita*, married the son of the pharmacist . . ."

"So I heard," said Weissman, but he realized immediately that he had spoken too casually in the belief that Viziru would approve. He blushed in embarrassment.

". . . to the desolation of Eleonora, my father's second wife," Stefan continued with a sad smile. "She'd been in love with that pharmacist's boy for a long time. The poor woman waited all those years for my

509

father to die so she could marry the man she loved, but the *Doctorita* intervened. She beat her to him. . . . The only ones for whom things are going badly are Adela and Raducu. I sent them some money before I left, but they refused it. They're both people of character. I hope they'll accept it later when they have nothing more to sell. If only Raducu is not arrested eventually. He can't keep his mouth shut. . . ."

The next day Weissman had let him sleep until ten. When he took him some coffee, he found him still in bed smoking.

"If you like, you may stay here. It gives me the greatest pleasure to accommodate you. Tell me how you're fixed for money."

"Thank you. For the present I have all I need."

"Let me know when you require more. With a little luck we'll become millionaires. I have an extraordinary transaction underway. I'll tell you about it later. . . . Now, drink your coffee—and after that tell me what else has happened at home."

They conversed that morning for two hours. Stefan did most of the talking, but he spoke with such excitement that Weissman couldn't always follow him. Finally he lost patience and stood up. "You'd better get dressed. We'll be going to eat in half an hour."

Stefan had just lit another cigarette. "Let me finish this," he said. "You don't know what it means to stay in bed till noon without a schedule and without a care—without the fear that at any moment someone will open the door and stand over you, asking you to account for what you have or haven't done."

"Yes, I do know. I left Romania for that same reason. . . ." He picked up the chair, holding it by the back, and carried it closer to the bed. "And if I'm sorry about anything it's that you don't have the least bit of faith in me," he continued, placing the chair directly in front of Stefan. "I'm not a curious man, but I expected that at least you'd tell me with whom you associated in Romania. . . ."

Stefan stared at him with wonder in his eyes. "I supposed that you knew," he replied. "It was Biris I saw most of the time."

"Well, he's the very one who interests me. I'd like to know now— this morning—what Biris thinks. How does he view events—the way they're developing?"

"He believes it would be the greatest crime, and stupid, too, to organize a resistance. . . ."

"Don't say that," interrupted Weissman nervously. "You're in danger of being overheard by other Romanians and then you'll really be suspected. . . ."

"Listen, Biris is right. It would be stupid to resist in the Western sense of the word—to provoke an irreparable bloodbath. We must just rediscover the technique of camouflaging ourselves, the art of lying and

510

deceiving. Let the victor think that he has converted us to his beliefs, that he has conquered us within. That's all. . . ."

"I like your optimism," said Weissman, smiling ironically. "One can see you're an intellectual. All intellectuals are optimists. You live in the clouds. . . ."

". . . That's all, but it's difficult and dangerous. This collective lying could last a great many decades, perhaps even a century. It's very hard to preserve the soul intact throughout a century of hibernating under a mask. So then we are faced with the problem of how to accomplish the preservation of our soul in the new Dark Age that's beginning for us."

Weissman regarded him again with intense curiosity. He rose suddenly and seized the back of his chair with both hands. "I like you! You know how to change the subject," he said with a wry smile. "But don't imagine you can trick me so easily. If you don't believe in the resistance, I might ask you why you fled the country. According to your theory you should have stayed there and camouflaged yourself."

"Of course I should have done that. But I realized I would be good for nothing until my life had regained its meaning. Many people throw themselves into politics in order to forget a personal tragedy or to fill an inner void. And probably that's why they are successful, at least on an exterior, historical level. When you no longer have anything left to lose, you can become a hero or a great political figure."

Weissman paused a moment, gazing at him, then shrugged and returned the chair to the desk, lifting it by the back. "Let's stick to the subject of politics," he said.

"Aren't you at all curious to know who this person is?" he inquired when he noticed that his guest stole a glance at his watch.

"What person?" asked Stefan, puzzled, starting slightly as though just awakened.

"The person I met last evening when I was with Vidrighin's friends. She said that she knew you very well. . . ."

At once Stefan looked up.

"No, it's not the one you think. It's someone else—a very beautiful woman. She knew you well. She'd like to see you again, to talk with you. . . ."

"Invite her. I'll be glad to receive her."

Weissman smiled at him. "I'd like to see how long it takes you to pry it out of me."

"Not long, because I don't have time. Today I'm going out very early."

"You're going to the Louvre, I presume?" Weissman teased him, bursting into laughter, in excellent spirits.

Stefan did not reply and for awhile they were both silent.

511

"Really, aren't you curious? Because I warn you, it's a question of someone who's very important. . . ."

"Invite her," Stefan repeated, getting up. "But now I must ask you to
excuse me. I have to be off. . . ." He held out his hand and started for the
door.

"You're terrific!" There was a trace of regret in Weissman's voice. "But
I'll share the blame," he added, slapping Stefan on the back. "I chose a bad
moment. I shouldn't have spoken to you at this time. I didn't know you were
leaving so early."

He stepped out on the balcony to see which way Stefan went. Vidrighin
was right, he said to himself. He's a strange man. But I have enough patience.
Eventually, I'll find out everything. . . .

He had been telling himself this for several weeks, ever since that rainy
morning when he heard Stefan speaking as usual about Ileana and
History.

"The delusion would be to believe that I'd be able to do anything
truly useful in the world—in History—without finding Ileana. Not only
could I do nothing, but I'd create confusion. My inner rift would affect
the whole world. . . ."

Weissman was beginning to feel that he could not listen to Stefan's
comments much longer when he suddenly heard him declare, "For a
long time I didn't realize that, at least in part, last year's drought was due
to the fact that I was out of balance—that I had not pursued Ileana."

He had uttered the last words in a faltering voice with a hint of fear
in it. Weissman could not refrain from remarking, "You're joking!" he
smiled.

"I speak in all seriousness. Bursuc understood this before I did. He
told me that I was partly responsible for the drought because my hands
were stained with blood."

"Bursuc's a rogue! A rogue and a traitor. . . ."

"But in my case he was right. The drought in Moldavia was in part
the consequence of our spiritual drought. It was precisely like that in the
legend of the Fisher King. Until Perceval came to ask the right
question—the only question which was imperative: What is the nature
of the Grail and where may it be found?—the wasting of the land
continued and the Fisher King couldn't recover. If I'd known how to ask
the right question, perhaps the drought would have ended. But I didn't
know what the true question was and I don't know it now. . . . I hope I'll
discover it when I find Ileana again. . . ."

Sipping his coffee from time to time, Weissman inspected Stefan
carefully.

512

"Listen closely and I'll tell you a great secret," continued his guest, approaching him and placing a hand on his shoulder. "In the depths of my soul I believe I'm responsible for everything that's happening in the world today. If I had sought for Ileana perhaps there would be at least one terrible thing less occurring in the world. . . ."

"You're joking, of course," repeated Weissman. "Still I'm not angry with you, because you're so likable."

"I began to understand all that when Biris told me a legend about a Chinese sage . . ."

Weissman raised his head suddenly and looked in Stefan's eyes. "I like you . . ." he began, but Viziru did not allow him to continue.

"As I was listening to Biris I began to understand. For everything that happens in the world I share the responsibility. Because I'm not a whole man—I'm not a harmonious unity. I'm an unbalanced individual without a center. Probably there are others too, tens of millions, like me. And since for modern societies 'the world' is getting to be less 'Cosmos' and more 'History,' you can realize what repercussions this interior lack of balance could have beyond ourselves. How could we, the tens of millions of unbalanced individuals, ever have been creators in History?"

Suddenly self-conscious, he lit a cigarette and began to smoke. Weissman had finished his coffee, and he set the cup on the tray resolutely.

"I'd like to speak seriously with you," he proposed. "I understand very well that you're discreet and cautious. Therefore I've waited for you to tell me if you caught them off-guard in Prague, if you were able to effect a transfer of important documents. Just that much! I wouldn't ask you to tell me the kind of documents—only a hint so I too can enjoy the trick you played on them. I know more about you than you think. I should have expected you to tell me at least what you think of Bursuc. I know that he's a scoundrel and a double agent, but I'd like to know with whom he's working on our side. It's very important to keep in contact with him, but it's also necessary to know precisely who's the intermediary. Have you heard of a certain Pantelimon? It seems that Bursuc is working with someone called Pantelimon, who says he's on our side. Have you heard of him?"

Stefan was embarrassed, but he smiled. "I've heard of him, although I can't tell you who he is. I don't know him. . . ."

"It's very important," Weissman continued, speaking more softly. "The man who has to get Biris across the border has made contact with Pantelimon. I must find out who this man is. . . ."

Stefan shrugged. "We'll learn someday. Meanwhile I have to find

513

Ileana. I suspect where she is—in Switzerland with the Valkyrie. But they won't give me a Swiss visa. I went to the Consulate and they told me they don't give visas to holders of Romanian passports."

H-m-m. He does know about Pantelimon, but he won't talk, reflected Weissman. Maybe he doesn't trust me, or else he's exceptionally discreet. But never mind, I'll find out eventually. . . .

Since then he had tried other stratagems. He would let Stefan talk and suddenly he would ask him a question entirely removed from the subject under discussion. Then he would steal a glance at Stefan to observe his reaction. He would have liked to do more—for instance, to follow him and find out whom he met—but Weissman had to leave the house every morning and he almost always went out before Stefan. He would have liked to know whom Stefan talked with on the telephone and what their conversations were about. Once he had retraced his steps and found the door locked and bolted. He had opened it very carefully, trying not to make any noise, and had entered the hallway walking on the tips of his toes. Stefan was speaking on the telephone. "Good. . . . Good. I'll come. . . ." Weissman began to tread heavily then and he coughed a few times before entering the study.

"Who was that?" he asked casually.

"You don't know him—a former classmate from the University."

"If you like I can take you in a taxi to your appointment. I have to take one anyway, since I'm late."

"I'm not meeting him today. I'm going to the Louvre. . . ."

This was frequently his response when he came home in the evenings and Weissman asked him how he had spent the afternoon. "I was at the Louvre," he would say. "You won't believe me, but I must confess that my only regret is that I'm not a painter. . . ."

Sometimes Misu found Stefan waiting for him on the balcony. The evenings were warm and serene, and he would be stretched out on the chaise longue, woolgathering, an unlighted cigarette between his fingers.

"I tried again today," he said once. "It's a vicious circle. They won't give me a visa on a diplomatic passport and I have to have an IRO* travel voucher, but the Swiss almost never give a visa on a travel voucher. . . ."

Weissman knew that Stefan told him all this just to make him think he had spent the afternoon at the Swiss Consulate. "If that's all, don't worry. Vidrighin has a friend who has assured me he can obtain a visa for you. But you'll have to go and see Vidrighin. . . ."

When Stefan remained silent, Weissman went closer to get a better

*International Refugee Organization.

look at his face. "Why so thoughtful?" he demanded. "Have you heard some bad news? Have you met someone?" It seemed to him that Stefan was embarrassed when he peered at him, but Weissman searched his eyes and insisted, "You can tell me. I'm like a tomb!"

"I haven't heard anything in a long time," Stefan finally replied. "I'm beginning to worry. . . ."

Weissman's smile was eloquent. He had observed that recently Stefan tried to maintain his reserve by responding that he was "worried," without specifying why. A few days before, very early in the morning, he had thought he heard him say on the telephone, "Good. Then you'll come to get me. . . ." Weissman did not divulge what he had heard but he left soon after, stopping at a cafe on boulevard Murat, where he found a seat at a table near the window. He prepared to wait. After about an hour had passed he saw Stefan come toward him accompanied by a thin, poorly clad young man with a sallow complexion. They walked along side by side without speaking. In front of the Métro station they separated, shaking hands warmly in a gesture of farewell. That evening Weissman listened with growing impatience to a prolonged oration about the Louvre, but finally, unable to restrain himself, he exclaimed, "You, *coane* Stefan—you like secrets and mysteries! You like to surround yourself with mystery. . . ."

"Really?" responded Stefan, astonished. "I thought the only mystery that ever excited me was *doamna* Zissu. You don't know the story of *doamna* Zissu. Or more precisely, it can't actually be called a story because I don't know anything about her. *Doamna* Zissu has remained just what she was from the first day I heard her name—a secret. . . . Why do you smile?" he asked suddenly, staring at Weissman, who was no longer trying to hide his smile. He allowed it to spread over his entire face, illuminating it. Raising his hand he motioned to Stefan to continue. "No. It's nothing. I was thinking of something else. Go on. . . ."

"The fact is there's almost nothing to tell about *doamna* Zissu. I heard about her from Vadastra when I had my secret room. We stayed in the same hotel. . . ."

He stopped and passed his hand across his face. "I don't know how many years have passed since then. I have to figure it out every time to be sure of how many years it's been. It was in 1935 or '36. That's eleven or twelve. . . . But why are you smiling?" he insisted again, and it seemed to Weissman that this time he was somewhat annoyed.

"While I was listening to you talk about the mystery of *doamna* Zissu I wanted to ask you something." He paused deliberately in order to regard Stefan more closely, and he thought that his friend had become slightly pale, as though he found it difficult to master his irritation.

515

"I wanted to ask you who the chap was you met this morning."

Confused, Stefan was silent for some time. He began to moisten his lips.

"If it's some big secret don't tell me."

"I'd rather not say. I'm a little worried. . . . But you'll find out later, when Biris comes. . . ."

Weissman watched him, suddenly amused. He seemed about to laugh. "You're right," he said at last. "I congratulate you. More than that, I take you for my example. I've already done that—made you my example. I've learned to surround myself with mystery too. But since you've brought up the subject of Biris—you can't imagine what mission he will have here or what his role in Paris will be!"

"We'll make philosophy together," was Stefan's rejoinder and for the first time that evening he grinned.

"Besides that," insisted Weissman. "He'll do that here as long as he stays with us, and at the sanatorium too. Because you'll agree that he must first spend some time in a sanatorium and be thoroughly cured. I've arranged to send him to a certain place. But that's not what I meant. I said that you've no idea what his mission here will be nor why I spend so much time with Vidrighin's friends."

Stefan felt reassured and he listened in amazement.

"Because Vidrighin's friends are well established in Paris. One of them knows everybody—all the writers, actors, journalists. . . ."

"I think I know what you're talking about . . ."

"Impossible!" Weissman announced with an air of triumph. "Biris will have a lot of work. There are several kilos of manuscripts." He pronounced the words slowly and distinctly, underscoring them by the stress in his voice. "You'll never guess whose they are."

"Bibicescu's?"

"Not only his. There are others too, just as priceless. Dan discovered them several years ago. If a book should be written about how he found them, you'd think it was a perfect novel. An adventure story!"

He stopped and looked at Stefan with an ample smile lighting his face, his eyes blinking constantly to clear his vision so he could enjoy Viziru's expression and everything he could read in it. After a moment Stefan remarked simply, "Interesting!"

"But you see, now I like to surround myself with mystery too. I can't tell you any more. You'll find out later. . . ."

As soon as the train began to move Biris felt gripped by fear. I'm a coward! he said to himself several times. I'll have to admit that I'm a coward and scared to death!... He waited a few moments to see if the mental repetition of these words would have any effect, but his body seemed fully as tense as it had before. He quivered inside, his mouth was dry, and there was a great void where his heart should have been. I'm a coward! he thought again and searched for his package of cigarettes. I flattered myself that I liked to feel History on the march around me, that I wanted to live only to see what happens in the world—and now I'm afraid because I'm going to Arad. I'm only going to Arad. That's all I'm doing. That's my whole adventure. And yet I'm scared.... When I arrive I'll get off the train, go to *aleea** Alexandru and ask for Doctor Vlad. I'll just say, "I'm the representative of the firm 'Home Industries,' of Bucharest. Do you need anything?" And Doctor Vlad will reply something in this vein, probably, "I believe my wife needs some curtains.... Come in, please." That's all. I'll spend the night with him, and the next day I'll go by car to the point of crossing. There's no risk of any kind. Hundreds of people have crossed over before me.... He repeated obstinately, *There's absolutely no risk of any kind,* and he underscored the words in his mind. Then why the devil am I afraid? I'm a coward. I flattered myself that...

His thoughts were interrupted by the sensation that he was about to choke on the cigarette smoke. He opened his mouth to allow the smoke to float out freely, making an effort to avoid coughing. The man opposite him in the compartment—an ageless man with a beard of several days growth and a face that was tanned and dry—looked at him in astonishment. When Biris felt that the danger of choking had passed, he swallowed a number of times and smiled. But when he observed that the man continued to stare at him, fascinated, he turned away and looked out the window. The train had left behind the last wretched remnants of the outlying areas and was now crossing the verdant plain, lightly gilded by the sunlight of the October morning.

"We're in luck," said the man across from him suddenly. "After so much rain...."

For about ten days it had been raining steadily. When he had received the postcard with its conventional message he had stood for awhile at the window, watching the rain fall and trying to quiet the pounding of his heart. More than once he had caught himself in a sigh as he glanced around the room. Good-bye, *strada* Macelari, he thought, trying to sustain his courage. He noticed that a few books still remained. I'll have to sell them too—except the one from Catalina. I'll take that with me.... Suddenly he was impatient to depart, and he went quickly into the kitchen.

"I've made up my mind," he declared, forcing himself to assume a casual tone. "I'll be leaving one of these days. They've written for me to come any time and stay until after the grape harvest." "Don't catch

*Avenue.

517

cold," *doamna* Porumbache warned, "after all that rain. Wait till the weather changes." "No, I'm leaving now. Maybe I'll find a seat on the train, more easily this way. I'll stay for several weeks and take advantage of the clean air." "Don't catch cold," *doamna* Porumbache insisted.

He had sold the last of his books. He searched his drawers carefully and burned all the papers and letters. "*Incipit vita nova!*" he said to himself again and again. And then one night he had very carefully sewn into the lining of his coat the dollars that Stefan had left with him. The rest—ten napoleons, a few hundred pengö and some Swiss francs, also given to him by Stefan—he had hidden in various pockets. The guide who was to take him across the border had already received half of the amount due him. The ten napoleons constituted the other half, and these Biris would give him after they reached Hungary.

He scarcely closed his eyes the night before he left. He kept hearing the sound of the fine rain as it struck against the glass of the window with all the monotony characteristic of late autumn storms. The room had become cold. He pulled the cover up to his chin and reminded himself, It's late—I have to go to sleep.... And he had slipped into ˙sleep without being aware of it. In the morning *doamna* Porumbache wakened him when she brought his cup of tea. The room was bathed in sunlight. "I'm in luck!" he said, and all of a sudden he realized he had started to tremble. "The weather's changed...."

When he set the empty cup on the tray he looked at his aunt once more and smiled. That's my last cup of tea on *strada* Macelari, he told himself. Then he dressed and put on his overcoat. His little valise, in which he had taken his books to the dealer, was waiting beside the bed. He picked it up and went out into the hall.

"Good-bye, keep well," he said, trying not to reveal how deeply moved he was. He put down his valise and kissed *doamna* Porumbache's hand. "Thank you for everything," he murmured softly. She accompanied him to the street, where he took leave of her, but after he had gone a few steps he turned around, went back, and kissed her on both cheeks.

"We're in great luck," the man continued, letting his gaze swing to the distant scene beyond the window. "The country's beautiful.... Are you going far?" He turned to Biris.

"To visit friends at their vineyard," Biris responded vaguely.

The man had begun to study him with curiosity. He seemed to be almost anxious, although he was making an effort to smile.

"... At their vineyard," repeated Biris, becoming timid suddenly. "It ought to be beautiful there now. I hope the fine weather will last...."

The man glanced furtively around and leaned toward Biris, indicating for him to come closer, motioning as if he wanted to show him something in the field.

"Straighten your tie," he whispered quickly as he pointed far away across the plain. "Your banknotes are showing. . . ."

Biris looked at him in alarm and put his hand to his necktie. The man smiled broadly and gave him an understanding wink.

At Arad he got off the train and stayed for a half hour in the restaurant at the station, trying to regain his strength. Why the devil am I afraid? he kept repeating to himself, watching his shaking hands. I knew long ago I was a coward, but I never suspected I was in such bad shape! I was glad that I was tubercular and wouldn't be sent to the Russian front. I was a coward then, but at least it made some sense. But now, why the devil am I afraid? I'll get into a carriage and go to *aleea* Alexandru. That's all. That's my whole adventure. . . . Maybe it would be wiser to go on foot, he reasoned, but he felt exhausted from twenty-two hours on the train and a second night without sleep, and he did not dare to attempt it. He drank several cups of tea and glanced repeatedly at his watch. When he saw that it was eight-thirty he paid for his tea, picked up his valise, and went out.

Aleea Alexandru was some distance from the station. Pulled by sleepy animals, the carriage proceeded slowly, and after about thirty minutes it stopped in front of a modest house that had a provincial air. God help me! Biris said to himself as he pulled the cord to ring the bell. Soon a man came out, rubbing his eyes as though the strong morning light annoyed him.

"I-I-I'm the representative of the Home Industries," Biris stammered. Immediately he remembered he should have begun differently, "I'm looking for Doctor Vlad," but he had no opportunity to correct himself.

"Please come in," the man said, still rubbing his eyes.

They entered a dark anteroom. A coatrack caught his attention. Several hats were hanging on it, and in a corner someone had left an Inverness cape. Biris set his suitcase down. The man promptly picked it up and kept it in his hand as he led him into another room, which they crossed. Neither spoke, but the man, switching the valise to his other hand, tapped timidly on a door. He listened for the response and opened the door wide to permit Biris to go in ahead of him.

The room was large, a sort of salon, with windows facing the garden. Biris stepped forward and felt suddenly a great emptiness within. Smiling, his hand extended, Mihai Duma advanced to greet him.

"You've become bald, Biris! You've aged considerably since we last saw each other. Sit down," he urged, indicating an armchair. "You must be tired...."

With a sudden burst of energy Biris turned and ran to the door, but he had scarcely managed to open it when he felt himself grasped by two strong arms. Another man, appearing unexpectedly, began to search his pockets to see if he were armed. Biris pulled away abruptly in an attempt to escape them, and one of the men thrust a fist in his face. He felt the blood start to accumulate in his nose. At the same moment he heard Duma's voice call from the salon, and he felt the man's arms tighten around him with a jerk, dragging him into the room.

"Don't beat me!" he pleaded, trying to avoid swallowing the blood that bathed his lips. "Don't beat me! I'll tell everything!"

With unexpected politeness the agent opened the door, stepped aside, and let him pass. Duma rose from the desk and came toward him, smiling cordially and holding out his hand. "I hope you had a good trip," he said. "Take a seat, please. My chief, *domnul* Protopopescu, wants to meet you...."

A tall, portly man with gray hair approached Biris and shook his hand warmly. "Delighted. Duma has spoken of you in the most complimentary terms. I'm happy to know you. Take a seat, please."

Both men accompanied Biris to an armchair and invited him insistently to be seated. At once *domnul* Protopopescu held out his silver cigarette case. "Cigarette?" He regarded Biris with a smile of extravagant sympathy and concern.

"Much obliged."

Duma had already struck a match and was waiting for Biris to select his cigarette, but he was unable to extract it from the case. His fingers trembled so violently that after a few minutes he became ashamed. He withdrew his hand and tried to hide it. Duma blew out the match. *Domnul* Protopopescu chose a cigarette and, with the same cordial smile, held it out to Biris, who seized it quickly—his hand still shaking as if someone were jerking his shoulder—and put it eagerly between his lips. Duma struck another match and leaned toward him.

"Thanks," said Biris after he had inhaled the first smoke. "I don't know why my hand shakes so.... Excitement," he added, trying to smile.

"Travel fatigue," said Protopopescu, seating himself in another chair nearby.

"I was sorry we couldn't make the trip together," said Duma, returning to the desk. "I had to stop at Brasov. But I trust that you had everything you needed. I reserved a compartment for you in first class. I hope you took all your meals in the dining car. As far as Iordan is concerned, I don't doubt that you got along very well. . . ."

"He's well-qualified," said Biris, smiling. "But he has one big shortcoming—he doesn't smoke."

Duma frowned as if he had communicated an extremely unpleasant piece of news.

"During the whole journey to Arad he didn't smoke one cigarette," Biris continued. "It was impossible for me to corrupt him."

"We must draw his attention to this," Protopopescu remarked to Duma. "He should always have cigarettes with him. . . . Anyway, please accept our apologies," he added, turning to Biris. "In the meantime, do me the pleasure of taking my pack."

"Thank you. You're very kind."

Duma opened a file and began leafing through it absently. "Now, tell us," he commenced abruptly without raising his eyes from the papers. "What were you going to do in Paris?"

"I was bringing a message," replied Biris with a smile. "A message from the labyrinth. . . ."

Duma scrutinized him distantly, his face almost void of expression.

"This is a formula of ours," continued Biris, "a coded formula that we invented—Stefan and I. It's our way of expressing ourselves when we refer to the predicament of being closed in without any apparent exit. . . ."

"Be more explicit," Duma interrupted. "I asked you what you were going to do in Paris. . . ."

"You know that I'm very much interested in Existentialism. According to what I've heard Existentialism is now in vogue in Paris—Jean-Paul Sartre and the others. I wanted to meet them, talk with them, explain to them about what it means in this part of Europe to be *en situation*, and to be faced with *le problème du choix*. I wanted to present them with a series of 'existential situations'. . . . I've a passion for philosophy," he added with a little laugh. "Up to slightly over a year ago I taught it, but now I'm a private philosopher, as Kierkegaard calls it. That's why Existentialism has such a strong attraction for me."

"When was the last time you saw Viziru?" asked *domnul* Protopopescu.

Biris turned his head fearfully. He hardly recognized the man's voice. It had become strange, harsh, menacing.

"Several days before his departure for Prague," he said, starting to tremble again. "I don't recall the exact date—the tenth or twelfth of August."

"What did he say to you?" demanded Duma.

Biris looked at him for a moment only and then drew deeply on the cigarette, swallowing all the smoke in the hope that it would induce a fit of coughing. But contrary to his expectations, his throat and chest felt entirely dry, even wooden, like borrowed foreign organs that did not fit him very well, but which he could tolerate because they did not irritate him or cause him to cough.

"Don't be afraid," added Duma, looking down at the dossier again. "We're not going to do anything to you. I am bound by the ties of an old friendship and I'm sure we'll get along perfectly. We need your testimony for an investigation. If you satisfy us we'll let you go."

"If you absolutely insist on going to Paris," Protopopescu declared, "we'll send you to Paris. We'll send you on a mission in a sleeping car. . . . Tell us what Viziru said to you."

It was at this point that Biris noticed the secretary who had come in unobtrusively sometime during the discussion. She had seated herself at a little table placed a step or two behind him and was recording the conversation in shorthand. When he saw her he inclined his head diffidently several times and murmured, "How-do-you-do?" The girl glanced down at her pad.

"We're listening," Duma said, continuing to leaf through the file. "What did you talk about with Viziru?"

"We discussed philosophy," Biris commenced. "He too is preoccupied by the problem of Time and History . . ."

"I didn't ask you about that," interrupted Duma. "We're interested exclusively in political questions. No doubt Viziru told you that he intended to defect from Prague. What else did he say to you? Didn't he tell you why he was leaving the country?"

"Certainly." Biris rubbed out his cigarette in the ashtray. "He told me himself, but I'd guessed it long before. He left to search for Ileana. . . ."

Duma raised his eyes from the dossier and tried to intercept Protopopescu's glance.

"Ileana Sideri," continued Biris. "He's been in love with her for ten years."

"What role did this *domnisoara* Sideri play in all this business?" Duma demanded, looking fixedly at Biris's eyes.

"I don't believe she could have had any role. He hasn't seen her since his stay in Portugal. That's why he left—to find her again. He looked for her everywhere he could think of in Romania—at Jassy, Zinca, all over Moldavia. When he became convinced she wasn't here, he decided to leave."

"He could have requested an exit visa," observed Duma, glancing down at the folder again. "I would have given him one. But Viziru preferred to desert to the enemy. We're interested in knowing what his motive was. . . ."

"I told you—to search for Ileana."

Protopopescu began to laugh heartily and lit another cigarette, putting his case back in his pocket absently. Biris blushed. He had been prepared to reach out and help himself to a cigarette, too.

"Maybe you don't know, so we'll tell you," said Protopopescu. "Viziru fled with a number of important documents."

"I don't believe it. The British said the same thing when they confiscated his diplomatic courier portfolio on his way home from London. They said that there was a quantity of important official documents in it. In reality the papers were without value."

"How do you know they were without value?" Duma inquired.

"He told me. And later on the others were convinced also. . . . May I ask you for another cigarette please?" Embarrassed, Biris turned to Protopopescu, who held out the case and the lighter with a preoccupied air.

Duma closed the file and crossed his arms on top of it, looking up slowly. "Listen to me, Biris. We're friends and I'd like to save you from the scrape you've got yourself into. But I can't do it without your cooperation. Viziru made off with a number of secret documents, which means that his flight was premeditated. You two were very good friends; therefore it's impossible that you didn't discuss together the preparations for it. The proof is that two months after his desertion you have tried also to cross the border clandestinely. The case is clear. It's futile for you to try to conceal anything. For your own good, tell us all you know. With whom did you meet and how did you work?"

Biris was strangely calm as he continued to smoke, listening to Duma. He kept glancing at his hands to see if they had begun to shake again. He could not understand what miracle had occurred, but the trembling had suddenly ceased—just when, he was not sure. Now he regarded his motionless hands with a sense of security and pride sweeping slowly over him.

"I don't know if you'll believe me," he declared in a firm voice, "but this is the way it was. I realized long ago that Viziru wanted to leave the country to search for Ileana. He had told me nothing, but I guessed. We met very often during the days before he left and he kept giving me money. He gave me dollars, Swiss francs, and gold. He told me to keep it because someday I'd need it. Then a few days before he left for Prague he told me that he wasn't coming back, and he asked me what I was planning to do, if I didn't want to go to Paris too. I answered that I'd be happy to go because I had nothing to do here in Romania. While I was a teacher I felt I had a tie with something and socially my existence had a meaning. Now, if he also left, I was condemned to die of hunger—that is, more precisely, of tuberculosis. Because, as you know, tuberculosis is a capitalistic malady—in order to be delivered from it you have to overeat. Viziru seemed very well satisfied that I had decided to leave. He told me that in principle the crossing of the border was already arranged, that a large group of people would cross in the course of the fall, and that I'd have to be ready to leave at the beginning of October."

He stopped and puffed again on his cigarette. Duma's roving eyes halted on Protopopescu's face, and he began to finger the dossier slowly. "Who else was in the group?" he asked.

"I don't know. He didn't mention any other name. He just said to be ready to leave and that a week at the latest after receiving the postcard to present myself at *aleea* Alexandru in Arad and ask for a Doctor Vlad. That was all. . . ."

"What kind of postcard?" asked Protopopescu. "What was written on it? Who signed it?"

"The signature wasn't important, but the text of the message was this, approximately, 'We are ready to harvest the grapes and we await you with pleasure.' Then there were a few conventional sentences about the weather."

"Why do you say that the signature wasn't important?" Protopopescu interjected. "Who signed it?"

"I give you my word of honor that the signature was indecipherable. It could have been Popeanu, Popescu, Topescu, Ionescu. . . . I couldn't figure it out."

"It wasn't Pantelimon by any chance?" questioned Duma, smiling, gazing directly into Biris's eyes.

The color left the other man's face and he felt himself begin to tremble again. Avidly he drew on his cigarette. "No, it wasn't that," he managed to articulate after a pause, and his voice sounded strangled.

"Then how do you know about Pantelimon?" demanded Duma, "and what do you know about him?"

"I don't know anything. Viziru told me that a man named Pantelimon is connected with the passing of this group across the border. That's all."

"What does this Pantelimon look like?" continued Duma. "Where did you meet him?"

"I've never met him. I thought that I was going to see him at Arad."

"Think carefully now." Smiling, Duma persisted. "It's to your advantage."

"I give you my word of honor . . ."

"All right, all right. Maybe you'll remember later," intervened Protopopescu. "Meanwhile tell us what message you were to take to Paris. You spoke a little while ago about a message from the labyrinth. What does it refer to?"

Biris turned his head and looked at him a long time. He seemed to be wondering whether *domnul* Protopopescu was joking or speaking seriously.

"I told you it was just a saying of ours. Stefan once sent me to Ileana with a message. He said that he had felt lost, as if he were in a labyrinth, but that nevertheless he had not let himself be overwhelmed by despair and finally he had discovered it was possible to get out. But I'm not sure this was the exact content of the message to Ileana because I was rather ill on the day he told me. I had just had a hemorrhage . . ."

"When did this happen?" asked Duma.

"Oh, a long time ago," Biris exclaimed, smiling. "Before the flood— before the war. In 1938 or 1939—I don't remember now. . . . That was the

524

message from the labyrinth," he concluded, seeing that both of the men were looking at him intently, waiting for him to proceed.

Domnul Protopopescu shook his head and ran his tongue around the inside of his mouth and over his teeth as though he had suddenly discovered a bitter taste that he wanted to be rid of. "Let us tell you what this message from the labyrinth means. The group in Paris claims that in the Carpathian Mountains an armed resistance has been organized which the government will never be able to annihilate. . . ." He paused a moment and then went on. "It can't be annihilated because the places where the guerillas are hiding are as difficult to conquer as a labyrinth. . . . And so the message that they expect from you must give them precise details about this armed resistance in the mountains."

Biris began to laugh. "That's absurd!" he exclaimed, shrugging. "I give you my word of honor that it's nothing more than an expression only the two of us know. It was the message Stefan addressed to Ileana through me. But this happened long ago, before the war. Probably even Viziru doesn't remember now what he said then, in 1938 or 1939. . . ."

"Let us remind you what the content of the message must be," Protopopescu resumed. "It had to do with the resistance organized by Pantelimon . . ."

"That's absurd!" Biris repeated after a greedy puff on his cigarette. "I haven't the slightest notion who Pantelimon is! And as far as armed resistance is concerned, Viziru and I were in full agreement that it would be absolutely stupid to organize anything like that. If I'd wanted a reason for going to Paris it would have been to tell everything I think about the resistance and all that. . . ."

"Approximately what did you want to say?" asked Duma, beginning to drum on the dossier with his fingers.

"You already know what I think—that it would be utter madness, that it's not only absurd but positively criminal to goad people to armed resistance. On the contrary, the Paris group should have explained to the Westerners that they have permanently lost this part of Europe and that they lost it precisely because of their policies. The Soviets didn't occupy the countries from Stettin to the Adriatic. The Allies *invited* them to establish themselves in this half of Europe. And at Teheran President Roosevelt didn't ask us, or the Czechs, or the Poles if we wanted to be occupied and educated by the Soviets. He took the initiative himself without consulting anyone. What right do the Americans have now to force resistance on us? They offered us as a gift to Russia. Very well. Let's draw the conclusions—they've lost over a hundred million Europeans who tomorrow will fight against them and will fight well. The Paris group ought to explain this to the Westerners, and they ought to tell them something else too—tell them they won't have things so good much longer, because soon their turn will come. Tell them that it's useless to hope

525

they'll escape or be able to continue to live in peace and quiet and capitalism just because they sacrificed a hundred million Europeans. They should bear in mind that soon their turn will come!"

"This is very interesting," Protopopescu declared. "And what did Viziru say?"

"He agrees with me entirely."

"Then why did he flee with the documents?" asked Duma. "Because we're friends I can tell you that they were documents relative to our war debts and economic agreements with the Soviets. Doesn't it seem to you that they're rather important?"

Biris shrugged his shoulders again, and Protopopescu broke in with "Let's drop that. . . . What connections do you have in Paris? Whom do you know?"

"Other than Viziru and *conu* Misu I don't know anyone."

Domnul Protopopescu caught Duma's eye for a moment and smiled. "Weissman knows a great many people. This could be interesting. . . ."

He rose from the armchair and held out his hand hastily. "We'll give you time to think it over. Maybe you'll remember Pantelimon's message. Then we'll send you to Paris by sleeping car. . . . We'll send you like Viziru," he added, smiling at Biris.

Generally they summoned him to the interrogation at three in the morning. The guard would lean over him, put his hand on his shoulder, and shake him. "Please! Up!" he would say.

Biris invariably found Duma seated at the desk with a dossier opened in front of him. He had ceased to rise in greeting or to shake his hand. In fact he hardly even looked at him. Biris remained on his feet in front of the desk and tried to guess what the first question would be. Would Duma ask him, "When did you last see Weissman?" or "What did Viziru tell you before he left for Prague?" Ordinarily Duma began with one or the other of these two questions in order to lead up to the meeting with Pantelimon and the content of the message of which Biris was supposed to be the bearer. At intervals he interrupted the conference to read Biris passages from his previous statements, which Duma kept before him and thumbed through continually as he listened. When Biris lapsed into silence Duma looked up slowly from the file.

"Go on! Keep talking! I'm listening."

After the second interrogation Biris had learned to respond with what he thought Duma wanted to hear. He would expound on what he planned to do in Paris, since the official seemed to be especially interested in this. When Biris spoke of St.-Germain-des-Prés and the Café Deux Magots, Duma would stop turning over the pages of the dossier and slowly raise his eyes from the papers, brightening visibly.

"Do you know Paris well?" he asked once.

"Only by hearsay and from literature. I've never been there."

"I have. It's very beautiful. . . ."

Still standing before the desk, Biris would continue his chronicle, stroking the top of his head from time to time. "I'd like to go to the Deux Magots at sunset. I've heard that the Existentialists gather there at that time. I'd like to get into a discussion with them, just to spoil their fun. 'Why don't you come and visit us behind the Iron Curtain?' I'd ask them. 'You'll see how we pose *le problème du choix* and what becomes of *le problème de la liberté*! Why don't you come visit us? You'll get acquainted with the true "historic moment."' I'd like to chat with them and afterward I'd shake hands warmly and say, 'When you're in the cattle car headed for the fields of progressive labor or standing before a firing squad you'll remember what I told you this evening. . . .'"

"Biris!" interrupted Duma, frowning slightly. "You're mad!"

"No, I'm not," smiled Biris. "Because I wouldn't have the courage to say that. I'm too much of a coward. I only tell it to you because we're friends. In Paris I'd be content to discuss philosophy. My obsession is philosophy. And now I realize why. It's because I'm a coward. I'm afraid of life. And not only life—I'm afraid of everything. You saw how I shook when you brought me for the first examination. I was quaking with fear. I was terrified that you might beat me, torture me. . . ."

"Don't be afraid," Duma soothed him. "We won't do anything to you. And if you want to go to Paris we'll send you there. But be honest with us. Tell us all you know."

"If you won't do anything to *coana* Viorica and if you promise not to beat me, and if you give me cigarettes, I'll tell you everything. . . . But now let me talk about Paris. I've seen a photograph of St.-Germain-des-Prés. I'd like to walk there in the evenings and meet the Existentialists. . . ."

He spoke thus for a long time, except when Duma interrupted him. He spoke about Paris and all he wanted to do there, about the discussions with the philosophers. He paused only long enough to beg for cigarettes, which he smoked greedily, choking and coughing, and asking for permission to be seated. But he discovered that the stenographer was half-asleep, looking at him with her hands in her lap and her pad closed in front of her. Disappointed, he turned to Duma and questioned him. "Then you're not interested in what I'm saying any longer? You're not recording my comments?"

Duma shook his head slowly in unconscious imitation of *domnul* Protopopescu. "We're linked by an old friendship and I want to help you go free," he said after a pause. "For half an hour you've been talking nonsense. A tenth of what you've said up to now would be enough to get you sentenced for life."

"Just give me time to contradict myself," replied Biris, becoming nervous again all at once. "I told you I'm a coward and I don't have the courage to defend my point of view to the end. I'm a teacher of philosophy. I can change my position—I can change it from one moment to the next!"

"Maybe tomorrow you'll be inspired," Duma suggested, pressing the button to call the guard. "Try to remember about Pantelimon. And bear this in mind—our patience is not without limit. . . ."

One night he awoke and saw Bursuc beside him dressed in ordinary street clothes. He was sitting on a chair at the foot of the bed.

"What have you done to me?" the monk exploded. "What've you got me into?"

Biris rubbed his eyes and glanced around the room. They were alone. "Where's the typist?" he demanded. "I want to make some important statements. . . ."

"I've come to save you," broke in Bursuc, lighting a cigarette. "We're alone. Don't forget that I'm a monk and I possess all the gifts of the Holy Spirit. I've come to fortify you spiritually. . . ."

He held out his package of cigarettes. Selecting one, Biris began to roll it around between his fingers. Then he carried it to his nose and sniffed it, savoring its aroma. "That's strange," he said. "I seem to have no desire to smoke. . . . What time is it?"

"Almost two. Duma told me I could stay as long as I like. They aren't going to take you to be interrogated tonight. They'll be satisfied with what I tell them. I've come to save you. . . . You're awfully naive," Bursuc added with a smile. "Whatever possessed you to spout political theories about the resistance, the West, Communism, and all that nonsense? They're just interested in one thing—what you know about Viziru and Pantelimon. Tell them, man! If you don't others will and they'll find out anyway. They've got their hands on the whole Arad network. They know more than you can imagine. . . ."

"What time did you say it was?"

"Two!" exclaimed Bursuc, getting up from his chair.

"That's strange. I don't seem to be aware of time anymore. It doesn't seem to be passing."

"Biris," said Bursuc, beginning to pace the floor, "I've come to save you. These people know all about Viziru and Pantelimon. Don't think that you'll be betraying someone if you tell them what you know too. After that they'll let you go and send you in a sleeping car to Paris . . ."

"With the Existentialists!" Biris interrupted, twisting the cigarette and

528

sniffing it again. "How wonderful that will be! Viziru told me about a hotel in St.-Germain-des-Prés. We'll discuss philosophy . . . ."

"These people just want to test you to see if you're a man of your word and trustworthy. Then they'll send you to Paris. They'll ask you to work for them, and you tell them you'll do it. What will it cost you? Agree to everything they ask. Once you reach Paris you can do as you please."

"But *coana* Viorica is still here," Biris said, suddenly troubled, "a hostage in their hands. Has she found out anything?"

"No, they haven't told her. But you know they've made a search. They ransacked your papers."

For awhile Biris was silent, musing. "Bursuc," he said impulsively, "I'm a lost man. I don't deserve to live. I have no dignity of any kind. I'm a coward. Because I was afraid, I've told them all I knew. I told them about Ileana and Stefan even before they threatened me. I told them all I knew, hoping they'd let me go. I'm a coward. . . ."

"You were unwise. You made political statements against the government."

"That's true. I was wrong. I felt too much hatred inside—the hatred of a weak man. I spoke hatefully against the Westerners because they abandoned us. That was a mistake. I ought to have made an effort to understand the free world too. Anyone else would have done what they did. When it's a matter of saving yourself you don't think about the other one. You simply sacrifice him. It's been that way since the world began. I'm sorry now for all I said."

"You said a lot of nonsense! Your hatred blinded you."

"If I should get to Paris I wouldn't tell them that. I'd tell them something different. I'd want to bring them a kind of message of love and farewell— something like this: 'Ave Occidens, we who are behind the Iron Curtain, we, *morituri te salutant!*'. . . How do you say in Latin 'We who are behind the Iron Curtain?' You've studied theology. You know Latin better than I do. *Salve Occidens, morituri te salutant!* It would be wonderful to go to Paris and tell them that. So they'll know that even though they've condemned us to death, we fools and paupers here still love and venerate them. Because the West is there—where the sun sets. That's where the true twilight is and it's more beautiful there than here. Only there, in the West, do people realize that they die. That's why in the West men love History—because it reminds them continually that men are mortal and civilizations are mortal. We who live here don't have much reason to love History. Why should we love it? For ten centuries History meant for us the barbarian invasions. For another five centuries it meant the Turkish terror, and now for I don't know how many centuries History will imply Soviet Russia. . . ."

"Biris!" cried Bursuc, "You're beginning to talk nonsense again. And I want to help you. I want to save you!"

529

"How do you say in Latin, 'We who are behind the Iron Curtain?' *Qui inlocunt . . . post parientem ferreum?*"

"I don't know!" responded Bursuc, losing his temper. "I came here to talk seriously with you . . ."

"Anyway I'd like to deliver a message to them in Latin. Occidentals are cultivated people. In Paris, at Oxford, at Cambridge, they still speak Latin. *Ave Occidens*, we Easterners, *morituri te salutant! Nos, qui habitant intra saepta ferrea . . .* or *qui habitant intra cancellos ferreos . . . morituri te salutant! . . .* It would be wonderful."

"You were a fool," declared Bursuc. "You got yourself into this mess through your stupidity. If you wanted to defect why didn't you tell me? You had to follow Viziru's advice."

"All this was because I was afraid and I was a coward. And I'm afraid now. I'm afraid they'll beat me."

Bursuc sat down again and sighed. "They promised me they won't do anything to you if I bring them your statement about Pantelimon. Let's make it together. What would you say this fellow looks like?"

Biris closed his eyes. Bursuc waited for some time in the belief that he was trying to remember, but when the interval of silence lengthened he reached over and shook him. "Hey, have you gone to sleep?" he asked sharply.

Biris regarded him thoughtfully and brushed his hand across his eyes. "What time is it?" he inquired in a whisper. "It's strange how I'm no longer aware of time at all. I think I'm very tired. . . ."

"All right!" exclaimed Bursuc, suddenly rising. "Don't say I didn't try to save you. I wash my hands of you. Go on—do whatever you want. If you want to become a martyr of the resistance, just keep it up! But if we should ever meet again don't complain."

Biris smiled. "Where do you think we might meet? Do you believe in the existence of Paradise? I'd like for us to meet again in the shadow of a lily in Paradise. . . . Too bad it doesn't exist!" he added sadly.

"Man, tell them who Pantelimon is!" Bursuc cried in exasperation.

"You spoke a moment ago about martyrs. I'd like to be able to be a martyr. Not for some cause, but just to protest against fate. I'd like to be able to have the faith of the Christian martyrs. To be a St. Sebastian. But I'm too cowardly. Even the idea of physical suffering terrifies me. I've heard that they beat you on the soles of your feet. When I think about it I begin to tremble. . . . If I had faith I'd pray. Perhaps prayer helps you to endure such pain. Can't you fortify me with something? Can't you give me some kind of prayer to keep me from being afraid? I swear to you, if I weren't afraid I'd tell everything I think to anyone and in any circumstance. But the way I am—a coward—I keep contradicting myself all the time. Give me a prayer that will strengthen me. . . ."

"Prayers are no good if you don't have faith," said Bursuc bitterly. "You have to have great faith and then God strengthens you. But *you* don't need that. Just tell who Pantelimon is and you'll be free. Tell them his name—his real name."

"Pantelimon!" Biris exclaimed with a smile. "Thy name is legion!"

Bursuc stared at him and then started for the door. "All right! I've done my duty and now I wash my hands of it. To each his own misfortune. . . ."

From that night onward he kept having this dream: he thought that it was the eve of Easter and he was standing on the deck of a ship, holding a lighted candle in his hand. It seemed to him that the flame lengthened and mounted ever higher, a slender filament of light. He followed it with his eyes as it touched the arch of the sky and pierced it. He tipped his head back in order to see it better, and there high above where the light penetrated the heavens a radiant face appeared. Undoubtedly it's God or Jesus Christ, he said to himself, and he awoke overcome with emotion, his spirit flooded with a happiness that was beyond belief.

Once when he awoke someone was sponging his face with a moist cloth. The next moment he realized what had occurred. I had a hemorrhage in my sleep! The cloth was red, and even though he did not feel the need to spit there was a taste of blood in his mouth. He heard Duma's voice.

"What do you say, Doctor? How do you explain it?"

"That depends on what you did to him," responded someone behind him whom Biris could not see. "It depends on whether the iron was warm or hot."

"It wasn't even lukewarm, *domnu'* Doctor," Biris heard another voice speak up, apparently coming from the wall. "I had just stretched him out when he began to bleed."

"You're exaggerating," suggested the doctor dryly. "You probably gave him a few vigorous slaps and stunned him."

"Only on the soles of the feet, *domnu'* Doctor. I swear by the heads of my children, I only touched him on the soles of his feet and he began to spit blood. . . ."

"Did he cry out?" demanded Duma. "Did he say anything?"

"He didn't make a sound, *domnule* Inspector. After I hit him the second time I looked to see what he was doing. He'd closed his eyes and he seemed to be smiling, but he was limp."

"He fainted," the doctor said. "Probably he won't last much longer. Besides, I've seen his X-rays. He has cavities as big as a fist."

"That doesn't mean anything," declared Duma. "Other consumptives have gone through here and they didn't faint. Some of them seemed to be even more resistant than the strong and healthy ones." He lowered his voice. "How long before the injection takes effect?"

"It ought to have taken effect already. . . . But if you want to be sure he doesn't die it would be better to leave him alone tonight. You can try again tomorrow."

"Impossible. We've received special orders. Give him another injection so he'll stay awake, and then we'll try the alternative method."

Biris smiled when he saw the doctor approach him with the syringe in one hand, questioning him. "How do you feel?" He began to rub Biris's arm with a piece of cotton saturated with alcohol.

"Well, thank you." He waited for the prick of the injection, but the doctor had already emptied the syringe, removed the needle with a deft gesture, and was again rubbing his arm with the sterilized cotton. Biris stared at him in amazement. My God, when did he do it? he wondered. Just a moment ago he was there with the syringe in his hand. . . .

"How do you feel?" asked Duma, approaching the bed.

"Thank you. I feel fine. My feet are a little cold."

"You'll have to warm him up," the doctor said to the man who was standing near the wall. "Wait fifteen minutes and then you can begin. . . ."

Duma put his hand on Biris's forehead and the sick man felt a peculiar warmth permeate his body, attended by a feeling of sympathy that moved him almost to tears. "You won't beat me?" he inquired with a smile.

"I told you that an old friendship binds us. . . ."

"Don't beat me. I'll tell you all I know. We were friends. I don't understand why you won't believe me. . . ."

Duma stared at him and tried to smile. "Biris," he said finally. "We've received special orders. It would be better if you'd tell us the content of the message. We know you had connections with Pantelimon. Many witnesses have testified. . . ."

Biris sighed in despair. "If you won't beat me I'll tell you everything you want me to, but I don't know Pantelimon. If you like I'll describe some man—any man—and I'll say that it's Pantelimon and I'll sign the statement. But I swear to you I don't know him."

Duma said no more and withdrew slowly. When Biris tried to raise himself he realized that he was strapped to the bed.

"Don't beat me!" he cried, his voice unexpectedly sharp. He waited. He heard footsteps departing, and he heard the door close. Then a face that seemed familiar bent over him. The man was robust and swarthy, with a thick black moustache that almost covered his upper lip.

"Talk, *domnule* Professor, say something!" he begged. "I've got orders to use the alternative . . ."

"What alternative?"

"I have children," the other insisted. "Say something! If you know, say

532

something! Like *domnul* Inspector asked you. He has orders. I pray you as I pray to God! I have five children. . . ." He looked at Biris and wiped his face again and again with a gaudy handkerchief.

"What alternative?"

The man was embarrassed, but he smiled. Wiping his hands on his handkerchief, he thrust it into his pocket. Then he leaned toward Biris and suddenly his face seemed sinister.

"Talk! You good-for-nothing little professor!" he whistled through his teeth. "Say something, because if you don't you'll die under the red hot iron, and all my life I'll have you on my conscience!"

"Don't beat me!" cried Biris, frightened.

Exasperated, the man raised his hand. A moment later Biris found himself again aboard the ship that was advancing over the sea on the eve of Easter. Again he held the lighted candle, clasping it tightly with both hands, exhilarated, fearful that someone might snatch it from him. Around him on the deck as far as he could see people were kneeling with candles burning in their hands. He waited a few moments for his flame to ascend, but the tiny tongue of fire hesitated and faltered. Finally it began to rise, and then it sank down again, wavering and threatening to go out. The ship was speeding forward in the night and Biris began to fear that the ribbon of light would not have enough force to reach the vault of heaven and break through it. A great sadness overwhelmed him and, moved, he began to pray, his eyes fixed on the flame. Then unexpectedly it flared with sudden brilliance, and joyfully Biris threw back his head so his eyes could follow its ascent. He watched it touch the sky, and there again was the shining golden face, waiting for him in the luminous opening. It's God! he said to himself, marveling that he could still think, so lost was he in the incomparable bliss that engulfed him.

"What have you done to him, Barsane?" he heard a familiar voice say. "He has three doses of oil of camphor and three of strychnine in him. How the devil could he faint again?"

"I didn't even touch him, *domnu'* Doctor!" said the man by the wall.

So his name is Barsan, Biris thought as he awoke, and he smiled. He has five children. And in order to give them tea and black bread every morning he has to beat people on the soles of their feet and burn them with a hot iron. . . . And yet he can only give them tea and black bread. . . . His eyes filled with tears of pity, and he began to blink rapidly to clear them. When he tried to sit up he felt the tug of the straps that encircled his body. Duma was speaking.

"What's the matter with him, Doctor? Why did he faint?"

"*Consolamentum,*" said Biris, smiling. "You studied at the University—don't you remember? *Consolamentum* . . . the Albigenes. . . ."

At once Duma went to him and looked intently into his eyes. "I didn't study philosophy," he said, and Biris thought that his voice broke with sadness.

"Ask Bursuc. He'll explain it to you. He's a theologian. . . ."

533

After a long silence Duma asked him, "Did you feel anything? Did you suffer?"

"I don't think so. I don't remember. . . ."

Duma looked steadily into his eyes. He seemed to be waiting for Biris to continue. He brought his hand to his forehead. "Let him alone," he said after awhile. "I'm going upstairs to make a telephone call."

Biris listened to the sound of footsteps as the doctor walked to the door, and he heard him whisper before he left the room, "I don't believe he'll last long. A specialist ought to see him."

For days—Biris did not know how many—they had not summoned him to the interrogation. Whenever he woke up he would immediately ask the time. He did not always receive an answer. Often he awakened alone, and then he was afraid. He would close his eyes quickly in order to recover the bliss of the dream. The ship continued its voyage in the night—always the same night that had no beginning and no end. But there were not so many lights and Biris did not always have the candle in his hands. Once he stayed a long time on the deck, trying to understand what was happening to him, how he had come to be on board this ship and where the journey would end. He began to walk, but the darkness was so impenetrable that very soon he abandoned his efforts and halted. He heard only the noise of the motors and the sound of the waves as the prow cut through them. When he longed to see the lighted candles again his wish seemed sufficient to start them burning, for suddenly the entire deck was aglow with the points of light. He opened his eyes wide and looked around. Barsan was kneeling by the bed, imploring him with clasped hands, "Talk, *domnule* Professor, my children are destitute! I pray you as I pray to God! I have five children. . . ."

Biris began to weep, unaware of his tears. Someone always has to pay, he thought. And this time Barsan will pay. In order that he, Biris, can know bliss, Barsan has to suffer. He was overcome by a feeling of infinite compassion and he smiled as he wept. "Barsane," he whispered. "Don't be afraid of God. He won't do anything to us. We'll all go to Paris. . . ."

"I pray you as I pray to God, *domnule* Professor," Barsan continued without rising from his knees. "Talk!"

"What must I say?" asked Biris, making an effort to rouse himself.

"What they told you to say—the contents of the message. I'll be saved, and you too. . . .

Troubled, Biris stared at him. "If it will save you, Barsane, I'll say it. I'll say it just for your sake. Inform Duma that I'll tell everything. Have him bring a stenographer—I'll tell everything. . . ." Then he closed his eyes and waited.

Presently he heard Duma's voice very near. "It would have been better if you'd decided this long ago. You wouldn't have suffered so much."

534

"Did you bring the stenographer?" Biris asked without opening his eyes.
"She's here beside me. You may begin."

"I ask you to record that I'm doing this only for Barsan's sake, to save him. . . ."

He paused a few moments, his eyes still closed, frowning as though he were making a great effort to remember. Then he began to recite, his voice almost choking with despair:

> "Down from the flowering
> Wild mountain garden
> Threshold of paradise
> Three flocks of sheep
> Come along the path
> Decending to the valley
> With their shepherds three . . .*

'With their shepherds three . . .' What comes next?"

"Biris!" he heard Duma say harshly, "are you making fun of us?"

He opened his eyes, but he did not look at them. His unfaltering gaze was on the ceiling. "No. It's very serious. You'll soon see why. It's a code language. This is the way the message from the labyrinth begins."

It was suddenly quiet in the cell.

"Tell me what comes next," said Biris, continuing to regard the ceiling. "It has to do with the message. It's from the Mountain."

"Do you know what comes next?" demanded Duma of the stenographer.

Biris heard the girl's timid voice. "I think so." She approached the bed and continued the poem.

> "See how the two
> The alien ones
> Plot and scheme together
> Confer with one another.
> At sunset they will kill
> The Moldavian, the mighty,
> For he has many sheep
> Old and splendid with horns.
> He has well-trained horses
> And fine strong dogs. . . ."

After a while, seeing that Biris was listening with his eyes closed and saying nothing, Duma interrupted the girl. "Do you remember now?" he asked Biris.

"Yes. Set it down carefully because I might forget it again. It's a coded

---

*Opening lines of the celebrated Romanian folk ballad: Miorita (The Little Ewe Lamb).

535

message. This code was chosen precisely because it's very simple. Everybody knows it. We learn it in primary school."

"Be more explicit," commanded Duma.

"This is the message. They sing it on the Mountain, but the people on the ship know it too. Only, on the ship no one sings it anymore. . . ."

"Biris," Duma interrupted again, "this is in your own interest. Speak clearly. To whom is the message addressed?"

"It's a coded message, and it's for Paris. All messages go to Paris. The ships take them. They only travel at night, without lights, but they all go to Paris. To the West. *Salve Occidens!*"

"You're mad!" cried Duma. "You're ridiculing us!"

"All messages begin like this—'Down from the flowering wild mountain garden, threshold of paradise. . . .' But you can't decipher them if you don't have the key, and you won't find the key except on the ship. When you wake up on the ship, you realize that you're going to Paris. Everyone will be there in the shadow of the lily—in Paris—and then this message was invented which even children in primary school know. But it's a coded message. It has to do with Paris. . . ."

"Who invented it?" insisted Duma.

"Pantelimon."

An eerie silence crept over the room. Biris hesitated, his lips parted.

"Go on," Duma urged. "Who is Pantelimon? What sort of man is he? Describe him as precisely as you can."

"He's a tall handsome man with black, fiery eyes. He seems ageless. He's not like an ordinary person. They say that he's from the Mountain. When you get near him you realize it's too late—you can't resist him. You're his. It happens to everyone. Once you've met him you can never leave him. He takes us all to Paris . . ." His voice faltered and he did not resume his account.

"Barsane," he heard Duma say then, "the next time you see he's raving, don't bother us. . . ."

Biris waited. When he heard the door close he opened his eyes slowly and smiled at Barsan, who approached him menacingly. "You no-good blasted little professor! You make a fool out of me and get me fired and throw my children out on the streets! But never mind, just wait, I'll squeeze the fat out of you, you damned consumptive! You won't forget me!"

The flock of sparrows had flown away again, darting up from directly beneath the balcony, scattering in fright, twittering sharply, shrilly, and reassembling in a few moments about ten meters in front of him on the cemetery wall. St. Martin's summer, Stefan found himself thinking. It's absurd! Absurd! Absurd!

536

The black trees, bare of leaves, dampened by the dew, seemed to sparkle like glass in the clear, bright glow of the autumn twilight. Stefan blinked his eyes repeatedly and declared to himself, It's absurd! Everything's absurd—absolutely without meaning. . . . He heard Weissman speaking.

"Perhaps it's not true. The same thing was said about the others. He ought to. . ." Misu did not venture to finish the sentence. He seemed to realize suddenly how ridiculous and vain his thought was.

"I told him." he began again presently. "I warned him to stay away from Bursuc."

Stefan left his place near the balcony door, and as he passed the desk, he extinguished his cigarette among the stubs that almost filled the ashtray. He sat down on the sofa and bent his head, his eyes tracing the patterns in the carpet.

"At first, when we hardly knew each other, he talked to me constantly about Partenie. He was obsessed by Partenie's destiny. It seemed to him that Partenie had a premonition of something and that was why he wrote in such haste. If he really did have a premonition he was the only intelligent man among us all."

Weissman gave a sudden sigh and rose from the armchair, almost springing to his feet. He circled the desk several times and strode resolutely to the balcony door. Opening it wide, he breathed deeply through his nose, grinding his teeth in exasperated, puerile fury, as the sparrows flashed in front of the windows with an abrupt and deafening clatter. They chased each other in brief disorderly flight to the end of the street.

"There's no God, no justice, no anything!" exclaimed Weissman. "There's nothing but luck. You don't need anything else. Whoever doesn't have luck is better off not born—or dead in his cradle! It's better not to know anything."

Stefan glanced up from the carpet and smiled involuntarily. He searched in his pockets for a package of cigarettes. "If what you say is true it would have been better for the Romanian people not to have been born at all, or to have died in infancy. Our whole nation is a luckless lot."

"I'm not thinking of nations," said Weissman without turning his head. "I was thinking of men, of individuals. If you don't have luck there's no use being born. You just don't get anywhere. There's nothing else besides luck. If God existed. . ." He interrupted himself again with an embarrassed air, as though he had realized, just a moment before uttering the irretrievable phrase, that he was about to say something foolish. He returned to the middle of the room and let himself slip into the armchair, giving the impression of being exhausted by a tremendous exertion. He was like a different man. His rather fleshy hands at the end of his short arms—those hands that he rubbed together so expressively when he wished to make an important pronouncement—now rested slackly on his lap.

537

"Maybe . . . just the same . . ." he murmured after a pause, a little fearfully, "God might permit him to escape. . . . Everything depends on what sort of man Pantelimon is."

Stefan shrugged his shoulders, incapable of controlling his impatience. "It's preposterous!" he cried. "There's no connection between the two. Biris has absolutely no idea who Pantelimon is. It was a stupid thing that his name was ever mentioned in connection with the crossing of the border. The imbecile or scoundrel who did that will have hundreds of innocent lives on his conscience. Pantelimon has nothing to do with it. This is the concern of the others." He got up from the sofa and began to walk about the room.

"Do you know him?" inquired Weissman with diffidence.

"No. And I hope no one knows him."

"So do I. People are so indiscreet . . ."

Stefan stopped abruptly before Weissman and stared at him. "St. Martin's summer," he said suddenly. "How incongruous! I keep trying to remember what Biris said to me once when we had barely met. It's remarkable how I forget things now."

"Was it something about the summer of St. Martin?"

"I don't think so, but I'm not sure. I don't remember. It was in the summer of 1936 in Bucharest, shortly after I had met him at Casa Pestera. I ran into him by chance on the boulevard one evening. I recall that it had been quite hot that day, and since I didn't know him very well yet, I thought he was a little drunk. But he wasn't. He told me then a lot of important things. . . ."

"In connection with the summer of St. Martin?"

"I simply can't remember. How absurd!" He began to pace the floor again. *Mother! What was it that happened one autumn during the summer of St. Martin? . . .* I wonder what prompted me to ask Mother that? he questioned himself a moment later when he became aware of his thought. It has no bearing on this case. Biris didn't know her. He didn't even know his own mother—or I think he knew her, but he was too young when she died and he didn't remember her. . . .

"I ought to tell you something," Weissman ventured timidly, after stealing a glance at his watch. "Someone's coming. She ought to arrive any minute now. . . ."

I haven't thought of Mother for a long time. It's as though I'd forgotten her. I don't think about Father either. I'm afraid to remember them. I keep trying to cling to something living—something that will be in the future. . . . It's preposterous. . . .

"Do you hear me?" demanded Weissman. "I told you that one evening when I was with friends of Vidrighin I met a very beautiful woman who said she knows you . . . She was *doamna* Wainwright—the former *domnisoara* Zissu," he added hesitantly.

538

"Stella Zissu?" Stefan stopped in the middle of the room and turned to face his friend.

"I wanted to surprise you, but I didn't know. . . . I hadn't found out about Biris. . . . She ought to arrive any minute," he repeated, glancing again at his watch. "Perhaps it would be better not to receive her. I'll telephone her tomorrow and tell her that some friends took us out in their car this morning and we had a breakdown and didn't get back until after midnight. . . ."

"That's interesting. She got married then."

"She was lucky." Weissman sounded somewhat envious. "She caught a millionaire. Now she has an apartment at the Georges V, a car at the curb. . . . But we can't receive her. She wouldn't understand. Our grief is no concern of hers. . . ."

"She was a beautiful woman." Stefan went back to his place on the sofa. "And she was lucky."

"She was eager to see you. She said she met you in Lisbon and that she was in love with you once. Oh, she's quite indiscreet! She told everything. Vidrighin's friends were there, foreigners, and she told the whole story—how the English stripped you to the skin—and she made a big joke of it. She said, 'He stood there naked. But he's a handsome man and he has a fine figure. . . .'"

"She could tell us a lot," Stefan mused, staring absently at the pattern in the rug. "She knows a great many things."

"I say let's not receive her," insisted Weissman. "We'll invite her another time. She'll notice we're sad and she'll ask questions. Then she'll spread it all over Paris. . . . But after all," he added, seeing that Stefan was silent and pensive, "we'll do as you wish. She's coming to see you. She admitted in front of all Vidrighin's friends that you two had a big romance, that you were ready to commit I don't know what folly for her—that you were going to run away to America together. . . . I know a lot about you, so I didn't believe her, but the others, Vidrighin's friends . . ."

"I'm very curious to meet her again," commented Stefan presently with a smile. "She might be very useful to us."

"As you wish," said Weissman, looking once more at his watch. "She ought to arrive at any moment—now, in fact. She said she'd come at four-thirty or a quarter to five. She's a little late. . . ."

That night he awoke suddenly to find his entire being overflowing with a happiness he had never known. His body seemed renewed and full of vigor, bursting with health. He had not felt so well in years. When he opened his

539

eyes and was confronted with the darkness of the cell, he was not afraid. He did not hesitate but sprang from the bed and stood up without a stagger, calling "Barsane!" in a whisper. No one answered. He's resting, Biris guessed, and he smiled. He sleeps at night too, like everyone else. Immediately he recalled the message and began to shake with excitement. If no one were there to tell it to he would forget it again. Groping, he went in the direction of the door, his hands extended in front of him in the dark. He knew why he had awakened. It was because he had to tell the others—those who remained— what it had been his privilege to understand, although the circumstances of this comprehension, or whose assistance might have come to his aid, he did not know. But now everything was perfectly clear. The simplicity of it all was extraordinary. He was ashamed not to have understood it sooner, since it was exactly as it should be. Even children would understand it.

His hands touched the cold damp wall of the cell, and he began to grope along it to the right and then to the left. Yes, it was exactly as it should be. At a certain moment the ship stops, the gangway is extended, and crossing over it, you disembark. Your feet scarcely touch dry land when you realize that up to that moment you have been traveling continuously, that you never have stayed in one place, and that even the idea of stopping would have been inconceivable. At the instant of touching the ground, when *you have finally stopped*, all your life—all the lives of others, all that has happened to you until then— appears to you now as it really is and not as it once seemed to be.

Although he continued to feel his way through the darkness he did not come upon the wet iron of the door. He decided then to circle the room, staying close to the wall. He could feel the beating of his heart, the throb of life in his body, and this euphoria began to trouble him. He must hurry so that he would not forget. Again he whispered, "Barsane! Barsane!" and stopped to listen. But he could hear only his heartbeat and the sound of his breathing, which was somewhat labored, as though he had been running long and fast. If Barsan had been here he would have told him, and Barsan would have repeated it the next day to Duma or to his children. He has five. . . . People would have found out—those who remained here—and their lives would have begun again from the beginning as if they had been born a second time.

After awhile he stopped, his hopes dissipated. He thought he must be dreaming. It seemed to him that he had groped endlessly through the darkness, circling the walls of the cell, and that he ought to have reached the door. He could hardly have missed it. It was made of iron and it was wet and cold. He could not have failed to feel it under his fingers. If he had found the door he would have begun to beat on it with his fists until he woke up the guard in the corridor. He would have told him first. He would have said it as succinctly as possible and in the simplest words, so that he could understand too. Then he would have told him he wanted to make a statement. At the same time, as he waited for Barsan to return, he would have repeated the message over and over in his mind to be sure that he would remember it. He felt his heart beat faster and he set off again, walking rapidly, keeping one hand on the wall and moving the other constantly back and forth in the darkness around him. He seemed to be afraid of colliding with something or someone. Suppose he did not find the door? He might forget. It was childishly simple, but he could forget it at any moment.

He paused again and began to beat on the wall with both fists. But at once he realized the futility of his gesture. His clenched hands struck noiselessly on the cold, mouldy stone. It was like pounding on sand. Panic seized him then and he left the wall, running toward what he thought was the middle of the cell. He began to shout. "Barsane!" he cried and then stopped because the loudness of his voice frightened him. It was much stronger than he had expected. I've got to deliver the message while there's still time! he found himself thinking. He called out again several times and was deafened by the clamor of the interminable echoes awakened by his cry. He put his hands over his ears. They've locked me in another cell, he said to himself, shaken by fear, a special cell without an iron door, without any exit. They locked me in here while I was asleep. They must have lowered my bed by a special apparatus, through an opening in the ceiling, through a trapdoor that's closed so tightly no noise can penetrate it—like being sealed up in a tomb! They've shut me in here alive! As if they knew I'd be entrusted with a message!

Standing motionless, he listened, his arms hanging limply, wearily at his sides. He felt despair engulf him. His life might have had a meaning, a fulfillment—and they had prevented it! He had something to say, something very important, the only thing that needed to be said. All the rest—philosophy, politics, love—were games played by children. He had squandered his life playing them. Everyone else too, without exception, had done the same thing. What he had discovered that night was the only thing worth knowing. Something that began on the ship. . . .

He became alarmed again and put both hands to his face frantically, feeling his cheeks, trying to prod his memory. There was something about a ship, but there were other things besides—things that were much more important. The ship was just at the beginning. It was only after the ship stopped that the true revelation commenced! He must say something about what happened after the ship stopped. He moistened his lips several times and breathed very deeply, but he no longer remembered. He only recalled the ship.

In his despair tears gathered in his eyes. He hastened through the darkness, extending his hands before him, and in a few moments he found the wall again. He wanted to lean on it, to rest his head upon his arms so that he could weep without restraint, but suddenly he felt an intense burning deep within his chest. He clenched his jaws together tightly in a desperate attempt to halt the swift rush of blood, but in a moment it began to stream from the

541

corners of his mouth and from his nostrils. Weakly he let his mouth drop open wide, unaware that he had fallen on his knees. His chin, his neck, his chest felt wet and sticky. A cold sweat covered his body. Defeated, he closed his eyes and collapsed on the concrete floor. At the same time he remembered again all that had been revealed in the moment when the ship stopped and the gangway was noiselessly lowered. He smiled.

Even before he was fully awake he recognized the strong odor of the hospital, and he heard a deep voice that sounded far away. "He's been in a coma for several days. He hasn't regained consciousness since. The doctor was amazed at such stamina. . . ."

"The women have come to ask for the body," he heard Bursuc say. "They're waiting in the courtyard. At Police Headquarters they were told he had died. They came to the Patriarchate and fell on their knees imploring me, as if I were God, to intervene so they could have the body. . . ."

"He should have died the day before yesterday, according to the doctor."

Biris opened his eyes and saw Bursuc. The monk was dressed in his surplice. "Your blessing, Father!" the sick man whispered.

"I've come to get you," said Bursuc, his voice quavering slightly. He went quickly to the bed and laid his hand on Biris's forehead. "You're saved. The women are in the courtyard waiting for you."

"*Coana* Viorica?" It was difficult for Biris to speak.

"And Irina. They came in a car. I told them to wait."

"I'd like to see them . . ."

"We're taking you home," interrupted Bursuc. "We're going in the car."

"I'd like to see them now," insisted Biris.

"I don't know if they'll let them come in. I'll go ask." He started to leave the bedside, but Biris caught his sleeve.

"Stay with me. Send someone else. I just want to see them. Otherwise I can't . . . I see that I can't die. . . ."

"Don't be childish. You're safe now. We're going to take you home and you'll get well."

"I know. But there's no more time. . . . I'd like to ask you something. I don't know when this was. I think it was last night. I understood it then. . . . Come closer. Listen carefully. I understood. It's something very simple. Tell them all that it's very simple. Tell Barsan, too, not to worry. It's very simple. I've forgotten the rest now, but assure them all that that's the way it is. Tell them not to be afraid. . . ."

He stopped in order to swallow. His mouth seemed to have become dry. Bursuc turned and called to someone who was waiting in the doorway of the sickroom. "Go to the Chief and tell him to let the women in. Tell him I request it. Tell him why." Frightened, he moved his hand in a vague gesture.

"Tell *coana* Viorica too," said Biris, "but don't tell it to her like that. Don't tell her what it was like when you saw me. Don't alarm her. Just tell her that it was tuberculosis, like Mother. That's the way Mother died—with tuberculosis. I was condemned long ago. . . ."

Bursuc rubbed his eyes with his left hand. "They promised me they wouldn't do anything to you," he began, and his voice faltered. "I'm a monk. They shouldn't have lied to me. I was always honest with them. I never lied to them. They shouldn't have deceived me and mocked me. . . ." Tears ran down his cheeks and he searched the pockets of his surplice until he found a handkerchief. He dabbed at his eyes and face.

"It's not their fault," Biris went on. "It's no one's fault. . . . And now I want to make a request. Tell Stefan when you see him . . ."

"I'll tell him nothing!" cried Bursuc, with a shudder. "It's on account of him you're here. I don't want to hear anything!"

"Just tell him this—that he's right. There *is* a way out. Tell him to look for it. . . ." He stopped speaking and gazed fixedly, very intently, at some spot directly in front of him, at something that seemed to be difficult for him to see. "And now . . . hurry! . . . hurry!" he whispered.

Bursuc leaned over him, alarmed. "What's the matter? What do you want?"

Biris was silent, still staring straight ahead.

"Nurse!" cried Bursuc.

"*Coana* Viorica," murmured Biris. "Tell her I wanted to go to Paris." He smiled and turned to face the monk. Reaching for his hand, he held it tightly in both of his. "Absolve me, Father," he said in a surprisingly clear voice. "Hurry!"

"I'm not worthy," Bursuc exclaimed, bursting into tears. "I'm more sinful than you. I'm a thief, a criminal. I'm not worthy to absolve you." He dropped to his knees and began to sob. His head lay on Biris's hands.

"A prayer," Biris whispered. "Say a prayer. . . . Hurry. . . ."

"You say it too." Bursuc raised his head slowly. "Say it with me . . . 'Our Father, which art in Heaven . . .'"

Biris nodded assent, repeating the words slowly and with increasing effort. When the door opened and *doamna* Porumbache rushed into the room he tried to raise himself on his elbows. His face brightened suddenly and he smiled. *Doamna* Porumbache screamed—a startled cry that was stifled as she froze with her hand over her mouth. Irina fell on her knees beside the bed. Happy, at peace, Biris gazed at them with eyes that saw no more.

7

STEFAN CLOSED THE DOOR BEHIND HIM, AND WITHOUT TURNING ON THE LIGHT he stood for a moment listening intently. They're not at home, he said to himself. Maybe they've gone to see a motion picture. Then I have at least two hours ahead of me. . . . Tiptoeing to the window, he opened the shutters. When he rested his arms on the windowsill, as he did so often, he was greeted by the cool freshness of the summer night, and he leaned out to look at rue Vaneau, a street not entirely unfamiliar to him. He had read about it in *La Cousine Bette* long ago, even before his first visit to Paris twenty-five years earlier.

In February, when he had spent his first night on the fourth floor of this hotel, time had somehow reversed itself mysteriously and he had felt that he was once again in his secret room. There were thin wooden doors on each side and the walls seemed as insubstantial as screens. The slightest sound could be heard—every footstep, all his neighbors' discussions. Stefan had listened rather absently at first. His thoughts kept turning back twelve or thirteen years to the time of the secret room in Bucharest when he had overheard the conversations between Vadastra and Arethia.

During the first few weeks he seldom slept at the hotel, and when he did spend a night there it was necessary for him to put Boules Quiess in his ears so that he could go to sleep, since it was always late, after midnight, when the last of his neighbors went to bed. He quickly learned to know these people, even before he met them on the stairs or in the hallway. The room on the right was occupied in February by a young couple who prepared their meals on an alcohol stove. He heard them take the silverware out of a suitcase they kept under the bed and he listened as they washed their pots and pans. They

544

talked all the time about the apartment that they would soon occupy. The sound of meat sizzling in the frying pan would reach his ears, and soon the odor of *côte de mouton* began to filter under the door. Then Stefan would go to the window and open it noisily in order to inform his neighbors that his room was being invaded by the smell of fried mutton. No matter how many newspapers he stuffed around the door, the kitchen smells always found their way into his quarters.

Fortunately, in a short time the young couple succeeded in securing the apartment, and their place was taken by a woman whose age was difficult to determine—she was probably younger than she looked—and a little girl of nine or ten who had a bandage over half of her face. Stefan had met them in the lobby on the evening of their arrival. The woman was completing the registration form, and the girl, seated on a suitcase, was waiting for her with a resigned air. The child had regarded Stefan sternly with her one unbandaged eye. Stefan found out later from the porter that the girl had had an accident in which one side of her face had been burned. They had come to Paris so the child could enter a hospital for plastic surgery. He did not know, the porter had said, if the woman were her mother or her aunt or only a friend of the family. They did not have the same name, but the little girl called her "Mama." Every night when the woman changed the dressing and bathed the wound before they went to bed, the girl would moan and stamp her feet. Sometimes she screamed and tried to run away.

The first time he heard her scream Stefan had just returned from a long walk in the company of Baragan, whom he had met that afternoon as he was waiting on rue Copernic for the IRO office to open. It was always a varied assortment of individuals who found themselves thrown together in the queue, which grew rapidly in length before two o'clock. Stefan leaned against the wall and looked at the people around him, trying to guess their nationalities before they spoke. Some were wearing clothes that had once been military uniforms, which, in order not to arouse suspicion, had been altered unskillfully and concealed under a cloak or a faded trench coat. There were also those whose garb bespoke elegance. Freshly shaved, they smoked their American cigarettes as they talked among themselves, without a glance at the others in the line. They seemed to be trying to create the impression that their having to stand on the sidewalk of rue Copernic was due to an error—that they had mistaken the hour and for that reason had to wait with all the riffraff, but everything would be arranged once they spoke to Monsieur X. . . . Near Stefan a young man leaned on the wall, smoking. His thick black eyebrows almost grew together and he had a deep scar across his cheek. He inhaled the smoke of his cigarette insatiably, and from time to time he took out a handkerchief and wiped his mouth. Presently he

545

turned to Stefan and asked in Romanian if he knew M. Brémont, the man who was in charge of questioning the Romanians and assembling their dossiers. In this way they entered into conversation.

The young man said his name was Baragan and that he had come there from Hungary, where he had been imprisoned for six months for crossing the border illegally. He had been released on the morning of January 1, 1948, and the first thing he discovered upon leaving prison was that King Mihai had abdicated the night before. From that time—from New Year's Day until that very afternoon late in February when he met Stefan—Baragan had been pondering a plan of action. He had come to Paris to recruit resolute volunteers and to put his plan into operation that spring. After he filled out the questionnaire he waited on the street for Stefan to talk with him and try to persuade him to join his cause. They set off on foot from rue Copernic, and all the way to la place de la Concorde he talked constantly. Stefan suggested a cup of coffee in Montparnasse, and they descended into the Métro station. The only time that Baragan ceased to expound on the subject of his plan was while they were in the crowded subway. He contented himself with eyeing his traveling companions curiously, wiping his mouth with his handkerchief from time to time. In the cafe he listened cautiously for a moment to be sure no Romanian was being spoken at the tables near them, and then he revealed the final details of the plan.

It would take fifteen, or at the most twenty, volunteers. But the men must be committed, because there was not the slightest chance of their surviving. Furthermore, he must draft a message addressed to all the leaders of Europe and America. Days or weeks in advance he would type one or two hundred copies of it, which would be signed by all the volunteers. Then he would send the statement to political figures, writers, major journalists, and church leaders. In the message he would explain that it was not their intention for this gesture to have any immediate political repercussions. It was just a last desperate, futile cry of peoples who were condemned to death. For that reason Baragan wanted to locate volunteers from all the countries occupied by the Soviets. Their deed then would become a collective symbol of protest from those parts of Europe that had been sacrificed in a few spectacular meetings of the Allies. Since no means of escape from this situation existed, there was nothing left to do except make a non-political gesture that would focus the attention of the Westerners on the tragedy of the sacrificed nations. Baragan's plan was simple—he would post the letters to the leaders of Europe and the United States so they would all arrive on the same day as those mailed to the Parisians. Then in the middle of the night at la place de la Concorde the volunteers would blow themselves to pieces with dynamite. Baragan, Stefan learned, had studied

546

industrial chemistry for three years and had worked in a munitions factory under the Communists. He claimed to know how to prepare the charge of dynamite so precisely that there would be no chance any of them would live through it. "So far I've found two volunteers," he confessed, lowering his voice, "a Romanian and a Hungarian. But to really impress world opinion there must be at least fifteen. . . . I'm not putting pressure on anyone," he added, a little embarrassed, almost apologetic. "It's just an invitation to an examination of conscience. . . ."

That evening when he returned to his hotel Stefan had heard the girl screaming, and he stood astounded in the middle of the room wondering what to do. Perhaps he should knock on the door to see if they needed something. He thought the woman was struggling with the girl, because he could hear her heavy breathing. She might have been straining to hold the child with one arm in an effort to keep the other hand free. A little later he heard her talking and whispering to the little one, kissing her, pleading with her to forgive her. The girl had begun to cry. Stefan relaxed and stretched out on the bed.

"You're plan is not a bad one," he had said on leaving Baragan. "I regret that I'm not free, as I was a few years ago. It would be a beautiful death and a purposeful one. I had a friend once, a playwright. He dreamed of writing a kind of tragedy inspired by the agony of the *Nibelungen*. He would have liked your plan very much. . . . But I'm not free. I'm searching for someone." "Please don't tell anyone," Baragan had said. "If the police find out they'll expel all of us. . . ."

The little girl sobbed quietly. From the room on the left came the constant and regular tramp of footsteps. The man had become impatient and had begun to pace about in agitation. "He must be waiting for his girl friend," guessed Stefan. He was a Greek who had a family somewhere nearby in that quarter of Paris. When it was time for dinner a car stopped in front of the hotel and Stefan heard the horn blow. His neighbor quickly opened his window and signaled to the occupants. In his haste he almost ran all the way down the three flights of stairs. Stefan had seen them all several times—the mother, a sister, and an uncle who was constantly scowling, wore dark glasses, and hardly ever spoke. He simply blew the horn whenever his nephew seemed to be delayed.

Once Stefan had questioned Stella Wainwright, "Does your husband, by any chance, have among his numerous friends a Greek millionaire, a very dark-skinned man who wears sunglasses? A man of indefinite age, stern, sullen, who never smiles and is always impatient? A man who likes to be silent and who delights in prolonging his silence if he thinks that the others—above all his sister and his nephew—suspect that he's angry, especially at them?" Stefan was not being serious when he asked her this. He knew he was painting an exaggerated portrait, that he was constructing a character. He knew too that there could be no possible connection between Wainwright and the man with the dark glasses who lived somewhere in the shadow of the Invalides. But he liked to cut short Stella's frenzied chronicle of life in New York, of her conquests among the multimillionaires, of the receptions at the Georges V. It pleased him to interrupt her just when her narration had become most animated. He would ask her an absurd question concerning Mr. Wainwright. Stella would give him a long hard look, then slightly lowering her lashes she would smile in satisfaction. "You're jealous!" she would say. "You envy me. All Romanians envy me for having millions, for being beautiful, for having an American passport!" Sometimes she would add, "I'm sorry, but you're not what you used to be. You've aged. . . ."

She repeated this to him whenever she had the opportunity ever since she had gone to see him on boulevard Murat. "Stefan, you've aged! You have too much gray hair!" She had remained unaltered. She was just a little too elegantly dressed, a little too well-groomed. "I forgave you," she told him once. "And yet I regret that I did! It would have pleased me to take revenge!" "Have you been in Switzerland?" asked Stefan abruptly. "Do you know anyone in the American Embassy in Berne? I have to go to Switzerland and they won't give me a visa. . . ." Stella had seated herself on the sofa. She stared at him a long time without attempting to hide her disappointment. "I can't get over how much you've changed," she said. "You were a handsome man." "Do you know anyone at the Swiss Consulate?" Stefan insisted. "That depends on what you're going to do in Switzerland." "I have to search for Ileana." Stella was thoughtful for a moment and she smiled. "Ileana? Are you still involved with her?" "Do me a very great favor," Stefan continued. "If you'll introduce me to Wainwright, I'll ask him myself. Americans are sentimental. Perhaps I can persuade him. . . ."

Since that afternoon early in November he had seen her repeatedly, but it was not until January that he succeeded in making the acquaintance of Wainwright. "He's gone," she would tell him when they met. "They called him on the telephone from London this morning. . . ." Or, another time, "He took a plane for New York yesterday. He promised me he'd be back next week. . . ." Stefan didn't always believe her. He would stay near the door of her apartment at the Georges V, close to the wall, smiling, embarrassed. "Are you afraid?" She came closer. "Are you afraid of me?" "I know you want to get even with me," he said. "I'm protecting myself." "I hated you for several years, but now that's past. You're lucky. . . ." "Don't think I'm giving in to you," she warned him once as she walked slowly across the salon. "Don't harbor any illusions. I like you because you're Romanian and you're unhappy. You're a drifter, and tomorrow or the next day you'll have to find work in the market, like the others. Or else you'll emigrate to Canada to chop wood in the forest, or you'll go to Argentina or Australia. That's why I like you. I like to remember the time when we were together, when you teased me. Tell me a story. I like to listen to you. Tell me what else happened in Paris. . . ."

He sat on the sofa and watched her as she walked around the room, his eyes constantly seeking hers in an effort to read her thoughts—to divine what she was planning to do—and he talked to her. "It was in 1928," he began once, "the year I took my doctorate here in Paris. I had a friend who was a theologian . . ." "No," Stella interrupted him. "Romanians don't interest me. I'm tired of hearing about nothing but tragedies and misfortunes. Tell me something else." "Hear me out and you'll discover how I decided to study political economy after I made friends with a theologian. Because you may not know this—I came here to Paris to study theology. . . ." Suddenly he relaxed and beamed at her, unconsciously recovering the freshness of his youth. Stella studied him attentively, her eyes slightly closed, and waited eagerly for him to continue. He often invented characters from his student days in Paris, but then he wondered what he would do with them. How would he carry them through the world for twenty years and through what circumstances would he be able to bring them to the present? "Tell me something else," Stella would break in from time to time, her patience at an end, and she would get up abruptly to search for a package of cigarettes or to go to the window and look out on the street. "Tell me something interesting!" "Just listen!" he would say. "In those days when I went into a Romanian restaurant . . ." He knew that this always held her attention. She wanted to know what went on in the Romanian restaurants.

Often she invited him to dinner in the evening. "Oh, no!" he would protest, "this evening you're my guest. . . ." "You'll spend all your money!" Stella would tell him, and he thought he detected a gleam of wickedness in her eyes. "You won't have a cent left and you'll have to go to work nights at the market like a common laborer. . . . Let's go to a Romanian restaurant," she added, smiling. "I'd enjoy disgracing you." "Shall I tell you what else happened to my theologian friend?" he went on as though he had not heard.

As they entered the restaurant Stella would glance around her conspicuously, laughing and chattering in a loud voice until she felt herself the center of attention. Then she would lean close to Stefan and whisper to him. Once she stated, "All these people think you're my lover. And since they know you're a poor devil of a refugee, they

549

imagine that I'm supporting you!" She brought her face close to his. "Let's find out what happened to my friend the theologian," he suggested again, unruffled.

Usually Misu Weissman would remark when he came in with the coffee in the morning, "You were with Stella again. I found out from Vidrighin's friends." And a few minutes later he would add, "You told her again about the theologian. . . . You were unwise. She's extremely indiscreet." "You won't misunderstand me," Stefan would interrupt. "You know why I left the country. . . ." Misu Weissman would regard him with an embarrassed smile. "Vidrighin's friends say that you're living with Stella. I had an argument with one of them last night." "The only serious thing . . ." Stefan would continue as though he had heard nothing. "The only thing that worries me is that I can't get to meet Wainwright. Probably Stella doesn't want me to. . . ."

But one day he met him unexpectedly in the lobby of the Georges V. A fat man, becoming bald, but still rather young, he wore gold-rimmed glasses that concealed his eyes in a curious manner. You could not recognize their color or even discern in which direction he was looking, and this gave you the disconcerting impression of talking with someone who did not see you. He was sitting with a group of men around a low table. Stella led Stefan by the hand and presented him as if she thought him a rare and exotic animal. "How do you do?" said Wainwright in English, shaking Stefan's hand vigorously without looking at him. Then he turned back to his companion and they resumed their conversation. "He adores me," Stella said. "He doesn't refuse me any caprice. . . . We're dining together this evening," she added. "Everybody's invited. You can talk to him. . . ." But it was impossible to talk to him that evening. Wainwright had approached Stella and put his hand on her shoulder. "You will excuse me, my dear," he apologized, speaking in English, and he nodded to Stefan several times and smiled. "This evening you're my guest," Stella had said. "Friends of Vidrighin will be there, and *conu* Misu too."

A few weeks later, when he was finally able to speak with Wainwright, he realized that no matter what he might say Wainwright did not listen. He nodded his head approvingly all the time and he smiled, but he was unable to listen, regardless of his good intentions. "Don't worry," Stella assured him. "If he made a promise, he'll get you your visa." This was in March. Several days before that Misu Weissman had come home preoccupied and troubled. "Some difficulties have arisen," he said, "and I can't persuade Vidrighin. He's obstinate and suspicious. It's the business I told you about."

Actually he had spoken only very vaguely about the matter he was working on with Vidrighin and a Belgian syndicate. All that Stefan had

550

learned was that it concerned the redemption of stock of a Romanian petroleum corporation which had recently been absorbed by Sovrompetrol. "But don't let it bother you," Misu had continued. "The deal's all set, with or without Vidrighin. There are plenty of other interested people. I told you eventually we'll be millionaires. . . ." And since he noticed that Stefan remained silent and thoughtful, Weissman began to talk again, simulating a cheerfulness he did not feel. "I mentioned you again to Stella. She's remarkably curious and wants to know all about you. 'I don't understand him,' she said to me," and before he was aware of it he had started to imitate her. " 'It's impossible to understand him. Do you understand him? What sort of man is he? Sometimes I have the impression he's crazy. Or perhaps he wants to play the fool, but I don't understand why. He's a very strange creature. I'd like to know what goes on in his mind—what he's thinking. Because he's always thinking!' " "You imitate her very well," Stefan commented with a smile. "I might be listening to her. I didn't know you were such a good mimic. . . ." Flattered, Weissman began to laugh, but he must have remembered Vidrighin, for a shadow crossed his face. He made an effort to banish the thought and rubbed his hands together in agitation. "Yes, she's very curious," he began again, seating himself on the sofa. "And it seems to me that she's a little jealous too. 'Who's his girl friend?' she asked me. 'Ileana,' I answered, 'Ileana Sideri. He left Romania to search for her. . . .' " He stopped, suddenly embarrassed, and glanced apprehensively at Stefan, who hastened to reassure him. "You answered her very properly. It's no secret. . . ." "That's just what I told her—it's no secret. It's better for people to know why you came here so they won't make all kinds of accusations. But Stella wouldn't believe me. 'I didn't ask you about Ileana,' she said. 'I want to know who his girl friend is here in Paris.' I answered that I don't know, that I'm not acquainted with her. Did I say the right thing?" he asked, looking directly in Stefan's eyes. "You know the other Romanians are asking the same question, but they think that you're Stella's. . . . I told her that too and she laughed. She seemed delighted. 'Do you think this puts him in an embarrassing position?' she asked me. 'Do you think the Romanians are convinced that I'm supporting him?' I looked at her a long time and answered, 'You're too young and too beautiful to find it necessary to support a man.' Do you think that was a good answer?" "Perfect!" Stefan assured him. "I have the impression that she still loves you and is terribly jealous," Weissman added after awhile. "We ought to speak seriously with her one of these days. . . ." And when he observed that Stefan did not appear to understand, he explained, lowering his eyes in embarrassment and wondering what to do with his hands, "To tell her that some difficulties have arisen, but that if someone with a lot of money

551

would step in—for instance, Wainwright—we'd become multimillionaires in a few weeks. . . ."

Several times after that Stefan tried to sway her. He would let her get involved in telling him about her conquests and then, unexpectedly, he would interrupt. "You can persuade Wainwright to participate in *conu* Misu's business deal." Stella would gaze at him with half-closed eyes. She wondered if he could be speaking seriously. Or was this a joke uttered simply for the purpose of cutting her off? "Have you some interest in the deal?" she asked him one day. "None." ". . . Fortunately for Misu. Otherwise it would come to nothing. I'd even sell my jewels to destroy it and then I'd be sorry, because I find the old man quite personable. . . ." "Can I tell *conu* Misu all this?" he had asked her, but Stella did not reply. "I'd like for you to be rich." She had continued to pursue this thought dreamily, "Very rich, but with all your money invested in one big business. And then in a single day I'd destroy you! I'd reduce you to zero, so you wouldn't even have enough to pay your hotel bill! And you'd come to beg Wainwright to lend you a few thousand francs, but of course I'd be there and I'd signal him to refuse. Probably you'd commit suicide, because you're too proud to beg. Or maybe it would be more serious—you'd be put in jail. And after that you'd inevitably commit suicide. . . ."

She was silent then for some time, smiling absently, as though she could not bear to abandon her dream. Suddenly she demanded, "Will you have dinner with me tonight? I was invited to eat with Vidrighin's friends, but I can decline." She waited a moment in front of him, impatient, fidgeting. It seemed a considerable struggle for her to keep from throwing herself at him and ripping him to shreds. "You're my guest," Stefan said, "but we can't go to the Romanian restaurant or Vidrighin's friends will find out about it." "Let's go to St.-Germain-des-Prés then, so I can see the Existentialists. . . ."

Later, after they had left the restaurant and had stopped in a number of cafes, they were walking toward the Georges V when Stella caught his arm and whispered to him, "How happy we'd have been together! I'd have had money and we'd have been happy. I was crazy about you. I thought you loved me too a little . . ." "I never said I loved you." "I thought you were too proud to tell me." She was silent, musing, clinging to his arm. "And yet you've changed since you became an American citizen," he said some time later. "When I first knew you, you used different expressions. You were always saying 'You're a pig!' Now you don't say it at all. You've changed." Stella had sought his eyes in the dark, leaning her head closer to his, and she had smiled with visible effort. "If you only knew how much I hate you!" she murmured. "I never thought I could hate anyone so much! I keep trying

552

to think of something horrible to do, something that will destroy you completely. . . ." But he continued to accompany her very amicably, talking to her without stopping until they reached the lobby of the Georges V, where he kissed her hand courteously. "You've been a dear!" was her parting thrust. "See you soon!"

On the first night that he spent in the hotel it was very late when he went to sleep, since he was forced to listen to the conversations in the adjoining rooms and he struggled with the memories of his secret room in Bucharest. He pressed the pillow over his head and finally managed to drop off, but the next morning he bought a box of Boules Quiess. After that whenever he heard his neighbors come in at night he stuffed these in his ears so that the noise was at least muffled. At this time he was still living with Misu Weissman on boulevard Murat, spending only his afternoons and evenings at the hotel. Sometime later Weissman said to him, "You ought to give notice of your change of address." "I'd rather not if I can avoid it. I'd like my address to remain secret." "Impossible!" interrupted Weissman. "You don't have that right and the police are very strict. They might make a search. Yes, a search!" he insisted. "The supervision of aliens. Don't forget that ours is a special situation." "Then I'll report the change, but I ask you in all seriousness not to tell anyone where I've moved. Especially, don't tell Stella or Vidrighin's friends." Weissman concealed a quick glance at Stefan, a sly smile on his lips. "With respect to me don't worry, but at the same time let me call your attention to the necessity for caution. If you happen to have any important meetings—I mean political ones—it would be better for you to come here to my place. Give me a call and I'll leave you the key."

At the beginning of March Stefan installed himself permanently in the hotel. Shortly after that the woman and the little girl with the burned face moved to the floor below and in their place a family from Sweden arrived for a stay of two weeks. Early in the morning Stefan heard the man working at his typewriter, while the woman sat near the window most of the time, humming to her little son, whom she held on her lap. In the room on the left there was almost no sign of life from the Greek during the course of the morning. "He's studying for his exam-inations," the porter said. "His family rented the room for him so he could work undisturbed." The uncle with the dark glasses continued to come regularly at the dinner hour, blowing his horn as soon as he stopped the car in front of the hotel. Sometimes in the afternoon Stefan could tell that the Greek was waiting for his girl friend, because he tramped impatiently about the room and kept opening the window to look out at the street. When Weissman came the first time to see Stefan, the girl had just arrived and the man was quarreling with her. For nearly three-quarters of an hour he berated her for being late. Weissman stood amazed in the middle of the room. He had not imagined that one could hear the voices of the other tenants so distinctly. "Let's go," he whispered. "I have important things to tell you and your neighbor might understand Romanian. . . ."

As they went downstairs and set off for a nearby cafe Weissman seemed more preoccupied than usual. He had found out long since that Stella would not intercede with Wainwright. "I'll surprise them yet," he had said then, and now as he walked along absently beside Stefan, staring vaguely ahead with his hands in the pockets of his overcoat, he repeated it, "You'll see, *coane* Stefan, I'll give them all a surprise! I'll surprise you too. . . . Because you're skeptical," he added, turning to Stefan with laughter in his voice.

It's true, I am skeptical, Stefan started to answer. He had wondered many times how Weissman could still have money. He maintained the same life-style—always riding in taxis, issuing frequent invitations to everyone to dine in expensive restaurants, never failing to send flowers to Stella whenever she invited him to dinner. "He's head over heels in debt and yet he borrows constantly," she had told Stefan once. "That's why Vidrighin withdrew from his business deal. . . ."

"I figured you out a long time ago," Weissman continued. "You're skeptical. But I'll give you a surprise too." Then, unexpectedly, he broke into a laugh. "That creature!" he exclaimed finally. "She sends us both greetings from Italy on the same postcard! She ran off without a word. . . ."

He hunted nervously in his pocket and showed Stefan a picture postcard from Naples. "Greetings from both of us, Stella." "She didn't say anything to anyone," Weissman went on, disturbed. "What will Vidrighin's friends think? I'd just arranged some dinners with his friends and the Belgians. Stella was to have been there too. You can imagine—a woman as beautiful as she always makes an impression." Stefan tried vainly to get Misu to confide in him, to inform him of the current status of the transaction, but Weissman replied evasively, "I'll give everyone a surprise. . . ." He thrust his hands angrily into his overcoat pockets.

In April, with the aid of a former university classmate, Stefan found work at an economic agency. Three times a week he went to the office, read the Russian and Romanian journals and magazines on economics and made resumés for an information bulletin. He had not told anyone, and when Weissman came to see him one morning he caught sight of the pile of materials and questioned him casually, "Do you read Russian all the time? You're fortunate! You're keeping up with what's going on in Romania. . . ." He sat down on the edge of the bed and ran his hand over his face. Stefan looked at him in alarm. Misu seemed to grow old before his eyes. But the next moment he managed to smile again, and this effort made his countenance appear infinitely sad. Stefan tried to persuade him to stay for lunch, but Weissman refused. He was invited elsewhere. He always answered him like that—he was invited, or he was having guests for dinner, in which case he would insist that Stefan join them. When he came to visit in the morning he always seemed pressed for time. He would sit down absently on the sofa, but after a few moments he would get up again to look out the window or pace the floor without speaking. Stefan kept trying to get him to talk about the business negotiations. "I know a little about such things. I was an economic adviser. . . . Why don't you tell me about it?" "I'll tell you. I'll tell you someday very soon," promised Misu. Then one morning, much embarrassed, with a sudden blush, Weissman asked Stefan to loan him ten thousand francs. "I'm expecting a draft from Belgium," he said. "I'll return this in the evening." He telephoned Stefan that night and announced triumphantly, "I'm calling from the Georges V. Stella's back and wants to see you without fail. She insists that we dine together this evening."

It was early in May. That evening was the first one that had felt truly like spring, and the sky was clear and sparkling. A sizable group of people was gathered in the lobby around a small table of aperitifs. Immediately Stella grasped his arm and drew him into a corner. "I have a lover," she whispered. "He's here. See if you can guess. I'll give you a quarter of an hour." Then, smiling and clinging to his arm, she brought him back into the midst of the group. Stefan surprised an expression on Weissman's face that contained a mixture of joy and fear. He seemed delighted at the intimacy Stella was displaying toward Stefan, as though all his hopes depended upon it, and yet he was afraid to rejoice too much in case he should become the victim of an illusion. "She's dying for you, *coane* Stefan," he whispered a few minutes later, approaching him to fill his glass. "You've devastated her. . . ." Embarrassed, Stefan smiled.

Fifteen minutes later Stella pulled him into a corner of the room again. Stefan indicated one of the young men with a glance. She was ecstatic and murmured, "You didn't guess! I told you he's more than a lover! I told you I adore him!" "Stella," Stefan interrupted, taking her hand in his, "you don't know how much it pleases me to hear you say that. I'll venture to make one request of you . . ." "You didn't guess!"

Stella whispered again in agitation. "He's terribly nice. Look again, now. Maybe you'll guess this time...." He glanced around and thought that he saw who it was. One of the young men was standing silently apart, turning his glass around in his fingers, gazing morosely at the carpet. "Is it he?" Stella nodded. "I have a request to make," Stefan insisted. "It doesn't have anything to do with me. It's *conu* Misu's affair. Intercede with Wainwright for him. It's a very serious matter...." Frowning, Stella stared at him. She seemed to be wondering for a moment what it was he was trying to tell her. Then she took his arm and led him to a chair. "I'm simply mad about him!" she whispered, and then she added, "Don't worry. He doesn't understand Romanian. He's from South America...." Weissman approached him once more, with the same mixture of happiness and fear still showing in his eyes. "You're terrific!" he whispered. "She's in a good mood to give in tonight!" "*Coane* Misule," Stefan confided presently, "it's not what you think. There's nothing between us. We're just friends. I asked her once more tonight to intercede with Wainwright and I'll ask her again. But don't imagine that between us... She has a lover...." Speechless, Weissman considered him for a long time. "I'm just beginning to have some hope," Stefan said in an effort to reassure him. "Now that she's not furious with me I may be able to persuade her to speak to Wainwright...."

After that time he saw Weissman less often. Once Misu told him on the telephone that he had found a new silent partner. He seemed cheerful enough, but when they met that afternoon the expression on his face worried Stefan. He appeared both frightened and humiliated, and his humiliation arose from the fact that he seemed unable to master his panic. After that he talked constantly of going to Belgium, but Stefan simply did not believe him. He ran into him once coming out of the Métro. Weissman was embarrassed. He wore an expression of guilty surprise. "I forgot to phone you that I postponed my departure," he said, and he blushed. But Stefan had never been informed definitely that he was leaving. Perhaps Misu had mentioned it to his other friends without recalling exactly whom. In any case, he looked tired and had not shaved. The fact that he had ridden on the subway—he who always traveled in a taxi—seemed ominous to Stefan. "Have you seen Stella lately?" Misu asked once. "I heard that she's been disgracing herself with that new man of hers. Her life's one big orgy, going from bar to bar. She's not interested in seeing Romanians anymore. She says she's bored with us poor devils...."

The Greek moved at the end of May and after that the room on the left was occupied again by transients. A traveling salesman, a Lebanese student, and several Englishmen slept there, in that order. After the

Swedish family left, the room on the right was taken by a woman of indefinite age whose distinguished face was almost beautiful but lacked expression. She had come from one of the provinces, the porter told him, and was in the process of getting a divorce. She was almost always away. When she returned in the evening she was generally accompanied by a friend with whom she would remain closeted for a long time in her room, absorbed in conversation.

Weissman came once again at the beginning of June to borrow another ten thousand francs. "Can you imagine? On my way into the city this morning I lost my briefcase, or perhaps it was stolen on the Métro. I don't know. Fortunately I didn't have too much money and my identification card wasn't in it. . . ." He seemed confused and smiled without ceasing, moving his hands helplessly, as though he were afraid that Stefan would not believe him. "I wouldn't ask you for so much, but I've invited some Belgian friends to dinner and I don't have time to go to the bank. I'll return it to you this evening. Or rather, to be certain, give me until lunch tomorrow. If I don't have time to come, I'll telegraph it to you. . . ."

It was a week before he received it. The porter handed it to him in an envelope. Weissman had left it at the hotel when Stefan was away.

When he came home at night he liked to remain for awhile in the darkness contemplating the street as he leaned on the windowsill. It was almost ten when he returned to his room. At that time there were fewer people passing by, and before eleven rue Vaneau seemed deserted. But it suddenly came to life again an hour later when the neighborhood motion picture theaters closed their doors.

If they've gone to the cinema I have two hours ahead of me, he said to himself. He had work to do, but that night he seemed unable to tear himself away from the window. I have time, he repeated. I've two good hours. . . .

He thought he heard a knock at his door, and he stepped back, startled. With rapid strides he crossed the room, and locating the wall switch, he turned on the light. The knocking sounded again. "Come in!" he cried.

Immediately the porter opened the door, but he did not enter. From the doorway he held out a rather large package wrapped in brown paper and bound very securely with several strands of cord.

"An errand boy brought it just now," he said. "I gave him a hundred francs. . . ."

Stefan searched nervously in his billfold and held out two hundred-franc notes without a word. Biris! he remembered suddenly, and the thought trou-

557

bled him. On that evening the porter knocked on the door, and then we met on *bulevardul* Dinicu Golescu and we talked about Partenie—about an article of Partenie's. That was in 1936—in August—I remember very well. . . .

"Thanks, and good night," said the porter, withdrawing.

Stefan stood perplexed on the threshold with the package under his arm. No, it wasn't then, he corrected himself. That wasn't the evening I met Biris. He felt his heart leap. *I gave him a hundred lei. . . . He said that he came back from the Bratianu Statue. . . .* That's what the porter said to me another time, earlier, when he came up to my room and brought me the gloves. On the Night of St. John, when I met Ileana. *He said that they belong to the young lady who was with you,* Stefan recalled, and he took a deep breath, holding it as if he wished to suppress a sigh. He closed the door and started to go to the desk with the package still under his arm, but changed his mind and sat down on the bed. The bundle was heavy. He turned it from one side to the other trying to untie the string, but he grew impatient and got up to search on the washstand for a discarded razor blade. He had never found out definitely if they were her gloves and he didn't even know what had become of them. He was carrying them in his pocket on that evening when he met Biris on *bulevardul* Dinicu Golescu and Biris had spoken about Partenie.

Now the details of that meeting returned to him with greater clarity. *The behavior of men is like the functioning of an organ—like a kidney, for instance, or the genitals. . . .* He cut the cords with difficulty because they were stout and tightly tied, and he began to unwrap the package. After removing the brown paper, he noticed that there was a sealed parcel inside with an envelope on top, open and unaddressed. It contained a single sheet of paper with a few lines on it penned by Weissman. "This was the surprise," read the note, and he had signed his name, then added as a postscript, "They are the master-pieces of the Romanian literature of tomorrow. Take care of them. Yours, with all confidence and friendship." He had signed it again. Bibicescu's manuscripts, surmised Stefan. But why would he send them to me? he wondered somewhat fearfully. What can have happened to him?

He rose from the bed and went to close the window. Picking up the package again he placed it on the desk. Why would he send them to me? Carefully he cut the seals of the inner wrapper and took out a bundle of notebooks and loose pages covered with writing. They're Bibicescu's manu-scripts, he continued to repeat to himself in an effort to quiet his growing apprehension. He began to thumb through the papers hurriedly, reading only the titles. He found a typewritten copy of *The Wake*. "By Ciru Partenie and Dan Bibicescu" was written on the first page. There was a sheaf of hand-written pages inscribed, *"The Return from Stalingrad,* A Modern Myth in Five Acts, by Dan Bibicescu." A penciled notation in Bibicescu's handwriting was in one corner. "Provisional and unfinished version." Stefan glanced at page one. "The scene represents the ruins of a blockhouse in Stalingrad. . . . A

558

few moments later a colonel appears. Colonel: What's happened here?...
Don't you hear me? Where's the sergeant?...." There were more bundles of
pages clipped together and these Stefan set aside without looking through
them. Why would he send them to me? he found himself wondering again.

He saw a thick copybook with a short note in Bibicescu's handwriting
attached to the cover with a pin. It bore the date 15/X/1945 Bucharest.
"Found by me at Ciulnita in house ____, together with other papers of less
importance. It is a copybook of intimate notes and memoirs belonging to Ciru
Partenie (may be considered a fragment of a journal, the only one which has
been preserved for us)." Stefan was disturbed. He hesitated. Perhaps it would
be better if I didn't read it, he told himself. Nevertheless he opened the
notebook and was struck immediately by the many obliterations that had been
made with ink of a different color. Here a series of words, there even an entire
. line, had been crossed out, obviously by another hand. "Today ____ was
here," and the name had been deleted. "She has not come to see me for
several weeks. I had hoped that the break was final." Stefan felt the hand that
held the manuscript shake slightly, and he laid the notebook on the desk.
Farther down on the same page he saw the line, "She asked me if I still love
____," and again the name was marked out. "'Of course I love her,' I
answered." Stefan lifted the book and held the page closer to the light, trying
to decipher the name that had been expunged. He heard his own agitated
breathing. His efforts were unsuccessful, and he began to read from the
beginning of the page. There was no date on it, nor any other explanatory
note. "I find myself again in that same strange landscape which seems to me
to possess a clarity, a beauty, that is utterly remote and futile. I feel that I have
wandered for a long time alone, that I have been borne..." The sentence
remained uncompleted. Perhaps it's part of a literary work, Stefan thought.
Or maybe someone came in upon him as he sat at his desk and interrupted his
writing. Later when he reopened the notebook, he no longer remembered
what he had meant to say or it didn't interest him. Because a few lines farther
on he starts something else. "The difficulty with intellectual characters—they
all resemble one another. They all speak the same way. Ultimately they're
uninteresting. The golden rule: to avoid characters presumed to belong to an
educated class. Hard to convince the reader that an intellectual can have
strong passions." Next there were some truncated phrases. "____ was here
today. She asked me if I still love ____. 'Of course I love her,' I replied. I was
afraid that she would not understand me, that she would imagine I had
replied to her in this way in order to reconfirm our separation. In fact this was
so. I did want to do just that. Fortunately she believed me. Very sentimentally
she begged me with tears in her eyes to remain on friendly terms with her. I
promised."

Stefan turned the page. "In literature simple people with powerful
passions dominated by a single vice or some mania seem *alive* and *authentic*.

The others, especially the good, kind, intelligent people, and above all people preoccupied with moral problems, seem insipid, amorphous, devoid of personality. Basically, from the point of view of literature, they are uninteresting. What contemporary novelist would dare to choose as a principal character an individual who, let's say, longs for 'perfection'? Such characters seem artificial, bookish. A false perspective on the passionate personality has been created and what is most amusing is that the cerebral, erudite, cloistered writers have been responsible for this. . . ."

Interrupting his reading to light a cigarette, Stefan glanced ahead in the manuscript. There followed an entire page of observations concerning fictional characters and the technique of the novel. He skipped over this. Next came some personal notations. "Ten days with X. I discover a lot of sensational particulars about her grandfather—about his last affair, when he was over seventy, and the scandal he caused when he went to the magistrate to acknowledge the child. X implores me not to utilize these confidences. She tells me that rumor has it that I only write about what has happened to me or what I've heard has happened to others. I ask her: what else could I write about? She replies quite candidly, 'A writer ought to have imagination'. . . ."

Stefan was more calm now as he leafed through the pages, smoking. There was a lengthy sketch for a story. "At a name-day celebration in the house of a bourgeois family. (I use the house of X, the families of Y and Z) The son has invited several classmates. Descriptions. In particular, V, ugly, with wire-rimmed glasses, freckles. The story opens with his cry—'Doamna, Niculaie won't come out of the cellar!'" Stefan glanced absently over the summary of Niculaie's adventures. Several pages of descriptions and dialogues followed. Here and there he noticed many corrections, as if Partenie might have worked over this outline before undertaking the writing of the story. As he turned the pages Stefan paid special attention to the lines that contained excised names. "Presented to ____ my last memoir of Mangalia." "____ or The Journal of Retrospective Jealousy. I'd thought about writing that for a long time. I found out today that____ is preparing a novel with this title. . . ." Stefan skimmed through the notebook without reading the observations and reflections concerning the art of the novel that he was continually running across. Only once, when his eye halted by chance on the word "myth"—a term that he did not expect to find under the pen of Partenie—he read the entire notation. "I am a member of a generation of sacrificed writers. None of us will be able to write in a major style. We suffer from psychological tics, from the clichés of our recent literary experiences, etc. We must rediscover the mythical narrative, but it will not be done by someone like me—a rationalist devoid of a taste for myths."

As he turned the pages Stefan absently extinguished his cigarette. Several sheets had been torn out and for a few seconds he eyed with sudden uneasiness the bits of paper that still adhered to the back of the binding. "Could it have been *conu* Misu who tore them out?" he wondered. Toward the middle of the notebook the entries became fuller. They seemed to have been transformed gradually into little essays or fragments of memoirs, as if once having started to write, Partenie had forgotten that this was an intimate journal and had allowed himself to be carried away by his inspiration. Certain pages were crossed out with a blue pencil and a notation, "used," was scribbled in an upper corner. He had begun one page with a tale about someone who had spoken to him that day about La Veuve Cliquot. The person's name had been obliterated, but when Partenie asked naively, "Who's that?" he had been informed that it was a brand of pink champagne. He had not known that there was such a thing as pink champagne and had become the target of much teasing. In relating this event Partenie permitted himself to become involved in recollections about his first glass of champagne. He was still in the *liceu*, and he and his schoolmates had gone one evening to a bar, the Olympia, where they had ordered a bottle, first taking the precaution to determine its cost. After this there were memories of his classmates of that time and of a meeting at Constanta ten or fifteen years later. It read almost like a story. The descriptions became increasingly precise and full, the dialogues more lively, and on page after page one could discern how the writer intervened more directly in the narrative. The tale broke off abruptly, and Partenie had made the notation in blue pencil, "To be resumed."

A few pages farther on, a confession interested Stefan. "Speaking with ———— about the Journal of Jules Renard, she asks me if I also am writing a journal. I reply that I wrote one earlier, but I only kept those pages that can serve directly or indirectly for literature. All the rest could be burned—'and that's what I did with them,' I added."

Stefan stopped and reread the last lines. During the past half hour his mind had been occupied subliminally with the task of pinpointing, by means of allusions in the text the year in which it had been written. He made another attempt. Partenie had died in 1939 at the age of thirty-six. If he had burned all the other notebooks it meant that this one before him was the last in which he had made entries. And there were blank pages still remaining in this book. Hence he had written it a few years before his death, perhaps sometime between 1933 and 1939. But up to this point Stefan had come across no precise references to Ioana, nor did Partenie refer to the books he was writing or to those he had completed. He began to turn the pages again. Several times he found notations in blue pencil, "plan for a novel," "used," "to be developed." Stefan thought that something more revealing might appear toward the end of the copybook, and he turned to the last notes. Here he found what seemed to be a portion of an uninterrupted passage about a woman, Lenora. He was surprised that the name had been allowed to remain. He turned back a few pages to find the beginning, and glancing over the first lines, he gathered that they consisted of recollections from the author's early youth concerning certain romantic encounters. In this section no names had been obliterated. Whoever had undertaken this task must have grown tired of it or had not had time to continue to the end.

"While walking today along *calea* Mosilor I thought I saw Fanny. I stared at her and at last she recognized me. We are very nearly the same age. When I was seventeen she was an apprentice at the shop and was about fourteen or fifteen. Today she looked like a middle-aged woman who might be anywhere between thirty-five and fifty, and yet she could not be more than twenty-seven or twenty-eight." Stefan stopped reading and made a rapid calculation. If Partenie was thirty-six in 1939 and the meeting with Fanny had taken place, say, five or six years before, in 1933 or 1934 when he was thirty, then he had known Ioana at that time. Perhaps they were engaged or had just broken off their engagement.

"'Do you remember me? I was with *duduia* Eleonora . . .' she said. I thought then that she gave me a sad smile, revealing several gold teeth. 'I remember perfectly,' I answered. 'How could I forget Lenora?' I realized that I had spoken with unwarranted familiarity and as usual I aggravated the situation further. 'How could I forget my first love?' I exclaimed and even broke into a laugh. 'I was seventeen and I'll never be that again!' 'Ah, youth!' She sighed. 'It was beautiful. It seems like a different life. Poor *duduia* Eleonora! I heard that she fell very low in her last days. She died in a hospital. She'd even sold her piano. . . .' 'I heard that too,' I said and tried to change the subject quickly. I asked her if she knew anything about the other girls—Anicuta, Puia, Sofia. Without any effort all those names which had been buried for so many years came to my mind again. Fanny seemed surprised by the accuracy of my memories. She told me something about Anicuta—she was her best friend—but I did not listen. At that moment I was thinking about my novel. I was sorry that I had burned it. Undoubtedly it was detestable—a pseudo-autobiographical tale written when I was about nineteen or twenty. But it would have amused me to reread it now to see what Fanny, Anicuta, and the other girls had become in my fictionalization of them. I remembered only the destiny that I bestowed on *duduia* Eleonora. She had become Lenora, the *femme fatale*. The hero was not seventeen, like me, nor was he a student in the first year of college. He had become Doctor V, the misunderstood and rebellious genius, a bit demoniacal, a bit fatalistic, pursued by misfortune—as I liked to picture myself at that time.

"Until I reached home I kept thinking about that one thing. How could I have produced such a monstrosity? The actual situation was extraordinary and it did not lack a certain tragic grandeur. I was seventeen and she was thirty-five or thirty-six. My passion for her was deep and true, and it consumed me. I ran away from home. I was ready to commit any folly, even to kill myself. Then how—wishing to write all this and wishing especially to write it as an autobiography in the first person singular—how had I produced such a terrible

562

novel? It was altogether insipid, dull, false, grandiloquent—although almost nothing that I had written was exaggerated. I had not only lived it—I had lived it with fiery ardor. But I was not yet twenty and I had not learned even so simple a thing as this: that in transforming *duduia* Eleonora into Lenora I had completely annuled the authenticity of the events, and that by turning myself into Doctor V, who was in love with Lenora—not *duduia* Eleonora—I had written the autobiography of a puppet. . . ."

Stefan did not know just when he ceased to read the lines although his eyes still followed them. He had heard the door open in the room on the left. Someone murmured a few words whose sense he did not catch, but the voice sounded familiar. He raised his eyes from the notebook, listening, holding his breath. The footsteps of his new neighbor headed for the window. He drew the blind. An exclamation in Romanian followed. "Five hundred francs!" Suddenly Stefan thought that he must be dreaming. "Five hundred francs a night!" he heard again in Romanian, and then the man said in English, "Half a pound! It seems extravagant!"

It was Vadastra's voice! For some time Stefan sat motionless, his hand on Partenie's notebook, his head turned toward room 16. He had not changed his position after the moment when he had begun to listen. He heard the man walk about the room, thrust aside a chair, utter an exclamation. Stefan thought that Vadastra halted then in one spot, listening, but he realized immediately that he had entered the washroom and turned on the faucet. He heard him rinse out a glass as he continued to mutter to himself.

Suddenly Stefan made up his mind. He crossed the room on tiptoe in order to make as little noise as possible and went out into the hallway. After a moment's hesitation while he tried to rouse himself by alternately clenching and opening his fists, he started downstairs.

"He's an Englishman," the porter informed him. "He arrived this evening from London."

"What's his name? I heard him speak and I seemed to recognize his voice."

The porter opened the register and read aloud, "Harry Johnston, born in 1907, resident of Birmingham."

"I think it's he," said Stefan, and he went back up the stairs, consulting his watch. Past eleven. He began again to walk on the tips of his toes before he reached the fourth floor, and when he came to room 16 he hesitated, holding his breath, waiting. He heard footsteps inside the room and decided to knock, but then he heard nothing more. During an interval that seemed very long to him there was no sound. The footsteps had ceased. He knocked again and the next instant a stern, raucous voice boomed out from directly behind the door. The man must have been standing there with his ear against the panel.

"What's the matter? Who is it?" the new tenant demanded in English.

"*C'est le concierge,*" Stefan responded, suddenly intimidated. "Somebody is asking for you," he concluded, also in English.

He heard the key turn in the lock, and slowly, cautiously, the door began to open. Stefan recognized him at once as he appeared before him with his hand resting on the door handle, poised to draw back immediately. He knew it was Vadastra in spite of his dark glasses, his moustache that had grown thicker, his altered face. It was a little asymmetrical. One temple seemed to be higher than the other.

"I heard you speak some words in Romanian a little while ago," Stefan said, "and I thought that I recognized your voice, *domnule* Vadastra. I thought that you . . ."

Vadastra turned his head a little to the left, glancing toward the corridor leading to the rooms that overlooked the courtyard, and he asked, speaking in a Romanian that was touched slightly with a foreign accent, "What do you want?"

"I thought you were killed in the air raid. I searched everywhere for you. Perhaps you remember me . . ."

"*Domnule consilier* Viziru," said Vadastra with a smile. "I know you very well. I know all about you."

"It's incredible!" cried Stefan, and then he realized why one temple seemed higher than the other. It was due to a horizontal scar that followed his hairline. "There wasn't a sign of life from you. Irina knew nothing . . ."

"Please. Come in." Vadastra opened the door wide and stepped back to let Stefan pass. "Do you know Irina well?" he asked, sitting down on the edge of the bed. "When did you see her last?"

"Shortly before my departure last summer. I saw Gheorghita too. He had passed into the second class at the primary school."

Vadastra moistened his lips and smiled absently. "I'm perfectly informed about them. Gheorghita is exceptional. Irina has remained what she was, a model wife."

"Everyone thinks she's a widow. She even thinks so herself . . ."

"That's not so certain," Vadastra interrupted. "She was informed in good time."

"I don't think she knows anything," insisted Stefan. "She'd have told me. She'd have given me some hint."

Vadastra shrugged and smiled again with obvious satisfaction. "Perhaps she received special instructions. Possibly she . . ." He interrupted himself and frowned, and suddenly severe, suspicious, he peered at Stefan. "Actually," he added, "how do you know that I'm Vadastra? Perhaps I've let you believe so because this confusion is advantageous to me. I know a lot about you, but you

564

know nothing about me. You think I'm Vadastra and I let you believe this for motives which you don't suspect. But presuming I am Vadastra, what conclusions would you draw?"

Licking his lips constantly, he got up from the edge of the bed and approached his caller. Even through his dark glasses his eye seemed to probe deep into Stefan, who suddenly felt awkward and shifted in his chair as though he were trying to recall something. At last he slipped his hand into his pocket and searched for his package of cigarettes. But he had left them in his room on the desk and he smiled at Vadastra, inquiring, "You don't smoke, do you?"

"No, thank you. . . . But presuming I am the man whom you think I am, what would you conclude?"

"It's hard to say. I haven't recovered yet. . . . I imagine that you were gravely wounded on the night of the air raid and you had amnesia. Such cases occurred frequently during the war. I suppose that. . ." Stefan broke off in embarrassment when he noticed that Vadastra was surveying him with an expression at once triumphant and contemptuous.

"Continue, please. Continue. I'm listening with the greatest interest. A plausible enough hypothesis. It's good to consider all hypotheses."

"You had amnesia. . . . Although in this case I don't understand why no one knew about it at the Legation. Especially after the death of Antim. . . ." Stefan hesitated again.

"I know. I know the story," Vadastra said, raising his hand in a brief signal to Stefan to skip that detail and get on with his account. "Continue please."

"Of course England was at war, and we could assume that one amnesia victim more or less would constitute no problem. You spent years in a hospital somewhere in the country and everybody thought you were dead. And when you recovered your memory you found that Romania was engaged in a war with the Soviet Union, that she was on the point of losing the war, or was even occupied by the Russians already, and you preferred to stay where you were in England, under another name and living another life. I understand . . ."

"Interesting," declared Vadastra, beginning to pace the floor. "This is one hypothesis. I confess it doesn't seem convincing to me. It's too simple, almost banal. It would have been much too trite a life for the man you believe to be Vadastra. But we could also form other hypotheses. For instance let's assume—it's just a conjecture, you understand—that the person you are thinking of did not have amnesia, but that for various reasons he was afraid to go home and he lived for several weeks under an assumed name. You will ask me how this could be done in London in wartime. Very simply—if you find some identification papers. There were plenty of dead that night. But let's take a look at another hypothesis. Your Vadastra, let's say, wanted to fight on the

565

side of the Allies, and Romania was occupied that autumn by German troops. All you members of the Legation were suspected of being pro-Nazi. The man you believe to be Vadastra might have presented himself at a military office and declared that he wanted to enlist in the British Army, but only on condition that the Legation not be informed. Perhaps you don't know, but a large number of Romanian seamen enlisted in that way and the Legation never was the wiser. But although he joined the British Army there were certain reasons why your man could not go to the front. However, he could be useful in other services—classified as auxiliary but infinitely more important. Think of it! He was a Romanian. He was believed dead by all his people. He could have been very useful if he had been dropped by parachute into Romania. With his false papers he could have lived for the duration of the war a life filled with dangers and adventures. Not, of course, at Bucharest, because he would have risked being recognized, as he was here this evening by you. Not at Bucharest, but, let's suppose, at Ploesti in the region of the oil fields, or at Campina at the refineries.

"But let's assume something else. Let's make another hypothesis. Say, for instance, that we're in London on the night of September 9, 1940, the night of the bombing. By some miracle your man, Vadastra, was saved at the last moment, but he was not evacuated by ambulance. Suppose, rather, that he was rescued by someone who was passing by in a car on his way out of London that very morning, and that he picked up Vadastra and took him with him to some place in the country. That man was an officer. Vadastra, for personal reasons, didn't tell him that he was Romanian, but said—let's assume—that he was Greek, or Serb. But sometime during the days that ·followed he was addressed in Greek or Serb and he did not understand it. Then, of course, he became suspect and might even have been placed under arrest. Those who questioned him knew well enough that the Legation had announced the disappearance of a Romanian citizen named Vadastra, but the interrogators did not inform the Legation about the Romanian whom they had arrested, because they wondered if perhaps it might have been contrived, a matter of something else entirely—espionage, perhaps. And then your man was in prison for months and months, perhaps even years, until the English convinced themselves that he was not engaged in spying. Or maybe, on the contrary, they discovered in questioning him some very important things concerned precisely with espionage, and they thought that they could use Vadastra as a double agent. So they sent him someplace where he could be of use to them, say the Near East or even Romania!"

Stefan listened to him fascinated, although he could not always follow the man's thoughts, because Vadastra would frequently lower his voice almost to the point of whispering. Then Stefan would realize that he had lost an entire phrase or sentence, and his own thoughts kept running back to London

566

at the time of the blitz, or to the evening he spent in Antim's flat, or even still further to his secret room in Bucharest.

"Yes, it's true," Stefan agreed. "One can make a lot of hypotheses. And yet you should have informed Irina . . ."

"Wait! I haven't finished," Vadastra interrupted, becoming suddenly agitated. "The number of hypotheses is infinite, but I haven't yet told you the most interesting one. It might be that everything that seems so complex and remarkable to you was in reality much simpler. We could imagine that in his youth Vadastra had an ideal concerning which he had never spoken to anyone and that this ideal had been destroyed by his superior, a certain Popescu. We could imagine that this Vadastra, as anyone would expect, had sworn to avenge himself, to destroy someday the man who had humiliated him and had prevented him from realizing this ideal. Unfortunately that man, his one-time superior, was invulnerable. Let's assume that he was a major political figure or a general or someone who guides things from behind the scenes, and you have no way of striking him. Let's assume further that this man, Vadastra's erstwhile superior, is placed one day in the service of enemies of Romania, say the Nazis or the Communists. Then Vadastra's revenge acquires great importance, becoming almost a sublime idea, a patriotic duty. Because to vanquish that man no sacrifice is too great. For he—let's call him Popescu—is a deadly enemy. He sells out his country pure and simple. He sells out to the enemy in order to save his skin. . . . Then you'll understand why Vadastra sacrificed everything—family, peace, happiness—to track him down and eventually destroy him. . . ." His voice dropped suddenly. "To destroy him utterly. . . ." He was thoughtful for a moment, brooding.

"Yes, it's true," Stefan admitted, and he rubbed his face in an effort to awaken himself from what seemed to him like a dream. "All those hypotheses are plausible."

"And then one evening," Vadastra resumed, looking directly ahead of him as if he were speaking to someone else, "you meet someone in the room next to yours whom you take to be Vadastra, the man whom you and everyone else considered dead eight years before. In a moment of weakness the man you believe to be Vadastra replies to you in Romanian and confirms your opinion that he *is* Vadastra, whom you thought lost. Like all Romanians you are indiscreet, and tomorrow all Paris will find out what happened. Of course you have no proof that the man with whom you're now conversing is one and the same with your Vadastra, but you'll persist in believing this because it pleases you to have something extraordinary happen to you. And the whole world will find out that Vadastra lives."

"No, I won't tell anyone . . ." Stefan began.

"Just let me finish!" Vadastra interrupted rudely. "This would be no serious matter if it had happened to someone else. But let's imagine that the man you consider to be Vadastra is here on a very important secret mission. We could make several hypotheses. Let's assume, for instance, that he had come to Paris to investigate why one of the networks of information and counterespionage that operate in Romania was discovered by the villain Popescu. No one could do this better than he, because he alone knows Popescu's methods of working. But we can assume something more. Let's imagine that the man you consider to be Vadastra has to go farther, perhaps even so far as to be parachuted into Romania. Let's imagine that he has to fulfill an important mission in the homeland. But what will happen now? Tomorrow you'll tell all Paris that you met me, and Popescu will find out inside of twenty-four hours. . . ."

"I give you my word of honor that no one will find out anything . . ."

"Of course you'll pay dearly for your indiscretion, because it's unnecessary to add that you won't survive for long! But what good would it be for me to know that if I fail in my mission you'll be found dead somewhere in the vicinity of Paris? The important thing for me would be not to have met you at all, or having met you, not to be recognized. It's true, you don't know where I'm going or what I intend to do, but the simple fact that you suspect Vadastra is alive is a very serious matter . . . in my present situation," he added, meditatively.

"For my part you can be certain," declared Stefan. "I know how to keep a secret. I understand very well how serious it is . . ."

"You can't understand," continued Vadastra, "because I've told you nothing. All I've related to you were simply hypotheses to test you, to observe your reactions. Actually you know nothing about me. You don't even know if I'm really Vadastra. . . . But let's assume that I am . . ." He paused a moment and his voice altered, "But no, let's not. Let's not assume anything for the present. I'm tired. We'll talk again tomorrow morning. I'll put you on trial then to see how discreet you can be. . . ."

He conducted Stefan ceremoniously to the door, opened it, and as he stood there he spoke suddenly and very loudly in English, "I was very glad to meet you, sir. . . ."

Stefan was almost grateful to him for unexpectedly putting an end to the conversation. He felt that he would not have been able to listen much longer. As he entered his own room his glance fell on the manuscripts and he smiled. In haste he lighted a cigarette and puffed it feverishly for a moment. Then he threw himself on the bed. He ought to have informed Irina, Stefan found himself thinking, and he discovered that he had already finished his cigarette. He looked at his watch. It was after midnight. He really should have informed

Irina. And Ileana too ought to have informed me, given me some sign of life, just a word—a signature on a postcard—to let me know she's still alive. Vadastra ought to have done this for Irina.

He realized how different this Spiridon Vadastra was from the man he had known. He was not like the same person, not so ridiculous as in former years. Something's happened to him and he's changed. He's become another man. Almost eight years have gone by, and with the passage of time he's become someone else. 'Poor *doamna* Zissu!' he said then on the night of the air raid. Maybe he doesn't remember now who *doamna* Zissu was. When I question him tomorrow morning he may not be able to remember. If he did suffer from amnesia he may never again remember anything from his youth or *doamna* Zissu. Or maybe he just won't want to tell me and he'll say that he no longer remembers her or that it doesn't matter anymore. . . ."

He sprang from the bed and went to open the window. Mechanically he lit another cigarette, and then a moment later he noticed that he was still holding the box of matches in his hand. He looked at it, undecided, wondering what to do with it, and finally thrust it into his pocket. Seating himself at the desk, he glanced at the manuscript and saw that it was open to the page beginning ". . . the autobiography of a puppet. . . ."

He thought he heard a sound from the room next door and he turned his head, listening intently. Vadastra was snoring softly as he slept. It was like a gentle moan. Suddenly Stefan felt ridiculous. All his actions since he had returned to his room seemed pointless and absurd. He felt like a frightened child who is aware of being watched and does not know how to behave. I can't sleep, he said to himself. I've got to do something. . . . He gathered up the manuscripts, wrapped them in the paper in which they had been packed, and placed them in the closet. Then he turned off the light and went out on tiptoe. The porter was dozing with his head resting on his arms.

"I'm not sleepy," said Stefan. "I'm going to take a little walk. . . ."

When he awoke he glanced at his watch in dismay. It was nearly nine o'clock. He bathed hurriedly, controlling his impatience with difficulty, and put on his dressing gown. Taking his cigarettes with him he left the room. He knocked timidly on Vadastra's door, but there was no answer and, worried now, he went downstairs to question the porter. He learned that Vadastra had requested his bill early in the morning and had left before seven. "He explained that he had to catch a train to the provinces."

Returning to his room Stefan felt that the whole situation was preposterous, absurd. I should have expected this. I should have kept an eye on him. I shouldn't have slept. He lit a cigarette and lay down on the bed. Why did

569

Misu have those things delivered to me? he found himself suddenly wondering. He went downstairs again to telephone Weissman, and he listened for a long time to the bell ringing in the study on boulevard Murat. Perhaps he wanted to surprise me. He suspected I'd read Partenie's notebook first. He's waiting for my impressions, my reactions. Maybe he even spent the evenings this fall shut up in his room crossing out the names with a pen while I was asleep next door. Probably Ioana's name was among them. . . .

"No one answers," said the porter seeing that Stefan made no move to replace the receiver. "He's not at home. Try later. . . ."

He tried again several times that morning. And after he came back from lunch he went down every hour and telephoned, listening as if spellbound to the bell sounding in the empty room. The afternoon was warm and Stefan drew the blinds at his window. He relaxed on the bed and waited, although he did not know what he was waiting for. He checked the time now and then, lit a cigarette, and descended regularly, obstinately, to use the telephone.

"What did the delivery boy say?" he asked the porter. "Did he say when the package was given to him?"

"He didn't say anything. He asked for you and started to go upstairs, but I didn't let him. I told him that after nine o'clock in the evening tradesmen can't go up to the rooms. I understood what he wanted and I gave him a hundred francs. . . ."

The sun descended slowly, unnoticed, behind the Invalides. Stefan searched through the package of manuscripts, selected Partenie's notebook and laid it on the desk. ". . . I had written the autobiography of a puppet." He reread the passage, trying to arouse again the interest with which he had perused it the night before. But Vadastra's words, the explanations of the porter, and Misu Weissman's mysterious allusions kept coming into his mind. "I'll give them all a surprise. I'll surprise you too, *coane* Stefan, because you're skeptical!" He sat for awhile staring at the page that he had begun to read. Then, as though he were ashamed of his reflections, he decided abruptly to continue.

"While writing I told myself that I do so in order to heal myself, but probably I was healed long ago. I see no fever in the novel anymore. And yet, what a wonderful theme! Not as I conceived it at nineteen, but the way it deserved to be seen by a writer. The dramatic tale of Doctor V was not interesting, nor was he himself—that rebellious genius—absorbing. The story of the piano was far more provocative, although I almost failed to mention it at all in the novel. By transforming *duduia* Eleonora into Lenora and her dressmaking shop into the salon of the widow of a war profiteer, the piano lost its essential function as a symbol of an existence that seemed to her then, in 1920, to be enchanted. It was the only souvenir she had kept from the apartment the captain had rented for her ten years before on *bulevardul* Elisabeta and had furnished so luxuriously—'like the palace of an oriental princess,' *duduia* Eleonora would say. That morning the captain had signaled the coachman to stop on the boulevard in front of a new house that was several stories high. Taking her hand he drew her after him into the elevator. 'It was like a palace!' Eleonora exclaimed. 'When I went in and caught sight of the piano I threw my arms around his neck and began to cry!' 'Do you want to make me jealous again?' I interrupted her in a tone of false irony, although it was true that I was insanely jealous of that poor shadow—the captain. 'There was nothing but expensive furniture, nothing but silk and gold,' she continued rapturously, 'but above all there was my dear piano! And when my fortunes declined, I sold and pawned everything, but I couldn't part with the piano. . . .'

"But there was no place for the piano in my novel. *Duduia* Eleonora had become Lenora, widow of a war profiteer. In her dressmaking establishment the piano was imposing, just as she had preserved it—out of tune, covered with brocades, adorned with photographs of herself at twenty and two large vases full of artificial flowers that were dusty and faded. It was burdened with memories and dead illusions. In renouncing the true Eleonora I lost from the outset more than half of the epic substance of the novel, because without the piano I could not justify Mitica's jealousy. . . ."

"It's she! It's *doamna* Zissu!" exclaimed Stefan. "It's Mitica Porum- bache's Zisuleasca!" Suddenly he was aware that he had known this all the time. He had known it when he had begun to read again. Possibly he had suspected it even the evening before when the word "piano" first caught his attention. "She'd even sold her piano!" Vadastra's piano, he said to himself. Vadastra's *doamna* Zissu!

He wanted to savor his discovery, but now a vague sadness numbed him. A feeling of disillusionment that he could not explain gripped him slowly. Vadastra's *doamna* Zissu, he repeated to himself. Vadastra's *doamna* Zissu . . . as if this would dispel the troubled mélange of melancholy and disappointment that threatened him. He began to make rapid calculations, hoping that the mental juggling of destinies and fragments of time could unfetter the joy that he knew was caught somewhere in the depths of his being, caught and shackled there—for what reason he could not comprehend. In 1920-21 *doamna* Zissu would have been about thirty-five or thirty-six years old, while he was a mere youth of seventeen. She had been his first love, just as she was also Vadastra's a few years later. When she met Vadastra, he was in the *liceu* and was probably fifteen or sixteen, while *doamna* Zissu would have been forty. "The distinguished *doamna* Zissu, a beautiful woman who loved me. . . ." Perhaps he had been her last lover, because soon after that she had died in misery after having sold all her possessions, even the piano.

Everything seemed clear to him now and he longed almost desperately to enjoy his discovery, his enlightenment. The captain, Mitica Porumbache, then Partenie, then Vadastra—all had loved her. To each of them she had

571

been either his first or his last love. Probably this accounted for Stefan's obsession with the mystery of *doamna* Zissu. Partenie had loved her first and then he had loved Ioana. Perhaps Stefan should have met her too and loved her after Partenie, just as he had met Ioana and loved her when she was the writer's fiancée. But instead it was Vadastra who had met her. "The distinguished *doamna* Zissu, a beautiful woman who loved me. . . ." This must have been why those words had disturbed him so much when he heard them through the flimsy wall of his secret room. Why had they obsessed him for so many years in such an incomprehensible manner? Possibly he had discerned in them a part of his destiny that he had betrayed, a fragment of his own life that had been assigned to him but that he had not lived, although he did not understand why. It had remained unfulfilled and had followed him therefore like a ghost, demanding actualization, pursuing him, driving him to probe until he found the answer.

So this was *doamna* Zissu, Mitica Porumbache's Zisuleasca, he reminded himself, smiling—a dressmaker who had once known the idleness and prestige of being kept in grand style. Then her fortunes had declined, and she had again taken up her life as a seamstress. But she was still very beautiful and had undoubtedly a great deal of charm if at seventeen Partenie had run away from home because of her and even contemplated suicide. It might have happened to me. . . . It *should* have happened to me, he corrected himself. And now it seemed that his agitation and impatience subsided strangely. He felt reconciled, resigned.

I ought to do something, he thought. Perhaps I should pray. I should tell someone that *something* has happened to me, that all the events of my life have had a meaning but I didn't understand it. I didn't know how to look for it. That's why this name pursued me—*doamna* Zissu. I must tell someone. . . . "Lord, thy will be done." He spoke aloud, suddenly. "Thy will be done," he repeated more softly. He had never before experienced such a feeling of great peace, and yet it was tinged with fear. I could die now that I've found out. I could die without meeting her again, without being able to tell her that I know who *doamna* Zissu was, that my obsession wasn't absurd, that it had a meaning. . . . It had a meaning. I must tell Ileana that everything that's happened had a meaning. . . . "Thy will be done!" he said aloud again, suddenly, fearfully. He sat unmoving for some time, as though listening for something he could not hear. Then he began to read again.

"Because without the piano I could not justify Mitica's jealousy, and so I abandoned those sensational scenes that I reconstructed from Eleonora's tales. Long after midnight, sometimes in the morning, Mitica and Eleonora would return from the Garden of Gaiety and go up to the apartment furnished and paid for by the captain. When Mitica, who was almost always drunk, caught sight of the piano he would begin to swear—at first through his teeth and then, abandoning all restraint, he would become increasingly louder and more vulgar. At last Eleonora would burst into tears, and he would caress her and beg her forgiveness, saying that he had only meant to tease her. But after she moved from *bulevardul* Elisabeta and sold all her furnishings, keeping only the piano, Mitica would declare whenever he came to see her that this was the last time he would set foot in her house if she did not sell that piano. He would go to it and slap the lid or the wooden side with his open hand, listening to it resound and shouting, 'Hear how it sings when you touch it!' All these details I had no way to relate in the novel. Mitica had been changed— he, my predecessor in the heart from which Eleonora had not managed to evict the captain even after he had died. Nor could I hope to dispel his memory. Among the many gestures that legendary characters make, the captain had chosen the most romantic, the gesture *par excellence*—he had committed suicide. 'He killed himself because of me! I sent him to his grave! And he had become a major!' And so, in the novel, Mitica had become a bank clerk, methodical and stodgy with no depth of character, reduced to tics and clichés, because in my great naiveté I believed that this was the only way to heighten the contrast between his mediocrity and the pathetic genius of Doctor V.

"Then too the whole episode at the Garden of Gaiety had to be dropped. I replaced it with a rendezvous in a summer garden restaurant frequented by the *nouveaux riches*, the war profiteers. The scene of the meeting between the captain and Mitica had begun under circumstances that I did not exactly understand. Eleonora had been reluctant to tell me about it. She said that she didn't like to recall such sad things. That scene had become in my novel a banal episode of bourgeois jealousy. However, it seems that there was an unforgettable row that night at the Garden that was mentioned in the newspapers and talked about in the neighborhood for years. The captain had arrived unexpectedly from Jassy and found Eleonora at the table, dining in the company of Mitica and surrounded by the musicians. 'Is the boy mine?' he demanded, very pale but calm. Eleonora claimed that she screamed indignantly. 'Is he mine? Like the children of the tailor!—her former husband— 'are his?' Then up jumped Mitica and the fight began. Eleonora had fainted, and she remembered nothing more. She said she only remembered the finale, which was like a story by Pushkin. A patrol came, and the officer in charge lifted the captain from the gravel, where he had fallen unconscious after receiving a blow on the head with a bottle of seltzer. All the participants in the scuffle had pounced on him. The officer helped him up—bloody, disfigured, his uniform in tatters—supported him with difficulty under his arm because he was wobbling like a drunken man, and said to him, 'Captain Sideri, you're under arrest!' "

Stefan raised his eyes from the notebook. Captain Sideri, you're under arrest! Dear *domnule* Weissman, you have no way of knowing. For many years I've loved a girl—Ileana. Ileana Sideri. *Captain Sideri, you're under arrest*! Maybe he was her uncle. Maybe he was even her father! I'll have to do some figuring. . . . " 'Who's his girl friend?' she asked me. 'Ileana,' I answered. 'Ileana Sideri. He left Romania in order to search for her. . . . It's no secret!' " This was what Weissman had told him one morning when he brought the coffee. *Ileana Sideri. He left the country. It's no secret. . . .*

He looked at his watch, surprised, as if he had just wakened, and he saw that it was after nine. With a feeling of apprehension he left the desk and went down all the flights of stairs on the run. The porter saw him coming and smiled. "Trying again?"

I gave him a hundred francs. He said that he came from the Bratianu Statue. He asked for you and wanted to go up to your room. I told him that after nine o'clock in the evening . . . Captain Sideri. . . .

"No one answers." He heard the porter speaking. "He's not at home. He hasn't come back."

He fled Romania to search for her. It's no secret. Stefan listened patiently to the bell resounding shrilly in the study on boulevard Murat.

After the motor coach had left Paris he remembered that he had not eaten. And I'd have had time to eat—there was a cafe on the corner. I could have eaten a sandwich. *Nel mezzo del cammin di vita nostra. . . .* The line came back to him. He had been repeating it constantly—he did not know why— while walking the streets from place de la Muette to Etoile. And then near Etoile he thought he understood why. It was to avoid the absurd refrain that also kept recurring in his mind. *But his body hasn't been found!*

When he had gone downstairs in the morning the porter had indicated with a slight inclination of his head a man who was seated at the little table in the lobby, turning the pages of the telephone directory. His face was blank, expressionless. He rose from his chair and smiled awkwardly. "Monsieur Stefan Viziru? You lived for awhile on boulevard Murat at the apartment of Monsieur Weissman . . ."

"Has something happened to him?" interrupted Stefan.

"No. That is . . . To be more precise, we don't know. Be so good, please, as to come with me and give us some information."

The taxi had left them in front of a police station somewhere near boulevard Murat. Stefan had emerged from it nervously, lighting another cigarette at the last moment, and then he had sat on a bench near the door and waited while the inspector was talking on the telephone.

His body hasn't been found! Stefan's sudden strange lighthearted-

574

ness, he realized, had its source in this apparently insignificant detail. Although circumstances pointed to Weissman's suicide on a beach in Belgium, the fact that his body still was missing placed in doubt everything one might conclude from his mysterious disappearance. The same thing had happened to Vadastra. Only Antim had understood: "No one has seen him dead . . ." he had declared without ceasing, sitting ensconced in his armchair in the salon of the Embassy in Belgrave Square. He had not dared to go out alone on the street because no one had been able to prove that Vadastra was dead by showing him his body.

He supposed it was unreasonable for him to believe that Weissman had not killed himself, but he liked to imagine him somewhere free of the terror of his debts, liberated from the obsession of his great business enterprise, dressed in the apparel of a vagabond and setting off for some distant spot in the wide world. And one day he would send Stefan a sign of life, a few words on a postcard. The inspector had listened with attention and then thanked Stefan affably. "No, they haven't found his body yet," he had repeated once again in the doorway, smiling. He was somewhat baffled by Stefan's insistent return to this question in the course of their conversation.

At Etoile he stopped in front of a kiosk and purchased the noon editions of the papers. He glanced through them quickly, seized by a sudden excitement, to see if perhaps . . . There was no information relative to the disappearance of Weissman. *Aujourd'hui été*, he read on the front page and it puzzled him until he had almost reached la place des Ternes. Of course. The summer solstice. St. John's Eve. *His body hasn't been found. Nel mezzo del cammin di vita nostra . . .* He rolled up the papers, laid them on a window ledge, and hurried on.

Parc Monceau was almost deserted at about one o'clock. A woman sat on a bench absently eating a sandwich. There were a few children lingering at their play, and a pair of lovers. The warmth of the day was making itself felt even here in the shade of the trees. *Una selva oscura* . . . Proceeding idly, he paid little attention to his surroundings as he went through the park and emerged on the sidewalk again. He hastened his steps.

On boulevard des Courcelles he was about to cross over to the other side of the street when he saw the three motor coaches in a row some distance ahead of him. Without curiosity he went toward them, but he walked faster as if he were afraid that the moment before he reached them they would leave. They were standing in front of a large courtyard. Stefan read the inscription on the building. "Club des Etudiants." Leaning against the wall he wiped his face with his handkerchief. Groups of young people were waiting in the courtyard and on the sidewalk, and seated around the tables at the cafe on the corner. As the afternoon became hotter Stefan took off his jacket and draped it over his shoulders. He lit a cigarette and smoked it tranquilly, his eyes fixed on the pavement before him. Finally a girl with a book of tickets in her hand came out of the courtyard and approached the nearest group. He saw the young people take out their billfolds and from his own he selected a five-hundred-franc note, which he handed to the girl when she stopped in front of him. She gave him a ticket and two hundred francs in change. "Third bus," she said.

I'd have had time to eat a sandwich. There was a cafe on the corner in the shade. . . . The coach was proceeding now between fields of grain dotted with poppies. It's like this at home in Romania, he found himself thinking. He had been looking out of the window ever since they left Paris. "Destiny is the fragment of Time . . ." He remembered Bibicescu's words. ". . . the fragment of Time that History allows us. . . ." What exactly did he mean by that? Stefan did not try to understand. His thoughts took him more deeply into the past, a time long, long before. When was it? In his youth? In his childhood? In a time long past he had been on a train and had looked out of the window upon a similar landscape of gently waving wheat and barley fields scattered with poppies. Then as now the road wound between the hills and the woods of beeches and locusts.

They passed through several villages and small towns, and as the bus went by them he tried to read the names, wondering where the caravan was going. About a quarter of an hour after they left the last village he began to perceive the outline of a forest in the distance. While he gazed at it, the bus seemed to change course as though the road were going to take them around it. Sadly, he turned his head to keep it in view—that forest so dense and dark, composed of great tall trees. But he noticed shortly that it was again in front of them on the right. They were going directly into it! Now he thought he had known this from the beginning. The day was warm. On such a summer noon, clear and hot, these busses with their burden of young people could only be going into a forest.

"In these places there were once marshes," he said suddenly to the youth beside him. The boy was tall and blond and wore glasses, and he had smiled at Stefan as they were leaving the coach. Adjusting his step to Stefan's he had walked along with him and told him about the concert and who would be performing. But Stefan was not listening. He was gazing far ahead of him at the walls of the monastery. "Where this forest is now there used to be marshes," Stefan repeated.

"There still are marshes," said the youth, "but they're on the other side of the forest."

The young people hurried along the walk in a compact group, for the concert was to begin at three-thirty. They reached the entrance and Stefan hesitated. In the shade he saw the cars parked one after another in a row.

"I'm going to walk a little longer," he said. "This is my first visit to Royaumont."

The young man smiled and promptly disappeared, swallowed by the throng. Stefan watched them enter the courtyard, augmenting the crowded lines of people converging on the building. "Only a few rooms and the chapel are left," the boy had told him. "The monastery was destroyed during the Revolution, but the concerts are held in the former chapel. It has a certain atmosphere, an atmosphere . . ." he had begun in a clear voice surprisingly masculine, shaded with emotion. But at that point Stefan had ceased to listen.

After the last group disappeared behind the ruined wing which was all that still remained of the monastery, Stefan set off alone down the walk. Whatever possessed me to tell him there used to be marshes here? he asked himself suddenly. If we'd spent another half-hour together, undoubtedly I'd have told him about Snagov and how Mia called out and how . . . At that moment he realized that this was what he had been thinking about when he had mentioned the marshes near Bucharest where he had gone to swim as a boy, where the tall shady trees had grown in later years. His mind had reverted also to that summer afternoon at Snagov when he had heard Mia calling and had seen her for the last time, trying to raise her head. But then a wave had struck against her face and the warm water of the lake had engulfed her. Almost thirty years have passed since then, he thought, attempting to free himself from this nightmare. It's still frightful. . . .

Here under the tall trees the heat of the summer afternoon had not yet penetrated. Aloud he repeated, *"Nel mezzo del cammin di vita nostra . . . Una selva oscura . . ."* Suddenly he felt as though someone were watching him and he smiled in embarrassment. He was aware that he was repeating these words to help him drive away the memory of the marshes and his childhood and Mia's blond hair floating for a single endless moment on the gently rocking surface of the warm lake. He began again, *"Una selva oscura . . ."* and he tried to shake off the strange sensation of childish fear that someone unseen and very near was following him and watching him and reading his soul like a book, knowing his outrageous childish hope that he could escape all those memories by reciting the one verse of the *Inferno* that he knew. He wandered deeper and deeper into the forest, always accompanied by that obscure and implacable presence that divined all his thoughts and caused him to smile with chagrin. He felt like a small boy surprised at his play by the eye of a stranger. The game cannot be resumed, but he must wait with a guilty grin on his face, catching his breath timidly, until the alien eye disappears and he is alone once more with the mystery of the play that only he understands.

He saw her in the distance and his heart began to race even before he identified her. He started to run. The car was standing by the side of the lane under the light shade of a maple. The door was open. Ileana was bending over the back seat of the car, trying to fit a stack of magazines between two small valises. When she heard his heavy steps she turned around, startled, then suddenly became very pale.

"This was it," Stefan said as he ran. "This was the car!" He stopped in order to quiet the pounding of his heart and swallowed several times with great effort. What a stupid thing to say! It was an absurd and incredible greeting. He had been rehearsing this conversation for years, imagining the many possible circumstances of their reunion. He had heard himself innumerable times pronouncing the first words he would say to her, and they had never been anything like these. And yet, although he saw her from afar and ran to meet her, although he guessed that it was she before he recognized her, he was incapable of any other utterance. He had seen the car.

"It's the car I told you about," he explained. Why did he allow this to continue? Why did he let someone else speak for him, in his name, before he could speak, before he could say what he wished to say? "It's the one I thought would disappear, the one that would vanish exactly at midnight. . . ."

Ileana leaned on the open door. She looked just the same as when he had left her—tanned by the sun, with eyes the color of that rare species of pansy. No, he thought a moment later, it was not when he had last seen her that she had looked like that, not when he had left her in their room at Bussaco on New Year's Eve. This was the way she had looked when he saw her for the first time at Baneasa, turning her head to see who was following her through the grass. "In these places there were once marshes," he had told her then. Those were the first words he had said to her. Although he had known about the car at that time too, he had not spoken of it until later. He had talked to her about the marshes, about the trees he had planted when he was in the *liceu*, about the hedgehog, about the heavens that open on the Night of St. John. But even then he had known from the beginning about her car.

"It was exactly like this," he continued. "You had a small ring with a Yale key and several other little keys. . . ."

With some effort he managed to smile and he looked into her eyes. "This time it's not a hallucination. It's real. . . ."

For years she had not permitted herself to recall the night at Bussaco. It seemed like a petrified time transformed in some mysterious manner into a sort of fortress with high stone walls. When she returned in reverie to the past, she saw from a distance the walls of the night at Bussaco and she fled from them, she detoured around them. She immersed herself in other memories—the fisherman's house at Cascais, the last years she had spent on *strada* Batistei; or she went back even farther to the vacations at Zinca, the summers of her childhood. The petrified time had assumed the appearance of the room at Bussaco. It had become sinister, like a room in which someone had died, before the wreaths and black draperies had been brought in. She had begun to dress. "I'm not trembling!" she repeated constantly to herself. "I'm not trembling!" When the car moved silently out of the courtyard of the hotel and entered the forest, she had noticed the wisps of fog hanging among the trees like gloomy shrouds, and an undefined feeling of futility settled upon her. All the life around her seemed suddenly to have been snuffed out. "I'm not crying," she repeated to herself. "I'm not crying!"

"When I saw you at Baneasa in the distance, I knew you'd come in a car. I wasn't crazy. It wasn't a hallucination. It was this car, this very car. . . ."

Entroncamento, Madrid, the telegram to the Valkyrie. The hours spent in the waiting room of the railroad station, hiding her eyes in the newspaper so that she wouldn't be recognized by someone from the Legation. The night on the sleeping car going to Barcelona. *"Est-ce que Madame désire encore quelque chose?"* the steward had asked her.

"I knew I'd find you. I went to Zinca too. The peasants had burned the mansion. Marina had died. But I knew I'd find you. . . ."

Ileana did not turn her eyes away from his. She was frightened. She did not know what other things he might say, what other words would leave his lips, but she feared them.

"I knew it," Stefan resumed, "when I understood all that has happened, when I found out who *doamna* Zissu was. . . ."

Suddenly troubled, he was silent. Ileana released her grip on the car and stepped to the edge of the lane, seating herself on the grass. She encircled her knees with her arms and bent her head. He approached her slowly, anxiously, thinking that she was crying, and stood self-consciously before her.

579

Sometimes at night despair would awaken her. I've nothing from him, nothing. She would press the pillow over her mouth so the Valkyrie would not be disturbed, and she would sob. But the Valkyrie always heard her, and a few minutes later she would tap lightly on the door and come in, embarrassed, with fear in her eyes, not knowing what to say. "He left me nothing," Ileana would moan. "I wish I had something from him—a flower, at least, or a handkerchief, or an envelope with the address written by him. Anything... just something of his...." One night she had said, "I'd like to have a baby. I hope I have a baby...." And after that she kept repeating, "I'm going to have a baby...." Her Portuguese friend in Lisbon wrote to her almost daily. She mentioned that Stefan had sent flowers several times, that he had looked for her at Cascais, he had telephoned to Madrid. Then she wrote that he had taken a plane to Bucharest. He'll go to see *Tante* Alice, Ileana had said to herself. He'll find out where I am and in a few days he'll be here. He'll come with a bouquet of lilies of the valley, with his hair wet from the rain, without a raincoat. He'll ring the doorbell and he'll have a bouquet of lilies of the valley in the rain and I'll open the door and we'll look at each other.... He'll smile at me...." She told the Valkyrie, "This is what he always does. He disappears for weeks or months and then he shows up again unexpectedly in the rain with a bouquet of flowers in his hand, and he smiles in an embarrassed way, like a child." Then she would add quickly, "I want a child by him. I'm expecting a baby...."

"Stefan," she murmured without raising her eyes, "what do you want from me?"

At once he dropped down beside her on the grass and stared at her, incredulous, but he did not presume to touch her. "Ileana! It's I, Stefan.... How I've searched for you! I knew I'd find you again...." He heard himself speaking, but it seemed to him that his words faltered impotently, as though spoken by someone else in his place—someone who tried to imitate him but did not succeed because a very slight, almost imperceptible falseness betrayed him the very moment he pronounced the words. "It's I, Stefan!" he repeated with anguish in his voice.

That winter her days had been spent in waiting. *Tante* Alice wrote to her regularly, but she never mentioned Stefan. One day Ileana decided to inquire about him, and after some time *Tante* Alice replied, "I've heard that he's at the front in Russia...."

She heard him continue to repeat, "It's I... It's I...."

She kept to her room all the time, smoking incessantly and gazing out at the lake. Whenever the Valkyrie came in she found her with a cigarette between her lips and she would hasten to open the window. "I knew from the start that it would be like this," Ileana told her. "I knew I wouldn't have a baby. I knew that nothing would be left to me from him. I knew it as soon as I saw him. From the moment I set eyes on him in the forest I knew it would be this way, that I'd have nothing from him. This was my fate—to have nothing. . . ." "Ileana!" the Valkyrie exclaimed one night, and her own cry startled her, "you won't be able to live without him. Go to Romania after him, search for him!" "Probably he died in Russia," Ileana responded. "In any event he's dead to me. If he didn't go to *Tante* Alice's to look for me, it means that I've died so far as he's concerned, and now he's dead for me too. And I have nothing left from him, not even an envelope addressed by his hand."

Often when the Valkyrie entered the room she found Ileana stretched out on the divan, still smoking. "He told me only three times that he loved me. Three times in six years! He talked to me more about Vadastra and *doamna* Zissu. He talked about Time and about the car that ought to have disappeared at midnight, about the room *Sambo* and about the heavens that could open. He talked to me about everything, even about the war and Vidrighin's intrigues—but he never spoke to me about his love. I'm not even sure he loved me. He just said that I was his destiny. I've loved him ever since I saw him. He was walking behind me in the forest and I turned my head and I knew then that he was the one—that I'd love this man all my life. I knew it, but I didn't want to admit it. He was married; he adored his wife; soon they had a baby. But I knew that I'd love him all my life, even though I didn't want to admit it. I kept trying to forget him. And maybe eventually I would have forgotten him if he hadn't reappeared unexpectedly so many times. Suddenly he would come to see me or telephone me, and then I'd realize that I hadn't forgotten him yet. But I didn't want to admit it."

"Ileana!" the Valkyrie had said, taking her hand, "go and look for him!" "He'll look for me," she cried, jumping up abruptly from the divan. "He'll search for me on his knees to the end of the earth and he won't find me! If he hasn't died in Russia, he'll search for me for the rest of his life, but he'll never find me! Only . . . I wish I'd have a child by him. . . ."

"Ileana, what's wrong with you?" Stefan asked her, his voice dropping suddenly to a whisper, for he feared that he could no longer trust it not to betray him.

"I wish I'd have a baby," she would repeat to herself whenever she felt like crying. These words would bring the tears to her eyes, because they reminded her of what might have been but was not. The Valkyrie would hear her sobbing with the pillow over her mouth and would get out of bed. But then she would hesitate and wait timidly, uncertainly, wondering if she should go to her and try to comfort her. One morning Ileana remarked, "I hope he's not dead, because then I have a reason to live: to get even with him! This is all I ask—to bear his child and avenge myself. Is this too much, Val? I don't ask for anything else—just to have a baby and get even with him. . . ."

"I knew this was how it would happen," he whispered. He had noticed the wedding ring on her finger, but he had looked at it without seeing it, refusing to acknowledge it. He drew closer to her.

"I went to Zinca," he began tentatively, after a pause, trying to escape from his own voice, to separate himself from it, to extract it and throw it behind him somewhere so that finally he could be alone with Ileana.

But all his efforts suddenly seemed in vain and he fell silent. At that moment everything seemed vain. There was that wedding ring on Ileana's finger, and the warm gleam of the burnished gold reminded him of the fruitlessness of his striving. He turned away and his glance fell upon the car.

All at once he felt as though the blood were draining from his veins and spreading over the ground at his feet. *It was the car!* It was not his love for Ileana but the car that was his destiny! There it was, exactly as he had seen it in the Forest of Baneasa, exactly like all those other cars that had jarred his consciousness. It was like that taxi he had found on New Year's Eve, almost buried under the snow, while Ioana waited impatiently for him, her mind intent on the festivities already underway in the house in Cotroceni. It was like the car whose picture he had tried to paint, and like the one that he had seen wrecked on the road to Ciuc when he had heard Ileana cry, "My fiancé. . . Maybe he's still alive!" This was the car he had pictured in his mind when Filimon told him about the cyclone. It was somewhere on the highway between Lisbon and Estoril, overturned by the waves and wind. "*Mon cher,*" Filimon had exclaimed, "a car turned over right in front of me . . . struck by the waves in the middle of the road. . . . Imagine!"

Would his life have taken a different course if Filimon had not told him about this? Perhaps he would have remained much longer under the spell of Circe, of Stella Zissu, for undoubtedly he had been enchanted. He could not have left her. He might have gone with her to New York, continuing to insist that he did not love her, continuing to talk about Ioana and Ileana, but incapable of breaking her spell. He would have had to follow her everywhere and wait fearfully for her to approach him with her parted lips, her white teeth gleaming menacingly.

It was the same car.

"I have to leave," Ileana said, suddenly rising from the grass. "I've delayed too long already. I have to reach Lausanne tonight."

He wanted to tell her, Nonsense! Don't you realize that it's absurd?

We've scarcely met again. I looked for you for six years—on the front in Russia and in the Crimea. I went to *strada* Batistei, I went to Zinca. Don't you see how absurd it is?

But he only said, "The Valkyrie hasn't sung yet," and he was amazed at the calmness of his voice. He too had stood up abruptly, and Ileana looked at him in wonder, a faint smile tugging at her lips.

"How did you know she was singing?"

"I imagined it."

He wanted to say, I knew it at once when by chance I discovered on the bus that there was a concert at Royaumont and there would be foreign artists. I knew.

"I imagined it," he repeated. "I thought that was why you came—to hear her. You came together..."

"I have to leave," said Ileana. "I should have left long ago. I'd started to leave, but I thought something was wrong with the motor and I stopped. It wasn't anything.... To your misfortune," she added with an uncertain smile. "It gave you a chance to meet me again.... What are you smoking?" she inquired unexpectedly, searching his eyes, her lips trembling slightly.

"Gauloises Bleues."

How quiet he felt now. He took out his cigarettes and offered her one, striking a match. He wanted to say, This is incredible! Haven't you understood yet? Haven't you understood anything except that you don't love me anymore? But this is serious only for me. You still have your whole life ahead of you. Don't you realize what you're doing is absurd? Haven't I told you that I recognized the car?

"I like to smoke a Gauloise now and then." She turned upon him a smile that was sad and distant, heavy with melancholy, but it was a smile and Stefan's face brightened to see it.

"I'm glad that we met again, Stefan. I'm glad you're alive. I knew you were alive. I'd heard it, and now I'm glad I saw you again.... You haven't changed," she added after a moment.

"I've grown older."

"I'm not aware of it. For me, in any case..."

"Yes. I understand," Stefan interrupted, smiling. "I know what you mean. For you I've stayed the same because I died long ago."

"Yes."

"I ought to have known that. I left for the front because I knew that if I didn't die there things would be even worse for me. I would have to find out someday, directly from your own lips, that I had been dead to you for a long time...."

"You mustn't do that,"Ileana hastened to tell him. "I mean you mustn't think... You mustn't think of that...." She paused. "Are you living in Paris?"

583

"Yes."

"I can let you off on the way, but we must leave now. I've waited too long already. Whenever you wish we'll leave."

"Probably if I should ask you—if I should beg you not to leave today, or at any rate not to go in this automobile . . . Probably if I should say . . ."

"No, Stefan," she interrupted, with a smile. "Now, I'm asking you—I beg you, if you prefer—don't ask me anything. Don't tell me anything."

"You don't understand," began Stefan, troubled. "I meant that this car . . ."

"I know, I know!" She sounded exasperated, discouraged. "You think that this car . . . Oh, I don't want to remember. All I ask of you is this: be so kind as not to remind me! After six and a half years the first thing you said to me was something about that car." She tried to smile. "You haven't changed."

"I only wanted to tell you . . . It's not what you think. If you were to leave another day, or if you were to go back by train . . ."

"No, Stefan. I have a terribly nervous husband. He won't be able to sleep until I'm home. . . . He phoned me a few hours ago." She spoke wistfully. "I'd hoped that at least at the Abbey of Royaumont there wouldn't be a telephone, but I wasn't that lucky. There's one here. . . . He's waiting for me." She seemed resigned and annoyed. "I've taught him to think that I'm an ideal wife. . . . We'd better go," she said in haste and threw away her cigarette. "I'll leave you in Paris."

"If you could put up with me, I'd ask you to let me go a little farther with you. You could drop me off later wherever you like . . . at a railway station along the way . . ."

"I'd rather . . ." she began. Her voice trembled slightly and, frightened, she lowered her eyes.

"Ileana!" Stefan whispered, seizing her hand. "I don't ask anything else of you. Maybe we'll never see each other again. I'll never ask you for anything more. . . ."

She had said to the Valkyrie, "Ask him not to insist any longer. I know I make him suffer, but it's impossible for me to call him by any other name. I learned to call him 'Doctor.' I can't call him Bernard. He's so good . . . he's been so kind to me—but I can't call him Bernard. He's been a saint. The first time he asked me to call him Bernard I said 'St. Bernard' and we both laughed. But now he's very upset. He insists. And it's impossible for me. He's my doctor, my savior. I can't call him Bernard." "But he loves you," the Valkyrie exclaimed. "I know. He's told me so. I know I love him too. I've told him. I love him more than I love my own self. I love him the way I believe the saints are loved. That's why I can't call him Bernard."

584

"What do you think of him?" the Valkyrie had asked her in the beginning. She had seen him only a few times. His kindness, his distinction, his intelligence shone in his eyes, and she had liked this at once. "He's a remarkable man," the Valkyrie had continued. "He's a doctor, a psychologist, an artist all in one. He's a genius. He's a very remarkable man. . . ." When she had met him he had two children, and a little while after that he came one evening to tell them that he had one more, a boy. He seemed to be happy. He invited them to his villa a few kilometers from Lausanne on the shore of the lake. It was a Sunday afternoon. His wife was waiting for them on the terrace with the elder of the two little girls. She seemed to radiate a happiness that was simple and calm.

"The truth is that he saved me," she said later to the Valkyrie. "Because of him I've begun to live again." And another time, "He told me, teasing, that he was afraid he was falling in love with me. I reassured him. 'Don't worry, Doctor. I'm unlucky in love.' He reminded me of a dream I'd told him a year earlier. 'It means that you've resolved your crisis,' he said then, and he repeated it to me again. 'Don't be afraid of Stefan anymore. You've accepted and are reconciled to his death—physical death or spiritual death, it's the same thing. You've accepted this fact, this evidence that Stefan has died so far as you're concerned. You've become reconciled to life and now you begin a new one.' 'Of course,' I replied. 'I owe this to you.' 'But you must go further. You must make peace with him—with Stefan, the man you loved who made you suffer and who is now dead to you. You must. . . .' 'I know,' I answered. 'I've done it already.'" "You ought to tell him how you waken at night from your sleep," the Valkyrie had interrupted. "You ought to tell him you wake up screaming and calling for Stefan." "I've told him. He's known that for a long time."

Then after a year had gone by she found out that there was persistent talk at the clinic about the two of them, the doctor and herself, about their friendship which was much too intimate, even incriminating. "I should see him less frequently," she had said to the Valkyrie. "It will be hard, because I've grown accustomed to being with him. I need his friendship. He's been like a saint." "I have the impression that he loves you," remarked the Valkyrie, "that he's terribly in love with you." "No, it's not that," declared Ileana quickly. "It's a different kind of love. It's affection of an entirely different sort. Something else. . . ."

One evening after dinner he had come to see her unexpectedly. He seemed to be much disturbed. "Ileana," he said, "will you be my wife?" He was suddenly pale and he looked deeply into her eyes. "But, Doctor. . ." "Call me Bernard." "I feel terrible. . . . What about Claire?" "I told her," he said promptly. "I had to tell her and she understood.

585

We're separating. She left this morning with the children." "How awful!" Ileana exclaimed. "But it would have been a hell." His words came faster. "I'd be living a lie. I'd destroy her life and eventually mine as well. Will you be my wife?" he asked again. "Whatever your answer is you must realize that I can no longer turn back. I cannot live a lie. . . ." "How awful!" repeated Ileana. "Claire . . ."

"Ask him not to insist," she said to the Valkyrie. "It's impossible for me. I can't accept. I can't call him Bernard. I can't be his wife." "But he loves you. He's obtained his divorce. This is driving him out of his mind. Do you want him to lose his reason completely? You're destroying him. You've told me you love him, that he's the only man you love and ever will love. You've said that he's been like a saint to you. . . ." "I can't!" Ileana insisted. "I can't lie to him!"

Finally she told Bernard. "I can't lie. I love you too much to lie to you. But you know what's in my heart. You're the man I love most in the world. You're the only person I really love. I loved *Tante* Alice, but now she's gone. Yet I can't lie to you. You know what's in my heart." "It's just your imagination," he said, taking her hand and holding it in his own. "You're wrestling with a shadow, something that's been dead a long time, but you persist in giving it life through your imagination, your own life. It's only a shadow." "I still call to him, even now, in my dreams at night," she whispered in despair. "That doesn't matter. For twenty years I've called out in my sleep the name of the teacher who slapped me once when I was a child—slapped me so hard the blood came. It has absolutely no significance. . . ."

They were married in January 1946. When she sometimes awoke with a scream at night, she heard him beside her, comforting her. "You were frightened," he would say, "you had a bad dream." "How kind you are," was her answer, and she started to bring his hand to her lips, but he quickly bent and kissed her hand instead. "I'd like for us to have a child," he said to her once. "How kind you are," she whispered. And often after that he repeated, "I'd like for us to have a child." Several months later he told her, "Probably you're still not persuaded that we must have a child. We both need it, or at least I do. I need to have that to look forward to. . . ."

Sometimes in the night she would awake and find him beside her, gazing at her with a smile that was not always convincing. It was an expression that had begun to appear weary. "I'm not sleepy," he would say. "I can't sleep." "Doctor!" she cried on one occasion. "You're not happy!" "Call me Bernard," he begged her. "Learn to call me Bernard." "You aren't happy," she repeated, "because of me, because of me. . . ." She wanted at least to be able to cry, to show him it grieved her that she could not make him happy. But her eyelids were hot and dry and rough, and she did not look at him but kept repeating, "because of me, because of me...." "But what about you?" he asked her once. She turned to him, wondering. What did he mean? "I?" she meant to smile, but instead she shrugged her shoulders. "No. That's no answer," he insisted. "I know what's gnawing at you and consuming you like an invisible cancer, but it's preposterous! It only exists in your imagination. You also have to want to do something about it. You have to want to live. There's absolutely nothing wrong with you otherwise. You've recognized for yourself that Stefan no longer means anything to you, that he's just a shadow you nourish with your imagination. But now you have to *want* to conquer it, you have to *want* it...."

"What's the matter with Bernard?" the Valkyrie asked her. "What's wrong with him?" "Ileana," she cried one day, "what's happened between you? Don't you love each other anymore?" "Yes, yes, of course," Ileana assured her. "It's something else. He's tired. He works too much and suffers from insomnia. I've told him he has to take a long vacation, a very long one. We must go somewhere together, far away...." "Are you serious? Why are you crying?" "No, you're mistaken, I'm not crying. But I'm sorry. I was afraid it would be like this. You know very well that I didn't want... that I resisted as much as I could. I told him, 'Doctor, you must stay as you are.... For me you'll always be a saint.' 'That's ridiculous,' he answered. 'These are images that you yourself project, and then you believe they actually exist. You believe that I'm the way you imagine me, a St. Bernard....'"

But the Valkyrie continued to ask, "What's happened to you two? What's the matter with Bernard?" Once she had begun, "I heard a colleague of his saying..." "I don't want to hear about it," Ileana had interrupted. "Please, I implore you, don't tell me anything...." In the night she heard him walking about in his room. Waking, she lit a cigarette and smoked it absently, listening to the footsteps on the other side of the wall. Sometimes she called to him, "Doctor! Doctor!" His lips still wore the same strained smile when he entered. "I'm sorry..." "It's nothing," he quieted her, "it's nothing." Once she said, "But you know if you want me to I can disappear. I'd be happy to be able to do something for you. I'll go home to Romania. It's impossible for anyone to come back from there." "Ileana!" He was alarmed. "Are you mad? You're all I have! I live only for you!"

They spent that winter on the Côte d'Azur, determined to appear happy together, to enjoy their vacation, their wealth. In the spring they went to Sicily. One evening at Taormina he asked her suddenly, "Do you know that Viziru's in Paris?" They were walking in the park and Ileana stopped. The color left her face and she stared at him for a long time. "His name is Viziru, isn't it? Stefan Viziru, former *consilier* in the

587

Ministry of the Economy. I inquired through a university classmate who's stationed now at the Swiss Legation in Bucharest. It was very simple. Besides I ought to have done this long ago. Maybe it was a mistake that I didn't." She continued to gaze at him, pale, mute. "Yes, he's in Paris. He defected last summer when he was on a mission to Prague. And now here's what I've been thinking..." "Bernard!" she whispered, "I beg you, I implore you...." "No, my dear, it's very serious." Stern, unmoved, he watched her eyes. "An image in your mind prevents you from living, so the problem is very simple—you must go and confront the image." "Bernard!" she pleaded. "You'll have to confront it and see for yourself that Stefan Viziru is simply a phantom without life, or blood, or soul. It owes its existence to your imagination, which animates it...." "Bernard!" She grasped his arm and both were silent for a long time. They did not look at each other.

"You'll have to hurry," he reminded her all that day. "It's out of the question!" she protested. "I swore that he'd never see me again, that he wouldn't find me even if he searched on his knees to the ends of the earth...." "That's nonsense!" the doctor interrupted. "You must hurry. I've inquired and he's still in Paris, but we can't wait much longer. He may leave. He's a refugee now." "Impossible!" "I have perfect confidence in you," he had said on a later occasion. "I know what will happen. You'll simply confront him and be cured." Another day he suggested, "Go with Anne-Marie. Go by car...." He must have found out about the concert at Royaumont and arranged through the office of Swiss Cultural Affairs in Paris for the Valkyrie to be invited. "Now you have to go," he pressed her. "Take Anne-Marie so you won't be alone. Stay in Paris for several days. I know his address. Send him a note by special messenger and make an appointment to meet him at a cafe. Or no, it would be better to meet him in a garden—the Luxembourg, for instance. Ask him to come there. Insist. And after two hours Anne-Marie will come to get you. I'll phone you in the evening and you can tell me the details of the interview. I believe I'll be able to determine then if you'll need to see him a second time...."

Then suddenly early in the afternoon she had been summoned to the telephone. "Lausanne calling," they told her. He had tried to locate her in the morning at her hotel, but she had been invited to lunch at Royaumont with the director of the concert. "Have you written to him?" he asked. "Not yet." "I'm glad," he said precipitately. "It's not necessary. I've thought it over and it was a stupid idea...." "I won't write him," Ileana whispered. "But I have one request to make," he continued, "a big favor...." "Say it." "I've never asked anything of you before, but today I have this one request...." "Say it," repeated Ileana. "Maybe you'll smile and think that..." "What is it?" A note of anxiety had entered her voice. "What's the matter?" "Nothing . . . except that I feel extremely nervous. I couldn't close my eyes all night. I realized that I'd made a foolish mistake for which both of us might have to pay very dearly. Even now I still feel terribly nervous. My heart . . ." "Bernard!" "No, it's nothing serious, it's just because of the insomnia. But I'd like you to come back immediately. If you leave now you could reach the border before midnight. . . . Are you sorry I've asked you this?" "No," whispered Ileana. "I'm glad." "Is that true?" "I'm glad," she repeated. "I'll tell you why when I get home." "Ileana! That's the first time you've told me that. . . ." "I'm glad," she murmured again. "My darling!" She could tell that he was deeply moved.

"Talk to me," she urged at intervals. The silence between them seemed to assume a tangible form and it frightened her.

He held his gaze straight ahead of him where the highway stretched away endlessly, rising slightly between a double line of poplars. Very near them the sun went down behind a hill.

"It's extremely hard for me to talk about myself," Stefan began after awhile. "I think you know the most important thing. The rest isn't interesting."

"Just talk to me. Tell me again about the most important thing. . . ."

"I think you know. It's appallingly simple. It can be reduced to a name and an image, that's all. An image . . ."

"An image?" echoed Ileana, distressed.

"Yes. I calculated the time—I've always had this mania for computing. For almost fourteen years I was obsessed by a name: *doamna* Zissu. And for twelve years—exactly twelve—I was obsessed by an image. An automobile."

"I understand," Ileana murmured, watching the point where the highway lost itself in the distance.

"I don't think you do," said Stefan with a tormented smile. "Until yesterday even I didn't understand. Until yesterday . . . no, to be more precise, until just a few hours ago."

"I know," Ileana rejoined. "It's a question of the car. Always something about the car! An image. Without life, without blood, without soul. An image."

"Yes, an image. But now I understand." Maybe I should try again to tell her, he thought. We still have time. She has her whole life before her. She has her life. . . .

"An image," resumed Ileana, musing. "You haven't changed. A hallucination that even you didn't believe in at first. . . . But you've persisted in

589

clinging to it stubbornly, furiously, desperately. You've nurtured it with your own life, giving your blood and your soul to keep it alive. You've held it constantly before you, always near you, until . . . until you believed that you could no longer live without it. That image is your life, your fortune, your happiness. It's your fate. . . ."

"Yes. That's the way it was. But now I understand why."

"Only an image," Ileana went on, "a hallucination. And for that you destroyed your life. You made those who were dear to you suffer and you destroyed their lives too."

"Yes. That's so. Everyone fails in life. Except the saints."

"Why do you say that?" asked Ileana, irked. "Why are you always talking to me about saints? Ever since I've known you you've never stopped talking about the saints. Why? Why?"

The highway emerged from between the rows of widely spaced poplars and skirted the slope of a hill planted with grapevines.

"I'm not sure myself. Maybe it's because, like everyone else, I've had a longing for an unbroken kind of existence. Only a saint can live both in time and outside of time, in eternity. Only such an existence, full, rounded . . ."

"An image and a name," Ileana broke in again. "A name you heard once long ago through a wall."

"It wasn't just a simple wall like any other. It was . . ."

"I know. It was a part of your secret room. You heard it there in your sanctuary. . . ."

"It wasn't a sanctuary. It was simply my secret room."

". . . Your sanctuary that you yourself created in your imagination," continued Ileana hopelessly. "An image that you superimposed on another image—that of the room *Sambo* of your childhood. And because of that name and that image you destroyed your life. You lived an illusion and you destroyed your life!"

"Yes. But now I understand why. I found out who *doamna* Zissu was. Partenie loved her. And before him Mitica Porumbache loved her. And before him . . ." He hesitated. *Captain Sideri, you're under arrest!*

"Stefan!" she whispered suddenly without turning her head, continuing to look straight before her over the highway. "I'm sorry I have to tell you this, but my heart aches for you—it's breaking with pity. I pity you terribly . . ."

"I understand."

Here in the shadow of the beech and maple forest the evening seemed further advanced. It was already night under the trees.

"Talk to me," entreated Ileana again. "We don't have much more time together. Talk to me. . . ."

"It smells like home," Stefan said. "You'd think we were in a forest in Romania."

"It's true," said Ileana in a voice that was suddenly soft. "I didn't notice it at first but it's so. It has a fragrance like the woods at home. . . ."

"Like the woods at home."

"Yes, it's true. It was like this."

"But not at Zinca," Stefan resumed after a pause. "You didn't have such great forests at Zinca."

"There was one there, very old and very large, but it was some distance away from our place. It was beyond *Tante* Cecile's land. I remember it very well."

"Nothing is left of it now. The peasants cut it down the same winter they burned the mansion. It was a very hard winter and many died of the cold or typhus or of hunger."

"I know," whispered Ileana. "I heard."

Captain Sideri, you're under arrest! remembered Stefan. I ought to tell her. She has her whole life ahead of her. She has her life. . . .

The restaurant had been built near a mill and the tables stood in a row along the bank of the stream under an arbor of ivy and wisteria.

"There's something familiar about this place," Stefan began tentatively, "something I've known, but I can't remember what."

"Yes, that's so. It resembles something in Romania."

After a long silence Stefan remarked, "I can't quite recall what. . . ."

"Don't think of it anymore," interrupted Ileana with a smile. "Don't be always remembering things—what used to be, what might have been. Don't keep living in the past!"

"You're right. It's our greatest sin that we can't live in the present. . . . Only the saints live continually in the present."

Ileana stared at him and smiled again, absently crushing her cigarette in the ashtray. Idly she deciphered the letters on it: *Souvenir*. . . . "Stefan," she said, "you haven't changed. You've stayed just the same."

"I've grown older."

"No, you haven't. You'll never be able to grow old."

"It's very strange. . . . This water that flows so fast, this water flowing and falling out of the mill, reminds me of something."

"Yes—and me. How beautiful it is, incomparably beautiful. . . . And the beauty of the night is so haunting! Everything's so beautiful. . . ."

I ought to tell her now, he thought. She has her life before her. "Ileana," he began, suddenly troubled. "If I request something of you, if I implore you to listen to me to the end and not interrupt me . . ."

"No, Stefan, don't say anything. It's better—much better—not to say anything."

"No, you don't understand. I want to tell you something entirely different. It has no connection with me, or if you insist it has only a very insignificant connection. It's something that only concerns you . . ."

"Please, Stefan!" she whispered, looking at him fearfully. "Please!"

". . . something that concerns you and you alone. It's about your life . . ."

"Then I'm leaving!"

". . . and your future . . ."

She started to rise from her chair, but Stefan caught her arm and stopped her. "All right, I'll do as you ask. I won't say anything more. Stay. Please stay. . . ."

Ileana's eyes searched his again and she laid her hand on his arm. "Don't be angry, Stefan. I don't want to hurt you. But this is better." She paused thoughtfully. "It's so beautiful here. I'm sorry we can't stay longer. I don't like to think about leaving. The night's so beautiful. . . ."

"It's like something . . ." mused Stefan, and he seemed reconciled. He smiled. "We still have time."

She glanced hastily at her watch and the color receded from her face. Reaching for the glass that had been left almost untouched on the table, she drained it suddenly.

"It's late. In ten or fifteen minutes I have to leave. We'll part. . . ." Her voice was grave and it faltered and was lost in the ubiquitous sound of the turbulent water. "I'd like to say something. But I want to be sure that you'll listen and not interrupt me no matter what I say. Stefan, what do you hold most dear in all the world?"

"You," he said simply, averting his eyes. "Forgive me for saying it."

"That's all right, that's all right. It doesn't matter," responded Ileana impatiently. "I'm asking you to swear to me by that which you hold most dear. I want you to swear to me that you'll do what I'm going to ask you to do. Do you swear it?" She turned and looked directly at him, and in that moment Stefan saw that she had become again the woman he remembered. This was the way he had always seen her, ever since they had walked side by side through the grass, ever since she had shaken her head at him and told him with a smile, "I don't understand you. I'm sorry. Probably you're saying some very interesting things but I don't understand you. . . ."

"I swear," he said. "It's unthinkable for me to do it, but I swear."

"You've sworn to me, Stefan, you've sworn by me! There's nothing more to do. . . . And now this is what I ask. Don't search for me anymore, don't even think of me! Or think of me as someone who has died. This is really what happened to me—I died long ago. Remember whatever you wish, but don't think of me anymore as someone living in the present—in the time that God still gives me to live. . . ."

"God . . ." Stefan repeated, his voice scarcely audible.

"I ask you to forget me. But before you do, I'd like to inform you of one more thing. I don't tell you this to torture you and make you regret everything that might have happened and did not. Maybe it wasn't your fault—but neither was it mine—that I met you and fell in love with you, that I loved you and couldn't forget you. It was my destiny. Probably when I was born a Fate came who had not been invited, and she predestined misfortune for me. Listen to me, please!" she cried, raising her hand in alarm when he tried to speak. "You swore you'd listen to me. This was destined for me. Probably you were not at fault at all. But I'd like you to know this—that I've remained faithful to my destiny. I let you believe I didn't love you anymore, but I lied. I've never stopped loving you for a moment. Maybe I didn't always want to, but this was the way it was. I've loved you ever since I saw you the first time twelve years ago in the Forest of Baneasa, and I love you today. I was condemned to love you. I'll love you, probably, until the last moment of my life. This I was condemned to do. It was my fate. If I live fifty or a hundred years longer and if I have children and my children have children, and after fifty or a hundred years I die surrounded by my children and grandchildren, in the moment of death I'll call the name that I've called for the past twelve years— 'Stefan!' And I'll declare then, as I do now every night when the thought of you wakens me, that I've loved only you. And if—which is probable—I live exiled among strangers, with children and grandchildren who will know not a word of Romanian . . . if as an old woman I remember scarcely anything of the language which once was mine, in the moment of death I'll tell you in Romanian that I love you. . . . Don't interrupt me, please! You swore you'd listen to me. Let me say it all! I want you to know everything. I want you to know that when I first realized I loved you, a few weeks after I met you, it seemed incredible that I could love you after seeing you just a few times. That was in 1936. I ridiculed myself in order to bring me to my senses. I told myself repeatedly that this was unheard of. It was like *Tristan und Isolde*. . . . Stefan, for me it was like that story. On that night, perhaps without intention and without knowing it, you must have given me some magic potion to drink. You entered my blood, my soul, and since that time I've lived only because of you. I haven't lived like a person who is alive and wide awake, but as a shade . . . perhaps as the dead live only in memories. Unfortunately I've had such meager memories to live in—the brief disastrous quarter hours you gave me when you appeared with a bouquet of lilies of the valley to tell me that you were in love with me. But you told me this once, or at most, twice in a year, and all the rest of those precious minutes you gave me were devoted to talking about the car in which I ought to have come but did not. . . ."

"Ileana! It's *this* car!" Stefan exclaimed in a whisper. He leaned toward her and grasped her hand in a gesture of despair.

593

"Please, let me finish! Let me finish!" she said, pulling her hand away, frightened. "You swore that you'd let me finish. . . . You—my heart, my fortune, my tormenting demon—came a few times a year, stayed a quarter of an hour or once in awhile perhaps thirty minutes. You talked about a car that ought to disappear at midnight, or else about the mystery of *doamna* Zissu. Stefan," she whispered, looking in his eyes, smiling with difficulty, "if you ever love me again, if you ever love anyone again, don't do that! It's horrible. I've lived in the memories of a few hours. If I put together all the hours and minutes you've given me perhaps they'd amount to a day and a night. I've lived in them in the way that shades live on their memories of an entire and full lifetime. You gave me a magic potion to drink, Stefan. You never knew what you did . . ."

"Ileana," Stefan murmured. "Let me . . ."

"You swore by me, Stefan! You swore to do as I asked. And all I ask is this—don't say anything! Just let me look at you. We don't have much more time to be together. Just let me look at you. . . ."

She said to him, "I'll leave you at the station. I'll let you off at the first one. Probably there'll be a train to Paris before midnight."

"Ileana . . ."

"You swore to me, Stefan!" She did not let him continue. "You swore that you'd listen to me, that you'd never search for me again, that you'd think of me as someone who died a long time ago . . ."

"I swear it now . . . I swear it again," whispered Stefan. "I swear by all I have left in the world that this is the last night I'll ask you to let me sit beside you in this car," and he repeated, emphasizing the words, *"In this car.* I swear it. . . ."

When they had left the last lights of the town behind them Ileana said, "Stefan, tell me a story. Tell me about your childhood. Tell me about the hedgehog and the butterflies in the forest. I like to hear you talk about your childhood. I like to imagine you as a child. . . ."

He stole a glance at his watch. "Soon we'll part," he said suddenly. "I swore to you, I swore by you, and I'll keep my word. But there's no judge in the world who would not allow me, without exceeding the letter of the oath, a few words—very brief—and I'll ask you too not to interrupt me. I have very little to tell you. I'll say it in a few words."

"That's the way you are," Ileana remarked quietly and she smiled.

"I was a fool. No, more precisely, I was blind. For twelve years I didn't understand. It was not until this afternoon that I understood. I knew from the beginning, ever since I first saw you, that I loved you, and that I'd love you all my life..."

"Stefan!"

"... that you were destined for me, that we had drunk the same potion together..."

Frightened, Ileana turned to look at him. "Stefan!"

"Be careful! There's a truck ahead..." He felt his heart racing. It's not yet midnight. She has her whole life before her....

"You swore to me!" He heard the hopeless catch in her voice. "You swore to me! Have at least a little pity...."

"Just a few words," he pleaded. "Careful!" he cried in alarm a moment later. "If you'll let me, I'll take the wheel...."

"No. It's all right. Don't be frightened. But I begged you not to tell me.... Give me a cigarette, please. Light it for me."

Stefan obeyed and drew the first puff of smoke for her, then he placed it with a trembling hand between her lips.

"That's good.... It's a Gauloise," she said softly. "Talk to me. Tell me more. Forgive me for screaming. I was frightened...."

"Ileana, be careful!" Stefan cried again.

"Are you afraid?" she asked, turning her head and smiling. "Don't be. I'm very calm. I'm quite cool behind the wheel."

But it's not yet midnight, he continued to tell himself mechanically. I should still have time to tell her....

"Just a few words," he began again, "but please, I beg of you, I implore you, listen to me. Soon, very soon, we'll part."

"That's so. I'll listen. I know you'll make me suffer and I'll remember these few words my whole life, but I've never been able to refuse you...."

"I was blind. I knew all the time that you were destined for me, but I didn't understand why. Ileana, if I ask you... Watch out! What are you doing? Let me drive awhile!"

"Don't be afraid." Smiling, she soothed him. "If you will, please, throw away my cigarette...."

Taking it, he touched her hand and began to tremble. He thought that she was trembling too. I must tell her everything. I must tell her now. "Ileana!" he whispered, "my love, my bride..."

"Stefan!" She seemed to lack the strength to cry out, to oppose him. Her voice choked with exhaustion.

"My bride," Stefan continued quickly, as if he no longer heard her. "I have loved you as you loved me, irrationally, like a restless spirit that cannot die, not understanding, not comprehending what was happening to us, why we were fated to love and yet not be able to love, why we were destined to search for each other, never to meet . . ."

In the beam of the headlights of an approaching car he saw her face for a moment, and he saw that she was crying. She was looking straight ahead like a blind person, her eyes wide, unblinking, unseeing.

"I want to tell you this, but not to make you suffer. I want to confess that I've loved no one but you. Perhaps I've never shown it, but I've loved no one but you. And this afternoon I understood why. There was something that I'd forgotten, and I was a fool. I was blind, I never should have forgotten. And now I have to tell you. I loved only you and I must tell you. I've loved only you, and I'll love you too in the last moment when . . ."

He was suddenly silent. His strength deserted him. I must tell her now while there's still time, he reminded himself, watching her cry. I must implore her to stop here, to telephone Lausanne, to take the train. I must fall on my knees and plead with her . . .

"My darling!" he heard her whisper.

"I just want you to know this," he began again with great effort. "I want you to know . . ."

"My darling!"

He saw the parapet, and beyond it he could picture the abyss that yawned in the darkness. He began to tremble. I have to tell her. I still have time to tell her! But the headlights of a car lifted them out of the darkness, blinding him, and instinctively he drew closer to Ileana. That moment—unique, infinite— revealed to him the total beatitude he had yearned for so many years. It was there in the glance she bestowed on him, bathed in tears. He had known from the beginning this was the way it would be. He had known that, feeling him very near her, she would turn her head and look at him. He had known that this last moment, this moment without end, would suffice.

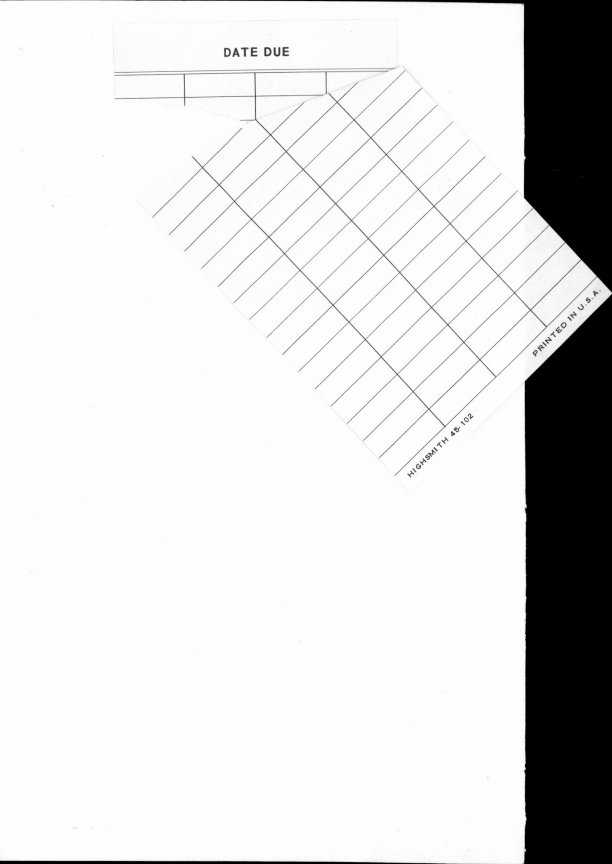

DATE DUE

HIGHSMITH 45-102

PRINTED IN U.S.A.